Charles Allen is a renowned histo~~rian~~ ~~of the British Raj~~ who first made his name with *Plain Tales from the Raj*. His most recent books include *Duel in the Snows: The True Story of the Younghusband Mission to Lhasa*; *The Buddha and the Sahibs: The Men Who Discovered India's Lost Religion*; *Soldier Sahibs: The Men Who Made the North-West Frontier*; *God's Terrorists: The Wahhabi Cult and the Hidden Roots of Modern Jihad* and *Kipling Sahib: India and the Making of Rudyard Kipling*.

HAT DEPARTMENT—contd.

Child's Pith Helmet.
Covered White Cotton 11/6

Lady's Pith "Connaught."
Covered White Drill and Pugri 21/0

Lady's Pith "Connaught."
Covered Drab Felt (to order only) 30/0

"Cawnpore Tent Club."
Pith, with Quilted Khaki Cover 19/6
(English Finish.)

"Cawnpore Tent Club" 22/0

Wolseley Helmet 29/0

The "Curzon."
Pith, covered Felt, and blue silk Pugri ... 30/0
„   „   Drill, „ white   „ ... 17/0
To order only.

Ellwood's Cork Polo Helmet.
Covered White Drill and Pugri 25/0
Hawkes's ditto 30/0

Regulation Naval Cap 34/6

Undress Forage Cap, R.M.L.I.
Complete 53/6

R.A. Undress Cap.
Complete 39/6

R.A.F. Cap.
Complete 70/0

ALL PRICES ARE SUBJECT TO MARKET FLUCTUATIONS.

Plain Tales
from the British Empire

Images of the British in India,
Africa and South-East Asia

Collected and edited by
Charles Allen

This omnibus edition first published in Great Britain in 2008 by Abacus

Plain Tales from the British Empire copyright © 2008 by Charles Allen

Previously published separately:

Plain Tales from the Raj first published in Great Britain by André Deutsch and the
British Broadcasting Corporation
Copyright © 1975 by Charles Allen and the British Broadcasting Corporation
Introduction © 1975 by Philip Mason
Tales from the Dark Continent first published in Great Britain in 1980 by Futura
Copyright © 1979 by Charles Allen
Tales from the South China Seas first published in Great Britain in 1984 by Futura
Copyright © 1983 by Charles Allen and the British Broadcasting Corporation

A CIP catalogue record for this book is available from the British Library.

ISBN 978-0-349-11920-5

Papers used by Abacus are natural, recyclable products made from wood grown in
sustainable forests and certified in accordance with the rules of the Forest
Stewardship Council.

Typeset in Baskerville by Hewer Text UK Ltd, Edinburgh
Printed and bound in Great Britain by Clays Ltd, St Ives plc
Paper supplied by Hellefoss AS, Norway

Abacus
An imprint of
Little, Brown Book Group
100 Victoria Embankment
London EC4Y 0DY

An Hachette Livre UK Company

www.littlebrown.co.uk

What shall we tell you? Tales, marvellous tales
Of ships and stars and isles where good men rest.

J. E. Flecker, *The Golden Road to Samarkand*

With special thanks to Michael Mason (producer of the BBC Radio 4 series *Plain Tales from the Raj, More Plain Tales from the Raj* and *Tales from the South China Seas*), Helen Fry (producer of the BBC Radio 4 series *Tales from the Dark Continent*) and Faith Evans, my editor at André Deutsch.

Contents

Preface

This trilogy began as a series for BBC Radio 4. In 1974, having been repeatedly warned that the British Empire was of little interest to listeners, the BBC radio producer Michael Mason finally secured permission for a series to be based on the taped reminiscences of British men and women who had lived in India under British rule. The initial broadcast series of *Plain Tales from the Raj* is now widely recognized as a radio classic. It also touched a chord with the listening public in a quite remarkable way, revealing what had long been overlooked: that you have but to scratch the surface of the average British family to find any number of links if not with India then with other corners of the British Empire where forebears went out to try their luck in one capacity or another.

At the start of the Second World War the British Empire was the most extensive the world had ever known, with approximately a quarter of the world's population under its sway. Within three decades that empire had been almost totally dismembered. As newly decolonized countries set out to recover their national identities or to construct new ones, beginning with India and Pakistan in 1947, it was inevitable that those who had been associated with colonial rule took on the role of scapegoats, to be vilified as oppressors or mocked as stock figures of fun. *Plain Tales from the Raj* and *More Plain Tales from the Raj* challenged these simplistic attitudes – not by glorifying or mythologizing the Raj but by humanising the colonial experience. British rule in India was made up of many constituent parts, some negative and damaging, others positive and beneficial. Yes, it was a self-serving exercise in throwing national weight about, but it was also about people and the gambles they took with their lives, their interaction with other cultures and the subsequent cross-fertilization which continues to affect us to this day. As a contributor to a subsequent radio series (*Tales from the South China Seas*) put it, 'So many Englishmen gave their hearts and very often their health and their lives. It is a very great grief to me that so much of this is not known to the young people of today – and that a great deal of it has been forgotten.'

Plain Tales from the Raj set out to preserve some small part of Britain's involvement in India as remembered by the last generation of Britons who had lived there under Crown rule. Here it was my good luck to attend Michael Mason, rather as a *chela* to his *guru*, serving my apprenticeship as an oral historian by being sent out with a bulky tape-recorder to disarm and then interview 'survivors' of the British Raj in their homes, former *koi-hais* and *memsahibs* whose collective experiences Mason then winnowed, sifted and blended into eleven magical radio programmes. We were well advised by Philip Mason and Sir Penderel Moon, two former members of the Indian Civil Service turned historians, and by Evan Charlton, former editor of the *Statesman* of Calcutta. The first was kind enough to provide an introduction to the book that followed the radio series, which is reprinted here unchanged. In its talk of toasts to King-Emperors, of duty and service, it wonderfully conveys the ethos of that now far-removed world of imperial loyalties.

These were the men who helped shape *Plain Tales from the Raj*, yet the real progenitors were our 'survivors' – the sixty-six men and women I interviewed. This was how I described them back in 1975:

Widely separated by age, rank, occupation, geography and personal character, these Survivors all share the experience of British India in the twentieth century. In this sense they are representatives of their age. Accordingly, I have not always identified quotations where commonly expressed attitudes or experiences are given. Similarly, whether well known or relatively unknown, I have referred to my Survivors in the text as they were then. Brief details of their careers and distinctions can be found in the appended biographical notes.

In structure, this anthology follows the general experience of the great majority of its contributors, most of whom were born at the turn of this century, many into the India of Curzon and Minto, with forebears whose service in India already stretched back a hundred years and more. Exiled from India as children, they returned as adults – together with the newcomers to India – after the Great War, which stands as a divide between the old imperial India of the Edwardian age and the newly self-conscious India of the 1920s. They grew to their maturity in the inter-war years and saw the Raj through to its decline and sudden end in their late middle-age.

Not all these Survivors fit this pattern. Some were already in India as adults long before the First World War: Claude Auchinleck, whose father fought in the Indian Mutiny and who himself rose to preside over the bisection of the Indian Army, came out in 1903; H. T. Wickham joined the Indian Police in the Punjab in 1904; Kenneth Warren followed family footsteps into Assam as a tea-planter in 1906. Outdating them all is Mrs Grace Norie – ninety-nine years old at the time of writing – who was born in Roorkee in 1876 and retired to England in 1919 – only one year after the youngest Survivor represented here was born [that was Terence 'Spike' Milligan, born in Ahmednagar in 1918]. Young and old, in India they lived out their lives – as we all do – without self-conscious regard to their times and the great events that shaped them – and this is how I have presented them. It is not a romantically idealised picture; the speakers themselves have been remarkably frank and self-critical – and yet, when told about it 'warts and all', I for one find their Raj no less impressive.

Tales from the Dark Continent followed five years later. Again, the project began as a radio series for BBC Radio 4, my radio producer in this instance being Helen Fry and our adviser the historian and former member of the Colonial Service Anthony Kirk-Greene. We soon realized that British Africa was a far more diverse, less cohesive subject than British India. The chequer-board of colonies, protectorates, mandated territories and one condominium that until the mid-1950s and early 1960s made up the sum of Britain's African Empire had little in common beyond the imposed system of government that – very briefly – linked them together. Accordingly, we concentrated on the general form of Crown rule itself and on the shared experiences rather than the differences or the distinctiveness of each territory. The one common presence in all these territories was the colonial officer, usually in the form of a member of the Colonial Service, so it was that cadre, along with their wives, which became the main focus of the radio series and the book that followed.

Another significant difference between this second exercise and the first was that Britain's colonial involvement in Africa was so remarkably short-lived and so recently brought to an end that in 1977–8, when the interviews were conducted, it was still possible to find witnesses to what was almost the complete colonial cycle of occupation, consolidation, emancipation and withdrawal. At one end of the time-scale were the last survivors of what was known – from a somewhat partisan point of view – as the era of pacification: the years before the Great War when men like Angus Gillan (born in 1885) and Alan Burns (b. 1887) went out to the Sudan and to Southern Nigeria as pioneer administrators, and Mrs Sylvia Leith-Ross (b. 1883) became one of the first white women to enter Northern Nigeria. At the other end were those like Patrick Mullins and Noel Harvey who barely had time to learn the administrative ropes before the dependencies to which they had been posted, the Gold Coast and Nyasaland, gained their independence as Ghana (1957) and Malawi (1964).

Glaringly absent from this record was the British settler in Kenya and Central Africa – for the simple reason that the BBC was not prepared to pay for me to go out there. With hindsight, I think it was also an error of judgement to use the term 'Dark Continent' but then this was the 1970s and racial sensitivities were not as sharp as they are today. Indeed, there are some statements and assumptions that new readers will find distasteful, such as the widespread British view that the Mau Mau were little better than beasts of the jungle and deserved to be treated as such. Such attitudes have to be set against the surprisingly enlightened thinking of the last generation of colonial civil servants who saw it as their duty to do themselves out of their jobs.

Finally, there was *Tales from the South China Seas*, first broadcast and published in book form in 1983, when I again had the pleasure and benefit of working with Michael Mason. This time the BBC part-funded my travels, which allowed me to wander through Malaysia collecting interviews from a number of old colonials who had chosen to stay on in the country in which they spent both the best and worst years of their lives.

Here our central theme was no longer that of one supremely successful (in purely colonial terms) racial minority imposing itself upon a rather unsuccessful (again, speaking in colonial terms) majority – as in India and Africa – but of several races drawn to the same watery crossroads by the lure of trade; competing as rivals but coexisting more or less as equals. The main image now was a shifting one: in place of continental land-masses, islands and archipelagos and casuarina-fringed sands backed by rain forest. In a phrase, the South China Seas. Indeed, the original scheme was to include the British in China and a number of such interviews were gathered only to fall foul of the limits of broadcasting time and space – with one striking exception: Captain Robert Williamson's account of four years as ship's master on the Upper Yangtse from 1921 to 1924, so Conradesque as to demand inclusion.

Like its predecessors, *Tales from the South China Seas* made no attempt to confront the political issues of colonialism. It was, first and foremost, a social history: the details of their lives as remembered by ordinary people placed in what many of us would regard as extraordinary places and times. My oldest 'survivor' here was Alan Morkill, born in 1890, who began his career in the Malayan Civil Service in the newly created Unfederated Malay State of Kelantan. Morkill was one of the last of that pioneering wave of administrators who helped establish British rule in the Malayan peninsula. By contrast, the youngest contributor was born almost forty years later, one of four daughters of a rubber planter in the 1920s. Susan Whitley's childhood experiences, along with those of her three elder sisters, are set down in the same form in which they were originally broadcast.

In compiling this final volume I felt there was no need to go over again the common ground of public administration and day-to-day routines of the British colonial experience, already detailed in the first two volumes. Instead, I focused on what struck me as the special features of British rule in South East Asia: the curiously distanced (to modern sensibilities) relationships between the different races; the striking contrasts between life in the big towns and life up-river in what was known as the *ulu*; the bizarre phenomenon of the Sarawak of the White Rajahs; the self-contained world of the rubber planters; the sea captains' lives aboard the little steamers that plied the archipelago; and, inescapably, the terrible nemesis that descended upon this most peaceful corner of the British Empire as the thirties drew to a close.

It was here in the South China Seas that the disintegration of Western imperialism began, beginning with the fall of Hong Kong to the Japanese forces on Christmas Day 1941, swiftly followed by the surrender of 'Fortress Singapore' six weeks later. These events signalled to every corner of the world the ending of white supremacy and forecast the end of Rule Britannia. The traumatic years that followed affected directly, and often cruelly, the lives of every one of those who contributed to this last volume. It was the last chapter of British rule in South East Asia and for this reason I have extended what was never intended to be more than social history to include some part of their experiences in the war years and a little of what followed in the years leading up to *Merdeka* (Independence). In a fourth volume of oral history not included here, *The Savage Wars of Peace* (1990), I gave some account of the little wars that accompanied Britain's painful process of colonial disengagement.

Inevitably, gaps remain that can now never be completely filled due to the passage of time and the laws of nature. Of these, the most glaring is that what is told here is only one side of the story.

Charles Allen, Somerset, September 2007

Introduction to Plain Tales from the Raj

Philip Mason (1975)

It is now nearly thirty years since the partition and independence of India. That means that any Briton who was once accustomed to drinking the toast of the King-Emperor is likely to be over fifty. Two generations have grown up in Britain who have no first-hand knowledge of the life their countrymen lived in that strangely alien part of the Crown's dominions, not even that second-hand knowledge from brothers, sisters and cousins that was once widespread. It was therefore an admirable idea of the BBC's to record on tape the memories of as many as possible of the survivors.

There have, it is true, been quite a few books in the last fifteen years which attempt to reconstruct some aspect of British life in India. But most of those that have come my way have had their origin in a post-graduate thesis; they are usually heavily tied to written sources – and such sources tend to recount the breaks in routine, whereas it is the everyday detail that is so fascinating to a later generation. 'Strange encounter with a bandicoot' will go in the memoir-writer's chapter heading but what we really want to know is what he had for breakfast. Nor have the kind of books I am thinking of always been written with much concern for the general reader. A most distinguished member of my former service once remarked with dry realism: 'No one will ever read anything that I write unless he is paid to.' And some of the recent academic books have been rather like that.

Charles Allen's pot-pourri from the conversations he recorded with survivors of the Empire – I cannot bring myself to use the expression 'Raj' of which the BBC are so enamoured – has come down firmly on the side of being readable rather than pedantic. I am sure this is right. The purpose of his book is to give the general reader some feeling of the flavour of a life that has gone for ever. A serious historian can go to the tapes themselves where he will identify each remark in its context. And in the same spirit I think he is right to use what he calls 'basic' spelling of Indian words rather than be phonetically accurate. I was taught Urdu at Oxford by a most accomplished linguist who hated the use of English words in Indian languages and prided himself on the accuracy of his pronunciation. He was an examiner in Urdu (and other languages) and it was said that he once found himself sitting at lunch at the Naini Tal Club next to a subaltern whom he had that morning failed in Urdu. He wanted a tomato but there is no word for tomato of Arabic, Persian or Sanscritic origin so he used an expression of the purest linguistic respectability meaning 'a round red fruit that grows on a small plant not a tree' and the *khidmatgar* was puzzled. 'Can I help you, sir?' asked the subaltern politely. 'Want a tomato? Oh, yes, I see. Boy! Tamata *lao*.' And of course it came at once.

This book would have been less readable if it had been arranged by provinces or periods – although either method would have been more helpful to a historian. Arranged, as it is, by subjects, it has to blur the differences between different parts of India and different periods. And the very fact that Charles Allen was so successful at getting the confidence of the people he talked to has encouraged them, talking at their unbuttoned ease, to utter generalities that they would not have put in writing. We, who served in a particular district at a particular moment, are bound to grumble at *something*; it wasn't, we are bound to say at some point, like *that* in my time and in my province. For example, I am astonished to find someone saying that many posts in the police were reserved for Anglo-Indians. I don't think there was one Anglo-Indian in the police in Bareilly, a fairly average UP district. It is asserted that it was a rule of pig-sticking never to hunt alone – and I remember one of my first commissioners who maintained that hunting a pig alone when in camp was the cream of the sport. I am shocked to hear of a memsahib who allowed a sweeper to handle bacon which she meant to eat – but I suppose we were more infected by Hindu prejudice than most.

None the less, I think this book, in which most of the talking is done by people who were actually there, gives a total effect much more like the India we knew than any of the more learned productions I have referred to. It is sometimes a trifle Turneresque – but then *Rail, Steam and Speed* is alive, while a drawing of a locomotive in a shed by a mechanical engineer is likely to be dead.

Apart from details, the aspect in which this picture differs most from my own experience is in regard to the lives of women. No doubt there were many who did find life dull; perhaps it is inevitable that those I remember best should be those who always found plenty to do. I recall for instance one formidable old lady – she seemed old in those days – who after her morning ride and her inspection of the stables and the garden, the cook-house and the cook, would then be off to her maternity centre and child welfare clinic in the city and would fit in a purdah party for Indian ladies before her dinner party for the brigadier. *She* told the cook exactly what to do; she saw that his pans were properly scoured and the kitchen table scrubbed; she inspected the dishcloths. She told me that when the camping season began, the first thing to start was the cold weather stock-pot – a huge iron pot into which must go a hare, a duck, a quail, a snipe and a partridge; it travelled from camp to camp every other day in a bullock cart and it must be brought to a simmer every day – and she must see it simmer,

just as she saw the water boiled and the cow milked. She had
done twenty-five Hot Weathers in the plains – and I silently
resolved that my still problematical wife should not! She really
was the platonic idea of a memsahib. And another, who always
comes to mind very elegant in camping or riding clothes, made
herself a most accomplished water-colourist and experimented
with coloured lino-cuts. And another, an army wife, took as a
ruling passion her clinic for soldiers' wives. But it is odd that so
few ladies since Fanny Parks – who was interested in everything – have left lively memoirs.

The life of the British in India, even in 1939, was still
Victorian. Clothes had changed, some customs a little, but the
framework of life had been settled in the last years of the old
Queen. And since it was a country ruled by an official
hierarchy, it was socially conservative. Seniority played a
big part in promotion and senior officials do not usually
undervalue the wisdom that experience has brought them.
In social matters they are likely to prefer the standards of their
youth and long before the young men of their day have
become old enough to change things they too have accepted
the standards of their seniors. Of course this was not the same
everywhere; Delhi was less behind the times than a provincial
capital and broadly speaking the further you went from
headquarters the more Victorian survivals you would find.
Here and there in the UP in the thirties you might find a little
old lady, altogether Indian in features and complexion, a
descendant of the Hearseys, the Skinners or the Gardners,
heroes of the early days of the Company. She might be ruling
two or three villages with feudal autocracy but in her front
parlour she would sit among her sofas and antimacassars,
modelling herself on the Great Queen. And again, the time-
lag was greater with the ICS and the Indian Army than with
officers of the British service, who were often more aware of
modifications in the social climate in England – but then they
seldom stayed in India long enough to have much influence.

The time has come, I think, to look at this fragment of the

Victorian world – stranded in time, like a lost world – with some attempt at a more kindly understanding. The Victorians themselves were inclined to be contemptuous of other cultures and often took it for granted that any custom different from their own was wrong or barbarous or even wicked. Today anthropologists have taught us to look more enquiringly at the habits of other people and also of ourselves. What exactly is it that they do, we begin to ask, and why do they do it? What is the effect of this custom on their society and economy? And surely it is with no less sympathy that we should look at fragments of our own past too.

In the fifties, even in the thirties, it was enough to raise a guffaw to mention dressing for dinner in the jungle. But there were three good reasons for keeping up in India a custom which was obsolescent in Esher or Weybridge. For a great part of the year, it was a matter of elementary comfort and cleanliness to change clothes in the evening and, since the bearer, who put them out for you, had nothing like enough to do, it was no more trouble to put on one kind of clothes than another. But there was also the more complex feeling that it was necessary to 'keep up standards'. This of course did influence us a good deal and it is easy to make fun of it. But there was a good reason. Aldous Huxley, on a tourist's visit, noticed that many of the inhabitants of India might have sat as models for the old man of Thermopylae who never did anything properly. And in a sense it was by doing things properly – more often at least than most Indians – that the British had established themselves in India and that so few ruled so many with so slight a use of overt force. There was a subconscious awareness of this that involved us in continual effort and expressed itself in all kinds of ways – from insisting on absolute precision in military drill to the punctilious observance of outdated etiquette, or a meticulous insistence on a knife-edge crease to khaki shorts.

The effort was all-pervading and probably more exhausting than we realized at the time. My first responsible job was as sub-divisional magistrate in Bareilly. When I went in to the court room where I was to try cases I saw that the immensely lofty ceiling – perhaps thirty feet high – was draped and festooned with cobwebs – stalactites and stalagmites of cobweb, hanging curtains of cobweb six feet deep. I told the clerk of the court to see that they were removed and he said that of course it should be as I wished. Three days later it was just the same. The court clerk had passed my orders to the *nazir*, who was a kind of quartermaster to the headquarters of the district. I sent for the *nazir*; he, too, had passed on the order, to the head messenger. I told him to make sure it was carried out. Three days later, the cobwebs still stirred sluggishly in the increasing heat of March. I sent for the head messenger; he too had duly passed on my order to someone else. It took about a fortnight to reach the final link in the chain of command. This man, I resolved grimly, would *have* to be punished. But they led in an old, old man, hardly able to walk. He had been a messenger fifty years, on ten rupees a month, and since his pension was only two rupees a month he had been given the job of dusting the court for another two rupees. It would be only the walls of the court he was expected to dust and the furniture; no one but a sweeper could do the floor and messengers were often men of high caste. But even that was beyond him and probably a grandson actually did dust the court for eight annas. Of course, the old man couldn't be punished, so we found a contractor with ladders and strong young men and made a special occasion of it.

That was the kind of thing that made us a little fussy about doing things properly. But there was another side to it. Most of us – soldiers and civilians alike – had far more responsible jobs than we could have expected at our age anywhere else in the world and off duty – out of our own district, away from the regiment – we were sometimes a trifle irresponsible. Even the ics played rugger in the ballroom after their annual dinner in Lucknow; two young officers from Delhi who had to wait at a wayside railway station on their way to my Christmas camp in

Garhwal passed the time with rifle practice at the insulators on the telegraph posts – but it was outside my district and I conveniently forgot that they had told me. Youthful high spirits often merged subtly into middle-aged eccentricity – both perhaps as a reaction against too much insistence on doing things properly. Eccentricity indeed – as Ian Stephens says in this book – was one of the pillars of the Empire. It was the lubricant that enabled the machine to work. It sprang from confidence; you can afford to be eccentric if you know that you can get away with it and that is why it was common among English aristocrats and Indian bureaucrats. I have perhaps in other books told enough stories about eccentrics in India but I have so often been asked about something to which I merely alluded – the Gambit of the Second Reminder, said to have been an infallible recipe for disobeying the orders of higher authority – that perhaps it should now be released.

Huish Edye, who invented the device, was a determined district officer, well known for his witticisms at the expense of the secretariat. But when he received instructions of a general kind of which he did not approve, he would – he alleged – write an effusive letter to the chief secretary congratulating him on this far-sighted measure but adding in a postscript: 'Of course I assume this is not meant to apply in this district.' Warmed by the unexpected tribute, the chief secretary would mildly ask the reason for the exemption. This letter should be left unanswered, and preferably concealed in some unlikely place. The secretariat clerks had precise instructions as to the interval before they should send a reminder; when it elapsed, off would go the first reminder. This Edye would ruthlessly destroy. After the prescribed interval, the secretariat clerks would send the second reminder. The head clerk in the district would be puzzled that he had no first reminder and would feel his professional efficiency aspersed. He would indignantly point out that there had been no first reminder – and he and his colleague in the secretariat office could be trusted – Edye maintained – to argue about that for a couple of years.

He cannot really have used the ploy very often but it does illustrate that humorous, confident, essentially aristocratic aspect of British rule in India which sweetened the whole and might not – one suspects – have been so much in evidence if the officials had been French or German or Japanese.

No one who wasn't there will ever really understand what it was like – but this book may be a step on the way towards understanding.

Plain Tales from the Raj

1

The Shrine of the 'Baba-Log'

She will be zealous in guarding her children from promiscuous intimacy with the native servants, whose propensity to worship at the shrine of the Baba-log is unhappily apt to demoralize the small gods and goddesses they serve . . . The sooner after the fifth year a child can leave India, the better for its future welfare. One after one the babies grow into companionable children. One after one England claims them, till the mother's heart and house are left unto her desolate.

MAUD DIVER *The Englishwoman in India* 1909

'I grew up in bright sunshine, I grew up with tremendous space, I grew up with animals, I grew up with excitement, I grew up believing that white people were superior.' Every *chota* sahib or missy *baba* whose first years were spent in India would echo such sentiments – be they the sons and daughters of state governors or, as in this instance, the son of a British army corporal. The extra dimensions of India took immediate effect. First memories are of mosquito nets, of ponies rather than prams, of a father 'killing a snake in my bathroom,' of 'nanny getting smallpox'. The youngest in a distinguished line of Napiers, Rosamund Napier, is admonished with, 'Soldiers' daughters never cry!' and the infant John Rivett-Carnac, whose family is mentioned by Kipling, is informed by servants that 'without doubt the captain's little son will be an officer in the army'. Their first common image is of ayah.

The figure of the native nurse dominates the 'Anglo-Indian'* nursery, usually in sari and blouse and 'covered in nose-rings with bangles on her wrists and ankles: when she was moving about you could hear her a mile off'. Archetypal ayahs are always 'very gentle, sweet-natured women with beautiful hands, very gentle and beautiful in their movements'. They had their own hierarchy, headed by the Madrassi ayah, the cream of ayahs, mission-educated and thus given 'a good many civilized ideas'. The virtues of the trained ayah were considerable. 'They had this capacity to completely identify with the children they looked after,' explains Vere Birdwood, 'and it seemed as if they could switch on love in an extraordinary way. They were so dedicated to their work, in a sense so possessive of their children that it was almost impossible for a good ayah to yield up her charge even for a few hours.' One such paragon was Lewis Le Marchand's ayah in South India:

> She was very fat and Madrassi and very, very oily about the hair. Her toes were quite enormous and cracked like dry wickets that had had the sun on them for a few days. If the day *chokidar* didn't give me another biscuit with my early morning tea or if there was any sort of trouble, I used to go to her and she usually managed to solve it. I didn't know her name; I called her ayah. Sometimes, being a fairly naughty boy, I would anger her, but she'd never show it. She'd turn her back and go and sit down cross-legged on the floor of the verandah and take out her knitting, and the more I called her or the more I was naughty or rude, the more she ignored me, until

* The word 'Anglo-Indian' was applied originally to all the British in India but was officially adopted in 1900 to describe persons of mixed descent, then known as Eurasians. However, since 'Anglo-Indian' continued to be used in both contexts for the next forty years, I have used inverted commas to differentiate between 'Anglo-Indian' (British in India), and Anglo-Indian (person of mixed descent).

finally I would come along and say, 'Ayah, I'm sorry,' and then all would be well.

Ayah ministered after me during the day and very often during the evening, but it was mother's privilege – heaven knows why – to bath me and put me to bed. Ayah used to wait and, if necessary, sleep outside the doors of her children's rooms, lying down outside on the mat until such time as my mother would come along and say, 'You can go, ayah, little master's asleep.'

Ayah was the open door through which contact with India was made. 'One of the most charming things I've ever seen,' declares Reginald Savory, 'was the ayah squatting down on her haunches on the verandah with a little child, saying their rhymes together. Most of them they had translated into a kind of curious Anglo-Indian patois. There was "Pussy-cat, pussy-cat where have you been? I've come out from under the Ranee's chair". Another one was "*Humpti-tumpti gir giya phat*". Then there was "*Mafti-mai*": Muffety mother was eating her curds and whey on the grass . . .' There were also the Urdu songs and rhymes that ayahs sang to put their charges to sleep and which many never forgot: '*Roti, makan, chini, chota baba nini*' [Bread, butter, sugar, little baby sleep] and:

Talli, talli badja baba,	Clap, clap hands baby,
Ucha roti schat banaya.	They make good bread in the market.
Tora mummy *kido.*	Give some to your mummy.
Tora daddy *kido.*	Give some to your daddy.
Jo or baki hai.	What is left over
Burya ayah kido.	Give to your old ayah.

As well as nursery rhymes there were the stories that began '*Ecco burra bili da* . . .' (There was a large cat then) and, for older children, tales that took a more sinister turn. John Rivett-Carnac remembers a story about a leg-eater which lived under one's bed, and if a small boy got out of bed the leg-eater snapped off his leg. We were terrified of getting out of bed and once we'd been put to bed we stayed there. The other story was about an old man of the wood, black and hairy, who used to come from the jungle into small children's bedrooms and tickle them to death. This proved even more frightening than the leg-eaters and one evening we got so terrified that we leapt from our beds – jumping as far as possible away from the bed so as not to lose our legs – and dashed into the dining room where my parents were having a big dinner party. We took a great deal of persuading to go back to bed.'

More often it was the children who had the upper hand: 'Ayah would pat us gently until she thought we were asleep and then creep silently to the door, and just as she reached the door we would open our eyes and say, "Ayah!" and she had to come back and pat us again.'

If ayahs had a fault it was that they spoilt their charges, that they never said no. Nor was this lack of discipline confined to ayahs. 'This is the one thing over which the Indian fell out badly. Because he loved children he was quite incapable of exercising any sort of discipline over them, and therefore children brought up entirely by Indian servants were reputed to be extremely undisciplined.' There was also the largely unspoken fear – a hangover from Victorian 'curry and rice' days – that an ayah would give a child some opium on the tip of her finger to make it go to sleep.

England provided both temporary and final solutions; imported nannies or governesses . . . and exported children. But before this last drastic step there were the years of temporary reprieve. Outside the nursery a host of followers stood ready to serve and spoil: 'If nanny or mummy was busy, one of the Indian manservants was detailed to look after us, which meant that he would devote the whole of his time to entertaining us, to making sandpies or whatever it was that we were doing, and this of course was simply wonderful because boredom was completely eliminated from our lives.' Indian servants had the capacity 'to become children at the time they were playing with children', and to forget their own differences. Radclyffe Sidebottom recalls seeing his 'six foot four Pathan bearer and the sweeper, who was of a different religion, each carrying a child on his shoulders, with the sweeper chasing the Pathan round the drawing room'.

Outside the bungalow there was the compound and yet more followers. Nancy Foster, the youngest of three sisters, remembers that 'the *malis*, the gardeners, were always getting into difficulties with my parents for coming and helping us build houses in trees or set up a bazaar or to make wreaths from flowers that they would never normally think of picking – or perhaps for pulling up vegetables and bringing them to us to sell in mock bazaars'. There was also the man at the gate: 'The *dewan* was perhaps one of our greatest friends and he used to join us in our games whenever he possibly could. One of the games that we used to have again and again was collecting various flowers and making up a brew and dyeing things, and he joined in to such an extent that he let us have all his clothes and his white uniform, which was dyed yellow – and he got into great trouble for this.'

When the children ventured beyond the compound there were eager escorts, as Nancy Vernede remembers from her childhood in Allahabad: 'The *syce* was probably the servant I knew best, because I used to ride my pony every day. All I really did was either walk or trot or canter slowly up and down the road outside our house while the *syce* either walked or jogged along by my side. I think we carried on a non-stop conversation. I learnt nearly all my languages from him and he was one of my best friends.'

For the *baba-log* language was the least of barriers: 'We used to talk to our servants in Hindustani. In fact most children learnt Hindustani before they learnt English.' Adults had their reasons for wishing their children to speak to Indians in their own language: 'My parents always told the servants to speak to us in their own language,' explains Nancy Vernede, 'partly so that we could learn the language, and partly because they didn't want us to keep the *chee-chee* English accent, a singsong accent rather like Welsh which I believe originated from the original missionaries in India who were Welsh and were the first people to teach English.'

For all the familiarity and affection there remained 'a friendly barrier between us and the servants', so that 'you were always treated with respect. You were called little master and you just took it for granted.' The *chota* sahib, in particular, enjoyed a special status: 'In talking to a small English boy the Indian servants used to use the same word that they themselves used when speaking to an old man, particularly a religious old man or a *saddhu*.' Not surprisingly, such respect led to abuse. The young George Carroll remembers ruefully how he kicked his *chaprassi*, an ex-soldier who had served with Lord Roberts at Kandahar, 'just to show that I was master'. Being born of the sahib-*log* had given him strange notions: 'I remember my utter disappointment when I learnt that the great Queen Victoria, who was known as the Great White Queen to all Indians, was not omnipotent and she could not, of her own will, order any person to be shot or killed or hanged.'

For John Rivett-Carnac this early deference 'made me have a great opinion of myself. There were many servants and orderlies who treated me as if I was an adult, with the same respect as they treated my father. The result was that I got a very great idea of my own importance, so much so that in later life it never crossed my mind that I could be killed or be in any danger from an Indian.' Even when playing the *chota* sahib could not forget his privileged status: 'Games were rigged so that we always won,' recalls Terence 'Spike' Milligan, whose first years were spent in the Poona military cantonments. If the games were not rigged the results were always the same: 'Even though I had a fine hockey stick from Timothy Whites, the English stores in Poona, they would win the game with a stick taken out of a tree. They beat me at everything – yet I never thought of anything else except the Indians being inferior. I was born to believe that we were the top people.'

But even subordinates had rights and chief among them was caste, as the young Joan Allen discovered when she attempted to water her garden: 'Outside the gardener's hut I saw a nice little earthenware bowl so I picked it up. The *mali* came rushing out of his hut and he was furious. He picked this bowl out of my hands and dashed it to the ground. This was his bowl, and by touching it I had made it untouchable for him, and so he broke it.'

Other restrictions had also to be observed. Neither parents nor children would think of entering the servants' quarters without warning or permission. The native bazaar was also out of bounds and was thus a constant source of fascination to all European children, as Deborah Dring asserts:

Our parents always thought we'd catch something if we went down to the bazaar. But my brothers and I always looked upon the bazaar as being too exciting. All those lovely stalls covered with sticky sweets and silver paper and piles of fruit and those little flares they lit, the old boys sitting stitching clothes or boiling things in huge *dekshis*. I'll never forget the smell – partly a very strong spice, an incensy smell – and all the heat and the movement and the people and the colour. There was a little temple which had rows and rows of little brass bells all round. If you were a good Hindu you jingled all the bells as you passed, and I remember thinking, 'Now that's marvellous! If only I could go past and jangle a few bells.' But no, the bazaar was a forbidden land when I was a child.

Daily routines were always well established. The children woke early to the sound of crows, had their *chota hazri* – a banana, perhaps, or a glass of fruit juice – and took morning exercise. Prams were soon abandoned. Instead: 'You were placed in a saddle which had a ring round it so you couldn't fall out, and you were led by a *syce* and taken out for a walk.'

After an hour's ride there was a bath and a change of clothes –
a complicated process if you were a girl. 'White starchy
petticoats, white starchy knickers, starchy cotton frock, all of
which were pulled up on tapes round one's neck and were so
hot. Hats made of cotton or muslin which were starched and
then hauled up like a mob cap on a string to fit over your *topee*.
When they got the slightest bit damp they flopped all over
your face.'

Breakfast was taken with one's parents, often on the verandah or under a shady tree. The older children started
lessons and the younger ones played in the garden until it
got too hot. Out with the sun came – invariably – the topee:
'We were never allowed out in the sun without a topee on our
heads, and we were very severely punished if we forgot our
topees. They were very pretty, but very uncomfortable.'

A light lunch would be taken early and then, after a long
siesta, more dressing up; 'It didn't matter how hot it was in the
afternoons,' continues Nancy Foster, 'we were always changed
into white, frilly dresses, usually starched with big sashes. Very
pretty but intolerable in the heat. In the morning we were
allowed to have our hair screwed up in a bun on the top of our
heads for coolness, but for some reason in the afternoons we
had to have our hair hanging down over our shoulders and
very well brushed and this was very hot indeed. We were full of
envy of the little Indian children running about with almost
nothing on.'

At teatime one's father might be expected to put in an
appearance, to 'collapse into a chair which had legs sticking
out and a cane bottom and put his feet up and savour a cup of
tea and anchovy on buttered toast, before changing and going
off to the club to play his game of squash or tennis'. If the
children went out to tea they took their own milk 'because
nobody trusted any other mother to boil the milk properly.
Everyone was very germ conscious because of typhoid and
dysentery and all the various things you could catch. So all the
children used to go out to tea with their bottles of milk

wrapped in tissue paper.' The milk usually came from the nursery cow which, in Iris Portal's household, 'was brought round to the verandah every morning by the *gai-wallah*. He used to milk it in front of our Scottish nanny who was supposed to watch over the milking to make sure first, that his hands were clean and secondly, that he didn't put water in the milk.'

If the children lived up-country and the station was large enough, tea might be taken at its focal point. 'We generally used to meet other children at the club. Most English clubs in India had very good gardens so all our nannies used to like going there and chin-wagging to each other outside the club.' In smaller stations the children might well have only adult company. 'I think the nearest European child must have been twenty miles away,' remembers Joan Allen, the only daughter of an indigo planter, 'with another about thirty miles away. It was very, very seldom that we met. One was a little boy who was about four when I was about nine, and yet I used to be frightfully pleased when he came over and played with me.' Similarly, there were other children, the sons and daughters of forest officers, perhaps, or of those whose jobs took them deep into the *mofussil*, who grew up as close to nature as any latterday Mowgli. John Rivett-Carnac grew up in the jungles of Bengal, surrounded by wild animals: 'We ran completely wild, climbing trees, shooting small birds, looking for birds' nests and seeing how far into the forest we could go. We used to set traps for wild cats at night with a hill boy from a jungle tribe who helped to look after us and taught us jungle lore. He showed us what was dangerous and what was not. We used to get a lot of fun turning stones over for dangerous snakes, which we killed.'

Although snakes presented no major threat to Europeans in India, they had still to be avoided. A pet mongoose often helped. Another well-established manner of ridding oneself of snakes was snake-charming. Lewis Le Marchand remembers how a king cobra was once observed under his father's office and a snake-charmer sent for: 'I can remember the fellow playing this extraordinary flute instrument for hour after hour after hour. This went on for several days but nothing happened and the servants would say, "Oh, yes, it will happen, we'll get him out." Then finally this huge snake, a hamadryad probably about six feet long, was piped out, literally, from its lair underneath my father's office. It came out swaying to the music and by that time my father and his assistant were both there with 12-bore guns and despatched it.'

A much greater threat to European children was rabies. 'We were never allowed to stroke dogs; there was always the fear of rabies. For a long time we weren't allowed to have dogs because of this.' Sometimes the fear became a reality. F. C. Hart was five when he was bitten: 'This dog came into our house one morning while I was having breakfast and bit me on the shin under the table. Later in the afternoon it returned and attacked my younger brother, biting him rather severely. Eventually the dog was killed and found to have rabies. We were immediately ordered up to the only Pasteur Institute in India, at Kasauli in the Simla hills, and we left that night. This was a distance of about four hundred miles.' Treatment lasted three weeks and involved a course of very long hypodermic syringes driven into the stomach. Even then the Hart family's troubles were far from over. On the day before he was due to leave hospital the younger boy was asked to stay on another night: 'That night the nurses had some custard pudding for their dinner and, liking my brother, they asked him if he would have some. Being a child he said yes, so they gave him some pudding and some also to the little girl who was in the bed alongside his. That night fourteen nurses and these two children died of Asiatic cholera.'

Disease and death were a constant preoccupation: 'There were many, many sights that you never forgot. The armless and legless beggars and the lepers. You would see them and your servant would take you away.' Sometimes you could not be shielded, as in the year of the world influenza epidemic, when Vere Birdwood rode to school in Simla with the road-side ditches full of unburied corpses: 'I had a *syce* of about nineteen of whom I was very fond and we used to chat as we went along the Simla roads to school, and then one day I heard that he had been struck down and, two days later, he was dead. In a strange way the piled-up corpses meant much less to me than the death of my *syce*.'

Diversions came at regular intervals with the festivals, both Indian and British. 'We loved the Indian festivals,' says Nancy Foster. 'Some were very frightening, like the *Holi* festivals in which we were never allowed to join. We used to watch from the top of the house, rather fascinated but rather frightened. Some of the goddesses were beautiful, some were terrible. We used to ride out on our ponies and watch them being made in the villages from wire and straw and clay, very cleverly and beautifully modelled. I think the only one that put any terror into us was *Kali*. We never liked *Kali*, she was grotesque in our eyes, but the others were very beautiful.' As well as the spring festival of *Holi* there was the Mohammedan festival of *Mohurram*, originally a festival of mourning, but to Deborah Dring and her sisters more in the nature of a carnival: 'We looked forward to the *Mohurram* far more than Christmas or Easter. Men used to come gambolling into our garden dressed up as horses and do a most extraordinary dance in front of our house. They used to give us sweets – which was absolutely forbidden – which we used to eat. It seemed quite the most perfect festival.' After the Rains came *Diwali*, the festival of light, when the children copied the servants and 'lit lights in little clay dishes with oil in them and a twist of cotton, and placed these lights on the gateways, along the walls, along the sides of the houses, windows, steps, anywhere'.

Christmas was heralded with catalogues from the big Calcutta emporia, the Army and Navy Stores, Whiteaway's and Laidlaw's, Hall and Anderson's. Best of all, from the young Spike Milligan's point of view, was the big Army and Navy catalogue:

It used to arrive three months before Christmas which was just enough time for you to rush through it and order things for Christmas. A large part was devoted to the military services and I remember this complete page of how to go on a military picnic. There was the tent and there was a gentleman opposite with this picnic outfit on, which consisted of shorts, gaiters up to the knee, boots and a topee. There was a lady with a hat and a great net over her face to stop the mosquitoes, with two children likewise garbed. And then there was a series of stools, one made very large to take the bustle of the lady. And there was a servant's tent, much smaller and inferior, with a hole in the side through which you could shout, 'I want so and so!'

I found it more interesting to look through this book than the Boy's Own Annual. I used to mark with a red pencil all the toy soldiers I wanted and then on Christmas morning there would be a parcel from the Army and Navy Stores with the band of the Royal Marines in a red box, all with blue and white helmets, a box of Cameron Highlanders charging and Arab horsemen at the gallop.

Attempts to reproduce an English Christmas were rarely a success. In Western India Father Christmas arrived on a camel, elsewhere, on an elephant. In the railway communities he very often came on a loco engine. In the bigger stations there would be picnics and, of course, fancy dress parties, but the one local Christmas tradition that suited India perfectly was the Christmas Camp: 'The Christmas we liked best of all was when we used to go up into the jungle camping with my father. We used to go out on the elephants and watch the shooting, and we'd camp and fish. That was the best Christmas present.'

Camps were a feature of the cold weather, as were the tours undertaken by a great many fathers in their official duties. Touring in the days before the widespread use of motorcars had a leisurely pace of its own, as Iris Portal recalls from her own childhood:

I can remember the sun just rising, pink on the huge, great plain and being wrapped up in a quilted Rajput dressing-grown and put into the cart pulled by two ponies called Peter and Polly, while my parents rode. We proceeded slowly along because the camp kit had to be put on camels. We had a special nursery camel and the man who drove it had a red *puggaree*, and there was a terrible day when the nursery camel fell down and everything was broken.

An advance party would have struck a few tents for us at the next stopping place and we would get there in time for a late breakfast. Then my father would set up his table for petitions and we would be turned out with our toys to play among the tents, with nanny keeping an eye on us – although she and my mother also did a lot of first aid and medical work for villagers who came in. We were always told not to slide down the tents but, of course, it was a great temptation to scramble up part of the tent flap and come sliding down.

I can remember watching my father sitting under a tree with this crowd of petitioners around him and thinking what an important person he must be because he had all these people standing round the table. But it was the simplest thing, just a tree in the middle of an open plain and a wooden table underneath it, and that was how a district officer did his job in those days.

Towards the end of the day he and mother would go out with a gun to shoot something extra for our meals, because in those days game abounded. I can remember one camp on the edge of the jungle where father went out and shot a bear and I was made to stand beside it holding the rifle. I was very frightened because I didn't feel quite sure that the bear was dead. I remember the smell of the bear and the cordite of the rifle, which made a great impression on me One had toy bears and it seemed so sad that the bear should be shot.

Another daughter of an ICS officer was Nancy Vernede: 'We seemed to travel mostly on elephants from camp to camp. We had a rough mattress thrown across the elephant's back and tied with a rope and we just sat on top. If we ever went into the real jungle the grass would be well above our heads and the elephant would move through slowly and very, very quietly and one could see many more wild animals.' At night, lying under a mosquito net, which 'gave you a great feeling of security', the children heard the sounds of the jungle and, in particular, the sounds of the jackals, which were said to howl, 'I smell the body of a dead Hindu! Where? Where? Here! Here! Here!'

The cold weather ended abruptly in mid-March. Then, as Nancy Forster describes, the annual migration of mothers and children to the Hills began: 'We usually left about the end of March and came back when the monsoon had broken, so we were usually away for the very hot months. But even then it got so hot sometimes that you got terrible prickly heat, and that was a thing you never forgot at night. You would wake up with sweat pouring down your face and you'd hang over the side of the bed trying to get cool.' To reach the nearest hill station could mean a journey of several days and nights in a train: 'Usually you had a whole carriage to yourself, a first class carriage with four bunks in it, two up, two down. You'd have a tin bath in the centre of the floor with a great big block of ice which used to be renewed at the stations, and there would be two small fans that used to blow down on the ice and keep you really very, very cool. We loved these journeys. At night when you stopped at the stations and you looked out you saw the vendors going up and down past all the forms asleep on the platforms and heard the various calls they used to make.'

For Spike Milligan, too, the train journey, which could be a tedious business for parents, was 'a golden experience. One time we were going along and we came across a whole British regiment bathing stark naked in a river. I remember my mother saying to my Aunty Eileen, "Don't look, Eileen, don't look, they're all males." Then one dark night I was lying looking up at this chain and I thought, "I wonder what it's for?" and I just pulled it. The train came to a grinding halt in the middle of some mountainous area of India and there was a slow walk of footsteps and the Goanese guard said, "Did somebody here pull the chain?" My mother was terrified.'

Each district had its hill station to which wives and children and senior officials retreated and sat out the hot weather and the rains; Ootacamund in the south and, in the Himalayas – 'which seemed to stretch for millions of miles' – Mussourie, Simla, Naini Tal and Darjeeling. Towards the end of the hot weather came the rains, tremendous downpours that would ease off for a while and then return as endless torrential rain, bringing only temporary relief from the heat. 'We used to rush out,' says Deborah Dring, 'and stand in it and let it pour over us, and we were soaked to the skin. If we could take our clothes off so much the better. We'd be soaked and probably come in to a jolly good spanking.'

For the first years of childhood there were few shadows. The more observant children of officials would have noticed their parents' preoccupation with saving and their fears of the family being left penniless in the event of the father's death; fears which undoubtedly left their mark. But the real threat to happiness was something that no English parent with children born in India could ever forget. 'When my first son arrived,' recalls Kathleen Griffiths, 'I looked at him and I thought, "Oh dear, you'll soon be five or six and then I will have to take you home and leave you there and be separated from you." This is always at the back of your mind, that separation has to come eventually.' Some saw this separation as 'a sacrifice made by children to fulfil the aims – and very worthy aims – of their parents'. But not so the children: 'We never thought of England as home,' recalls Nancy Foster. 'It never occured to us that our home wasn't India.' England was a land of 'straw-berries everywhere', or, as Spike Milligan imagined it, 'a land of milk and honey that used to send us Cadbury's military chocolates in a sealed tin once every four months. England was the land that sent us the *Daily Mirror* and *Tiger*

Tim comics. England was a land where you could get chocolate and cream together for a penny, that's what my mother
told me. But it never happened like that – England was a
gloomy, dull, grey land.'

'When I brought my two children home,' remembers
Kathleen Griffiths, 'we got into the train and the younger
one, aged five, piped up in front of a carriage full of people,
"Mummy, why hasn't the guard come along and asked your
permission to start the train?" and I replied, "Darling, we are
not in daddy's district now! They do not come along and ask
me if they may start the train here. This is England, you must
get used to English customs now!"' And now the children
learnt that most dreaded and incomprehensible of 'Anglo-
Indian' customs – separation from one's parents at an early
age. If it was hard for the parents it was twice as hard on their
children. Not only were they deprived of their parents, but
they were deprived of all the life they had become used to. 'We
had nothing in common with our new friends,' explains Nancy
Vernede. 'They'd never heard of the brain fever bird or the
sound of jackals, and they'd never ridden on an elephant. We
just had nothing in common.'

The regular exchange of weekly mail provided a frail link
between parents and children that weakened as every month
and year of separation went by. 'When they came back on
leave,' says Frances Smyth of her parents, 'they were like
beings from another world – but it wasn't my world.' On the
other hand, as Vere Birdwood observes, 'separation made us
immensely independent, and to some extent independent of
love. I think it probably hardened us. My brother, I remember, would pack his school trunk alone from about the age of
eight. We got used very early on to making our own arrangements for travelling or doing whatever it was. Perhaps it also
helped young men to go out to India at the age of nineteen and
immediately take control of vast districts, take on enormous
responsibilities, far and away beyond anything which their
contemporaries were experiencing in England, because they

had been conditioned earlier at a very vital age to managing on their own, coping with life.'

But India was never forgotten. 'All through the time I was at school and growing up,' recalls Iris Portal, 'India was a land of promise, something I would go back to. One was sustained throughout all those years by the thought that one would go back.'

2

The Tomb of His Ancestors

If there were but a single loaf of bread in all India, it would be divided equally between the Plowdens, the Trevors, the Beadons and the Rivett-Carnacs.

RUDYARD KIPLING *The Tomb of His Ancestors*

At the close of the nineteenth century a powerful tradition of service continued to dictate a choice of career. Few who went into one or other of the Indian services could fail to claim an 'Anglo-Indian' ancestor. It was a fact of Empire: 'One's brothers, one's friends' brothers and so on were all either in the civil service in some part of India, or in the forces or the police or in something else. The men of the family served the Empire as a matter of course.'

In many families a connection with India had been established with Clive and reinforced many times over thereafter. The Rivetts joined forces with the Carnacs to become one of the best-known families of 'Anglo-India'. The Maynes 'flocked into India' from 1761 onwards, leaving 'two graves in Darjeeling, two in Allahabad, one in Saharastra, one in Meerut, one in Bangalore, one in Achola and another in Lucknow'. The first Ogilvies landed four years later in 1765. When Vere Ogilvie married Christopher Birdwood, the 'boy next door' –

and the son of the Commander-in-Chief – their offspring became in due course 'the sixth and seventh generation of children who had started their lives in India'. Some families specialized. When Rosamund Napier married Henry Lawrence in 1914 it was an alliance between two great families of soldiers and administrators. When John Cotton entered the Political Service in 1934 he was the sixth generation in an unbroken male line to serve the East India Company prior to 1858 and the Indian Civil Service thereafter.

The 'Anglo-Indian' family cherished its ancestors, whose achievements and eccentricities coloured and influenced the lives of its youngest members. The Maynes remembered Augustus Ottoway, killed at the Relief of Lucknow in 1857 and found dead on a *dooly* by Lord Roberts who 'took his dear friend Mayne out at early dawn and dug his grave and buried him in his frock-coat and top boots, and as they laid him there leant down and fixed his eye-glass into his eye as he always wore it in the heat of the fray'. His grave now lies on the seventh fairway of Lucknow Golf Course, 'a cause of great frustration to golfers'.

Vere Ogilvie heard stories of her grandmother, who went out as the young bride of Ogilvie *Dandi mar* or 'Ogilvie Beat-with-a-stick': 'The first thing that confronted her in this very lonely station in the Punjab was a compound full of native women with whom he had solaced his solitude, and several suspiciously pale-faced children running about. In keeping with the mores of the period, once my grandmother had arrived the native women were put aside. Nevertheless, it was not exactly a happy beginning for the bride and the story goes that my grandmother found a little comfort in the friendship of a very good-looking Pathan orderly who appears in many family photographs and is reputed to be the father of my eldest aunt, long since dead.'

Grandfathers and even fathers, exiled from home for many years on end, often seemed larger than life to their estranged children and grandchildren. Olivia Hamilton's grandfather,

Resident in Kashmir during the Mutiny, was said to have drawn a line round a great deal of Kashmir and told the Rajahs that if they allowed their women to throw themselves on to funeral pyres the English would take that much of their country. Geoffrey Allen's grandfather had taken the young Kipling under his wing to work on his Lahore newspaper, the *Civil and Military Gazette*. Kenneth Warren's grandfather had pioneered tea growing in the tropical jungles of Assam, and was followed by a son who travelled alone for three months up the Brahmaputra river after being told that he would never come out alive. Kenneth Mason's uncle, who had taken part in the Great Game as an intelligence officer on the North-West Frontier, was said to be part of the make-up of Colonel Creighton in Kipling's *Kim*.

Few families were as packed with legends, both dead and living, as the Butlers. There was Uncle Charles, known as 'Smith of Asia', Uncle Willy who led a lonely life as an Assam tea planter and 'kept a tame bear which used to hurry people off the estate', and Uncle Harcourt, an outsize figure in every way, of whom Indian mothers in the *terai* sang to their babies, 'All is peace and quiet because the great Harcourt Butler Sahib is taking care of us, so my baby can rest in peace'.

If certain families made India their vocation so, too, did certain peoples: 'Anybody with a Celtic streak was immediately more at home in India. They seemed to integrate better than the very conventional English.' Ever since the late eighteenth century, when India proved 'a godsend for the younger sons of the Manse', Scots and, to a lesser extent, Ulstermen had dominated the administration, continuing to provide nearly half the ICS well into the twentieth century. They also provided engineers and planters. According to Kenneth Warren, threequarters of the Europeans in Assam came from Aberdeen or elsewhere in Scotland.

The pattern of generation succeeding generation continued almost without diminution into the twenties and thirties. But there were other factors – romantic, practical, even involuntary – that caused this last generation of young men and women to strike out for India, knowing full well that Independence was going to come and that 'we were really there to guide it on its way'.

The romantics were those who were early 'victims of propaganda' and of the Empire's chief propagandist. 'The answer to why I went to India is Kipling,' explains Philip Mason, who went out as a member of the Indian Civil Service. 'When I was a small boy I had an absolute passion for Kipling and read everything I could get hold of. Something in those stories appealed to me enormously and gave me a romantic desire to go to this country.' This appeal reached far beyond the usual range of readership. The common soldier, whose enforced service in India Rudyard Kipling chronicled with such humour and sympathy, held him in rare esteem. Many of those who followed in the footsteps of Privates Ortheris, Learoyd and Mulvaney knew by heart 'Boots' or 'Gunga Din' or some other barrack room ballad. 'His soldier poetry and his Imperial stuff fired something in me and drew me to India,' remembers Stephen Bentley, a serving soldier in the Seaforths. Kenneth Mason who followed his uncle's footsteps and, in his turn, played the Great Game in the Karakoram, was a self-confessed disciple of Kipling: 'Kim was an atmosphere I lived in from about the time I was fourteen till I went out to India.' Others were fired by the writings of Flora Annie Steele or Maud Diver, or by the tales that old soldiers brought back of leaning out of barrack room windows and 'picking bananas and oranges off a tree', or 'shooting tigers from one's bed either before or after breakfast'.

Also to be numbered among the romantics were those thousands of young girls who went out to find love and marriage and willingly – sometimes blindly – followed fiancés and husbands into an unknown sub-continent beyond the splendidly marbled Gates of India that stood on Bombay's waterfront.

Realists chose India either because it promised them a life they could not lead elsewhere or because it came nearest to unattainable goals. For Arthur Hamilton, who went into the Indian Forest Service, India could satisfy his love of mountains and woods; for 'Jackie' Smyth, India offered campaigns on the Frontier and for John Morris, then with the Leicestershire Regiment in France, the very opposite – a chance to escape from the trenches of France. Others with military leanings had ambitions that could not be realized in England. 'I wanted to go into the cavalry,' states Reginald Savory, 'and my father, who was not a poor man by any means, nevertheless said he couldn't afford to put me through a good British cavalry regiment and if I wanted to join the Cavalry I'd have to go to the Indian Army and join the Bengal Lancers.' It was also a question of finance for Claude Auchinleck: 'In those days you couldn't live in an ordinary British Infantry regiment unless you had about a hundred a year, which today would be about six hundred a year. I had to either get into the Gunners or the Sappers – in which you could live on your means – or join the Indian Army.'

Money, and the lack of it, pushed many young men towards India. H. T. Wickham was told by his guardian to go and earn a living: 'He threw me a civil service book and said, "Take your choice." I saw the Indian Police and I saw the subjects for examination and I decided that I would go for it, although I had no leanings towards India or even the police for that matter.' Despite the legends that persisted, the prospect of making money and of shaking the pagoda trees of Calcutta and Bombay was no longer a realistic one. The days of quick fortunes made by men who risked much had gone with the John Company Nabobs and the importation of Victorian standards of rectitude and incorruptibility. Yet the established trading houses could still offer adventure and prospects to the right sort of public schoolboy, one who was ready to take on early responsibility and could survive the harsh baptism of a 'first tour' of four or even five years deep in the *mofussil* without a home leave.

The massive unemployment of the inter-war period meant good recruiting for the British Army, which provided India with a substantial if steadily decreasing garrison of British County and Cavalry regiments. 'The situation in '27 was very poor,' remembers Ed Davis, 'so one day my father said, "Would you like to join the army, because we can't afford to keep you in clothing." So I joined the Dorset Regiment and that was the start of my career in the army.' The recruits were not always given a choice: 'We were lined up on the square and they numbered us all. Numbers one to six went into one regiment, seven to twelve into another.' For these young Britons the Indian 'tour' was a rather bad legal joke: 'A soldier contracted to serve four years in India but there was a clause whereby the four years could be extended under certain circumstances, such as transport difficulty or what have you. As a matter of hard fact those circumstances invariably arose and so the soldier served what he bitterly called his *buckshee* year.' The British soldier's India was a very different one from that experienced by most 'Anglo-Indians'. Service in India would prove that caste applied as much to Britons as to Indians.

Nearly all the young men joining the Indian civil and military services – as well as those who went into business – shared the common background of the English public schools. When John Rivett-Carnac applied to join the Indian Police Service he observed that 'the mentality of the applicants was that of the public school prefect. We were very innocent of life in general. We were straight from public school, we had had no contact with adults but for the occasional schoolmaster. We had no idea at all about sex, we had no experience of English people who told lies and we never doubted the word of a fellow Englishman.' Yet it was precisely this innocence that made them ideal officers to govern a country like India, because they had the strictest ideas of truth, honesty, fair play and decency.

The better public schools – in particular Rugby, Marlborough and Wellington – supplied the Indian Army with its officer material. Since the Indian regiment had fewer British officers than the British regiment, vacancies were limited and the competition among those entering or passing out from Sandhurst was correspondingly fiercer: 'The stock of the Indian Army was so high that they could afford to give us an extra six months training and then only take the top twenty-five.'

The Indian Civil Service, which provided India with its administrators, magistrates and judges, sought out its recruits chiefly from Oxford and Cambridge. 'You couldn't read Kipling,' remembers Philip Mason, 'without knowing that the ICS was the premier service and that it ran the place.' It was an elite service, few in numbers, and could afford to pick and choose. Indeed, it was said with only slight exaggeration that nobody without a first class honours degree stood a chance. Successful applicants took a further year to learn both a vernacular and a classical language as well as 'something about the history of India and the law'. Some found this extra study 'an atrocious waste of time'. Penderel Moon had an 'efficient though eccentric teacher at Oxford who used to delight in counting backwards from one hundred in Urdu and seeing the shortest space of time he could do it in. We were never informed that the language of the Punjab was Punjabi and rather different from Urdu, with the result that when I got there I was most upset to find that I couldn't understand a word of what was being said. We went out totally unprepared.'

With fourteen provinces to choose from most recruits for the civil services put down the Punjab or the United Provinces. Penderel Moon chose the Punjab 'because that was the fashionable thing to do'. On the advice of a friend Philip Mason went for the United Provinces, because it had 'nicer people'. Less successful or bolder candidates got the 'undesirable' provinces like Bengal. A privileged few followed their fathers, so that 'a young man coming out before the First World War, being the son of a man who'd been in the ICS before him, was greeted in the station that he went to by people who'd known him as a baby, and they would give that man utter and complete loyalty, because he was the son of his father'.

Before final appointment there was a covenant or contract to be drawn up with the Secretary of State for India: 'A declaration that you would obey the Viceroy and behave as a decent chap and agree to the conditions laid down under the regulations of that present government.'

Having committed themselves, the young men had to kit themselves up and prepare for embarkation. Those who sought advice from old India hands were told to get 'one good pair of riding breeches and get them copied out there by a *derzi*, and to take a shotgun and a saddle'. The less well advised allowed themselves to be fitted up by Gieves of Old Bond Street with pith helmet and palm beach suits and duck clothes – half of which they discarded when they got there. Edwin Pratt, going out to join the Calcutta branch of the Army and Navy Stores, was persuaded to buy a tropical suit in the form of tussore: 'It was a bright yellow and I was told that that was what people wore out there. When I put it on people laughed at it and said, "Where the hell did you get that?" It was the bane of my life!'

None were put to more expense than the newly commissioned subalterns, who were required to buy their own uniforms, together with a sword and a revolver. Since British officers in Indian infantry regiments were mounted they were also expected to buy their own saddlery and, in due course, their own horses. 'The military tailors had a very expensive monopoly on providing kits for officers,' recalls Jackie Smyth. 'The fitting-out came to something like £150, which my mother couldn't possibly afford, but it was understood that every officer had to have all these things. If it hadn't been for my old headmaster who got together one or two people to pay the bill, I would never have gone. When I got out there I found that an Indian *derzi* would rig up all the things that you wanted for practically nothing. At least half the bill, if not threequarters, was quite unnecessary.'

The enlisted man in the British Army – the British Other Ranker – had no such problems, since everything was decided for him. Drafts were sent out at intervals and when names appeared on the notice board it was a great source of excitement. After a month's embarkation leave the men drew their new tropical kit: 'You were fitted with a cork helmet, a spinepad which hung over the back of the helmet to protect the back of your neck from the sun, and the usual khaki shorts and jackets.' In the traditional army manner 'the kits you were issued with at home were never suitable for the regiment you were joining. The khaki was a different shade, your hose wasn't the right colour, the puttees weren't the right shape or size and everything had to be bought afresh, out of your own money, of course, from the *derzi* shop.' The men were also issued with pith helmets and topees. 'I saw the difference immediately,' says Ed Davies, 'the pith helmet was a clumsy looking contraption, very thick but very light, whereas the topee was very sophisticated and smart, with a *puggaree* wrapped round it bearing the green flash of our regiment. It was much heavier as it was solid cork.'

Others were also given topees – and parental advice. 'The three most dangerous things that I had to watch out for in the East were wine, women and the sun,' remembers Rupert Mayne, 'and I had to keep my topee on after Port Said, the self-same topee which my father had brought back when he retired and which had resided in the attic in its tin topee case. I also gave an oath to my father that I would never shoot East of Suez without cartridges of sufficient calibre to be able to defend myself against a dangerous animal. My father had been attacked by a panther near Meerut when he was partridge shooting; a fellow officer had shot at it with No. 5 12-bore cartridges and it had attacked my father and got him in the shoulder.'

The British troops were also given advice. Before final embarkation they were issued with a booklet which told them 'not to go down to the brothels, to wear a pith helmet or topee at all times during the day and not to drink water outside the cantonment, as it would be contaminated with typhoid, diphtheria and all the rest of the diseases prevalent in India.' At the dockside others were equally free with advice, as Stephen Bentley describes: 'You couldn't move but there was some do-gooder at your elbow. There was the Salvation Army, there were the Army welfare workers, there were Christian Union people, all handing you tracts and pamphlets not about India or anything connected with India, but about the way of life that you should lead – on a much greater spiritual plane than you were ever likely to encounter in any part of India. The troops were embarrassed but they didn't show it and they took all the literature as they always did and stuffed it in their pockets and never read it.'

Some were seen off in style: 'I had an uncle who was an admiral who happened at that time to be director of transport, and he, no less, came along to see me off. The result was that Second Lieutenant Savory, when he boarded Her Majesty's Transport *Dongola*, was seen off by this gold-braided gentleman who put the fear of God into the Captain and the Officer Commanding Troops and everybody else!' Others went with less ceremony: 'The last thing an old corporal said to me as he gave me my packet of biscuits and bar of chocolate was, "Now look after yourself and keep away from the women."'

3

Posh

It's so easy to love a little, flirt a little on a big ship, even if a husband or a bridegroom or duty with a big 'D' is waiting on the quay at the other end.
AMY J. BAKER *Six Merry Mummers* 1931

'There was the weekly P & O on which both officers and civilians were supposed to travel. You were thought rather badly of if you didn't support the British line.' Up to the early forties the standard mode of travel to India was on board the P & O 'travelling hotel' from Tilbury or Southampton to Bombay. Those going to South India or seeking to avoid a tedious train journey across India to Calcutta took a BI boat. Wealthy passengers and those prone to sea-sickness bypassed the Bay of Biscay by travelling through France on the 'Blue' train and catching the steamer at Marseilles.

Seasoned travellers had their passages booked on the port side of the ship going out and starboard home, travelling POSH and so avoiding the worst of the sun. The accepted time for 'coming out' was in the autumn. 'The ship was mainly full of people returning from leave,' recalls Kenneth Warren of his first voyage out, 'either civil servants or military or business people and quite a number of young girls going out for the Christmas holidays to stay for two or three months during the

Cold Weather with their relations or friends. In those days they were known in India as the Fishing Fleet.' The Fishing Fleet was by long-established custom made up of the 'highly eligible, beautiful daughters of wealthy people living in India. This was the only way in which they could come out under the protection of their parents, to meet eligible young men and marry.' Those who failed returned to England in the spring and were known as the Returned Empties.

Besides members of the Fishing Fleet, there would be other women on board the outgoing liner. Norah Bowder was following another tradition by going out to be married in Bombay by special government dispensation. Her companion was the wife of a friend of her future husband who spent her nights weeping, because she had left her little girl behind in boarding school. Sometimes the mothers stayed behind and saw their children settled into school and then it was the fathers who returned alone from home leave. Some of the young men, too, were less than cheerful. 'Leaving England was really worse than going back to school,' recalls Penderel Moon. With him on board the *Viceroy of India* were a number of new ICS recruits, both Indian and English. 'Amongst many topics we discussed on the voyage out was how long the Raj was going to last. This was in 1929 and the general consensus was, "Well, at any rate it'll last about twenty-five years, which will entitle us to proportionate pensions." We were fully conscious that we were on a sinking ship, as it were.' Yet there was also the idealism of youth. 'We were all for conferring self-government on India,' declares David Symington, another ICS recruit, 'I visualized myself very rapidly achieving the ambition of becoming a viceroy and handing over the government of India to its elected representatives at some kind of big *durbar*.'

These young men who went out after the Great War regarded themselves as different from their predecessors, the 'funny old boys' who came back from India: 'We were quite clear we weren't going to be like that.' None the less, the codes of behaviour established by their predecessors continued to make themselves felt on board, as John Morris soon observed: 'The protocol which went on in most military cantonments was carried onto the P & O. If you saw a major or a colonel in front of you, you naturally stepped aside to let him pass, and if you were late coming back when we called at various ports you were sent for by the Captain of the ship and asked why you hadn't come back when you heard the ship's siren going.' The social divisions of 'Anglo-Indian' were also quick to establish themselves. Rosalie Roberts, going out as a missionary nurse, noticed immediately that there were different groups: 'The military were separate, the ICS and government people were definitely on their own, and the planters, and then there were mothers with children going out to join their husbands. The purser arranged the tables very carefully for all the different groups.' Not always successfully, however, since her husband-to-be, the Reverend Arfon Roberts, found himself seated at a table of hard-drinking planters, one of whom, on hearing that a missionary's salary was £165 a year, informed him that he spent that amount in one month on drink alone.

Norman Watney, going out with one of the last groups of British recruits to the Indian State Railways, soon found himself observing another 'Anglo-Indian' convention: 'We had come to the signing of chits, which meant that everything was signed for and at the end of the week the cabin steward put on your table a nice bunch of notes, ringed by a rubber band which invited you to pay the total at the purser's office at the first opportunity. This signing of chits was a pleasant business because no money was needed and every time you signed you felt a feeling of affluence creeping over you. But as time went on and hotter weather came, drinking increased, the bills increased and it was difficult to restrict this signing, particularly if you were with others probably richer than yourself!'

As the voyage progressed it was also observed that 'evening dress was not now just plain black. Some were wearing black trousers and white dinner jackets, some were wearing the opposite. Enquiries soon revealed that the more important clubs in India had their own ideas of what should be worn. For instance, it seemed that the Punjab Club members must wear white jackets and black trousers, and Calcutta Club members black coats and white trousers, and so on. All this struck us as rather peculiar at the time because we had neither.'

Nevertheless, life on board the passenger liner was, as Rosamund Lawrence remembers, 'very pleasant and lazy – and I was very much intrigued by a young man who'd taken possession of a girl. These two simply couldn't be parted from one another; she'd go and knock on the door of the smoking room and he'd come out and then they would spend their time dancing together on a threepenny bit. I was only a young girl, about seventeen, and I was rather shocked with this – and very fascinated.'

Shipboard romance was a predictable feature of every voyage. But here, too, as Frederick Radclyffe Sidebottom observed, protocol had its place: 'I can remember one famous occasion when a governor's daughter happened to be a passenger aboard the ship. The first class was full of very stuffy people and she took a fancy to a very handsome young second class steward and when the fancy-dress ball was being held she danced with him all night, and the next morning – they having parted, perhaps, only half an hour beforehand – he approached her and she froze him absolutely stiff in his tracks and said, "In the circle in which I move, sleeping with a woman does not constitute an introduction."'

Some shipboard romances were rather happier. Kathleen Griffiths, going out to India as a governess, rose early one morning to see the sun rise: 'There by the side of me was a young man to whom I had not then spoken also admiring the sunrise. We had a few words, and after this we discovered that we'd been drawn in a deck game together. And from there on our acquaintance developed. In a few days under a full moon on the Red Sea we became engaged, much to the delight and interest of many people on board ship. In my cabin there was a rather senior lady who, rather looking down upon me as a governess, said, "Oh, I hear you've got engaged to young Griffiths. You've done well for yourself, haven't you. Don't you know? He's one of the heaven-born – the Indian Civil Service!"'

For one minor but significant section of the 'Anglo-Indian' community the voyage out was anything but a romance. The British troops went out on small, over-crowded 'vomit-buckets'. 'I don't think there will be one man who went to India on a troop-ship who won't remember it as one of the most sordid memories of his life,' declares Stephen Bentley. 'The officers got three-quarters of the ship with their lounges and smoke rooms and luxurious cabins, and the troops got only the troop-deck.' Troubles began with accommodation. Some men found that there simply wasn't any, so the unfortunate ones had to pick up their baggage and get up on deck, a favourite place being round the funnel, where it was warm, or under the boat deck. Then there was the problem of hammocks, as another soldier, E. S. Humphries, explains: 'On the very first night out from England two or three men lost their hammocks – and it grew like a snowball. Each night more and more people lost their hammocks and more and more people had to sit up and lie awake until they managed to pinch someone else's hammock because no one could face the indignity of being the sucker in the battalion who arrived in Bombay minus his hammock.'

But it was the Bay of Biscay that very often set the seal on the voyage:

When you see a thousand men in the throes of the most appalling sea-sickness and realize what it entails, then you have some idea of how awful it was. The whole administration just went to pieces. No one came round to see that the men were fed, no one came round to see if the men were really ill or just sea-sick. No one came to see that the latrines were working – and they weren't, so that the overflow from the latrines was swishing all over the middle deck. There was very little water. You couldn't get into a wash place, you couldn't get to your kit and worst of all, you couldn't get to your hammock. It looked like the carnage of a battlefield. I can honestly say that in the first five or six days I never saw an officer on the troop-deck. I don't think the troops resented it, because that was the sort of thing that you got in those days.

Once into the Mediterranean, however, prospects improved. There were concerts, with a wealth of talent available on every troop-ship, and there was housey-housey, the army version of bingo, run by members of the crew, who would make money out of it. There were also the unofficial gambling schools. 'The crown and anchor board boys who used to perform down in the bowels of the ship, with look-outs posted all the way up to watch out for the military police coming round.' Then there was PT every morning, and lectures from a medical officer on every danger to life in India from cholera and snake bites downwards, adding almost as an afterthought that 'On the other hand, you'll be much healthier than you were in England, because you won't catch colds.'

The East began at Port Said, where 'the bumboat men came alongside and tried to sell you things. They used to throw a rope up to the ship's side with a basket attached. You'd pull it up, put your money in the basket, lower it down to them and they'd put in oranges, apples, bananas or whatever it was.' Port Said was also where little boys dived for pennies and where the 'gully-gully' man came aboard. 'The gully-gully business was a family affair,' explains Kenneth Mason. 'Before finishing a trick he used to say "Gully, gully, gully, gully, gully." The people on board were gathered round and when he was going to produce a chicken from some lady he would say, "Now come on, Little Langtry, what are you doing with a chicken?" It was his patter. The last time I went out East Mrs Simpson had taken over from Lillie Langtry.'

The men who went ashore – always in parties since it was dangerous 'even for British people' – were introduced to the unsavoury aspects of the East: 'We went to a casino where we were duly robbed of our few odd shillings, we were taken to a brothel from which we had to drag one of our number and, of course, there were the smutty postcards.' For both sexes there was also the ritual of topee-buying at Simon Artz, since 'when one arrived at Port Said it was the accepted thing for every newcomer to buy a topee'. As Percival Griffiths recalls: 'No young civilian ever got out to India by sea without falling into the clutches of Simon Artz, where you were always inveigled into buying a Curzon topee which you probably never wore the rest of your life, because what you did wear was an old pig-sticking topee that you probably bought in Calcutta or when you first got to your station.'

Through the Suez Canal, too narrow for ships to pass unless one was tied up to the shore, and a halt for coal at Aden where 'coolies carried small buckets on their heads, up planks from the shore'. Then 'sharks, flying fish and no land for miles around for days on end', the routine only broken by an occasional passing ship. Ed Davies remembers the excitement on board at 'the sight of a troop-ship passing our own, going back to Blighty. We all rushed to the side shouting, "Troop-ship! Troop-ship!" and we felt our ship list. They could hear our cheers and we could hear theirs. So there were two ships nearly sinking, as we shouted hysterically at each other.' In the meantime it would be growing palpably hotter on board ship. The troops now wore tropical uniform on deck and a pair of shorts below deck. 'Even those travelling on P & O liners before the advent of the electric fan had to sleep on deck,' remembers Kenneth Warren. 'The cabin steward took your bedding up and put it on deck. The men all slept on one side and the women all slept on the other side. If possible you had your bedding put on one of the hatchways so that when they came to wash the decks down early the next morning you weren't disturbed.'

The voyage drew to a close: 'During the last few days a feeling of excitement did begin to build up. There was the hot, sunny weather, the flying fish dropping little droplets of water onto the smooth sea – everything seemed to be beautiful.' There came 'a difference in the air or in the atmosphere or in the heat or in the way the wind blew or possibly even in the smell,' and then the smell of India, 'difficult to pinpoint, partly the populace, partly the different vegetation, partly the very rapid fall of dusk and the cooling off which leads to a most lovely scent just after sundown.'

Then landfall: 'The *ghats* leading up to the Deccan mountains rising to three or four or five thousand feet, and all the foothills very green after the monsoon, the sea very blue, the buildings mostly white and looking rather gorgeous from the sea, and altogether a feeling of opulence and luxuriance.' Finally, disembarkation and first impressions. 'I felt happy,' recalls Ian Stephens, 'that somehow or other I belonged here, that this was the sort of place for me, and I've often wondered whether something like an ancestral memory wasn't ticking over, whether my great-grandfather and my grandfather and my uncle weren't in me in the reactions I had to the Indian scene.' Other reactions, like those of John Morris, were less favourable: 'I thought what a terrible place it was, with rather shabby Victorian buildings; architecture once described by Aldous Huxley as "a collection of architectural cads and bounders". It did seem like that.' Reginald Savory, expecting to find something full of magic, found instead 'a very ordinary, rather unpleasant, dusty country'. Even so, 'that was the first time in my life I saw an officer dressed up in khaki drill, which thrilled me to the marrow. I had visions of Piper Finlayson and Kipling and all those chaps'. Similarly, to drummer-boy Ed Brown, then just fourteen years old, 'it seemed as though the dream world I'd read about had come true; waving palms, coloured people, beautiful coasts, rock pools with mother-of-pearl flashing. I thought it was a dream land.' But not for long: 'An Indian woman holding a baby came up to me and said, "You're the father of my child, Sahib, give me some money, I want *baksheesh*." '

"PUKKA" LUGGAGE.

The absolute reliability of which is guaranteed to each purchaser by a bond supplied with every article, undertaking to keep same in repair free of charge for 5 years, and replace gratis if beyond repair. No complicated conditions but a simple, straightforward guarantee

"PUKKA" SUIT CASE.

No. G.G.44.

Covered with brown flax-canvas, fitted with leather straps inside. Two good locks and clip in centre.
Registered design.

Size 22 by 15	by 7½ in.	£3 15 0
„ 24 by 15½	by 8 in.	4 2 0
„ 26 by 16	by 8½ in.	4 9 0
„ 27 by 16½	by 9 in.	4 12 0
„ 30 by 17	by 9½ in.	5 10 0

"PUKKA" IMPERIAL.

No. G.G. 45.

Covered with brown flax canvas, fitted with tray 4½ in. deep, with 2 web straps in tray and body of trunk. Two good locks and clip in centre.

Registered design.
Supplied to order.

Size 30 by 19 by 17 in.	£9 4 0
„ 33 by 20 by 18 in.	10 2 0
„ 36 by 21 by 19 in.	11 0 0
„ 39 by 22 by 20 in.	11 12 0
„ 42 by 22½ by 21 in.	12 19 0

"PUKKA" WARDROBE TRUNK.
No. G.G. 46.

Covered with brown vulcanised fibre, fitted with drawers, garment hangers, coiled linen bag and shoe box. Strong clips, lock, brassed corners, locking bar to secure drawers.

Fitted with airtight waterproof and dustproof adjustment.
Covered green Williesden canvas.
To order.

"PUKKA" WARDROBE TRUNKS.

"PUKKA" HAT-BOX.
(Ladies'.)

No. G.G. 47.

Covered with brown flax canvas, fitted with removable wire fittings on which to fix hats or bonnets. One good lock and two clips.
Registered design.
Supplied to order.

Size 20 by 16 by 16 in.	£5 19 0
„ 23 by 18 by 18 in.	6 9 0
„ 24 by 20 by 20 in.	7 3 0

"PUKKA" CABIN.

No. G.G. 48.

Covered with brown flax canvas, fitted with tray 4 in. deep, with 2 web straps in tray and body of trunk. Two good locks and clips in centre.
Registered design.

Size 30 by 19 by 14 in.	£7 7 6
„ 33 by 20 by 14 in.	8 2 6
„ 36 by 21 by 14 in.	8 17 0
„ 39 by 22 by 14 in.	9 12 0
„ 42 by 23 by 14 in.	10 6 6

"PUKKA" WARDROBE TRUNK.

Size 37½ by 21 by 14 in. (6 hangers and 5 drawers) (supplied to order)	£13 14 6
„ 40 by 21 by 14 in. (6 hangers and 5 drawers)	13 13 6
„ 40 by 21 by 16 in. (6 hangers and 6 drawers)	14 5 6
42 by 21 by 21 in. (10 hangers and 6 drawers)	16 13 6

ALL PRICES ARE SUBJECT TO MARKET FLUCTUATIONS.

The native population – 'thousands of people moving, moving, moving' – could hardly be ignored. 'There were people in the streets and people working in the fields and your house was full of servants. Wherever you turned your head there were servants.' Nor could the sun be ignored: 'When you walk out of the customs shed into the sun of India it hits you like a blow, and it continues to do that all through the years you're in India. Every time you walk out of doors during the middle of the day you feel as if you've been hit by something. It's a mistake to think that people get used to heat – they don't. When they first meet it it doesn't worry them, but when they go on encountering it year in year out, then it begins to wear them down.' From the moment they set foot in India BORs were commanded 'never to move anywhere between sunrise and sunset without your topee. If you were ever found out in the sun without your topee you got fourteen days confined to barracks.' In the event, a topee was not enough: 'After a couple of hours the whole of our necks were red, all our arms were red and our knees were red and beginning to blister. That's how hot it was in Bombay, and if it hadn't been for a cool breeze blowing in from the sea we would surely have been roasted alive.'

Receptions varied according to status and connections. Those of high degree or with connections were garlanded and their luggage seized by *chaprassis* in scarlet uniforms. Some were met by shipping agents and shepherded through customs. Others had less auspicious introductions. The troops' baggage was loaded on to supply and transport – or 'shit and treacle' – wagons and while they waited on the quayside they began to understand why India was known to seasoned veterans as 'the land of shit and shankers'. Stephen Bentley met his first beggar, whose head was a mass of running sores: 'I thought it was his hair at first, but it was black with flies, and it came to me very forcibly in that moment that this was the East and one of the things you are going to live with in the East is flies.'

E. S. Humphries, disembarking with the 1st Battalion, Royal Scots, met the 2nd Battalion about to embark: 'The 2nd Battalion were all spick and span, upright, soldierly-looking people, lithe and suntanned, many of them wearing moustaches. We poor souls, just off the ship after weeks of lolling about on deck and with no opportunity to shave, to wash properly or wash our clothes, looked a decrepit-looking lot by comparison. However, on further inspection it was seen that two out of three of these fine, stalwart-looking, lithe fellows were in fact sufferers from malaria. This could be seen by their yellowish skins, their sunken cheeks and their fleshless limbs.'

After inevitable delays at the docks – 'They gave us a couple of packets of cigarettes and a meal and said, "You're on your own for today"' – troops were often moved to Deolali transit camp, where mental patients on their way to Netley Mental Hospital had their papers stamped. Thus 'Doolally tap' came to mean 'someone a bit round the bend'.

At the transit camp the British soldier made his acquaintance with the kite-hawk, known familiarly as the 'shite-hawk'. 'There used to be thousands of them,' remembers Charles Wright. 'When one drew one's food from the cook-house and went to take it across to the dining room to eat at the tables underneath the sheds, these kite-hawks would swoop down and take the lot off your plate if you weren't careful. So you had to walk waving your arms above the plate until you got in under cover.'

For the great majority of travellers Bombay, Karachi or Colombo was only a staging-post in their journey. But before proceeding up-country some further – more practical – kitting-up was often required, as Norman Watney describes:

> We were recommended to go to an emporium called White-away and Laidlaw, known universally as 'Right away and paid for' because of the necessity of paying in ready cash. White-away's had acquired the distinction of being solely for those

with small purses and had a large clientele of junior officers such as ourselves. Others in a more senior position used to go down the road about a quarter of a mile away to the Army and Navy Stores.

We went along in a four-wheeled Victoria, a musty-smelling apparatus with a driver who must have been at least ninety, and eventually landed at this rather imposing building. The doors were thrown open by stalwart Pathans in grandiose uniforms and we were directed to a counter where we obtained all the necessities required by the junior officer during his first tour of duty. The assistant was able to tell us that it was not expected of people in our position to buy indigenous articles; it would not look good for us to be seen to have inferior equipment and for this reason only the best would do.

First we had to have a canvas hold-all fitted with two heavy straps with internal flaps. Into this were put sheets and pillows, together with a sort of mattress filled with kapok. This was the *bistra*, or bedding roll. In addition we had to have an enamel basin, together with a top cover made of leather with straps running underneath. With these two articles you could travel the length and breadth of India.

4

Aliens Under One Sky

English men and women in India are, as it were, members of one great family, aliens under one sky.

MAUD DIVER *The Englishwoman in India* 1909

Frequent transfers and movements over great distance were recurrent themes in the 'Anglo-Indian' experience: 'As official people we were constantly on the move,' recalls Vere Birdwood. 'After I married we moved fourteen times in fourteen months, and a move was not just packing a couple of suitcases. It had to be planned like a major operation.' With the exception of the *pukka* Grand Trunk Roads that linked the larger stations of upper India, the road systems of India were best suited to the bullock cart. The natural lifelines of India were its great rivers, familiar to Nancy Foster both as child and adult: 'The river was vast, almost a sea at certain places. It could be very cruel, very dangerous with sudden storms, or it could be very calm and beautiful. It had a great many moods. You could see for miles from the decks of the steamers. You'd see fishermen with their long, slim boats, shaped like the new moon. You'd see the much bigger dhow type of boat with huge patched sails, sometimes made of matting. Then there'd be the humans packed solid in small boats crossing from one side to

the other. Then you'd see the river steamers with their big
paddles, taking the jute down to Calcutta. At times the river
was so narrow that the jungle almost brushed you as you went
past, endless birds, endless animals. Then you'd come to great
wastes of marshland and nothing much there, just sky and very
beautiful.'

If the rivers were the old lifelines of India, the railways were
the new. A criss-cross of broad-gauge railway lines united
India with a tediously slow but efficient system of communication that blended most agreeably with both Indian and
British life styles. Before the Indian train journey all other
forms of travel paled into insignificance: 'To people who lived
in backwaters, leading very quiet, humdrum lives and not
really seeing an awful lot of the country it was like going to the
cinema nowadays, the complete panorama of India.' The
Indian railway station was part of the social fabric of India.
At night 'every platform was a mass of sleeping forms wrapped
in cloth, always heads covered with the feet sticking out', over
which passengers changing trains had to pick their way. By day
'you'll find beggars curled up in the shade, you'll find the odd
pi-dog wandering around looking for food, the stationmaster
would be having his afternoon snooze and the whole place is
dead. But the people are there just the same, all curled up,
waiting. They've probably waited for their trains for a couple
of days.' Trains drew in to a crescendo of excitement and
sound, as the station came to life: 'A terrific gabble in either
Hindustani or Tamil or Telegu, probably all of them. Men
with *dhotis* running along with things on their heads, men with
broken-down umbrellas trying to get onto the train. You'd see
people clinging on the carriage, even on the roof, and the
stationmaster trying to pull them off.' There were also the
station vendors and sweetmeat sellers with their hawkers' cries
that quickly became familiar to the traveller: '*Hindi pani,
Mussulman pani,*' from the water carriers who sold water to
Hindus and Muslims separately; '*tahsa char, garumi garum*', hot
fresh tea from the tea vendors; '*pahn biri*', cigarettes and betel

nut, even 'Beecham *Sahib ki gooli*', Beecham's pills for those
who required them. Less attractive were the child beggars who
hung on to carriage windows as the train pulled out, 'screeching and looking at us with great big spaniel's eyes until you had
to tap their knuckles, so that they would drop off all along the
platform like little flies'.

The railway carriages themselves were 'highly hierarchical',
reflecting the social structure of British India. Yet if they were
'very luxurious in the upper classes, the distances were great
and the fatigue great and, in summer, the heat great'. As a
newly appointed assistant superintendent on the Indian State
Railways bound for Lahore, Norman Watney's first experience of Indian trains was made aboard the Frontier Mail: 'A
four-berth carriage had been reserved for us with a self-
contained toilet compartment with a shower. All Indian railway carriages had the doors fitted with a throw-over catch
which effectively bars entry from the outside. Furthermore, the
windows, which were in triplicate – glass, venetian blinds and
gauze – were also latched, so you were in a pretty impregnable
position. We asked what would happen if anybody else tried to
come into our compartment and were assured that nobody
would turn up. No Indian would dare to attempt to come into
our compartment so long as he saw more than one European
therein.

'To break the monotony of the journey it was possible to go
and have a meal in the European dining cars, which were run
only on the mail trains and only between certain junctions. If
you wanted a meal you had to get down from your carriage,
lock it up, go down the track, jump into the dining car and stay
there till the next stop.'

Indian trains were not free from dirt or disease. Seasoned
travellers brought their own bedding and ensured that the
floors of their carriages were swabbed down with disinfectant.
Some even went so far as to take a bottle of Evian water with
which to clean their teeth, because the water on the trains was
considered to be impure. If the travellers were of some rank

they might well be approached by the stationmaster for permission to proceed.

There were also troop-trains and once again, as Stephen Bentley records, the contrast was extreme:

We were put in six to a compartment and told to settle down. Which is just about the last thing you can do in any compartment on an Indian military train. They were about ten feet by eight feet in area and in each compartment there were racks, slotted like park benches and about two feet apart. You had all your kit, you had all your equipment, you had your blankets, you even had your greatcoat rolled up – and it all had to be stowed away. Having no room it was absolute chaos.

Like everything else in the army, we had been taught to make the best of a bad job. We had our emergency rations and we ate them and, as night falls very quickly in India, it was dark by the time the train got on its way and we were only too anxious to get the racks down and go to sleep. The train had been left in a siding all day and the heat in the compartment was fearsome. So, of course, we pulled all the windows down and set the fan going at full speed and went to sleep. Within the space of minutes the temperature had gone from hot to almost zero and we were nearly freezing. I never heard such cursing up and down the carriage.

Meals had been arranged at predetermined stations along the line, so that the train couldn't get there before time and couldn't get there after time. It had to get there military fashion, dead on time. You got out and there would be a group of military cooks on the platform with all their pots and pans and stewpots. In all my years in India I don't think I ever ate a meal on a station that wasn't smoked. It was nearly always stew and rice pudding, of such poor quality that very few of the troops ever ate it, and most of it was given to the begging Indians, of which there were usually scores, or to the pariah dogs that always seemed to be waiting for troop trains.

Nothing so clearly demonstrated the depth of India as that first train journey. Its size was brought home to Christopher Masterman as he crossed the Madras presidency: 'It took us two days and nights to get up to Madras, and there's more of the presidency north of Madras than there is in the south.' Travelling across central India to Bengal, Percival Griffiths was struck by the enormous variety of the country: 'Long before one knew one type or one caste from another, the variety hit you in the eye. You felt you weren't going to a country, you were going to a continent.'

Frances Smyth saw this 'continent' with a painter's eye:

> The country stretched to eternity. The sky was immense and the whole horizon was far away. And you were very small in this immensity and in some curious way this gave you a heightened awareness of everything about you. There was this visual pleasure of great dun flat landscapes, no colour practically, and then against this beige, the trees. You would see the sudden flaming patch of scarlet, which was a gold mohur tree. The tree is the most important thing in India – a green shade. There are great big trees, banyans, with roots that grow down from the branches so that you get a kind of forest of roots. The old men of the village sit there and everybody comes and life goes on under this tree.

First impressions of the terrain were not always encouraging. Penderel Moon, travelling northwards into the Punjab, thought it 'a terribly dry, unproductive, unattractive country. Endless rocky hills with a few brambles or prickly bushes, no nice green verdure or waving crops. And when I got to the Punjab I was aghast at the flat, featureless character of the countryside and the constant wastes of sand and cactus bushes.' By contrast others moved across landscapes rich with fields of blue linseed and yellow mustard and backed by acres of sugar-cane. Others, yet again, found themselves in tropical jungles, in marshy alluvial plains, in snow-capped mountain ranges.

Yet the land also had its common elements: 'the curious, perfectly horizontal lines of fire smoke near a village in the sunset and the cows coming back to the village in the evening, with pale, pale golden dust hanging over the slow movement of the cows.' The evening, rich in scents and sunsets, and turned by dust 'into a sort of bowl of rosy milk', brought with it a sense of affinity. Even if the day seemed to take out most of the charm, 'when you got to the evenings you could begin to feel, "Well now, this is a country which I could belong to – if I didn't belong to a nicer one."'

The Indian sub-continent contained two Indias. One third of the land – scarcely known to any but a few British 'politicals' – was fragmented into 562 nominally independent princely states. The other two thirds of India came under the direct administration of the British Raj and were divided into four-teen provinces, each subdivided into districts. Thus, the United Provinces were divided into forty-seven different dis-tricts and in each the key man was the district magistrate, the deputy commissioner or the collector.

Socially, British India was divided in a far simpler manner: 'There were two areas of life, one of which was life in the big cities – Bombay, Calcutta and, to a slightly lesser extent, places like Delhi and Lahore – and the other the vast *mofussil* – "up-country" – which really embraced all the other stations to which Europeans were sent. This could be some really remote part of the country where perhaps you and your family were the only Europeans, or it could be a small military or civil station with perhaps fifty or one hundred Europeans living outside.' Those who lived up-country generally had a low opinion of those who did not: 'We considered the Europeans in Bombay or Calcutta, who dwelled only on business matters and dealt with Indians who were equally interested only in commerce, to be ignorant of the real India, whereas we in upper India had a much more intimate connection in the form of administration through the police, roads, buildings, the ics and so on.'

Although the political axis shifted from Calcutta to Delhi in 1912, the former remained pre-eminent as the business centre of India. The old East India Company had been replaced by a handful of managing agencies, which had built up small empires of their own and ran their companies from head offices in Calcutta. As 'the most revolting' or 'the most horrible' city in Asia, Calcutta had no serious rivals. To Percival Griffiths, one of the very few to move from admin-istration into commerce, it was 'a city of gulfs' where 'nobody knew anybody outside their own particular sphere. The civil servant didn't hob-nob with the businessman. The Indian businessman didn't hob-nob with the British businessman. The Bengali businessman didn't mix in with the Marwari businessman. It was a city of four or five quite separate communities which hardly mixed at all.'

For newcomers like Edwin Pratt, joining the Calcutta branch of the Army and Navy Stores, the extremes of Calcutta began at Howrah Railway Station, which 'was smothered with human forms all in very primitive attire, sitting and standing and wandering about, some eating, some cooking and some just sleeping'. Outside there was Howrah Bridge, 'a mass of moving humanity and merchandise jolting over the humps where the pontoon sections were joined together, in bullock carts, buffalo carts, rickshaws, gharries, taxis, buses and private cars, quite apart from the hundreds of pedestrians on either side'.

On the other side of the Hoogly River 'British' Calcutta was almost a world apart; its splendid Maidan flanked by palatial government buildings – a racecourse, cathedral and an os-tentatious memorial to Maharanee Victoria. To the south there was Chowringee with such European emporia as the Army and Navy Stores, Hall and Anderson's, and Newman's. There was also the Great Eastern Hotel, the first place in Calcutta to be air-conditioned, and the Grand Hotel, which was said to be 'over-run with rats but comfortable'. There was Spence's, a small planter's hotel mainly frequented by men

and an 'absolute gem of India' where, as Radclyffe Sidebottom describes, 'you could get exceedingly good food and
with a vast billiard room where you could play billiards and
snooker. The decor was entirely early Victorian, the various
rooms being divided by lattice-work teak and cherry wood and
with *punkahs* pulled by *punkah-wallahs*.' There was also Firpos, a
smart Italian restaurant where, if you ordered whisky – 'which
you could any hour of the day or night – you were not
measured a peg, you were given the bottle. You went on
drinking that bottle and when the bill finally came along the
servant stood in front of you with a thumb against the mark
where the drink had gone down to and you were charged by
that amount and it was never, ever questioned.' Another
famous lunching place was Peliti's, in Old Court House Street,
where on Fridays 'you could guzzle yourself to death on just
one rupee'.

Calcutta also had its residential areas, which reflected its
social divisions: 'There were the old parts of central Calcutta
where the old palatial *burra* sahibs' houses had been built, left
as a legacy to those who came on afterwards, and around them
came the new buildings, blocks of flats where the young sahibs
lived when they first came out. But as you became more senior
and you wanted tennis courts and more servants, you moved
into what would be called the suburbs. Ballygunge was the
second stage, and Alipore, built under the wing of Belvedere,
which had been the old vice-regal lodge and which therefore
contained that air of sanctity, was the final stage.'

Up-country the social – and racial – divisions were even
more clearly marked. Each district had as its focal point the
Station, consisting of 'the cantonment where the military
personnel lived and worked, the civil lines where the civilians
such as the ICS and canal people and the police and forest
officer and so on lived, and then the city, which was just a mass
of small shops and rather smelly drains and was very densely
populated. In the civil lines one had the Club, which was the
meeting place for both army and civilian personnel of officer

status and was a wonderful forum for gossip and games of all kinds, dinner, dancing, swimming, golf, squash, polo and so on.'

Military cantonments on the larger stations contained barracks for both British and Indian regiments, with their own family lines near by. Such stations were classified as first, second or third class. Ed Davies' first station at Meerut was a first-class station where 'everything was clean, white-washed and red-ochered, so that if you looked at it too long it sort of blinded you. The bungalows were all well separated with bits of green in the front, and were very spacious with big verandahs.' Meerut had special associations for the British for it was the 'Mutiny Station'. Iris Portal, married to a cavalry officer, lived for four years in the lines where the Sepoy Mutiny first began:

> On the gates of the bungalows were plaques which said, 'Here Mrs So and So and her three children were killed and thrown down a well,' or 'Here Captain and Mrs So and So were found hiding and killed' and so on. There was one bungalow near by where they had to take their beds out into the garden, not only for the heat but because things happened, like doors blowing open when there was no wind. Dogs would never stay in the house, and it was emphatically haunted. They all felt it and they all hated it, and that was one of the Mutiny bungalows with a plaque on it. In the church, where both my children were christened, you could see the places at either side of the pews where the side-arms were stacked.

By contrast, Jhansi was a third-class station. 'I don't think there were many stations in India worse than Jhansi,' declares Stephen Bentley, whose detachment of Seaforth Highlanders found themselves in this 'punishment station' because they had celebrated Hogmanay back in Aldershot rather too enthusiast-ically:

The barracks were miles away from the town and what town there was was really only a small railway settlement. There was only a very poor bazaar of about ten or twenty shops. There was one corrugated-iron cinema. There were no cafes, no shops, no civilian population except the population of this railway settlement which was principally Anglo-Indian or half-caste. As soon as we got to Jhansi the first order that appeared was that you shan't go into an Indian village. Then they put the civilian lines – this settlement of Anglo-Indians, which would have provided some diversion or change – out of bounds. So anyone coming to Jhansi realized that hence-forth for as many years as he had to serve in Jhansi – which in my case was four – his life was the barracks, the canteen, the regimental institute or a walk round the roads immediately surrounding the cantonment.

In addition to its quota of British civilians and military personnel, any station that was on the railway line had a 'railway colony' composed for the most part of Eurasians – officially termed Anglo-Indian – and domiciled Europeans. A specific number of subordinate posts in the central services – the police, customs, railways and telegraphs – had been set aside for this twilight community, which saw itself very much as the 'back-bone of the British administration'.

Outside the main stations there were the lesser outposts of British society, such as Darbhanga – 'a complete backwater that had once been a thriving community of indigo planters' – where John Morris was marooned for a year:

The times had gone forward and left it behind. It was full of huge bungalows, mostly unoccupied, and nearly every one had a curious little outhouse attached to it which used to be known in the early days as the *bibi-khana*, the place where the lady was kept – the lady being the planter's Indian mistress – a practice that went out with the arrival of the memsahib. I could have lived like a white rajah in one of these huge, decaying bungalows, but I decided instead to live in a tent in the camp where the troops were quartered. The first result of this was that my bearer – an ancient who had been in the regiment for many years – resigned because he thought that my doing this was not behaving in the way that a sahib should. The curious thing about Darbhanga was that there was a huge club there with a polo ground, all beautifully kept up. And one day an ancient gentleman with a hennaed beard, apparently a servant of the club, asked me if I wished to join. And I said, 'Well, what goes on in the Club?' And he said, 'Oh, the sahibs from the plantations come in at Christmas every year.' I didn't really think that was sufficient reason for joining the Darbhanga Club so I never did. The whole place was a ghost club really. The cloth on the billiard tables had faded to a sort of bilious yellow. There were a lot of books, mostly Victorian novels, mouldering away and the whole place was really most depressing.

The architecture of 'Anglo-India' came in three basic forms and was rarely distinguished. Palaces, public buildings and the larger railway termini were frequently 'unsuccessful Victorian attempts to synthesize Gothic with Saracenic'. Rather more successful was the 'English Palladian style adapted to India in the latter part of the eighteenth century', such as the British Residency in the native principality of Hyderabad, which reminded Olaf Caroe – then a very junior army officer – of the London Athenaeum and made him wonder if there wasn't something to be said for the Indian Civil Service if its political members could live in such dignity. In Southern India and Calcutta senior officials still inhabited relics of the first British settlements. Christopher Masterman, living in the Collector's bungalow in Cuddalore, where Clive had lived, found it 'architecturally very fine but very unsuitable as a modern residence, with walls six feet thick or more and very small windows on the ground floor – and vast rooms on the first floor which were impossible to furnish'.

Equally historic, but of a far simpler architectural design, was the Deputy Commissioner's bungalow in Peshawar, where Olaf Caroe followed in the footsteps of Edwardes and Nicholson, two of the great nineteenth-century Bayards of British India: 'A very pleasant mud brick bungalow with high, cool rooms and a wide verandah standing in wide lawns with huge banyan trees that dropped branches down to the ground.' This was the archetypal up-country bungalow, to be found in Eastern and Upper India and in the smaller stations, built 'facing the north-east, the coolest aspect, the rooms very high and very large in order to remain cool during the hot weather. There was no sitting room, only the verandah. In the old days the walls were simply a skeleton of timber framework with reed rushes plastered over with earth mixed with cow dung, then painted with whitewash; very suitable from an earthquake point of view. With most bungalows you got a thatched roof and then the ceiling of each room was a hessian cloth painted with whitewash. Between the hessian cloth ceiling and the thatch roof was a space which was usually inhabited by bats and often by snakes – you could look up and sometimes see a snake wriggling along the other side of the cloth.'

In Assam and Bengal a local variation, known as the *chung* bungalow, put the bungalows on pillars to avoid floods, with a bathroom under each bedroom, entered through a trap door. Percival Griffiths recalls that, before taking a bath, 'it was advisable to take a tennis racket with you, because bats used to come in and always seemed to want to have a splash in the bath beside you'.

The third form of residence, the *pukka* bungalow, most often found on the larger stations, was an evolved version of the country bungalow; often a two-storeyed structure, flat-roofed and incorporating arcades with Tuscan columns and round Renaissance-style arches. Variations on these basic themes were limited, 'so that one knew exactly what sort of accommodation to expect when one moved on transfer'.

Backing up these three basic forms of housing were the government *dak* bungalows, situated at strategic points throughout the countryside and which themselves came in three forms: 'The plains inspection bungalow consisted mainly of a living room which was flanked by two bedroom suites complete with bathrooms. The hills bungalows were double-storeyed and basically consisted of the same accommodation but on two floors. And the old forts were very old buildings dating back to 1700 or 1800, commandeered and made into very comfortable inspection bungalows.'

Against this topography of set and identifiable structures the *chokra*, the young man fresh from home, set out to make a *burra nam* for himself.

5

Learning the Ropes

No deep division severed then
The Powers that Be from other men;
But all was friendly to the core,
When Thompson ruled in Thompsonpore.
SENEX *The Golden Age* 1933

Philip Mason's arrival at Saharanpur typified the introduction
to the civil station that many young men experienced:

I arrived in the middle of the night, which one almost always did in
India. I don't know how they managed to arrange this on the
railways, but it was very cunningly arrived at. I was met by a man
two years older than myself, who was killed playing polo about a
year later. He met me at the station and drove me to the
Collector's house, where I was put into a tent, a great big
marquee. Its floor was covered with straw, with a *dhurri* laid over
it and there was a bathroom at the back. I was astonished at how
comfortable it was and how fresh and clean and pure the night was
in December up in that corner of the UP. In the morning I looked
out and I saw trees which looked so like English trees stretching in
every direction, the most delightful landscape. There was a feeling
of freshness and vigour which I have never forgotten.

I met my Collector for the first time at breakfast. He came in from his morning ride and said, 'Hello, Mason, I've got a pony for you that you can buy immediately after breakfast if you like. There's a dealer here and you might like to buy it. Work? . . . no, you don't need to do any work your first year. Here's a book about polo, you can read that and I'll examine you on it this evening.' Also that first morning, very early, there came a long procession of officials who said, 'Sir, I am the *nazir*, have you any orders for me?' and 'Sir, I am the *tahsildar*, have you any orders for me?' I simply couldn't think what to do with any of these people, and I only gradually found out who they all were and how they all fitted into the hierarchy.

Young subalterns joining the Indian Army spent their first year attached to a British regiment: 'The object was to see whether under service conditions you were really fit to be an officer of the Indian Army – which entailed a good deal more responsibility than in the British Army. It also gave you a year to get used to the country and the people.' Some British regiments made their attached officers feel at home, others made them feel that they were 'outcasts and a nuisance'. John Dring's introduction to life in a cavalry regiment was characteristic – if a little abrupt:

The little train puffed into Mardan before light. I was met by the adjutant in a *tonga* and we rattled off to the mess where I was accommodated in the guest quarters. I had a bath and some breakfast and then I was taken up to the lines by the adjutant and put on a horse. He said, 'Follow me over some jumps,' and put me down a jumping lane, then more or less said, 'That'll do. Come along with me and see the remounts.' So we went over and saw some horses and the adjutant said, 'Take on one of these and go through with the training.' I selected a chestnut mare which looked very nice. The next morning I went out to mount the animal for my first parade and I'd hardly got in the saddle before it was all over the place; I was on the ground, the horse was on the way to the lines and I arrived at my first parade on foot.

Rather less typical was Kenneth Warren's first taste of plantation life in Assam:

Having had lunch, Bertie Fraser – with whom I was to share the bungalow – went off to play polo and I was left sitting on the verandah with nothing to do. I couldn't speak the language so I couldn't talk to the servants and I got more and more hungry. It was not until about eight o'clock that night that Bertie Fraser returned, having played two or three chukkas of polo and having spent the rest of the evening at the bar. He came home full of good cheer and called for dinner and we sat down for a meal. He seemed to be rather a queer sort of fellow; he was telling me all about various matters of which I had no knowledge whatever when he suddenly leapt to his feet, seized the lamp from the middle of the table and rushed out of the room, leaving me in complete darkness. I thought, 'Well, he is mad after all!' Then he started shouting at me from the lawn in front of the bungalow saying, 'Come out, you fool!' Then I suddenly realized that the bungalow was swinging about. I got halfway down the steps when the bungalow gave an extra heave and I slid down the remaining steps. That was my first earthquake.

Geoffrey Allen's beginnings as an assistant manager working for the Maharajah of Darbhanga were equally inauspicious:

Almost my first job was to bury my manager. He had been a very famous, very skilful polo player, a very nice person indeed and very happily married. Unfortunately he had taken to drink and this culminated in him being off work for about a week, when the general manager sent me out to take charge. I was let in to see him and I saw at once that he was very drunk.

The A.-D.-C. ON DUTY.

THE MANAGER HOTEL,

Please order me a

horse	घोड़ा
carriage	बग्गी
Motor	मोटर
elephant	हाथी

at_____ o'clock_____ to take me

to_____

One hour's notice should be given and for Elephant one and a half hour's.

*Signature*_____

Place :—

*Room No.*_____ We found this in. the Guest House at Gwalior.

*Date*_____192

Elephant order form; guest house, Gwalior, 1931

He cursed me up and down and said, 'You can get out of my room. I know you've come out to do me down.' Eventually with very ill grace he handed over his office keys and I took over. One evening, about three weeks later a *chaprassi* arrived on a cycle with a note saying that he had died from the DTS. This was the hot weather and anyone who died had to be buried within twenty-four hours. The graveyard was just beyond my house in a little grove, so I went out that night with a couple of labourers and two lanterns and spent the whole of the night digging by the light of the hurricane lamps. The extraordinary thing was that in this particular graveyard there were also buried the last three managers before this one. He was the fourth, all of them had died from DTS and all had been buried in this same little graveyard.

Other newcomers up-country made their first acquaintance with the land and its people. In Western India David Symington encountered the characteristic smell of the Sind plain, the smell of the salt land cooling off at evening combined with the tamarisks, 'an ammoniac odour which more or less grips you by the throat'. Meeting with 'great respect from the great majority of the inhabitants', he found it 'absolutely right and not surprising'. Kenneth Mason, posted to Meerut, found such respect unnerving: 'An Indian passing me got off his pony and salaamed me. I said to him, "What on earth did you do that for?" and he said, "Sahib, you are a young man. You will realize that in India we salaam those we respect. We do it to our Brahmins, we do it to our rulers." My comment was, "Well, you needn't do it for me."'

Some were temporarily disillusioned. Conrad Corfield, faced with an outside temperature of 115 degrees upon his arrival in Lahore, was lying on his bed trying to keep cool when a sleepy hornet dropped through the ceiling and stung him furiously, making him wonder whether he would not do better as a schoolmaster in England. Others had suspicions that required to be dispelled. Ian Stephens, coming to the

Delhi Secretariat as 'a Cambridge prig', expected to be 'enmeshed in the administrative machine' and instead found his companions 'liberal-minded and far-seeing'. Penderel Moon, assigned to a remote district of the Punjab where there was no European except himself and no Indian officer who spoke English, disliked India at first but found – like so many others – that it grew on him.

For bachelors in the larger stations the problems of accommodation were simplified by the *chummery*, a household shared by three or four persons, with a cook 'who had to be accustomed to all sorts of late hours and producing a meal for any number of friends who might come at a moment's notice'. Since furniture was usually rented, the younger bachelor tended to live in considerable discomfort with only basic furniture; a *charpoy* bed and its mosquito canopy and perhaps some Roorkee chairs, made of canvas stretched on wood – and for the verandah, planter's long-sleevers, with long leg-rests and drink stands attached to the sides. Philip Mason recalls how when some young ladies came to stay in his bachelor *chummery* in Bareilly they were somewhat put out to find no curtains: 'We'd never thought of having curtains on the windows.'

Where there was no memsahib the running of the household devolved upon the bearer. 'The first thing I had to do on arrival in Lahore,' recalls H. T. Wickham, 'was to engage a bearer. There was no end of choice because bearers wanting situations would present themselves in queues with their chits or certificates of recommendation, and one had to choose from that.' Others, like Ian Stephens' Abdul Aziz, 'polished, humorous and excellent with my many guests,' were inherited from predecessors. The bachelor's bearer did the lot. 'When I was a bachelor,' recalls Percival Griffiths, 'I left everything to my bearer. A nice hot chicken curry for lunch and a mulligatawny soup and roast chicken for the evening, and that was the menu every day. He'd bring up the cook book at the end of the week and I handed out the money.' Ghulam Rasul, 'slave of the prophet', would tell his sahib, Penderel Moon, to get his hair cut: 'He used to say, "Your hair's getting long, I'll call the barber." Then I'd sit on the verandah and the barber would cut my hair while he stood and supervised.' Jackie Smyth's bearer was 'a frightful worrier' who never had enough to eat because he wouldn't take enough time off for his meals and made a point of sleeping outside his master's door when in hostile country.

This combination of devotion and personal service culminated with the dressing and undressing of those sahibs who could tolerate it. Cuthbert Bowder put up with it because 'if I hadn't he would have considered it not quite the thing. So my bearer used to undress me before I went into my bath and dress me when I came out of it and this literally meant putting on my socks, holding out my vest and shirt and helping me to put on my trousers and jacket.' Some would not be dressed. 'I found this highly repulsive,' recalls Norman Watney, 'and after two days of being a tailor's dummy I told my bearer to desist.' With a few exceptions – Radclyffe Sidebottom's bearer once enraged him so much that he 'picked him up by the seat of his pants and the neck of his shirt and dropped him down the lift shaft' – most bearers and their bachelor employers built up a close personal relationship that lasted until their employers married. Few such relationships survived the transition, 'because deep down they didn't like to see a European memsahib ruling her husband'. Rupert Mayne's bearer, Abdul, was 'a quite magnificent man but, as so often happens, he was a bachelor's bearer and after I got married we had to start afresh'.

While some sections of the British community – notably officers in British regiments and city businessmen – neither required nor made the effort to learn a native language, elsewhere it was an essential and even a compulsory requirement, encouraged by financial rewards or threats. In the Indian Army, where no soldier was – in theory, at least – allowed to speak English to an officer and no officer was allowed to speak English to a soldier, financial inducements made language study a 'paying proposition'. When George Wood, an officer in the Dorset Regiment, passed the Urdu examination in 1931 he got 'the princely reward of seventy gold sovereigns, which was the price of a pony that I badly wanted'. For Rupert Mayne, in the jute trade, it was a case of having to learn both Hindi and Bengali, as 'in our business contracts we had the ominous words that failure to do so would be taken into consideration in renewing our contracts'. In fact, learning a native language was perhaps 'the best thing that ever happened' to people who went out to India and those who failed to do so remained for ever at a distance from the land and its people.

The man who taught languages was the *munshi*, sometimes a scholar of considerable learning. Olaf Caroe remembers 'a very sweet old man with long eye-lashes and a beard, rather saintly to look at', with whom he had great arguments about Emperor Aurangzeb. 'I used to say that he was a tyrant who had overborne his Hindu subjects and undone the good which his predecessor Akbar had done. The *munshi* wouldn't agree at all. Our argument was a precursor of the deep-rooted Hindu-Muslim differences which have torn the sub-continent apart.' David Symington's *munshi* was Mr Chiplunkar,

> A very dear old boy who used to dress in a white coat, a long *dhoti* hanging low towards his ankles, which was a sign of his high social status, a tight little purple turban wound round the head and a pair of steel-rimmed spectacles. He would come in carrying my yesterday's exercise with him which he wouldn't hand to me, but dropped on my table because, in spite of being a sahib, I was untouchable. We often went for evening walks together so that we could talk Marathi, which we did for a bit, then both of us got tired of my Marathi, and we would speak in English. I learnt a great deal from him about the Brahmin's view of life and about

Indian habits of thought and their views of political and religious matters. In fact he taught me a very great deal of what I've learnt about India.

The *chokra* also learned from his *burra*-sahib. Christopher Masterman, newly arrived in his district, was immediately taken on tour by his Collector, Charles Todhunter:

> We started off very early in the morning and rode through the land inspecting things on the way, and all the time I was being given instructions by the Collector as to what these crops were, when they grew, what their seasons were, how they were irrigated and so on. After these long rides we returned to our camp and had the main meal of the day, which was a combination of breakfast and lunch, generally called brunch. All during lunch Todhunter was still examining me as to what I had learnt during the course of the morning's ride. And then after lunch I was despatched to my small tent to study the Tamil language. Well, after a long ride in the morning and going into a very hot, small tent, I'm afraid that my Tamil studies didn't improve very much. In fact I generally fell asleep.

Conrad Corfield, another junior Indian civil servant, also learned much from example, watching his superior officer on one occasion move into a crowd of Congress demonstrators and 'gaze thoughtfully from face to face as though to mark well the features of each individual and bear them in his memory. No word was spoken but one by one the crowd began to melt till only a few loyal citizens remained.' He also watched him charm the villagers: 'I noticed that each gathering ended in loud chuckles of delight and I soon learnt the reason. He had a fund of Punjabi wisecracks of which few could be translated, most were proverbial and nearly all rude.' Learning 'by being put on a job and requested to get on with it' was another strong feature of the Raj: 'One had an initiative at a young age

which one could never have got in England'. As a newly
appointed assistant chief of police, John Rivett-Carnac 'was
immediately put in charge of up to half the district with every
possible case, including murder, robbery with violence and
riot cases on my hands. The responsibility was very great.' The
responsibilities of the young sub-divisional district officer were
even greater; within a year of arrival and with two depart-
mental examinations behind him he could be dispensing
justice as a magistrate, first class, to some three-quarters of
a million people.

Although 'built on European lines, with the same kind of
taboos and snobberies', British social life in India was different in one major respect: 'It was twenty years behind the
times.' It had also developed customs of its own. For the
newcomer the first and most important of these was dropping
cards on the station. The protocol for this 'absolutely ridiculous custom' was rigidly laid down: George Carroll remembers 'going out in the afternoon and dropping cards on
various *burra* memsahibs, all dressed in my full Indian Police
regalia, travelling in a bullock cart with trotting bullocks, my
legs sticking out at the back with the full sun on my dress
Wellingtons'. It was not enough, as Norman Watney discovered, simply to drop a card at every bungalow: 'As a bachelor
I was to put two of my visiting cards in a little black box that
always appeared on the outsides of my senior officers' bungalows. If the senior officer had a daughter it was the
procedure to put in a third card with the right hand corner
tip turned down. The reason for this always baffled me. You
never got an invitation to dinner unless you had dropped a
card.' Rupert Mayne, sharing a *chummery* with four others,
failed to drop cards on a married couple: 'It wasn't until
they'd been to the house on several occasions that one evening
the lady said to me, "Oh, I do wish that you'd drop cards on
us so that we could ask you back."'

The officers of John Morris' Gurkha regiment, newly
returned from the war, had no cards and as a result 'were

more or less ostracized by the local people because we didn't call on them'. The practice of calling reached absurd proportions in the larger stations, where 'You dressed for the occasion even though you never expected to meet anybody – in fact, it was socially improper that they should notice that you were there.' John Morris recalls how, when his regiment moved to Delhi; 'we were expected to call on all the senior officers at army headquarters and there were hundreds of them, so we used to parcel areas out between ourselves and drop each other's cards'. Just as you left cards when you first arrived, so you left them when you departed, writing PPC in the corner – *pour prendre congé* – which made it clear that you were going away.

The next item on the social agenda was joining the Club. For Norman Watney 'this meant the local Gymkhana Club, as against the Sind Club which was for the higher-ups. Armed with an application for membership my boss took me to the bar and I signed here and I signed there. Then he rushed around and found two other members who put their names on the application. Having now become a member I found that the usual custom was for the *burra* sahib to offer you a drink and without asking me whether I wanted it he ordered two *chotapegs*.' The next move was to revisit the club 'to see whether your cards had been returned. This meant that the senior officers had taken their cards, written your name on the top left hand corner and slipped it into the notice board in the club annexe.' One more essential had still to be completed: 'The Divisional Superintendent announced that he expected all new officers to join the Auxiliary Force of India. Considering it to be part of the white man's burden I had to go. Thus I became a private in the Northwestern Railway Regiment of the AFI.' Local detachments of the AFI, often in the form of Light Horse Cavalry, were to be found in all the stations of India. The Mutiny was not entirely forgotten; only Europeans or part-Europeans were allowed to join this local equivalent of the Home Guard.

The newcomer was also expected to conform to certain social standards. 'The British reputation in India was extraordinarily high,' declares Kenneth Mason who joined the Survey of India Department in 1909, 'I would have been the first to have told a man off if I thought he was lowering our prestige. We had to rule by prestige; there's no question about it. It wasn't conceit. We were there to rule, and we did our best.'

Kenneth Warren, isolated on a tea garden in upper Assam some years before the Great War, always made a point of dressing for dinner: 'If you lost your self-respect you were not looked upon in a respectful and proper manner. So in order to maintain my self-respect I put on a dinner jacket and dressed for dinner and I said to my servants, who were quite likely to get a bit slack just looking after a man by himself in the middle of the jungle, "Now this is a dinner party and every night is a dinner party and you will serve my dinner as though there are other people at the dinner table."' While such staunch attitudes softened considerably in the next two decades 'the attempt to push one into a mould' really only ended with the emancipation that came with the Second World War. Then it was best symbolized by the abandonment of the topee, leaving this 'status symbol of the European community' to be adopted by the Anglo-Indians, 'who practically wore topees in their bedrooms, because of the need to show that they were of European descent'.

The concern with maintaining standards was also reflected in the degree of 'vetting' that went on: 'I was full aware that my background, my actions and my manners were under careful scrutiny,' recalls Conrad Corfield, 'but as my family had connections with India, the name of my public school was known and I'd been through the discipline of an officer's mess, no obvious gaffes occurred.' John Morris remembers that over the question of newcomers joining his regiment 'the most tremendous argument used to go on for days over whether or not the candidate was a sahib and a gentleman.

If he was the most fearful cad that didn't matter – so long as he'd been to the right public school.' This social snobbery could be extremely cruel. Irene Edwards, an Anglo-Indian nursing sister, had to overcome the 'terrible handicap' of a *chee-chee* accent and 'country-bred' manners; 'I had to learn not to offer my hand. I had to learn not to say, "Pleased to meet you." I had to learn to just bow and say, "How do you do?" I had to learn to say "Goodbye" and not "Cheerio" or "chin-chin".' She also had to face the supposed test of mixed blood: 'I remember a young subaltern coming up to me and asking me to open my mouth. I didn't know what he was after, but he looked at my gums and then he inspected my finger-nails. Later on I was told that this young man was looking for the tell-tale blue gums and blue marks in the fingernails found in people of mixed races.'

Lord Linlithgow, Viceroy of India from 1936 to 1943, once admitted to Gilbert Laithwaite, his private secretary, that he had never seen an Indian rupee. Yet even those on less exalted planes rarely carried money about: 'It was like royalty. Everything was done by chit. If you went into a shop to buy something you signed a chit. Practically the only time you ever gave anybody any money was when you gave it to the caddy on the golf course, or to the cook in the morning when he had to go and do the shopping.' The great danger of the chit system was that it was all too easy to be given credit: 'At the end of the month you got a bill. Even though it might frighten you, the fright didn't last for very long. You either paid part of it or none of it and carried on to the next month. You weren't bothered by these chaps; they liked to get you into debt. They knew that sooner or later you'd pay up, to your detriment, perhaps, but you would. And ninety-nine per cent of officers, British Army or Indian, would pay up.' But if you didn't, you were in trouble because the non-payment of bills was looked upon by commanding officers as a slight on their regiment and by employers as a slight on the employing company.

The unfortunate defaulters could, on occasion, be asked to transfer or even to resign.

None the less, the young Englishman, required to live to a certain standard and return hospitality on inadequate pay, was very often obliged to live beyond his means. Herein lay the basis of one more unwritten rule: 'In those days we all married very much later,' says John Cotton, who went out to India in 1929 and married eight years later. 'First of all, we couldn't afford the luxury of a wife and family because our pay wasn't sufficient. Secondly, there was always a scarcity of marriage-able girls and, thirdly, it was actively discouraged in certain walks of life and particularly in my own service. In the Political Service we joined at the age of twenty-six or so and then there ensued three probationary years during which time one was not allowed to get married. If one did get married then one was returned either to one's regiment or, in the case of civil service officers, back to one's province.' Similarly in Assam, as Kenneth Warren recalls, 'it just wasn't done to get married until you were a manager. Then you had a bungalow to yourself and you were in a position to get married. So it was only managers – and senior ones at that – who ever got married in those days.' When a newly promoted assistant manager on Kenneth Warren's tea garden 'had the cheek' to go and get married, the other assistants objected in the strongest possible terms.

Who one married was quite as important as when one married: 'There was one club in Calcutta where you had to come up for re-election if you married, merely for the noble committee and the balloting committee to ensure that your wife was of the requisite material and would not let down the side.' In one of the British regiments in India 'an unfortunate senior subaltern was greeted by every one of his friends about twenty times a day with, "Sam, you're not going to marry that girl" – and Sam didn't marry that girl. The regiment was just making it quite clear that *that* girl was not going to come into the circle.'

But the young sahib did eventually marry. Though he may have kept to the pattern and returned single from his first home leave, thereafter he was free from social restrictions. Before the end of his second furlough the sahib had – usually – found his memsahib.

6

Household

Save for arranging a wealth of cut flowers laid to her hand by a faithful mali, an 'Anglo-Indian' girl's domestic duties are practically nil. All things conspire to develop the emotional, pleasure-loving side of her nature, to blur her girlish visions of higher aims and sterner self-discipline.

MAUD DIVER *The Englishwoman in India* 1909

There was a great shortage of potential wives in India. The Fishing Fleet did something to redress the balance but England remained the chief source of brides: 'Men went home on leave and got engaged and either married during their leave or a year or two later, when the brides would come out to meet their husbands at Bombay and get married within a couple of hours of setting foot on Indian soil. This was made possible by a special act of Parliament which did away with the premarital residential requirements.' Such arrangements did not always go to plan. It sometimes happened that a man went to meet his fiancée off the boat only to find that she had already left with someone she had met on the voyage.

The English bride, as Vere Birdwood describes here, did not always transplant well:

They never entirely integrated with India and this was terribly important as far as the whole ethos of the Raj was concerned. The men were very closely integrated but not their wives. We were in India, we were looked after by Indian servants and we met a great many Indians, and some of us undoubtedly made a very close study of India and Indian customs, but once you stepped inside the home you were back in Cheltenham or Bath. We brought with us in our home lives almost exact replicas of the sort of life that upper middle class people lived in England at that time. It was very homogenous in the sense that nearly everyone in official India sprang from precisely the same educational and cultural background. You went from bungalow to bungalow and you found the same sort of furniture, the same sort of dinner table set, the same kind of conversation. We read the same books, mostly imported by post from England, and I can't really say that we took an awful lot from India.

It was a shock to be met after a calm and lengthy voyage by 'the mass of humanity, the shouting and the jabbering, the smells and the noise, the poverty and the squalor, the cries of "*Bunby, bunby*"'. Mary Carroll, returning to the land of her children, thought it 'perfectly normal' to find a human bone dropped by a vulture on her doorstep in Bombay. But others were frightened and also lonely. 'Take a girl from a background which has no connection with India at all, to whom it's a totally strange country, and it is a frightening country. India frightened people, especially women. They'd been told you caught awful diseases, things like smallpox and so on, and they were all told about snakes and tigers and things which you don't really need to be too worried about in India.'

Since most brides married fairly junior officers or civilians their first homes were often far up-country. Thus, after meeting up with her husband and his colleagues in the Forest Service in Lahore, Olivia Hamilton was required to follow him to his headquarters in the hills, first to the railhead by train and thereafter on horseback: 'My husband brought me a waler – one of those huge Australian things – and he had the funniest little pony I've ever seen, roughly twelve hands I suppose. It either walked or it cantered. We had seven days of riding, anything between ten and sixteen miles a day, so you can imagine me bumping like a sack of potatoes and arriving at the other end barely able to sit down for my supper. But we arrived at what was going to be our little home, a very simple bungalow with just the necessities of life – no cupboards, but tables and chairs and two *charpoys* – and a lovely garden full of fruit and beautiful mountain scenery.' Olivia Hamilton soon found that her husband 'lived on the country. Only *chapattis* and home-made porridge or wheat ground on stones – and therefore full of stones – chicken and rice and no biscuits except ship's biscuits, which he seemed very fond of. If I wanted a plain biscuit or a cup of cocoa I had to write all the way to Lahore, and it took a fortnight to get a parcel and cost the earth.'

Some brides arrived in greater style, as did Rosamund Lawrence when she married the newly appointed Commissioner of Belgaum in 1914:

When we got to the station there was a band playing and banners saying 'Welcome to our new Commissioner' and rows of police on arabs all drawn up in the brilliant sunshine, looking very spick and span in dark blue uniforms with red caps on their heads. They brought garlands of roses and put them round our necks. Then my husband said, 'You'd better do just what I do,' and I saw him shaking hands. There were a lot of messengers and servants in dazzling white starched clothes with scarlet and gold bands all looking much grander than the others, so I started shaking hands with them, which seemed to surprise them. Then we got into a four-wheeled bullock cart painted white outside, with tigers and leopards painted inside, and drawn by great big bullocks with garlands of roses round their necks. We just sat there and rattled along

with rows of people lining the road any saying 'Salaam,
salaam.' I felt like Queen Alexandra driving through Hyde
Park, don't you know!

A decade later, Kathleen Griffiths' introduction to her husband's first sub-division in Bengal was rather less grand. After
losing the bearer and all the luggage on the way they arrived at
Kontai Road Station where the only transport was a lorry:

Halfway along the road, after being smothered in red dust
which blew up from all quarters, we had a rainstorm and a
puncture. We all had to get out on to the side of the road
where I was drenched in rain over the red dust. Eventually we
proceeded to Kontai. Our furniture was supposed to have
arrived but unfortunately it had been loaned to someone who
had not sent it on to us, so for several days we had to stay in a
dak-bungalow. My husband went straight into court and got
on with his business while I borrowed a sheet and sent all my
clothes to the *dhobi* to be laundered. There wasn't another
European in the place within sixty miles of me. I had a week of
this; then we moved into our bungalow and the furniture
arrived – and much to my horror it arrived in pieces. There
wasn't a leg on a table or a chair, the dining table was split
right across, the mirrors were broken, not a glass or a cup was
unbroken; they were all smashed. I felt like sitting down and
weeping, trying to make up my mind whether I was going to
stay in Bengal or pack my trunk and go back to England.
However, I made up my mind. I told myself, 'Well, I fell in
love with this man and I've married him; I'd better make the
best of it.' So I decided to learn the language.

It took time for English culture to re-establish itself. As soon
as the sahib left the house in the morning the new memsahib
was on her own. Servants came for instructions and could not
be answered. Rosamund Lawrence found that she was not
allowed to pick up her scissors when they fell to the floor.

Kathleen Griffiths attempted to plant seeds with a little fork
and trowel, causing a deputation of *chaprassis*, clerks and *babus*
to call upon her husband to say that it was not allowed: 'We
will bring you ten coolies tomorrow to do the digging.'
Wherever Norah Bowder moved in the garden a *chaprassi*
followed her with a deck-chair. She also found – 'to my horror'
– that her husband was being dressed and undressed by his
bearer, 'even to the point of having his bath water poured over
him. I found this extraordinary because when I first met him in
England he was doing everything himself quite competently.'

Some, of course, felt perfectly at home and, indeed, regarded themselves as being back at home. They were the girls
of seventeen and eighteen, not yet memsahibs but with the
probabilities very much in mind, for whom education in
England was merely an interruption of their 'Anglo-Indian'
lives. Having only just arrived at her father's bungalow, Mary
Carroll was killing a centipede in the bath when she heard her
father running round the bungalow downstairs: 'He shouted,
"Lock yourself in your room!" so I did, and then I heard the
most extraordinary noises and a shot every now and then. I
asked what was the matter and he shouted out, "There's a
mad dog. Stay where you are." Eventually he shot it and I
came out and saw this awful, mangy yellow thing and I
thought, "Good old India. This is really it!" '

Similarly, Iris Portal found her father's bungalow perfectly
familiar: 'It was exactly the same sort of bungalow we'd had in
Lahore, and the thing that was very much India to me were
the pots of chrysanthemums. An Indian winter garden in the
north of India always has rows and rows of pots of chrysanthemums. Gokhal, my father's bearer whom I'd known as a
child was still there, and far from welcoming me with cries of
delight – the little missy *baba* come back – he was completely
impassive. But there he was, and that was continuity.' Yet
there was a significant change of attitude: 'Whenever my
father came in Gokhal always bent down and dusted his shoes
with a duster on the steps before he entered the house, and

there was something worrying to me – I suppose I was the beginning of the new age – about any human being bowing right down to the ground before another. But it was an Indian custom and not imposed by the British.'

The memsahib's domain was contained within the compound, generally enclosed by a wall or a raised *bund* and containing garden, bungalow and servants' quarters: 'There was no kitchen as such in the bungalow because the cooking was all done by the natives in the cookhouse, which was part of the servants' quarters. The food had to be brought in from there and kept in a hot-case in the pantry which was in the bungalow. The memsahib did not do her own cooking, it was always done by an Indian cook on an Indian type oven.' In Eastern India where rainfall was frequent a covered gangway often ran between bobajee-*khana* and bungalow. Elsewhere a hazardous gap remained: 'We were having wild duck for lunch,' recalls Rupert Mayne, 'but when it reached the table there was a mound of chips but no duck, because a kite had swooped down and gone away with it.'

The bathroom was equally un-English: 'Now see that hole in the corner there,' Rosamund Lawrence was told by her husband, 'that is to let the water out. Snakes will come in from there, so you must always keep your eyes skinned.' The two main features in the bathroom were the earth closet – 'In the ordinary household you sat on a thing called a "thunder box" for your daily task and the sweeper removed the remains' – and the hip bath – 'You soon got used to folding yourself up in a tub with your knees up to your chin.' Water for the bath was heated up over a wood fire and carried to the *gussal-khana* 'in kerosene tins slung two to each person, rather like an old milkmaid'.

By comparison with the English home, the simple up-country bungalow with its primitive bathroom, white-washed walls and muslin cloth ceilings was an unattractive living quarter. Not surprisingly, memsahibs 'took a great deal of trouble to have nice English rooms, the same as in England'.

Their first difficulty lay with the furniture: 'Just cushions and bamboo furniture and very little else.' What there was might well be standing in saucers of water to prevent the ants climbing up. Many memsahibs had still to familiarize themselves with the *punkah*, 'a long pole which hung across the room with a deep frill of material on it. A rope attached to it ran through a window to a man on your verandah who pulled it and made the fan move the air in the room. As a rule he lay on his back on the verandah with the string attached to his big toe, pulling this string and going to sleep at intervals.' Despite the advent of electricity the *punkah* and the *punkah-wallah* persisted in many outlying districts well into the forties.

The great difficulty with household furnishing was that so many Europeans were constantly moving. Because of this there was 'a feeling of impermanence. For instance, flowers grew very beautifully in the north of India but you knew when you planted some daffodil bulbs that you'd never see them come up. One did plant, and you even occasionally brought some furniture and certainly hung a few curtains, but it was all very transient.' Movement or the lack of it underlined the differences between the various sections of the British community: 'Whereas we in the army were on a mobile basis and hired our furniture, the businessmen stayed in one place year after year and of course they furnished their houses on a much more lavish and solid scale, many bringing out their furniture from England.' Others found it less expensive to have furniture made for them locally. It was considered 'rather smart' to have your own furniture: 'it showed you were better off than your neighbours.' Those forced by occupation to move frequently from one rented bungalow to another had also to hire their furniture. To do so they went, as Deborah Dring describes, to the furniture-*wallahs*: 'marvellous men who had whole *godowns* full of English furniture. We used to say, "I'll have that table, I'll have those two chairs, I'll have that sofa and those beds." If you were lucky and came down from the hills very early in the winter you probably picked out some jolly nice bits of furniture. If your move was delayed until later in the winter, then everybody else would have got there first.'

Most memsahibs added something of their own to soften the effect: 'I used to own all our curtains and all the material that covered the chairs. I used to buy printed linens and things in England and bring it out. It was rather nice to see a nice bit of printed linen on your chairs.' Gardens posed the same problems; 'Great efforts were made to grow English flowers, which generally looked rather sickly in the Indian climate. We could have had the most marvellous gardens with orchids and all sorts of things, but no, they must be English flowers.' Yet, as Deborah Dring explains, English gardens were terribly important:

> You wanted to be surrounded by something that wasn't just dust and dead leaves. You could only hope to get a winter garden really. We had all the annuals, things like phlox and nasturtiums, and all those grew most wonderfully. It was wonderful how they grew – just to be ruined by the first blast of really hot weather. The hot weather used to destroy any garden that you'd made, so when you came back again at the beginning of the winter you had to pull up your socks and begin again. Of course, the great thing was pots. We had pots and pots and pots all along the edges of our verandahs. And very often when you left and went somewhere else the person who took over from you took over all your pots.

An Indian attempt at the English lawn was assiduously cultivated. 'Our lawns were made of a special kind of creeping grass, which we used to call *doob* grass. It made the most lovely lawn, so close it smothered most of the weeds. Of course, very often the rest of the compound was bare and hard.' Most lawns required constant irrigation and attendance: 'A little party of three or four men would spread out with a yard or two between them and go up and down the lawn on their hunkers, each man picking out a weed, with another man behind him with a basket egging him on. It was a nice way of mowing one's lawn.'

The memsahib's strongest link with India was through her servants in a feudal relationship that was clear-cut and long-established. 'Be very fair to your servants,' Olivia Hamilton was told by her mother before she left England. 'Always be very firm. Unless you're firm at the beginning, and also fair, they won't respect you.' Attitudes towards servants varied greatly, depending very much on the occupation of the employer, but were always double-edged. On the one hand 'one's attitude was that they were menials. You shouted "*Koi-hai*! Is anybody there?" and somebody came at once.' It was also perfectly true that 'the memsahib shouted and screamed at her servants – but then everybody shouted at the servants. They were the most frustrating people. They always had some very good reasons for why something wasn't done, which you knew – and they knew you knew – to be an absolute lie.' Yet at the same time there was 'a great deal of respect between master and servant and you felt very responsible for them. You were the person who knew whether they were ill, whether they had to be sent to the doctor or whether a dose of castor oil would do the trick. If you found that one of your servants appeared worried or distressed you said to him, "What's the matter?" And then he would perhaps tell you that his brother was in trouble with the moneylender and you would either have the brother up or perhaps lend him money to pay off his debt. They gave you the most wonderful service in the world and in return you felt that they were your people and that you jolly well had to look after them.' This same feudal attitude allowed one to ignore the presence of servants, even when changing, as Radclyffe Sidebottom recalls: 'My wife would have the bath first and the ayah would dress her. I would go in and have my bath and my personal servant would bring in a drink and give it to me in the bathroom and my wife and I would carry on a conversation as if the two servants in the room weren't there.'

The question of how to address the servants varied with status. 'It was a point of honour with us in the established civil services never to talk to the servants in anything but their own language,' states John Cotton, 'the result was that he who spoke the language had a much better type of servant.' In much the same way Iris Portal was taught that 'you must never have an English-speaking servant. My father's attitude was that if you, an educated woman, can't speak the language of a man who is illiterate you really aren't fit to employ him.' English-speaking servants were very often thought to be untrustworthy. In the Indian Army it was generally held that British Army wives got 'scallywags' for servants, because 'you couldn't expect British Army wives to know enough to treat them well'. Although the government gave a grant to army wives who passed a test in rudimentary Urdu 'it just wasn't done'. Wives who knew the customs and languages of India 'would never think of asking a servant to do a thing that was beneath him or was in any way contrary to his religion'. The *pukka* memsahib was never 'tactless enough to bring back bacon from the Club and hand it to a bearer who was a very strict Mohammedan. One put it upon a table and the sweeper would come and take it away, because he was a Hindu and didn't mind touching bacon.'

The extraordinary number of servants required for every European household was very largely due to caste restrictions. When Marjorie Cashmore – newly arrived in Ranchi – asked a *mali* to remove a dead bird from the compound she was informed that he was forbidden to touch dead birds: 'So I told the bearer to call the *masalchee*, but the *masalchee* wouldn't touch it. Then I called for the sweeper and he wouldn't touch it, so I asked the bearer who could move it and he told me to send to the bazaar for a *dome*, a man of very low caste. So we had to pay to get this lad to come and take the bird away.' Status – and a highly developed sense of demarcation – also contributed to the general superabundance of domestics, who were there 'not because you needed them but because they were very strict about their own little trade unions. The man who waited at table might not be prepared to bring your tea in the morning; the cook would perhaps cook but he wouldn't wash up; there would be a special man to dust the floor; another special man to sweep out the verandah and so on. If you had a man to look after the horses he would need to have an assistant who went and cut the grass. As you rose in your career so the number of servants increased, not because you wanted them but because they insisted on it.'

But if seniority required more servants – and Gilbert Laithwaite recalls that on one of the Viceroy's tours in the thirties it was officially noted that there were 'also about two hundred inferior servants' – the easing of caste barriers and the rise in wages had the opposite effect. The household that employed two dozen servants prior to the Great War would probably have cut back to half that number before the Second World War. Average salaries in the thirties ranged from some 25 rupees a month (worth about £2) for the bearer, to 15 rupees for the sweeper, which was sufficient 'because nothing cooked was ever used again. It went out to the sweeper and his family.'

All household servants wore uniforms, usually white with bands on their turbans and cummerbunds in the colours of their sahib's service. Inside the house they went barefoot, 'the question of them wearing their shoes in the house never arose'. In earlier days – up to the threshold of the Great War – it was 'not considered right to inspect the servants' quarters, because of the purdah system'. In time this became the exception rather than the rule, with wives making regular tours of inspection. Nor was it customary for the memsahib to go into the bobajee-*khana*.

While a senior servant such as the head bearer or the *khit-magar* might be known and addressed by his name, the others were referred to by their occupations only. The servants had their own hierarchy dominated by the twin figures of the head bearer and the cook: 'The key to the whole thing was a good bearer who was a sort of majordomo, and who was generally a Mohammedan. He would follow you around wherever you went on your moves and he would be the man who engaged all the other servants. When you went on home leave you paid him a retaining fee, which was half pay. You kept in touch with him and eventually he met you at the quayside, smiling broadly.' Wives who inherited their husband's bearers were well advised to leave the running of the household alone. 'I always found that if I left things to him the whole camp went like clockwork,' says Norah Bowder. 'Friends of mine who used to take the reins into their own hands had continual trouble.' Some bearers – even if they stayed on when the sahib married – never really accepted the dominant role of the new memsahib. George Wood's bearer, Mohammed Ishak, 'fought an endless war' with his new memsahib: 'I decided that my husband's grey homburg hat was rather nice for going out in the midday sun in, so I used to take it and push up the crown and turn down the brim, put it on my head and go out. In the evening Mohammed would rescue it from my room, knock in the crown, turn up the brim and put it back in the Major-sahib's dressing room. And every day this went on. It was not my hat and he did not approve.'

The cook was the great 'I am' of the staff, 'capable of culinary wonders at short notice and usually aided by an unpaid apprentice known as a cook's matey'. The best cooks had learned 'from our grandfathers and grandmothers. Their fathers had been with our grandparents, and they had passed the recipes down. Hence you got some recipes that even you didn't know. They learnt them all by ear and remembered them.' Olivia Hamilton recalls how even in the wilds her cook, 'a most splendid, devoted servant, could produce meals at any time of the day or night. Whenever you got into camp, the first thing he did was to make his fireplace, build his fire, get his charcoal from the village and get our meal ready for us. It was always three courses, it was always beautifully served, and almost anything I ordered he would be able to produce.'

It was not customary for the memsahib to intrude into the bobajee-*khana*. Instead, cook appeared armed with his account book every morning, to be followed by other members of staff in strict order of seniority. 'This magnificent figure,' recalls Mary Wood, 'would come in and we would gravely do the accounts for the day before. We had had so many plates of soup at one anna, we had had chicken for four, fish for four and so much fruit – and I would pay for that. We'd then decide what we would eat that day; whether anyone was coming to dinner. He would then produce a pile of plates and on these plates he would say he wanted flour, sultanas, this, that or the other.' Cook also did the shopping and always took his perk: 'If you tried to go down to the shop to do your own purchasing you were just asking for another twenty-five per cent more to be added to your bill. If your cook brought things for you he just put a little more on the list than he had paid, but that was his *dastur*.' *Dastur*, as Kathleen Griffiths explains, was an immutable fact of Indian life: 'You could leave your jewellery, your money, your bungalow wide open and nothing would ever be taken from it. Their devotion and honesty to you personally was absolutely amazing, but as regards their little perquisites in the way of food or making a little bit on the bazaar, all this was taken as part of their daily life and you accepted it. If I thought the cook was adding on a little too much I would say to him, "Oh, cook, I think you've made a little mistake; you'd better go into the cook-house and reckon it up again and then come back to me and tell me." And he would come back and say, "Oh, yes, memsahib, I wrote five rupees instead of five annas." ' June Norie, faced with a similar situation, observed that her cook cracked his toes under stress: 'I noticed that when there was a large number of eggs or something coming up he'd stop suddenly and I'd hear him crack his big toe and I'd know, "Aha, you've got a guilty conscience over that!" '

Apart from his *dastur* the Indian servant was scrupulously honest and, in turn, 'you trusted your servants implicitly. Once you'd got your servants round you they usually stayed until you went, and you left them with a pension after you'd gone.' Characteristic of the close relationship between master and servant was the behaviour of Dorothy Crichton's bearer when his first son was born: 'He came to tell us about it. He was very, very happy but he didn't say, "I've got a son!" He said, "The little sahib's bearer is born!", referring to *my* son.'

7

The Order of Precedence

FOURTH CLASS

74 *Members of the Indian Civil Service of 12 years' standing and Majors.*
District Judges in Lower Burma and Judge of the Small Case Court, Rangoon, when without their respective charges.

75 *Lieutenants of over eight years' standing, and Chief Engineers of the Royal Indian Marine.*

76 *Government Solicitors.*

77 *Inspector-General of Registration.*
Sanitary Commissioners.
Directors of Land Records and Agriculture under Local Administrations.

78 *Officers in the 3rd Class Graded List of Civil Officers not reserved for members of the Indian Civil Service.*
Agricultural Chemists.
Assistant Directors of Dairy Farms.
Assistant Inspector-General of Forests.

Excerpt from *The Warrant of Precedence* 1921

'Precedence in India was most important.' The stress on protocol and hierarchy that characterized the British Raj had its roots as much in Hindu and Muslim culture as in the British. Conrad Corfield, who spent many years in the native states, saw its origins in Mogul times when 'precedence was your place in court. Where you sat in the row or where you were greeted on arrival was the most important thing. For instance, if you were greeting a prince of a certain standing you had to go down to the bottom of the steps outside to meet him. With one of less standing you would greet him at the top steps and one of no standing you would probably greet while you sat in your study – and that meant everything to the prince. Another way of expressing this protocol was through the gun salutes. In fact, very often before a prince arrived a special envoy would be sent in advance to count the number of booms.' Protocol was important on both sides. As official representative of the Viceroy in a native state, the Resident could not be kept waiting: 'I was shown into the drawing room where I sat down. No ruler. I waited for a quarter of an hour and still no ruler. I thought, well, this isn't good enough, he's trying it on. So I said, "Do you know, I've heard from His Highness that the garden is vastly improved recently, I'd just like to go and see it." The ADC said, "Oh, no, it's perfectly all right, Sir, he'll be here any minute." But I said, "No, I'd like to go." And I went and walked away from the house through the gardens as far as I could on a very hot morning. I'd gone at least half a mile before His Highness came running up behind pouring with perspiration. The next time I arrived there he was standing at the bottom of the steps to greet me.'

Ian Stephens, who as a journalist moved in all sections of British and Indian society, found a strong Hindu influence in the hierarchy of 'Anglo-India':

The Brahmins, the so-called heaven-born, were the members of the topmost British Government service, the Indian Civil Service. They were the *pukka* Brahmins and below them were the semi-Brahmins, the various other covenanted services – the provincial civil services and so on. Then you had the military caste, composed partly of members of the British

Army and partly of members of the Indian Army. They all strikingly resembled the Hindu warrior caste, the *Kshatrias*. The British businessmen, very wealthy and powerful in places like Calcutta but fairly low caste, were analogous to the wealthy but also low caste mercantile and moneylending caste, the *Vaisyas*. These were the *box-wallahs*, a term of contempt applied quite freely by the two upper British castes to the British mercantile community. They might be merchant princes of the very highest quality but they were quite inferior to the covenanted services and the military caste. This mercantile class subdivided willingly – even strongly – into two. The upper people said that they were in commerce, the lower people said that they were in trade and there was a hard division between them. A member of the trade sub-caste, for example, would find it impossible to get elected to the best British clubs. They were inferior, they were people who actually traded and worked in shops, which was very demeaning. Then you went lower down to the menials, the so-called Eurasians or Anglo-Indians, people of mixed blood analogous to the despised Hindu lower castes. Another category here was the unfortunate domiciled community, people of pure British race whose parents, for one reason or another, had elected to settle in India.

Indeed there was no need to look to Hindu society for parallels. 'Most ICS people would have been the sons of moderately well-to-do people and would have come from the greater public schools,' asserts Percival Griffiths. 'That gradually changed and by the time that I went in possibly two-thirds came from the big public schools and the others came, as I myself came, from an ordinary grammar school and had then gone on to university with scholarships. The Forest Service had very much the same background as the Indian Civil Service and the Police Service would nearly always be boys who had not gone on to universities, probably the same social class as the ICS but recruited straight from school. There were from time to time what we used to call domiciled Europeans who came into some of these services. They were very, very few in number. I think we must be honest and say that there was a feeling that they were not quite out of the top drawer.'

The 'strong attitude' of the ICS towards *box-wallahs* was said to have had its origins in the old East India Company's hostility towards interlopers. 'It's true,' continues Percival Griffiths, 'we did regard ourselves as being a cut above the *box-wallahs*. When heads of big business houses came to my district, while I was polite to them, I was apt to regard them with a great deal of suspicion – with very much more suspicion than I regarded the ordinary Indians I was dealing with.' Accusations of excessive arrogance, of being 'the pedestal mob' and 'tin gods on wheels' were frequently levelled against the ICS. 'People did call us the heaven-born and I suspect that most of us felt heaven-born from time to time. If British rule in India was good for India, it wasn't always good for the British. No doubt we did tend to get aloof and perhaps a little bit conceited.' Nevertheless, this 'ruling class was never much more than a thousand strong the whole of the time we were in India – and it had great power, far more power than the civil services in Britain. The Indian civil servant, whether he was in district administration, in the secretariat of the provinces or the secretariat of the Government of India or working in one of the Indian states, had a much wider responsibility and a more testing one. He had to deal with people, with problems of famine and hunger and administration in a way which would not fall to the lot of the civil servant at home.' The result was 'probably the finest civil service that ever existed'. Even if 'they were sometimes pompous and stuffy, they were the heaven-born to many people, not in an offensive way but in an affectionate way. I think everybody realized that they were completely incorruptible and also that they really were the people who ran India.' The ICS was also 'one of the best paid services in the realm and the pension was always considered very remarkable: "a thousand pounds dead or alive" was how it was described'.

Standing between the army and the ICS and drawn from both pools was another even smaller elite, the Viceroy's corps diplomatique, known as the Indian Political Service. As agents or residents these politicals represented the British Raj in the more important native states and principalities scattered through India.

If a Resident became on occasion 'very pompous indeed' it was hardly surprising, since his power, exercised independently and depending much on his influence and personality, could be very great indeed. As a last resort he might even bring about the deposition of a prince or a rajah. As representative of the Viceroy he often moved in atmospheres thick with protocol and formality. Even exchanging calls with a maharajah was a complex business that required a junior officer – in this instance Conrad Corfield – to prepare the way:

I journeyed solemnly through the city to the palace in a cocked hat and a one-horse Victoria which had lost most of its springs. The reception room was an octagonal chamber on the palace roof surrounded by a pillared arcade. There were two chairs, on one of which His Highness sat, and all round the room were senior ministers of state and palace officials seated on the marble floor. My spurs clinked as I walked across to pay my respects. There was silence until I was ensconced on my chair. His Highness then turned to his courtiers and said to them in a deep, commanding voice, 'You may go.' They all got up, bowed deeply and moved three yards behind the pillars of the arcade. I presented the Resident's compliments, which the Maharajah accepted with a gracious bow. We then sat in dignified silence, after which His Highness turned to the arcade and said, 'You may return.' They all did and sat on the floor again, whereupon I took my leave. Protocol being thus completed, the Maharajah set out to call on the Resident and he later returned the call.

GOVERNOR'S CAMP,
UNITED PROVINCES.

November 6, 1933.

Dear Mrs Kendall

His Excellency will be very
pleased if you will reserve Dance No.1
for him on Thursday the 9th of November,
at Government House, Allahabad. If you
will please be near the dais at the
beginning of this dance, I will be there
to introduce you to His Excellency.

Yours sincerely,

Mrs. Kendall,

　　7, Hastings Road,

　　　　Allahabad.

ADC's note, United Provinces, 1933

If pomp and ceremony dominated the native court it was no less in evidence in the higher circles of the British Raj. The Prince of Wales was reported to have said that he had never realized what royalty really was until he stayed at Government House, Bombay, in 1921: 'If the Governor was entertaining, all the guests would be arranged in a circle and he and his lady would be led round the circle and each would be introduced. The ladies would bob to him and the men would bow their heads, and the Governor and his lady would then lead the way into the meal.' Here, too, hierarchy was clearly displayed. 'At any formal dinner at Government House the precedence was of the utmost importance,' explains Christopher Masterman. 'I once attended three dinners running at Government House and got the same lady beside me each time, strictly according to precedence. I was in the secretariat, he was a fellow secretary, so his wife was always invited to the same dinner as myself and I always got her as a partner. I really got very knowledgeable about her family.'

To assist in the proper ordering of official society the Government published a warrant of precedence which was added to from time to time as new posts were created. This Civil List, variously known as the Blue, Green or even the Red Book, was to be found on every civil official's desk. 'The Warrant of Precedence,' declares David Symington, 'was a very humorous document if read in the right spirit. It occupied about ten closely printed pages and showed the relative precedence of various jobs. If you wanted to know whether an Inspector of Smoke Nuisances was a bit higher than a Junior Settlement Officer you had only to look it up and you'd find out what their relative position was.' Armed with his book the junior official or the ADC could plan the seating for a *burra khana* in full confidence. Only those outside the system created problems, as Christopher Masterman once discovered: 'A Mr Abrahams had written his name in the Governor's book and the police reported to me that he was a very important international financier who was making a tour of India. So

Mr and Mrs Abrahams were invited to a state dinner. As Collector I was also invited and when I arrived I was greeted by a member of the staff who said, "You must go and see your Mr and Mrs Abrahams." So I went to see them and I found they were very black, and he was improperly dressed in a blue serge suit. So I had the rather difficult job of telling them we were very sorry but they couldn't come into dinner, but they would be invited to the garden party. They took it very well.'

If slip-ups did occur it was often the memsahib who objected. 'Women,' says Vere Birdwood, 'have a way of being more vocal about these matters. The husband might accept with a shrug of his shoulders that he had not been placed in quite the right position, but his wife would certainly be extremely put out.' In much the same way honours were extremely important. 'In the rather lonely life of the memsahib it became a very great thing for her to think that one day she would become Lady So and So. In those days it mattered terribly because there was not an awful lot else. They were the only critical record of a successful career. When the Birthday Honours or the New Year passed and there was nothing in the list there was quite a marked depression in the household for a few days.'

Although the ICS might not have agreed, the army certainly thought of itself as on a par with the ICS: 'British society in India was represented by the Army and the Indian Civil Service. Others were not admitted to this inner circle of good society.' From the army point of view there was a certain fellow-feeling between these two groups: 'We keep the law and they do the governing.' This was strengthened by the fact that whereas 'the business people concentrated in the great ports and cities, the army served up-country where the only British we came into contact with were members of the ICS and the Indian Services.' Although life in the Indian Army was 'a real gentleman's life', there were gentlemen and gentlemen, and while rank eliminated all problems of hierarchy there remained the hotly disputed question of regimental status.

'There was a curious snobbery about regiments,' recalls John Morris, himself a Gurkha officer. 'The Indian Cavalry considered themselves the cream of the Indian Army and so far as the infantry was concerned the Gurkhas were considered the *corps d'elite*. The Royal Ordnance Corps and the Royal Service Corps, upon which we all depended for the necessities of everyday life, were looked upon as tradesmen. The greatest punishment that could be handed out would be a transfer from a Gurkha regiment into the Royal Indian Service Corps.'

Nor was there much fellow feeling between officers of the British Army and the Indian Army. Claude Auchinleck recalls how before the Great War the Indian Army was looked upon as a 'Jim Crow' army by certain British army officers, although not among the 'good' regiments: 'It was ridiculous because very often the officer in the Indian Army came from the same school and had passed out higher at Sandhurst.' Indian army officers retaliated by looking down on British army officers as birds of passage: 'Few of them learnt the language or learnt to understand the native way of life, particularly the cavalry regiments which were more interested in their training and their polo.' The British cavalry were considered to be the 'real snobs'. Iris Portal, married to an Indian cavalry officer, observed them at close quarters at Meerut: 'They were, of course, richer than anybody else. They had the most beautiful houses all down the Mall at Meerut; lovely gardens and beautiful horses. But they did tend to keep among themselves because they were able to live a kind of life that the rest of us couldn't always keep up with. There was a bit of jealousy, I must admit, but we accepted it in the Indian Army because we enjoyed despising them for knowing so little about India. We got our own back that way. We used to say to each other in sniffy voices, "Tut, tut, they have English-speaking servants who, of course, cheat them very much, we're quite sure."'

The *box-wallah* was properly the Indian commercial traveller who came round on a bicycle with 'lots of silks and shawls in a tin trunk which he laid out on the verandah and said, "No need to buy, madam, just look." ' The European connection was said to have begun with a certain Mrs Wood, living in Calcutta, who prepared boxes of babies' and women's clothes and sent them up-country. In time the term had been extended to include all European businessmen in India: 'The army, who were always jealous of the supposed prosperity of the man in commerce, got back at him by referring to him as the *box-wallah*.' It was said against the *box-wallahs* that they 'did not get to know the real India' and that they lived in the cities and rarely left them. This was certainly true of the average person who lived around his office: 'He played his regular games of tennis. He played his regular games of golf. He rode, played polo, went out paper-chasing. He was a member of the clubs and had a fairly routine existence – the same golf four on Sunday, so many pink gins, the inevitable curry lunch, the afternoon siesta and, often, the same seats booked in the cinema for the six o'clock performance throughout the year, followed by a buffet supper and more drinks.' Perhaps some of the feeling against the *box-wallah* had its roots in class prejudice, since the commercial sector of the business community was curiously divided. There were a great many Scots from the Lowlands who had made good, or whose families 'had made their own way up from the bottom' but whose companies were leavened by young men from a higher social background. These two very distinct types were also to be found among the planters. Curiously, while tea-planters and indigo-planters enjoyed considerable status, sugar-planters and jute-*wallahs* did not. The latter were classified as trade and not allowed to join the clubs of the *box-wallahs*. Rupert Mayne, with a foot in each community, recalls asking a *box-wallah* to come to dinner with three jute-*wallahs* and warning him in advance about his guests – 'that was how deeply engrained this feeling was'.

Edwin Pratt, whose association with the Army and Navy Stores placed him firmly in trade, was 'disturbed by the way one section of a small European community could treat another'. In his Auxiliary Forces Unit all sections of the business community were equals and got on well together 'but once one got outside, the barrier seemed to creep up'. In his opinion it was a division 'greatly accentuated and maintained by the wives, who insisted that the social groups remained apart. Men by themselves are inclined to accept each other for what they're worth. Women never will.'

The British soldier had very little status among his own kind. As far as the Indians were concerned he was 'a proud person and always walked about ten foot tall', but 'if you were a (European) civilian your status was far above that of a soldier. If people were seen talking to soldiers they'd be written down in the same way as a soldier would be written down for speaking to a native.' As a result 'there was absolutely no contact between the white element in India and the British soldier. We were less than the dust and it is well established that Lady Curzon thought so too, because she is reported to have said that the two ugliest things in India are a water buffalo and a British soldier dressed in his white uniform.'

At the bottom of the pyramid, caught between two strongly hierarchical cultures and looked down upon by both was the Eurasian, who was traditionally said 'to have acquired the worst characteristics of both races'. The attitude of the British towards the Anglo-Indian was in keeping with the age and, according to one view, was 'tempered by the fact that while the earlier generation of Anglo-Indians, going back over one hundred years, came from good stock – where it was a perfectly done thing for good quality Europeans to marry good quality Indians – in the last fifty years many Anglo-Indians were the result of sometimes pretty trashy Europeans and undoubtedly trashy Indians, prostitutes and women of the bazaar and so on. So that while there was a category of Anglo-Indian that was of high quality, there were a very large number who were pretty wishy-washy. They had no strength of personality, they were accustomed to being underdogs and they had that hangdog "chip on the shoulder" attitude to life.

Some of them on the railways did first class jobs, and some of them as individuals were delightful. But not many companies were prepared to regard them as high management quality.'

When observed from a different point of view this attitude appeared in a much harsher light. 'There was a very strong colour bar,' declares Eugene Pierce. 'Conditions in those days strongly resembled present conditions in South Africa, with this difference: that while in South Africa it is imposed by government, in India it was accepted by a mutual arrangement and by tacit consensus.' This colour prejudice diminished as the years went on, but it remained one of the least attractive features of British India.

8

The Land of the Open Door

It is part of the immemorial order of things, in the land of the Open Door,
where the wandering bachelor – sure of his welcome – drops into any meal
of the four . . . India is the land of dinners, as England is the land of five
o'clock teas.

MAUD DIVER *The Englishwoman in India* 1909

The memsahib's household duties were not onerous: 'Half the
women in India left everything to their servants.' The morning
consultation with cook, the refilling of the decanters and
cigarette boxes brought by the bearer, the issuing of clean
dusters; these and other similar routines did not take very long.
'One would go and do one's flowers which were always there,
an enormous pile laid ready with the vases already filled with
water. Where the flowers came from I don't know, never from
my own garden. One didn't enquire. After that the day was
yours. You could very easily get bored.' With her children in
the hands of the ayah or the nanny or even packed off home
for schooling, the memsahib's day was long and difficult to fill:
'After about eleven o'clock in the morning there was nothing
to do except have people come to bridge or to coffee – and
then the gossip started; scandal, gossip and conjecture. The
husband came home to lunch and after lunch you went to your

siesta. After that you went to play tennis at the Club. Then you sat at the Club drinking until you came home to dinner, and then you may have gone to a dance or a party. That was the life. That was how it went on every day.'

With few outside diversions and the same small circle of acquaintances, with whom 'one became too intimate', the average station or cantonment memsahib 'got into the habit of doing the same thing every day and never bothered to break it'. Unless she was a woman of considerable character or force of personality she could easily 'shut out the great world outside the station, the Indian world'. When India intruded it was often to conspire to make the memsahib's life more indolent still. 'One nice thing was handing out all the laundry in the morning and finding it all ironed and neatly folded on the bed in the afternoon.' The man responsible was the dhobi, who came with his donkey and 'took away the washing to a water point where the dirt was literally bashed out'. Rosalie Roberts recalls how he sometimes 'turned up in a most smart shirt and it was obvious it was the police sahib's shirt he was wearing'.

Even more important from the memsahib's point of view, and very often shared between several households, was the *derzi*: 'He'd come along and squat on your verandah on a little rug with his own sewing machine, and you'd give him a shirt or a coat or a pair of trousers to copy and there he would sit with half a dozen needles stuck in his turban, each one with a different size or different coloured thread, which he'd pull out when he wanted.' In a land where new or fashionable clothes were not readily obtainable the value of a personal tailor was immense. 'If you were dressing and you suddenly found you'd torn your frock all you did was throw it out of the window and say to the *derzi*, "*maramut karo*!" [mend it!] and you wouldn't see it again until it was all complete.' The *derzi* could also alter and copy: 'If you gave him a dress and said, "Now make me one like that," he was too clever for words. He altered things awfully well and made something out of nothing magnificently.' But he was not perfect: 'If you gave him an old thing that you'd worn before, he'd reproduce it exactly and if by any chance you'd patched it you had to be very careful or the *derzi* would copy the whole thing – including the patch.'

Where there were small children in the sahib's household a *ghai-wallah* and his cow were often in attendance. Memsahibs were well advised to watch while the cow was milked. 'I found all sorts of tricks,' remembers Marjorie Cashmore. 'You would make him turn the pail over so that you knew it was empty when he started, but then he squeezed water in using a goatskin up his arm.'

Less frequently there would be traders who came to call: 'the Chinaman, who made very good shoes to measure – you would stand on a piece of paper and he would draw round your foot – and the Kashmiri merchant who would arrive laden with bales of beautiful silken underclothes and Kashmiri shawls and rugs and delightfully embroidered cloth.' Chits would be sent round to friends and 'we would spend the morning trying on, holding up, examining and bargaining for the most delectable articles'. There would be other itinerants: The snake charmer with his cobras and his mongoose, the shaggy brown bear that 'used to come regularly every winter and dance pathetically in the compound'. Norah Bowder also recalls 'a nice old gentleman, well thought of in the neighbour-hood' who used to share the well in her garden – 'a *sadhu*, naked except for a G-string and painted all over, who used to astonish my mother when she was staying with us'.

In many other respects the memsahibs tended to forgo the little luxuries of life. Outside the major cities there was no such thing as a hairdresser. Army wives could draw upon the services of the regimental barber but elsewhere 'either you didn't have your hair done or you did it yourself'. Dentists were also a problem: 'There was very often a doctor but never a dentist, although there were occasional itinerant dentists, mainly Americans or Australians who used to travel round the up-country places and set up a dispensary in a rest house for perhaps a couple of days.' Since telephones were rarely to be found outside the larger stations 'life went on with chits. If you wanted to communicate you sent one of your servants with a chit.' In the absence of telephones *dak* became a word of great significance. 'We relied a great deal on the post,' explains Vere Birdwood. 'Our books were posted, our newspapers were posted. Everything was sent for, everything had to be imported. We existed on the Army and Navy Stores catalogue from which we used to order a great deal to be sent up.' The mail order catalogue was a major institution: 'Everybody spent many hours browsing through it and one acquired all sorts of useless junk over the years.' Two means of payment were available. With VPP or Value Payable Post, you paid the postman the value of the goods in the parcel. Alternatively, you paid only for what you consumed during a particular month. Reginald Savory recalls, 'a well-known firm in Bombay called Phipson's who had an enormous stock of every imaginable English, Scottish or French drink, and ran what they called a Cellar Account. They would send us up so many dozen of each and we paid for it as we consumed it. Once a year one of Phipson's men would come round and say, "Six dozen bottles of whisky. You've only got half a dozen left so pay up for the rest." Then he'd make up the numbers to six dozen or so for the next year.' The most surprising feature of the mail order service was its range, which included perishable goods packed on ice and sent on special trains to arrive at destinations on specified dates and at specified times. Ice itself was a valuable commodity. It could be bought 'when the mail train came through' from Bombay, or, if the station was large enough, from the local ice factory: 'It used to arrive in large blocks which you threw into a thing called an ice box and it would last for a day. Ice was essential, particularly in the Hot Weather. A drink without ice was not in the least refreshing.'

Despite the lengthy time lag, links with home were strenuously maintained. Bundles of newspapers arrived weekly in specially bound editions, as well as the more popular magazines. *Blackwood's* and *The Tatler* enjoyed a special popularity.

Local newspapers were read avidly. The *Statesman* – 'the *Manchester Guardian* of the East, liberal and outspoken in a high-minded Victorian way and respected as such by the Indian public' – was perhaps the most important, although equally influential in Upper India was the *Times of India*, published in Bombay. 'Circulation may not have been large,' recalls Ian Stephens, former editor of the *Statesman* of India, 'but copies were passed round from hand to hand and widely read. All the big cities had English-language newspapers.' As the only major source of communication and opinion the influence of these local papers was considerable.

With so many limitations and restrictions to equable living and with an 'alien' culture constantly lurking in the background it was not surprising that some turned – where they could – to a rather frivolous social life and others, prevented from doing so by seniority or isolation, to the preservation of English conventions: 'One always had to behave in a comparatively circumspect manner in the matter of drink or flirtations, because servants were constantly hovering around – and one felt that one must show the flag.' In fact, in terms of sexual behaviour the British in India were probably no more immoral than in any other place in the world but 'whereas in England you could be immoral and get away with it, you could be immoral in India and everybody knew exactly what was going on. Your bearer would pass the word to another bearer and soon it would be known that Mr So and So sahib was having an affair with such and such a memsahib.' In the small up-country station or cantonment 'the opportunities just were not there'. In the cities or in the hill stations standards were rather different and varied with the seasons.

English conventions were also preserved in the preference for expensive British goods rather than the cheaper 'country-made' versions. In the same way, food was often made 'as much like English food as possible' even if attempts to Anglicize the cuisine beyond a certain point were much frustrated by India. Meat had to be eaten on the day it was killed and so it was always tough. Since the slaughtering of cows gave great offence to Hindus there were many places where beef was unobtainable: 'The result was that we had to fall back on mutton, usually very tough, or the equally tough chicken which was the staple diet of many of us in India.' Chicken, usually not much bigger than a pigeon, was 'always dished up in restaurants, in *dak* bungalows or anywhere else where one happened to be on tour. One got sick to death of chicken, whether curried or done in some other way designed to make it attractive.' Preceding the chicken there would, in all probability, be mulligatawny soup and, following it, caramel custard, known as 'custel brun' among Indian servants. Currying – 'the men always liked it' – helped to make meat tastier, and many thought that 'you got the best curry in English households'. Eggs – 'the size of pigeon's eggs' – became 'rumble tumble' when scrambled and 'craggy toast' when taken with tomatoes. Bread was made with yeast that 'came by parcel post every month from somewhere near Bombay and was appalling'. Butter came in cases of thirty-six tins and was always oily, 'except around Christmas time when it just about set'. Where it was unobtainable, buffalo butter, with added colouring to make it pass for the real thing, was an adequate substitute. Vegetables, salads and fruit had always to be washed – preferably in the presence of the memsahib – in bowls of water mixed with potassium permanganate. Drinking water was always boiled and some memsahibs insisted that this, too, should be done in their presence – although it was unwise to be too watchful. One of the standard 'Anglo-Indian' jokes concerns the memsahib who visited the kitchen before every meal until one day she found the cook straining the soup through a sock: 'She was horrified and said, "Bobajee, what are you doing? That's one of the master's socks!" "It's all right, memsahib," he said, "it's not one of his clean ones." '

The memsahib of the twenties and thirties did her best to keep up with her English counterpart. Fashions were followed as far as the climate allowed. The inappropriate costumes of the previous decade – 'lots of underclothes and heavy skirts down to the ankles' – had been abandoned for practical informality. 'I look back,' recalls Mrs Lee of the Edwardian era, 'and marvel how we survived.' Now slacks, jodhpurs and breeches were worn, perhaps 'because we were perpetually jumping on and off horses', together with shirts, sweaters, and tweed coats in the cold weather. Such bold innovations did not always meet with approval. Vere Bird-wood's cook deplored the fact that memsahibs now came in trousers to do the morning chores. 'He thought this was really quite indecent. As far as he was concerned some great dignity had gone out of English life.' Only headgear failed to move with the times. As long as the British remained 'very much afraid of the sun' the topee kept its place, although double-*terais*, 'two felt hats, one on top of the other,' provided a more casual alternative.

Old-fashioned convention made itself felt most obviously in company, and most often at dinner, for 'it was in the evenings that old traditions were maintained'. Thus 'it was absolutely *de rigueur* to change for dinner. It was only natural to change after the day's work and what was more easy to change into than a dinner jacket. If you did not want to do this then you could "dine dirty", but it was not looked upon with favour.' Even this represented a major social revolution, as Reginald Savory describes: 'If you dined out pre-1914 anywhere in India privately, it was a tail coat, a boiled shirt and a white waistcoat, with a stiff collar and a white tie. Long after they gave this up in England we continued to do it in India. I even remember up in the Himalayas where we had to ride about five miles to get from our camp to the station club where we danced, we would ride in on ponies in our tail coats. We'd put our tails into our trouser pockets and trot in and dance there. Then we'd stick our tails back into our trouser pockets and gallop home in tails, white waistcoats and boiled shirts, the lot!'

It was not done to wear gloves in the jungle. 'After the first time I did this,' remarks Iris Portal, 'my husband said to me, "If you wear gloves in the jungle again I will divorce you." ' But on more formal occasions it was still thought correct to wear gloves, preferably kid gloves. Rosamund Lawrence thought this 'a perfect nonsense. To wear long, white wrinkled gloves for an ordinary dinner was simply absurd. It cost a frightful amount, it was very hot and uncomfortable and it was impossible to get them cleaned.' As the wife of the Collector of the district she could do something about it. 'The Lady Commissioner sahib is the head of the station and she can do what she likes – so white gloves disappeared and everybody was relieved.' Only a Senior Lady, a *sakt burra Mem*, could comfortably afford to flout convention. Mary Wood, going out to dine in Simla in borrowed white gloves with 'a very exalted old dear, the wife of a very senior army officer', arrived to find 'her very dignified bearer on his knees on the floor solemnly using a flit spray up the old darling's petticoats. She looked at me and said, "Quite all right, my dear, quite all right. I find this very efficacious for the mosquitoes." ' By tradition the Senior Lady also 'dined the station' at least once a year, inviting in turn every senior official in her husband's district to dinner. 'As a bride and newcomer I found this very difficult to begin with,' recalls Kathleen Griffiths. 'When you were giving a big dinner party you always consulted what was called the Blue Book. You had to do this most carefully as they all had a definite precedence. I've seen memsahibs extremely annoyed when they thought they were being put in the wrong place.' John Morris was once inadvertently placed on the wrong side of his hostess and next day received a note from her 'apologizing for not realizing that I was senior to the other man and for having put me on the wrong side'.

The *burra khana* brought out the best in the Indian servants. Unexpected guests were always catered for, even though 'the soup may have been a little thinner'. Extra places could always be laid. Cutlery and utensils passed along the servants' grapevine from bungalow to bungalow as the need arose and guests frequently found their own dishes – 'sometimes even your own vegetables' – laid out before them at the dinner table. 'You never had to worry about the meal. You came to the dinner table and it was always beautifully laid.' Table decorations proliferated. 'The *malis* were all perfect marvels. They would take all day arranging flowers and making beautiful arrangements on the table. In every finger bowl there would be a sprig of sweet-smelling lavender or scented verbena.' The cook also contributed: 'Cooks absolutely adored to decorate everything with lots of colour, especially in mashed potato. They'd make it into a motor-car with little lights or a bird of some kind – usually with an egg stuck on the back to make it more realistic.' The 'toffee-basket' was another great favourite: 'They used to make the most wonderful pudding out of transparent toffee in the shape of a basket which they used to fill with tinned fruit and cream.'

Nancy Vernede's father was High Court Judge in Allahabad and when she came out to join her parents in 1931 she found herself involved in frequent formal dinner parties for perhaps sixteen or eighteen people:

> Guests would arrive at 'eight for half-past eight' with drinks beforehand in the drawing room. The bearer would bring in the drinks and the head *khitmagar*, who looked like Moses, would preside in the dining room and see that all the other *khitmagars* waiting on the table were ready at their places. Then we would all proceed in at about half-past eight. The ICS were supposed to be the senior service and it could be rather difficult because if you were a young bride married to one you were officially senior to someone old enough to be your grandmother, simply because you were ICS and the so-called Senior Lady. She'd go in with the host and sit on his right-hand side while the hostess would have the senior man on her right. You had to arrange the dinner party just so. The table was very carefully arranged. Everyone had their names printed and you just looked for yours and sat down. A lot

of the older memsahibs became very grand indeed – ships with full sail – and took themselves very seriously. They were very fussy about position, but not so much our own generation. Everyone knew it was just a little bit of play-acting.

I can remember being very nervous of the conversation when I first went out to India. My mother would say, 'You must make conversation. You must talk first to the man on your right and then to the one on your left – and you must talk. You must never close a conversation.'

We'd have about five or six courses and it always took a very long time. After the savoury the bowli-glasses were brought out with the dessert plate, little bowls with water to wash your fingers in, and chocolates and little oranges in a sort of syrup, and all types of dessert and fruit and nuts. Port and Madeira would be passed round and then finally at the end of dinner the ladies would all go into the drawing room, leaving the men with their port. They would have their coffee in the next room and then about half an hour later they'd be joined by the men and one would carry on a fairly formal conversation, I suppose, until half-past ten, which was the magic hour. The Senior Lady had then to get up and say she had to go home now. Until she'd done that no one could move. The Senior Lady had to make the first move and sometimes she wouldn't realize it. She'd be new to India and just wouldn't know, and everyone would hang on and on and people would get sleepier and sleepier until someone had to pass her the hint. But half-past eight was the time of the dinner, and half-past ten was the official time of departure.

After the guests had departed everything could be left to the servants. The host and hostess could retire to their beds – but not to the silence of the night. There were always the night sounds of India, in season the cicadas and bullfrogs, and all the year round the nightly accompaniment of the jackals. 'Some people disliked this,' remarks Raymond Vernede. 'I can't understand why. I thought it was a most enchanting sound, very comforting and familiar. There was something homely about it.' The last sound of all would be the night *chowkidar* 'moving around at night, clearing his throat and spitting'.

9

The Club

*In any town in India the European Club is the spiritual citadel, the real
seat of the British power, the Nirvana for which native officials and
millionaires pine in vain.*

GEORGE ORWELL *Burmese Days* 1935

Any member shooting a pig be expelled the Club.
Rule Eleven, Nuggur and Deccan Tent Club

The Club was a peculiarly 'Anglo-Indian' institution. 'A lot of
fun has been poked at club life in India, without those who
indulged in this sort of sport realizing how vital a part of the
life it was. Getting together for games and exercise and talk
was really a very important part of our life. It was the social
centre of the civil and military station.' A club was to be found
in all but the very smallest stations: 'The ordinary station had a
club of sorts, at least a meeting place, with a few old books and
some drinks. The bigger stations added tennis courts, a golf
course, even a squash court. It was of particular importance to
the odd civilian who had not got the officers' mess behind
him.' It also provided 'a sort of get-together place for the
women-folk,' even though they had no official standing and
their names did not appear on its list of members. The Club

represented the 'hub of local society', principally of senior officials. 'There would be the Collector, the headquarters Sub-Collector, the Sessions Judge, the District Forest Officer, the District Superintendent of Police, the Excise Assistant Commissioner and several other officials from the public works department and so on.' Not surprisingly, 'there were only a limited number of places at which there were any Europeans who weren't officials'. At such places army officers swelled the list of members and the club provided 'a meeting place between the Civil and the Military'.

Many of the up-country clubs had their origins in sporting institutions. When Kenneth Warren first went to Assam all the clubs were polo clubs and it was only in later times that these clubs became more social clubs. This mixing of sport and social activities was a feature in all but the largest stations: 'You had to belong to the club before you could play any games.' Those who could join were not expected to do otherwise. 'It was considered obligatory to belong, even if one never went,' says John Morris. 'I certainly paid my subscription over a number of years but I shouldn't think I went to the club more than half a dozen times during the whole of my military service.' Others, like Philip Mason's first Collector, felt obliged to go to the club: ' "I regard it as a duty to go to the club at least every other night," he used to say. He was a very light drinker and always used to drink what was called a *pau-peg* or a quarter of whisky when he got there.'

Some men, usually by virtue of their occupations, made poor 'club men'. 'My life was so different from theirs,' recalls Arthur Hamilton. 'When a forest officer returned from a tour and came to the club he was looked upon rather as a jungle-*wallah*. And, of course, he was a jungle-*wallah*. That was his job.' Olivia Hamilton, returning briefly to society after months in the jungle 'used to be absolutely petrified. One put on an evening dress every night but one felt rather like a sort of Cinderella. You'd never seen any of the theatres, you'd never been to a cinema, you didn't know any of the people they talked about, who was the "Belle of Lahore" and who was the most popular person, and I just felt that I couldn't fit in.' Nevertheless, you were unwise not to become a club member if you could. 'If you didn't belong to the Club you were an outcast,' says Reginald Savory. 'Some people refused to kowtow to all these social things and refused to belong to the Club, intellectuals very largely, who'd rather spend their evenings studying history or the Indian language or the classics and who thought the Club was a waste of time. Either you were a rebel, and a rather courageous rebel, who didn't belong to the Club, or else you were a social outcast who wanted to belong to the Club and couldn't get in.'

Club membership was dependent almost entirely upon occupation. Thus F. C. Hart, who was 'country bred' and so prevented from joining the Indian Police at the same level as his public school contemporaries, was able to play hockey and cricket with them but could not join their clubs. Similarly, in a district dominated by cotton mills 'all the office people – nearly all Europeans but some Indians – were all allowed to be members of the club, but the technical people, the men who mended the looms, who were also Europeans and skilled workmen drawing much higher pay than most of the white-collar workers, were on no account admitted as members'. Christopher Masterman recalls an extended committee meeting to decide the status of 'a new man whom they called a coolie-catcher, whose job was to recruit Tamil coolies for the Ceylon tea estates. We eventually decided that he was eligible.' One section of the community whose status was indeterminate was the missionaries. In practice 'not many missionaries were members, partly because they couldn't afford to be members, and partly because they had moral scruples.'

In the cities discrimination over status was preserved but softened by a range of clubs: 'In Calcutta there were quite a large number of clubs solely confined to the European com-

munity and even confined to categories within that community.' These clubs were 'very carefully ruled', as Kenneth
Mason observed. 'As an army officer I would not have been
eligible for the Bengal Club, which was mainly commercial,
nor would a man in commerce have been eligible for the
United Service Club. On one occasion two brothers came out.
One was in commerce and eligible for the Bengal Club but the
other was not, being in trade and a distributor of imported
wines. He joined the Calcutta Light Horse and so became
eligible for the United Service Club.' Europeans in trade in
Calcutta found themselves in an invidious position, as Ridgeby
Foster explains:

> People who worked in shops were known as 'counter-jumpers'
> and even the general manager of one of the biggest stores in
> Calcutta could not get into the more select clubs. If he was in
> commerce and therefore acceptable the first club which the
> young man joined was the Saturday Club, which was a social
> club for dancing and squash and swimming and a generally
> active social life. Next there was the Tollygunge Club on the
> outskirts of Calcutta, a very select club with a six-year waiting
> list, which had a golf course, a racecourse and a swimming
> pool. Many people used to ride from it out into the country-
> side and come back and have their breakfast in the club. Then,
> when a young man got more senior there was the Bengal
> Club, which was famous for its cuisine and was quite a
> landmark.

The subject of Indian membership of clubs 'almost split the
Empire'. Reginald Savory maintains that 'one of the greatest
mistakes we ever made was to frown upon Indians becoming
members of the Club. Certain clubs would not allow Indians
to be members. They had it written down in their constitution.
When one considers that it was not every Englishman who
came to India who came out of the top drawer, and that there
were in India some of the most highly bred and cultivated and

ALLAHABAD CLUB

List of Members present in Allahabad—October, 1934

Name	M for Married Member	Address	Remarks
A			
Allsop, Hon. Mr. Justice J. J. W. ...	M	16, Hastings Road.	
Alston, Sir Charles Ross ...	M	5, Edmonstone Road.	
Anketell-Jones, Major S. W. (I.A.O.C.)	M	4, Napier Lines.	
Apps, Capt. E. H. (R.A.O.C.)	M	No. 11 Quarters, The Fort.	
B			
Bennet, Hon. Mr. Justice E. }	M	7, Thornhill Road.	
Miss M. Collett White }	...		
Biggane, P. (I.P.)	...	No. 6, The Club.	
Bishop, T. B. W.	M	Collector's House ...	Tel. 214.
Bomford, H.	M	Commissioner's House ...	Tel. 203.
Botley, T. M. (P.W.V.)	...	Officers' Mess, 2nd P. W. Vols.	
Bowden, F. H.	...	Mirzapur.	
Bradley, T. A.	...	15, Thornhill Road.	
Braide, Major R. W. (P.W.V.)	...	49, Napier Road.	
Bretherton, Capt. W. (P.W.V.)	...	Officers' Mess, 2nd P. W. Vols.	
Brooke-Edwards, L.	M	Dufferin Hospital ...	Tel. 335.
Burmester, Capt. A. C. (I.A.O.C.)	...	5, Club Road.	

Will members kindly notify the Secretary of any alterations or corrections to the above list!

Club list, Allahabad, 1934; few Indians and fewer women

educated men in the world, to keep them out and allow the
Englishman in was nonsense.' Yet there was a case to be made
for segregation in clubs: 'We spent our time watching our step
and watching what we said – and there was a certain relief to
go amongst people of our own race and let our hair down.' At
the time 'it didn't appear to us to be anything particularly
reprehensible and nor, I think, did the Indians feel badly about
it'. Indian objections were equally understandable: 'It was
unfortunate and unpleasant that the rulers should gather
together and spend their leisure time together, presumably
hatching up further methods of enforcing their rule and things
of that kind.'

The controversy over Indian membership, usually presented
in terms of a colour-bar, began with the ending of the First
World War and was still going strong in the big cities well into
the Second World War. H. T. Wickham remembers how the
question of allowing Indians to join the club came up when he
was a Superintendent of Police at Bishraw in 1921: 'The club
was a purely private club supported by subscriptions from
members who had to be elected and when the question of
permitting Indians to join arose a large number of the members
didn't like it. Their chief objection was the fact that the Indians,
if they joined the club, would consort with the female members
of the club, while their own female members were prohibited
from coming, because they would be in purdah and could not
therefore mix with people while unveiled.'

The 'Indianization' of both the civil and military services
made it difficult for all but the largest station clubs to preserve
their exclusiveness. Up-country, where Indian membership of
the civil services made itself most felt, the racial barriers fell
easily and with only an occasional upset. In Deradoon Kenneth Mason was asked by an Indian IMS doctor if he would put
him up for the Club:

There were Indian members of the club, but a restricted
number, many of them descendants of Indians who had been

loyal in the Mutiny days. I went to the ICS Superintendent of the 'Doon and asked if he would second this Indian officer. The members of the club then voted. They had to write their names in a book and then put a white ball or a black ball into the ballot box. A certain number of names were already in the book and the balls in the boxes when I invited the officer to dine with me in the club. He was quite nice to everybody but halfway through he cleared his throat, turned round and spat on the floor. He had only forgotten his manners for a fraction of a second, but I knew that he would not be elected to the club so afterwards I deliberately made the ballot void by shovelling a handful of balls into both boxes, far more than the number of names likely to appear in the book. The officer was then politely informed that the ballot was void, but that he would be at liberty to come up again for election in six months. Unfortunately he got someone else to put him up again. He got two white balls and all the rest were black. There was a frightful outcry and we got a raspberry from Simla saying that this was not the way to behave. Fortunately, we had a list of people who had voted and every Indian who was a member of the club had blackballed that man.

In the cities mixed clubs – such as the Willingdon Club in Bombay and the Calcutta Club in Calcutta – attempted to bypass the problem. Elsewhere a head-on clash became inevitable, reaching crisis point during the Second World War. President of the Madras Club at that time was Christopher Masterman: 'We had admitted all European officers as temporary members of the Madras Club, but the General commanding the Madras district said that he would not allow European officers to become members unless we also agreed to allow Indian officers to be members. The commercial element out-voted the officials and by a very small majority it was decided to still refuse to admit Indians as members. The result was that the European officers were also not admitted under the orders of the General.' Other attempts to break the bar were more successful: 'I had an officer in my regiment who had been a cadet at the Indian Military Academy under me,' recalls Reginald Savory. 'I put him up for the club and they turned him down. I put the club out of bounds to all my officers from that minute. Eventually the penny dropped and this man was allowed to become a member of the club.'

The Anglo-Indians had their own clubs – and their own restrictions. Wherever there was a sizeable railway colony there were two separate institutions – one for the Anglo-Indians and another for the Indians. Anglo-Indians, in their turn, were 'allowed into corporals' messes, even some ser-geants' messes, but the Officers' Club was absolutely out of the question. We were not bitter about this because not only the colour bar but the class bar cut right across India and we as Anglo-Indians did not allow the Indians into our institutes.' Nevertheless, it was with regard to the Anglo-Indian that colour prejudice showed itself in its rawest form, as Irene Edwards describes: 'I knew an Anglo-Indian girl in Peshawar, white with blue eyes, who was known to be Anglo-Indian because her parents lived in Peshawar. She knew I used to go to the club because I used to talk about the parties there and she wanted to join. I asked a lady doctor who had influence to try and get Celia in and she told me it was no use trying "because everybody round here knows Celia is an Anglo-Indian". I told this lady doctor, "Well, so am I." "Yes, but people don't know it here. You have passed in the crowd, but Celia won't." The club was taboo.'

Despite the external controversies the club itself re-mained 'a very friendly place where you danced or talked or looked at the papers or played cards'. Most were old buildings of no architectural merit, and were hung with pictures of 'dead and gone cricket teams'. The Madras Club was exceptional both in its fine architecture and for what was said to be the longest bar in India. In other respects it was true to the norm: 'Up above the bar was the dining room and the reading room; really one huge long room. On one side were rows and rows of single chambers of residence and some married quarters. On the other side was a very good library and another small dining room. It had a large verandah where people met and talked. Then the men generally drifted off to the billiard room or to the bridge room.' A number of minor conventions had to be observed, for instance it was not considered at all the right thing to go to the club wearing a topee in the evening, and the bar was a male preserve. 'No women were allowed near the bar. They had a special area reserved for them called the *moorghi-khana*, which inter-preted means the hen house.'

As a social spot the club verandah on a large station had few rivals. 'On almost any evening you would see the club verandah, usually a long deep area which was cool and in the shade and fitted out with cane chairs and tables, occupied by literally hundreds of people in groups of two, four and upwards. They would be busily chatting among themselves, drinks would be flowing freely and you would repeatedly hear the exclamation "*Koi-Hai!*" which was the call for one of the servants to come and attend.' Within these 'basket chair circles' the conversation was said to be 'trivial in the extreme'. A small community continually re-meeting could not be very original: 'People talked shop a great deal and women talked about servants and children.' Gossip of the 'most personal kind' was kept for the 'intimate little dinner party among a group of your friends'. In mixed clubs 'politics was not discussed with Indians' and it was considered 'injudicious to talk too freely about women' – except in the hot weather when, with the womenfolk safely up in the Hills, 'the conversation was uninhibited'. Tales of *shikar* were frequently exchanged and 'a great deal of the conversation consisted in talking about So and So, some-body whom everybody knew in the UP and of stories of his eccentricities'.

While the expression *Koi-Hai* was used principally to call for servants, it had another meaning; the '*Koi-Hai*' was the old India hand, the 'character' to be found on every station, like the man who 'kept a tame cobra on his office table to discourage thieves and whose wife left him because he used to go to bed in his boots', or the Chief Medical Officer who 'fired all six rounds of his revolver into the bonnet of his car when it broke down on a lonely road', or even the sugar planter who 'used to turn out every morning with a hunting horn, immaculately dressed in a well-cut riding coat and a cravat and a riding whip, and go off to inspect the cane on his horse blowing his hunting horn and shouting "Yoiks, Tally Ho!"'

If British India abounded in – and made much of – its characters there were good reasons for it. Eccentricity frequently grew out of isolation, from loneliness of the kind that forced a colourful character of Percival Griffiths' acquaintance – later shot by Bengali terrorists – 'to play bridge with his cook'. Similarly, John Morris recalls touring in Gilgit and being asked to dinner by a local political officer who added at the end of his note: ' "P.S. Black tie." Fortunately I had been warned about this man and told that he was a terrific stickler for the correct costume and so had carried my dinner jacket for miles and miles on porters' backs all the way up through Hunza and Kashmir and on to the Pamirs.' For many officials there was the added strain of having 'to be very careful not to mix too freely or make individual friends'. It was also true that eccentricity appealed to the Indians. The night before he reached Bombay Ian Stephens was told by an Indian acquaintance that he would probably do well in India 'for a reason which may sound rude to express. You are a little eccentric and eccentric Englishmen in India – provided they don't get all walled up in the system within their first five years – tend to do very well.' Undoubtedly those officials who got on best – and were longest remembered – were those 'queer Englishmen who usually arrived at the truth', like a Collector under whom Christopher Masterman served in Madras who 'impounded a village headman in the village cattle pound and wouldn't release him until he'd paid the ordinary fee for release, on the grounds that he was no better than a buffalo'. This same Collector scandalized the local European population by 'driving from his residence to the Club in the evening in a horse-drawn barouche while his wife was made to bicycle behind him'.

Perhaps because it was such a conventional society 'Anglo-India' both fostered and made much of its characters. Among Indians too legends were assiduously fostered in life and preserved after death. Thus the *dacoit*-catching exploits of Freddie Young sahib of the UP police, remembered by George Caroll as 'an enormous man of nineteen or twenty stone who wore an eyeglass which didn't suit him at all and whose compound was always full of Indians', were embroidered into plays put on by wandering Indian actors. Olaf Caroe recalls how, on one of his tours on the North-West Frontier in 1927, an old man was brought out to recount how Abbott, a famous deputy commissioner, had told his people to stand firm against the Sikhs in 1845.

In a land where 'sociability was gauged in very large measure by drinking habits' and where whisky came at less than three rupees a bottle, it was nevertheless a severe crime 'to drink too much or to be seen to drink too much before your Indian servants'. Some saw this as 'a reaction against the heavy drinking of earlier generations'. If there was to be any hard drinking the club was certainly not the place for it, and 'if a chap showed any signs of being half-intoxicated he was hustled out by his friends. Every club had a secretary, usually an ex-army man who knew how to cope with that sort of thing.' Those who indulged to excess did so in the privacy of their own bungalows. A plantation manager dismissed by Kenneth Warren was found to have 'replaced one of the panels in his dining room with hessian cloth painted to look like the rest of the dining room. Through a hole in this hessian cloth went a tube which led from a cask of beer in the dining room to the bedroom.' Public drunkenness was exceedingly rare, although Kenneth Mason recalls 'a lady in the club at Dehra Dun who was so intoxicated that she walked off the end of the verandah and landed among some ferns and screamed for help from an officer who wasn't her husband'.

Even if the cities may have had the conventional habit of 'short drinks before lunch', up-country 'the custom was that at six o'clock sundown you had your first drink. We were very often quite punctual – but never before. You'd say "No, no, another ten minutes," and that was that. There was no drinking at all during the day. The normal life was to go down in the afternoon, play three or four chukkas of polo, come in and change – because you were soaking wet – and then have a good, long drink.' Right up to the Second World War it was still generally accepted that 'the way to avoid heatstroke was to replace the moisture content of our bodies'. A great deal of drinking was done in consequence – but not in the manner commonly supposed: 'Whisky was the great drink, but drunk very diluted with soda water and ice.' Wines were 'not readily available', although popular in messes. There was also 'the gimlet, really a gin and lime, a long drink very much liked by both the men and the women. But mostly in the evening it was Scotch which was drunk – *chotapegs* or *burrapegs*, as we used to call them. The *chotapeg* being two fingers of whisky and the *burrapeg* three.'

At the larger stations dinner on Saturday night would be followed by a dance at the club. 'In Allahabad we had one every Saturday,' recalls Nancy Vernede, 'and on Thursdays dances which were held just between tea and supper.' The Thursday tea dance was less formal than the Saturday dance, although 'there was always a band playing, either a military band or a police band and sometimes Anglo-Indian bands'. But on most nights at the club the 'evening get-together' ended at eight o'clock or nine o'clock, when everybody returned home for 'a thumping big dinner'. Those who lived near at hand might be escorted, as Rosamund Lawrence was, by *hath-butti-wallahs* 'who met us with lamps and sticks which they banged on the ground to keep away snakes as we walked through the darkness'.

10

Hazard and Sport

Horsemanship and physical fitness were the only gods he knew.
GEORGE ORWELL *Burmese Days* 1935

'Sport was the great thing in the old India', an obsession that had its roots in the dread that unless one kept fit one would catch 'some dreadful disease or other'. It thus became a credo of British India that to indulge in some sort of physical exercise was essential – particularly in the hot weather – and the result was 'a generation or two of enormously fit people' who went in for every sort of game and every sort of sport, all of it cheap and very procurable: 'This played an enormously important part in our lives. To have missed taking exercise in the afternoon you would have had to have been really quite ill.' Sport was something that both sahib and memsahib could indulge in equally. In fact, in Iris Portal's opinion 'women took far too much exercise in India. One was always told that one ought to take a lot of exercise. One was told that a jolly good sweat was a tremendously good thing to do in India, but I think it was very much overdone for women. They used to play violent tennis, or even squash in later days, or gallop about in the hot sun and get exhausted, and probably have to have a fairly strong whisky and soda at the end of the day to pull them

round. I don't think that that sort of thing is very good for a
woman's constitution in a hot climate.'

Sport not only brought the sexes together. It could also
bring British and Indian together. 'Playing games was of great
importance in your relationship with educated Hindus,' declares Christopher Masterman. 'I got to know Hindus of the
educated classes by playing tennis with them.' In the Indian
Army and the police, where there was always some sort of
exercise between five and dinner in the evening, games
provided valuable opportunities for British officers to exercise
and mix informally with their men. In mixed cantonments
casual games also provided a link between British and Indian
other ranks: 'In the evening we used to go along and have a
chat with the Gurkha boys,' recalls E. S. Humphries. 'We
would invariably find them playing football and they would
immediately split up and demand that we should join them.
From then on it was everyone for himself, with about forty
Gurkhas on each side, each having two or three British ranks
playing with them and with the ball being passed to the British
ranks by every Gurkha on their side.' In the hill country British
and Gurkha also competed in *khud*-racing, 'starting at the top
of a small mountain and making your way to the bottom and
then running up another one'. It was a sport in which 'the
little, tiny Gurkha men could lick the best of our British boys to
a frazzle'.

Very few individuals totally evaded the usual patterns of
sporting orthodoxy. Ian Stephens was probably unique in his
time in taking up yoga and cycling to his office in khaki shorts,
singlet and *chapplis*, followed by his bodyguard-orderly on
another cycle with a change of clothing: 'When one got to
the traffic blocks there were one's friends, the more conven-
tionally minded *burra*-sahibs. They'd have no ventilation to
speak of in their cars and the armpits of their suits would be
drenched with sweat.'

Many clubs had golf courses of varying quality laid out,
complete with local hazards: 'Crows would come down and

pick your ball up and fly away with it.' Squash and 'club tennis' was a feature of sporting life in all but the smallest stations. But the 'man's country' demanded more practical and more aggressive sports, involving either the horse or the gun. 'I went riding every morning of my life as far as I can remember,' declares John Dring. 'I always kept a couple of horses. I used them for touring as a district officer or just for exercise out in the early morning. When polo was available I used them to play polo or to hunt if there was a hunt available.' There were many areas where the horse was of great practical value. In the earlier days on tea gardens it was often the only means of communication. 'A married senior manager or superintendent had a buggy, and could drive about, but anybody else – an ordinary assistant tea planter or a junior manager – was expected to ride rather than drive. Your company always gave you an advance to buy the pony because you had to be able to get around on a thousand-acre garden.'

Rather better financial arrangements were available for army officers: 'Every officer in the Indian Army was supposed to have his private charger. It didn't cost him very much and it was fed free by the Government, and was used by him for his military purposes. In addition to that, you could always get from the local cavalry regiment a thing they called a seven-eighter. You paid the princely sum of seven-and-a-half rupees to hire one of His Majesty's chargers for one month.' Not surprisingly, the Indian Army was the most horse-oriented section of the British community. This 'tyranny of the horse, which was regarded as a sort of object of worship', reached its peak in cavalry regiments, where 'one lived and talked horses. Although a rule existed that shop could not be talked in the mess, it was accepted that horses did not constitute shop.'

The horse was also a great liberating influence for the memsahib. 'It took you where you'd never get in any other way,' says Nancy Foster. 'You always rode early before break-fast, riding for miles across country, riding out into the paddy-fields. You went through miles of mustard fields or beans with the most wonderful scent. You'd meet peacocks strutting about, you'd go through the villages and all the people were very friendly; they'd offer you a glass of milk or some fruit and they'd chat. I usually rode completely alone and never at any time, even at the difficult times, did I meet any unpleasantness or rudeness.' The ride was a rare opportunity for the mem-sahib to explore and make contact with the real India, as Iris Portal describes:

I used to ride out in the morning, very often alone, out into the blue, straight out into the plain and across the rivers. I took any little path I could find. It was the most beautiful country, not at all as people imagine India, but all up and down like downland with big fields and little villages dotted about. If you rode through a village the dogs would all rush out and bark and scream round your pony's legs and you'd crack your whip at them and they'd run away. You'd meet the villagers out in the blue coming home from the fields, or as you came near the villages. I must have looked very peculiar, a white woman with a pith helmet on a big, black pony, but they'd come out and put their hands together and say '*Ram, ram,*' and you'd say '*Ram, ram.*' As you went along the edges of the fields you would see a little tiny shrine, or perhaps a little tiny stone, a sort of lingam with red paint on it. I used to ride past these and I always touched my hat to the gods of the country as I went by – because they're there.

The early morning often saw other sporting activities get under way, some transplanted direct from the English sporting scene: 'In Lahore and Peshawar we had a hunt. We didn't hunt foxes but jackals. The jackals gave you as good a run as the fox – in fact rather better. We had fox-hounds imported from England, and we had marvellous days, just as good as a hunt in England except that there weren't many hedges to jump. You jumped over ditches mostly, irrigation ditches, and it was more like hunting in Ireland.' A certain degree of informality was allowed: 'Only the hunt staff wore a pink coat and white breeches. Some of the field wore a black tailcoat, but hardly anyone wore a pink coat and most wore an ordinary jacket. Everyone in the cantonment joined in; elements from the judicial side and the army, from the public works department, and some of the locals – the landlords used to come out mounted. The Viceroy invariably hunted when he came to Peshawar.' Girls from the Fishing Fleet were always enthusiastic followers of the hunt: 'They rode anything with four legs and fell into every river and had to be pulled out and generally speaking added an enormous amount of sparkle to our lives.' The big cities were by no means excluded from the early morning meets. In Delhi the Viceroy and his staff rode regularly to hounds and in Calcutta, paper-chasing provided a popular alternative. Specially designed courses and jumps were prepared, a paper trail was laid and 'you went out at half-past five or six in the cool of the morning. The Calcutta Light Horse and various different clubs would have their teams and you would go paper-chasing through the jungle.' Ridgely Foster recalls how Calcutta in the early morning 'was just teeming with high-quality horse flesh. The sight of the Calcutta Race Course on a December morning was quite tremendous. All the main princely houses, Kashmir, Jaipur, Bhopal, would have their strings of polo ponies and they would be ridden round, each one with his syce on, each one with the distinctive *puggaree* of the prince concerned. People would be doing "stick and ball" in the middle of the race course and horses would be having practice gallops.'

'Stick and Ball' – 'cantering around, tapping the ball, practising shots, getting your pony accustomed to shots on either side, under the neck and under the quarters and so on' – was in preparation for the one local sport which the British took up with enthusiasm. 'The obvious thing was to play polo,' explains Kenneth Warren. 'Everybody else played polo and you were expected to, and if you didn't like it, well you'd jolly well got to lump it. I once had an assistant who came and said he didn't want to play, he wasn't keen on playing polo, so I told him, "Well, if you can't play polo you're not much use to me. I'll have to find somebody who can." And that was the sort of attitude in those days.' Polo was played all year round, but with its high season in the cold weather, when the tournaments and the polo weeks were held. In the hot weather 'station polo would be a pretty low standard affair. One played to get exercise and one played only slow chukkas because it was too hot for the horses to play fast polo. There might be a number of the ICS, a couple of military officers, a policeman and perhaps an Indian superintendent policeman if one couldn't make up the numbers. We bought our ponies from Afghan dealers in the local fairs or we might buy one – and sometimes regret it – from a senior officer in our own service who wanted to get rid of one.'

A remarkable feature of the sport was that the more senior the sahib the better his game. Younger men lacked the means to support more than one pony: 'You had to ride it down to polo, you played it in a couple of chukkas, and that was about all it could do because you'd had it out all day and then you'd have to ride it home again. But as you got older and had a little more money you'd buy a second or perhaps even a third pony. Later on you could perhaps have one in a buggy and drive down and send your polo ponies down to the club ahead of you.' Here again the army enjoyed a great advantage. Whereas in other services it often proved that 'matrimony and polo were incompatible', this was rarely so in the army – and never in the Indian cavalry where horses for the Indian troopers were smaller than the troop horses used by the British cavalry and thus suitable for training as polo ponies. As John Dring recalls, 'When the remounts had arrived at my regiment we British officers all paraded under the Colonel to see which of the newly arrived remounts might make suitable polo ponies for our own use. Our argument was that if a troop horse developed into a good polo pony he was, by the nature of the thing, a good troop horse.' The game itself was 'rather similar to bob-sleighing, in the sense that you move at very great speed on something else, with the added excitement that you're very often riding somebody off or hitting the ball with someone trying to stop you. You got so excited that you shouted things like "Damn you, get out of the light!" or "Stop sticking your elbows into my ribs, you bastard!" – without knowing that you were doing it.'

It was only a small step from polo to pig-sticking, which some rated as 'the most dangerous sport of all. You can't see the country you're riding over because the long grass hides where you are going, and you have to go at a gallop to keep up with the boar. The horse may put its foot in a hole or a hollow and turn a somersault, and the spear itself is also a danger because of the heavy lead weight at its base.' John Rivett-Carnac recalls an instance of a rider who dropped his spear: 'The lead butt went forward, the point entered the horse's chest and came out behind his saddle, just missing the rider.' The boar itself was a formidable quarry: 'I had several horses cut and on one occasion a big boar charged me on and got right through my riding-boot. The tusk broke off in the bones of my instep and made quite a nasty wound. I had my boot cut off, disinfected the wound, then tied the boot on again and went on pig-sticking – which shows how keen we were in those days.'

The first rule of pig-sticking was never to do it alone. John Rivett-Carnac had a friend who broke the rule: 'The boar got him and stood over him and went on cutting his back as he lay with his arms along his sides. He was cut to bits and had to have over a hundred stitches in his back.' In more orthodox situations 'hog hunters' armed with 'hog-spears' rode in groups of four. 'It was a cruel sport,' admits Raymond Vernede, 'but the boar is a very valiant animal and he very often got away. When he died he died gamely, charging you, and this was why it was so important to have a really sharp spear to finish him off quickly. I can remember being charged by a pig head-on and getting my spear stuck in the front of his

"Whoof whoof"
A clever old horse taking care of a novice

'Whoof whoof' by 'Snaffles',
a popular illustrator of Indian sporting scenes in the twenties

head, and as we passed each other I was carried clean out of the saddle and ended up sitting on the ground still holding the butt of the spear with the pig in front of me stone dead.'

Pig-sticking meets were held in the cold weather 'when the crops had all been cut and the land was fairly bare'. The largest of these meets was on the flat alluvial plain of the

Ganges near Meerut, when teams and individuals competed for the Kadir Cup: 'One of the sights of dawn, just before starting the first beat, was that regular sight of all the chaps standing round holding their spears up and sharpening the blades to razor sharp with a small stone. Immediately a pig broke the horseman nearest the pig was traditionally the first on and would normally have the first chance of spearing it. The first spear got alongside the pig and tried to make it charge him. This was the moment you waited for. You held the spear under your arm in the traditional tent-pegging manner and you depended on the pig charging to drive your spear into the shoulder of the pig. If you didn't get the pig on to the point of your spear and it grazed off, of course the pig could cut your horse terribly.' Not everybody took to pig-sticking. 'I was persuaded to go out pig-sticking one Sunday morning,' recalls John Morris, 'on a horse which was lent to me by someone I'd never met in my life. While we were waiting in a sort of thicket for the pigs to break out the Master saw me on this rather restive white horse and shouted at me in a rather offensive way; "Take that bloody horse under cover!" When the pig finally appeared the horse I was on simply shot away like a streak of lightning. It had a mouth like iron and I was totally unable to control it, but I managed to stick on to it somehow or other until we arrived at its stable, by which time I'd lost all interest in pig-sticking and never indulged in it again!'

Riding after sows or leopards was frowned upon, the latter for reasons which soon became apparent to John Rivett-Carnac when he and three others went after one: 'I was going full gallop when the leopard leapt at me with his mouth open and his claws out. He just missed my thigh and landed on the back of my horse, made claw marks all down the rump of the horse and fell off. Somebody else charged it and speared it and finally it laid down and died.'

Both hunting and pig-sticking were never more than minority interests and not strictly a part of the great pursuit known as *shikar*. Up to the early twenties the Indian countryside was still 'teeming with game. Along the road you could shoot peafowl, deer, partridge, anything. Of course, it later on got shot out.' The opportunities for *shikar* seemed almost unlimited. 'More than once we got bags of more than a thousand duck in a day with eight guns,' recalls Kenneth Mason. 'One's gun got so hot that you had to have a second gun because you could no longer hold the first.' The general attitude to this overshooting was that 'there was so much game that there was no harm in it'. In time a new attitude began to take over. 'Having spent a year in the trenches in France I had no desire to kill or be killed,' declares John Morris. 'I paid lip service to *shikar* to the extent that I owned a shotgun and a rifle, but I don't think I ever fired off either of them.' Conrad Corfield was similarly affected by the Great War and never found any pleasure in shooting: 'I shall never forget seeing a German wounded and apparently blinded by a shell. He ran straight for us and of course was shot before he reached our trenches.' Others tried it and found that they did not always enjoy it, like the man who shot a brown bear and 'thought of all the little teddy bears that I'd ever seen before and hated myself'.

Despite the example set by viceregal and princely shoots, where game was 'slain literally by the hundreds and scores were kept to show how one viceroy had fared compared with a viceroy on an earlier occasion', trophy hunting and killing to excess was gradually being replaced by a more natural philosophy: 'It was in stalking and in hunting that you had your fun. The actual shooting meant nothing really. The only thing was to kill outright.' Chief among its rules was the unwritten law – 'never leave a wounded animal.' Equally important was 'the surrounding of the *shikar*, the camp and the camp fire mentality, which was more important to us than the actual killing of the animal'. Part of that surrounding was the 'complete quiet and absolute stillness' of the jungles and the hills. Here *shikar* assumed a very practical role, as Olivia Hamilton recalls: 'When I first went to the mountains I'd never used either a shotgun or a rifle but my husband said I must learn to shoot. The first thing he taught me to shoot with was a rifle, then he introduced me to a shotgun. This was very necessary because often we couldn't get either a sheep or a goat to kill so I'd go out into the jungle and shoot some green pigeon or a pheasant for supper, something to fill the pot.' *Shikar* was not a sport from which women were excluded: 'It was commonplace and usual for the women, the wives and the grown-up daughters, to shoot and some of them were very good.' Geoffrey Allen's mother was an All-India Rifle Champion, adept at shooting crocodiles on the Ganges – 'In those days full of crocodiles'. A far more common experience was sitting up at night for a tiger or leopard over a kill, as June Norie recounts: 'I had no idea that the forest could be so absolutely quiet, not a sound except for the wind and the dead leaves on the ground. I felt my face swelling every minute from all the mosquito bites. And then suddenly I heard a rustle and then this noise, a kind of woof, and I remember my heart beating as I thought, "Ooh, he's there." He came right up against the tree we were sitting on and I could almost feel his warmth as he walked round and round the trunk of the tree.' Olivia Hamilton, in much the same position, had no such warning: 'Suddenly I felt the tree dip. I couldn't believe it. Something shook the tree. So I cast my eyes down and there was the panther sitting right under my knees. I couldn't do a thing, I couldn't move, I couldn't get to my rifle. All I could see was those whiskers twitching, the eyes glaring, looking to and fro to see what was around. I just froze. I prayed that my husband would shoot the beast. Suddenly he jumped down and went very slowly to his kill. So then I got my hands out of my mackintosh and I raised my sights and I thought, "I must kill and not wound." I took a neck shot and fired – and with two or three bounds he was away. I heard my husband's voice say, "You've missed him, you've missed him." But as I stood up I saw him fall back, stone dead.'

The tiger, the very symbol of India, suffered greatly at the hands of the amateur *shikari*, its skin becoming too commonplace even to be put on display in the bungalow. Yet it was every young sportsman's dream to bag a tiger as soon as means or opportunity allowed. Geoffrey Allen shot his first tiger at the age of seventeen: 'It was Christmas Day, I remember. They'd all started dinner and I walked in and said, "I've shot the tiger," and nobody believed me.' Yet 'shooting from a *machan*, once you knew all about it, was not very sporting'. Very often it was simply a matter of holding the rifle straight and there was no danger to anybody – 'except the beaters of course'. By the early thirties shooting tiger 'for the hell of it' had largely disappeared: 'you shot a tiger because he was being a nuisance or because he was a man-eater.' Only in the princely states did the custom of laying on tiger on a lavish and totally unsporting scale persist, with an often docile prey being shot from elephants' backs or 'absolutely surrounded by *shikaris*' by viceroys, governors or visiting VIPs. Viceregal tigers were usually bigger than other tigers 'because when they measured tigers shot by eminent people they pressed the tape down every four inches as they went along instead of taking the measurements, as true sportsmen did, from nose to tail'.

Where tigers or leopards were cattle-lifters or man-eaters villagers continued to turn to the nearest European for help: 'They had tremendous faith in the European, to such an extent that they looked upon him as utterly fearless and a dead shot.' Sometimes this faith was misplaced. The Reverend Thomas Cashmore was once 'shaken by his toe at four in the morning and told, "*Sahibji*, in my house there is a very big tiger."' He sent for a friend of his, a policeman, who had one shot and missed completely, 'which upset the tiger quite a lot. The second shot just seared the tiger's temple, cutting its fur and sending it into a rage. I said, "You're a mug, you know, you really are. What are we going to do, leave it?" "You can't leave it," he said, "it's a wounded tiger. You borrow one of the villager's axes and crawl in, and I'll shoot the tiger over your shoulder." I thought this was a very bad show altogether, but I crawled in and he came in after me. It was one of the most magnificent sights I've ever seen; the eyes of the tiger glaring viciously and the muscles all rippling as he got ready for the spring. Then Alfie shot and fortunately for us hit him and dropped him like that. I went outside and said, "The tiger is dead."'

11

The Hot Weather

If Fate cast her lot in the North she is called upon year after year to face that pitiless destroyer of youth and beauty – the Punjab hot weather.
MAUD DIVER *The Englishwoman in India* 1909

The new year always began with a burst of military splendour, the King-Emperor's Parade on New Year's Day, when on every parade ground in India cavalry and infantry were to be observed 'marching past, trotting past or even galloping past in lines of squadrons'. This was 'the Army in India seen in all its glory', a sight that few watched unmoved, as Vere Bird-wood describes in recalling the scene as her husband's cavalry regiment passed the saluting base: 'There was a great deal of jingling harness, the cavalry regiments with pennants flying from their lances and their horses tossing their heads, all beautifully groomed. I doubt if there was a man in the regiment who was under six foot. They were all physically perfectly made and handsome to the nth degree, with a tremendous martial sense, a tremendous way of wearing their uniforms, a tremendous pride in what they were doing.' From a child's viewpoint the parade was 'a continuous conveyor belt of different music and colours – and all the time the dust rising up from the *maidan* and settling – like a dream picture seen through a gauze curtain!' In fact, this dream picture was the Armistice Day Parade on the polo grounds at Poona and the child in question, Spike Milligan, the youngest Survivor represented here, witnessing what was perhaps the last blaze of Imperial pomp before the slow eclipse:

> The most exciting sound for me was the sound of the Irregular Punjabi Regiment playing the *dhol* and *surmai* – one beat was dum-da-da-dum, dum-da-da-dum, dum-da-da-dum! They wore these great long pantaloons, a gold dome to their turbans, khaki shirts with banded waistcoats, double-cross bandoliers, leather sandals, and they used to march very fast, I remember, bursting in through the dust on the heels of an English regiment. They used to come in with trailed arms and they'd throw their rifles up into the air, catch it with their left hand – always to this dum-da-da-dum, dum-da-da-dum – and then stamp their feet and fire one round, synchronizing with the drums. They'd go left, right, left, right, *shabash*! *Hai*! Bang! Dum-da-da-dum – It was sensational!

Also in the parade were the elephant gun-batteries, which came on 'in a phalanx of six in line, all polished up, all their little toes whitened up. They had leather harness and the regimental banner was hung on the forehead of the one in the middle. The *mahouts* wore a striped turban, dark blue with a narrow red stripe, and they came in to the drum beat – ba *dum* . . . ba *dum* . . . ba *dum* . . . ba *dum* – and when they got in line with the Governor-General's box the *mahouts* would put their knees behind their ears and they'd all raise their trunks and go "Uuerghhh!" '

The New Year's Day Parade did not always proceed without incident. Charles Wright remembers 'one particular occasion in Quetta when we fell in and the right hand man was a corporal and a pretty wild boy. Now when they give the command "Fix bayonets" the right hand man takes three paces forward to give the timing for the other people to fix their bayonets. When the company commander called "Fix" this corporal took not three paces forward, but ran right through the bungalows into a carriage that was waiting there and drove off to the city and that was the last we saw of him.'

During the early months of the year the major social activities of the cold weather, which had reached their peak over Christmas week, gradually diminished in scale and frequency. In early March 'the Fishing Fleet left, complete with the Returned Empties who had tried their best and failed'. An early blossoming of summer flowers ensured that most stations had a flower show at least once a year, and just before the end of the cold weather the 'outstanding social event of the year' took place in Delhi, with garden parties, polo and tennis tournaments and horse shows, played out against the background of the Red Fort – 'a superabundance of gaiety and pleasure' that culminated in the Viceroy's Ball, 'like something out of the Prisoner of Zenda'.

India's climate followed an annual cycle of three distinct seasons: Cold Weather, Hot Weather and Rains. In South India the climate was said to be 'hot part of the year and hotter the rest of the year. It was never pleasantly cool in the so-called Cold Weather, but the temperature never rose as high in the Hot Weather as it does in Central or North India.' In Upper India the extremes and the effect on life styles were more dramatic. There was no spring to speak of: 'You go straight from a quite tolerable climate into an intolerable one.' In mid-April, 'something happens' as Reginald Savory describes:

> The wind drops, the sun gets sharper, the shadows go black and you know you're in for five months of utter physical discomfort. Mentally you have to battle against this heat. Physically you try and shut it out. When I first went out there was no electric light, there were no fridges and no electric fans – and to live in those conditions is pretty foul. We talked about 'shutting out' the heat. Hurdles of dried straw called *khas-khas tatties* were put across the open doors and the verandah, and a

man would be kept outside to fling water on them now and again, so that such air as did come into the bungalow was mildly cooled. I can smell to this day the nasty, mildew smell of the water on these *khas-khas tatties*.

We never slept indoors in the hot weather. We always slept outside on the lawn under a mosquito net, with a little table by our sides with a thermos flask or something with cold water in it – and with our shoes always on a chair because if you left them on the ground they might be occupied by a snake or a scorpion. One used to lie and look through the top of one's mosquito net at the stars. It was peaceful, but very hot. Then in the early morning it would start cooling down. At about four o'clock you'd drop off to sleep. And then up the sun came over the horizon and hit you a crack with its heat. The result was you took up your bed and walked into a bungalow which was still over-heated from the night before and which was oozing heat.

The glare was one of the things that I found most trying. It used to strike right through your eyes into the back of your head. The first rays of sun that came through the windows struck the floor almost like a searchlight. One would wander round outside when one had to with half-shut eyes. Heat, light, headaches – right up to September. You think it's never going to finish. Then one day you hear, miles up in the skies, the honk honk of geese or wild cranes, and you know that they are the advance guard of the cool weather coming down from wherever it may be – Siberia or somewhere. It's the most wonderful sound in the world. And you say to yourself. 'Thank God the *kulang* know it's cooling down. It'll be all right in another fortnight or three weeks' time.'

Until the advent of air-conditioning the hot weather had to be suffered 'like toothache'. Penderel Moon recalls how 'as the year came round and you got to April you began to think, "Hell, another six months!" About the first week of May when you thought, "Now we're in it" my bearer would suddenly produce a mango, and that was the one redeeming feature. Then you knew you'd got this fearful grind of work throughout the hot weather with no relief, no let up.' It was a time when 'you longed for a grey English day', with 'the heat coming off the ground and up your shorts and hitting you in an un- believable manner'. Unbelievable temperatures by day – the heat registering over a hundred and thirty degrees under a banyan tree – torrid afternoons with 'the air so still that if you ran a razor blade down it you could almost part it and walk through', and sleeping by night in the garden 'in a foretaste of Hades'.

The hot weather had its own characteristic accompani- ments. There were the *koels* and brain-fever birds whose calls went right up the scale 'rather like a man describing a race, though it was never regular. You waited for those last few notes and they would always come a few half-beats off.' Another 'very monotonous and very trying sound' was that of the tin-pot bird, 'a hammer sound all the time like a small cotton-ginning factory'. A night sound which disturbed those trying to sleep outside on their lawns was the sound of jackals howling 'like babies being torn limb from limb' and in town- ships there was the incessant barking of pariahs. It was a time of year when 'mad dogs often came around' and stray dogs were destroyed on sight.

'I lost four dogs from rabies,' states Jackie Smyth. 'It was a very dangerous affair because if you had a dog that died of rabies you had to make up your mind whether you'd been licked by the dog.' The vital need for treatment at an early stage and the impossibility of knowing for certain whether rabies had been transmitted could turn a brush with the disease into a frightening gamble with death. In Delhi Jackie Smyth's dog, named Kim, was frequently taken for walks by one of the daughters of the Adjutant-General: 'Kim con- tracted rabies and died and I couldn't think of anyone who'd been in contact with him the week before he died. Shortly after the time limit for treatment had passed I was round at the

Adjutant-General's house when the girl said, "Oh, Jackie, I forgot to tell you. I took Kim out last week and he was so glad to see me he licked me all over my face." My heart stood still – because at that stage nothing could be done about it. I had to make up my mind whether I was going to tell her father or anyone at all, and I came to the conclusion that it was quite useless and I'd got to bear it myself. I started to come round to call at their house almost every other day and they began to think that I had intentions with regard to the daughter, because I was always asking how she was. I knew it was all right if the rabies didn't come out within another week – and thank goodness, it was all right.'

The hot weather saw the employment of *punkah-wallahs*, for the hand-pulled fans in those bungalows without electricity, and at evening time there appeared the *bheesti* with his goat-skin bag, going round the bungalow sprinkling water into the dust and, with it, the unforgettable smell of evening: 'the smell of the grass when the heat has gone off it, dry heat and a quick cooling'. There were other ways of making the best of the hot weather. The first of these was to work and take exercise in the cool of the morning. Fitness was all-important and 'the only way to keep yourself fit is constant and regular exercise, being careful in your diet and your drink'. When the nights became intolerable 'we used to wrap ourselves in a wet sheet and lie down in it, so as to get the evaporation to cool us off a bit'. In the days before refrigerators there were simpler devices for keeping food and drinks cool. There was the ice box, which required replenishing every day and, where there was no ice, earthenware pots hung from trees in wetted straw-matting bags. Wherever possible movement and travel were avoided. 'I knew it was going to be a hot day,' recalls Norman Watney, 'because for the last thirty miles in the train I had stood up with my topee on, quite unable to sit on the hot seats.' Those forced to travel by train did well to secure a large block of ice so that 'you could sit with your feet on it until it melted away'.

The only sure way of beating the hot weather entirely was to avoid it. The time-honoured custom of taking refuge in the Hills persisted till the Second World War. Central and state secretariats retired annually to the nearest hill stations and wives and children followed suit, with a number of husbands taking local leave to join them for a month or two. 'Bachelors helped out by taking their leave in the cold weather so that they could be present in the hot weather to allow married officers to get away up to the Hills. It was done quite willingly, with great camaraderie.' Not all the womenfolk retired to the Hills. In the twenties and thirties an increasing number took to staying behind with their husbands. 'I always stayed behind if I could,' Frances Smyth recounts. 'The great thing was not to take any notice of the hot weather. I loved the hot weather because it was a challenge. I remember I used to say, "A wife's place is with her husband," but it was really because I wanted to stay in the plains myself. When all the women and children left, India heaved a deep sigh of relief and became herself. You really felt that you were getting to know the real India and not just the superficial British cantonment type of India.'

For those who stayed behind life continued, but in a more subdued manner. 'In the small district you had no companionship, you had no women, no club life. You did your work, you had your meals, if there was any shooting you would go out and do some shooting, you then had dinner and went to bed.' For John Rivett-Carnac 'the hot weather was quite the worst period of my life. Whenever I feel bored or lonely now. I cast my mind back to what I went through and realize that I'm in heaven by comparison.' Where there was a club its role became doubly important. 'One lived in one's house – which was darkened to keep out the heat – in the gloom rather like a prison, and you just felt in the evening that you must escape.' In darkened offices and courts work went on throughout the summer: 'We had fans but even a fan couldn't cope with the climate after midday. It was really a struggle to keep awake, your papers were flying all over the place and your arms were covered with sweat. If you inadvertently put your arm down on something which had been written in ink, the ink was blurred and your arm was dirtied. It was not until we got air-conditioning that one realized just what a difference it made.' In the cities a certain social life also continued, as Radclyffe Sidebottom recounts of Calcutta: 'When the Fishing Fleet left you became freer. The weather was hot and passions were high and you behaved in quite a different way. The girls that you couldn't be seen with during the cold weather, the Eurasians and the "poor whites" who were absolutely riddled with sex and very beautiful, were comparatively fair game. You hadn't got to marry them and they courted you. Moonlight picnics were a very common event. You drove your cars or you rode your horses out until you came to a peepul tree. There you took out your cold chicken and your champagne or whatever it was and you had your party.'

Of those forced to endure the hot weather, few were worse off than the ordinary British soldier. 'You longed to go to the Hills,' states Ed Brown, 'but it was only the married people or boys who went to the Hills. The ordinary soldier was left on the plains. In the really hot weather he used to finish at nine a.m. and for the rest of the day had to occupy himself as best he could. You weren't allowed to go out, except to the latrine, and from then on you were incarcerated in your bungalow. It became dreadfully monotonous. The soldier sweated it out in one long torment of heat.' Spike Milligan remembers the soldiers on their *charpoys* in the barrack-rooms: 'They'd lie there, many of them naked, under a mosquito net to keep the flies off, and the only thing moving was the *punkah* above them going backwards and forwards, backwards and forwards. Many a man just sat there and watched the *punkahs*. I suppose there was little else one could do but just watch.' The army attitude to the hot weather was simple: 'It was just not recognized.' The daily routines continued barely modified: 'I remember seeing regiments go by starting a route march and I thought they were wearing a different colour uniform at the back because they were just soaked with sweat. There was a spine-pad parade first thing in the morning and these spine-pads used to get soaked through with sweat and transfer it on to their uniforms. But you never saw them slacking. They were very fit indeed and there was no surplus of fat on any soldier I ever saw.' It was a time when tempers frayed, when 'many arguments used to go on and sometimes blows were struck'. Charles Wright recalls how in Multan it was 'so hot and so dusty and so boring that it got on people's nerves. I remember one sergeant, he may have had bad news from home, I don't know, but he got his rifle and put a bullet through his head in his bunk.' Mental illness had no place in the army vocabulary. 'It was all just bad discipline,' says Stephen Bentley. 'Where a weak-minded chap's mind snapped in the heat then, of course, they said, "This is a breakdown of discipline. Court martial him and put him in detention for three months, four months, six months." This was commonplace.'

Towards the end of the hot weather there was always a great sense of expectancy. Living by the Arabian Sea at Ratnagiri, Anne Symington recalls how 'we used to go out every evening for a walk from Thibaw's Palace. It was right on the sea and you could see the monsoon coming, you could see it miles away coming over the sea.'

The coming of the rains was always dramatic: 'Hot wind blew through our bungalow day and night from this huge open plain, and then the clouds began to bank up and bank up and there was an unbearable feeling of pressure. Then the rains came down with a terrific force such as you hardly ever see in Europe, and probably for two or three days this would go on, and within those two or three days the whole area round the house turned green. We used to plant seeds of cosmea and zinneas and in no time at all they were up and flowering, and an extraordinary life burst out, with frogs and toads hopping about the paths. At first it was absolutely wonderful.'

Nowhere was the monsoon more eagerly anticipated than in military barracks up and down the plains. 'When it did start men used to rush out absolutely naked, dancing about in the rain after being confined in the heat for such a long time. There was so little to do that even the rain was an event, something to be welcomed, looked forward to and enjoyed.'

Those living in the old country bungalows had special problems, as Rosamund Lawrence recalls: 'Everything gets dried up with the intense heat and the bamboo poles shrink, so there are gaps. When the monsoon comes the rain simply crashes in. It's like living under a waterfall. During the first days of the monsoon my husband and I went to bed holding up umbrellas.'

Relief from the heat was always short-lived. If the hot weather was bad it was far worse in the rains, when a hot, dry climate was simply replaced by a humid one and 'the air got very, very sticky, with more or less constant rain for six weeks or a couple of months'. Stephen Bentley asserts that it was even possible to *see* the humidity: 'When it stopped raining the vapour used to rise out of the ground up to a height of about a foot and remain static. I saw a chap get a shovel and stick it into one of these banks of vapour, and it stayed on the shovel as he picked it up and took it right through the bungalow to the other side, where he just shook the shovel to release it.'

This humidity was at its worst in Eastern India: 'Because of its humidity the Calcutta hot weather was a horror,' says Ian Stephens. 'I look back upon it with loathing and astonishment.' It was a time of universal sickness, 'a period when one's children invariably got ill,' when even the healthiest people suffered. 'It made me feel tired and slack,' remembers Raymond Vernede, 'as if my blood had been diluted. I nearly always got boils. I wasn't half the man that I had been in the hot weather.' Skin infections – eczema, impetigo and prickly-heat – became commonplace. In the army there was dhobi-*itch*, which was said to result from bad laundering: 'The dhobis would bring back your shirts ironed with knife-edge creases. Probably the seams inside were stiff with starch, and this resulted in the itch.' Prickly heat was a dreaded complaint: 'Little pimples rising over every inch of the body so that you couldn't put a pin between a pimple.' According to Ed Davies 'most soldiers had it. A chap would be playing cards and begin to scratch lightly. By the time the evening was out he'd be rushing round like a madman, tearing himself to pieces trying to quieten the irritation. I've seen one or two people tear themselves to ribbons, tearing their chests down till all the skin was hanging down in layers. We had to restrain people, otherwise they'd have done themselves further injury.'

The rains also brought out snakes, cockroaches, mosquitoes and a multitude of insects. In Bengal there was a month when 'you had nothing but large, repulsive greenfly over everything. They went just as suddenly as they came, and then you had a small black beetle, commonly known as the stink bug. It was in your soup at a meal, it was in your ink when you tried to write a letter. It was everywhere and was quite innocuous unless you squashed it and then it deserved its name. That again suddenly vanished, and then you had the small, white jute-moth which – again – was quite innocuous unless you knocked it and then you got a weal of eczema down your hand.' It was the rains above all other things that made India 'the land of sudden death'. Rosamund Lawrence recalls how, during the monsoon, 'we were giving a dinner party and I suddenly noticed a most awful smell. I thought, "Good heavens, whatever is this?" I was sitting next to a colonel of the IMS and he said, "For God's sake don't touch the fish, it's stinking." So I said, "Yes, but how embarrassing, what am I to do?" and I went on shovelling these bits of fish about and he said, "Oh, you can't possibly touch it; it's death." In India you could be ill one day and dead the next.'

12

The Hills

Up in the hills young men are rare; down in the plains young women are rare. Young men are spoiled in the hills and lost in the plains.
AMY BAKER *Six Merry Mummers* 1931

The great refuges of India were the Hills and in Northern India, as Olaf Caroe describes, the proximity of the Himalayas:

> You get these burning plains right across India, fifteen hundred miles of them, absolutely flat with rivers wandering through them fed by the snows, and behind them the greatest range of mountains in the world. You gradually go up from tropical and sub-tropical climbs, through European and Alpine flora until you get right up into the snows. I don't think there is anything in life which is such a relief and such a physical delight as going from the heat of the plains in the hot weather up into the mountains, gradually feeling it getting cooler. I remember the first time one gets to a base in the hills and the water is cold; what a delicious feeling to have cold water on your hands!

The same sense of relief and delight was to be found among the lucky ones among the British troops as they marched up into the Hills: 'We'd halt at these wayside camps; there'd be a rushing stream close by the camp, and you'd wake up in the morning in the darkness before daylight to hear the bullock-cart drivers getting their beasts on to the carts. You'd smell the smoke from the fires, you know, with the stream rushing by and then the piper would play reveille and it was rather wonderful.'

Even for the privileged the hill stations that the British built were often unapproachable except on foot or on ponies. 'Where the cars stopped,' remembers Nancy Vernede, 'we would get into our *dandys* or on to our ponies. A *dandy* for an adult would be carried by four men, and a child's *dandy* would be carried by two.' Earlier still, as Mrs Lee remembers, 'the wives and children went up to the hills in *doolies*, long box-like arrangements with a door that you draw back and crawl into. You take your bed-roll with you and you can barely sit up in it. All you can do is lie down.' On arrival visitors found 'a jumble of houses of every imaginable semi-suburban British kind perched on the top of a ridge,' houses with 'a sort of English feeling about them. The smell was English, the houses were furnished in a much more English kind of way and there were fires in the evening.'

The Hills provided a brief escape from the extremes of India's climate and culture – and something more: 'No Englishman of sensitivity who's been to India and loved the hills can deny the Hindu inspiration that the Gods live in the hills somehow.' The Hills had an atmosphere that 'stirred the imagination, something almost verging on the religious'. Part of the magic lay in the sounds; the doves, the barbets and the cuckoo, sounding 'even more beautiful than it does in England'. There were the sounds of water, 'a sort of pulsating coming up from the valleys below, the sound of the river rising as pulsating waves of air,' and the human sounds: 'A passerby singing at the top of his voice, or those little penny pipe whistles they made which would come right across the valley from where they were being played.' There was also the majesty of the Himalayan snowscapes, often veiled in summer but occasionally revealing tantalizing glimpses of themselves through the clouds, as in Darjeeling where 'you could look across miles and miles of tea gardens in the valley and then suddenly see this enormous great mass of ice and snow almost hanging in the sky, rather like a Chinese print.'

The retreat to the Hills in summer was part of an old tradition: 'The headquarters of government used to move up to the hill stations, taking with them all their files, an annual migration which cost thousands of rupees. And this of course set the standard. If government moved up a lot of officers had to move up, and so there was a social life. Wives moved up mainly because of the heat down below, and of course other wives weren't going to stay, so they all went. There was a considerable attraction in this annual exodus and they managed to have a pretty gay time.' At places like Simla, Mussourie, Naini Tal and Darjeeling the European womenfolk would 'take a house and share it with another wife or live in a flat or in a hostel and their husbands would take their short leave and join them for a week or a fortnight.' Of all the hill stations of India Simla was by far the most glamorous, so much so that some critics considered it 'not really part of India'. Simla provided a summer residence for the Viceroy and the Commander-in-Chief as well as for the Delhi and Punjab secretariats: 'It was plastered against the side of one of the lower ranges of the Himalayas. You came up and found yourself on these ledges, one ledge above the other, nothing but narrow paths everywhere and these appalling drops. You were constantly looking over an edge of some kind or up at a great towering hill. If you take a community and jam it on to this series of ledges at 8,000 feet you will get a claustrophobic and enclosed society.' Within this society that was 'unlike any place in India', the images of Kipling lingered on. 'I found it so like Kipling as not to be quite true,' recalls Mary Wood. 'It was what you expected Simla to be. One felt one might meet Mrs Hauksbee around any corner, especially when you walked down the Mall. I don't think it had changed very much.'

Sheltered though it was, Simla was one of those places in India where there was 'a tremendous feeling of the supernatural'. In Simla and elsewhere 'many people felt they had experiences at houses reputed to be haunted and there were many stories about hauntings. All around us there was death and that led on naturally to a feeling for ghosts.' In Mount Abu Vere Birdwood had a room in which both she and her mother's ayah felt 'something evil'. An old *chokidar* had the answer: 'In 1913 a young memsahib had died in that room and ever since her ghost had walked there. In the winter months when the house was empty he had seen this memsahib walking about this room. Many years later when I went back to Mount Abu I found out from the church register who the woman who had died there was, and sure enough she was the young wife of a British officer. And I went to her grave in the churchyard and I stood by this grave and I said to her, "You gave me a very bad summer."'

Ann Symington's encounter with the supernatural was even more sinister. Shortly after her marriage she took up residence in an enormous palace built for the exiled King Thibaw of Burma and his ill-reputed Queen Supalayat, known to the British soldiers as 'soup plate'. 'One night I was fast asleep under my mosquito net when something made me wake up,' she relates. 'I looked at the foot of my bed and there was a grey, misty figure indented into the mosquito net with a knife in his mouth leering at me. I couldn't scream but I went, "Ohhhh . . . ohhhh . . ." My mother heard me and came running along and I said, "Oh, I've just seen the most awful man and he's just disappeared!" And he did, he actually faded away! Some months afterwards when I went to another station someone said to me, "By the way, did you ever see the ghost in Thibaw's Palace?" And I said, "Yes I did!"'

Part of the nineteenth-century atmosphere of Simla was due to the absence of the motorcar. 'The annual move to Simla was romantic but rather horrifying,' remembers Ian Stephens. 'The memory that sticks in my mind is of these coolies pulling and humping terribly heavy loads on their backs up hill slopes. I felt the same repugnance to travelling around Simla in a rickshaw. Eventually one got accustomed to it, but never quite used to it. I always made a point of paying my rickshaw men very well which somehow satisfied my conscience – and thereby had the pleasure of a very fast rickshaw team to get me quickly to dances.' In summer, as in all the more popular hill stations, 'the sex ratio was reversed. There were a lot of married women and there were very few men – and most of the men were in the secretariat or some sort of office job and were, as a rule, rather sober sorts of characters. On the other hand, the young men who came up for brief periods were on holiday and on the loose.' This was the 'rather different kind of atmosphere' in which the Simla Season took place: 'Depending on their rank, they either came to dinner, lunch or a tennis party. You could get rid of an awful lot by a garden party. We used to reckon on three to four dinner parties per week, and the same with luncheon parties. It was a whirl of entertainment, interspersed with some quite gorgeous ceremonial and pomp, particularly in the Viceroy's house.'

As assistant private secretary to the Viceroy, Conrad Corfield observed court etiquette at first hand: 'One of the first things I learnt was that the court bow was only made from the neck, it was much easier than the curtsey, which everyone knows is a terror for the ladies, especially the elderly. Dinner every night at Viceregal Lodge was an occasion for full evening dress. At its close His Excellency would rise from his place at the dinner table and all the men would follow suit. The ladies then departed, led by Her Excellency, and one by one as they reached the door were required to turn and curtsey; an awkward manœuvre which was watched in fascinated silence by the men. At one time we used to have bets on the number of cracks which could be heard – the maximum was four, one by each knee at the dip and the same for the recoil.' A more active participant in this ritual was Sylvia Hadow, later Lady Corfield: 'There was a step just in the doorway and you had to be very careful when you did your curtsey to put your heel either below the step, which was the safest place, or the other side of it. Jordan, the butler, knew all about this and he stood behind the curtain waiting to catch any lady who made a mistake. We had a little rhyme about this: "A lovely party, dinner ended, Jordan passed."'

It was on one such occasion that the most famous faux pas of the inter-war years was made. Like the stock *babu* jokes and the one about the well-dined brigadier who tried to light his cigar with a geranium, it became one of the fixtures of the period, to be repeated almost ad nauseam throughout 'Anglo-India': 'The Viceroy had his own orchestra which used to play most evenings during dinner, and on one occasion Her Excellency enquired the title of the tune that was being played. No one could remember so an ADC was sent to enquire from the bandmaster. The conversation at the table changed to another subject during his absence. He slipped into his seat on return and waited for an opportunity to impart his information. At the next silence he leapt forward and in a penetrating voice said, "I Will Remember Your Kisses, Your Excellency, When You Have Forgotten My Name."'

Iris Portal, who was born in Simla and lived there as a child, returned as a teenager:

In the two summers I spent at Simla I never thought about doing anything but amusing myself. It was excessively gay. My record was twenty-six nights dancing running, at the end of which I could hardly keep awake, but I had to attend an official dinner that my mother was giving and was severely reprimanded for falling asleep in the middle when talking to a very woolly old judge.

You had to ride everywhere in Simla, or go in a rickshaw, which was expensive. So one used to ride out to lunch and to race meetings in one's best dress hitched round one's waist with a blanket tied round you, and a big floppy hat. You used a horse as you would a vehicle and the *syce* ran on ahead and waited for you and held your pony while you attended your function. Then you rode home again. During the summer this was all very well, but as soon as the rains began these poor men were drenched.

We were always meeting the same people. Everyone knew rather too much about everyone else's affairs, and it was a staple topic of conversation – what was going on, who was going out with so-and-so. If there was a very big party you always knew about it and if you hadn't been invited you took that very seriously.

There was the most marvellous Black Hearts fancy dress ball one year. They even went so far as to send for some of the prizes from Paris, which we thought was very exciting indeed. They always took the real tennis court of the United Services Club for their ballroom and did it all up with special Black Hearts decorations and coloured lights and so on. The British in India had a curious convention at all dances where sitting places known as *kala juggas* were constructed. These were coy little sheltered-off places where you were allowed to disappear with your partner. You were not allowed to go to the party unless you were chaperoned but it was understood that once you disappeared into the *kala jugga* you were left alone. Of course, you were never there very long because the next dance started. You did your dances in blocks. There were certain people you always had the same dance with, but if you had a blank space in your programme you hung about at the door for a bit hoping for the best. If nobody came to ask you to dance you went off to the Ladies and had a wait until the next item on your programme. At every one of the Black Hearts parties they had two sets of Lancers and the top set of Lancers, which the Viceroy danced in, was always girls, with the married women in the second set.

The Black Hearts were 'very rich bachelors', who in time became White Hearts – 'Black Hearts who had got married

and whose wives were at home'. There was also the Gloom
Club, made up of 'bachelors who wished to return hospitality'.
Their invitations were all black-lined and couched something
like: 'Chief Mourner and attendants of the Gloom Club
request the pleasure of So-and-So to their wake which is to
be held at the club on some-such day.' The dance programmes
were shaped in the form of a coffin with a skull and crossbones
and, of course, a black border. The Gloom Club members
decorated the club in the most funereal drapings and everybody had to be in a costume dictated by the Chief Mourner.

Another popular source of entertainment and a major
feature in Simla social life was amateur theatricals. The Simla
Amateur Dramatic Company, composed of 'officers and their
wives and sweethearts and anybody who aspired to act', put on
five or six productions every summer: 'We didn't do Shake-
speare or anything like that. We did Frederick Lonsdale and
Barrie and Pinero and so on.' The plays were put on at the
Gaiety, 'an enchanting little theatre, beautifully built, like a
little tiny jewel of a theatre in some small German principality.
Everybody came, including the Viceroy, the Commander-in-
Chief and the Governor who all had their special boxes.
Everybody came in full evening dress, usually after dinner
parties which they'd got up before the show. The rickshaws all
roared up and down outside the theatre and it was very gay
indeed. At the end of the run there was a great assemblage on
the stage and then all the bouquets came pouring in and you
looked enviously to see if anybody else had got more bouquets
than you, and then you had a riotous party on the stage, which
was awful fun.'

Within this marked holiday atmosphere and absence of
officialdom, where 'wives very often got bored without their
husbands', flirtations were inevitable: 'There were certain hill
stations to which colonels of Indian Army regiments would not
allow their subalterns to go on leave. Poodle-faking stations,
they were called.' Those who went after the ladies were known
as 'poodle-fakers' and were said to come down from the Hills

'fighting rearguard actions against the husbands coming up'. The husbands, in their turn, were 'fairly broadminded and wouldn't really expect their wives to go up and live in monastic seclusion'. Both circumstances and surroundings were highly conducive to romance. 'It's difficult to convey how enormously romantic the atmosphere was in Simla,' says Iris Portal, 'the warm starlit nights and bright, huge moon, those towering hills and mountains stretching away, silence and strange exotic smells. Very often coming home from dances the current boyfriend used to walk by the side of the rickshaw, murmuring sweet nothings and holding hands over the side of the hood, nothing much more than that, but it was very romantic. Everything was intensely romantic – and a lot of people were lonely.' As an army officer explains: 'When they were bored and we were bored we used to meet up together. There was no harm done. There weren't many scandals and ninety-nine per cent of those little liaisons in the Hills were as harmless as you can think of.'

Yet there was 'a frightful lot of chitter-chat – most of it completely bogus'. One constant belief was that at the Charleville Hotel in Mussourie 'a separation bell was rung by the manager at four o'clock in the morning'. In actual fact, within this permissive atmosphere 'a strong sort of Edwardian morality prevailed. If a young officer wanted a bit of fun he would pay court to a married woman, not to a girl.' Unmarried girls, 'brought up in an atmosphere of innocence', were not considered 'fair game'. There was also the fact that 'you were looking for a husband – and so you knew where to draw the line.' It was what Iris Portal describes as 'the last remnants of the Kipling business. I was never allowed to go out with a young man alone. It always had to be in a party with at least one married woman in it, even though she might be only a few years older than oneself and certainly not terribly moral or virtuous. That didn't matter a bit, provided she was married. The married women had an edge on one because they could go out alone with a man and they could give parties as they pleased. And they did very often pinch the most attractive young men.'

But for most people these sojourns in the Hills were brief and uneventful. Many wives came down to join their husbands in the plains at the earliest opportunity and without waiting for the rains to end, 'then there was the main exodus in about September or October when everything was wound up in the Hills and they all came down'. Those who had stayed on in the plains waited for the first signs of change. 'Every year there seemed to be a miracle. After humid nights and weeks and weeks of rains you wake up one morning, go out on the verandah and there's just that hint of freshness. The rains are ending, the autumn is coming.'

13

The Cold Weather

*The arrival of a cargo (if I dare term it so) of young damsels from England
is one of the exciting events that mark the advent of the Cold Season.*
LADY FALKLAND Chow Chow 1857

The Cold Weather was heralded by greenfly hatching in
millions, autumn breezes and the 'cold weather line' that
appeared in the plains at sunset, 'this long flat line of smoke
just above the tops of the houses, and as you passed you would
get a waft of something, a whole range of scents'. It was the
time of year when 'one could think of planting seeds, because
those were the months when one could grow English flowers'.
For India autumn was the season of festivals, beginning with
Dashera, which in Gurkha regiments was celebrated with
animal sacrifices: 'British officers were supposed to attend
and did attend but nobody liked it very much. If the bullock's
head was severed with one blow that meant good luck for the
regiment for the rest of the year.'

But the British had their own autumn rituals. The first was
the arrival in September of the catalogues, sent round in good
time 'to enable customers to choose what they would like
despatched from London for Christmas'. In October this was
followed in the larger stations by the already familiar ritual of

dropping cards: 'We started off by going to Government House and writing our names in the book there, then we went on to the Deputy Commissioner's wife, and on down the ladder to the Colonels' wives and Majors' wives and so on, dropping our pasteboard cards into the little wooden boxes hung outside the gatepost of each house.' This annual ceremony had its origins in the days of the old East India Company 'when all the people who had been senior enough and wealthy enough to move up to the hill stations to avoid the unhealthy hot weather came back in October. The ones left alive among those who had had to stay down in the plains went to call on them at the beginning of the cold weather to show that they were still alive – and this became a tradition. On the fifth of October you put on your morning suit and you went and called on them.' Accompanying this formal acknowledgement of autumn was an abrupt change of attire from light summer to heavier winter wear.

Next came the arrival of the Fishing Fleet and the changing of partners: 'In the hot weather you took out what was called the "B" class girl, usually Anglo-Indians, who were dears in every way and the greatest fun. But the moment the cold weather started they were taboo, because all the young girls from Roedean, Cheltenham and the great schools of Britain came out in the P & O liners and you were expected to toe the line. You kept your nose clean and if you were unwary you caught yourself a wife.' In the cities and the larger stations the cold weather's sporting and social activities were 'absolutely endless'. Nobody enjoyed them more than the young girls fresh from England. 'I lived in a whirl and I thoroughly enjoyed it,' remembers Deborah Dring. 'Every day we went to something, a tea dance or a dance or a ball or a dinner party.'

With six months of almost perfect weather ahead, elaborate 'weeks' could be planned: 'Most stations had their "weeks" during which various dances and balls were held and various games were played, polo and hockey tournaments,

tent-pegging and pig-sticking and so on.' The season reached
its peak with Christmas week, distinguished in Calcutta by the
visit of the Viceroy. At Belvedere, the old Viceregal Lodge,
there was always a fancy dress ball and a children's party
where Father Christmas entered on an elephant.

Christmas in India was celebrated by the European community in its own style. 'Everybody made an effort' at
Christmas; the Christmas dinner and the Christmas cake
followed the familiar pattern, although pea-fowl – 'beautifully
white flesh but very, very dry' – frequently took the place of
tinned turkey. Christmas up-country was often spent in camp
in or on the edge of the jungle, sometimes in tents, sometimes
in *dak* or forest bungalows. These camps were mostly simple
affairs; 'usually two or three families would join together and
bring their tents and elephants – if they had any – and pool
things to eat.' There would be rough shooting by day, then 'a
bath in the round tin tub at the back of the tent,' followed by
quiet suppers – '*dal* and rice perhaps, with a poached egg on it'
– round a roaring camp fire. The campers slept surrounded by
the sounds of the jungle, hearing 'the rasping saw of a panther
prowling round the camp'. This was 'the natural India' that
many loved.

Other camps were more sophisticated; governors' and
viceroys' camps that remained highly formal, and maharajahs'
camps that were lavish in the extreme, as Geoffrey Allen
recalls of Darbhanga Raj: 'Hundreds of tents were put up and
the guest house was absolutely full of VIPs. People from
hundreds of miles all round Bihar were asked. Hospitality
was lavish. Firpo's, the caterers from Calcutta, used to come
up and very good food and drink was laid on, with Firpo's
servants, dressed up in livery, passing the food round. Hall and
Anderson's, the furnishing firm from Calcutta, used to bring
up literally hundreds of wardrobes, beds, mirrors and dressing
tables by train to furnish all these tents.' Instead of rough
shoots there were elephant drives against big game with
'elephants and beaters all out in a very long line, driving

through the long grass, with dozens of cars coming and going,
bringing food and provisions in and out of the camp. In the
evening there was usually a big dance and for these dances, of
course, one changed into evening dress. The men always wore
stiff, white shirt fronts and the ladies all had to wear gloves.
The band used to come up from Calcutta to play.'

The cold weather provided maximum opportunity for movement in comfort and style. If 'the key note of British rule was
indeed personal rule' it was best characterized by the Tour. Not
only was this an essential duty for every official in the district,
but it featured in one form or another in nearly every trade and
occupation; policemen, canal workers, *box-wallahs*, missionaries
– even soldiers – had their tour or its equivalent. Sometimes its
purpose was obscure: 'It was never explained to me,' declares
Penderel Moon, 'what you were supposed to do, so I had to
invent objects for myself.' Yet the end result was very clear. 'It
allowed two widely separated cultures to meet in friendship and
affection,' and it depended for its effect on slowing down to
meet the pace of India, 'the pace of the bullock cart'. The
motorcar remained 'an alien thing' in India; roads were strewn
with hazards and pock-marked with holes gouged out by the
steel-rimmed wheels of bullock carts. In hot weather the
wooden spokes of the wheels of the earlier motorcars tended
to work loose and 'one had to tie a special kind of grass around
them and keep it wet the whole time'. Wherever possible 'you
reverted to the coaching age'.

The duration of the tour varied with occupation and
district. 'I'd go out on tour for four or five weeks,' says
Cuthbert Bowder, who worked in the irrigation branch of
the pwd in the United Provinces, 'and then come back to my
base for about ten days' rest. Then I'd be off again. I should
think that I toured for about nine months of the whole year.'
The same pattern was followed by those working in the forest
or agriculture services or in other branches of the public works
department. Elsewhere it was a matter of weeks rather than
months: 'Some skimped it a bit, others would make every

possible excuse to extend the period for as long as possible.' Some used the tour for sport, arranging it so as to cover the best parts of *shikar* in their districts; others used it as a way of adding to their incomes 'because there was a system of extra payment for travelling allowance or, as we called it, TA. If you went on tour you used to say, "I'm going hunting the TA bird."' Very few failed to enjoy it, perhaps because 'you were completely independent'. For Percival Griffiths it was 'the best part of one's life in one's early days. You camped outside a particular village for four or five days, dealing with all its problems and its disputes, and then moved on to the next village perhaps ten or fifteen miles away. In a district where the paperwork was heavy, it would follow after you, probably by bullock cart, and when you'd done your active work during the day you sat up at night and disposed of your file.'

Modes of transport varied from district to district. In the Sind, as David Symington recalls, it was the camel: 'As an assistant collector I used to have seven baggage camels and a riding camel. They were all provided by a contractor, and the contractor was also the man who had the honourable job of driving my riding camel. These camels were hired out on a peculiarly Sind idea of the rate for the job; the assistant collector used to pay seven rupees a month for each camel, the collector used to pay nine rupees and the commissioner in Sind used to pay about ten or twelve rupees. This seemed absolutely right to everybody!'

Accompanying her husband from one camp to another, Norah Bowder often travelled on an elephant 'with the baby and the ayah and the cook and the bearer. We used to all sit back very comfortably on one elephant. Sometimes the *mahout* would have the baby sitting in front, on the elephant's head. When it got warm it would fill its trunk and spray us with water to keep us cool, and if we were eating an orange it would put its trunk back and take the orange and eat it. It would stand there and my little boy would put his bricks underneath the elephant and nobody ever worried. Ayah used to sit leaning up against the elephant's leg.'

BRITISH OFFICER'S DISTRICT TOUR 1936—37.

బ్రిటిష్ ఆఫీసరులు జిల్లా చుట్టు ప్రయాణం.

Place.	చోటు.		Date. తేది.	Time. కాలము.	Address.	విలాసము
Rajahmundry	రాజమండ్రి.	...	30-10-36	0900—1300	Traveller's Bungalow	ప్రయాణికుల బంగ్లా
Cocanada	కాకినాడ	...	31-10-36	0900—1600	,,	,,
Samalkot	సామల్ కోట్	...	2-11-36	0800—0930	Railway Station	రైల్వే స్టేషన్
Pithapuram	పిఠాపురం	...	2-11-36	1100—1600	Dy. Tahsildar's Office	డిప్టి తహసీల్దార్ జారి ఆఫీసు
Tuni	తుని	...	3-11-36	0900—1100	,,	,,
Anakapalli	అనకాపల్లి	...	3-11-36	1400—1700	Traveller's Bungalow	ప్రయాణికుల బంగ్లా
Vizagapatam	విశాఖపట్నం	...	4-11-36	1100—1600	,,	,,
			5-11-36	0900—1200	,,	,,
Vizianagaram	విజయనగరం	...	6-11-36	0900—1200	,,	,,
Chipurupalle	చిపురుపల్లె	...	6-11-36	1530—1700	,,	,,
Chicacole	చీకాకోల్	...	7-11-36	1300—1600	,,	,,
Ichapuram	ఇచ్ఛాపురం	...	8-11-36	1300—1600	,,	,,

I hope that all ex-service and serving Viceroy's Commissioned Officers, N.C.O's and men, who wish to, will come and meet me at the above places and times.

All should bring their Discharge Certificates and Civil Employment Forms with them when they report to me, and correspondence connected with grievances where necessary.

It is emphasised however that while I will be pleased to see any ex-soldier, there is no obligation for men to come unless they have grievances or suggestions to make or prospective recruits to bring forward.

నోటీసు.

పటాలమునుండి డిశ్చార్జులో వచ్చినవారును, తత్సమయం సేవవృత్తిలోవుంటుగల వైస్రాయ్ కమిషన్డ్ ఆఫీసరులూ, నన్ కమిషన్డ్ ఆఫీసరులూ, సిపాయిలూ ఇష్టపడినవారలను మరియు పటాలమువార చేరనూనున్నూ క్రింట కాలములలో కనవచ్చును.

సేవవృత్తిని నిడిచియుండు వైస్రాయ్ కమిషన్డ్ ఆఫీసరులూ, నన్ కమిషన్డ్ ఆఫీసరులూ, సిపాయిలూ వారి డిశ్చార్జి సర్టిఫికేట్, సివిల్ పనికొసంబడిన కాగితములూ మరియు చేరే కాగితములనుసంబడిదానిని తేవలె యూను. నన్న వయులు యిదిచెప్పనొడిన దానిని తేవచ్చును.

నాక్ష చూసినసిపాయిలని చూడ ప్రియముండినను, విన్నపములేని వారు అసావశ్యకముగా రాకూడదు కాగా జాగర్ చేయు రిక్రూటలువుండిన తేవచ్చును.

Bangalore,
October 1936.

H. E. M. COTTON, *Lieut.*, R.E.,
Q. V. O. Madras Sappers and Miners.
Q. V. O. మద్రాస్ సాపర్స్ ఆండ్ మైనర్స్.

British officer's Cold Weather Tour, Bangalore, 1936

Up on the North-East Frontier Geoffrey Allen toured the Himalayas on foot:

You carried all your rations and took hundreds of porters with you, and you went out into areas which were unmapped. You recorded the names of the villages and the populations. You tried to make friends with sometimes hostile tribes, and generally showed the flag. You handed them a little pinch of salt and you took a little on your finger, ate it and said, 'This is Government salt. Would you like to become a Government servant? You eat salt, too, if you want to be friendly to Government.' And normally they ate the salt.

A lot of your tour consisted of dropping right down very steeply into a valley and then climbing very steeply up the other side again. We lost quite a number of porters over the years who slipped off the track and fell with their loads into the rivers below. The usual method of crossing rivers was over a thick, twisted rope made of plaited canes stretching from high up on one bank to low down on the other. There was a thick wishbone-shaped piece of wood made from a tree root, and suspended from this was a leather thong in which you sat. You backed into this, sat in it very uncomfortably, put your hands above your head and held on to this wishbone. Then they gave you a push and you shot down this sloping bamboo cable, with the cane rope smoking furiously, to the other side. They were very clever at landing without bashing their brains out on the other side. Eventually you got quite used to crossing in this manner.

In contrast, most touring in the plains was carried out in some style, as Cuthbert Bowder describes:

As soon as you had had dinner on the night before all the kitchen was packed up, with only sufficient pots and pans left out for breakfast the following morning. Your office equipment was also packed up and loaded on to carts or camels and they travelled during the night to your first stopping place, about ten miles distant. After breakfast the following morning the remainder of your gear was packed up, and that reached your destination at about five or six o'clock in the evening. When you arrived at your office table the following morning everything was exactly as you'd left it before leaving. If you had been reading a book, for instance, on some abstruse point of canal law, it was there again at exactly the same angle on the table.

The tents were rather like big tops. The floor was strewn with straw and over the straw you had a *dhurri*, a cotton carpet. They were well furnished with easy chairs known as Roorkee chairs, and when it was cold enough for a fire there was a stove in the tent which made it extraordinarily comfortable. After breakfast you got on to your horse and you rode off to inspect the canals. Then you came back at about one o'clock and lunch would be ready for you. You'd probably have a pink gin or something just before, and then you'd read the papers and rest until half-past two when you went to your office table and conducted interviews with various people, peasants and the landed gentry, until four o'clock. At four o'clock you took the gun and a couple of men and you got the odd partridge or pea-fowl or hare, just enough to keep the pot boiling, without any trouble at all. Then you came back and had a grand tea of hot buttered toast before a roaring fire. The sunsets were very beautiful but very short-lived and almost immediately after darkness clamped down. After tea, back again to the office table where I used to work until dinner, and very often work again after dinner.

On tour the district official was never off duty, as Philip Mason explains: 'When you were walking round in camp in the evening a villager would come to one with some story he wanted to tell. He would try to ingratiate himself in the first place by telling you that there were some duck on a pond a little way off, or that a partridge was hiding in the next bush.

But after a bit you would say, "Now tell me, what's the story? What's it all about?" Sometimes the only thing to do was to sit down on the ground and say to him, "Sit down, brother," and then it would all come out.' Contact was also to be made in other ways. 'We used to have two little rival surgeries, my wife and I. My prescriptions were usually rum, castor oil and aspirin, and hers were quinine and aspirin – and we did a little very rough surgery.' In return the official could be sure of the warmest hospitality. 'They would probably offer you refreshments, almost certainly hot milk or a boiled egg, which the headman would peel with rather grimy fingers as a special mark of honour and offer to you.' This hospitality reached an extreme on the North-West Frontier, where travellers might be required to sit and talk 'while a goat was slaughtered and cooked'. Even where there was no food to be offered there were other forms of hospitality, as George Wood discovered when he sat down with a circle of village headmen and found 'one rolling up the trouser of my right leg and one rolling up the trouser of my left leg. Then two pairs of horny hands began to massage my muscles as a traditional welcome to the tired traveller.'

Sometimes hospitality – often with a mis-spelt WELLCOME writ large upon a triumphal arch – was a little more formal. Kathleen Griffiths remembers how 'many a time when we've been on a long, weary tour and are returning very late at night, a little primary school has heard that we were passing and they've had the whole school decorated with marigolds and garlands, and they have kept open because they knew that we could not pass them by. I cannot count the number of times I have listened to the repetition of the story of the Maharanee Victoria.' Only in one respect – Penderel Moon saw it as a 'grave defect' of British rule – was this personal form of government visibly at fault: 'There was all this emphasis on village touring but it was never suggested that you should do what I call urban touring. Yet it was in the towns that there was most discontent with the

British Raj. There was nothing to bring officers into direct touch with the city populace.'

Both the British and the Indian Army had their forms of touring. The Indian Army had the recruiting tour, undertaken by its officers in the area from which the regiment drew its recruits: 'It gave one a chance of keeping one's finger on the pulse,' explains Reginald Savory, 'and we got to know our own men very well indeed, not only those serving but their fathers and, in some cases, their grandfathers and their uncles.' A measuring-stick – 'almost as much a sign of India as the spinning wheel' – was always carried, 'the kind of thing vets used to use for measuring horses. We used to measure our men in the same way. You knew how tall they were but they liked being measured, and if you thought they were good enough then the local sub-assistant surgeon would feel the man to see if he had an enlarged spleen and then he was told to come along behind us.' As the recruiting tour proceeded it would assume the proportions of a triumphal procession:

At the entrance to the village you'd probably be met by the local village band, big drum, pipes, side-drums, many of them retired drummers from the regiment. Then you'd be received by your head host, generally one of the senior ex-army officers, and brought out under the great village tree, the peepul tree, under which the whole village would come and sit and keep out of the rain or the sun. There'd be a table with a white cloth on it and I would sit there with the senior Indian ex-officer and hear complaints, because our job was not only to pick up recruits but also to keep in touch with the recruiting area, so one was able to do a tremendous amount.

In front of the recruiting officer there was always a bottle of whisky. They'd pour you out enormous tots into very thick glasses and they saw to it that you drank as much as you possibly could. While you were turning away talking to a chap on your left your glass was being surreptitiously filled. You'd turn round and find two or three glasses waiting for you.

Eventually one got to know what was happening and one used to hand one's glass over to somebody else. But it was a very, very warm reception. We'd sit and we'd talk and we'd discuss old friends and all the old times, all the old regimental stuff that nobody else could understand, but it was the breath of life to these chaps.

When I left in the morning they would all come out. They'd take you off with the band to the village boundary and as I left they'd all cry the Sikh war cry, '*Sat Sri Akal!*' and I would shout back, '*Sat Sri Akal!*'

There was also the route march, common to both armies; movements from the plains to the Hills and vice versa, from one station to another, to and from the North-West Frontier – often along the Grand Trunk Road, one of the lifelines of India upon which soldiers had marched since the days before the Mutiny and which had altered little since Kipling's day, with its 'traffic of bullock carts, of cattle being driven to pasture, the continual stream of pedestrians, staging posts usually marked by the *dak* bungalow, and the groves of mango trees which gave shelter from the sun'. The route march might well cover a distance of five hundred miles 'which at fifteen to twenty miles a day would take a month. After the first day or two the blisters wore off and it was sheer enjoyment, and, of course, we saw much more of the country moving at a walking pace.'

To the British soldier the extended route march was certainly 'no joke'. Many BORs dreaded foot-slogging in India. 'Your feet would be so blistered they felt like hot water bottles,' recalls Ed Davies. 'As you walked along a fine dust would rise in vast clouds and get up your nose, into your eyes, into your ears. Drinking water on the march was taboo. It was strictly forbidden. I used to suck a pebble all the way, which is what my dad told me to do, and found it very soothing. The officers used to ride up and down seeing everyone was all right saying, "Are you all right, Smith? Are you all right, Jones?" and we used to rally round and continue the march. Sometimes we used to carry the equipment of someone who'd weakened. We'd say, "Here y'are, Smudger, let's have yer bundle, let's have yer rifle, or let's have yer pack." ' To help pass the time the regimental band played and in both armies the traditional songs – 'very repetitive and most of them unprintable' – were sung. Francis Dillon recalls how the troops in his Indian Mountain Battery sang 'the famous Pushtu song called "The Wounded Heart": "There's a boy across the river with a bottom like a peach but, alas, I cannot swim." '

For all its discomforts the route march was one of the 'great experiences' of India and there was always the feeling 'that you were with friends,' as Charles Wright describes:

You fell in with your rifle and pack by company, mules in the rear and bullocks with the baggage waiting behind, and you marched at the rate of three miles an hour. The first halt was always twenty minutes after leaving camp when the troops relieved themselves on the side of the road. That was march discipline: always go out on the left of the road, take off your pack and rifle, sit there until two minutes before you were due to fall in. The whistle would blow, you'd don your pack and rifle and fall in in threes. The band would strike up and you'd march happily along for fifty minutes, off for ten minutes, on again until you arrived at camp. You passed flat expanses on either side, fields of sugar cane, a village on a high mound with the well worked by a bullock or a camel where all the villagers used to collect to bring the water in. They would pull their saris over to hide their faces and sneak into their huts, but the children would come out to dance along with you. On the road bullock carts passed by, axles creaking and groaning, the boy drivers shouting at the beasts, prodding them with sticks. We'd arrive in camp, each man absolutely red, the dust caked on his face with the sweat. The tents would be unloaded and placed on their respective places and when everything was ready the commanding officer would blow a whistle and all the tents would come up like a lightning stroke, as if a little town had sprung into being at once. The mess marquee and odd tents here and there were pitched and the campers settled down to housey-housey or a snooze in the sun. You'd finished your day's marching, you'd have a couple of beers in the canteen and lay down your bedding roll under the stars. Night would come very suddenly, velvet night, very peaceful – and it was marvellous!

14

The Mess

> *Have you had any word*
> *Of that bloke in the 'Third',*
> *Was it Southerby, Sedgewick or Sim?*
> *They had him thrown out of the Club in Bombay*
> *For, apart from his mess bills exceeding his pay,*
> *He took to pig-sticking in* quite *the wrong way.*
> *I wonder what happened to him!*
>
> NOËL COWARD
> *I Wonder What Happened to Him* 1945

'India was the soldier's paradise. If you were in the Army you could do anything.' The British officer in India had privileges of rank and regiment, rare opportunities for sport and action in the field. But from the civilian's point of view his life was circumscribed. 'The Army in India led a life which was quite different from ours,' says David Symington. 'They lived in messes, and they had their troops to drill and exercise and look after. They lived in a smaller world than ours.' This smaller world centred on the military cantonment: 'Cantonment life and village life had certain similarities. An Indian Army regiment in cantonments lived very, very much unto itself. It did not encourage visits from outside. In fact it discouraged them. The moment a stranger appeared in barracks a report was sent at once to the adjutant.' This insularity was heightened by the code by which the British officer lived. 'The British officer was very different from his contemporaries in civil life,' says George Wood. 'By force of circumstance we were separated from our contemporaries and as time went on foreign service broke childhood friendships and replaced them with service friendships. The result was that we became ingrown, we were godfathers to each other's children, we had the usual family quarrels and special friendships. We felt ourselves more and more a class apart, a samurai class. We were a family of brother officers, and there is no other word to express our relationship.' It was an attitude that the army wife shared – as far as she could: 'It was that lovely feeling of being part of a very closely knit family. They weren't strangers. Some you liked better than others, but they were the family, so that was that.' In the Indian Army the word extended to include the men as much as their officers. 'It was very much a family affair,' echoes Claude Auchinleck, 'and that was the charm of it. Son followed father and nephew followed uncle. That was what made the Indian Army so popular and so beloved by the British officers who served in it; because they felt they belonged to the family.' This sense of family – *bhai-bund* – was brought home to Rupert Mayne, not an army man himself but nevertheless a Mayne, on the centenary celebration of the 6th Lancers, known as Mayne's Horse: 'In the midst of the pensioners a very old man came up to me, buried his white beard in my chest and sobbed. I could not make out what he was saying so I patted him on the shoulders – and then the truth came out. He pulled up his trousers and showed a very badly wounded knee. And he explained to me that in a charge in Mesopotamia he had been hit by a Turkish bullet, had fallen off his horse and that my uncle had dismounted and carried him off the field.'

Before joining an Indian regiment the 'unattached' subaltern had his year to serve with a British regiment. He studied

Urdu, learnt the ways of India and was 'vetted' by the regiment of his first or second choice. This could involve an invitation to stay with the regiment for a few days. 'I thought I'd try for the Guides because they had cavalry and infantry,' recalls Reginald Savory. 'That would have enabled me, if I fell off my horse too much, to swap from one to the other. The Guides were one of the most famous regiments in the Indian Army, they were *It*. As my second string I put down the Gurkhas; they were also very smart, very *pukka* indeed, and I spent a week with them in their mess. However, I was not selected – and I only found out the reason why after I had retired. I sent them a cheque in payment of my mess bill and I forgot to sign it. It was sheer forgetfulness but I think the Gurkhas thought, "Here's a pretty crooked sort of chap, we don't want him!" ' For Lewis Le Marchand the procedure was rather easier; he joined his uncle's regiment, the 5th Royal Gurkha Rifles: 'At last, after years at Sandhurst and another year in a regiment which, as much as you loved it you couldn't call "My regiment", you found yourself in your own regiment, allowed to wear its button, its uniform, its mess kit, its particular flashes on the topee and its shoulder badges. You spoke of it as "My regiment. I joined my regiment," and, after a number of years, that is the first thing that you have.'

Whichever regiment you joined the same institution dominated the cantonment. 'The Officer's Mess was the centre of regimental life,' recalls John Morris. 'Here the unmarried officers spent a great deal of their time and had their meals and in particular, dined together every night.' Most messes conformed both architecturally and socially to the same pattern. The 3rd Gurkha Rifles Mess at Landsdowne was no exception: 'It was completely jerry-built, with bricks, wood, bits of stone, and without architectural merit of any kind whatsoever, designed by the officers and built by the troops themselves. And it was furnished similarly, with every sort of local-made jerry-built furniture. One entered the mess through a foyer which was furnished with rapidly decaying heads of animals which had been stuffed. On one side was the billiard room, the walls of which were also adorned with stuffed animal heads. All round the walls of the dining room were arranged the portraits of previous commanding officers. We always used to talk among ourselves and say that when an unpopular commanding officer left we would in no circumstances allow his portrait to be hung in the dining room – but tradition always won.'

Attached or unattached, joining one's first mess could be, as Reginald Savory recalls, a pretty 'rigid' affair: 'I remember the night we joined after a long and dusty train journey from Calcutta. We were allowed to dine in the mess in our plain clothes because we hadn't had time to unpack our mess kit, but we dined in what was in those days called the "dirty dining room". The mess was pretty stuffy. I was terrified of the commanding officer, we all were. I was equally terrified of the majors. The captains we treated with some respect and the senior subaltern put the fear of God into us. Altogether we were a little bit – to use a civilian word – regimental, but then all this was pre-1914, when the army was a little bit more blimpish than it was later on. The war taught us a thing or two.'

But even after the Great War there were routines that remained set and unbending, as John Morris describes:

One arrived in the Mess about half-past seven, dressed in full regimentals – stiff shirt, skin-tight trousers, skin-tight jacket and all the rest of it. One had a glass of sherry and as soon as dinner was ready the mess sergeant or mess havildar saluted the senior officer and announced that dinner was served. Then we trooped into the dining room in order of rank.

Dinner in the Mess was a most extraordinary meal because although we were living in fairly primitive surroundings we always had a most elaborate dinner. You invariably started with what was called a first toast. This was generally a sardine or half a boiled egg on a piece of soggy toast. You then went on to tinned fish. Then you had a joint and then pudding and a savoury, which was more or less the same as the first course and was called the second toast.

As soon as the last course had been served the mess sergeant placed three decanters in front of the senior officer; port, madeira and marsala. These were circulated and on Saturday nights, which was guest night, it was obligatory to drink the health of the King Emperor. After the royal toast the regimental pipe band was brought in and paraded round the table. The noise was absolutely deafening but it was considered the done thing to say how good it was. As soon as the senior officer had lit his cigar or cigarette or cheroot, one was free to smoke. But one was not free to leave the table until the senior officer did so and this frequently resulted in a great many boring evenings, especially with some of those old gentlemen who insisted on telling their stories of prowess in the hunting field which we'd heard innumerable times.

Conversation was informal but a certain protocol was observed: 'It was assumed automatically that a captain was more intelligent than a lieutenant, and a major more than a captain and so on. As for expressing an opinion which differed from the general point of view, that was almost unheard of. It would have been considered very bad manners not to agree with the senior officer and, of course, one was not allowed to mention a lady's name. If you mentioned a lady by mistake you had to pay for a round of drinks. The usual topics at table were the goings on in the regiment; who had done well in the football competition, who had shot well and so forth. This sort of thing was necessary for good discipline in a good regiment.' At breakfast the conventions took a different form: 'One just wasn't supposed to speak to one's fellow officers at breakfast time. In front of each place was a wire reading frame on which you could prop a book or newspaper. They weren't much use because the newspaper didn't arrive until the late afternoon. We subscribed to various papers and magazines in the mess, the chief of which was the *Field*, which was regarded almost as a sort of bible of sport. But one day it was discovered that we also subscribed to the *New Statesman*, so a special meeting was called and *La Vie Parisienne* was ordered in its place.'

The mess was where the unmarried officers ate and slept and so a certain easing of formality was quite in order: 'The mess is your home, so a subaltern has as much right as a senior major or the colonel. Whereas on parade you'd be addressed by your surname, in the mess you're Pat or George or whatever the name might be. It's your home and you do exactly as you please in it.' But it was 'home' with one important qualification: 'Except on guest nights women were not allowed in the mess.' For the army wife the mess was 'a place to which you did not go. In the same way, you did not walk about the parade ground. That was holy ground.' So while the mess was 'a place of refuge for the bachelor officers of the regiment, it was also a refuge for married officers who wanted to get away from their wives'. Nor were ladies necessarily welcome on guest nights, which were welcome opportunities to 'let yourself go'. After the band had played off and the anteroom had been cleared, games were played: 'High-Jinks', described as 'a fairly rowdy affair', or 'High Cockalorum', which began with six or eight people bending down and a similar number jumping on their backs; cock-fighting, with 'two officers sitting on the floor trying to throw one another over', or contests that involved 'people jumping from ibex's horns on to the mantelpiece and then on to a bison's horns and so on all the way round the room'. Senior officers were always fair game. Visiting generals would be shot off the ends of mess tables wrapped in blankets and if, in full flight 'you could not succeed in striking a match it was a misfire and you were shot again'. Occasionally limbs were broken – and quantities of furniture. In John Cotton's Light Cavalry Regiment 'the Mess had a ballroom which used to be cleared and used as a race track for bicycle races. This nearly always ended with a large number of windows being broken. The following day we would persuade one of the senior officers to certify that there had been a storm the previous night.' Guest night was also the occasion for 'a good deal of drinking. Drink was very cheap, with whisky at about six rupees a bottle, but that was offset against the small salaries we were all paid. Nevertheless, the senior officers certainly drank a great deal more in those days. What always surprised me was their capacity for holding their drink. One might have a very riotous guest night, finishing at three in the morning, but at six o'clock mounted parade the same officers would be there, impeccably turned out and able to sit on their horses without any sign of having been the worse for wear a few hours earlier.'

Before joining the 15th Ludhiana Sikhs, Jackie Smyth spent his unattached year with the Green Howards, who 'played hard and drank quite hard – at guest night you were always charged for two glasses of port even if you didn't drink any'. As a new officer and guest of honour, he created an enormous sensation when he asked for a lemonade: 'Everyone looked up as though some sort of strange animal had been introduced into the mess.' Certain regiments – British or Irish rather than Indian – prided themselves on being 'hard-drinking regiments'. Reginald Savory remembers one such regiment, 'hard-drinkers to a man, from the colonel downwards'. On the night before their departure for Europe in September 1914 they were 'drunk to a man. The next morning I went to the railway station to see them off. They were led by their band – poor devils, how they managed to play I don't quite know. They were followed by the colonel and his adjutant on horses, and about twenty or thirty private soldiers. The rest were either carried along behind the regiment in bullock carts or left drunk on the parade ground. They were shovelled into the train and some of them, who were more drunk than the others, actually died in the train on their way to Karachi.'

Every regiment had its own standards. In the Bengal Lancers a high price was put on horsemanship: 'The absolute height of success was if you were a good polo player and played in the regimental team. Nothing else really mattered, neither your military competence nor anything else, but if you played in the regimental polo team you were tantamount to a god!' Whatever its code, regimental esprit was dependent upon shared values: 'There was always this threat that if you didn't conform you'd be shunted off somewhere.' Those who fitted in got on, the misfits were quickly eased out: 'When it became noticed that a young officer was never going to make it, it was suggested to him that he should transfer to one of the Service Corps or the Remount Depot, where he would find a larger scope for his slightly different personality and talent. Many people transferred, generally for financial reasons and without being misfits, so it was no disgrace.' The greatest crime of all was letting the regiment down – and the final arbiter was always the colonel, who was, as Lewis Le Marchand explains, 'the man that keeps you on the straight and narrow. I remember my colonel saying to me, "I don't mind a bit what you do on leave out of this country, but what you do in this country is my concern and the regiment's concern. Any dud cheques, any unpaid club bills and any foot wrong socially in this country is very much my concern and the concern of the regiment." The Indian Army officer's word must be his bond, his behaviour must be beyond all criticism, because if it isn't he won't get the best out of his men.'

The honouring of bills was regarded as all-important: 'No officer was allowed to let the seventh of the month pass without paying his mess bill.' Despite that, 'most young officers lived beyond their means. The Army hadn't recovered from the idea that to be an officer in the Army you had to have private means. The result was you pretended you had private means and you lived as if you had, but you hadn't.' Sometimes the only solution was a visit from the regimental *banya*; 'Very very surreptitiously so as not to let anyone know – but of course they all did – you would arrange for him to let you have a thousand rupees. He'd come round to your bungalow in the evening through the back door. Your bearer would say,

"There's a gentleman to see you," knowing full well who he was. The *banya* would bring out wads of notes from his pocket and you would sign a chit and you probably wouldn't even ask what interest was going to be paid.' The general impecuniosity of junior officers was only one of the impediments to early marriage: 'You didn't get a marriage allowance until you were twenty-six years of age. If you got yourself embroiled with a young lady as a young officer the colonel would put his foot down and say, "You're not getting married yet."' There was also the question of suitability. 'In my regiment,' recalls John Morris, 'it was customary to ask the colonel's permission to marry. There would be a great many questions asked as to who the lady was, her background and so forth. In a small, closed community it was desirable that anybody coming into it should fit in with the people already there.' Sometimes the advice of other members of the regimental 'family' was also sought. 'In Lansdowne we had the most superb example of a memsahib you could find anywhere in India. She was the widow of an officer and had gradually become over the years the sort of super-colonel of the regiment. Nothing was done without reference to her and she provided in her day a great many wives for various officers – nieces and so on brought out from home. Nobody would have been so bold as to get married without asking Mrs Fizzer's permission or advice as to the suitability of the proposed bride.'

Marrying into the army required a major readjustment on the part of the bride. The army was a male-oriented society, dominated by military discipline, where 'wives tended to acquire the rank of their husbands. The colonel's lady regarded herself as a sort of colonel and certainly she commanded all the other wives of the regiment.' Although she was now part of a 'close-knit family' the army wife lacked a positive role to play. Only in the last decade of the British Raj did the military memsahib – largely through her own perseverance – really establish herself within the military community and find a genuinely creative outlet for her energies. Until then, many probably felt, as Vere Birdwood did when she married into Probyn's Horse, that at least 'it was a total loss of the quality of life, at any rate for the women. The life itself was excessively boring, trivial, claustrophobic, confined and totally male-oriented. The army wife was not expected to do anything or be anything except a decorative chattel or appendage of her husband. Nothing else was required of her whatsoever. She was not expected to be clever. It didn't even matter if she wasn't beautiful, so long as she looked reasonable and dressed reasonably and didn't let her husband down by making out-rageous remarks at the dinner table. She certainly had wonderful opportunities for riding and for participating in all sorts of horse sports, but apart from that and looking after her children and running a fairly decent dinner party, there her role ended.'

Life was made no easier by the frequency of military postings and the long separations that came with active service. With two years as the average duration of a posting the army wife had little opportunity to put a home together. She had also to endure the absolute lack of privacy in regimental life where 'every facet of your life was known – with the side result that there was virtually no immorality whatsoever because of the extraordinary communal life that we lived. So it had a sort of bonus of an extremely moral existence – but, oh my goodness, it was dull!' Not all military life was so dull – or so moral. The 'Fornicating Fifth' was said to be blatant in its wife-swapping, but elsewhere a discretion prevailed. 'There were love affairs going on in every station,' declares Frances Smyth, 'but it was a question of . . . "You mustn't be discovered."' Vere Bird-wood recalls the 'very strong unwritten law that regimental officers could have little affairs with wives of other regiments, but to do so with a wife in your own regiment was much frowned upon. So strongly was this law obeyed that in a Frontier station, when the husband was away campaigning, it was generally considered wise for the wife left behind to have a young officer to sleep overnight in the bungalow as a guard. As far as I know this privilege, if you can call it that, was never abused.'

Yet military life had many compensations. There was always that 'tremendous sense of community that you get from being one of a crowd, of the same lot and the same spirit'. What wife could fail to respond to the splendour of a ceremonial march past – 'and of course, if your husband is leading the parade – this very handsome man, beautifully dressed and waving a sword – it is extremely moving.' And for the husbands themselves, there was 'no finer feeling than being at the head of six hundred men, all marching behind you, probably fifteen miles and nobody falling out. You never feel it again after you leave a regiment.'

15

The Barracks

The men could only wait and wait and wait, and watch the shadow of the barracks creeping across the blinding white dust.

RUDYARD KIPLING *Soldiers Three*

'We used to think of India as a place of stations, never as a place where people had homes and where they lived.' Of all sections of the British community the circumstances of the BORs had changed least since Kipling's day. They remained the least privileged and the most restricted. A German businessman visiting India just before the Second World War remarked to his host that on his journey from Calcutta he had failed to see a single British soldier: 'Where are all your troops? How do you rule here?' The answer lay partly in the 'great segregation' that Stephen Bentley became conscious of when he and his comrades in the Seaforth Highlanders first landed in Bombay and which they were 'going to feel in ever-increasing intensity as life wore on'. It was a characteristic of British rule in India that 'the military were never to the fore' and, in fact, they were spread very thin across the land. As far as possible the military cantonment was self-contained – with its own approved bazaar – and access to the local community limited. 'The first order that appeared when you got to a new station usually stated that all Indian villages, Indian shops, Indian bazaars and the civil lines were out of bounds to all troops.' The BOR was thus all but confined to barracks, barracks which were 'the same everywhere, drab, very widely spaced with no signs of greenery around to break the monotony. Just sand, sand and sand again.'

Within these confines military duties continued in the usual way: 'You paraded for your meals. You paraded to see the doctor. You paraded to draw your rations. You paraded to draw your stores. You paraded to draw your ammunition. You paraded on Sundays because Church Parade was compulsory. It was parades 365 days a year. Any hour of the day or night the call would come up, "On Parade, On Parade."' But parades and military duties took up only a small proportion of the BOR's time. Most of his off-duty hours he spent in his 'bungalow'. These were not bungalows in the usual sense 'but more in the nature of aircraft hangars, very solidly built, about 250 feet long, about 100 feet wide and between 30 and 40 feet high. They were very light, very cool and well ventilated. The cook-house, latrines and other parts of the barracks were all separate. In many cases the cook-houses and the latrines were as far as two hundred yards away from the bungalows.'

Since the bungalow was shared by a platoon of anything up to fifty men, the ordinary soldier had little privacy: 'All he could lay claim to was perhaps one hundred cubic feet for ninety per cent of his life.' He had his own bed and his own kit box. 'This bed was the centre of his life. He used it for everything. He used it as a writing desk, as a cleaning room, as a work bench, as a card table, and when he wasn't doing anything on the bed he was sleeping on it. A great part of the time in India he slept, principally because he had nothing else to do.' The kit box contained all the soldier's worldly goods. 'You weren't allowed to have anything that couldn't go into that kit box. It had always to be locked and your lock had to be burnished and always shining brightly because it was inspected every day.' A vital item of equipment, as Ed Davies, a soldier in the Dorset Regiment, explains, was the 'mozzie net' with 'four poles at each corner of the bed and reclining over the top and right the way down a net like a queen's bedchamber. We used to lower it down before the mozzies came in the evening after the sun went down and keep it well tucked all the way round.'

The tedium of daily routine for the ordinary soldier was softened by the services of the camp followers, known as *wallahs*, the first of which began before reveille, with the visit of the *nappy-wallah*: 'He'd shave you and you never had an idea until you woke up all nice and cleanshaven and with a face like a baby's bottom, and he'd charge you at the end of the week.' With sun-up came reveille and the sound of the morning gun, which used to 'echo all round the quiet barracks and startle the crows. You'd hear "Boom . . . quark, ark, ark!"' The *char-wallah* came round with a big silver urn and poured out tea into the mugs at the side of each bed. This was paid for by the annaworth and was reckoned to be 'good stuff'. Then came physical training on the barrack square, cold showers and a change into uniforms 'pressed the night before by one of the *chokras*'. These 'boys', often elderly men, looked after the needs of a number of soldiers in return for a rupee a week from each man. Breakfast was usually 'what we called a khaki steak, very tough meat worked to a frazzle' and had to be fetched from the cook-house and taken over to the dining-hall, with the ubiquitous kite-hawks waiting to swoop down upon some unsuspecting rookie out from Blighty: 'He'd come out so unconcerned, whistling, with his plate of grub in his hand, and all of a sudden the kite-hawk would swoop down and leave him with nothing.'

Army rations were not thought to be adequate. 'All the years I remained in the ranks,' recalls E. S. Humphries, who served in the Royal Scots, 'I spent the whole of my money to provide myself with sufficient food to prevent malnutrition.' Vendors were always on hand to make up the deficiencies. 'The egg-*wallah* frying eggs in a large pan, the *dudh-wallah* with his little pats of butter and milk, and the ham-*wallah*, a fellow with a board with a roll of ham on it which he cut.' The most exotic of the vendors was the sweet-*wallah*, 'usually a fat and cheerful man who would announce his arrival by chanting in a loud, strong voice, "Jimmy Kelly good for belly, take and try before you buy. Sweetie! Sweetie!" He would put his tin box on the verandah and before one's very eyes display vast amounts of white, sugary sweets mixed with coconut, all for the price of four ounces for one penny.' All the camp followers had to be licensed by the regimental quartermaster. Some were specialists of rare degree:

You'd get the fellow who came round the verandah of the bungalow shouting 'Corn-cuttit *wallah*!' He'd cut your corns with a nice, horn-shaped little tube that was put on the corn and would draw it out. If the battalion was on the move you'd get a fellow coming round who'd call out, 'Names-to-put-on-the-kitbag *wallah*' and he would paint your name and number on your kit bag. There was the Bombay-oyster *wallah*. He'd bring round raw eggs which he'd break into a glass with vinegar or sauce and which used to be swallowed with a gulp. As well as the dhobi, who took the weekly washing, there was also the man known as the flying dhobi. If you were going on guard that night he would pick up your drill in the morning and bring it back that evening beautifully laundered and starched ready to put on.

The net result of these auxiliary services was a remarkable improvement in the turn-out of the British soldier. Under the Indian sun 'a speck you got away with on parade at Aldershot was like an ink stain on the parade ground at Poona.' Yet the almost unlimited workforce allowed 'bulling' to reach new heights: 'The turn-out of the battalion when I first saw it dazzled me. I had never seen such smart soldiers, because I had never seen soldiers whose uniforms were washed and ironed every day.' On top of this the British soldier in India enjoyed considerable status: 'He was the soldier-*sahib* and was addressed as such by the humbler Indians and insisted on being addressed as such.' The effect on the BORS' morale was considerable: 'After about a year in India they were four feet off the ground.'

One group of camp followers earned a special place in the affections of the British soldier. These were the *bheestis*, the regimental water-carriers whose reputations Kipling had done much to enhance, and the sweepers – known as *mehtars* – whose virtues remained unsung. The *mehtar*'s job was a vital one: 'Latrines in those days used to mean a hole in a board behind corrugated iron sheeting. Occasionally whilst sitting there you'd find a black arm snaking out from under you and taking the tin away. This was a bit frightening at first but you got used to it.' Waste from the latrines was collected by the sweepers and removed in a conveyance drawn by a pair of oxen and known as the 'Bombay milk-cart'. Because it served several bungalows the privy was an important social centre as well as a haven for scroungers, since 'when you were in the privy you were inviolate'. A certain fellow-feeling grew up between the British soldier and the sweepers, 'the only caste of Indian that we had the opportunity of meeting or conversing with'.

The interaction between the British soldier and the camp-follower led to a strange mixture of British and Indian camp slang that both sides mispronounced and mis-used. For the most part such communication took a brisk and no-nonsense approach, as Ed Davies explains: 'If you wanted one of the vendors for something you used to say to him, "*Idder ow jeldi*" – come here quickly. It had to be "*jeldi*" because he got a kick up the backside if he didn't run. We'd say to him, "*Kitna pice?*" – How much? He'd probably say "*Das anna, sahib*" which is ten pence, and we used to say "*Das annas? Hum marcaro jeldi*" – in other words, "I'll give you one across the skull." If you were determined to let them know you weren't going to let them muck you about you used to look them straight in the eye and say "*Malum?*" and that was enough. They'd say, "*Achah*, sahib, *malum*".' Amongst themselves the BORs frequently used their own Anglo-Indian argot: 'If anybody got a bit obstreperous we used to say to him, "Don't be *bobbery* – don't be mad," and we used to say, "What about cleaning your *bundook*, then?" That's his rifle. And, "Oh, I see you've been *charpoy*-bashing again," sleeping on your bed.'

As a rule, military duties were not arduous. In the hot weather activities were restricted to early morning parades and sports and exercise in the evening. Thursday was always a buckshee day, or old soldiers' day, when all parades were cancelled and the day given over to sport and other leisure activities: 'We had one great weapon against boredom. The answer was sport, sport, sport. We were games mad and that was an enormous help.' After games the men showered: 'then you'd don long slacks, khaki shirts with sleeves right down to your wrists so that the mozzies wouldn't get at you, and a side hat, and away you used to go to a club or a bar for a couple of pints, or to your own canteen.' Beer was cheap – about two or three annas a pint – and it was good and strong, but the troops knew that 'when they came out of the wet canteen they didn't have to be offensive, they didn't have to be uproarious, they didn't have to be helpless, they just had to stagger and someone on duty outside the canteen would put them in the guard room for being drunk'.

More adventurous activities beyond the cantonments, even if allowed, were restricted by lack of money. 'When I first enlisted,' remembers Ed Brown, 'the pay was 8d a day, less stoppages. One week I would draw 3s 3d, the next week 2s od and the funny part about this was that as you came away from the pay station the orderly sergeant would stop and ask you if you wanted to buy any war loans. You were then marched to the canteen where you were compelled to spend tenpence on cleaning materials.' Stoppages were a perpetual source of grievances among the BORs. 'There were some legitimate stoppages such as laundry and shoe repairs, but there was one which was neither fair nor reasonable called "barrack damages". It recurred month after month and this was one of the causes of the soldier drawing such poor pay in India.'

The BOR was entitled to a fortnight's leave every year – if he could afford it: 'He was stopped by one element alone and this was money.' As a result most troops stayed put with their regiment. A few made the effort and got away on leave: 'We used to team up with two or three mates, making it a four-some, and save up like billy-o to get the fare and the amount that the hotel wanted and enough spending money for a few fags.' YMCA hotels and the Sandys Homes for Soldiers provided cheap lodgings, even if in return you had 'to sing a couple of hymns – which we used to do out of courtesy'. Staying in a Sandys Home in Landaur, E. S. Humphries recalls that 'there for the first time I learnt something of the graces of good living, of kindly culture and good manners'. But such homes – and such hospitality – were few and far between. 'We'd served in Sudan before coming to India,' remembers George Wood, then an officer in the Dorset Regiment, 'and the men were very bitter on the subject of the kindness they had met with in the Sudan from the civilian population, as opposed to the way the British population in India ignored their existence.'

In the absence of support from outside, the regiment looked to itself – and to its officers. 'An officer's life we knew was the finest thing that was ever invented, but we never felt jealous,' says Ed Davies. 'During my whole service in India I never heard one person say, "Look at old Smith, he's living a life of luxury, look at what we've got." ' The reason for this deference was that 'the private soldier was taught to believe that the officer was a better man'. The officers came from 'the privileged classes and the common soldiery from the common people of England. These people were born leaders and born gentlemen. They never did a thing that transgressed the code of gentlemen. I've seen these officers in action on the Frontier. They were always in front. It would've been a dereliction of their duty not to have done it, and their duty was always paramount.'

As a child in army barracks, Spike Milligan very soon became aware of the superiority of officers. 'I really thought they were the gods and never got very close to them without being terrified out of my life. They had very loud voices, very proper, were very well turned out and always on horses, always taller than me, doing things with tremendous panache. If you heard the click of heels you knew the officer was somewhere near and somebody was standing to attention. They used to stand to attention like ramrods. I watched my father salute and I thought his arm would drop off with the ferocity of his salute.' Even more remote than the officers were their wives, 'always very pale and very beautiful and well-gowned and never moving very fast if they were on horses'.

The remoteness of women was perhaps the most frustrating aspect of a soldier's life in India: 'Complete segregation, not only from British women but from any sort of woman.' Ed Brown states that 'when I got home – apart from perhaps three women in the married quarters who were the wives of the bandmasters or band-sergeants – I hadn't spoken to a woman for nearly nine years'. This was certainly no isolated instance. 'I suppose I was in India for five or six years without speaking to a woman of any sort,' declares E. S. Humphries. 'We were inclined to place women on pedestals and this provided a sort of barrier against our licentious thoughts. Those of us who could not restrain ourselves were lectured by our unit medical officer regarding the dangers of venereal disease. He would beg us, if we were unable to withstand our desires, to go to our brothels, saying that "if you go trundling off into the village fields it will bring you calamitous results."'

Although illicit, military brothels existed and 'regiments did make discreet arrangements with the contractor for sexual relief'. Nevertheless, 'the ghost of Lady Roberts and various churchmen still persisted in India, compelling us to make these arrangements in the most secret manner'. The red light districts in the larger cities – 'in Bombay it was known as the Cages, in Poona it was called the Nadge' – were strictly out of bounds. 'If any white soldier was seen in the area whistles were blown by the police, all traffic came to a standstill and the soldier would, of course, be caught.' Periodical medical checks, known as 'short arm inspections', ensured that any man who availed himself of the 'tree rats' or 'grass *bidis*' was properly dealt with. 'He was given a severe ticking-off, had his pay stopped and was sent to Number 13 Block, which was the dreaded treatment centre.' Many turned, as a last resort, to the 'five-fingered widow'.

The ordinary soldier was only permitted to marry if circumstances allowed: 'The most jealously watched list in the regimental archives was the married quarters roll, which permitted a soldier not only to have his wife with him but guaranteed a quarter for her. Naturally the warrant officers, being great men, were all on the married quarters roll and then it filtered down, fifty per cent of sergeants, twenty-five per cent of corporals, ten per cent of the privates.' This privileged section of the community was known as the 'Hunting Clan'. Some BORs fought both army regulations and prejudice to marry Eurasian girls, usually encountered at the Railway Institute dances that did much to lessen the isolation of the British soldier: 'Whenever you were dancing with an Anglo-Indian girl the first thing she did was to assail you with a great puff of garlic and cheap perfume, but you stuck to her, because she was beautiful and in any case probably the only girl available.'

There was one inevitable side-effect of enforced segregation: 'It wasn't widespread but it was there, it was practised and it did more good than harm.' The attitudes of other soldiers towards the 'Darby and Joans' of the regiment was generally good-natured and sympathetic. Spike Milligan records the case of a young soldier 'desperately in need of sex who ravished the sacred cow at the temple. The Hindus took great offence at this and he was prosecuted – and the officer who was representing the Crown opened the case by saying, "On the day of the alleged offence my client was grazing

contentedly in the field." ' The case was apparently dismissed
when it was pointed out that 'the cow had been cited in a
previous case'.

In fact, a great deal of the soldier's affections were transferred to dumb animals: 'Puppies, kittens, monkeys, parrots
grew in profusion in these regiments and to see a G.S. wagon
going to camp with about 20 dogs, 15 parrots and 14 monkeys
was really something.' Nearly every soldier had a dog, with
inevitable results, as Mrs Lee the wife of an army sergeant
remembers: 'Every now and then it would come in Army
Orders that all dogs had got to be on parade. They'd parade
all their dogs and then they were only allowed to keep one
each. All the others had got to be got rid of and the chief
marksman would shoot them. One soldier had been out for a
walk somewhere and he came back to find his dog had been
put up to be shot. So he went up to the officer in charge and
said, "Anyone shoots that dog, I shoot them, sir." The officer
asked him how many dogs he had. "Only that one." "Oh well,
take him off." ' The same rule applied when the regiment
moved to a new posting. 'It was a strict order that only the
regimental dogs would be allowed and they'd march off in the
morning with only regimental dogs. But once you got to the
other camp then you'd suddenly find dogs, cats, mongoose,
monkeys – the whole lot was there, brought up by the bearers
in the rear of the column.'

Time passed slowly for the British soldier in India: 'It was
too hard a life in those days and the slightest thing used to
stand out as a delight. A delight was being able to get off
parade, being able to go sick and say that you'd got three days
excused duties, or meeting up with someone you hadn't seen
for years.' But the men were still held together by common
interests. Housey-housey was played regularly and 'on count-
less occasions we sat up until two or three in the morning
playing either crown and anchor or pontoon by candlelight for
cigarette coupons which were negotiable in the bazaar for
three annas a thousand'. Occasionally troupes of dancing girls

Barrack Room PETS!

"One Monkey per regiment is sufficient," said a well known Commanding Officer, some years ago, when the question of "pets" in barracks arose, "Undoubtedly". he continued, "the animal said to be the nearest to man in its mannerisms, makes a very fascinating pet, but off its chain it's the devil's own mischief itself."

India offers an extensive choice of pets to those who love them, and in and around the various barracks (apart from the dignified "mascot" pets which sometimes accompany the band) may be seen strolling leisurely about the troops' bungalows, young deer, fully grown and long-horned "Black Buck", Nilghi (Blue Bull) or perhaps a stately Sarus, a grey, long-legged, five-foot bird of the stork family, with a scarlet head and an eighteen inch beak like a bayonet.

Tiger Cubs and young Bears are sometimes seen, but as they mature their ferocious nature asserts itself and the order comes "Get Rid of IT."

Smaller animals such as the Mongoose and Squirrel also make delightful pets if procured young. Parrots, of course, get their share of Government Quarters, and the daily morning screech "Wake up Gunner, make the tea, a cup for you, and a cup for me," is as good as any "reveille."

Fowls and pigeons, too, find a place on the pet's roll. But last though not least comes our canine pet the dog.

There are always a dozen or more dogs of all sizes,

Advice on pets in barracks;
cigarette manufacturer's leaflet, 1940

'with bells on their ankles and wrists', Chinese contortionists, jugglers, fortune-tellers or snake charmers would visit the camp; 'one in particular had a pencil-thin snake which he put through his nose and drew out through his mouth'.

Sundays were marred, from the troops' point of view, by church parades: 'Totally unnecessary, really a matter of showing-off to the native population.' Nevertheless, they were significant occasions, as Irene Edwards observed when in Peshawar: 'It was a sight to be seen when the Army marched down the Mall, the band leading; the sun always shining, the trees on either side all in flower. The *chokra* boys flocked and cheered and we Anglo-Indians swelled with pride because we were part of the British.' The Sunday ritual included arms in church. 'Even in my day,' explains Ed Davies, 'we still had to go to church with rifle and bayonet and twenty rounds of ammunition, with flags flying and all the natives looking on. The troops used to file into church with their sidearms and rifle and we had to place them into slots specially made for the purpose. When a long address was given and the troops got bored we used to rattle our rifles, very soft at first. And the more the parson carried on the more we rattled them. All the officers and the officers' wives used to look round, and if looks could kill we'd have died on the spot.'

This ready availability of arms and ammunition on Sundays sometimes had unforeseen consequences: 'I remember two tragedies that occurred during church parades. The chaps were very low in spirit, I suppose. They'd say they were not very well and "please, could they be excused," and they'd go back to the barrack room and blow their heads off.' Suicides among BORs in India were far from exceptional: 'Besides these two shootings we had a young boy who'd only been out two weeks before he hanged himself, and another lad, only seventeen, who considered himself tormented by the NCOs and drove himself insane and blew his brains out.' There were occasional desertions, rarely successful, and 'a new sort of disease that came into the language and was called "doolally tap", not so much a disease as a mental condition in which men went mad, went on the rampage, smashed things up. Or they would stand outside shouting at the sergeant-major, "I want to bloody well shoot you the moment you come out." '

England never ceased to beckon. 'We thought England was the greatest place on earth,' says Ed Davies. 'We were always talking about home and it was a glorious moment when the mail call was sounded. We used to call it "Letters from Lousy Lou, Letters from Lousy Liz," but it meant everything to everybody. The corporal in charge of the bungalow used to shout out, "Come on! Mail up, boys!" and we used to rush in and he would shout out, "Davies, Smith, Jones, Brown, Green." Some chaps would never have any, of course, and we'd say, "Cheer up. Better luck next time." ' Everybody in the regiment looked forward to the mail, perhaps nobody more than the army wives, as Mrs Wood describes: 'On Sunday morning after church parade we met under the trees on the lawn, the band played and it was very pleasant. Then at twelve o'clock the mail from home arrived and everybody would vanish. You would race back to your bungalow and there would be those longed-for letters from home, possibly photographs of a four-year-old on an English beach. You lived for that letter day.'

Towards the end of their tour of duty the men would become 'utterly apathetic'. Their officers would go to England for six months every two years while they had no option but to soldier on: 'They'd got no time for anything but this one fact, and it used to recur every minute of the day. No matter what little problem arose, they would meet it with, "Roll on the boat, roll on the boat." You would hear this from morning till night. That one phrase was used in India more frequently, with more force and vehemence than any other.' Another over-used phrase was 'Roll on my seven and five,' because 'a man's service was seven years before the colours and you usually landed up in India doing five.'

Finally the time came when the return draft was called.

'The draft paraded on the square and the whole regiment turned out and escorted us off, with beer and whisky and what have you.' The band played 'Rolling Home to Dear Old Blighty' and the draft marched off to the railway station: 'If you used to go with Indian girls they'd all congregate as you were marching away and sing a little ditty called "Oh doolally sahib", which means a mad gentleman. They'd sing:

Oh doolally sahib, fifteen years you've had my daughter,
and now you go to Blighty, sahib.
May the boat that takes you over
sink to the bottom of the *pani*, sahib!

They'd all sing that and then roll up with laughter.'

16

The Frontier

Probably no sign until the burst of fire, and then the swift rush with knives, the stripping of the dead, and the unhurried mutilation of the infidels.
GENERAL SIR ANDREW SKEEN *Passing It On: Short Talks on Tribal Fighting in the North-West Frontier* 1932

There were two frontiers of India, the North-West – 'full of romance and danger and deeds of derring do' – and the North-East, virtually ignored and, in many areas, unexplored up to the Second World War. The former had long been the scene of constant political and military activity, with 'this little air of danger, where there was always the chance of a stray bullet'. As a result it retained a powerful hold over the imaginations of the British both at home and in India.

To a great exponent of mountain warfare like Claude Auchinleck the Frontier was 'the one place where the new officer could hope to get on active service. Anybody who had a certain amount of ambition wanted to serve there. And you had to be on your toes the whole time. I never enjoyed anything more.' To a 'political' like Olaf Caroe, last in a line of great frontiersmen, there was much more: 'I remember Lord Ronaldshay saying that "the life of a frontiersman is hard and treads daily on the brink of eternity". That was the sort of

feeling one had about the landscape there, which was sometimes gloriously beautiful, green and lovely and verdant, and
sometimes stark and horrible and beset with dust storms. The
stage on which the Pathan lived out his life was at the same
time magnificent and harsh – and the Pathan was like his
background. Such a contrast was sometimes hard to bear but
perhaps it was this that put us in love with it. There was among
the Pathans something that called to the Englishman or the
Scotsman – partly that the people looked you straight in the
eye, that there was no equivocation and that you couldn't
browbeat them even if you wished to. When we crossed the
bridge at Attock we felt we'd come home.'

Few failed to respond to the picturesque figure of the
Pathan, 'a great chap for swagger'. Walter Crichton, who
served four years on the Frontier as a medical officer and very
nearly ended his days there, saw the Pathans as 'very fine
looking men with long bobbed hair and untidy looking turbans
tied loosely with loops coming down round their necks; then
sheepskin poshteens which they wore in winter, baggy trousers
and sandals – and a fearsome looking bandolier full of
cartridges either slung across the shoulder or round their
waists – and, inevitably, a rifle.' Like so many of his countrymen he found them 'a very nice lot of people on the whole,
whom we liked because they were tough fighters – whether
they played the game according to our rules or not – and very
good marksmen'.

The North-West Frontier Province consisted of a belt of
administered territory and, beyond that, an unadministered
tribal area, based on 'a kind of instinct that we didn't want to
have a common frontier of administered territory next door to
another power'. Administration of the tribal areas was 'merely
designed to see that the tribes did not commit nuisances either
in India or in Afghanistan'. These nuisances came in many
forms; some as manifestations of the 'blood feud' which
accounted for three hundred murders a year in the Peshawar
district alone, some based on the long-established custom of

raiding for cattle, women and guns, and some politically motivated. Following ancient Muslim ethics rather than the Indian Penal Code, the political officer tried wherever possible to make use of the tribal *jirga*, which was both a jury and a tribal assembly: 'They sit round you in a circle of two thousand men and you sit in the middle and have to talk. You have to be able to speak the language well enough to take up a running argument, make speeches and even know the proverbs.' Sometimes outside intervention became inevitable: 'We did interfere whenever they were a nuisance to us, and interference had to be by force.' Force came in the form of a punitive foray, a light bombing raid after advance warning or, as a last resort, a military column involving several brigades.

Life on the Frontier had its own special style, ranging 'from excitement to boredom and back again'. Entry into the tribal areas was by permit only, with special restrictions on women. Those who stepped off the government roads on to tribal territory did so at their own risk. Down these roads came the *kafilah*, the caravans from Bokhara and Samarkand, as Dolly Rowe describes: 'They come down head to tail, these camels, tramping along, plod, plod, plod, bellowing away, supercilious, some with bags round their faces, and froth . . . There are buffaloes, there are donkeys, there are sheep, and then the women; they tinkle, tinkle, tinkle as they walk past you, wearing huge earrings that wingle and wangle about and gold and silver on their fingers. Sometimes there's a woman in front, sometimes there's a man and sometimes there's a tiny little child, and away they go down to Peshawar.'

Despite opposition from family and friends, Irene Edwards went to nurse in Peshawar – 'the city of a thousand and one sins' – in 1929: 'The fort was on one side of us and the city on the other. It was very comforting to see the Union Jack flying on that fort and to see the British soldiers on the parapet. We used to have the wolf whistles but it was all very cheering and comforting, especially when the trouble started and the anti-British feeling grew. When the Redshirts started shouting "Up the revolution!" we used to look at those soldiers and that fort and really feel safe.' Nursing on the Frontier was unusual in many respects: 'I had heard about the family feuds, now I was to see the results. You would get a case coming in with all the intestines sticking out. They used to get the skin of a chicken and wrap the intestines in this skin to keep them fresh. We used to have to cut out parts of the intestine, pick out shrapnel and pellets from gunshot wounds and sew them up. We used to have jealous husbands cutting off their wives' noses, breasts amputated, even pregnant women with their abdomens ripped open.' Even the gardeners were out of the ordinary: 'Our gardeners were prisoners. These men had heavy chains round their waists, down each leg and round each ankle. The clanking of these chains used to be our waking bell as they came into our verandah watering the pots in gangs, always with an armed guard.'

Peshawar was a colourful and, for the most part, peaceful city, a family station 'where you played your games and lived the ordinary cantonment life'. But when trouble spilled down from the Hills, as it did in the Red Shirts Rebellion or the Peshawar Riots of 1930, then it could be as dangerous as anywhere on the Frontier. Walter Crichton recalls:

I was walking through the bazaar with my sub-assistant surgeon, a very nice little Hindu whose name was Tir' Ram, and going through these narrow crowded streets we were held up for a moment by a train of mules carrying timber. I bent over to talk to a little boy who was pounding chillis on the ground and in that instant I suddenly felt a blow, a terrific sock right in the back, and I thought that one of these mules had lashed out at me and caught me with its hoof. But when I turned round to see what had happened I realized it was not a mule at all, but that I was at the end of an axe which was stuck in my back and held at the other end by a rather fierce-looking Pathan who was doing his best to dislodge this axe from my back. Tir' Ram looked around, or I may have cried to him, and promptly leapt at this man, jerked the axe out of my back and then twined his little legs round him and tripped him so that they both fell to the ground in a cloud of dust. I staggered about in a rather drunken fashion with a lot of blood streaming down my back and into my boots. Then members of the militia came running up and seized the fellow and brought him away. They tried to carry me to the civil hospital but I said I'd walk. When I got there I more or less collapsed on to a *charpoy*. They got my clothes off and by the aid of a series of mirrors I told them what I thought should be done – and I was then stitched up.

In surviving the attack 'Crit' Crichton was luckier than one of his predecessors, a Captain Coldstream. Irene Edwards relates how she and he were having coffee and talking about golf:

He knew that I was very keen on golf and asked me if I'd like a lesson from him. I said yes, I'd be very grateful, and he arranged to pick me up at five that afternoon. Then he went downstairs. When he got to the bottom he waved to me and said, 'I'll pick you up then, at five.' I said, 'Right,' and I turned round to walk back to the duty room. Then I heard a peculiar sort of scuffling noise. Suddenly I heard shouts of 'Sister, Sister, come quickly!' I rushed to the top of the stairs and looked down and there were two of the *babus* carrying Captain Coldstream upstairs. I could see blood streaming from his neck and I said, 'What has happened?' 'He's been beaten,' one *babu* said. The other *babu* said in Hindustani, 'No, he has been knifed.' I looked down at Captain Coldstream and I knew that he was dying. When assistance came I went back into the duty room and I saw our coffee cups. I looked at Captain Coldstream's coffee cup and I picked up mine, which was still warm. I sat there and cried and cried, till another sister came and put her arms around me. We then walked out on to the verandah and we saw Abdul Rashid, the orderly, standing there with blood pouring down his arm. I went up to him and said, 'Oh, Abdul Rashid, have you been

hurt?' and they all looked at me queerly. I thought Abdul
Rashid had gone to Captain Coldstream's assistance. Actually,
he was the murderer.

Further up the Frontier there were smaller family stations
such as Palantrana, where 'the European community consisted
of the political agent and his wife and the OC of the Corps of
Militia and about half a dozen officers and the Agency
Surgeon.' Here the dangers of Frontier life were obvious. Crit
Crichton had a nice bungalow, 'large and commodious with a
very nice garden – but it was whispered to me as I got there that
my predecessor and his wife had actually been murdered there
by Pathans from across the border. On one occasion my wife
was fishing, and on the other side of the river there was a battle
going on between two sections of Pathans.'

In tribal territory there were non-family stations only, for-
tifications or large camps surrounded by barbed wire, where life
was 'great fun but terribly frustrating, and on occasion frightening'. For all that, every soldier jumped at the chance: 'It was an
adventure to go there and the British soldier was proud to go
there. Only good British regiments were sent to the Frontier and
they went there with a feeling of professional pride.' Separations
and hardships 'on the grim' – as the Frontier was known to the
British Ordinary Soldier – were inevitable. 'Before we could
leave,' recalls Reginald Savory, referring to his own regiment of
Sikhs, 'all the women had to be told to go, and they were put into
special carriages in one of the local mail trains and sent off under
the escort of trusted elderly men, because the Sikh is a lusty
chap!' On active service on the Frontier officers got three
months' leave a year on full pay – 'but we earned it. The
remaining nine months were spent surrounded by a barbed wire
fence, away from your wife, longing for the post to arrive. I lived
that kind of life for ten out of the twenty years which separated
World War One from World War Two.'

When Ed Brown's Royal Warwicks moved up to Landi
Kotal they followed the usual practice and marched: 'We

could see on the horizon a kind of battleship shimmering in the heat. This was a fort, looking just like a gunboat or a warship, shimmering grey in the heat of the day. And we never seemed to get much nearer to it, we had to keep on marching and marching. We passed a caravan, a thousand head of animals I should think, camels and donkeys laden with carpets from Persia and Afghanistan, and a lot of followers. We saw one of the men beating a woman with his camel whip and we had to suffer the sight of this poor lady being whipped cruelly as we left her in the distance.' After a night at the fort they continued to march: 'Horrible looking hills loomed nearer and nearer and then you saw some sort of crack going up through the hills – and this was the Khyber Pass; great slabs of rock towering up on either side of you.' Finally, at Landi Kotal itself, 'as you went through the gate there was a notice which read, "Abandon hope all ye who enter here," and that just about put the lid on it.'

Major G. Humphries of the Telegraph Department is permitted to visit Torkham on 12th February 1930 on duty.

It is clearly to be understood that no one except on duty is allowed to accompany him and in no circumstances whatever are any ladies allowed to proceed to the border.

PESHAWAR.   Lt.Col.,
12th February 1930.   Political Agent, Khyber.

Travel permit, North West Frontier, 1930

The restrictions of life on non-family stations were considerable yet George Wood, who spent two years on the Khyber as brigade-major, remembers that the British soldiers were never happier. Nevertheless, their isolation created certain difficulties: 'As we were all behind barbed wire, the ordinary punishment for defaulters seemed rather inappropriate. However, with the assistance of our engineer I set the defaulters to work with pick-axes and cold chisels to level a large area of virgin rock to a perfect level over which was spread a coating of fine cement. The contractor was then told to produce all the roller skates in India, fairy lights were slung over this area and all through the cold weather the British troops roller-skated and roller-skated.'

Campaigning on the Frontier required a rigid and constant adherence to a system that had been tried and tested for more than half a century. 'The advance into hostile country was an absolutely stereotyped performance,' explains Claude Auchinleck. 'Your line of advance was always up a river valley. As the column went along, the advance guard would put people up on either side of the valley on peaks or ridges from which the enemy might fire on the main column, and if it was properly done you got through. When you got to your camping ground pickets built themselves little forts with stone walls all round the camp to prevent the camp being fired into. Then you proceeded to make camp like the Romans did, with a wall all round it of stone and, if necessary, dug in a bit. If you failed to know how to picket the route – what places to put your men – then you were always liable to an attack on the baggage column or the transport mules by perhaps fifty or one hundred men who came down unseen. It was purely a matter of ground. You always had to have high ground and you had to know exactly where to put your men.'

Even on the best-regulated operations there were risks – 'the danger was there and it was an invisible danger.' Only when you were at your most vulnerable did the enemy show itself and that moment came most often when the picket was being withdrawn. 'The Pathan would very often be waiting in dead ground where you couldn't see him,' explains Reginald Savory, 'and when you were just ten yards or so off from the picket the Pathan would jump on top and have a shot at you at short range. So the moment the last man was off you brought down covering fire. The last man was generally your fittest man and carried a yellow or a red flag and as he got down below the crest he waved his flag and ran down the slope as quick as he could. When he was about twenty yards away the fire came down on the top. Withdrawing pickets along a ridge and running uphill to the next peak, with the enemy shooting at you from behind, was one of the most unpleasant experiences I've ever known. One used to get most frightfully conscious of the little dip between one's shoulder-blades.'

Those who failed to observe the rules of mountain warfare invariably paid a price, as John Dring witnessed when, as political agent in South Waziristan, he accompanied a punitive column into hostile territory: 'The hostiles were out in very large numbers; they got above the military pickets and disaster followed. Every single thing went wrong. One regiment came literally running from the hills into camp. We got bogged down seven miles from Razmak, all wires were cut and I spent no less than four and a half weeks in a hole in the ground utterly cut off. On that short march the column suffered at least eighty killed, including the British colonel of one of the regiments.' Sniping – 'the odd bang, bang at night and the whang of a bullet' – was a constant and trying feature of Frontier campaigning. Regiments new to the Frontier frequently returned fire: 'We used to rush and mount the Lewis guns, fire Verey Lights and spray the outside of the wire with fire and, of course, when the machine guns opened up they just slid back behind the ridge.' More experienced regiments held back: 'It was accepted practice in the Indian Army never to return fire. It was a sign of steadiness not to shoot back, to look for and spot the man but never fire back. If a regiment shot back against a sniper it was a mark against them – "Oh, they're the chaps who shoot back at snipers." '

Few regiments were as skilled in mountain warfare as the Gurkhas, and none more experienced than Lewis Le March-and's 5th (Frontier Force) Gurkhas. After being subjected to sniping every night – 'not many casualties, but very annoy-ing' – they retaliated by 'sending out the usual working party of possibly thirty odd men, Gurkhas in their off-parade clothes, baggy trousers and so on. They went out and cleared a little bit of the countryside and then came back after about an hour's work, but instead of thirty of them coming back, only twenty-five did. We left five men with rifles concealed in their long trousers hidden up where we thought the sniping was coming from. And sure enough, that night at about ten o'clock or so a couple of rounds of sniping started, and then there was a volley of shots and our five Gurkhas came in bearing the corpses of two Mahsuds, dead as mutton. The political agent came to see them the next morning and said, "Good God, I dined with that fellow last night!" It was one of the local Khans. He'd given the political agent dinner first and then decided to go down and have a few shots at him.'

It was a precept of Frontier warfare never to lose a rifle. 'The loss of a rifle was regarded as the most heinous crime and it generally meant a court of enquiry and sometimes a court martial. You were never allowed to forget it. You'd hear people say, "Oh, that regiment – oh yes, weren't they the ones who lost those rifles in Tirah in 1894?" That was the kind of disgrace which one feared much more than losing one's life or getting a bullet in the groin.' The Pathans coveted rifles greatly and were prepared to throw lives away in order to secure one. Most attempts, as in the following incident described by Reginald Savory, were unsuccessful: 'I was sending some men up to picket one of the heights when they were charged by a group of young chaps with knives. They went for them with the bayonet and killed the lot. We laid them out in a row – such a good-looking lot of young chaps they were – and one of the village elders came along, an old grey-bearded man. I showed him these four or five boys lying by the roadside and I don't think I've ever seen anybody quite so broken-hearted in my life.' More often rifle thieves, known to the BORS as 'loose-*wallahs*', naked and greased all over, attempted to steal rifles by night. To prevent this 'every man had to sleep with his rifle chained to him. The chain went through his trigger guard and round his waist. If you hadn't got a chain you dug a little pit the length and width of a rifle, you put the rifle in it and you slept on top of it.' Sometimes not even the most elaborate attempts to safeguard rifles were enough. 'We had to have folds stitched into the end of our blankets,' remembers Ed Brown. 'We used to thread the rifle into the fold and the sling outside it round your arm. But still they broke into the camp and stabbed a man numerous times to make him release his rifle. Eventually he did – and although that man was stabbed and hurt so badly he had a court martial. He was told that he should never have lost the rifle but in view of the circumstances his only punishment would be that he'd have to pay for the rifle. Eighty-one rupees, eight annas they charged him for it. He accepted it. It was all part of the way things were.'

The Frontier was never merciful: 'The Pathan is an attractive man but he had a very, very cruel streak in him, and if you left a wounded man behind he was not only killed but frequently mutilated in the most obscene manner. It became, therefore, a point of honour with us never to leave a wounded man behind. So if one of our men was wounded we counterattacked in order to get that wounded man back.' But above all the Frontier tested the man: 'To run away or to show cowardice on a Frontier campaign and come back and wine or dine with your brother officers in the evening was a far worse punishment than risking death.' There were occasional failures. 'I've seen a British officer lying in a hole and pulled him out of it – but not very often,' says Claude Auchinleck. 'Before one went into attack one was frightened, there's no doubt about it. You just had to put it away somewhere and go ahead.'

17

The Land of Regrets

*Sooner or later the lurking shadow of separation takes definite shape;
asserts itself as a harsh reality; a grim presence, whispering the inevitable
question; which shall it be? . . . the rival claims of India and England; of
husband and child.*

MAUD DIVER *The Englishwoman in India* 1909

Throughout its history one generation of British men and
women was always absent from the Raj: 'There were no old
people among the British in India. A man of sixty was
probably the oldest that one was likely to meet.' Early retirement was only partially responsible. Of the ten young officers
who went out with H. T. Wickham in 1904 to join the Indian
Police, two died within five months and another six within the
decade. Twenty years later India was still taking its toll of the
misfit – and the unfit. 'I made two friends on the voyage out,'
recalls Philip Mason, 'one of them died in his first summer. He
wasn't happy in India at all. Just before he reached Bombay he
said to me rather sadly, "I suppose I shall never again feel
really well," and he didn't. He was not merely critical of the
society he found himself in, but he felt he had to express his
criticism. He went out on Famine Duty in the hot weather in
June, and he got an appendix and by the time they got him

into headquarters, a two day journey in a bullock cart, that was that.' Similarly, an acquaintance of Rosamund Lawrence 'hated everything about India. She didn't like the servants and she didn't like the weather, she didn't like the food and she didn't like the people. She wouldn't learn to ride and she wouldn't learn to drive. She just grumbled all day long and hated everything. And then one day the doctor told me that she was ill. I said, "Oh, what's wrong with her?" and he said, "I don't know, but she's very ill." The next day she was dead. Her idea of happiness was a suburban villa.'

Sometimes India – and the standards that were demanded of the young men who went there – was too much for even the stoutest character. Olaf Caroe recalls an instance when he was governor of the North-West Frontier Province:

> In Waziristan there was a political agent who was the son of a man who had been in Waziristan before him. He was kidnapped and held by the Mahsuds and I had to harden my heart and take air action. It was taken and he was released. He came and stayed with me in Government House and I said to him, 'I think you'd better be moved. It's not fair to send you back again to this place.' And he begged me almost on his knees, with tears in his eyes, to send him back. He said he would never be able to stand up to himself or to anybody if he wasn't sent back. So I said, 'All right, I'll send you back for a short time, and then we'll move you on.' So I sent him back to his original station in South Waziristan and after six weeks or so I wrote him a letter and said, 'I think you've been there quite long enough. You must feel that you've proved yourself now, and I propose to move you to such and such a place.' Two days later I was rung up and told that he had shot himself, and my letter was lying unopened on his desk. He had found it too much for him.

Apart from the misfits, India took its toll in other ways. Speaking of the turn of the century, Mrs Norie recalls that 'life was so very short. When anybody got ill and died – and lots did – they were buried the same day. It made the parting so sudden and it made an awful impression upon people.' Nevertheless, it was characteristic: 'Everything is sudden in India, the sudden twilights, the sudden death. A man can be talking to you at breakfast and be dead in the afternoon – and this is one of the things you have to live with.' The old cemeteries of Calcutta and the UP, crowded with the graves of young men, younger women and their even younger offspring, were reminders of the fate that could still overtake those who failed to take the proper precautions.

While there were many noble and devoted exceptions – pioneers who fought through improvements in health and welfare in the face of hostile and even dangerous opposition, whether it was improving rickshaws in Simla or campaigning to stop cows being kept in houses in Delhi – the stock of the medical officer was not high. When Iris Portal fell ill up-country, her car was sent fifty miles for the nearest doctor: 'When it returned my husband was absolutely horrified to see emerging from the car first an enormous red nose, then a very pock-marked face, and then a very drunken doctor who said in muffled tones, "It must be malaria, or typhoid, or cholera. It obviously isn't cholera or typhoid, so it must be malaria. Give your wife thirty grains of quinine a day." Then he tossed the pills on the table and was driven away again. When I got back to headquarters I had various tests and was told that I had had typhus.' But whether good medical attention was available or not, 'gippy tummies', dengue and malaria continued to make life uncomfortable. 'We always used to take two grains of quinine every day,' remembers Kenneth Warren, 'and anybody who didn't take it was bound to go down with malaria.' For all the precautions, malaria in one form or another was virtually endemic in some areas. Kenneth Warren had the intermittent variety: 'I had two good days and then on the third it used to come on at about a quarter to twelve. I didn't want to be caught wandering about out of doors with this ague, so I used to go back to the bungalow just in time and then in about ten minutes I shook all over, my teeth chattered and I sweated. By next morning it had gone.' Even memsahibs took malaria in their stride: 'You go to dinner and you know your temperature's up at about a hundred and something, but you just don't bother.'

An abundance of insects added greatly to the general discomfort, not only those that bit or stung or stank when squashed, but others that destroyed – bored through books and ate through furniture. The bottoms of leather trunks fell away when lifted up and 'if you left your boots on the floor at night you lost the soles by the morning'. There was the potential threat of snakes, even though 'in nine cases out of ten the snake would try and avoid you and it was only when you were unfortunate enough to tread on it when it was asleep, or something like that, that you suffered any evil conse- quences'. It was even possible to spend a lifetime in India and never see a snake. 'I can remember months and months of not seeing a snake at all,' says Raymond Vernede. However, he was required to kill a cobra in his bathroom on one occasion and a krait was found under a cushion in the sitting room on another. For want of a better place to put it the latter was left tightly curled up in the calling box and forgotten. The following day the sweeper, 'a curious, inquisitive gentleman', opened the flap and 'the krait expanded and leapt out and there was a most fearful shriek'. The memsahib was rather more vulnerable than her husband. 'I hated snakes,' recalls Mrs Symington, though with some reason: 'The children's toy box had a snake in it one day and when I opened it out it popped. On another occasion I'd been sitting on a chair that had a loose cover, and when I got up the nanny went and sat on it and I suppose she was rather heavier than I was because a snake slithered out and went straight across the room to my little girl who was sitting in her chair.' Others had a more blasé attitude towards snakes. The men in Ed Brown's regiment, for instance, when stationed in the Rajputana desert, found numerous snakes sheltering in rat holes: 'We used to tee off with hockey sticks and golf balls and try and hit these snakes when they put their heads up out of the holes. Some of the snakes were cobras and I remember one of our fellows catching one with a piece of rag by letting him strike and catch his teeth in it. He put it in a bath of water in the washhouse and everyone crowded round to see what it was and whether it was dead – which it wasn't. It put its head over the rim of the bath and I've never seen such a stampede!'

The Pax Britannica gave both British and Indians a quite remarkable degree of safety in their daily lives. Hot weather after hot weather thousands of Europeans slept nightly out of doors, undisturbed and in perfect security. Nevertheless, the North-West Frontier had no special monopoly on violence. Violence directed against individuals was rare and isolated – but it occurred. When Percival Griffiths took over as magistrate in one particular district in Bengal, he did so in the knowledge that his three predecessors had all been shot by terrorists: 'It was rather sad because of those three, two were specially known for their fondness for the Bengali and for the tremendous amount of public work that they were doing for the Bengali. The shooting was not directed at them as persons, it was directed at them as representatives of the British Raj.' Even in the worst years, when the non-co-operation movements and the *swaraj* demonstrations were gathering in strength, few Europeans were in real physical danger. 'We were left alone,' says Mrs Symington. 'I never had any rudeness or hostility or was ever frightened about anything. When my husband went away to quell a disorder or a riot I used to feel a bit nervous but I never felt that any harm would come to him. The whole house was always open, because we never felt that we were going to be attacked.'

This was only part of the picture. Half a century earlier, when Claude Auchinleck had come out to India, the attitudes of many memsahibs were very different. The Mutiny had not been forgotten. Claude Auchinleck's father had himself fought in the Mutiny as a subaltern and 'it had left scars on the communal memory. So far as the men were concerned, the Mutiny meant nothing to them. But the Englishwomen out there remembered the Mutiny and they influenced to a certain extent the behaviour and the feelings of their menfolk.'

The English memsahib came in for a great deal of criticism. 'Most of them started out as perfectly reasonable, decent English girls,' states John Morris, 'and many of them in the course of time developed into what I can only describe as the most awful old harridans. And I think they were very largely responsible for the break-up of relations between the British and the Indians. In the early days, before the Englishwoman went out to India at all, British officers spent much of their time with Indians, got to know them better, got to know the language well and so on; whereas once the Englishwoman started to arrive in India she expected her husband to spend his time with her. She couldn't communicate with anybody except her cook who knew a few words of English, so she was forced to rely almost solely upon her husband for amusement and company. I don't think that she realized what a menace she was.' Others were also critical of the memsahib, but for different reasons. 'At one stage of my life in India,' recalls George Carroll, 'I was very much against the white women because I considered that they were apt to let us down in prestige by going off to the Hills every Hot Weather and leaving one down below. The general understanding was that they went up there to lead a life of immorality, and in many cases it was true.'

But even the critics agreed that attitudes were changing: 'Womenfolk before the First World War were definitely more reserved and more concerned with preserving their separation. After the war that began to disappear.' As hot weather conditions improved, more and more wives chose to stay down in the plains with their husbands. None the less, the image stuck – 'the mythical picture of the British memsahib which was started by Kipling and has lived in the annals ever since'.

Frances Smyth argues that this was a generalization with only a certain amount of truth in it: 'British women in India were like British women anywhere else, they were a lot of individuals. But there were certain attitudes which you took up, perhaps, from all the others. Such as, you don't mingle with Indians too much; you remember that you're British; and in the way you treat your servants. The older women would get together with you and say, "You know, you won't do your husband any good, my dear, by going and doing those sort of things," in a disapproving way. And so, if you were a good little wife, you probably thought, "Well, I'd better not." ' Such pressures were by no means the same everywhere: 'There was a great difference between the civilian wives and the military wives. The civilians were for the most part stuck out in small stations where the wives took a much closer part in their husbands' work, whereas the military wives really had nothing to do with their husbands' jobs.' It was here and in the big cities where the wives 'who lived a life far more English than the English' were most often to be found – 'more often than not, the real India passed them by'.

Other factors discouraged the Englishwoman in India from playing a full role in the country. As might be expected in this 'very extrovert society' the women conformed to the cultural expectations of the men. 'There was a very strong feeling that women were not supposed to be clever. They were supposed to be decorative and intelligent and good listeners, but they weren't supposed to be clever and, if by any conceivable chance anyone was, they kept it pretty dark.' They were also at a great disadvantage when it came to mixing with Indians, because Indian women 'didn't come into society. They were nearly all in purdah, so your chances of meeting them were fairly rare.' This imbalance remained virtually unaltered right up to Independence and it required considerable strength of character on the part of those many memsahibs who penetrated this wall of male supremacy by giving 'purdah-parties' and establishing friendships with Indian women. There was also the 'generally rather indifferent education given the middle-class Edwardian lady'. Like her sisters at home she was not trained to do more than read good books and run a house well – and in India the latter was very often taken care of for her. Yet despite these many handicaps the exceptions who began to break through the 'Anglo-Indian' ethos in the early twenties were fast becoming the rule by the end of the thirties. Wives were finding useful and valuable roles for themselves, not only in support of their husbands but as individuals and as pacemakers outside the British community, taking up nursing, guiding and many other forms of voluntary work.

The sahibs themselves were equally subject to the 'attempt to push everybody into a mould', and to the feeling of 'sticking together, that you must always back each other up, if necessary'. Some saw this conformity as yet another manifestation of the 'convention-ridden memsahibs, who tended to build up a kind of "little-England" protectively around their unfortunate husbands'. But whatever the cause, it was not an atmosphere that encouraged artistic or cultural pursuits. 'You found repeated the social patterns of the way people lived at home,' asserts Iris Portal, 'and the British were not in those days a very cultured race. It was not fashionable among upper-class people of the type who went into the services to be very cultural, although you did find in the ics very highly cultured, intellectual people who did get homesick for a more cultured life. I remember a very able member of the Indian Civil Service who shared a house with my father one winter and used to worry him by constantly playing gramophone records of Bach in his bathroom.'

At least one hardship was common to both sexes: 'The heartaches of separation are ever present in India,' declares Lewis Le Marchand. And this was particularly true of the army. 'Although the saying is "If you marry the drum you've got to follow it," there are many times when you simply cannot stay with it and you've got to be sent away. For the wife it is, "Goodbye, husband, I'll take the kids up to a hill station and we'll expect you on leave when we see you." ' Deborah Dring's experience was probably shared by many other army wives whose husbands were frequently 'up the line' on military duty: 'My husband and I were always being separated. I once worked out that in thirteen years we'd only spent three whole years together.'

The worst of these 'unending separations' and 'dreadful partings' were those that involved children. A time came when they had to be sent to England 'by convention, to be educated and to get them out of the Indian climate'. Every mother was forced to make a choice between children and husband – and with a major sacrifice either way. Those who chose to remain with their husbands did so at some cost to their children, as Marjorie Cashmore describes: 'We were told by our bishop that we mustn't keep our eldest child out over the age of five, so when she was only three we had to send her to her granny. That meant that for five years we didn't see her. In those days it took six weeks to get a letter and by the end of the five years when we got her back again she really was a stranger to us.' In the early years of service, separation and loneliness were much accentuated by poor pay and infrequent home passages. The assisted passage to and from England was a comparatively late innovation. Speaking of his own father, John Cotton recalls that 'between 1916 and 1926 he never came back to England at all, nor did we see him during any of those ten years'.

In striking contrast to the salaries of senior officers and – in the ics particularly – generous pensions, low pay to junior officers was common to all the services in India. One result of this was a 'terrible feeling of insecurity', and one of the most common characteristics of the life of the Raj was 'this feeling that the only possible way of ensuring some kind of security for the family was to save and save and save, and this is what the majority of officials in India did, with the result that the family went short in the early years of the father's service'. Only in one respect was this Spartan code not observed: 'the one thing that was never saved on was the children's education, because this was considered the greatest security of all'.

India was hard on the British and the British were often hard on themselves and on others, never more so than on those who stood uneasily between themselves and India. Irene Edwards remembers as a child that 'there were benches, one marked "Europeans Only", one marked "Indians Only". There were also the waiting rooms marked "Europeans Only" and "Indians Only". As an Anglo-Indian child I never knew which one to occupy.' Attitudes towards the Anglo-Indians varied: 'The lower classes and the Other Ranks welcomed the Anglo-Indians into their clubs and messes. They even married them. But the higher up you went the greater was the prejudice against the Anglo-Indians.' In retrospect these prejudices came to be seen as reprehensible. 'We can never be sufficiently blamed,' declares Iris Portal. 'When I was very young I took the conventional attitude which everybody took – even enlightened people like my parents – of making jokes about "blackie-whites" and "twelve annas in the rupee".' The prejudice came from both sides. According to Irene Edwards, 'the Indians looked down on the Anglo-Indians because to them you were neither one nor the other. They used to call us *kutcha butcha*, that is to say, half-baked bread, and depending on the shade of your colour they used to talk about the Anglo-Indian as being *teen pao*, three-quarters, or *adha seer*, half a pound, if you were nearly white.'

The Anglo-Indians co-existed in their own 'railway communities' beside the local British communities, with 'a deep gulf' in between: 'It wasn't that one was unfriendly; it was a sort of social taboo.' Outside work the point of social contact was the Railway Institute Dance. 'We used to go to these dances in rather a condescending manner,' admits Joan Allen. 'We'd go to be polite to them and it was like moving into a different world, a much more old-fashioned one, because the girls would never sit with their dancing partners but were always taken back to their parents. I'm afraid we used to rather laugh at them because they seemed to be such frumps. They always seemed to be dressed about several years back and never seemed to quite catch up with modern fashions.'

From the British point of view marriages between the British and Anglo-Indian communities were deeply frowned upon – but not from the Anglo-Indian: 'An unwritten rule was for the girls to try and marry the British soldier. Not to propagate the species but to improve the strain, so our aim was to marry British soldiers, not to marry Anglo-Indian men.' Given the isolation of the British soldier and his segregation from unmarried European women, this ambition was often realized. 'I met hundreds of Anglo-Indian girls and I can't think of one that was really unattractive,' declares Stephen Bentley. 'They had the virtues of the two nations. They were all wonderful dancers and you always saw them when they were made up for a dance. You never saw them when they were "off-parade".' The point is echoed by E. S. Humphries: 'The Eurasian girls were experts at making themselves up and the aroma from their bodies was tinged with the wonderful scent of jasmine which made them probably far more attractive than they really were. In some cases they managed to persuade a British soldier to become engaged and ultimately to marry. It was frowned upon by the British Command, but despite all the efforts to quash it a vast number did manage to get married. One of my own soldiers elected to become engaged to a lovely Eurasian who was almost as black as your hat. I took steps to warn him against it, and when he persisted I made arrangements for him to be transferred to another station.'

The Second World War changed many attitudes, including those towards Anglo-Indians. The impetus for this change came from the Anglo-Indians themselves who seized the opportunity to prove both their loyalty and their worth, as Iris Portal's own experience confirms: 'I changed my attitude completely in the Second World War when I went to nurse in the Indian hospitals in Delhi, where the only woman who could help me and came in and worked with me, was the Eurasian wife of a Eurasian doctor who became one of my best friends. And I realized then what nonsense it all was.'

18

The Day's Work

The life of the 'Anglo-Indian' officials is not all jam. In comfortless camps, in sweltering offices, in gloomy dak bungalows smelling of dust and earth-oil, they earn, perhaps, the right to be a little disagreeable.

GEORGE ORWELL *Burmese Days* 1935

'It was service, service, service every time.' The word runs like a response through the litanies of 'Anglo-India'. Even those outside the military or the civil administration used it when referring to the 'tour of service' by which they were contracted to their employers. It was part of an often unconscious attitude inherited, as David Symington suggests, by all those who made their careers in India: 'We realized that we were members of a very successful race. We belonged to a country that, in the world league, had done exceedingly well for a small island. And we also realized that we were working in a country which was as pre-eminently unsuccessful as we were successful. And I suppose that that produced a frame of mind in which we tacitly – not explicitly – felt ourselves to be rather superior people.' The superiority was stressed by authority at an early age, whether in the office, the tea garden or the court of law, and it was accepted without question. As Assistant Super-intendent of Police at nineteen, George Carroll had authority over hundreds of policemen in his district: 'The question of exercising my power never arose in my mind because it seemed so natural that, as an Englishman, I should have power over all my Indian subordinates.'

The prestige of the Raj enhanced the status of all the British in India, *box-wallahs* and BORS as well as those in authority. Its advantages in terms of respect and obedience were considerable, but it demanded a conscious sense of responsibility towards those under you. Geoffrey Allen, working as a junior assistant to a native *zemindar* in Bihar, found that the local population relied on him for justice: 'You were always being asked to try cases which were brought before you. It was much cheaper for tenants to come to you to decide cases than to go many miles away to the civil courts.' From the Indian point of view such authority was founded upon the *ma-bap* principle, as Kenneth Warren illustrates in the context of the tea-garden manager: 'It was customary for a member of the labour force who had a request to make to come to you and first of all address you as *Hazur* – Your Honour, and then *ma-bap* – you are my father and my mother, I have this, that and the other request to make.' While this open paternalism drew its authority from an Indian initiative, it was reinforced by the 'public school mentality' which required the school prefect to look after those under him:

We had an epidemic of ophthalmia in the garden where I was manager and a number of the labour had to come to hospital for treatment, among them a man who was three days in hospital under treatment and was cured. The next thing I heard at my early morning durbar was that this man's child had been taken to the hospital with her eyes burnt out. She had developed ophthalmia and her father, although he himself had been cured in the hospital, said he knew better and that he knew of a jungle cure, a mixture of certain herbs and jungle plants, which he mashed up and plastered on his daughter's eyes and burnt them out. She was a child of about fourteen, a charming little girl, and when I came into the hospital she heard my voice and fell on to her knees and held on to my legs and implored me to cure her saying, 'Sahib, I know you can cure me. You can do anything if you wish to.' It was a most distressing and terrible experience for me. I held the durbar the next morning. I had the father brought up to my office together with the whole of his clan. I told them what had happened and how disgraceful it was and what did they, the clan, suggest should be done. With one accord they said he should be beaten. They put their heads together and discussed it and then the head man turned to me and said, 'Sahib, we think it is right and proper that you should beat him and not us.' So I said, 'Well, if that's your decision all I can do is carry out your wish.' I came down from the verandah and I went up to this fellow and I hit him. I hit him so hard that I bruised my right hand and I had to have it in a sling for twenty-four hours afterwards.

The sense of duty was strongest in the civil administration. Its strength may be gauged by Rosamund Lawrence's comment that her husband was 'like the Duke of Wellington, always talking about duty. My husband's people, the Lawrences, were very religious and they were absolutely immersed in what they felt was their duty to India.' In Henry Lawrence's case the expression of his duty took the form of a *shauq*, an obsessive interest: 'My husband was absolutely heart and soul wrapped up in what he called the Sukkur Barrage. He was obsessed by it, by the amount of people there were and how they were all going to be fed by it, but he was only one of a chain of people, who had started it long before.' Duty of the order exercised by the ICS meant that 'an officer of the Raj could never say that his home was his castle. There never seemed to be a moment when you could be entirely free – unless you were on leave. You would find somebody waiting to see you on a Saturday evening or a Sunday, because he knew that that was the time you were free.' Accessibility to the humblest petitioner was a Mogul tradition inherited and maintained by the British. Its most significant expression was in the early morning queues of *mulaquatis* on the verandah of every district or political officer in the land. '*Mulaquatis* were divided into two classes,' explains Penderel Moon, 'the *mula-quati* proper was a person of some education and standing, an honorary magistrate, a municipal commissioner, a leading lawyer, the headman of a group of villages or a landowner, who'd come in to salaam-*wasti*, to say salaam to you. Generally they had some ulterior motive. I'd ask about their health, sit them down and have a general chat about the weather or the crops or the latest news, trying to bring them to the point as quickly and politely as one could. Then there was the second group, what my *chaprassi* called *feriadis*, which means "the humble petitioners", who simply came with grievances.'

The success of the interview was often dependent on fluency in both native languages and customs, as Olaf Caroe explains:

You had to be very careful in using the right honorifics in speaking to a gentleman. You had to call him Your Honour, 'Your Honour has brought himself to this place,' and you had to know all about '*ijazat o barkhast*', when to sit down and when to get up, and observe the oriental formalities of behaviour, shaking him by the hand and in the right way and with the right amount of cordiality. If you could quote a hackneyed verse which was appropriate to the occasion you'd probably get what you wanted. Whether it was Urdu or Punjabi or Pashtu, particularly, they had some very racy, meaty proverbs. I remember once someone said, 'You're very patient,' and I said in answer, 'Well, I remember a Pashtu proverb, Patience is Bitter, but the fruit of it is sweet.'

The interview was fraught with hazards. 'One was always very wary,' comments Raymond Vernede. 'Sometimes people came merely to indulge in backbiting and to insinuate against their enemies. Many people came because others would notice that they had been, and they could go back and say that they had seen the District Magistrate. I suffered a great deal of flattery, which I had to get accustomed to. You had to recognize that it was the tradition of the country. You were the God, the sun and so forth. "Defender, preserver of the poor," was a stock expression, but it was like saying "sir". I disliked that sort of thing but never paid very much attention to it.'

The administrative system of the Raj had its origins in Mogul rule and was based principally on the collection of land revenue. But this was only a part of the Collector's or Commissioner's work. He was also responsible for the administration of justice, either in makeshift form in the open air or in a proper court of law, often referred to as 'the halls of chance'. Many covenanted officers found work in the courts frustrating and tedious, most criminal complaints being 'either false, frivolous or futile' and with 'witness after witness telling obvious lies'. Some even felt that the British legal system was 'totally unsuited to India and had been completely perverted'. The sanctity of the law meant very little to most Indians. 'It was really rather a game,' asserts Percival Griffiths, 'and in order to win the game you had to get witnesses. As the people of the country were pretty poor, you didn't have to pay a very great deal to get a man to come and give evidence the way that you wanted. In fact, there used to be a Bengali saying, the *tetul gacch shakshi*, which means the tamarind-tree witness, because there was always a tamarind tree outside the court and the witnesses would be gathered and coached there under the tamarind tree before they came into court.' Most cases that came up before the sub-divisional or district officer concerned property – or criminal assaults arising out of disputes over property: 'The usual kind of story was that a buffalo had wandered into somebody's sugar-cane and a quarrel had arisen and someone had taken a stick and hit somebody over the head.' In the Sind crime arose from '*zana, zar, zamin; zana* meaning women, *zar* gold and *zamin* land,' and usually took the form of murder or cattle-thieving, which was 'more or less the national sport'. Armed with sessions powers as a special assistant agent in Madras, Christopher Masterman was sentencing men to death while still in his mid-twenties: 'The accused would invariably plead guilty. You asked him, "Did you kill this man?" He said, "Yes." "Did you mean to kill him?" "Yes, of course. He was stealing from my palmyra tree." Then you said, "Well, was he armed?" "Oh no, he wasn't armed." "Then why did you kill him?" "I killed him because he was stealing from my palmyra tree," and you couldn't get away from it.' Death sentences were invariably commuted to terms of gaol or transportation over the *kala pani* to the Andaman Islands.

The Indian court was more than a seat of justice. 'The courts were to the Indians the equivalent of the cinema to us,' explains Raymond Vernede. 'They were fascinated by it all, and they listened quietly in most cases. In the hot weather I'd go to the court in khaki shirt and shorts. Some of the police prosecuting officers would be rather overdressed in their uniforms and perspiring very unpleasantly; the lawyers would have their gowns but it was all pretty informal. In my day we had overhead fans which made it possible – except on bad days – to survive. But tempers could be rather short after sitting several hours on a difficult case.' Having heard all the evidence, the district magistrate was then required to respond with a judgement that would support the truth. This required getting to the *kutch-chahal*, 'the raw state of the case, what it was like before they'd prepared it for court', resorting if necessary to arbitrary methods that went beyond the rules of jurisprudence. 'When I was in doubt I did not hesitate to make extra-judicial enquiries from the police investigating officer,' admits Penderel Moon, 'or from other responsible people in the locality as to what they thought the truth of the case was – and I used to take into consideration these extra-judicial opinions in forming my judgement, which was quite irregular.' Nor was he alone in making his own adjustments to a much-abused system. 'I also made rules of the most arbitrary nature,' declares Philip Mason. 'I said that I wouldn't allow anyone to call more witnesses than the other side had called. I also said that nobody could cross-examine for longer than the main evidence. It was high-handed and arbitrary but one was so certain that one was doing the right thing that one didn't have any doubts.'

A certain prejudice in the courts was inevitable, showing itself most obviously in 'a bias on the side of the cultivator, the man who actually drove the plough, as against somebody rather distant who collected the rent from him'. In the ics there was traditionally 'a division between the people who protected the poor, the *gharib-parhwas*, and the *amir-parhwas*, the protectors of the rich'. Philip Mason recalls the case of a *banya* who 'didn't dare go into his village because he was so oppressive that they hated him. He came and asked me to pass orders against all the villagers because they wouldn't let him into his village and I said, "I'm going to pass orders against you, because you must have done something to provoke them." It was rather unjust, I must admit, but it showed my social bias at the time.'

A major impediment both to legal and social progress in India was corruption. *Dastur* – 'the custom of the country' – was a Mogul inheritance, perfectly acceptable to Englishmen in the days of John Company but combated thereafter with fierce Victorian zeal. Victorian ethics of 'honour, decency, truthfulness and running a good show' persisted in India to a quite remarkable degree. 'I would have no hesitation in saying that during the years I was in India, bribery and corruption were unknown among the British,' asserts John Morris, one of the fiercest critics of the moral codes of the Raj. It is an assertion that few have challenged – except in degree – and a great many have confirmed. 'It never entered my mind that lowness of pay or lack of cash could ever influence any British officer to take a bribe,' maintains George Carroll. 'It never entered my mind, and I was always quite convinced that no

British officer would ever take a bribe of any sort. Once when I was a superintendent of police a man who was accused in a certain case approached my bungalow and placed in front of me a large bag of cash. When I realized that he was offering me a bribe I chased him out of the compound. He ran like a hare to my gate and got into a tonga which was waiting and he got away. Had I caught him he would have had a jolly good thrashing.' One explanation of this innocence – the public school attitude – has already been offered. There was also the belief that 'we had inherited high standards which we had to maintain. Living in the public eye you felt you couldn't really afford to take risks – even if you had been tempted – which would not escape notice and would lower that standard.'

Such attitudes created an administration that was 'probably the most incorruptible ever known. A source of great amazement to many Indians but one that gave rise to a very great trust.' The truly remarkable feature of this incorruptibility was the background against which it was maintained. 'I was always amazed,' declares John Cotton, 'at one's moderation in the face of temptation – which was always present.' Some found corruption and bribery among the subordinate levels of the administration appalling. 'I was perhaps much too hot in trying to check it,' recalls Penderel Moon. 'I ran in a large number of people of almost every rank for corruption, from the highest to the lowest. Tips I didn't object to. It was harassment, refusing to do a thing unless the palm was greased.' For their own protection all government officers were subject to the *phal-phul* rule, by which they were forbidden to accept presents other than fruit and flowers. 'There was a comic aspect to this,' comments Percival Griffiths. 'If there were four or five European officers on a station and it was known they were all men of complete integrity who wouldn't accept presents, a chap would bring an expensive present along and offer it to the first man, knowing that he would say no, and then take it to the second and then to the third and then to the fourth. So he would get the goodwill resulting from offering presents to all of them, knowing that it wouldn't cost him anything in the end!'

Others attempted to get round the *phal-phul* rule in other ways. The presentation of trays of fruit and nuts, known as dollies, was deemed to be acceptable and was a special feature at Christmas time. But sometimes the dollies or the bouquets of flowers concealed something more, as John Morris recalls: 'I remember on Christmas morning the man who supplied the troops with food appeared to pay his respects to me and presented me with a cauliflower as a Christmas present, and I noticed when I took the cauliflower that out of it fell a gold sovereign. This was an understood practice, but it was also understood that one accepted the cauliflower or whatever it was and returned the sovereign.' Efforts to subvert were also made through the memsahib or the children. 'An old lady came to see me,' relates Rosamund Lawrence, 'and she brought some little varnished toys for my little boy which must have cost a few annas at the most. My boy was delighted with them so I sent a note in to Henry saying I was sure she would be terribly offended if I didn't take them, so what was I to do? "Better not," he said. The very next day there came a letter from her asking that a most valuable piece of land on the banks of the river should be accorded to her nephew.'

Raj gossip sometimes liked to hint that British residents in the native states did on occasion accept bribes from the rulers. Conrad Corfield's account of a new Resident who was presented with a Christmas dolly illustrates how such allegations could arise: 'An enormous dolly was brought in looking quite beautiful. He started picking at it and at the bottom of the tray he found one hundred and one gold mohurs. He was staggered and went into his office and wrote a furious letter to the Ruler. The Ruler wrote back and said, "I'm dreadfully sorry, but one hundred and one gold mohurs is what has been presented to the residency every year at Christmas and if the amount is not enough will you tell me what is?" Then they started to make enquiries and found that five of the gold mohurs were always kept by the servants of the residency and the rest went back to the state office, where it was distributed – while in the lists was put "Towards Christmas present for the Resident, 101 gold mohurs."'

In the business community bribery and corruption was quite a different matter – although there were always the established companies, well-stocked with public school boys, where it was virtually unknown. 'One would hear rumours that so-and-so was making a lot of money on the side,' relates Rupert Mayne. 'I can remember one man always known as "corkscrew" for the simple reason that he was in on it; and another person who earned some sixty rupees a month before the war and retired with a hundred thousand pounds which he made during the war.'

Elsewhere in business the moral code was 'something akin to that which existed in England at the time of Pitt. It was not considered immoral to have a cut in every contract.' Speaking of the railways, Eugene Pierce recalls that 'my father was a very honest man by any standard but he got so many thousands of rupees before a brick was even laid, when he gave the contract to the right parties. For orders to supply rails or sleepers or cement, contractors presented him with money and gold bangles and my mother was given jewellery. Stations used to be virtually sold. Your stationmaster used to give you a bribe to be placed at that particular station. His salary was negligible but the stations were allotted wagons which were the gift of the stationmaster to give to the merchants who booked them, so his income was enormous. He paid the district traffic superintendent and the company inspectors who'd go down their district once a month – when a brown envelope was slipped into their hands containing this tip.'

Despite its high standards, 'Anglo-India' was not a place of great religious principle or practice. That particular function was delegated to the missionaries, who were given a limited role on the fringes of 'Anglo-India' and were, by and large, left to their own devices. Few worked in India for more altruistic motives or faced greater difficulties. 'Travancore was a great centre for missionaries,' recalls Christopher Masterman, 'CMS, SPG, Canadian Baptists, American Missions, Medical Missions, Roman Catholics, Belgian Priests – and there was a great rivalry between the different sects. If the CMS had a beanfeast of some sort, half the SPG lot would go and join the CMS, and vice versa. I don't think they ever converted a caste Hindu but they got the scheduled classes, the depressed classes and the untouchables.' Yet, as Bishop Cashmore describes, in other parts of India the rivalry was less acute: 'We would not go into an area that the Baptists had or the Methodists or the CMS had without their permission, and they wouldn't come into ours without permission. So there was no sheep stealing.' In terms of genuine conversion, the missionaries made few inroads into Caste Hinduism or Islam, but their pioneering in education and medical work – in the face of widespread apathy and even hostility – was one of the great achievements of British India. Rosalie Roberts' account of midwifery in Bengal exemplifies the difficulties faced by pioneers in the field:

> They would wait five or six days with the woman in labour, hoping it would come all right. They didn't want to bring them into hospital. So I used to go out on my cycle, off into the jungle. I started going out in my white uniform but I soon stopped because all the cows and buffaloes in the jungle chased me and I changed over into khaki. Practically all the midwifery cases were on the mud floor. I tried to manage with as little as possible so as to show the village midwife that she could do it with what she had at hand. In some cases it was very difficult – while I was attending to the woman they'd be tying charms on her hair – but as time went on I got to know the village midwives and we got quite friendly and by the end of the five year period the delay had got down to two days or even one day, because they weren't afraid any more.

The missionaries had no monopoly on privation and hardship. Many young men suffered long and lonely first tours of

duty that lasted four years and more before a home leave and
provided as severe a test of stamina as any. There were a
handful of men in the Forest Service or the Survey of India
who spent month after month in the forests or in the mountains and for whom loneliness and discomfort were the norm.
Arthur Hamilton recalls how, after a long season of surveying,
'I was just longing to meet a European to talk to him. The
vastness of the mountains overcame me and I had an awful
feeling that I must throw myself over a cliff.' But for the great
majority actual hazards and privations were limited in duration and interspersed with generous periods of leave and a
great deal of leisure. When not on active service officers in the
Indian Army observed a far from uncomfortable routine. An
early morning parade was followed by breakfast and a change
into mufti before 'regimental office' when charges and grievances were dealt with. Lunch was usually followed by a long
siesta: 'Then in the late afternoon you either played games at
the club or, if you were so inclined, you played games with
your own men. Thursday was a whole day holiday. Saturday,
of course, was a half-holiday and Sunday was a holiday. You
had as a right ten days absence every month and you were also
entitled to an annual holiday of two months. Every three or
four years you got eight months furlough at home. So it really
cannot be said that any of us were greatly overworked.'

These were all the occupations of the minority. The ICS itself
was never more than 1,300 strong – of which many were
Indians – and although the Indian Army rose in wartime to be
the largest volunteer professional army in history, its British
officers were very few – no more than twelve per regiment –
and growing fewer each year as 'Indianization' slowly began to
take effect. The majority of the British in India – a fast-
increasing majority – were, in fact, businessmen, some contracted to the old-established trading companies or to newer
industrial concerns, some working in the large city emporia,
others working as managers or engineers in tea or coffee or
jute. It was often said that theirs was not the 'real' India, but in

terms of numbers they were in fact the most 'representative' of the British in India; young men who came out as junior assistants and probably spent one hard and uncomfortable tour in the *mofussil* before promotion to the company's air-conditioned offices or the chambers of commerce in Calcutta or Bombay. Again, it has to be remembered that most sahibs in India spent most of their working hours in darkened bungalows, sitting at desks surrounded by files, *babus* and *chaprassis*, contending with inordinate amounts of paper work and, in particular, with a system of minuting said – quite wrongly – to be derived from Lord Curzon, by which 'everybody from the lowest Indian clerk right up to the final authority wrote a minute enlarging on what had gone before'.

Until the air-conditioner turned the office into a refuge from the hot weather it was more often a shuttered, silent and somnolent place, where the only sounds were the creak or the whir of the *punkahs*, the fluttering of papers under large quantities of paper weights, the scratching pens of the *babus* and the soft padding of the *chaprassis*' bare feet as they circulated files or cups of sweet, milky tea. Extended lunch breaks and long siestas divided the day into manageable stints and the work itself was made easier by the presence of 'the most efficient and wonderful clerks in the world. If there was any grinding work to be done at a file, all this work could be done for you by your clerks and everything would be neatly set out on paper, and if it was done properly you had merely to reach a decision at the end and say either "Yes" or "No" or "Thanks very much".' The routine life of the office-*wallah* was not one of great remark or circumstance. It was often tedious and certainly not much fun – but it was undoubtedly the most common experience of a working life in the Raj.

19

Indians

The Indian gentleman, with all self-respect to himself, should not enter into a compartment reserved for Europeans, any more than he should enter a carriage set apart for ladies. Although you may have acquired the habits and manners of the European, have the courage to show that you are not ashamed of being an Indian, and in all such cases, identify yourself with the race to which you belong.

H. HARDLESS
The Indian Gentleman's Guide to Etiquette 1919

'I remember once returning from leave in England in the twenties,' says John Morris, 'I went on to the train in Bombay and discovered that the other berth was occupied by an Indian. I am sorry to say that by that time I had become affected by the mentality of the ruling class in India and I said to the stationmaster, "I want to have the gentleman ejected." He spoke absolutely perfect English and he could have taught me a great deal about India. It is one of the incidents of my life of which I am most ashamed. But you have to remember that in those days army officers did not associate with Indians of any class other than the servant class, to whom they just gave orders. I think that one of the chief reasons for the curious attitude of the British towards Indians – it may have been quite unconscious – was the fact that they were regarded as a subject race.'

The attitudes of the British towards Indians varied greatly according to the social circumstances of the parties concerned. It was frequently asserted that prejudice against Indians was greatest amongst those who came into contact with them least – that is to say, in the British Army and in the commercial community – and least amongst those who worked in close proximity to Indians up-country. Yet, there were many exceptions to the general rule: Anglo-Indians who made a point of referring to Indians as 'niggers' and, conversely, BORS who fraternized with the lowliest of the cantonment *wallahs*. In fact, BORS' attitudes were curiously ambivalent, for 'if a soldier was seen joking or talking to an Indian, especially the same Indian two or three times, he had to be jeered at and called a "white nigger".' Yet there was still a special camaraderie between British troops and certain Indian Army regiments, the Gurkhas in particular, who were 'full of jokes and fun and more like us in a way'. E. S. Humphries recounts how 'it was their great joy when they greeted a British soldier to hold up their little finger and, giving the full length of it as a measurement, say to the British soldier, "Aha, look, British Tommy so big!" Then, taking off a quarter of an inch from the bottom they would say, "There, Gurkha soldier nearly so good as British soldier!" Finally, putting their thumbs still higher up the little finger until it almost touched the nail they would say, "This is the other Indian soldiers!" '

Attitudes changed with time. Those who went out to India in the early years of the century found a marked lack of familiarity between the races, the strongest prejudice coming from 'senior officials, old die-hards and hesitant partners', with what Claude Auchinleck describes as 'an attitude of ensuring what you might call "white superiority". Supposing you were on leave in the Himalayas and riding along a mountain track. If an Indian came along the other way riding his mule or his pony, he was supposed to get off. Similarly, an Indian carrying an open umbrella was supposed to shut it. It sounds ridiculous but that attitude was still being imbued into the newcomer to the Indian services when I first went out.' The attitudes of the womenfolk in earlier days were similarly exclusive: 'We didn't mix with the Indians at all,' remembers Mrs Norie, who returned to India as an adult in 1893 and lived there throughout the prewar period. 'You mixed with a very high-up family perhaps, but you didn't really bother about the Indians.'

The changes brought about by the Great War emphasized the difference in attitude between the older generation and the new. 'Much as I loved and respected my father,' records Rupert Mayne, 'I abhorred the attitude adopted by my forebears, which culminated in him saying that he would never permit me to go into the Indian Army and serve under what he always called a native officer.' Frances Smyth, who returned to India in 1925, found a parallel between this change of attitude and the emancipation of women in England: 'In my day in India it was rather like that. We were just beginning to accept Indians as equals – just.' In one respect change was not for the better. Improved communications between India and Europe, assisted passages and the establishment of commercial airline services broke the close threads of communication between India and the Englishman, hitherto isolated by long periods of time from home. By bringing England nearer it drew India and British-India apart, breaking rather than making the necessary connections.

The psychology of the two races was often described as complementary rather than matching: 'The Indian was pliant and would say "yes" to everything whether he was going to do it or not, whereas the British were more obstinate, more obdurate people and they wouldn't undertake a thing unless they could see it through.' But if the British were 'a bit Olympian or perhaps a little squirearchical, this was complemented by the attitude of the Indians towards us. They expected the Europeans to be rather superior, encouraging us to behave in that way.' Sycophancy was not something the British enjoyed. 'There was certainly a lot of sucking-up to the British,' states Ian Stephens. 'All sorts of tricks which one had to be wary about. But the wariness itself was a danger because it mightn't be what you thought. What was being miscon-strued might really be genuine affection. A genuine desire for normal, human contact.'

Differing standards of morality and what often appeared, from the British point of view, to be a perverse sense of right and wrong in such matters as *dastur* often led to 'a lot of shouting and a lack of sympathy'. Nor was the Muslim or Hindu culture thought much of. Nineteenth-century evan-gelical attitudes effectively blocked any widespread study of Indian art and culture. Hindu art, in particular, with its close association with Hindu religion, was found to be particularly repellent. Rosalie Roberts recalls how she once visited a missionary colleague in South India and was duly shown the local sights: 'After we'd had a meal she took us down to a temple. It was a wonderful temple, very old, with hundreds of carvings and on every ledge was a tiny lamp. All these little lights were flickering and this huge gateway, like a four-storey building, was lit up. It looked like fairyland it was so beautiful. The next morning she took us inside the temple – and it was revolting. All the little niches had idols where there had been sacrifices and the blood was spilt there. There was the stench and the darkness, just the flickering light by the idols, and that was the picture inside.' The ethics of Hinduism did not appeal to the Christian: 'In Hinduism I saw no compassion. A beggar would come to the door and their religion would make them give alms. But if that beggar, through want of food or illness, collapsed on their doorstep, they would do nothing. They wouldn't touch him. Their religion forbade them to. They would lose caste.'

The Indians, in their turn, found aspects of British culture incomprehensible and, on occasion, shocking, as Iris Portal illustrates: 'When my husband commanded the Governor's

Bodyguard in Bombay I had a great time with all the wives of the troops, Sikhs and Mohammedans. I used to spend a great deal of time with them down in the lines, not only doing child welfare and first aid and hospital work, but just chatting. They used to give me their views about life and I used to give them mine, and I remember the wife of the *Jemadar* saying, "The *Jemadar*-Sahib tells me that English ladies run about in their underpants. Is it true?" I said, "Oh, no, of course they don't," and she said, "Oh yes they do. The *Jemadar*-Sahib says that he's been to the Willingdon Club on duty and he's seen them running about in pants. I think it's absolutely disgusting." Of course, they were just innocent English girls playing tennis in shorts.' Immodesty of dress and behaviour were not the only British habits that Indians found indecent. There was the Maharajah who 'refused to allow the railway from Bombay to Calcutta to pass through his capital, because travellers might be eating beef in the restaurant car'. There was the occasion, recalled by Charles Wright, during a British Army route march when the regimental cook slaughtered a cow and there was 'a terrible rumpus. The natives got to know about this and nearly stoned the camp and we had to turn out in a hurry to disperse them.' The British had also to be aware of other dietary prohibitions: 'The orthodox Hindu would not eat meat but was quite content to drink any liquor that you might offer him, while your Mohammedan friend would eat any kind of meat other than pork but, strictly speaking, would not drink any kind of liquor.'

Undoubtedly the greatest social stumbling block between the British and the Indians was purdah: 'If you can't have a *partie a quatre*, it's rather difficult to get to know people. If you only invite the man you don't make the same equation with people.' The bolder memsahibs gave 'purdah parties' or tea parties with screens erected on the lawns to protect the guests from male view. Others visited and encouraged: 'I had a great friend in Hyderabad whose husband was a close friend of my husband's,' recounts Iris Portal.

He was a very Westernized, very cultured, sophisticated man and she was old-fashioned and completely in purdah and didn't know any English at all. It took me a little time to make friends with her, chiefly because my Urdu was not good enough for her, but we did make friends eventually and we saw a good deal of each other. I used to go and visit her and have a *pahn* with her and smoke a cigarette. Then she wanted to meet my husband, so I arranged a meeting. We all sat round the tea table and she never spoke because, of course, a well brought-up Indian lady won't speak in front of her husband. I didn't speak much for the same reason. The men were very, very embarrassed and it wasn't a very lively party. But after it was over I asked her husband, 'What does *Begum-Sahiba* think of my husband?' 'Oh,' he said, 'I'm afraid all she will say is, "Very large and red!"'

Only in the very last years of the Raj did Indian women emerge into society. It was 'a revolutionary change and if it had occurred fifty years before the whole history of India would have been different'.

The movement towards Independence was characterized by the slow, often reluctant but inevitable progress towards power-sharing. The Amritsar Massacre of 1919 and 'Anglo-India's' support for General Dyer's determination to punish created an undercurrent of feeling on both sides that was never really eradicated. The 'Indianization' of the ICS and the Indian Army had been put on a more open footing immediately after the ending of the Great War, but in the Indian Army it was not sincerely applied. To avoid having British officers serving under Indians, special segregated units were set up. In Claude Auchinleck's opinion this had 'a very bad effect on Indian feelings. The Indian officers themselves realized that they were being put into units which might be reckoned as inferior to the British officers' units. The only result was that these Indian regiments became objects of contempt.' The establishment of an Indian 'Sandhurst' did much to improve matters. 'I regard my time at the Indian Military Academy as a watershed,' states Reginald Savory, one of its first instructors, 'not only in my military career but in my political thinking. For the first time I met young, middle-class Indians on level terms and I found all these young men fascinating. They were very outspoken, highly intelligent, and one of the first remarks I had levelled at me was this, "You British officers of the Indian Army don't know India. All you know are your servants and your sepoys."'

In commerce, as much as in the services, the lack of suitably qualified Indians and the fear of lowering standards was often cited as the reason for slow Indianization. It was said that 'Indians did not always produce the best managerial material'. As a result, putting Indians into higher management jobs was held back in the thirties in favour of 'the young Britisher who was prepared to take responsibility and was prepared to take his coat off and get on with the job. The feeling persisted that the young Indian was much more inclined to look round for someone menial to do the dirty work and wouldn't get on with the job in the same way that a young Britisher would. The astonishing transformation was after Independence when the young Indian was prepared to do all the things that one expected of a young Britisher. India now belonged to India and Indians were prepared to do whatever was required for India.'

In most spheres an initial reluctance was followed by a general acceptance of Indians as working partners. 'In the Bengal Pilot Service we had one Indian,' recalls Radclyffe Side-bottom, 'who joined in the teeth of what was anticipated to be great opposition. But so strange is the service and so deep is tradition that the moment he joined the vast majority of the pilots took no notice of the fact that he was Indian at all. After that there was fairly rapid Indianization.'

These were the general attitudes that concealed minor variations and exceptions. From the British point of view the maharajahas and princes, whose domains were for the most part outside British India, were themselves above the usual conventions. Many were of extreme sophistication, 'Brindians' with English standards and interests, often great sportsmen and great hosts – and more than equals. Even those who were not were left to indulge their own peculiarities of behaviour. The opening words of the political officer's rule book suggested that the good officer left well alone. Only in instances of gross maladministration or outrageous public conduct did the Resident openly interfere with the ruler and the running of his state. The maharajahs were free both to accumulate wealth and to spend it lavishly. Richest of them all was the Nizam of Hyderabad who was renowned both for his meanness – 'he used to go to auctions and bid for second-hand gramophones' – and for his bouts of spending. He was once observed buying up the entire stock of shoes at Spenser's in Madras so that he could choose the pair he wanted at his leisure. The Maharajah of Darbhanga was equally capricious in his spending habits: 'He would see that a particular dog had won at Cruft's and he would immediately buy this dog and import it into India. He was very keen to show you his dog and a man would follow regularly behind with a bottle of methylated spirits and a rag to wipe over the place as soon as the dog had left his calling card. Some of these bits of furniture – the most beautiful modern furniture – smelt terribly. It was really very sad because five or six dogs in favour at the time lived in the palace and were made a great fuss of, whereas the dogs that had been favourites last year were relegated to the kennels and never came out again. You'd see thirty or forty beautiful pedigree dogs in these kennels which were never bothered about.'

There were maharajahs who were great practical jokers, who enjoyed squirting guests with concealed lawn sprinklers or leaving wet paint on chairs. One ran a toy railway on his dinner table which carried wines and cigars round to his guests and which he speeded up occasionally, leaving 'a thirsty guest with an empty hand outstretched'. Some, like the Maharajah of Kashmir, made up their own rules of cricket, as H. T. Wickham relates:

> At three o'clock in the afternoon that Maharajah himself would come down to the ground, the band would play the Kashmir anthem, salaams were made and he then went off to a special tent where he sat for a time, smoking his long water-pipe. At four thirty or thereabouts he decided he would bat. It didn't matter which side was batting, his own team or ours. He was padded by two attendants and gloved by two more, somebody carried his bat and he walked out to the wicket looking very dignified, very small and with an enormous turban on his head. In one of the matches I happened to be bowling and my first ball hit his stumps, but the wicket keeper, quick as lightning, shouted 'No Ball!' and the match went on. The only way that the Maharajah could get out was by lbw. And after fifteen or twenty minutes batting he said he felt tired and he was duly given out lbw. What the scorers did about his innings, which was never less than half a century, goodness only knows.

British attitudes to other sections of Indian society were rather less tolerant. The British concept of benevolent paternalism ensured that a distinction was made between those 'whom we regarded as completely educated and the half-educated'. Shopkeepers, moneylenders and *vakils* were disliked principally because 'they were profiting from the lower classes and exploiting the rustic'. Equally disliked were the caste Hindus in areas such as South India where strict Brahminism clashed with good administration, as when non-caste Hindus were forbidden to drink from the same wells as caste Hindus. It was also the fashion to denigrate the *babu* type: 'We used to make fun of them, very unfairly, because they were interpreting rules which we had made.' *Babu* jokes, based on the English language either wrongly or over-effusively applied, were a constant source of amusements for all 'Anglo-India'.

Coupled with the denigration of the *babu* was a traditional distrust of the Bengali – 'litigious, very fond of an argument' – who was frequently seen as a trouble-maker: 'He doesn't appeal to many British people in the same way as the very much more manly, direct type from upper India.' Following directly from this general dislike of trouble-makers was a widespread antipathy towards politicians and Congress-*wallahs*, not only because of their aspirations for *Swaraj* or the methods by which they sought to effect those aspirations, but because 'they were often people of very poor mental calibre. It was very hard on the young Indians who had got into government service to find themselves put underneath people whom they regarded as layabouts and scallywags and failures.'

Then there were the preferences. 'One did find oneself liking the hillman more than the plainsman,' admits Philip Mason. 'British officers in colonial situations always do like the simple, unspoilt people. In the plains children would come out of school quiet, sober little creatures walking home, while in Garwhal they used to come out like puppies tumbling out of a basket. They would come roaring out, racing and fighting and pushing each other about just as children might do in England.'

Much the same attitude affected that unique and devoted relationship between British officers and Indians that characterized the Indian Army. 'It bordered on paternalism,' agrees Claude Auchinleck, 'but the difference was in your relationship with the men off duty. After a parade in the morning the men immediately got into their own native clothing. In the evening the officers would go down in plain clothes, in mufti. The discipline, the saluting and all that sort of thing was just the same but the atmosphere was quite different. There was no question of ordering them about. They were yeomen really, and that made all the difference.' Being head of the family, as F. J. Dillon explains, entailed certain responsibilities. 'From the day a man joined his unit and came under your command he became yours in a much more personal way than in the British Army. You knew all about him, where he came from, what his family was. You probably visited his village and actually knew his parents. And he certainly relied on you if ever he was in trouble. There was a pretty general custom in the Indian Army of durbar, when the Commanding Officer would meet the whole of his Viceroy's Commissioned Officers and NCOs and any of the men who wanted to attend. Any man could raise any question he liked there.' The Viceroy's Commissioned Officers were the middlemen, 'God's own gentlemen,' who stood at the elbow of every inexperienced British subaltern; the *subadars, risaldars* and *jemadars*: 'They feel absolutely for you and help you all along the line, but if they think you can do it without help they'll jolly well make you do it.'

The men themselves, the sepoys, represented the diversity of India, coming from what were held to be the martial races, each with their own characteristics:

Generally speaking the Gurkhas were very, very fine mountain soldiers. The Sikhs were very tenacious, very brave, and would carry out orders to the letter. The Punjabi Mohammedan troops, who formed something like fifty per cent of the Indian Army, were very biddable, very leadable and easily trained but never quite up to the standard of the Sikh or the Gurkha. Then came the Indian troops from further south; the Jat, very heavy, solid and wonderful in defence, very similar in outlook, speech and everything else to the Norfolk man. Then came the soldiers from the foothills, the Dogras, the Garhwalis and after them a big belt of soldiers from much further south based on and around Poona; the Maharattas, very brave and to be reckoned with but not quite as at home in the hills as the troops from further north. Then you got the Sappers and Miners, the Engineers, some from the Punjab, some from the UP and some from Madras, like the Madras Sappers and Miners who were descendants of our old Madras Army – all of them excellent troops.

After the Mutiny these racial groups had been split into mixed units, the idea being that 'if you had four companies of different religions there would be very much less chance of a mutiny'. Claude Auchinleck's 62nd Punjabis were one such mixed regiment, with 'a company of Rajputs, the descendants of the famous warrior tribes of Rajputana, a company of Sikhs from the Punjab, a company of Punjabi Muslims from the hills north of Rawalpindi and another company from the Frontier. Four completely separate companies. The Sikh never cuts his hair; he's allowed to drink but he's not allowed to smoke. The Muslim shaves his head and shaves his body and he smokes but doesn't drink. The Rajput smokes and drinks. They wouldn't eat together and each company lived its own separate life, but they got on very happily together.' Other regiments – principally those which had supported the British during the Mutiny, such as the Sikhs and Gurkhas – retained their racial unity and were known as Class Regiments. It was in these regiments, easier to command and administer, that the fiercest devotion grew up between officers and men and a terrific sense of pride that enabled the British officer to declare with absolute confidence that the men under his command were the best soldiers in the world. 'They were well known as being the finest mountain troops in the world,' asserts Lewis Le Marchand, describing the Gurkhas as 'very proud, very gay, very simple. He's as brave as a lion and he'll obey any order you like to give.' It was the same with Reginald Savory's Sikhs:

> They are physically as fine a race of men as the world can produce; one of the most interesting races of men in the world and one of the most difficult to command. I always felt that when they were shouting and you could hear them running about the place, then they were happy, they had something to do with themselves. When there was a silence in the line then I always had an idea that something was brewing and I used to

send for an Indian officer and say, 'You go down to the lines, it's too quiet for my liking, something is hatching.' And very often it proved to be true.

The Sikh with his turban and his long roll of beard is a man to whom personal looks mean a tremendous amount. You would see him looking at himself in the glass, picking his teeth or rolling his moustache and generally making the most of his looks. Sikhs use their conceit to show off to their rivals. For instance, it's a challenge to any other man if, as you walk down the platform of a railway station you twirl your moustache and say, 'Hmm, hmm,' to the man as you pass. We had many cases in the regiment of chaps who came to blows, very often with hockey sticks, broken heads and heaven knows what. You'd say, 'What's the trouble! Why did you hit him?' 'Oh,' he says, 'I was walking down the platform and he twirled his little moustache and went, "Hmm, hmm!"'

Until he knew you he was a little bit stiff. He stood to attention and he'd say, 'Yes, sir, no, sir.' But when you did get to know him and when you could reach the stage of being able to pull his leg and get a smile out of him, then you had him absolutely in the hollow of your hand. They had that spirit in them which was a wonderful thing amongst men you command. No wonder we were so proud of them.

20

'Quit India'

It is only when you get to see and realise what India really is – that she is the strength and greatness of England – it is only then that you feel that every nerve a man may strain, every energy he may put forward cannot be devoted to a nobler purpose than keeping tight the cords that hold India to ourselves.

LORD CURZON, Viceroy of India, 1899–1905

'There was a judge in Bengal, who was greatly loved by all the people of his district. He was their *ma-bap*, and they all came to him with their troubles. He loved India, he was devoted to India and like so many other men he worked long hours for India, and yet he met his end at the hands of two girls in saris. They came along to his bungalow and told his servant that they wanted to see the judge-*sahib*, as they had a petition to present to him. The judge came out on to the verandah and directly he got close to the girls with his hand out to receive the petition one of the girls pulled a pistol from her sari and killed him.' Like many of her compatriots, Marjorie Cashmore found such actions incomprehensible and sought an explanation from an Indian friend in the Congress Party: ' "Here you have devoted servants of India, giving their lives, sacrificing everything in order to serve your people. You have others who come out from England and don't understand India. They've only come out for a few years and they abuse the Indian. I can understand you wanting that type of person out of the country, but this person is serving you, doing more than anybody else for your people and yet you kill him." And he laughed and said, "Don't you understand? The judge and those like him are hindrances to our getting Home Rule. The other man we needn't bother about because he gives us a cause for kicking out the British." '

Self-government for India was an issue that pre-dated the Mutiny, yet the average Englishman in India did not look upon Indian nationalism with favour and, until the Great War forced the issue, did not give self-government much thought. Claude Auchinleck records the pre-war army view: 'I don't think the average subaltern thought much about British rule and, indeed, took it for granted that it would go on forever. I do remember when one of our Indian officers from the hills in the north said to me, "What is going to happen when the British leave India?" I looked at him and said, "Well, of course, the British are never going to leave India." ' Even to the young men joining the ICS, such as Christopher Masterman, it was not a serious issue. 'When I first went to India it never entered my head that India would one day be independent, but I saw a sign when the Montague-Chelmsford Reforms were introduced in 1921. I certainly felt then that Independence would come but I don't think we realized that it would be coming so soon. After the 1935 Act everyone realized that Independence was coming and was coming quite soon, and I don't think we resented it.'

The young men who joined the ICS after the Great War had very different views. 'I went to India clearly thinking that we were going there to lead India on the way to self-government,' declares Philip Mason. 'Although one constantly lost sight of this in the rough and tumble of a district, because you're always thinking all the time of stopping Mohammedans and Hindus from knocking each other on the head, or getting your land records right or getting your court up to date in its work, or stopping some oppression, none the less, I don't think one *really* lost sight of it.' Yet the tendency to be above politics was there: 'Political changes and political advancement had very little relevance to the happiness of the ordinary chap that we were dealing with, and it was his happiness that was our chief concern.'

A certain escapism also affected those outside government: 'If we thought about Gandhi at all it was really that he was just a bit of a nuisance and slightly absurd.' Vere Birdwood quotes from a series of minutes which she saw in 1941 added to a file: 'The most junior officer had written, "I don't think we'd better start this project, there may not be time to finish it." His senior officer had minuted on the file, "What nonsense. I was told this in 1919." And the most senior officer, the Governor, had minuted on that same file, "Absolute nonsense. I was told this in 1909."'

The inevitable consequence of this tendency to overlook India's future was that 'Indians never really believed that Britain had any intention of handing over power at all. They were convinced right up to the end that we were going to find some trick to avoid handing over power – and that was the foundation of their Non-Cooperation Movement.' Campaigns of non-cooperation and civil-disobedience grew in strength and frequency as the century proceeded. In urban areas it was impossible to ignore the changing circumstances, as Edwin Pratt remembers: 'When I first went to Calcutta you could walk down Chowringee and the Indians walking in the opposite direction would just get out of your way. Time came when they just continued to walk where they were and you got out of the way.' A very few met hostility, infrequently and uncharacteristically. During the Second World War Iris Portal cycled daily from her bungalow to the hospital where she was nursing: 'One day, bicycling along the road in a nurse's uniform I came on a row of young Indian boys who were right across the road arm in arm shouting "Quit India!" It was the first aggression that I had ever met in India, so I put my head down and rode straight at them on my bicycle, ringing the bell violently.' Many others remained untouched and virtually unaffected. In Bengal, where officials and policemen were being regularly assassinated, the Roberts could still feel untroubled 'for the first twenty or thirty years. We were on our own there, sleeping out on the verandah. The house was more or less open but I don't think we felt uneasy at all.'

Those who did meet trouble were the ones appointed to deal with it, and it came most often not in the form of political disturbances but in the 'endemic' inter-communal strife between Muslims and Hindus. This was 'the bugbear of a district officer. Once it broke out and you got Hindus and Muslims going for each other hammer and tongs really all you could do was turn out the police and try and separate the parties and drive them away from one another.' A great deal of effort was devoted to trying to anticipate the incidents – most frequently processions – that provoked these religious conflicts: 'There was a record kept in the police station which it was part of one's duty to keep up to date. This recorded all the customs in connection with festivals; the route which the *Mohurram* procession would follow, whether it went near a particular temple or not, whether it went near some particular peepul tree which might become holy in the course of time. You had to see that they followed the exact precedent.' It required only the slightest deviation, infringement or supposed provocation to create a full-scale riot: 'Some stupid little thing would happen, a rumour that Pathans were abducting Hindu girls, or that somebody had killed a Mohammedan. Usually it was quite untrue, but then the trouble, which was always smouldering in certain cities, started. You'd get some stabbing incidents at night, and then everybody was out trying to keep the score up; if five Mohammedans were stabbed one night, six Hindus would be murdered the next.' The conflict between Hindus and Muslims was a long-standing one. 'There was no answer to it,' declares Penderel Moon, 'you couldn't prevent it, but you might if you were sufficiently prompt and on the spot at the time, prevent it assuming a very serious form. I was a great believer in the maximum display of force at the very beginning to try and overawe people. I was also a great believer in using force effectively if you had to use it at all. I didn't believe in firing one or two rounds; I used to say to my magistrates, "If you ever have to open fire, fire at least five rounds. If you open fire make sure that it is effective, so that people are seen to fall and the mob takes fright." It didn't occur to me as ruthless. It occurred to me as plain commonsense.'

Raymond Vernede was district magistrate in Benares in 1939 when widespread rioting broke out during the Muslim festival of *Mohurram*:

I set out with a platoon under a very junior, recently joined subaltern and we found, as I'd rather feared, that the trouble had broken out in the most dangerous area in the city. Here there was a minority of Hindu spinners living right in the middle of a large number of Muslim weavers. We turned a corner and there in front of us all the houses were on fire. You couldn't hear anything for the roar of the flames, but outlined against the flames were literally hundreds of men looting the houses on both sides and throwing the stuff down to their friends below. It was impossible to issue the stock warnings to the crowd – nobody could have heard – so as pre-arranged with the subaltern I said I wanted him to fire to disperse this crowd. So he told a corporal to take three steps forward and fire one shot. He fired and although there were literally hundreds of men milling around, the shot went right through the whole lot without hitting anyone. But the effect was electric. The crowd was gone and the whole street was empty within a minute. We just went round the corner, about ten yards, and there the whole thing was repeated – flames and hundreds of men silently looting. So I said, 'You've got to stop this now, another round.' I pointed out to the corporal, who was their marksman, a man outlined very clearly against the flames on the cornice of a roof and I said, 'You shoot him.' The officer ordered him to shoot, because I couldn't order him to shoot, and he shot and killed the man. He fell off into the street and there was an absolute stampede. Within fifteen minutes the news of the firing was all round the city and had an astonishing effect.

Political demonstrations and the great majority of civil disobedience campaigns were of a very different order, being based on the Gandhian concept of *satyagraha* and passive resistance. In some instances the mere presence of the sahib was enough. 'I never allowed anyone to shout "Mahatma Gandhi" without giving him six on the bottom with a stick,' declares John Rivett-Carnac.

I found that if I went down myself, making quite an imposing figure in full uniform with a helmet and a revolver on each side and riding boots, I could overawe the crowd. I did this really through boredom and the desire for excitement, and considered it rather fun in a way. These mobs of about one or two or three thousand would converge on the market place. They would all have numerous flags and banners and would be shouting about Mother India, and they'd advance up to where I was standing. I would order a halt and tell the constable to take away all the flags and banners. I would then read out the names of five or six of the leading non-cooperators and they would be taken off with all the flags and banners by the constable, leaving myself with the sub-inspector. I would then speak to the foremost man and say to him, 'It's time for you to go home,' and he would refuse, whereupon I would give him a medium-sized blow on the chin. After about the second or third butt he would stagger off. I then did the same with the next man and the third man would turn and start retreating and I might help him along. Then the whole crowd would bolt out of the market place. This, as a rule, was a Hindu crowd; the Mohammedans I found very much more dangerous, but it

never crossed my mind that I could be killed under these
circumstances.

Another policeman, F. C. Hart, who served in the Special
Branch, recalls how it was possible to restrain the enthusiasm
of local Congress leaders in Bihar by dumping them naked by
the roadside rather than affording them the prestige of arrest
and gaol: 'In those days everybody wanted to get a gaol ticket.
Their whole political future depended on it.' The Indian sense
of modesty also gave the police an advantage when dealing
with women demonstrators: 'On one occasion in Patna City a
number of women laid themselves down on the ground right
across the street and held up all the traffic. When the Superintendent of Police arrived on the scene he was at first
nonplussed. If they had been men he could have sent in
policemen to lift them out bodily, but he daren't do it with
women. So he thought for a bit and then he called for fire
hoses and with the hoses they sprayed these women who were
lying on the ground. They only wore very thin saris and, of
course, when the water got on them all their figures could be
seen. The constables started cracking dirty jokes and immediately the women got up and ran.'

Only when it was quite clear that the police were unable to
contain the situation would the military be called in. 'We
didn't have to shoot anyone,' Charles Wright explains, 'when
the crowd were getting very angry and very unruly and
pressing up against us we would ease them back by gently
dropping the butts of our rifles on their toes, which did
eventually move them back'. This was usually followed by
what was known as 'showing the flag': 'The schoolmasters of
the villages would parade all the children outside to shout as
we passed by, "Three cheers for the Black Watch Regiment!"
and keep on repeating this till we got through the village.
However, I'm sure they didn't like us there.'

That the army did not relish 'coming to the aid of the civil
power' is well illustrated by Reginald Savory's letters, written

during the civil disturbances in Peshawar in 1930: 'I wrote to my wife on May 10 and said, "These civil disturbances are most unpleasant for both sides, and for me, I'd far rather be back in Gallipoli." On June 14 I wrote saying, "I'm wondering what the future has in store for the Indian Army; whether you and I will be in this country in four years' time," and ten days later I wrote to my wife in the following terms, "At times I feel like chucking it and taking my first pension. Living in a country in which, through no fault of one's own, one is hated, has few attractions and the future will probably deny us what little status we have at present."'

It says a lot for both sides that throughout this penultimate chapter of the Raj friendships between individual British and Indians not only survived but frequently prospered. David Symington recalls that 'the relations of members of my service with the Congress leaders were quite surprising. There was a time in 1942 in the Quit India Movement when we did experience a certain amount of unpleasantness, but that didn't last long. For all the rest of the time, although the Congress leaders were supposed to be in open hostility to the Raj, they would meet us on ordinary occasions as friends and we would exchange jokes about what they were going to do next. I remember the Congress leader in Sholapur who was going to offer individual *satyagraha* came along to me and said, "Oh, sir, I've come to say goodbye." I said, "Why, what's happening? Are you going away?" "No, I have got to offer myself for imprisonment today." So he said goodbye to me very politely and went out and got himself arrested on the road. They would go along shouting, "No help for the wars. Not a man, not a rupee!" and in due course, when they'd got it off their chests, the police would take them in and they'd be hauled up before a court and sentenced to a short term of imprisonment.' Anne Symington's friends in Congress included a leading political figure, Mrs Sarojini Naidu, with whom – even during the height of the Quit India troubles – she frequently had tea: 'I met everybody that was anybody in the political world there

and they used to say, "Is it all right to speak in front of Anne?"
and she'd say, "Oh yes, perfectly all right."'

Another leading figure of the Congress Party was Pandit
Nehru, with whom Raymond Vernede had a brief but
illuminating encounter:

> I received a coded telegram from the Government to say that
> they had released Pandit Nehru from gaol in Dehra Dun and
> they were sending him down to Naini Tal where his wife was
> also in prison and seriously ill. She had had a bad turn for the
> worse and they were very anxious that he should be released to
> see her – but they were not prepared to release him unless he
> would undertake not to take part in any political activities or
> make any political speeches while he was out. In the telegram
> they used the expression 'Release on Parole' and I was to use
> my discretion as to how to put this message across. Nehru
> arrived at about midnight at the narrow gauge station outside
> Allahabad and he was obviously very tired and very tense. I
> came up and met him and said I'd been deputed by the
> Government to meet him and that the Government wanted to
> release him on parole so that he could see his wife. It was the
> first he'd heard officially that his wife was seriously ill. I then
> plunged into my delicate task, saying that they would release
> him on parole provided he gave an undertaking. Immediately
> he stiffened and said, 'Oh, but I could never agree to that. It
> would be against all my principles to give such an undertaking.
> I have been in gaol for nearly three years. I want to be with my
> wife and the last thing I want to do is join in politics and make
> speeches – but I am not prepared to give an undertaking to the
> government.' All along the platform there were the shapes of
> Indians lying asleep in their white clothes and we walked up
> and down this platform for over half an hour, carefully
> stepping over these bodies, with a little group of bewildered
> policemen standing at the back wondering what it was all
> about. I tried to point out that releasing him on parole was an
> act of chivalry, that it was the highest honour you could pay

your enemy. 'That may have been all right in the Middle Ages, but it doesn't work in India,' he said. 'It doesn't apply any longer. It stinks.' Then I suddenly had a brainwave. I said, 'Well, look, if you won't give an undertaking to the Government, what about coming to a gentleman's agreement with me?' He stopped in his tracks and he looked at me and a delighted smile came over his face and he said, 'Ah, a gentleman's agreement with you? That would be different. I think I could accept that.'

As Independence approached, the changing political circumstances often placed former political prisoners in positions of authority over those who had gaoled them. Early in the 1930s Olaf Caroe was involved in the gaoling of the two Khan brothers, Dr Khan Sahib and his younger brother Abdul Ghaffar Khan, known as the 'Frontier Gandhi'. Within a few years both had become his close friends and 'when I was Governor and Dr Khan Sahib was my Chief Minister I remember we had a terrific quarrel once and he more or less lost his temper with me. So I said to him, "Doctor, if you don't retract that I shall put you in gaol again!" He looked at me in fury for a moment and then burst into laughter and embraced me.'

In the last years of the Raj 'the awful portent of Pakistan began to arise, and from 1939 this danger appeared before us and we could see no clear way of averting it'. To nearly all the British in India 'the idea of partition was horrifying'. Many saw it as 'the biggest disaster of the whole of British rule' which 'undid the greatest thing we had done during the Raj, which was to unify India'. Few had any doubts as to who was responsible. 'I first realized that partition was something more than a talking-point,' explains Percival Griffiths, 'when I dined with Mr Jinnah and he expounded his two-nation theory. He said, "You British people, you're good administrators, but you are very bad psychologists. You talk about Indian nationality but there is no such thing. I don't regard the Hindus as my fellow nationals at all, and they don't regard me as their fellow national. You talk about democracy, but you know there was never any such thing as democracy in India before you came. You have introduced a kind of democracy as a passing phase. It will pass with you."' The contrast between Jinnah and Nehru was marked. Olaf Caroe, who knew both well, found both arrogant, but Nehru's arrogance was 'shot through with charm, which Jinnah's certainly wasn't. He was very arrogant and very immovable and he is certainly not one of my heroes.' It was said at Viceregal Lodge that Jinnah was always five minutes late, whereas Mahatma Gandhi was always five minutes early.

Nowhere was partition more bitterly resented than in the Indian Army: 'To us it was the heartbreak of heartbreaks. We felt it beyond credence. We had united these dozens of different castes, creeds, colours, beliefs under one flag. We had united them under one regimental colour. It took us two hundred years to build that up, and for that to go literally at the stroke of a pen – it was something that one will never get over.' Perhaps no one felt this loss more than Claude Auchinleck, whose duty it was to divide the Indian Army into two: 'All Indian Army officers hated the idea but we did as we were told. They had to be split and then all the equipment had to be split with everything else. What it meant was that regiments like my own, half Hindu and half Muslim, were just torn in half – and they wept on each other's shoulders when it happened. It was moving for me and I think it was moving for them. The older officers like myself undoubtedly felt a sense of loss. You felt your life's work would be finished when what you had been working at all along was just torn in two pieces.'

With the exception of one battalion, the divided army remained 'staunch' through all the horrors that accompanied Independence. The slaughter that began in Calcutta in 1946 in what became known as the 'Great Calcutta Killing' was only the extension – on a much greater scale – of what had been going on between the rival communities of Hindus and Muslims for years: 'You could almost know that it was going to happen by a peculiar silence,' declares Radclyffe Sidebottom. 'But as tension grew the voice pitch went up and the high-pitched screaming of the rioting crowd was something that you could never forget. You'd hear the screaming coming towards you, they would commit some horrible act and then patter away without a sound. But it wasn't so much the sounds, it was the smell of fear – and you'd get the smell of fear not necessarily from those who were being killed, but from the rioting mobs that are doing the killing. The moment the crowd decided that one of the opposite religion had been killed, then everybody in one form of dress would turn on the others and in a matter of forty-eight hours there were three hundred, four hundred deaths a night. If you saw a man literally writhing in agony and you stopped your car and got out to help him – then you were finished.'

From the safety of a boat on the Hoogly River Radclyffe Sidebottom witnessed another side of the killing:

You could see a crop of one religion or another who had been captured and tied, brought down to the *bund* which went down to the river, being pushed down the bank into the water where dinghies with poles were pushing them under. You could see them being laid on their faces with their heads poking out over Howrah Bridge and being beheaded into the river, their bodies thrown in afterwards. After the riot the river was literally choked with dead bodies which floated for a while, sank for a while and then, when the internal gasses blew them up, floated again after three days. They were carried up and down the river by the tide, with vultures sitting on their bellies or their backs according to whether they were male or female – one floated one way, one floated the other – taking the gibbly bits and leaving the rest to float ashore to be eaten by the pi-dogs, the jackals and the ordinary vultures.

Another witness was Ian Stephens who, as a journalist, found himself numbed almost to callousness by the 'putrefying corpses stacked to the ceiling' in the morgues, but could 'never quite eradicate from the memory – though it was so small – a Hindu *chaprassi* who came to deliver papers to my bungalow, a funny little thing with a huge moustache. I remember his smile and, within five minutes, he'd been knifed to death in the street outside.' Mary Wood recalls a similarly personal, but happier incident: 'I was drying my hair when all hell was let loose outside my bedroom door. I shot out on to the balcony in my curlers and there was my poor little sweeper hanging on to one end of a long pole, while at the other end of the pole were four or five of the rest of the household who were intent on beating him up – and would certainly have done so except they were so startled by Memsahib gibbering with fury in hair curlers, that they fled. And I was left with my poor little sweeper who had flung himself at my feet and assured me I'd saved his life. I'm sure I hadn't, but one wonders what happened to people like that after the British all . . . went?'

21

Topees Overboard

The Englishman in India has no home and leaves no memory.
SIR WILLIAM HUNTER *The Old Missionary* 1895

When asked at his initial interview why he wanted to go to India Philip Mason had replied, 'Because it's such an exciting place politically. We have succeeded in devolving power to Canada, but to do this in India, where you have different religion and different culture and different race, is a very much more hazardous and difficult experiment, and it seems to me very exciting and I should like to be in on this.' Thirty years later this 'hazardous and difficult experiment' was completed – but not without a great many misgivings. 'I felt that the last chapter hadn't been worthy of the one hundred and fifty years that had gone before,' declares Olaf Caroe, echoing the feelings of many of his colleagues. 'The thing had been much too hurried.' Indeed, Independence Day came with such speed and in the midst of such turmoil that there was little opportunity either for preparation or reflection: 'We were at the centre of a vast typhoon which was going on all round us, but of which we were curiously unaware at the time.'

From the outbreak of war in 1939 the writing had been clearly on the wall – and yet a curious sense of timelessness had persisted: 'It seemed as if it would go on for ever.' Vere Birdwood had seen the change coming when the splendid cavalry regiments – 'pennants flying from their lances, their horses tossing their heads' – were hurriedly mechanized: 'One began to see that all that had gone before was a sort of dream. When we saw these splendid looking men crouched over the wheels of buses, driving round and round and trying to master gears when all that they had really mastered was how to ride a horse, it really did seem as if it had all been something that would never come again.'

Perhaps the least prepared were the Anglo-Indians, as Eugene Pierce describes: 'I don't believe any of us ever visualized that British rule would come to an end and certainly not as abruptly as it did. When it was announced that India was to get her independence we were very jittery about it. We immediately started discussing what we were going to do.' Now Anglo-Indians were called upon to decide once and for all where their loyalties and their identities lay. 'It was the end of our world,' asserts Irene Edwards, 'I remember once sitting on a platform in Mhou. You could just see the fort in the distance with the Union Jack flying, and a group of little India *chokras* were sitting and talking near by and one said to the other, "Do you see that flag up there? Do you know, there are a lot of people that want to see that flag come down? But that flag will never come down." And I, in my foolishness, agreed with them; I thought the flag would never come down. We were proud of being British. My father, when he heard "God Save the King" being sung, even away in the distance, stood up and we had to stand up with him. That is what we thought of the British Raj and it came as a shock to us when it ended. Now we did not know where we were, whether we were Indians or British or what.'

August 15, 1947, was celebrated in an atmosphere of remarkable good will. 'The day came,' recalls Rupert Mayne, 'and I can remember going round to the Viceroy's house in the evening. There were tens and tens of thousands, millions in the street, everybody patting you on the back and shaking you by the hand. We were the British heroes, the British who had given them Independence.' But with Independence came the great exodus, and with it the 'competition of retaliation' that ended with some one and a half million dead. Sylvia Corfield recalls how she waited in Simla for a military convoy to take her to safety, 'standing above the Mall just outside Christ Church and seeing all the shops being looted. I remember standing on the verandah of the United Services Club, which had opened its doors to women, standing there with the Bishop of Lahore and hearing the rickshaw coolies' quarters in the lower bazaar being bombed. We felt quite helpless listening to their cries and the dull thud of the explosions. We couldn't do anything.'

Rupert Mayne, travelling near the border between the two new countries, found himself equally helpless:

Amritsar was like one of the towns in Normandy after the bombardment. It was more or less decimated, and between there and Lahore there was mile upon mile of people going East and going West carrying their belongings. The Hindus and the Sikhs from Pakistan moving on one side of the road, the Mohammedans on the other. Every now and again some goat or something would run across the road and then there would be a beat-up trying to get it back again. Even the bark of the trees had been eaten up to a height of ten feet, as high as a person could stand upon another person's shoulders. The incident that, in my mind, epitomises the tragedy was when we stopped and were watching the people go by when a figure came out from the huge line of refugees, stood to attention and asked me to help him. He then said that he'd been with the 4th Indian Division through the desert and in Italy. What could I do to save him? All I could do was look at him and say, 'Your politicians asked for *Swaraj*, and this is *Swaraj*.'

'When I left India in December 1947 I felt we were leaving a task half finished,' declares Reginald Savory. It was a feeling that many shared. 'Our intention in India was to hand over a running show and I believe that if we could have held on for another ten years that would have been the case.' An extra decade would certainly have allowed the process of Indianization to have been completed – but 'the will was lacking'. By 1947 most officials and army officers had put up with eight years of extreme working conditions. Few had been able to take home leave and, as Ian Stephens observes, the pressure had begun to tell. 'A lot of them became almost drudges and when the great change of '47 came they were most of them too tired to take it all in. They were disillusioned; much of what they'd served for seemed to be breaking up and they pulled out fatigued and recognizing that they must rebuild their lives somehow and get re-adapted elsewhere.' Not all sections of the British community were required to 'rebuild their lives'. The *box-wallahs*, the businessmen and the planters went on as before, without major loss. The missionaries continued to play a leading role in health and education and many thousands of Anglo-Indians took the plunge to become Indian or Pakistani citizens. Large numbers of officials also stayed on for a year or two until an Indian replacement could be found.

Independence had opened the way for a greater friendship between the races. 'Both Europeans and Indians at that time held out their hands to each other in an extraordinarily easy way.' The new openness lasted and stood the test of distance and time. There was no longer 'that curious barrier that there used to be'.

Most directly affected by the break-up of the Raj were the ICS and the Indian Army; some went home because they had no choice, others because they preferred to. 'Much larger numbers of us would have stayed on and served under Indian governments,' says David Symington, 'if it hadn't been for three things. First of all, everybody was very tired and pretty browned off, disillusioned by all the political failure. Another reason was that the Government made it easy for us to go by offering us compensation. But most important of all was the fact that you either had to serve a Hindu Government or a Mohammedan Government, and you had either to be pro-Mohammedan or pro-Hindu accordingly, and that was contrary to everything that we thought right or possible.' The prospect of leaving India was accepted with fatalism: 'We all knew, like knowing that death is inevitable, that one day we would leave India. Most of us did not look forward to this day, but we knew it would come and, of course, everything was geared to this feeling in a queer sort of way.' A minority went with relief – 'without a thought, without a pang, without a qualm,' and were 'delighted to get away and lose India forever'. Many more were 'glad to get some rest', and eager to see their homes and families again – and yet went with great regret, taking with them 'a nostalgia for sights and sounds and smells and for the nice things' that would grow more acute as the years went by. 'I've only got to shut my eyes,' states Frances Smyth, 'and picture an evening in a village in India, with the smell of wood smoke, which is the most gorgeous smell in the world. There was a very sudden twilight in India always and when the twilight came it was dark and the mist would rise up in a sort of blue haze from the fields – and there would be this gorgeous smell drifting across the fields.' Others recall best the 'spicy, peppery smell of the shops in the bazaar' or 'the smell of dust after a long drought when the first rain falls' or being in the bazaar and 'talking with people, laughing with people, probably hot and sweaty and tired and thirsty – but all so very worthwhile'. For Vere Birdwood 'the most wonderful feeling of all was sleeping out under the stars; you could read by starlight in India'. For all of them India had moved deep into the blood. 'I never really got it out of my system,' declares Nancy Vernede, speaking for many.

Perhaps there was also a less demonstrable nostalgia; for Indian qualities that were not always appreciated in their time; the gentleness of the Indian, his courtesy and heightened sense of hospitality that so rarely allowed an Englishman to feel that he was not welcome in another man's land. 'We were walking back to our camp,' relates Philip Mason, 'and some people in the village we were passing saw us and came running out and said, "You can't go through our village like this, we must get you a bullock cart and you can go on that." I said, "No, no, I want to walk." "We'll get you a horse." "No, no, we want to walk." "Well, you must sit down and have some oranges or milk," and they joined hands and made a circle round us like children at a party and said, "We won't let you go until you have sat down."'

Even less tangible was the 'terrible nostalgia for having lost a skill'. The enormous self-confidence and the rare skills that so many had acquired – 'I went out rather a shy, diffident young man and I came away feeling I could turn my hand to anything' – would be regarded in the future with quite as much suspicion as favour. England itself would seem flat and characterless after India's extra dimensions and its 'sudden revelation of light'. Indeed, England seldom lived up to expectations. 'While I was in India England was always that wonderful country that I had known as a child,' remembers F. J. Dillon, who returned to find that 'the England I had always thought of didn't exist any more'.

Nor was it a grateful mother country that they were returning to. 'The English never cared,' states Claude Auchinleck, 'the politicians especially. I don't think they ever took any interest in India at all. I think they used it.' The lack of interest was not confined to politicians. Vere Birdwood remembers 'the total disinterest of the people in England to Indian affairs. I don't think any of us ever spoke about India for the six months or so we spent in England. We might occasionally be asked at a dinner, "Well now, what's all this about old Gandhi?" or something of that sort. Well, to try and settle down to a long dissertation on Indian politics between the soup and the fish was not really possible, so we just used to shrug our shoulders and our host or hostess or whoever might have felt obliged to put this question thankfully passed on to news of the latest theatre in London.' But even if 'you were a stranger when you came back to England', it was still home. The ties were too strong to be ignored. 'I was very fond of India,' remarks Kathleen Griffiths, 'and I found as the years went on that it grows on you. It becomes a part of your being, almost. But always at the back of my mind there was that thought that at the end of it all I want to return finally to England, back to my own country.'

The Raj had its critics. 'The psychology of the Raj was really based on a lie,' declares John Morris. 'The majority of the British in India were acting a part. They weren't really the people they were supposed to be. They were there for a very good reason; earning a living and making money – nothing ignoble about that – but I don't really feel that most people had a sense of vocation, that they were serving India.' Others also had their criticisms: 'English rule in India was very often called sarcastically *banya ki raj*, the rule of the moneylender, because all our laws enabled him to lend money to the illiterate people at vast interest. It was money for jam for the money-lender and the law was on his side.' Some disliked the Raj for a more basic reason. 'Cheap labour was another jewel in the crown of the Raj,' maintains Ed Brown. 'At the back of the jewel was the squalor, hunger, filth, disease and beggary. Only when I came out of the army could I see what a terrible thing it was that a country had been allowed to exist like this. Such snobbery, so many riches, so much starvation.' It was also said that if India made the British self-confident it was, perhaps, at the expense of the Indians, leading to 'the reduction of Indian self-confidence, to their self-criticism and their despair about themselves and their future'.

Such criticisms come with hindsight and, as such, are best left to the judgement of future historians. At the time 'Anglo-India' did not so much see faults or attributes in the Raj as simply take it for granted. 'I thought nothing about the Raj,' asserts Norman Watney. 'It seemed to me that I had a job, it was a tough one and that was all there was to it.' For those with ancestral roots in India the attitude was much more complex: 'I don't think we ever consciously thought about the British Raj as such. We simply accepted that this was where fate had placed us. We felt that this was our destiny – in many cases the destiny of our forebears – that we were there at some sacrifice to serve India. Those long partings from children were a great sacrifice, the loneliness was a sacrifice. There was absolutely no feeling of exploitation, no feeling of being wicked imperialists. In fact, in those days we didn't think imperialists were necessarily wicked.'

Certainly, on the personal level the benevolent paternalism had much to commend it: 'The fashion is to judge India by the few who made money out of it, and forget the devotion of the people who served it. The men who looked after the forests, the people who built hospitals, the people who made roads, who did the irrigation. It was their occupation, granted, but they did it with a love of India, a love of the people, and what they did and what they contributed is now forgotten to a large extent. They were the ordinary, plain little people, the ones in the middle who were never exalted, but who ran India really.' Certainly, it could also be argued that 'if we had not made a Raj in India, somebody else would have – and they would not have made such a good job at it'.

An assessment of the Raj and its worth has no real place in this present informal selection of images. Here let it be said only that the British found in the Mogul vacuum 'chaos and anarchy and the degradation of morals and standards', which they filled in time with a common language and legal system, a civil and administrative machine of rare quality and the 'great civilising effect' of the Indian Army. The Pax Britannica did indeed bring uninterrupted peace – though not prosperity – within India's borders and its power extended far beyond. Kenneth Mason, while exploring deep in the Pamirs, ran out of money and was lent some by a yak owner: 'I wrote out on half a sheet of notepaper to Cox's, Karachi: "Please pay bearer on receipt of this the sum of fifty pounds sterling." It must've been eight or nine months later that I heard from my bankers, Cox's at Karachi, that a greasy piece of paper had arrived and had been presented in the Peshawar bazaar and was said to be worth fifty pounds sterling. That piece of paper had gone from hand to hand all over Central Asia. It had marks of people that couldn't sign. It had thumb marks which had been dipped in ink. It had been to Samarkand and Kiva and God knows where, and it'd come over the Khyber Pass and was presented in Peshawar bazaar and was still said to be worth fifty pounds sterling.'

It could be said that the Raj also conferred indirect benefits upon India; the introduction of 'a new, galvanic impulse that gave Indians new ideas about liberty and a belief in the need for progress', and perhaps most important of all, the creation 'of the concept of patriotism for the Indian nation so that they thought of India as one nation and even talked of Mother India'. The end result was a 'synthesis of Eastern and Western civilizations which makes India different both from the West and from Asia', a synthesis which Penderel Moon saw as 'essentially a partnership; a government by Indians and British working together in close partnership – and its success arose partly from what I would call the intelligence of the Indians, their sense to accept what had happened to their country, that it had been conquered by foreigners, and to get the best out of it they could.' Penderel Moon was always, by his own admission, 'somewhat critical of the British Raj. I thought that many of the institutions we had brought to India were unsuited to India, that we had insufficiently built on Indian tradition and Indian ideas. But I also felt that the British Raj couldn't tackle the main problems of India, which were economic. I felt that a foreign power could not achieve the revolutionary steps that would be necessary to change the Indian peasant life. Then I asked myself, "Should one really try to change it?" I can't answer that question, but obviously Indian intelligentsia wanted to change it. And I felt that the British Raj must give place to Indian Raj if any change is to be effected.' Yet for all that, he concludes, 'the British Raj in years to come is going to be viewed as one of the wonders of the world!' A similarly critical but ultimately affectionate judgement comes from Ian Stephens. 'I'm so fond of it,' he declares. 'It was a great, lumbering, clumsy, brutal thing but, despite its flaws, this fusion, this contiguity between Britain and India worked, and there was much good in it.'

‑ For all their zeal in government and the benevolence of their intentions the British had no lasting place in India. In the last resort, argues Iris Portal, 'you must never take land away from people. People's land has a mystique. You can go and possibly order them about for a bit and introduce some new ideas and possibly dragoon an alien race into attitudes that are not quite familiar to them, but you must then go away and die in Cheltenham.'

And this the British proceeded to do. Most went with a sadness accentuated by tearful farewells from the most trusted of their retinues, who accompanied them on their last journey across India; ayahs who had fostered their children, bearers who had stayed with them for a quarter of a century and more. Pensions and gifts could not eradicate the fears that many felt for their future. Some slipped out ungarlanded and without ceremony, others took a more formal leave-taking. 'I can remember seeing the troops going up the gangway in pairs,' says Rupert Mayne, 'and finally their colonel, Colonel Blaire, standing and facing us, giving us a tremendously smart salute, about turn and up the gangway. Thus went the last British regiment. That was the Black Watch leaving Pakistan forever.'

The final, ritual farewell was made – as always – where the East ended and the West began: 'As we left Port Said and sailed into the open waters everyone was paraded with their topees on deck and at a given signal we all flung our topees into the sea and that was the last of India.'

Lastly, there was England and Home: 'The coast of England was green and white and the most beautiful sight I've ever seen in my life; little villages nestling in the folds of the hills, the white of the cliffs and, after being without colour for so long, the green of the grass – and to cap it all, when we got to South-ampton it was snowing.'

Tales from the Dark Continent

1

Running up the Flags

It was very largely individuals running up flags and saying, 'We are Residents' that brought the North under administration. And it was they that really gave substance to a somewhat extravagant boast within a few years of the occupation that a virgin could walk from Lake Chad to Sokoto with a bowl of eggs on her head and neither the virgin nor the eggs would be spoiled.

Britain's imperial rule in Africa was extraordinarily brief, as empires go. In Nigeria crown rule started in 1900 and finished in 1960, 'so that it was perfectly possible – as was, in fact, the case – for a number of old men to have lived to see the British come and go.' While collecting for Nigeria's museums at the time of Independence, Philip Allison once talked with an old chief of Benin: 'I'd called to look at some of his wood-carvings and brass castings and when I came to go he said, "I'm sorry we had to talk through an interpreter. When the British came I was out there on the Ologbo road, holding a gun for one of the chiefs when we were fighting the British. And when the British came we thought they wouldn't stay very long so none of us really bothered to learn English. I'm sorry now."' This same brief time-scale applied to almost every African territory that came under British control, with a beginning and an end within a single life-span, occupying the working lives of no more than three generations of its rulers.

But crown rule was not in itself the beginning of the British connection. In West Africa especially, British involvement went back over two centuries: 'There is a famous old quotation that "Trade follows the Flag" but in fact in West Africa and in most other parts of the Empire the reverse was true. After all, the East India Company first established British interests in India, and in Rhodesia the British South Africa Company, in East Africa it was the Imperial British East Africa Company and in Nigeria the Niger Company. These were really the first British presences.'

But long before these chartered empire-building companies there had been other interests, for 'the first signs of the white man that the African ever saw were the slavetraders and the early traders in the oil rivers; the most villainous, ghastly, dreadful people.' Relics of the trade in human lives could be found in almost every territory occupied by the British in Africa. In the West Coast it was to be seen in the big iron rings on the walls of the bank building in Bathurst where Bill Page worked as a cashier in the late 1920s and in the vast dungeons of the 'fairy-tale' Christiansborg Castle through which Gold Coast society danced congas in the 1950s. It was there in the demoralization and breakdown of tribal society and in the inter-tribal wars that were often cited as grounds for the assumption of white superiority in the early days of British rule.

In East Africa it was the flourishing traffic in slaves to the Middle East that first encouraged an active British interest in that region, while in the Islamic regions of the Sudan and Northern Nigeria the suppression of slavery was one of the declared objectives of the occupying British forces. Nor had the trade been entirely abandoned by the time that Angus Gillan came to the Sudan in 1909: 'Two or three of my servants were boys whom we managed to pick up being traded as slaves across to Jidda and Saudi Arabia. I know one little boy I had, he and his sister were being run across from some far remote part of the French Sudan and it was quite impossible to discover where one could send them back to, so one more or less had to take them on as servants.'

It was slavery and the anti-slavery movement that brought many of the early Christian missions upon the African scene. In the West Coast there was the Calabar Mission of the Church of Scotland, which had its roots in Jamaica following the emancipation of the slaves there in the 1830s:

> The urge of the slave people – a great number of whom had come from Nigeria – was made very clear to the early leaders of the Calabar Mission, who raised funds to send a team of Jamaicans and Scots and Irish to Calabar and they actually arrived and set up a mission in 1846. There were no mass conversions to Christianity, but they persisted and did a remarkable job translating the Bible into the ethnic languages. And that really was a great step forward because that led them to start schools, and really the main effort of the Christian thrust was through the schools, through the children – and that persisted right through until we were absorbed into the Nigerian Church.

Although the missionaries played no official part in government there were many regions where they blazed the trail and even – in some rare cases – assisted to some degree in maintaining law and order. An outstanding example was Miss Mary Slessor of Dundee, chiefly remembered for her efforts to suppress infanticide in the Calabar region, a 'very nice old lady' who 'had a great longing to explore and open up country further up the Cross river. Going up in canoes to Itu she started stations and collaborated very remarkably with the government District Officers of that time, who were so impressed by her influence over the chiefs that they gave her government status and she became a judge in the native courts, using a legal code that was very much her own.' When

the Reverend Bob Macdonald first came out to Calabar as a
missionary in 1929 Mary Slessor had been dead for fifteen
years:

> But of course a great number of the local people remembered
> her. On one occasion in a far-out village I was giving a lantern
> lecture, and I had a sheet up for a screen and a very doubtful
> kind of lantern which went on and off. But I happened to get a
> lot of old slides of Miss Slessor and her visitation and I showed
> one of this very town that I was in, and the old head chief came
> to me immediately afterwards and said, 'Give me that cloth,
> that was my friend. I want to keep it.' He had been one of her
> advisers and friends while she was opening up that area.

In East Africa the early pioneer whose name was best
remembered was David Livingstone. Some twenty years after
the Second World War Darrell Bates was caught in heavy rain
while on safari in his district of Tabora, in the middle of
Tanganyika:

> An old Arab asked me if I would like to come into his house to
> shelter from the rain, and he was very apologetic. He said,
> 'This is a very poor house but my house is thy house,' in the
> polite way that they have. And then he said, 'Many, many
> years ago *bwana mokolo*, the holy man, stayed here, the man
> that you call Living-stone. I'm an old man but I never met him
> of course – but my father met him, and I remember my father
> talking of him.' Now this was marvellous for me because
> Livingstone was in Tabora in 1872, I think it was, and so this
> went back seventy years and more. And he spoke about
> Livingstone as if he had met him only yesterday.

But Livingstone's main influence was concentrated further
inland – in Nyasaland, which was regarded very much as
Livingstone's creation:

It was he who first discovered Lake Nyasa in the late 1850s and was responsible for bringing out the University Mission to Central Africa in the 1860s, because he was quite convinced the future for Africa was to be British. It was an exclusively British dream that he had, to bring commerce and Christianity to that part of the world and he established this mission under conditions which were really almost intolerable for them to sustain, with slave-raiding going on all round them. The mission suffered disastrous casualties and had to be withdrawn after two years. The whole area was in chaos and practically depopulated by the 1870s, but the missionaries started to return and they were the first Europeans in the field. Gradually these missions developed in the 1880s, a small commercial centre grew up in Blantyre town and it was realized, with the Portuguese pressing at the southern end of the territory and the Germans in Tanganyika, that if there was to be a British presence in that part of the world, the United Kingdom Government would have to declare a Protectorate, and eventually in 1891 they did so. But all the early development and all the schools were set up by the missionaries. The Government didn't take over any responsibility for education in Nyasaland until the 1920s. The missionaries ran a great deal of the country in the early days and they were admirable people.

When Patrick Mullins came out to Nyasaland in 1952 the mission influence was still very strong: 'They lived on £30 a year and 7s 6d. a day messing allowance. They lived beside their African priests under very much the same conditions, they spoke the African languages, they understood the African better than anyone else in the country and they were entirely selfless, spending very little on themselves and devoting their lives to the people.'

But it was organized commerce rather than Christianity that really paved the way for crown rule. Here, too, the influence of the early days, the years of commercial freebooting and rivalry, continued well into the twentieth century. When Edwin Everett took up his first post at Badagri, close to Nigeria's border with Dahomey, in 1938, there was a relic of the past in the shape of the 'hulk' moored in the creek that served as both living quarters and police post. Although it was by then a two-storey structure built on a pontoon, it took its name from the days when other hulks had been moored permanently in the Badagri and other 'oil-river' creeks of Nigeria, providing homes and trading posts for the 'old coasters' and 'palm-oil ruffians' of Victorian times.

A more widespread legacy of those early trading days was the 'canteen', the up-country store operated by one or other of the many European trading companies – also known in the earlier days as 'barter-rooms' or 'factories'. Like many words in common usage in West Africa 'canteen' had its origins in the lingua franca of the coast, 'pidgin' or 'Kru-English', a basic trading language devised partly from Portuguese and partly from other sources. The spirit of nineteenth-century free enterprise also lingered on in the rival trading companies that continued to compete against one another until the economic realities of the Depression finally forced them to merge. When Donald Dunnet and Clifford Ruston came out to Nigeria after the First World War – to join rival companies which eventually became part of the United Africa Company – going into the West Africa trade was not so much a career as an adventure:

> If one's health failed one was fired and that was the end of it. There was no Provident Fund and there was no superannuation – although there was free medical attention for any complaint which wasn't caused by your own indulgence. The staff were more or less expendable. This was a relic of the old sailing-ship days when you signed on as crew in a schooner and if you got back you were lucky. And while you were there you made what you could for yourself. There was more or less an understanding going back to the old sailing-ship days when

the sailors up the masts, who had either to take the canvas in or put it out, had a motto: 'One hand for the owner and one hand for yourself'. And it was very much that sort of thing trading ashore – only in some cases it was two hands for yourself and nothing for the owner. There was no loyalty to the firm. They didn't deserve it.

Another feature that survived into the inter-war period was the intense competition between trading companies: 'This tradition of intense – almost insane – rivalry also dated back to the old sailing-ship days, when ships would arrive full of cargo which they were going to sell over the ship's side and buy produce to fill up the ship and sail away. And the quicker they got their business transacted and finished and got away, the less risk there was of dying. So when there were two or three ships, say, anchored in the Calabar river, there was intense competition to get away. And somehow or other that tradition had been passed on.'

West Africa's reputation as the White Man's Grave also lingered on well into the twentieth century – and with some cause. 'In the early twenties there was a great deal of illness,' recalls Clifford Ruston, 'malaria, yellow fever and black-water fever, and the mortality was quite severe. If a man was sick and died in the early morning he was buried the same day, for obvious reasons. Seldom a month went by without our attending a funeral of some member of the European community.'

The treatment for yellow fever was particularly unpleasant: 'They stuck a needle into the stomach of the patient, pumped in a large quantity of serum, unscrewed the syringe, refilled it with the needle still in the stomach of the patient and then did a further injection.' Other unpleasantnesses abounded in the form of a wide variety of afflictions that could strike the unsuspecting. There was the *guinea* worm – 'a water-borne parasite which laid its eggs in the water and if not properly filtered or boiled – or boiled and filtered as we used to do in

Nigeria – the egg hatched out inside you and the worm proceeded to wander around until it usually got stuck in one of the extremities – usually the leg, which then swelled up. Eventually the worm made a hole in the skin and the old way of getting rid of it was to wash yourself and when the tail projected you nipped it with a piece of bent straw strongly enough to prevent it drawing itself in and then each day you wound the worm out a small distance.' There was the *tumbo* fly, 'which tended to lay its eggs on wet grass or on the underside of leaves, places greatly favoured by Nigerian washerwomen for spreading clothes for drying', and whose worm manifested itself as a large boil; and the *filaria* fly, whose worms 'travelled about the body and when one got stuck in the wrist, for instance, a large bump rose up like half an orange and the fingers looked like a rubber glove that had been blown up. You also knew that if you had one you probably had lots of others and your only chance in those days of getting rid of it was if one day you suddenly began to see double, then you quickly called somebody who would look in your eye and, having seen the small worm gradually working its way across the eyeball, would pick it out with a needle or even a thorn – and that meant one worm less.'

Company rule in Nigeria – the fifteen-year administration of part of Southern Nigeria – under a royal charter by the Niger Company ended when the company's flag was hauled down at Lokoja on 31 December 1899. But there were other parts of Africa where this stage of colonial evolution continued through into the post-war period. When Bill Stubbs went out to Southern Rhodesia in 1921, that territory, as well as Northern Rhodesia, was still being governed by the British South Africa Company under a charter obtained by Cecil Rhodes in 1889: 'In fact the country was administered – and well administered – by a company and not by a crown.' Its paramilitary arm – and the service which Bill Stubbs joined – was the British South Africa Police, 'a mounted infantry regiment recruited in the first place by Cecil Rhodes or his agents in the 1890s. The advertisement used to appear in the paper – in the personal columns of *The Times*, I think it was – "Vacancies occur from time to time for the sons of gentlemen who can ride and shoot and are fond of an open-air life. Join the British South Africa Police!" '

Closely associated with Cecil Rhodes and his empire-building schemes was the Grenfell family. In 1896 Harry Grenfell's grandfather, Lord Grey, was appointed Administrator of Southern Rhodesia and brought his wife and daughter approximately a thousand miles in an ox-wagon from the railhead at Mafeking to Bulawayo: 'The result was that in August 1896 my grandfather, my grandmother and my mother were living in Government House at Bulawayo, a simple building built on the site of the *kraal* which had been occupied by Lobengula, who had been king of the Matabele before the pioneers entered Rhodesia with C. J. Rhodes.' In that same year the Matabele Uprising took place – the last, unsuccessful stand against the white settlement of Southern Rhodesia: 'As a girl of seventeen my mother rode on to the Matopo hills with C. J. Rhodes at one of the meetings which led to the making of peace with the Matabele.'

The other territory in which white settlement was promoted was Kenya and it was while serving there with the King's African Rifles in 1924 that Anthony Lytton took part in what may well have been the last great *vortrek* by covered wagon into the African interior:

Part of my task was to arrange for a boat to be despatched on ox-wagons in pieces together with four Indian carpenters, who were to put it together on the very unfriendly shores of Lake Rudolf. In order that matters should be properly done, we had imported a South African who was called a conductor, John Muller, a truly magnificent type of man who knew every one of his five or six hundred beasts and who himself, at night, in areas infested with tsetse fly, took through the *drifts* – that is to say, the river-beds – every single wagon. Now the wagons were relatively small affairs and there were nine yoke of oxen – that's eighteen in each of thirty wagons. Therefore a very considerable herd of animals and a very considerable cloud of dust and a very considerable journey stretching out over an area that had no proper road at all. The safari took place from six to ten in the morning, when we did eight miles; two miles an hour. Then we *outspanned*, that is to say we stopped in a place preferably with water and grazing. From four to six we went another four miles – a total of twelve miles a day, and therefore a very slow progress, with plenty of time to wander about the country and inspect the game.

Anthony Lytton was then on his way to take over a district 'about one-fifth the size of England' as its military Officer-in-Charge, a curious and possibly unique anomaly created by special circumstances – but one that harked back directly to the era of pacification, the period round about the turn of the century when a number of territories had been occupied by military force and governed by a military administration. So it was that in 1924 Anthony Lytton found himself acting very much as his military predecessors had done a quarter of a century earlier in such territories as Northern Nigeria and Uganda:

> All powers connected with administration were vested in the one white officer in any single post, such as the post I first went to at a place called Barseloy. All powers – of every sort – whether educational, medical, religious or anything else; they were all nominally vested in the Officer-in-Charge. As regards court matters and malefactors, I was a second class magistrate with power to imprison for up to two years. I rather think that in the period of fourteen or eighteen months that I was with the Samburu I dealt with no case at all – no case was brought before me; there was no crime. The chiefs were there and I suppose they exercised a certain amount of discipline. But there wasn't a civil administration at all, until – with the end of

my time there – District Commissioners came and took over in
the usual way.

In fact, he was governing in very much the manner
instituted by the father of the King's African Rifles, Frederick
Lugard – who first came to that region in 1890 with his own
military force of fifty Somalis and fifty Sudanese. It was Lord
Lugard, more than any other single individual, who set the
style for future crown rule throughout the British territories in
Africa. In particular, he was the architect of indirect rule, the
system of dual government which 'came about partly because
in various parts of Africa we'd bitten off more than we could
chew. We couldn't possibly administer all these people and
these vast territories closely. So our policy always was to leave
as much as possible to the people themselves and not to
interfere with their lives unless it was obvious that what they
were doing was wrong. If they could settle their own quarrels,
so much the better.'

The classic example of the application of the dual mandate
was in Northern Nigeria, where political officers, drawn
initially from Lord Lugard's occupying forces, left the running
of local affairs very much in the hands of the local emirs. As a
result there arose a marked division in the style of government
between North and South: 'In the South it was direct rule and
the District Commissioner really ran the show, whereas in the
North the chiefs ran it under the supervision of the district
staff.' Under Lord Lugard's direction these two separate
territories were eventually brought together as the two provinces of the Protectorate of Nigeria, together with a small
area around Lagos that was known as the Colony of Nigeria:
'So we talked of the Colony and Protectorate of Nigeria.'

One territory that was neither colony nor protectorate was
the Condominium of the Sudan, where the flags of Great Britain
and Egypt flew side by side outside every government building.
Although it continued to be administered by a political service
rather than a colonial service, its military administrators had

departed by the time that James Robertson came out in 1922. But there were still plenty of reminders of the past:

> At Omdurman the Mahdi's tomb was still unrepaired and there was a hole in the roof where a shell had gone through when one of Kitchener's gun-boats had shelled it. One of the things I did later in 1946 or '47 was to allow the Mahdi's son to rebuild his tomb. Quite a lot of the old men we met in these early days were people who had actually fought at the battle of Omdurman when Kitchener defeated the Khalifa's troops. There was one old gentleman in Western Kordofan who at the least provocation would pull up his pants and show you a hole in his leg which, he said, had been done by one of those 'Englezi' bullets; and there was an old gentleman called Ali Gula who used to tell me about Gordon and when Gordon used to ride through the country. Gordon was still quite a name in parts of Western Sudan.

The first generation of British administrators was drawn very largely from the ranks of the army or from such local paramilitary forces as the Royal Niger Constabulary or the British South Africa Police. One of the last to make this transition was Bill Stubbs, who transferred first to the Northern Rhodesia Police in 1924, just after that territory had been handed over to the Crown by the British South Africa Company, and then – with a little help from an influential uncle – into the civil administration:

> Nobody else was appointed in such a way after me until the end of the Second World War when recruiting became a slightly different matter. But the earliest native commissioners and magistrates were men of very varied abilities and experience, some had been soldiers and some had been more or less adventurers who had fitted into the local pattern and were taken on. Some of our more outstanding early native commissioners came in by this route. Characters like Bobo Young, for

example, a famous man in the early pioneer days who had started life as a pastry cook and then joined the army and saw service with the British Central Africa Company. All this, however, finished in about 1912 when the first batch of recruits came out direct from university.

Not all these early administrators were models of probity – as became apparent to Gerald Reece when he first came out to Kenya in 1925:

The Surest Protector of Health & Comfort in Tropical Countries

Wherever the Britisher pioneers or settles, Burberry Kit provides the most comfortable and protective equipment— dress that proves a standby for years against rough usage, hard wear and extreme climates.

Advertisement for colonial wear 1931, its two illustrations representing the *beaux idéals* of the soldier-pioneer and the civil administrator.

I'm afraid at the beginning I got a rather poor opinion of some of the older men. Their attitude to their job seemed to be different to those who'd just come out. For example, when they travelled – which they didn't do a very great deal – they would set up a Union Jack in their camp and rather tend to try and impress the natives with what wonderful things the British were doing for them; the whole idea of the White Man's Burden. I remember one of these old soldiers who, when he travelled north into the country of the Nilotic people, where the men are completely naked, always took with him an Indian trader with a large supply of khaki shorts, which he more or less forced the people to buy from the Indian by selling their goats. Now I thought that was a particularly bad thing to do because the Nilotic people have always been naked and are really very clean and, in their own way, a model people. But as soon as they put on khaki shorts, which were impossible for them to keep very clean, it was far less hygienic and healthy.

An equally unattractive manifestation not so much of the White Man's Burden as of the Black Man's Burden could still be observed in Zanzibar when William Addis first came there in 1925: 'If you were riding along and a man – even a long way off – saw you, he'd kneel down and start clapping and he'd go on doing this until you passed him. And if they came into the office the first thing they did was to kneel down and clap. They thought every white man was just perfect – and I never felt more like a tin god.'

Nevertheless, it was this early pioneer generation of administrators – the true contemporaries of Edgar Wallace's fictional character Sanders of the River – that created the legends which their successors savoured and enjoyed. One of the great characters of the pre-war period in Nigeria, about whom stories were still being told half a century later, was a man named Cockburn, known – no doubt for some sound reason – as Rustybuckle:

Many amusing stories are told about him and one of the best is
that he was on the river steamer when the Governor, Sir
Walter Edgerton, came up the river on a tour of inspection.
He had to reprimand Rustybuckle for one of his various
crimes and Rustybuckle listened for a while and then suddenly
said, 'I can't stand this any longer,' and dived over the side.
Everyone rushed to the side that he had gone over and a boat
was lowered and the Governor himself was very upset by this
and said that he would never have spoken to Rustybuckle in
that way if he had known that it would have this result. In the
meantime Rustybuckle, who was a very fine swimmer, had
dived under the ship and come up on the other side, and he
came up behind the Governor and said, 'I beg your pardon for
interrupting you, sir.'

Survivors from this generation could still be found in
nearly every territory in the inter-war period. In Somaliland
there was the somewhat pompous governor who, when he
got back from leave and landed at Berbera, 'got his houseboy to go down to the quay with an old gramophone to play
"God Save the King" as he stepped ashore.' In Tanganyika
there was the District Officer who 'woke up one morning to
find an ant-hill beside his bed, lopped the top off with a
panga, poured some paraffin over it and used it as a bedside
table.' In the Northern Province of Uganda there was a
well-known Provincial Commissioner who was said to wear
his dinner jacket while out on safari. Dick Stone met him in
1937 shortly before his retirement: 'He always used to say –
and he said this to me – "My boy, you must never have
more than one drink in the evening." And I thought this
seemed a bit extraordinary until I actually saw what he
poured into his glass. He filled his glass half full of whisky
and then added a touch of water – and that was his one
drink.' Dick Stone's own father had himself acquired some
local notoriety as a District Commissioner across the border
in Kenya: 'When he was DC of Embu and people wanted to

see him on what was called *shauri* – business of some kind – he made them walk up the hill where his office was with a large stone on their heads, and with these stones – after several thousand had been collected – he started building the *boma*, which became the district office.'

Eccentricity and foibles of character were qualities as much appreciated by Africans as by Europeans. Donald Dunnet recalls how in his early days in Nigeria 'it was common practice to give Europeans nicknames if they'd been long enough in the community to get reasonably well known. For example, we had one young chap who was very good-looking and he was known as *Ezecolobia*, which in Ibo is "king of the young men". There was another trading chap who had very slim hips and he was known as *Wengwela*, which means "lizard". The African women in that area had a custom of wearing strings of beads round their waists which protruded underneath their cloth and gave them a sort of bustle appearance. Well, one of our chaps had a bottom that stuck out like that so he was known as *Jigada*, which is the name for these beads. Knowing that so many people had got nicknames, I made enquiries about my own and I was rather sorry I did because I was particularly corpulent at that time and my native name turned out to be *Miliafu*, which is "waterbelly".'

Undoubtedly one factor in exaggerating personality traits or behaviour was the extreme living and working conditions that many of these early pioneers had to endure. These conditions varied very greatly both from one territory to another and within each territory. Viewed from a strictly Western point of view, social development was equally varied. From a very early date it was possible to find in Bathurst, the capital of Gambia, a black African society 'long accustomed to very easy social equality with their European counterparts in office' – whereas on the other side of Africa the social gulf between the races remained fixed for years to come. Coming out to Africa in 1932 as the wife of the new Governor of Uganda, having spent many years in India and Iraq, Violet Bourdillon was 'terribly depressed' by what she found:

> I remember a friend coming to stay with me from India. We went on tour and she said, 'Oh, do take me out and show me their things, their carpets and so on.' I said, 'What things? They haven't got any things. They haven't even got the wheel. They don't make their own pottery. They've got some straw mats but I can't show you anything.' And I remember saying to one of the officials, 'I wish I could see something old' – because we'd just come from Ur of the Chaldees, you see – and the official said, 'Oh, but you are going to.' I said, 'How delightful! What are we going to see?' and he said, 'You are going to see a very ancient fort.' And I said, 'Yes, and who built it?' and he said, 'Lord Lugard'.

The contrast between British Uganda and British India was particularly marked: 'There was no comparison at all. In India even in our junior days we toured far better than in Uganda. We travelled with an entourage of elephants and goodness knows what. But as a governor's wife I marched every bit of Uganda; we had two fly-tents that we slept under and everything was portered and done on the march.'

In 1935 when she and her husband moved on to Nigeria, Violet Bourdillon found Nigerian society very different. But even in West Africa, where colonial governors might reasonably have expected a certain standard of creature comforts, there were still surprising shortcomings. As late as 1941, when Alan Burns took over as Governor of the Gold Coast and moved into Christiansborg Castle, he found to his considerable astonishment that there was no plumbing. Indeed, the developing Colonial Service was 'a very austere service indeed' by comparison with the Indian Civil Service: 'All our colonial territories were hard up and there was none of the panoply of the Raj that had been accumulated over centuries in India against what had been basically a pretty wealthy background. None of this applied for us. The countries were wretchedly poor and the service, of course, was equally very poorly paid and poorly treated, by comparison with the ICS – all arising out of the financial circumstances which prevailed.'

Advertisement from the Colonial Office List Advertiser

Another obvious difference between India and Africa lay in communications. Even in 1927, when Martin Lindsay came out on attachment to the Nigeria Regiment, he found Nigeria to be 'a very primitive country' in this respect: 'There was only one railway line, from Lagos in the south to Kano in the north and, if you were stationed at one of the outposts like Sokoto in the north-west or Maiduguri in the north-east, from the moment you left the railhead you walked. You walked for three weeks to get to your post, with sixteen or twenty bearers carrying your kit on their heads, and then when you were due to go on leave you walked for another three weeks back to the railhead to take the train back again.'

In East or Central Africa the position was, if anything, worse. When an officer of the King's African Rifles was posted to a remote detachment like Wajir in Kenya's Northern Frontier District he had to take with him, as Brian Montgomery did in 1928, one year's supply of tinned food and other commodities:

> No facilities existed there and you couldn't buy anything at all in terms of tinned food and the like. So I went to the firm of Jacobs in Nairobi, the only departmental store of any size there at the time, and I purchased a year's supply of tinned food. I have the bill still, and looking through it I see that this included thirty-six tins of sausages, twenty-one pairs of socks, a plentiful supply of Eno's Fruit Salts, one table lamp, one iron kettle and things of that kind. The bill came to £175 for which I got an advance of pay, and it did not take long to pay that back, as up in the Northern Frontier District there was nothing whatever to spend one's pay on except the wages of one's boy or servant at 20s. a month, the cook at 30s. a month and his *mtoto* at 10s. a month.

Given such conditions it was inevitable that many territories remained very much 'a man's world', placed virtually out of bounds for European women for many years to come. 'I think in the whole of my eighteen months I only spoke to a white woman about three times,' declares Martin Lindsay, 'probably just to say good afternoon when she came to watch a polo game, and nothing more than that. No white woman spent more than nine months at a time there and, of course, there wasn't a single white child in the whole of the country.' The consequences of this shortage of European female company were predictable. 'There was one custom that I came across in Wajir which at the age of twenty-three I found rather strange,' recalls Brian Montgomery. 'Shortly after I'd joined, the officer commanding the detachment and the DC came up to me and said would I like them to provide me with a *bibi*? I was not entirely clear what they meant but it soon became apparent they were referring to the services of a Somali girl-friend or sleeping partner.' In East Africa it was generally believed that 'East African officers as a whole maintained a very much stricter code in the matter of sleeping with African women' – sometimes referred to as 'sleeping dictionaries', from their obvious advantages as language instructors – than did their fellow-officers in West Africa. No doubt those in West Africa thought the reverse. 'The convention was abstinence for most people for most of their tour,' asserts Martin Lindsay, 'and that was the position in the central stations like mine, but I think that in the outposts most people probably had an African girl living with them. She wouldn't have her meals with the officer, and she wouldn't be seen in the house. She would merely have her own house behind, along with his servants and his servants' wives, and she'd only come into the house after dark. That was the life of most lonely men in the lonely stations and, of course, they did learn to speak the language far better than those of us who lived a life of abstinence.'

One result of this early fraternization was the notorious affair of the Secret Circulars A and B, issued by the Secretary of State for the Colonies in 1909: The first declared that 'It had come to His Honour's attention that a certain number of

Airylight, yet strong and durable, Burberry Kit withstands the roughest wear, and is so closely-woven that even the dreaded wachteen-beetje thorns and spear-grass cannot penetrate its thin and flexible texture.

A curious advertisement that appeared in 1931, seeming to suggest that the advertised material withstood spears as well as *wachteen-beetje* thorns and spear-grass.

government officials were living in a state of concubinage with native women and a very serious view would be taken of people living under these circumstances.' Whereupon all sorts of unpleasantnesses beset the whole of the government service and a hurried Circular B was sent round saying that 'With regard to my last Secret Circular A, it now appears that *not* such a serious view will be taken of government officers living in a state of concubinage with native women.'

For District Officers like Nigel Cooke who followed this first generation, these early administrators laid up 'a capital of prestige and good will. One was very conscious all the time that in most places the British administrators were there and the people wanted them to be there because there was a need for law and order. And it was this capital on which my generation could draw and hopefully add to.'

2

White Man's Burden; White Man's Grave

> *Beware, take care of the Bight of Benin;*
> *One comes out though forty go in.*

From an early age historical events impelled Angus Gillan towards a life of service in the Sudan:

> The name of Gordon was still very familiar to us in the nursery and in our schooldays; the Kitchener expedition, of course, occurred while I was still at school and there was something which appealed to us rather directly. We had been mixed up in it and we felt, I think, that we owed something to Gordon. Then when I went up to Oxford and started really thinking about what I was going to do I was attracted by some form of life in what one is not ashamed to call the Empire – though, of course, strictly speaking the Sudan didn't belong to the Empire.

In 1908 he applied to join the Sudan Political Service, then the best-paid of all the Imperial Services, with a starting salary of £420 per annum:

> I have got to say that the Sudan appealed to one because there was no competitive examination. There was a current phrase

– I think it originated from the Warden of New College – that the Sudan was a country of blacks ruled by blues and there was just that essence of truth in it that these little stories convey. They wanted people who had had a share of responsibility, which I suppose comes to one if one is lucky enough to get on in the athletic world, and that is what Lord Cromer, who was the originator of the Sudan Political Service, really seemed to want – and I venture to think it worked reasonably well.

Angus Gillan himself was a notable oarsman who took time off during his third year in the Sudan to row in the 1912 Olympics. The same sporting prowess was evident in his fellow recruits:

Four of us went out together: two – myself and one other, Charles Dupuis, – from Oxford, and Robin Baily from Cambridge and Geoffrey Sarsfield-Hall from Trinity College, Dublin. I happened to have gained a certain notoriety in rowing, Charles Dupuis had rowed for his college and was a thoroughly all-round chap – I think he was president of his common-room – Robin Baily was one of the best wicket-keepers Cambridge had produced up to that time and Sars-field-Hall took a blue for hockey. So that we had a certain amount of athletic prowess between us, and I think our degrees varied between seconds and thirds.

After completing an additional year of training at Oxford, he and the other three probationer Deputy-Inspectors signed contracts, which laid down that 'we couldn't get married until we were taken on to pension, which roughly meant two years', and sailed to Alexandria. From there they proceeded to Cairo, where they bought themselves *tarbooshes*:

In those days it was part of the office kit, I don't say we liked them very much but there it was. Of course, outside one wore a pith helmet or something of that sort until, say, three o'clock in the afternoon, and then probably a homburg hat until sunset. There were a couple of chaps who in my day used to go about without helmets; one looked on them both as rather mad, but whether they were mad because they didn't wear helmets or whether they didn't wear helmets because they were mad I really wouldn't know.

Proceeding up the Nile by rail and steamer they finally reached Khartoum, which was just beginning to take shape as a modern town:

In fact the river frontage was a very civilized-looking place; nice houses, gardens and all the rest of it, with the native population by and large living across the White Nile in Omdurman. But Khartoum itself was being built on Western lines – though not on the same lines as I've heard of anywhere else – because Kitchener laid down that it should be built in the form of a Union Jack, and for quite a long time they did stick to that form, until gradually it proved to be impossible and you got funny rows of houses cutting across at angles which did not appear on the Union Jack. But that was the original idea.

Society ran on rather different lines to what it did twenty or thirty years later, naturally. The people in high office were very often the people who had come up with Kitchener on the expedition and it was still very much a military administration. Some of them looked on us rather as a new type of young man that they didn't approve of. There were very few women there. It was very much a club life in those days and it took some courage after lunch to walk around the verandah of the club with all those old men sitting with newspapers in front of them and some of them looking over the top; you almost heard them saying, 'Who's that blanketty civilian, eh?'

It was also a very much noisier place than it became even in the days of the motor-car because everyone had a donkey in one's yard. The high and mighty had their own traps with

ponies and a lot of people had riding ponies, but most of us
had a donkey to take us to the office – and when one donkey
started roaring, every donkey in the neighbourhood took it up
and one was awakened in the middle of the night two or three
times usually by a concerted choir of donkeys.

His first three months Angus Gillan spent at headquarters in
Khartoum and across the river at Omdurman where 'one still
felt the influence of previous history under the Mahdi and the
Khalifa's reign. Slattin, of course, was a power in the land. He
kindly asked the four of us to dinner one night and his
reminiscences were extraordinarily interesting. He had been
a prisoner of the Mahdi and became a Muslim not, I think, to
save himself, but for the benefit of his own people. But he was
wonderfully little embittered.' After spending a month in the
Khalifa's old house under the charge of the Inspector of the
District he began to go further afield. He learnt that Sudan
was really made up of two very different regions:

The North was entirely Muslim, Arabic-speaking nearly
everywhere except in the Red Sea hills where the Beggara
tribes talked their own languages – the Beggaras being the
fuzzy-wuzzies, the 'big, black bounding beggar that broke a
British square' – but apart from that all Arabic-speaking and
mostly Arab with a good deal of dark blood in them. And
desert almost entirely, except for the narrow Nile valley. Then
the South, beyond latitude 12, roughly, where you came into
entirely different country, a country of black tribes, generations behind in what we call civilization, from the six-foot-six
Nilotic Nuer to the squat forest people, pagan except where
Christian missions had made their influence felt – and talking
dozens of different languages. There were many parts where
one was still called a Turk, because they and the Egyptians
were the only whitish people they'd seen – and one didn't like
the name of Turk because it did seem at that time to have
connotations of slavery.

In due course Angus Gillan was posted to his first station, the headquarters of Kordofan Province at El Obeid:

I was dumped at Duein on the White Nile and there was allotted a number of hard camels to take me out to El Obeid, about five or six days journey. A good riding camel is one of the most comfortable means of locomotion I can possibly imagine; on the other hand a bad camel can make every bone of your body ache. So the ordinary hard handler was not a thing one would encourage, but still, it was the only thing one could get. From Duein to El Obeid it is typical scrub country; gum trees, various sorts of acacias – attractive country at sunset and sunrise, but it loses a good deal of its charm when the sun is beating down on your head. I was lucky enough to shoot a gazelle or two, which apart from being good for the pot made one feel that one really was going to be a game hunter. And I got up to El Obeid where I was welcomed by a very nice lot of chaps, mostly military.

Social life on what was still an entirely all-male station revolved around the mess, a simple rest-house where officers met for meals and drinks in the evening: 'Like all newly joined people, I was immediately made mess president, which meant that one did the donkey work.' Here he made the acquaintance of Uncle Zaid, the head waiter, who was many years later to become his personal servant – 'a grand old man and the best servant I ever had'. Uncle Zaid had been captured as a boy of seventeen at the Battle of Atbarah and had been with British officers ever since:

He had, like all of them, his eccentricities. You could bring anybody you liked to breakfast, lunch, dinner, it didn't matter, nor did it to the cook – somehow there was always something – but if I brought in anyone to tea he'd duly serve it but afterwards he'd come up and say, 'Mr So and So came to tea, I was not informed.' By and large one preferred servants

Menu

El Obeid, Kordofan.
Feb. 27th 1912

Caviar russe

Consommé aux pointes d'asperges

Soufflés de Saumon

Foie gras en aspic

Côtelettes de Mouton

Dindon farci, légumes

Macédoine de fruits

Crême aux cerises

Scotch Woodcock

The menu commemorates the completion of the new railway line from Khartoum to El Obeid in 1912, formally declared open by Lord Kitchener of Khartoum himself. From the album of Sir Angus Gillan.

who couldn't speak English – or who one thought couldn't speak English. This dear old Uncle Zaid never spoke to me in English at all, but he understood it all right. I remember once at some dinner party that the talk got on to some trouble in the Nuba mountains many years before and somebody said it was in such and such a month – 'Oh no, it couldn't have been because someone was on leave' – and so the talk went on with the usual chatter. Finally Uncle Zaid could bear it no longer. He bent down to my ear and said, 'It was 11 September 1904.'

As a Deputy Inspector in a station like El Obeid, Gillan found himself called upon to be a jack of all trades:

There was the Provincial Governor and then there were a few Inspectors and they looked after the executive staff who were mostly Egyptian, and gradually the Inspector assumed the more permanent duties of the District Commissioner – as he eventually became even in title. You had all sorts of jobs thrust on you. You were of course responsible for the taxation and you were a magistrate and in El Obeid you had to go around with a theodolite marking out people's homes for them – the sort of thing a survey department, a public works department and a land office would have to combine to do. In a rough and ready way the Inspector had to do the whole thing.

A good part of his time was taken up with touring the district:

There was a tremendous lot to be said for the old slow touring on a pony or on a camel. You could keep in much closer touch with the people. Usually some skeikh or a man of importance would be riding along with you and in ordinary chat one learnt a great deal more than you could however much you trekked around in a car.

One of the rather happy incidents which often happened when one was touring round, was that you'd go into a village and somebody would come up to you, shake you warmly by the hand and ask how you were. And often one didn't recognize them straight away and you'd say, 'When did we meet last?' 'Oh, don't you remember? You sentenced me to six months in prison in your jail.'

Of course travelling around in those days, and even living in one's own house, might well be pretty primitive. One depended very largely for light on what we called *shamardans* – rather on the lines of the old carriage lamp, with a spring to keep the candle up and a globe which withstood a great deal of wind. They've given place, of course first to the pressure lamp and then to electricity. All one's kit was simple; a camp bath, camp chairs and, of course, if one was going to visit anyone, one took one's bed with one, which was considered in a later period as rather insulting to one's host.

In 1916 Angus Gillan became a central participant in events that led to the last major annexation of territory of the period of pacification:

At the beginning of 1913 I was transferred from El Obeid to Nahud, the most western district of Kordofan and of the Sudan. Bordering on it was Darfur, which was originally part of the Sudan under Slattin, previous to the Mahdi. On the reoccupation of Sudan, Darfur was really too big a nut to crack and the effective government boundary ended at Nahud District. Beyond that the Sultan, Ali Dinar, paid a nominal tribute to the Sudan but nobody ever went across the border.

Soon after the outbreak of the First World War the Sultan stopped paying his tribute and announced that he wasn't going to pay any more: 'In January 1916 I was sitting in my office one morning when two obviously terrified men came crawling into the office – which was not the usual form for our petitioners to adopt – and handed over my desk two spears and two throwing-sticks engraved with texts from the Koran about the fate to be suffered by infidels – the obvious implication being a declaration of war.'

After unsuccessful attempts by the Sudan Government to defuse the situation, an expeditionary force was sent to Darfur. After a one-sided engagement outside El Fasher the Sultan fled south with the remains of his army. A small force of mounted infantry was sent after him, which Angus Gillan accompanied as Political Officer:

> We found the camp in which he'd been hiding for the last two or three months empty – but the pots were still boiling and we collected a very large number of rifles and such like. We were sitting at the next halt in the evening when two people came in who, I discovered, were Ali Dinar's spies, sent out to see where we were. Perhaps wisely they turned coat and told us where he was. So we set off that evening and at almost seven in the morning we found his camp and the machine-gun was playing on his camp before they had realized we were there. Off they scampered and off we scampered behind them from one little prominence to another. There was a series of little battles and at the site of the second or third we came across the body of a man, which was Ali Dinar with a bullet through his head. So the old gentleman eventually died in the field of battle, as I have no doubt he would have wished, and that finished the show. It took some time to get things settled down but on 1 January 1917, Darfur was declared to be an ordinary province of the Sudan.

Alan Burns came out to Nigeria in 1912, the same year in which Sir Frederick Lugard returned to unite the two separate regions of Northern and Southern Nigeria into the Protectorate of Nigeria. His background was rather exceptional:

> I was born in the West Indies – and practically into the Colonial Service, as my grandfather had been Auditor-General of the Leeward Islands and my father was Treasurer of St

Kitts. I also had an elder brother who was in the Colonial Service. My father's friends were all members of the civil service and it seemed to me the natural career for any young man.

After working in the local civil service for several years and seeing few prospects of advancement, he applied for promotion to the West Africa Service at a salary of £300 a year:

When I received my offer of an appointment to Nigeria, all my friends in the West Indies advised me strongly not to go there as it was almost certain death; West Africa was regarded as a White Man's Grave. However, I was determined to chance my arm and I went. Casualties *were* pretty heavy there and a lot of the men that went out at the same time as I did didn't survive; either they died or were invalided out of the service.

Arriving off Lagos in 1912, Burns was surprised to find that the entrance to the harbour was too shallow to allow steamers to enter. Instead passengers were lowered into surfboats in what were known as '*mammy*-chairs' – 'a wooden box suspended by a chain from the derrick on the steamer's deck'. After being transferred from the surf-boats to a tender, passengers were brought alongside the Customs wharf: 'I landed from the tender and I saw a white man. I went up to him and I said, "Can you tell me where I have to go and how to get there?" And he said, "Where have you come from?" So I said, "I've just come from England." He said, "Well, why don't you go back there?"'

As in the Sudan, Nigeria was divided both geographically and culturally into two distinct regions:

Along the coast were the mangrove swamps, including the Niger Delta which covered a considerable area, and behind the mangrove swamps were the tropical forests and behind that again a savannah area until you got up to the north of

Northern Nigeria where you come on to the Sahara Desert. The main communications in those days were along the rivers and creeks. There's a continual line of creeks all the way along the coast from Lagos to the far east of Nigeria and you could go by canoe or launch the whole distance without seeing the sea at all. There was also a railway which went up to Kano, and there were a few roads, but in those days the main means of communications were by river or creek in launches or canoes and, on the main rivers, the sternwheelers, which had engines heated by wood cut along the banks of the river and taken on board at various stopping places.

Lagos itself was still a comparatively small town:

The Europeans lived, as a rule, round the race course at one end of the town, and the African quarter was a huddle of buildings, with very few good streets and practically no amenities. But there was electricity, which was surprising to me. There were a number of bungalows, but I was living in a building called the 'chest of drawers' which consisted of six quarters, each of them having a bedroom and a ver- andah, and a common dining-room which very few of us used. There was a men's club, called the Gin Palace, which was a very popular resort of the white men in Lagos and also included three or four Africans – but there were no ladies admitted and it was really too expensive for the junior people to join. I remember a man from one of the outside provinces coming to Lagos and noticing there were several wives there as well as nursing sisters and remarking that Lagos was simply crawling with women.

Here, too, there were strong opinions about the best ways of keeping healthy: 'The principal danger was malaria and sunstroke. One thing that was compulsory was the taking of five grains of quinine a day, taken with a drink at midday just before lunch. And if you didn't take it and you got ill your

salary was liable to be stopped.' It was also virtually compulsory to wear a helmet if you went out into the sun:

> I remember one of the very early rebukes I received was
> because I walked for a few yards in the open air without my
> helmet and a messenger arrived from the Colonial Secretary
> to say that he wished to see me. I went trembling into the
> presence and, in a very rough voice, he said to me that it didn't
> matter very much whether I died or not but think of the
> trouble it would be to bury me and get another man out from
> England to take my place! We all had to wear, as well, a spine-
> pad on the back of our shirts, a thick material buttoned on to
> the back of one's bush shirt. And the women all had to wear
> double-*terais* and a veil hanging down the back of their necks.

'Dressing is a regular battle' – a light-hearted sketch from Capt
A. J. N. Tremearne's *Notes and Anecdotes* written in 1910,
showing something of the style of living in the Nigerian bush
at that time. The collapsible camp bath continued to be of
service for another half century.

After several months in Lagos, Alan Burns was posted to a Customs station at Kokotown on the Benin river:

I went through the creeks from Lagos to Kokotown by launch and when I got to Kokotown I saw a white man on the wharf – the man I was supposed to be relieving. When I had handed him my letter of introduction he read it and put it in his pocket and I said, 'Well, then, will it please you to hand over to me?' He said, 'Who are you?'' I said, 'My name is Burns. I'm the man referred to in that letter.' He said, 'Burns was referred to in the letter, but I don't know that you are Burns.' I then said, 'Well, look at my luggage, it's all marked Burns.' He said, 'Yes, I can see that, but it doesn't follow that it's your luggage.' I think the most charitable way to describe it is to say that he was mentally disturbed.

Having successfully relieved his fellow-officer of his post, Alan Burns settled down to his new job:

Kokotown at that time was a big trading centre and people spoke English of a sort, but generally pidgin English, which is a terrible language – but this was an old tradition from the sailing-ship days. It had curious words like 'live' that were used for everything. Instead of saying, 'That book is on the table' you'd say, 'That book live for table' and, instead of 'A man is dying', 'live for dying'!

My bungalow at Kokotown consisted of a bedroom and a sitting-room, and a wide verandah which in fact was used more than anything else. There was a store-room but there was no bathroom. I had my bath on the verandah in the evening and there was nobody there to see me because the bungalow stood in its own grounds on the banks of the river – and it was nothing unusual to see a crocodile perched on the bank sunning itself. There was no electric light in the bunga-low. We had oil lamps, *punkah* lamps with a fan instead of a chimney.

Whenever the opportunity arose Alan Burns went up-river to the district headquarters at Sapele, where white officials gathered at what was known as the 'Scotch club': 'We used to meet every evening after tennis on the banks of the river and our boys would bring out our own chairs and our own whisky and our own lamps and everything and we'd sit there and talk, generally about the work.' Kokotown itself had few social attractions:

There was nothing to do in the place, so some of the time I spent settling a land dispute for the District Commissioner with the chief, Nana, who was a very intelligent and pleasant man. In the old days he had been a principal slave-dealer in that part of the world and his town had only been captured after a considerable fight between four British cruisers and his own people. He was then tried and sentenced to deportation to Accra where he went for some time, and when he came back he settled in a town just below Kokotown, which he called America. When I went down to see him he invariably treated me to hot champagne.

This first 'tour of duty' lasted just one year, with very generous leave conditions 'due, very largely, to the health conditions in the colony. You got leave then of two weeks each way on a steamer going to and from England and four months in England.' After returning from leave Alan Burns was posted to the Chief Secretary's Office in the Secretariat Building in Lagos where 'they expected me to work very hard and we did work hard. But everybody was very willing to do it.' Here his duties brought him into contact with the Governor, Lord Lugard, who later invited him to become his aide-de-camp and part-time private secretary:

He was a tremendous worker, he'd work for hours in his office and very often until two or three in the morning. But his one fault, as I could see it, was that he would never depute anything to anyone else. He loved working and he hated anyone else doing the work that he himself could do. I remember once going into his office and seeing him checking a proof and I offered to do it myself for him. He turned to me with his usual sweet smile and said, 'My dear Burns, you could probably do it better than I can, but then, I like doing it' – and that was the end of that. On one occasion the doctor advised him to take more exercise and to play tennis so I fixed up a game for him and he was to play for an hour. He arrived at five o'clock and at six o'clock he put down his racquet in the middle of the game and went in back to his work. He was a very great man and in Nigeria at that time was regarded as really the creator of the country – and everybody admired him immensely.

Lord Lugard's retirement in 1918 marked the end of the era of pacification. Among the many whose lives he influenced to a marked degree was Sylvia Leith-Ross. When she first met her future husband, Captain Arthur Leith-Ross, he was serving with Lugard's West Africa Frontier Force in Northern Nigeria. But there was already in her family a remarkable association with West Africa:

My father had been in command of the sloop *Pandora* on the West Africa Station and had been at the taking of Lagos – and he had also captured the last Portuguese slaver. I still remember his description of what that slaver was like when his own people boarded it. There was one occasion when he must have gone up the Cross river to rescue some German traders who were trapped amongst very warlike natives and he went up and rescued them and they didn't even thank him – they didn't even give him a bottle of beer!

Her brother had also gone out to Nigeria, first with the Royal Niger Constabulary in 1898 and then as one of Lugard's administrators: 'My brother had met my husband out in Nigeria and had decided at once that he was the man that his little sister ought to marry. Both were having their leaves at the same time and so my brother brought him back with him and he stayed with us in our Sussex home.'

At that time wives were not allowed up to Northern Nigeria without the express permission of the then Sir Frederick Lugard:

Fortunately I passed all right. But as far as I can remember there were only three wives out in Northern Nigeria at that time. Nigeria was definitely known as a White Man's Grave – and actually it was. The mortality rate was very severe. Official statistics stated that one in five were either invalided or dead within a year. Yet somehow we went out quite carefree and it seemed somehow worthwhile to run the risk. My husband had a job there, I loved my husband and I followed him.

In the late summer of 1907 Mrs Leith-Ross sailed out to Nigeria with her husband on one of the passenger steamers of the Elder Dempster Line:

I remember that we had to take absolutely everything with us, all clothing, all drink, all food and almost all furniture. But the bulk of our luggage consisted I suppose of the *chop* boxes containing food for eighteen months. These were generally packed by wonderful firms like Whale and Co. or Griffiths McAllister, or the Army and Navy Stores. An officer was entitled to eighty carriers for his tour of eighteen months, eighty loads of fifty-six pounds, because fifty-six pounds was supposed to be the normal weight that a native carrier could carry with ease – although very often they carried a good deal more without a word of complaint. We had camp equipment, of course, which included things like a camp chair and a camp stool, and a camp bed with a cork mattress, and a bath – a tin bath with a cover and a wickerwork lining into which you packed all your toilet necessities. Of course, one had to take one's own lamps, too, especially the marvellous Lord's lamp, which was a kerosene lamp mounted upon four legs which could be set upon a sandbank, or on a rock, or in the middle of a river – wherever one wanted it. Mosquito nets, of course, had to be used everywhere and it was quite fatal not to do so.

We had as additional baggage an elegant, high-sprung dog-cart for which my husband hoped he would be able to train one of the native ponies. It was very elegant but on the whole rather useless as there wasn't a single road in the whole of Northern Nigeria. There were only carriers or camels or canoes or bullocks, or ponies or chiefly the human being, the marvellous Nigerian carrier.

The voyage out took three weeks, with the steamers then sailing nearer to the coast and calling at more ports.

Our fellow-passengers were nearly all government servants, a few agents going out for the trading firms and a missionary or two, that was all. But there was a very curious division among the passengers which even the ship's officers recognized. The purser would never have put at the same table officials going to Northern Nigeria and those going to Southern Nigeria. In fact we never spoke to each other. We looked upon each other with equal contempt, I think. We somehow took it for granted that all Southern officials were rather fat, rather flabby and that they started drinking at six o'clock while we never started before six-thirty. In the North you rode on horses, in the South they walked and, it is said, some officials were even carried in hammocks!

The approach to West Africa made itself felt by an extra-ordinary smell of swamp, hot and humid. We in the North did not land in Lagos, we stayed on board and transhipped into a sternwheeler which was to take us up the Niger. The transfer was done in the midst of shrieks and yells and a welter of luggage thrown in every direction, but somehow it all sorted itself out and eventually – there were only five of us by that time – we were more or less installed. The sternwheeler took a week to get up to Lokoja. It was an extraordinary craft, flat-bottomed, two decks and on the top deck there were, I think, three cabins which were just three boxes with no furniture at all. So your own camp furniture had to be put up. On the lower deck huddled African passengers, one's own servants and one's own cooks, and men and women and children and chickens and goats and great piles of foodstuffs. The captains of these sternwheelers were generally very aloof and there was a legend that they were all Swedish counts.

This first journey was a wonderful introduction to Nigeria; the sternwheeler progressed very slowly up the steaming river, high banks of copper-coloured vegetation cut off all view at the sides and for three or four days one saw nothing at all except the forest, a few sandbanks, a few crocodiles. And of course, we anchored at night. We drew in close to the bank, the engines stopped and an anchor or two was let down. Then the forest thinned and we came to more open country. Small villages appeared on the banks of the river and after eight days we reached Lokoja, which is at the junction of the Benue and the Niger river. A little further on we transhipped into native canoes to go up the Kaduna river. A little short of Zungeru the river narrowed and we disembarked and took an extraordinary little train which was really more like a tramway, for a few miles to Zungeru itself, which was the headquarters at that time of Northern Nigeria and consisted chiefly of the military barracks and a few bungalows. There was a small hospital, a fairly large cemetery, and Government House was nothing but a rather large bungalow, really not much better than those of the ordinary officials.

All these bungalows had been shipped out from England and erected by the Public Works Department using local labour. And they were all of one type:

One could find them anywhere with exactly the same lack of amenities. They consisted of three rooms and a wide verandah all round. I had realized exactly what the bungalows would be like so it seemed perfectly natural to me, but they were even uglier than I thought they would be, and devoid of any furniture except some large and heavy tables and a *punkah*, which was, so to speak, a petticoat attached to a long parallel pole which was swung back and forth by a small boy sitting on the verandah.

Mrs Leith-Ross's arrival in Zungeru caused something of a stir:

There were no wives there at all at that moment. There were two nursing sisters and the warden of a freed slaves home. I was the only wife. In fact, I think the officials were astonished to see that any white wife was allowed out, as I think there were only three others in the whole country. The white officials of course were few and far between themselves; I think I'm right in saying that there were altogether at that time forty administrative officers for the whole of Nigeria.

From the domestic point of view there were very few amenities to be found in Zungeru. But there were the servants:

Fortunately, my husband didn't lose his servants as sometimes happened when they saw a white woman coming – they stayed. The cook was a coast man – they came from Accra and were supposed to be the best ones – and my husband had a devoted steward for himself – although somehow the custom had grown up that all servants were called boy, no matter what their age was. Later they became a little more sophisticated and those who'd had a certain amount of training wished to be called steward. In addition to the boy there was the 'small boy' and the 'small-small boy'. And generally there was a gardener and, of course, the horse-boys. The water was brought by

prisoners from some distance away but had, of course, to be
boiled and filtered. It was kept cool to a certain degree in great
earthenware jars which were stood on the verandahs and these
coolers also served as our refrigerators, so boxes of any tinned
butter or any drinks were floated in the coolers. Meat had to
be eaten almost at once, although the Public Works Department provided a meat safe, which was a large box with muslin
sides hung from the ceiling.

Something that always surprised the newcomer was the
variety of insect life, which Sylvia Leith-Ross found quite
amazing:

From the point of view of the housewife I think the ants were
the worst enemies. They managed to damage almost everything, they even seemed able to eat through a tin, because all
our groceries had to come out in tins. Anything you put on the
table was immediately covered in ants, so everything had to be
either kept in a firmly closed tin or set in a receptacle placed in
a bowl of water.

Of course the evenings were the worst time because mosquitoes and flies of every description gathered round the
lamps. And in the evening everybody dressed for dinner,
whether you were at home or went out; you wouldn't dream
of doing otherwise. I remember very well having a bath towel
put over my side-saddle and riding off to dine in a long, low-
necked dress. Of course, the conversation was almost entirely
shop, but, all the same, of a high order; it wasn't only about
who was going to get promotion or who was going on leave. It
was nearly always in some form or other about the good of the
country at large. Their minds seemed to be really full of their
work, of what they were actually doing and what they meant
to do. But really, not much entertaining was done. For one
thing there were so few women and at the end of the day
everyone was very tired. The climate was abominable, the
heat intense, the glare was constant.

Ever since her arrival in Nigeria, Sylvia Leith-Ross had carried with her a premonition of tragedy: 'In the beginning it was not quite fear; although I had no fear for myself I had always had the feeling of an impending disaster and I could not get rid of it, therefore I dreaded Nigeria in an almost impersonal way.' Finally, when she and her husband had been in Zungeru for just one year disaster came:

My husband had had blackwater once before and had somehow survived, although he'd been completely alone. The second time it happened in Zungeru; one doesn't know why, it was just an infection, but at the time there was no known cure. He was at once taken to the small hospital and two doctors stayed with him day and night for two days, but he grew weaker and weaker and died within three days.

Of course, death was accepted as part of the day's work, but he had been so much liked that the whole of his colleagues and even the black clerks and the transport boys were all shocked deeply and were, in a way, not so sorry for me as sorry for themselves in that they'd lost a friend and an example. Everybody was kindness itself to me but the only thing to do was for me to go home. And when I left I found that of the five of us who had started for Northern Nigeria, I was the only one to return to England. The others were all dead.

This was only the beginning of Sylvia Leith-Ross's life in Nigeria, for 'it was only when she had done her worst that I realized how much I loved her.' She resolved to return and in due course she found a means to do so:

Quite suddenly I remembered a day when my husband and I had been riding out together and we passed a camp of Fulani herdsmen. The men were away but the women came out of their little house and looked at us very shyly, then they came a little nearer to me and smiled at me and I smiled back. It was dusk and the cattle were just coming home, with their wide horns and their great white flanks. We stayed a few moments amongst them and then rode away, but one Fulani woman must have known a few words in Hausa because she called out, 'Come back, come back again.' And I remembered their voices and the lilt of their lovely language and I suddenly thought I'll go back and study the Fulani language.

With Lord Lugard's permission Sylvia Leith-Ross eventually returned to Nigeria to begin a pioneer study of the Fulani language and culture that was to take her many years. In 1926 she became Nigeria's first Lady Superintendent of Education.

The Great War effectively brought to an end an era that had been characterized by supreme self-confidence. 'I don't know really how far one looked ahead,' acknowledges Angus Gillan. 'It was in the days when the Empire was, shall we say, cock of the world? And at that stage of one's career I don't think the young man thought a great deal as to when – even as to whether – the Sudan or an Indian state or Nigeria or whatever it might be would begin to demand Independence. It was only really after the First World War I think that one began seriously to consider these things.'

3

To Africa

The young men who went out between the wars to serve in the colonial administration or in the military services shared a common background. They were drawn from the middle classes and the great majority had been brought up in the 'British tradition of service' that was part and parcel of prep and public school education: 'One didn't go out carrying the banner of Wellington, but one did go out imbued with certain standards.' Chris Farmer, who joined the Administrative Service in Nigeria, saw himself as a typical product of 'the much-maligned public school system which, whatever you may say against it, did inculcate a sense of responsibility. I was head of my house, I was deputy head of the school, captain of rugger, and company sergeant-major in the Officer Training Corps, exercising responsibility and learning to use the authority which went with the responsibility, so that when eventually I found myself out in the bush in Nigeria on my own I wasn't worried about it in the slightest way.'

Only slightly less dominant a force was the tradition of family service that made a career in one or other of the Imperial Services almost inevitable. In some families this tradition flourished to a remarkable degree, as in Charles Meek's family:

The whole of my family, like so many British middle-class families in the nineteenth century, was very strongly connected with the forces and with Imperial administration in one form or another. My great-grandfather was General Sir Thomas Gordon, who was a notable figure in Indian administration, and was one of a remarkable pair of twin generals; they both took all their steps in the army on the same day, and ended up as generals on the same day and were knighted on the same day. I also had an uncle in India with a long connection with the Indian political service, my grandfather fought at Ulundi, the closing battle of the Zulu war, and my own father was in the Nigerian Administrative Service, so there's this long web of connection which certainly determined my future career. I never had any other thought of going into anything at all except the colonial civil service.

Brian Montgomery was similarly influenced: 'My grandfather, Sir Robert Montgomery, was Lieutenant-Governor of the Punjab, just after the Indian Mutiny. My father was born in Cawnpore and spent his boyhood up to the age of about eight in India. He entered the Church and became the Bishop of Tasmania. One of my uncles was Commissioner of Rawalpindi in India, and another was a Commissioner in Kenya.' As far as his own generation was concerned:

There was never any question but that most of us would have some connections in their professions with the British Empire. My eldest brother became a constable in the British South Africa Police, from which he gravitated up to Kenya and finished up as Chief Native Commissioner there. His younger brother next to him went out to Canada. My next brother to him was the one who served in India and became field-marshal. The next one after him became a parson, and was rector of Ladysmith in South Africa and later on a canon in the Arctic. It followed that when my time came – and I was the last of nine children – I should join the army. I joined the

King's African Rifles and later on transferred to the Indian Army.

In the nineteenth century and up to the outbreak of the First World War the main attraction for those seeking a colonial career was to be found in India, where the most prestigious position was occupied by the Indian Civil Service. But as demands for home rule in India grew, so its attraction diminished: 'My grandfather and my father served in India; they were merchants in Calcutta,' recalls James Robertson:

> So all my young life I was brought up to think of carrying on the tradition of going to India. My father had a great admiration for the Indian Civil Service and the idea was that when I had got my degree at Oxford I should go there. Well, of course, in 1921–2 conditions in India were a bit difficult. There were bandits, massacres and so forth. Meanwhile friends of mine had gone into the Colonial Service and into the Sudan Political Service and I heard quite a lot about that. Well, at the end of my academic time at Oxford I put my name in for the whole three and, in fact, the Sudan interview came off first and they took me.

For Darrell Bates, too, a career in the Indian Civil Service had been a boyhood ambition: 'But while I was at Oxford I came across people whose parents lived in India or who had an Indian background, and they gradually convinced me that India would become independent fairly soon and that if I went there I might find myself out of a job. And at that time the Sudan Political Service and the Colonial Service were becoming careers of tremendous interest to people at university who affected a sort of balance between brain and brawn – an intelligent man's outdoor life – and so I switched.'

Although the British colonization of Africa was still in the twenties and thirties too recent a phenomenon to have allowed any widespread ancestral pattern of son following father to have developed – as was the case in India – there were indeed some young men going out to territories where their fathers had been before them. Nigel Cooke's father had been in mining in Northern Nigeria since 1910 and Dick Symes-Thompson had been born in Kenya, where his father had bought a coffee plantation and settled in 1913: 'My mother also had African connections as she had been born in Basutoland where her father was a Resident, and for this reason I had always considered a job in Africa, possibly in the administration.' In Harry Grenfell's case the connection with Africa went back even further, to his grandfather's friendship with Cecil Rhodes and the white settlement of Rhodesia in the 1890s.

But there were many who had no such connections. Some of them, like Frank Lloyd, joined simply because it had been their childhood ambition to do so: 'From an early age I had thought in terms of joining the Colonial Service, even when I was still at prep school – and for some reason or other it stuck.' Many others had no such early ambitions and, like Anthony Kirk-Greene, who joined the Nigerian Administrative Service after the Second World War, knew virtually nothing about the Colonial Service: 'I even remember going out in the troopship during the war and being given a paperback which was called *Diary of a District Officer*. I had no idea what a District Officer was – if I thought of it at all it was as a sort of male variant of the district nurse – that was how ignorant I was.'

Although it was not published until 1942, Kenneth Bradley's *Diary of a District Officer* did, in fact, have a strong influence on a later generation of recruits. Earlier generations had to rely on Allan Quatermain and Edgar Wallace for their African reading.

Two other factors played a major part in shaping the decisions of those who were to go out to Africa. The first was the obvious attraction of an outdoor life, one that combined travel with sunshine and a strong element of human interest – and which was far removed from the 'rather stuffy, formal career structure' which most other young graduates would be doomed to follow. The second factor was rather more practical; the need to find a good job at a time when job prospects were far from secure, something that Nigel Cooke was very aware of in 1934: 'Going up to Cambridge at a time when the slump was very fresh in people's minds I was conscious all the time of the danger of arriving at the other end without a job, and in fact the salary that was offered to colonial cadets was very good indeed when you think that a schoolmaster was lucky to get £200, and we were on the princely sum of £400 a year.'

One of those young men who did arrive at the other end of his degree course without finding a job was Richard Turnbull who, by his own admission, joined the Colonial Service more or less by chance:

I'd taken my degree as a physical chemist and I'd hoped to get into industry but I failed to get a first; I was too interested in rowing and listening to music and making merry and I only got a second. Had I got a first I should almost certainly have been accepted by ICI and gone to the north country. As it was, I had to look for a job and there were thousands of us in 1929 looking for jobs and there were three million unemployed. Well, in the month of July I was walking down Whitehall on my way to the Abbey to hear a chorale that was being sung that day and I saw the name Richmond Terrace. And I knew I'd read it somewhere so I walked round Richmond Terrace and I came across the Colonial Office Appointments Board. And I banged on the door, walked in and the commissionaire said, 'If you're expecting to be appointed this year you're three months too late.' All the same, I got a collection of application forms, filled them in and presented them. Very much to my surprise, I was called up for an interview.

There were others who were also swayed by pressing financial needs, particularly in the army: 'Quite frankly, the reason why most army officers fifty years ago decided to serve in Africa was nearly always because they were in debt. No doubt there were cases where they were crossed in love or wanted adventure, but army officers were very badly paid in those days and it was very easy to get into debt – the debt usually taking the form of getting well behindhand with their payments to their tailor, because in those days regimental tailors gave officers unlimited credit – or else they had an overdraft at the bank.'

One such officer who found it impossible to live on his pay was Brian Montgomery, who applied for secondment to the King's African Rifles in 1927:

In the British Army of those days, and particularly in the infantry regiments of the line – what were called the unfashionable regiments – none of the officers, or very few, had any private means and therefore when the time came to compete with marriage, for instance, or other expenses, it was not possible to survive in England. And therefore many officers volunteered to join any of the colonial forces, which were paid for by the governments of those territories and provided much better pay. As my eldest brother was already Commissioner in Kenya it seemed quite natural that I should join the King's African Rifles, where the pay was £500 a year, which seemed a princely sum in those days, being in fact more than double the pay of a subaltern in the British Army in the UK.

It was the same basic reason that brought twenty-year-old Donald Dunnet into the West Africa trade:

I was on leave as a young soldier immediately after the armistice and I met a man who was working in Nigeria and was home on leave, and apparently it was quite a rewarding sort of job. There had been a boom in the West African trade just after the end of the war and he had earned very considerable commissions, and although I realized that work-

ing conditions in West Africa were supposed to be very bad, I
couldn't imagine that they were as bad as some of the foxholes
around Mount Kemel and the money was certainly better –
and I was rather attracted to the romance of mercantile
commerce. So I applied for a job with the people with whom
he was employed.

An escape, even if only a temporary one ('West Africa was
not a place where you went for a lifetime. You went there for
your tour or tours, and then you came back'), was what a job
as a cashier with the Bank of British West Africa offered Bill
Page in 1926 – as well as the opportunity to better himself:

I'd been working in Lloyds Bank for something like four years
and although I was no longer the junior junior but the senior
junior I found that the work was frightfully unedifying, just
listing cheques and adding them up, being everybody's dogs-
body. So I began thinking of a change – and the colonies and
India did afford an escape from the constricting circumstances
at home. And then there was the money; I'd been working for
four years and still getting about £2 a week – well, you
couldn't take your girl-friend to the pictures on that! So I
wrote to a firm in London that catered for people like me who
wanted jobs abroad and they sent me a number of forms to fill
in. I think I filled in a couple for India and then one came for
the Bank of British West Africa. Well, that sounded more
romantic. I'd just been to the Wembley Empire Exhibition
and there was a living model of an African village, all hot and
tropical and brown and that seemed to indicate that West
Africa wouldn't be a bad place, so I applied and had an
interview and got the job.

There was also a sizable body of young men – and women –
for whom Africa offered rewards that were anything but
financial. In 1929 Robert Macdonald became a member of
this dedicated band:

Although we were very much attached to the Church there was no tradition of missionary work in my family. But there was a missionary in the South Seas, Chalmers of New Guinea, a Scotsman whose life had fascinated me as a young boy. He was actually murdered and eaten, I believe, but that didn't deflect me from the idea. I'd wanted to be a missionary for as long as I can remember, but I was drawn to Africa because my cousin was already there doing interesting and exciting medical work, and two of my college colleagues were already there, and their letters and meeting them on leave confirmed my desire to make it the Calabar Mission in south-eastern Nigeria rather than anywhere else.

For some the process of selection seemed arbitrary, as Donald Dunnet found when he applied to the trading company of Miller Brothers of Liverpool: 'I don't think they were having too many applicants for the job because all they seemed to want to know about me was the size of my neck, as they were going to buy me some shirts – on a buy now, pay later sort of thing.' And when Clifford Ruston applied to join the Lagos Stores trading company in 1919 what his future employers seemed chiefly interested in was his sobriety: 'One of the clauses in the agreement for two years' service that I signed was that the clerk – I was always referred to as the clerk – would not indulge in alcoholic liquor save at meals or with the express written permission of the company's medical attendant. I may say that when I got to Lagos I found that this clause wasn't strictly adhered to.' But for those hoping to join the Colonial Administrative Service the selection process was anything but rudimentary. It began with references – from headmasters, commanding officers, college tutors, heads of houses – and a good, but not too good, degree: 'The standard laid down was that you had to have at least a second class honours degree or show (in the immediate post-war period) that had you gone to university you would have had second class honours.'

After the references there were the interviews. Here, as in every stage of the selection process, was to be found presiding the Patronage Secretary, Major – later Sir – Ralph Furse, who held the post for almost as long as anyone could remember. By the time that Kenneth Smith came to join his Appointments Department in 1945, Furse was practically stone deaf; but he was still very much an elder statesman – and his influence was still paramount:

> He had been since 1911, I think, head of that branch of the service as, in the first place, Patronage Secretary to the Secretary of State. He'd continued all through the post-war period of the construction of the Colonial Service – rather nicely, he had been joined by his brother-in-law, Captain Newbolt, the son of the poet, and it was these two who between them can be said to be responsible for creating a unified service for the administration of the Colonial Empire and the manner in which candidates for it were selected and trained.

Furse himself personally vetted thousands of young men in their first informal interviews before they faced the final interview board. Robin Short came up before him in 1949: 'I remember Sir Ralph Furse as a very benevolent old gentleman, asking me the time-honoured question, "Do you play cricket?" to which I am glad to say I was able to answer that I did. He also asked me, even in 1949, whether I would be prepared to ask Africans into my home, and I had, of course, to say, "Yes, I should be delighted, if they were friends of mine." '

It could well have been Furse who interviewed Richard Turnbull when he presented himself at the Colonial Office twenty years earlier and was questioned by 'a very charming and, I realize now, a very astute fellow. He asked any number of questions, most of which seemed to be pretty irrelevant. One I do remember was this: he said to me, "Do you think you could tell a smoking-room story to an African elder?" I said I was quite certain I could. It seemed to me at the time a ridiculous question but, of course, it wasn't. When I look back and think of the hours and hours I spent with dear old men swapping off-colour stories and both of us laughing ourselves silly and enjoying it immensely, I realize what a very, very profound chap my interviewer was.'

The final interview was usually a very formal affair. Darrell Bates recalls how 'I found myself one hot summer afternoon at Burlington House, and there on the other side of the table was a really alarming number of distinguished faces. None of them smiled when I came in and while I stood there waiting for someone to speak to me I felt as if they were taking my clothes off one by one and pricing them and having a look at how recently I had cut my hair and cut my fingernails. But once they started on the questions they were for the most part thoughtful and kind and wise.'

There was one particular line of questioning that remained as pertinent in the 1950s as it had been fifty years earlier: how would you really cope with what was likely to be a pretty lonely life? Questions about ultimate self-determination for the colonies regularly came up, but what was not considered, even as late as 1949, when Anthony Kirk-Greene faced his selection board, was the possibility that entrants to the Colonial Service might be embarking on a short-term career: 'If we had thought this our minds were very quickly put to rest by the selection board. Indeed the Governor of Nigeria two years later greeted one of his cadets by saying, "And how long do you think you'll be here?" The cadet, an extremely bright person, said, "Well, I suppose half a dozen years." And Governor MacPherson patted him on the knee and said, "Don't you worry, my boy, my son is just going into the Colonial Service and he has a career in front of him."'

This optimism about their career prospects was shared by the great majority of successful applicants as they began their year of training at either Oxford or Cambridge: 'Few if any of us on the Colonial Service Course at Oxford in 1935–6 thought that we should run out of time,' recalls George Sinclair. 'Most of us were so entranced by the idea of the job ahead and the opportunities and responsibilities that I doubt whether many of us thought much about the time-scale.'

By the time their courses had begun the ultimate destination of the newly appointed cadet probationers had been determined. Each applicant had listed his preferences, which had certainly been considered – even if they could not always be met: 'There was no specific purpose or method behind Colonial Office posting as far as we could see. A certain number of cadets were needed each year for each colony, and unless one had special connections in one colony or another I think somebody simply took a pin and selected one's name and sent one to that colony.'

Some had no preference, and were content to be sent wherever the Colonial Office decided. Others had preferences that were largely determined by the duration of the tour of duty, which varied greatly from one territory to another. It could be as short as twelve months in West Africa and as long as four years in the more temperate regions. This was certainly one of the reasons that prompted Frank Loyd to put Uganda down as his first choice rather than Kenya, 'because Uganda only had a two-and-a-half or perhaps a two-year tour, whereas Kenya had four, and for someone like myself the prospect of being away from England for as long as four years was rather awful. So I opted for the one with the briefest tour, which just shows how little I knew about Africa as a whole and East Africa in particular. I was, in fact, sent to Kenya, so the gods were with me.'

After the Indian Civil Service and the Sudan Political Service, Northern Nigeria probably occupied the most prestigious position on the Imperial list – although such a claim would be fiercely disputed by colonial officers whose loyalties lay elsewhere. But the fact that Nigeria was always the most popular choice among recruits was due as much to the fact of its being one of the largest and the best-known of the colonial territories as it was to anything else.

What had earlier been called the Tropical African Service Course and had been held at the Imperial Institute in London had expanded in the mid-twenties from a somewhat rudimentary training course into a well-organized Colonial Service Course run jointly at the two leading universities and embracing a wide variety of subjects. Other 'support' services and departments such as the Agricultural and Forest Services or the Colonial Police also ran their own specialized courses. For Darrell Bates, as for many others, this was a year of total freedom from responsibility:

> One had all the excitement of being at Oxford without having the pressure of an exam and one had all the joys of an Oxford which one had got to know without the constant worry about whether you would get a job at the end of it. And now they were actually paying me to take a course, so it was tremendous fun. But the course itself was designed perhaps to produce a whole set of poobahs. One had a tremendous variety of function and one got to know a little about a lot of things and not very much about anything in particular.

Part of the training was practical, 'designed to teach you the rural agriculture, anti-erosion techniques, rural hygiene and elementary public engineering', but there was also training that 'took you through the rules of law and evidence, with a view to your being able to sit in a court from the day of your arrival'. Then there was a part of the course that was related directly to the region to which the cadet would be sent. George Sinclair, expecting to be sent to Ashanti, considered himself to be particularly fortunate to have as his tutor Captain R. S. Rattray, one of the great characters of West Africa:

Rattray had been in West Africa since he was about seventeen or eighteen. He had left school in Scotland to serve in the South African war. After that he became an elephant hunter and as he moved northwards through Africa he recorded languages and folklore on his way. Finally he came in to the northern territories of the Gold Coast where he became a District Commissioner, later a Provincial Commissioner and then a government anthropologist. He then began to publish his books about the laws, religion, customs, folk-stories and proverbs of the Ashanti people – to whom he was known as *mako*, which means 'pepper', because he was so quick. I spent a year with him and was completely entranced with his approach to people as individuals and his respect for the people amongst whom he worked.

Behind the language courses and the law studies and the practical training there was also a clear-cut philosophy that was symbolized by the required reading of Lord Lugard's *Dual Mandate*. Its general tenor was that 'your job is to learn how they govern themselves and assist that process. You'll be there for a very long time, you're there to give support to existing native structures, to enable them to evolve naturally – and there is no immediate necessity either to understand urban politics or transpose Westminster models of government.'

Although it was enjoyed, this year of training was not always considered useful either by those who received it or by those for whom they worked, as Anthony Kirk-Greene found when it came to putting theory into practice:

Looking through my notebooks I see that on the administrative and political side, what I learnt would have been useful if I'd been appointed governor straight away rather than a mere Assistant District Officer – and my superiors didn't hesitate to point this out to me pretty quickly. My first Resident said to me, 'I suppose you, too, have wasted this year at Cambridge.' He didn't really mean this because I was

wearing a Hawks tie, having got a blue, and he, too, was
wearing the same tie, but I asked him, 'Well, what would have
been useful?' and he said, 'There are only two things needed to
make that course worthwhile; if you can do native treasury
accounts and if you can type. Anything else – you've wasted
your time!'

Once the course was completed the cadets had a few weeks
leave in which to prepare themselves for departure. For those
uncertain as to how to equip themselves there were the services
of such rival firms of colonial outfitters as Griffiths McAllister
of Regent Street, Messrs F. P. Baker of Golden Square and in
Oxford, Walters and Co. of 10 The Turl, who descended
upon all colonial appointees, offering exceptionally generous
terms of credit that could be spread over the first tour of
service or even longer. Although the days of *chop* boxes and
self-sufficiency had largely ended, there was still a tendency
among those outfitters to over-supply and to think in somewhat old-fashioned terms. 'Tropical outfitters were very keen
on nineteenth-century pith helmets,' recalls Darrell Bates.
'They had a tremendous variety of "Bombay bowlers" and
there was one I remember with a flap at the back like the thing
that a tortoise has. So, of course, when I got to Africa I arrived
fully equipped with Bombay bowlers and pith helmets. In the
end I gave them all away and bought a panama.'
Two other relics of the past that were still being supplied
well into the inter-war period were the cholera-belt and the
spine-pad, the latter an ominously coffin-shaped piece of cloth
fitted with buttons and worn down the back. The position had
scarcely changed even when Charles Meek went along with his
father to buy his kit from F. P. Baker in wartime London in
1941:

My father had retired from Nigeria in 1932 and it was at once
apparent to me how very old-fashioned his ideas were as he
tried to persuade me to buy spine-pads, red flannel and all that

kind of thing. And I was very successful in rejecting his advice until he scored one notable triumph with the help of Baker's assistant. This was in the form of a portable lavatory seat, which I felt must be a very old-fashioned bit of equipment and certainly not needed in these modern days – and I resisted very strongly until the shop assistant trumped my ace by saying, 'Look here, sir, I'll put it up for you.' And as a young man of twenty I was so abashed and red in the face at the very thought of this lavatory seat being erected in the middle of Baker's emporium that I said, 'No, no, I'll take it.' And in the end I'm bound to confess that it was one of the most splendid bits of safari equipment I ever had.

Other apparently outmoded pieces of equipment similarly turned out to be invaluable in the field: mosquito boots made of leather or white canvas and worn in the evenings to protect ankles and calves, and what was known in East Africa as the *jilumchi* or *chilumchi* – 'a most extraordinary thing, an ordinary tin basin with a canvas cover which was strapped down over the top and in that you kept all your washing kit and your sponges and razors and also pyjamas, so that when you travelled light you had no other piece of luggage, apart from your bedding roll, and you required nothing else.' There was also a larger version of the *jilumchi*, a tin bath with 'a very splendid wicker basket affair that went inside and was meant to contain all one's dirty clothes'.

Then there was the problem of what the well-dressed colonial official ought to wear. 'I remember having anxious moments looking at photographs in old books of District Officers,' says Anthony Kirk-Greene. 'Did one wear a uniform? Did one wear short or long stockings? Did one wear very long shorts? Could you wear an open-necked shirt? Did you have a tie? I remember going through all sorts of advertisements and brochures from the Colonial Office about our man in so-and-so, trying to work this out.' There was indeed an Administrative Service uniform – a white one with

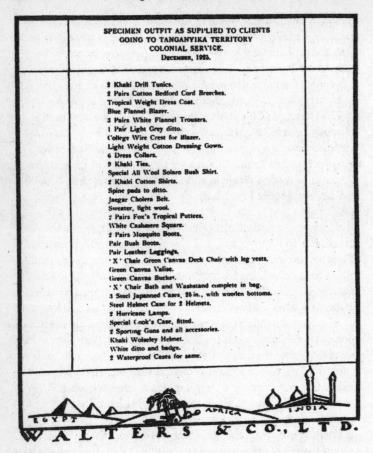

**SPECIMEN OUTFIT AS SUPPLIED TO CLIENTS
GOING TO TANGANYIKA TERRITORY
COLONIAL SERVICE.**
DECEMBER, 1925.

2 Khaki Drill Tunics.
2 Pairs Cotton Bedford Cord Breeches.
Tropical Weight Dress Coat.
Blue Flannel Blazer.
3 Pairs White Flannel Trousers.
1 Pair Light Grey ditto.
College Wire Crest for Blazer.
Light Weight Cotton Dressing Gown.
6 Dress Collars.
9 Khaki Ties.
Special All Wool Solaro Bush Shirt.
2 Khaki Cotton Shirts.
Spine pads to ditto.
Jaegar Cholera Belt.
Sweater, light wool.
2 Pairs Fox's Tropical Puttees.
White Cashmere Square.
2 Pairs Mosquito Boots.
Pair Bush Boots.
Pair Leather Leggings.
'X' Chair Green Canvas Deck Chair with leg rests.
Green Canvas Valise.
Green Canvas Bucket.
'X' Chair Bath and Washstand complete in bag.
3 Steel Japanned Cases, 28 in., with wooden bottoms.
Steel Helmet Case for 2 Helmets.
2 Hurricane Lamps.
Special Cook's Case, fitted.
2 Sporting Guns and all accessories.
Khaki Wolseley Helmet.
White ditto and badge.
2 Waterproof Cases for same.

EGYPT   AFRICA   INDIA

WALTERS & CO., LTD.

A specimen list from *Suggestions for Tropical Outfit and Equipment* as supplied by Walters and Co. to newly appointed Cadets, 1925.

gold buttons and a Wolseley helmet to match, to be worn on 'splendid occasions' but otherwise to be avoided: 'Uniforms in tropical Africa are not the ideal way of being comfortable and although for the Africans a uniform is a splendid thing and something they quite rightly enjoy and admire, for ourselves we would only wear these things when we had to and were much happier dressed as ordinary members of the public.' Officers in the Sudan and in Kenya stuck to a khaki uniform – in Kenya they had their own idiosyncratic system of rings worn on the sleeve which was said to go back to some obscure naval connection – but for the most part District Officers preferred to go about in khaki shorts with stockings up to the knee, worn with an open-necked bush shirt.

The traditional port of embarkation for Africa was Liverpool. It was from here that ships of the Elder Dempster fleet sailed on alternate Wednesdays for the West Africa Coast, leaving the British India and the Union Castle lines, departing from Tilbury, to serve the East Coast. Elder Dempster was a major institution on the coast, the 'big canoe man pass all', celebrated in the working songs of the Kru boatmen from Cape Coast Castle to Calabar, but as passenger liners went Elder Dempster ships were modest in size and far from luxurious in their fittings, reflecting the fact that their passenger lists were made up very largely of government servants, traders and missionaries – nearly all of whom travelled saloon or first class, leaving the second class to B class officials and the third class to Africans.

Donald Dunnet sailed for Nigeria aboard the Elder Dempster mail steamer the S.S. *Abinsi* in June 1920, after being given a brief once-over by his employers, which was done 'just to see that the men were sober before they actually sailed, because there were cases when people had turned up very drunk and the sailing had been cancelled on the spot'. He had bought himself a dinner suit 'because I understood it to be *de rigueur* to wear one on board, and I was very anxious to put this on. But as time came on for dinner I looked round anxiously and I couldn't see anybody wearing one so I thought, well, perhaps you don't do it on the first night – and that turned out to be the case.' On subsequent nights everybody in the first class dressed for dinner, the men wearing dinner suits or – in the thirties – white shell jackets, with officers in the Colonial Service sporting cummerbunds of different colours – green for Nigeria, blue for the Gambians, red for Sierra Leone and, of course, gold for the Gold Coast.

Although the different professions tended to seek out each other's company, perhaps the strongest division was between 'old coasters' and 'first-timers' or 'first-tour men'. Seated among old coasters at the Purser's table, Donald Dunnet felt himself to be very insignificant: 'The Purser was a great big chap, a pretty imposing figure, who had a pint of cold lager with his breakfast, and he strode round the deck looking very, very important, and he was very patronizing and made me feel very humble. In an endeavour to make up some conversation I asked him about the native quarter in Lagos, and he looked very superciliously at me and said, "Well, it's all native quarter in Lagos." So I didn't get very far with the conversation.'

It was almost a tradition that old coasters regaled newcomers during the two-week run across the 'Elder Dempster boneyard' with tall tales about the White Man's Grave, designed, as George Sinclair states, 'partly as lessons but mainly to horrify us with the prospect ahead. These stories were highlighted when we reached Sierra Leone and somebody came on board to meet Sierra Leone officers. The conversation ran like this: "Poor old Cocky." "Yes, indeed, poor old Cocky. Snake-bite, wasn't it?" We turned round and sought the bar.'

It was at the ship's bar, bound for Mombasa via the Suez Canal, that Captain Montgomery – and no doubt many other young gentlemen – first made the acquaintance of pink gin, as well as of the practice of signing chits rather than paying up on the spot, a dangerous custom as some found to their cost at the end of the voyage. David Allen was on board the steamship *Accra* when it was torpedoed in 1940. The morale of the passengers received a mighty boost when they observed the chief steward standing on the bridge: 'He shouted to us all and then out of his pocket he took all the chits that we'd signed,

and he held them up and he tore them up in his hand and
threw them into the sea!'

The first port of call on the African mainland was generally
Freetown, first visited by Hugh Moresby-White in 1915:

> Looking at it through the porthole of my cabin I thought what
> a lovely little place it was, with its picturesque little harbour –
> though it was very, very hot. And I remember a wreck, an old
> slaver, stranded on a rock at the entrance to the harbour. It
> was there for years. And there was a familiar figure, too, in the
> harbour – an African in a canoe wearing just a loin-cloth
> round his middle and a battered top hat on his head. He
> would sing English popular songs – a very cheerful chap, as
> Africans are – and the passengers would be leaning over the
> rail looking down at him and what he was waiting for was for
> coins to be thrown overboard. When the coin was thrown into
> the water he'd take his hat off and put it down in the canoe and
> dive down and collect the penny before it had gone very far.
> He was always there – for years and years.

Very much the same sight met Philip Allison as his ship lay off
Freetown in 1931. 'There were a lot of locals in canoes playing
about down below and diving for pennies and so on, and I was
on one of the upper decks and I leant out of the shadow of the
deck above and stuck my head out into the sun, and an old
missionary lady tapped me on the shoulder and said, "You must
be careful. You are in the tropics now, young man!" '

On the East African coast, as the British India and Union
Castle steamers sailed on down past Mombasa, the approach
to the island of Zanzibar was heralded from many miles away
by the exotic scent of cloves and spices: 'But over and above
the smell of cloves there was the smell of shark, one of the
imports brought by the annual dhow trade which they'd
caught on their way to Zanzibar and which were then
deposited in great vats while they were salted and then
reexported largely to the African mainland.' The main gate-

way to the mainland was the port of Dar es Salaam, which was, for Darrell Bates, the realization of a dream: 'It was a beautiful harbour, landlocked completely with a very narrow entrance lined with palm trees and white buildings, and it was how one had imagined it to be. And it was a great moment, really, because almost ten years of my life had been devoted to this as an objective.'

Every landfall had its own never to be forgotten flavour. On the West Coast the Reverend Robert MacDonald had continued on down past the Slave Coast to the Bight of Benin, where his ship arrived off Calabar at nightfall: 'It was a kind of fortnightly run of the Elder Dempster liner; a gun was fired when the anchor dropped in the Calabar river and it happened that it was night just as we anchored and I remember being tremendously impressed by the first sounds of Africa. The crickets came out with their long whistling noises, and with the fireflies illuminating the whole area it was almost like a show of fireworks – and I wondered if I'd ever get accustomed to this kind of thing.'

But there could have been no more romantic or exciting introduction to Africa than that experienced by Bill Page – as well as by all those who came to Accra by sea between the wars – as he was brought ashore by the Kru boatmen of the Gold Coast:

The steamers anchored a couple of miles offshore and there they rode gently rocking to and fro as the breakers came rolling in. And there we waited until the canoes – which they call surf-boats – came out. These were dug-out canoes made from one solid tree, with four men with paddles sitting along each side and one chanter at the back with a long oar to guide it and steady it. When they got alongside they would wait down below and on deck the *mammy*-chair would be got out. There were two seats facing each other in it and you could step in and then sit there. And this was winched up off the deck and then swung overboard and you were then suspended over the surf-boat below. Then they lowered the *mammy*-chair to within about four feet of the boat and as the surf-boat was resting in the trough of a wave they would let out the rope and you'd go down bang into the bottom of the surf-boat and step out. Then the Africans bent to their work and dug into the waves and got us travelling along well and of course the chanter at the back did his singing and they all joined in.

The surf-boat would go down into the trough between the huge rollers and you'd be completely out of sight of land, and nothing but waves around you. Then gradually you would mount again on to a crest and there you would see the shore again and slide down the other side. It was extremely hard work for these chaps and I was told that they didn't last long on this job, but they were of magnificent physique, with brown, shining and rippling muscles. As we got closer to the shore they would hold the vessel back until we were right on the crest of a breaking wave and then all together they would bend to it and drive us right up the shore. Then you had to nip out pretty quickly as the wave receded and the next one came in and, of course, the women were carried ashore by the boys. And so you went up the beach – and as you landed the heat hit you, like being hit in the face.

4

Taking up the Ropes

You would know you were in Africa if you woke up suddenly and found yourself there by the look of the sky, the clouds in particular, always brilliantly lit from the top with a dark line underneath. The sky and general colours are all of a very high key, very brilliant, so that the contrasts are very great and at the same time there is no softening. There are no soft greens, no grey, and shadows are equally dark, sometimes chocolate and sometimes a dark blue-grey.

If Africa had a characteristic appearance and a characteristic heat it also had a characteristic smell. It was the 'quite unacceptable' odour of rancid palm oil that first impressed itself on Nigel Cooke when he arrived in Nigeria – that and the 'extreme vivacity of the African, which gave an atmosphere of great cheerfulness that sustained many Europeans apart from myself through many years of service'.

There were others whose first impressions were equally mixed. Seeing Freetown for the first time, Kenneth Smith was 'very dismayed at the little that seemed to have been achieved by a hundred years or more of continual British administration there. The town seemed to me to be a run-down shanty town and I went back on board ship considerably dismayed at the prospect of serving in what seemed to be the impoverished, run-down

world of Africa.' Arriving in the Northern Rhodesian capital of
Lusaka after a four-day rail journey up from the Cape, Robin
Short took the 'rudimentary' local conditions for granted. Not
until some years later was he able to make any sort of valid
comparison: 'My parents, who had been in India, came out on a
visit and were appalled by the disgracefully primitive conditions
in which government servants were expected to live. They found
the contrast between India and Africa very great, but, not
knowing any better, we simply soldiered on.'

Almost by tradition, first-tour men spent a couple of days or
more in government headquarters, while their seniors dispersed without delay to their various provinces and up-
country stations, often catching the special evening boat-train
that met their ship as it docked – in Lagos it left at 9 p.m. Nigel
Cooke gained an early insight into what life as an Assistant
District Officer would be like as his ship arrived at Lagos and
the postings went up on the ship: 'I remember particularly an
ADO who was coming back for his fourth tour, looking with
amazement and disappointment to find that he was going back
to the same station yet again – and this was a station on the
Mambila plateau, the most remote in the whole of Northern
Nigeria and very lonely indeed.'

After landing and proceeding through Customs there were
certain conventions to be observed without delay. The most
vital of these was still the dose of five grains of quinine a day.
According to Martin Lindsay it was taken every evening with a
pink gin and soda-water:

Even when you were out to dinner with somebody else the
servant who brought the pink gin on a tray always brought a
bottle of quinine with it so that nobody should forget to take
his five grains a day. In spite of that most of us got malaria
once or twice, although probably very slightly. The people
who got it really badly were the second class – in the official
sense of the word – white men, such as the foreman plate-
layers and the engine-drivers who were miles away up-country

living a very lonely life and who were often heavy drinkers. Their antimalaria discipline was not good, and they used to get malaria very much worse than we did, which very often turned into blackwater fever.

Almost equally important – especially for those in government service – was the observation of protocol. Nigel Cooke had been warned and so he knew the form: 'When we arrived in Lagos we were taken to sign the Governor's book, the Chief Justice's book, the Chief Secretary's book. And furthermore, when one got to one's station not only did you have to sign the Resident's book but you had to leave cards in the appropriate places. I'd been told that a Resident should have a card and, furthermore, that any married couple should have two cards, but it was not obligatory to drop cards on married men who had not got their wives with them, or alternatively, bachelors without wives. And indeed, I left cards accordingly.' Edwin Everett was not so well informed:

It was the custom to leave cards very soon after your arrival. In fact we found this out when we were hauled up to headquarters and asked why we hadn't done it. The explanation that we didn't know anybody, we didn't know where they lived and in fact we hadn't managed to finish unpacking yet didn't get us anywhere. We were merely told that an officer would call that afternoon and drive us around so that we could leave cards, so we had to dash off into town and buy some blanks and fill them in and that evening a car arrived with an African police orderly who drove us around and kept stopping at various doors. And we just walked up the garden path and rang or knocked, and when the steward boy answered we said, 'Master in?' 'No' – we issued him with one card. 'Master get Missus?' 'Yes' – we gave him another card. Next day we were up on the mat again. 'Why did you leave only one card at Mr So and So's house?' 'But the steward boy said madam no here.' 'You silly fools, she was at the club.'

This custom of dropping and the returning of cards that followed it was not entirely without purpose, since it resulted in a considerable number of invitations to drinks and dinner. The practice was already on the decline when war broke out in 1939 and it was stopped by governmental directive for the duration of the war – never to be revived. But up to that time the extent of protocol continued to surprise many newcomers, including David Allen when he came to the Gold Coast in 1938: 'Everybody was really horribly and terribly aware of seniority in the civil service, so naturally at dinner parties you were very much seated in accordance with your status. There was this very firm feeling of status and seniority which went on for a very long time indeed though it got less and less as time went on.' The means by which this seniority was proclaimed was through the medium of the Staff or Civil Service List, known irreverently as the 'stud book'. This listed every official in the territory in order of seniority, together with such details as his salary, age, qualifications and his present posting: 'All formal entertaining was largely conducted with the Civil List in mind; the hostess was very conscious of where in the List the various guests appeared and took punctilious care to make sure that seniority was perfectly matched in the placing of her guests.'

The Civil List was also useful in other ways: 'One knew exactly where one stood with regard to all one's colleagues and how senior they were and how likely it was that they would get promoted and what one's own chances of promotion were and so on.' Going hand in hand with this status-consciousness was a certain formality of address. Very soon after his arrival in Lagos – 'my seniority at that state was only about six hours old' – Nigel Cooke was addressed by the wife of a more senior official who expressed surprise 'that we cadets were so brash as to address an ADO of seven years standing by his Christian name. When I got to Bornu I don't think my Resident ever addressed me by anything other than my surname and, indeed, no one in that province addressed him by any other title than "Sir", and this included the senior DO. However, all the younger members of the Service and indeed quite a large proportion of those who'd come through the First World War were calling each other by their Christian names.' This observation of protocol was by no means confined to the European community:

> When I went to my first council meeting the Resident told me exactly how many steps to take forward to greet the Shehu of Bornu when he entered the room. No steps were taken forward for the members of the council, and indeed they were not even sat in chairs, they sat on the ground. During the years that followed getting the chiefs to agree to their council sitting on chairs was one of the things which we were constantly pressing for, and of course, achieved in the end.
>
> Before the war, and for several years after the war, it was not customary for administrative officers to shake hands with any Native Authority official other than a chief. This was not because we objected to doing so, but because it was assumed that the chief would object to your doing so. I remember the acute embarrassment of the Waziri of Bornu, who after all was the most senior person in the whole of Bornu Emirate after the Shehu, when I, in my greenness, shook his hand.

But if protocol was a little heavy-handed and the atmosphere 'strenuous' at times, it was offset by a tradition of hospitality towards junior officers. David Allen's first few days in Accra were very typical:

> Every day we had a detailed programme laid out for us which involved going out and meeting senior civil servants and hearing what they'd got to say to us. And then various social events were laid on for us. I remember one afternoon we went out and had a game of golf. In the evenings we were invited out to dinner by senior civil servants and I remember very well one dinner party we went to – I think it was with the Deputy

Colonial Secretary – there was a lovely round mahogany table and no tablecloth on it, with everybody sitting round. What I remember is that the table was absolutely covered with ants; they just ran all over the place and nobody paid the slightest attention to this, and I thought, 'My God, for the rest of my time in the Gold Coast have I got to have ants running around on the table?'

Over and above their hierarchical structure the administrators had other minor social divisions. There was the good-humoured contempt expressed by those in Northern Nigeria – the 'holy Northerners' – and Northern Kenya for those in the South; the suspicion of men in the field, the district, for the men in the centre, the secretariat; the natural irritation of the experienced old hand for the inexperienced youngster, who would be told many times over that 'you've got to be two years in this country before you are any use to anyone'. Yet the administrators were themselves a group that was set not only above but also apart from the rest. There was, particularly in the early days, 'a great division, unfortunately, between government officials and commercials and also between A class officials and B class officials'. The division between A and B class officials was the same as that found between officers and men in the services. On the one side were the administrators and, as time went on, more and more officers from the various support services. On the other side, with their own B class or second class clubs – and leading very different lives – there were the white 'NCOS', the Public Works Department foremen, railway engineers, civil contractors and other Europeans, usually out on short-time contracts.

The division between officials and non-officials was less marked but it was there all the same. 'Our lives didn't coincide,' states Donald Dunnet. 'Trading was trading and we had no connection with administration. We had no authority or powers. We were simply there, and we were rather looked down upon by some of the government people. We had terrific cuts in salary when the slump came on, and I remember one government officer saying, "Well, of course, you are traders." ' Within the trading community itself there were other fine lines of social division and, as always, the first-tour man was at the bottom: 'Lagos society was very difficult for an assistant. First of all, trading assistants were not allowed to join the club, and there was a social division between assistants and what were called agents in those days – what we would call managers today. Having survived the rigours and all the ailments of West Africa and immeasurable quantities of alcohol, they had achieved this exalted state and they had no time for a first-timer. A first-timer was a term of contempt and derision – and a first-timer was left very much to his own devices.'

Attitudes towards Africans varied greatly between these different groups of Europeans – as indeed they varied greatly from colony to colony. Almost the first piece of advice that Bill Page received when he came to Accra in the mid-twenties was to 'keep them in their place – and their place was obviously below! In those days the division between the races was very marked, but it wasn't unpleasant for the most part, and for the most part both sides accepted it.' As a convinced socialist, Bill Page was naturally critical of British Colonial rule:

> I didn't think that our rule there was oppressive but I thought it was wrong and that it established the wrong relationships between people. But I also found that the government people I met were first class and far more friendly and prepared to mix with the Africans than the commercial community there. At Government House garden parties you'd see the higher people, particularly those who were commissioners from up-country, mixing very easily with the Africans and so would the missionaries, whereas the commercial people, and perhaps the lower civil servants, would be standing around, whites in one place and the Africans in another and not mixing at all.

Major differences in attitude towards Africans between one territory and another were due partly to the very different forms of social development within these territories, partly to the length and the nature of contact with Europe. In Nyasaland, for instance, which had come under exceptionally strong missionary influence since the days of Livingstone, the concept of partnership was implicit even if it was not greatly advanced. Administrators who served in this 'very small, very poor, not very important country' accepted that they were in something of a colonial backwater, yet shared a strong sense of family feeling, where 'everybody did tend to know everybody'. By contrast, the neighbouring territory of Tanganyika was the land of the 'tough German colonialists' where the inherited assumption was that 'an African or a wog was an inferior being, almost incapable of being taught, a first class liar and someone to whom one tried to be kind and at the same time train'.

When Robert and Mercedes Mackay came out to Tanganyika in 1934 they found 'layer upon layer' of snobbery:

> For instance, we met some very charming railway people on the way and we said, 'We'll be meeting you, of course. We'll be meeting you at the club, I expect.' And they said, 'Oh no, you won't. We're not allowed to join your club. We have to have our own club.' The social layers and the social snobbery were almost unbelievable and unfortunately it particularly hit at people like doctors, forest officers and geologists – my husband was one. People like that who had gone to universities and had tremendous years of training and who knew practically everything about their subject, were ordered about by and practically had to kow-tow to a little boy with his mother's milk hardly off his teeth who drove around with a flag in front of his car because he represented the King! Now that was very galling.

First-tour men were almost by definition bachelors. If they were staying either in the capitals or in the larger stations they usually moved into civilian messes, where three or four young men could sleep under the same roof and share certain amenities. Such a mess was provided by the bank for which Bill Page worked in Lagos:

> It was very pleasant if you had companions that were congenial – then it was absolutely first class, but if you didn't get on, you were in such close quarters that it was rather miserable. The heavy drinkers usually got into a mess on their own and therefore lived their own particular way of life without disturbing anybody else very much, but when you got a mixed mess then the non-drinkers would have their dinner at about half-past seven and go off to bed, and at about eleven o'clock the drinkers would come in very happy and noisy, call the boys to bring out their dinner and disturb us generally which was rather an irritation. Each mess provided its own food. We shared a cook, but one member of the mess would be *chop* master, looking after the *chop* for a month. He kept careful accounts of all that was bought, instructed the cook to buy the food and paid him for it and made the menus. I found the food very dull, with a tremendous amount of minced beef. The cattle were bred up in the areas free from tsetse fly, which were hundreds of miles away, and were driven down by road and so were fairly tough when they got down to the coast and then of course you had to eat the meat fairly soon after it was slaughtered. So it tended to be rather tough and hence the minced beef and rissoles day after day, and if you had a *chop* master who had no imagination you would get banana fritters three or four times a week as well.

The institution of the mess was also to be found operating along rather more conventional lines among the various military units scattered through the colonial territories; the West Africa Frontier Force on the West Coast with small detachments in Gambia and Sierra Leone, a larger formation in the Gold Coast and in Nigeria the Nigeria Regiment with four battalions and a battery – and in East Africa the King's African Rifles, with six battalions spread through Kenya, Uganda, Tanganyika and Nyasaland. The officers in these units were drawn from every regiment and corps in the British Army and included cavalry officers and gunners as well as those from the infantry. Whatever their origins all served as infantry officers and wore the same standard khaki drill uniform of an officer in the tropics: 'The only occasions when our regimental identity was evident was at night when we all dined in the regimental mess kits of our own corps, so that sitting at the mess table at dinner in Nairobi, the headquarters of the Kenya battalion, you had an astonishing scene of blue, green and scarlet mess kits of every corps.' In the regimental mess at Nairobi Brian Montgomery found that the conversation was 'almost entirely about experiences on safari, particularly the big game shooting. There was a very fine pair of elephant tusks, maybe fifty or sixty pounds in each tusk, in the mess and there were the heads of buck of various kinds also on the walls. And the prestige of a man who had shot a lion and an elephant, rhino and buffalo was very great. But the officer who'd never shot anything did not have much prestige and therefore, like other newly joined officers, I longed for the day when I would be sent on safari, with the independence and command of a detachment.'

When Brian Montgomery woke up on his first morning in his mess bungalow in Nairobi he heard for the first time the reveille, the 'Turkish rise' of the King's African Rifles. 'This bugle call was not the standard reveille of the British Army, but the Turkish reveille, a very tuneful call which none of us who served there will ever forget and which originated from the father of the KAR, Lord Lugard.' In addition to Lugard's original Sudanese and Somalis, the King's African Rifles drew its *askaris* from many other East African tribes – but not from the Kikuyu, who were considered to be lacking in the necessary martial spirit. What astonished Brian Montgomery when he first saw his *askaris* on parade was that they wore no foot gear: 'The uniform was a khaki drill tunic, khaki shorts, a *tarboosh* with a black tassel derived from the Sudanese origins of the KAR, blue puttees and no foot gear at all; the *askari* never wore boots. Their feet were iron-hard and the ground literally shook when they were given such orders as stand at ease – and the noise was tremendous.'

Another officer who had a period of service with the King's African Rifles was Anthony Lytton, who found the 'flesh-pots' of Nairobi to be 'insidious and most liable to corrupt'. Playing squash and polo took up much of his time and 'several times a year there was a polo week when the settlers descended in their cars from their remote ranches and farms from far and wide and gathered together and one danced from 10 p.m. to 6 a.m. One thought not at all, or very little, of the people up-country in remote posts, either alone or in twos and threes.' The Kenya settlers, of course, provided an element of society that was entirely absent from most colonies. Anthony Lytton found them to be distinguished by 'their enterprise, their energy and their resourcefulness in dealing with nature in its rawest and most difficult state. They were people of tremendous character – and their club gave an indication of what they were like by its rules and its customs. Muthaiga Country Club at one stage would not admit an official because the officials were always the brake on what the settlers thought it right to do and therefore for a very long time, right up to my period, there was a discord between the settler element and the officials.'

If Muthaiga was the most notorious club in Africa – 'full of rumour, intrigue and amorous occasions' – the English Club in Zanzibar was probably the oldest, set in an old Arab merchant's house with great brass-studded doors and catering for a 'very closed' English community. Although even the most junior members of the administration were accepted automatically, club membership was only open to the most senior members of the commercial and trading firms. The same distinction was made in such places as Lagos, where the Polo

Club was open to managers and agents but not to their assistants – who had to be content with their own B class clubs, where they could go for a game of tennis or to play cards and where 'you just sat and drank and that made it a bit more tolerable – because there wasn't much else to do'.

Perhaps it was just as well that most young men, whether they were officials or 'unofficials', were soon packed off up-country. Darrell Bates had two days in Dar es Salaam before he was sent off to the small coastal station of Bagamoyo to which he had been posted:

I went out in an old lorry, surrounded by all the packages which I'd brought out from England, the tin bath and the camp chairs and the boxes and the shotgun and a few stores, and it was a long and very exciting journey through the bush. We didn't see very much – very few people, practically no animals – and it was the emptiness which struck me first of all, the emptiness and, to some extent, the poverty. And then suddenly, we were there; the driver said, 'There is the place.' There was a fringe of bush along the road, there were a few patches of cultivation, fields of maize, and there were a few scattered huts made of coconut leaves plaited and sewn with twine. And we turned a corner and there suddenly between the coconut trees I saw a Union Jack flying, rather tattered and forlorn on top of a very unpretentious white building. It was forlorn and lonely but it had a certain smack of authority and order. There was a flight of steps which led up from the road and on top of it a tall, thin angular figure stood with crumpled white trousers and a white shirt, and his face was long and lean and rather grey. 'Well, here you are,' he said. I didn't know what to say and I stood there probably looking rather foolish. 'Well,' he said, 'I'm off for my evening walk,' and off he went. I noticed that he had a fly switch made from the mane of a lion in his thin, bony hands and he twitched it to brush the flies off his face – and though I didn't know it at the time, it was to become a badge of office.

For officers whose postings directed them deeper into the interior, the journey could often take days and even, in some areas, weeks. As late as 1950 it took Anthony Kirk-Greene ten days to reach his district, culminating in the crossing of a river that had neither bridge nor ferry:

I arrived at the edge of the river and could see about two hundred yards the other side, sitting on a Roorkee chair, a gentleman with a large hat on, a pair of shorts and a shirt – no uniform in Nigeria, of course, and no tie in the bush. And he was shaking hands with a young Assistant District Officer who was the man I was relieving. And we then – each from our respective sides – started to wade in. I had a puppy on my shoulder which I'd picked up in Yola from a veterinary officer, and when we got half-way and it was well up to my shoulders this other man reached me and said his name was Roger DuBoulay and I said, 'That's a great coincidence because I'm Anthony Kirk-Greene and my grandmother said I might meet you somewhere in Africa. She knew your father very well indeed in India.' So then we passed on, he to his side and I to my side, and there was the Senior District Officer, who greeted me and said, 'Well, don't bother to dry out. Just get into the car,' and off we went for the last stage of this journey.

Bill Page had the unfortunate – and not altogether unchar-acteristic – experience of relieving a man who had 'rather gone to seed. The three weeks while we were waiting for his boat to come and take him away were some of the most miserable I've had to experience, because it was very close quarters and you couldn't get away from him. He had a glass in his hand from nine o'clock in the morning and by the time the evening came it was more or less running out of his eyes and his mouth, and he would throw down the end of his drink on the floor or up the wall, wherever took his fancy.'

Most first-timers were luckier in their introductions to their first stations – even if the accommodation was somewhat stark.

Few can have lived quite as uncomfortably as Bill Stubbs when he first began his police duties in Southern Rhodesia:

> My hut was an ordinary native hut, wattle and daub with a thatched roof, about twelve feet in diameter and no door or window. I had no furniture, I had my tin office box which I used as a table and sat on a native stool to eat my meals. My bed consisted of two logs laid on the floor with a stack of grass between them over which I had my groundsheet and then over that one of my most useful purchases before I left England – a rolled-up valise affair of green canvas which is one of the things that the white ants don't eat, and one's blankets and pillow fitted inside it. I was quite content with this.

Philip Allison's first house was rather closer to the standard Public Works Department bungalow:

> My first station was at Onitsha on the Niger, where I lived in a very attractive situation in a house with a splendid view down the river. My predecessor who had built this house had spent nearly all the money in erecting a solid concrete platform and hadn't got any money left to do anything except put up an erection of bamboo poles and palm-leaf mats to keep the rain out. It was a very attractive place, but terribly bad for mosquitoes and you used to sit up there at nights and hear the drumming coming over the water from Asaba and hear the frogs croaking down in the Niger swamps. And then the mosquitoes would drive you under the mosquito net. So I used to sit up in bed with the bush lamp outside trying to read *War and Peace* – or perhaps I'd go down to the club and drink beer instead.

It was said that wherever there were two Englishmen there was a club – and certainly, by the twenties, the old Scotch clubs where local Europeans gathered at a mutually convenient spot for drinks in the evening were being replaced by club-houses; sometimes station clubs that were little more than a meeting place with a bar and a snooker or billiards table, sometimes gymkhana clubs where officials and non-officials alike could gather in the late afternoon to play scratch polo or a game of tennis or squash – or even a round of golf on a rough course that had browns instead of greens. It was always considered vital for one's health to keep fit and active, however unsuitable the season might be for violent exercise, and sport in one form or another provided the means, coming naturally to young men who had been brought up to regard sporting activity as an integral part of their social life. What was just as important from a health point of view was that the club provided the opportunity to drink in company – because 'drink was unquestionably a major factor in life in the tropics; it was a very pleasant thing after the heat and burden of the day to rest and to have a long whisky and this was a very common form of relaxation. Drinks parties were almost invariably sitting-down drinks parties, but there was not the same feeling of having one glass after another in quick succession as you do at drinks parties in this country.'

The verandah of the station club also provided a natural setting for the exchange of shop and station news. At Lira in Northern Uganda, where Dick Stone was posted in 1938, it was where 'all the local officials – the DC and the ADCs, the District Medical Officer, the OC Police, the Agricultural Officer, the vet, the Community Development Officer and so on – gathered on Saturday mornings. We'd drink large quantities of beer and gin, and discuss absolutely informally the problems of the district – to see if we could work out a district solution to the current problems of the day. Perhaps these gatherings at the Lira Club were the forerunners to the more formal – and very successful – District Teams which were started a few years later by the Governor, Sir Andrew Cohen.'

But for the newcomer probably the club's greatest value was that it filled the 'rather difficult hour in the tropics between six thirty and seven thirty', a melancholy hour which could be passed in congenial company before he returned through the darkness to his own bungalow to have a bath and a late supper before retiring to bed. 'A house was something which one didn't ever occupy in the latter part of the day if one could avoid it,' recalls Nigel Cooke, 'because it was in the nature of a storage heater. In my early years I never slept inside the house, I always slept not only outside but wherever possible away from it, so much so that on one occasion when my steward brought my morning tea, I heard him tut-tutting with amazement because he could see the pad marks of a leopard that had gone round my bed more than once during the night.'

For a young man living on his own, servants played an extremely important role. They came to him by various means. Some were selected more or less at random from servants' parades held at headquarters, some were inherited from previous incumbents, some were brought in by other servants, some simply turned up on the verandah with their 'books', the testimonials or 'chits' from previous employers that always featured prominently in expatriate folklore. Here would be found such old colonial chestnuts as 'I'm sure this boy will do you as well as he has done me', and 'This cook leaves me on account of illness – mine, not his'. Mocked though they were by employers, these 'books' were held in high regard by their servants, as Bob MacDonald found when he went down with a severe bout of malaria: 'I was very down and moaning a bit too much and I said to my steward boy, "Harrison, I go die." Harrison said, "Give me book first." In other words, give me my testimonial before you go.'

In the bachelor household the steward or house-boy was always the key figure, since the running of the household was left very largely in his hands. To assist him he had his assistant or 'small boy' – 'a youth who had to do all the menial jobs, like de-ticking the dog and cleaning the lamps and when you went from one house to another after dark he'd go in front of you waving his paraffin lamp to drive off the snakes and scorpions from the pathway'. There was always a cook and possibly his assistant or *mtoto*, and for those in horse country – as in Northern Nigeria – there would also be a groom and perhaps a water-boy. Very close and long-lasting relationships often developed between master and servant. Hugh Moresby-White's steward, Nduku – 'a most faithful servant' – came to him as a 'small boy' in 1916 and remained with him until he retired in 1944. Donald Dunnet's steward, Alexander, began in the same way: 'Living in grass huts as I did there was an awful lot of dust about and I used to get asthma and it was pretty painful. Well, he used to sleep at the end of my bed and make me hot tea during the night and look after me and really, apart from my wife, there's nobody who has done more for me in my life than this boy.'

Like most bachelors, Chris Farmer was content to leave the details of the catering up to his cook: 'It was up to him to produce my breakfast and my lunch and my evening meal as best he could and, after all, he knew better than I did what was available in the market. What I used to do was give him *chop* money, market money, enough for a week at a time and the meals would turn up. Sometimes he would use his imagination, sometimes he wouldn't. Occasionally I would get to the stage where if I saw another egg custard or another so-called pancake I would feel like screaming.'

Beyond a few unpretentious pieces of regulation furniture provided by the PWD, the bush bungalow offered few comforts. Lighting was mostly by Tilley or pressure lamp and paraffin refrigerators did not become widely available until well into the 1930s. 'You cannot imagine how primitive many aspects of life were,' asserts Clifford Ruston. Latrines – almost always cleaned out by prisoners from the local jail – often consisted of no more than 'a small mud hut with an open door, two upright pieces of wood with a horizontal piece and a small earthenware bowl and a pile of sand. And it was by no means unusual in the early morning to find a villager on his way to the well greeting one and wishing one a happy day's work!' In the bush supplies were always hard to come by. 'You might go into an up-country store and find nothing but cabin biscuits and bully beef and sardines,' recalls Edwin Everett, 'so you had to live off the country with its rather stringy chickens, the odd goat and anything more was considered a bonus. There was always rice, of course, and if you were really in the bush there would be a lot of bush fowl, partridge-like creatures infesting the African farms, and if you were lucky there would be anything from antelope to fish. But in some stations you just had to exist on tins and, therefore, if you were going to visit somebody either as a friend or on inspection, you'd take something with you. Even if it was only half a pound of

Civilian outfit as worn by officials and 'non-officials'.
Walters and Co., 1925.

butter, it would be gratefully received.' For those stationed near the coast or a railway line, newly imported supplies, known as steamer *chop* in West Africa, provided a welcome break in an otherwise monotonous diet.

In West Africa – where all food was referred to as *chop*, with canapés before dinner being referred to as small *chop* or (for some unaccountable reason) as *gadgets* – local foodstuffs and recipes made up only a small part of the European diet. The closest that most whites came to following native custom was in the eating of the two great West African dishes of groundnut stew and palm-oil *chop*. Much of Philip Allison's first tour was spent in country where 'palm oil was king' – along the creeks of the Niger river:

> The whole life of the creeks was palm oil and the food was palm oil and there was this glorified native dish called palm-oil *chop* which used to be served in European households on Sunday lunch-time, which was chicken stewed in palm oil, which had a golden-red colour – a bit like engine oil but more golden – and then served with peppers and rice and all sorts of side dishes which the cooks called *gadgets*, consisting of fried onions, raw onions, chopped-up coconut, fried bananas, plain bananas, stink fish – which were fried shrimps – and all this was consumed with a lot of beer and gin to follow and lunch-time was liable to go on to four or five in the evening.

Other than at weekends, heavy eating – and drinking – was strictly confined to the evenings: 'You weren't allowed to drink until the sun went down and then you had your sundowners,' recalls Gerald Reece, who went out to his first district at Kakamega in Western Kenya in 1925. 'It was almost ridiculous the way they waited until the sun disappeared completely before they would touch a drink. I remember when I called one day on an old settler and he asked me to have a drink and apologized very politely – "If you don't mind, we'll have to wait, because the sun isn't yet down" – and kept popping out to make sure that the sun wasn't down. And after doing that three or four times he came back and said, "We're all right now, the sun has gone down and we can have a whisky." '

5

Keepers of the King's Peace

I suppose the District Commissioner under the old system of colonial administration exercised more authority than anybody exercises in any job I can think of. We really were – as the Africans always called us – 'father and mother of the people', we really were.

Every province of every colonial territory was divided into districts, each administered by its own District Commissioner supported by a number of assistants and providing a system of dual government that underpinned to a greater or lesser degree various forms of Native Authority, ranging from the Northern Nigerian emirates where the power vested in the local rulers was paramount, to 'pagan' regions where local chiefs acted in subordinate roles and acknowledged the absolute authority of the DC. But whether his authority rested purely on his powers of persuasion or on a government mandate to rule, the District Commissioner was still the key figure in his district – a figure from whom every new cadet could learn.

In the event this was not always the case. Cadets very often found themselves thrown in at the deep end, where they learnt their jobs as they went along and as much by trial and error as anything else. But much depended on the personality of the DC himself. 'There were plenty of District Commissioners who would no doubt have been excellent guides in those early days, but I didn't have one of them,' remembers Charles Meek:

> I had a chap called Cecil Stiebel, an eccentric figure who in his early days had, I believe, been a chucker-out for Mrs Merrick, who was a notable figure in the night-club world of London in the early twenties. He was certainly built that way; a great, strong, robust, broad chap. I got on with him very well indeed but instruction came there none. In Tanganyika we were great proponents of the system of indirect rule which had been introduced by Cameron, and I had that explained to me in very short order. We had *liwalis* as headmen in charge of the areas within the district and I remember Cecil Stiebel on, I suppose, my first day in the office sitting me down and pulling a sheet of paper towards himself and saying, 'This is the way it works, Meek, you have a *liwali* here and a *liwali* there and a *liwali* in the other place' – and he drew a series of small circles around the perimeter of the paper. Then he said, 'Here in the middle you've got me,' and he drew a large circle in the middle of the paper and said, 'You see, that's the way it works.' And so it did.

Pat Mullins's first mentor on the Gold Coast was rather more helpful – but he, too, had his eccentricities:

> My first District Commissioner was Harry MacGiffin and he was a real education in himself. He was a lively Northern Irishman, then in his late thirties, and an unconventional character, a man with a great sense of humour and a very good idea of what was important in district administration and what wasn't, and among the things that were not important in district administration in Harry's eyes was anything at all to do with paperwork. When he got paper from any source he chucked it in the 'Out' tray. Harry would specialize in not answering letters and regional headquarters in Tamale would

bombard him with requests for replies and Harry was quite unmoved. I can remember him ringing up his neighbouring DC at Wa and talking on this very bad telephone line and saying, 'Gerard, I've had a seventh reminder from Tamale. I don't think you've ever had a seventh reminder, 'ave you?' On the other hand, outside the office he knew everything that was going on in the district and he could travel for miles and suddenly stop a man and ask him why he was carrying a stick, because he'd never seen him carrying a stick before and had he got an evil thought in his head? And this intimate knowledge of the African people in the area was incredible and I quite rapidly realized that I'd got to try and acquire a similar understanding of everything that went on in the locality.

In Ashanti, the central territory of the Gold Coast, George Sinclair and a fellow cadet considered themselves fortunate to be sharing an office with a District Commissioner who always set aside an hour at the start of a working day in which to receive petitions and complaints:

To us some of these complaints seemed trivial and some important, while others seemed to show that the complainant was a bit bonkers. But when the hour for complaints was over he turned to us and said, 'I know you two lads have been watching me very carefully. You may well have thought that I was wasting a whole hour going into these small matters when there was so much more important and urgent work to be done. But, I tell you, when the day comes when you no longer make time to listen to individual complaints, I hope you'll have the guts to go back to your bungalow, have a pint of cold beer, then write to your Chief Commissioner saying you feel you must resign as you are no longer fit to remain a member of the Colonial Service.'

Not only did we watch him at work, but occasionally, when he went out for meetings in various parts of the district, we went with him. But not for long, because he began to hand us the simpler tasks. We were sent off to inspect villages, to look at the water supplies and health arrangements. We were made responsible for the upkeep of a network of district roads; we had to look after the bridges and order cement and timber for their repair, and we had to pay the road-gangs and see that they were working properly and had the tools they needed. We were also sent out into villages to look into disputes that had been brought into the district office for our DC, and he would say, 'You had better go out and spend a few days in this area and listen to what people have to say and then come back and tell me what you think we should do about it.'

In addition to his European colleagues the cadet could also learn from the subordinate staff in the district or divisional headquarters. In East Africa these offices were known as *boma* and were almost invariably staffed by Goans from India:

There were Goan court clerks, there were Goan cashiers, and Goan district clerks. They were the most wonderful people; kind, generous and helpful and so superbly honest that one could scarcely believe that they came from the East. It has often been said that the Goans had a great graft and their graft was honesty; it was a matter upon which you simply could not fault them. Every young District Officer learnt one side of his trade from the Goans. He learnt how the government accounting system worked, how cash should be handled and how the records should be kept and he learnt about the office filing system.

As well as clerks there were also the African district messengers, 'the backbone of the administration', who acted not only as messengers but also as orderlies and bodyguards, 'a very fine body of hand-picked men, all from that district and varying tribes, but all completely loyal. They were a smart body under a head messenger and second messenger, neatly uniformed, unarmed and utterly reliable. Many a young

District Officer learnt more from his district messenger than he ever did from the Colonial Service Course at Oxford.'

But it was no use having help on hand if one was unable to communicate, and here the Colonial Service Course began to assume real practical value – as James Robertson found in the Sudan: 'In my first district office there was only one English-speaking clerk and one could hardly take him away from his essential duties to interpret what the local people were saying to you and the result was that one staggered along trying to remember what one had learnt in London and trying to understand what the people were saying and I found this very difficult to begin with. But after I'd been there for a few weeks I was trekking round the villages with nobody speaking English at all and I soon learnt enough to get on – because it was the only way one could live.' Another way to learn the language was to employ somebody to teach you, in Muslim areas a *mallam* or learned man. This was how Clifford Ruston learnt Hausa: 'The usual process was to read from Frank Edgar's *Litafi na Tatsuniyoyi na Hausa*, which was a collection of folk-stories going deep into Hausa history, and he would then correct my pronunciation and elucidate any unfamiliar words. And one would consult Dr Walter Miller's *Hausa Grammar*. This and Robinson's *Grammar* were the only text-books on the language.'

An additional spur to the learning of local languages was the requirement that all newly appointed officers should pass a government lower standard language examination within a certain period – since success brought with it a cash increment and failure could result in dismissal from the service. The same regulation applied to officers of the King's African Rifles who were examined in Ki-Swahili – the lingua franca of East Africa – six months after they joined and risked being sent home as unfit for service if they failed to satisfy their examiners. This strong emphasis on language requirements was of obvious practical value, but it could never overcome a widespread, and obviously unsatisfactory, reliance on interpreters. Such dependence on a third party was almost inevitable, partly because of the nature of the service, where transfers from one district to another took place every few years. After studying Hausa and Twi in the Gold Coast, Patrick Mullins was transferred to Nyasaland:

> I went to the Northern Province where the local language was Chitumbuka, so I got a sufficient standard to pass my lower standard government examination in Chitumbuka after about a year out there, and within two hours of doing so I was transferred to the Southern Province where no Chitumbuka was spoken at all and I was told that I had to take a second government language. So eventually I learnt Chinyanja and passed the language examination in that and shortly after doing that I went to Fort Johnston District where the Bishop of Nyasaland, an old-style missionary and a charming man, was insistent that I learn the local language which was Chiyao, and at that point I rebelled.

The need to have enough fluency in the local native tongue to be able to by-pass the official court interpreter was particularly acute when it came to taking on the role of district magistrate, the most obvious of the powers assumed by the cadet administrator. Authority to act came in the form of a judicial warrant handed over in a ceremony 'as solemn as a civil marriage service'. Hugh Moresby-White received his warrant from the Chief Justice of Nigeria: 'I remember he said to me, "Now one piece of advice I would like to give you. When you give your judgments never give your reasons. Your judgments will probably be right, but your reasons will probably be wrong."' Armed with this piece of advice and with a second class magistrate's powers to impose fines up to £10 and fifteen days imprisonment he duly went to court, which – as was very often the case – happened also to be his office: 'The accused in a criminal case would be brought in by a native policeman. I would be told what the offence was and the witnesses would be brought in one by one and I would listen to what they said and then pronounce a verdict.'

As his experience grew, so – provided he passed the appropriate law exams – did the magistrate's powers, although not all District Officers were required to act as magistrates, especially in those areas where an efficient native court system, such as that operated by the Muslim *alkalis* of Northern Nigeria, was already operating. But when they did hear court cases magistrates were bound to follow the standard codes of criminal procedure, which – even if 'you had virtually to be judge and prosecutor and defence as well' – went some way towards ensuring that the accused got a fair trial. 'There was no prosecution in my time,' recalls James Robertson.

> There were no lawyers and the magistrate just had to try the best he could to get the truth and find the man guilty or not guilty. But there were none of the niceties of legal procedure which one would have expected in a court, and the language was of course the language of the people. The accused occasionally interrupted and was brought to order by the sentry and then when you'd heard all the evidence and asked questions you asked the accused if he had any questions to ask the witness and usually he said the witness was a liar. Then you heard what the accused had to say, you asked if the accused had any witnesses and if he had then you summoned his witnesses and at the end you wrote out what you thought the whole thing was about and the reasons for your finding. You found him guilty or not guilty and then the accused was allowed to produce evidence of character, which you took, and then you had to consider what sentence you were going to give. It was mandatory that if you found the chap guilty of murder then you sentenced him to death.

There were some who regarded the British legal system as both out of place and unsuited to the African temperament. On the East Coast, magistrates were plagued by an excessive fondness for *fitina*, the making of false accusations, which was said to be 'almost as widespread and universal as football pools in England'. There was, too, an irritatingly disrespectful attitude towards the majesty of the law, as illustrated by the well-known – and probably apocryphal – story of the Nigerian who went to a European friend and in the course of conversation revealed that he had a court case coming up before a British judge: 'He told his European friend that he was going to send the judge a gift of six cattle to incline his heart in the right direction. The European said, "For goodness' sake, don't do that. The judges are incorruptible. If you send the cattle you'll lose the case. Go to court, tell your story truthfully and you'll get the right verdict." Six months later the two met again and the European said, "Well, Adu, how did you get on?" And the other man said, "I sent the cattle, but I sent them in the name of my adversary." '

Nepotism, bribery and corruption could be found in one form or another at most levels of society. The official attitude was unbending. If government officers were offered a gift which they were bound to accept in order not to give offence, then they were required to return a gift of equal value. 'When you arrived at a station on tour it was the custom for a gift, a bowl of eggs or perhaps some meat, to be presented to you,' explains Edwin Everett. 'Now quite often this gift was the delegated duty of some minor official and he wasn't paid for it, so it was customary to pay the local market value, not directly to the donor but to give it to him as a gift. And if you were touring rapidly such gifts could mount up. I mean, at the end of a week, what do you do with five bowls of eggs?' Faced with this situation, officers took the precaution of taking with them supplies of tobacco or objects suitable for presentation as gifts. But sometimes there were situations when gifts were not returned. While issuing motor-vehicle licences Edwin Everett once noticed a £5 note at his elbow. 'It hadn't been there before so I said, "What's this? Take it away." And the trader in the office said, "Oh, that's not mine." So I said, "Well, it's not mine, take it away." – "No, sir, no, sir, it's not mine. It must be yours." So I produced a box of matches and burnt it and for some reason I never found money lying about the table after that.'

Perhaps the most serious problem for law officers was the sheer volume of paperwork involved, which made it almost impossible to comply with the requirements of court procedure. Faced with such a situation, and a mounting backlog of court cases waiting to be heard, some officers tended to take a rather more flexible approach when it came to handling the less serious cases, as Kenneth Smith explains:

Now take a very typical offence – a fight which might very well involve ten to fifteen witnesses. One knew that at the end of the matter it was going to be either an acquittal or a fine of the order of five to ten shillings. But to have copied down the evidence of the witnesses would have virtually meant that your list was brought to a stop. So I discovered for myself a routine whereby I listened in silence to the entire case and if I found the accused guilty I firmly entered on the appropriate form a plea of guilty. If, on the contrary, the accused was acquitted, I simply wrote on the form 'Charge withdrawn by leave of court', which meant, in fact, that there was no written record of these tediously prolonged debates.

Closely associated with the work in court were certain unpleasant duties associated with the execution of justice. District magistrates were required to witness punishments ordered by the court, perhaps in the form of six to twelve strokes of a cane, but very occasionally the hanging of a condemned man, which had to be witnessed in the company of a medical officer 'to see that all was tidy'. It was a judicial chore that most District Officers dreaded and went to great lengths to avoid if they possibly could. Very frequently Assistant District Officers were appointed superintendents of the local jail and in this capacity they would be required to see the prisoners turned out to work in gangs every morning and sent off to do various jobs about the station – cutting grass, digging ditches and, of course, emptying out the thunderboxes from the bungalows. Sometimes this workforce could be put to other use. Dick Stone used his prisoners at Lira to build a squash court: 'This, I think, was the first squash court to be built in an up-country station in Uganda and I remember that I built this squash court, including a little gallery, with the invaluable aid of a Sikh mason imprisoned for some heinous offence, for the princely sum of £26.'

Being a district magistrate was only a part of the work of the District Officer. Coming to Tanganyika as a 'brand new cadet', Frank Loyd was surprised by the immense variety of the work that had to be done each day:

> There were petty court cases, there were matters affecting the African courts, there were things connected with the prison. But there was also road-building, tree-planting, the collection of tax, the exemption of tax from some of the older people or the sick; there were things like trading licences, matters connected with hygiene and extensions of the health service which the medical officer couldn't possibly cope with himself. All this together with endless miscellaneous things connected with schools, churches, and various individual problems that people themselves would bring forward because they rightly regarded the DO as the person to whom to bring their complaints and their problems.

Among the miscellaneous tasks that Frank Loyd found himself performing within his first few months were blowing up rocks in order to build a road through a rocky escarpment, laying on emergency relief following a flood – and dealing with a plague of locusts:

> Locusts are a peculiar and rather frightening phenomenon of Africa, and when one thinks of them one still hears that awful

noise that they make as millions of jaws chump away at the maize or whatever they are consuming at the time. When you are driving a car through locusts it is even more terrifying because you've got the windscreen wipers on and the locusts are so thick that the wipers won't really work; the whole windscreen becomes a sort of squishy mass and you can't really see anything through it. The stories about the trains getting stopped are perfectly true. Of course, we principally had to try to cope with them in the desert where the locusts themselves bred; the trick was to try and prevent them from ever getting away from the desert and becoming the destructive hordes that they did when they went further south.

Another essential part of a District Officer's job was dealing with petitioners. For Bill Stubbs the question of 'being available and willing to lend an ear' was the most important part of his duties: 'It was a nuisance sometimes when people turned up with a long story when one had other things to do, but, although sometimes one could do nothing to help, the fact that one was there and able to listen was a comfort to the person – and taught one a great deal about the African mind and how it worked and what was going on around one.' In regions where intrigue and corruption were endemic the need to be seen to be impartial was all-important. James Robertson's first District Commissioner at Rufa'a, Sam Budget, did this by having his petitioners in all at once:

They all sat in a mass on the office floor and he'd pick them out one by one. His idea was that in this way they would see what was being done and what was being said and there would be no accusations that the DC had favoured this man or that man – and also it meant that the *murasala*, the messenger at the door, wouldn't get any perk for letting so and so in before so and so. It had its advantages in that way, but it meant a frightful clutter of people, most of them spitting on the floor and coughing.

The new District Officer soon learnt that he was never really off-duty. 'We were the most accessible administrators you can imagine,' declares Charles Meek. 'We were always open at any time for even the most humble villager to come in and see us and talk to us and put his troubles before us. Not only in the office; one's home was an almost equally open forum and many a time in the evening when I had been wanting to sit down and have a quiet drink or was playing a game of bridge with friends, I was interrupted by somebody who felt he wasn't getting a square deal or somebody who had a nasty emergency on his hands – asking for help and getting it.'

Not only did the law have to be upheld, public order had also to be maintained. Two potential sources of trouble in many otherwise peaceful and law-abiding districts were disputes between villages or neighbouring clans over land and quarrels over the succession to chieftainships. In Ashanti George Sinclair observed that, 'You remained a chief only while you carried the consent of the people, otherwise they would find good cause for "de-stooling you", as it was known, and finding a successor – and of course this led to deep quarrels between those who were in favour of a chief in power and those who wanted to replace him.' Occasionally these quarrels led to serious outbreaks of violence:

I can remember in my first few months being sent out with one other administrative officer, with one tour's experience greater than mine, to quite a serious riot. Two sides of one big division in Ashanti, called Igissu, quarrelled over the de-stoolment or retention of a chief, with the queen-mother being on one side with her faction and the chief and his supporters on the other and eventually with the help of the police and very little violence we got the two sides separated. We took three lorry-loads of cudgels, cutlasses and flintlock guns from the contestants. I remember keeping the two sides apart by sitting in the middle of the village street and having our lunch of two pineapples and one pint of beer – until one side yelled some very far-reaching insults at the other side and we found that the two groups were mixed up completely and we were in the middle. It took about an hour of talking, with the use of the few police we had, to get them separated again but that 'riot' went on roughly for three days.

Sometimes the disturbance of the peace was directed against the authorities, but it was seldom of a violent nature. There was the famous story of the Lieutenant Governor of the Southern Province of Nigeria in the 1920s, who was in the secretariat offices one day when a large crowd assembled outside: 'He went out and raised his hand and silence followed and he said, "What do you want?" They said, "Please, sir, we are a riot." He said, "I'm too busy for you to riot today, you must come back tomorrow." They said, "Very well, sir," and they went away quietly. The next morning they turned up and the Lieutenant-Governor sat down in a chair in the secretariat compound surrounded by a few officials and they told him what they objected to and he spoke to them and they went away quietly.'

But very occasionally there was rioting on a far more serious scale – as occurred in 1936 in Zanzibar in a dispute over the grading of copra. William Addis was with the Sultan of Zanzibar when news of the disturbance reached him:

I was in the palace when a man came rushing up very excitedly saying in Swahili to the Sultan, 'They are killing Europeans.' So I jumped up and said to the Sultan, 'I think I'd better go and see what's happening.' I ran back out and jumped into my car, which was a Morris Minor tourer with an open top, and as I was leaving my Provincial Commissioner arrived and said, 'Will you take me down, too?' So we both went down, neither of us armed, not even a walking stick in our hands, and as we turned the corner by the Customs we saw a large crowd of Arabs with their long double-bladed swords, all shouting. I spotted the Assistant District Commissioner and the Commis-

sioner of Police being attacked so I drove into the crowd and
told these two to jump into my car. Then one of the Arabs
came up to me with a long curved knife and looked as if he was
going to plunge it into my heart. He stared at me and plunged
it into my tyres instead; he must have recognized me, that's the
only explanation I have. So I had to back out with flat tyres
with all the crowd rushing after us. The Commissioner of
Police was badly wounded in the head and the District
Commissioner had lost all his fingers. He was a keen cricketer
and he said, 'Oh, well, I'll never be able to bowl again.' In fact,
he had thirty-six wounds on him and he died that night from
loss of blood and shock.

Leaving his wounded passengers at the hospital, Addis
collected some armed police and returned to the Customs
sheds. After opening fire and dispersing the mob he found the
body of another colleague, 'a very pleasant Indian police
inspector, with his stomach absolutely ripped open by those
horrible curved knives they had and I remember so well how I
went home covered with blood – because I'd carried this man
– and said to my wife, "It's all right. I'm still alive." She said,
"What do you mean?" "Didn't you hear the rioting?" "No."
And she was only about a mile away.'

As a symbol of government and the keeper of the King's
peace, the District Officer was a natural object of respect and
flattery, addressed as *bwana makuba* (great master) or *zaki* (lion),
or in such terms as 'you are our father and our mother – please
help me in this . . .' As well as the flattery there was the
awareness that he exercised a quite remarkable degree of
authority – which he took for granted: 'One assumed a
superiority and capacities which make one surprised now that
we didn't have a bit more humility. But it induced a sense of
responsibility which tended to bring the best out of one rather
than the worst.' Any feeling of superiority was also tempered
by the knowledge that the effectiveness of indirect rule depended on the co-operation and consent of others – and by the

realization that power itself was something of an illusion, as Patrick Mullins acknowledges:

> The simple people in the villages looked upon you too much as a 'fixer'. 'The Government is our father and mother,' they used to say, but the father and mother couldn't do very much for them. And so one felt a bit of a humbug, in a way. Sometimes one had local successes and one traced a missing relative in South Africa or one found that it was possible to send medicine to a particular village for distribution by the Native Authority, tiny little local successes like this. But most of the time they were asking you to do things for them and it was terribly difficult either to say no or say yes with a conviction that you were able to do much to assist. The whole country of Nyasaland was running on a few million pounds a year. And when you got down to the district level this was split up into penny packets. If one got a hut established as a native dispensary this was quite a major success. If one got a small wooden bridge erected over a river so that the population didn't have to go around a long distance to cross that river you'd achieved a considerable success. There was also a sharp contrast between one's own living standards and those of the people you were living with and so any feelings of pride were pretty shallow and short-lived.

And yet, for all that, it was still, as Charles Meek observes:

> . . . the most exciting job you could do if you liked to wield authority as many of us do – not in a bullying way, not in a rough way, but always close to the people, always week to week, day to day with pressing decisions to make, not terribly difficult decisions because I think the simpler the society the more clear-cut the decisions are, but always with the weight of responsibility on you, from, in my case, the age of twenty. It didn't matter how old you were. I suppose I gained a bit by being lucky enough to start going bald at a very early age, and

that was good and helpful. But the authority was always there. It was something you couldn't divest yourself of; all the weight of so many decisions, so many worries of other people, everything from their domestic worries – stolen goats, the row with the wife – to the question of who inherited the chieftainship, sorting out the border raids between the Barabaig and the Wanyaturu, stopping the Masai lifting cattle from the Sukuma. All this was the web and woof of our daily life.

However rich the experience, there were always drawbacks, particularly for inexperienced young men on their first or second tours in the outlying bush-stations: 'The worst part of it was isolation and loneliness. It affected some people more than others. Some people used to spend their free time hunting, others reading, others painting their houses. Others occasionally, but not often, took to drink. But then if they took to drink they were obviously no good at their job – and if they took to African women that also would have an adverse effect on their position and their duty. But some people obviously had reserves and it didn't seem to affect them.' Probably the least affected of the different expatriate groups in Africa were the missionaries. Their isolation was often as severe and their tours certainly lasted far longer than those of their contemporaries in other walks of life – but their commitment to a cause was undoubtedly greater. 'I never really felt lonely in any circumstance,' asserts Bob MacDonald, 'it was all too exciting. After all, I was right in the midst of first-century Christianity with all the problems that faced the early Christians. The people were by no means saints but their faith was tremendous and inspiring, and one just couldn't go wrong or feel lonely or neglected in a situation like that.'

There were, of course, others besides missionaries for whom loneliness and isolation held no terrors. Bill Stubbs also found that it was impossible to be lonely, particularly 'if one had an observant eye and enjoyed what one saw. But it was a great help if one could take a dog and I have always had a dog, generally small ones. They were very good company although of course in tsetse fly country you couldn't take a dog. I also almost lost one dog which was taken by a leopard but fortunately escaped owing to a thick collar which protected its throat – although it was badly mauled.' Stuck for six months in a remote Rhodesian post, 'in complete solitude' except for his servant Willie and the local Africans, Bill Stubbs went down with his first bout of malaria:

> When I was unable to shoot game because of my fever, Willie killed off the last remaining fowls and for a short time we had no meat and we had to resort, on his advice, to his lining up a line of maize, and I would shoot from my bed into the horde of doves that came down for it and these were made into soup. Luckily for me a fellow-policeman who was on patrol in the area dropped in to see me and he had quinine and dosed me heavily with it and I was carried out from that place in a scotch-cart, which is a two-wheeled cart pulled by oxen, a journey of about a hundred and fifty miles. By the time I got to the police post I was quite fit again, but it was an unpleasant experience.

Loneliness sometimes proved to be fatal. There was the District Officer in Northern Rhodesia, remembered by Robin Short, who cut his throat 'because he couldn't stand it any longer – luckily he recovered. Then there was an earlier DC on a particularly hot and unpleasant station who shot himself – and then there was a legendary DO who had been posted many years before at one of the more remote stations of the territory by himself who had gone mad and who was still in a lunatic asylum in Cape Town. But I emphasize that these were the exceptions.' Nevertheless, Robin Short himself on his first tour in Northern Rhodesia became unaccustomed to speaking his own language – except sometimes to himself: 'I remember on my first local leave arriving at a big European store in Chingola where I wanted some chocolate very badly – but I was unaccustomed to speaking in English. There was a great pile of chocolate behind this girl at her counter, and I approached her slowly and carefully and I chose my words with care. I said to her, "Do-you-have-any-chocolate?" and the unfortunate girl was extremely worried and said, "Oh, oh yes, yes, yes! Take as much as you like!" ' Placed in a similarly isolated position up the Nile, where the steamers came only once a month, James Robertson was regularly supplied with a month's copies of *The Times* newspaper: 'I never made up my mind what was the right thing to do about this. Did I start methodically from the beginning and wade through day by day until the next lot came? I think I usually cheated and looked at the last one or two first and then waded casually through the rest.'

Two images of the District Officer in the bush.
From the Walters Catalogue, 1936.

There was only one sure way for the first-tour man to overcome loneliness, and that was to keep busy. In time, as

Nigel Cooke's first Resident in Bornu Province taught him, the newcomer developed a natural resistance: 'You are lonely for the first three months. For the second three months you don't care and for the third three months if you hear there's a European in the neighbourhood you take off in the opposite direction.' As a prediction it was not so very far removed from Nigel Cooke's own experience:

> For some time within the first three months that I was in Maiduguri I was heartily wishing that I'd never come. This might have been due to my being very young, to my suffering very greatly from the assaults of the mosquitoes and from the fact that I didn't feel terribly in rapport with the other members of the station, who were all that bit older than myself. I think it was probably at Christmas 1938 that I began to feel that I liked the place. Every administrative officer in the whole province came into headquarters and every European in the station was invited to dinner by the Resident, and one did feel that one belonged to something worthwhile. That year the Alou river came down and cut off the station from the native town, creating a broad expanse of water, and I was rowing about in it in a canoe with another ADO when he said, 'You know, Africa is an old bitch; it gets you in the end.'

6

Going to Bush

Most of us had seen a film called Sanders of the River, *based on Edgar Wallace's book, before we went out and suddenly here was this thing, it was real; one was walking behind a long line of porters and the sun got up in the morning glinting on the spears of the porters – and it was just like the films.*

From the administrator's point of view the essence of rule was that it should be based on trust. Any suggestion of ruling by force was out of the question: the means to do so were not there. In the district in Nyasaland where Noel Harvey began his service in the early 1950s there were, in addition to the District Commissioner and his two assistants, one European policeman, one African sub-inspector, two sergeants and a dozen police – and an African population of a hundred thousand. His situation was entirely typical. In the absence of military support 'what power, what influence, what effectiveness you had was entirely through trust and trust came through knowledge, because Africans will not trust somebody they don't know. So it was very important that they knew you and you knew them.'

This knowledge was acquired by touring through the district, a process that was known as a safari in east Africa, as *ulendo* in Central Africa and as 'going to bush' or 'going on trek' in West Africa. Whatever it was called, travelling about the district had a mystique about it that was to be found in every territory and 'the mystique was completely justified, because although everything might be fine around the *boma* or station, it was only by going from village to village, looking round the houses, looking at the people, talking to them, looking at their crops, taking their tax census, all the routine jobs, it was only by doing that that one could find out how they were thinking and feeling.'

Touring was always held in the highest regard by senior officers, who saw it as the most important single aspect of ordinary administration – 'returns were called for; how many days under canvas one had done in each quarter – and if one had not fulfilled a fair number there were questions asked.' This was an attitude that the younger men soon came to appreciate and to share. 'I was told by my bosses that one ought to spend half one's time at least in touring,' recalls James Robertson, 'and so I tried to do that; half the time in head-quarters and half the time going round one's district.' It didn't matter so much what you did on tour, Tony Kirk-Greene was told by his District Commissioner, so long as 'you were seen, you were accessible and – I remember his words – that it was a visit and not a visitation.'

There were few unmarried officers who did not find touring 'a very satisfying thing to do'. There was indeed the 'un-doubted element of escapism' as well as the fact that travel and bush allowances added considerably to one's income. But there was also a powerful sense of romance about it all – something that immediately conveyed itself to Tony Kirk-Greene as he began his first tour:

> Stepping out at the head of my line, with one policeman in front of me and a government messenger behind me and the Emir's representatives behind him, all in single line with a string of carriers. Early dawn had not yet broken at half past

five, I'd had a cup of coffee and I was thinking what a good advertisement it would be for Nescafé; twenty-six miles a day on a cup of coffee. The carriers were piping and neither then nor now would I be ashamed of the real romance, the *Sanders of the River* touch. And I was always conscious of this, even in later years, riding out in the early morning with the heat of the day to come. There was something very exciting indeed about it.

Others besides officials found opportunities and reasons for touring. Military officers in the King's African Rifles and West Africa Frontier Force went out on recruiting tours to the tribal areas from which they drew their recruits, traders went from one prospective supplier or customer to another – and, of course, the missionaries went proselytizing. But for Bob MacDonald it was not the image of Sanders that came to mind: 'It was the old idea of a great long line like David Livingstone's, a whole line of head porters with boxes on their heads. The villagers in each of the villages we passed through supplied the carriers for this and when the first lot reached the second village they'd dump everything in the market place and go right back without a word. We would rest a while, the chiefs would tell small boys to go and bring us coconuts from the trees and we would drink the coconut water and meantime there would be a great row while they would be marshalling the new carriers to take us on.' But not all his touring was done in this classical manner: 'I've started off in a truck with a motor-bike and a push bike in the back, going as far as I could with the truck, leaving it and my driver there and going on the motor-bike, with a boy following me on the push bike. When the motor-bike was no longer possible the push bike could still go a bit, and might get me to the side of the river where a canoe would be ready to take me on the rest of the way. That was the kind of progress we made on quite a number of our visits, both on church work and on school work.'

In West Africa, where the routine of 'going to bush' was well established, it was customary to travel from one rest-house to another, rarely camping under canvas – except where the rest-houses, often no more than simple circular huts with thatched roofs, were found to be bat- or bug-infested. In Northern Nigeria the travelling was mostly done on horseback, as Chris Farmer describes:

> What would usually happen is that one would go out on a lorry with one's servants and the Emir's representative and a government messenger to the first take-off point of your tour, and you'd stay there in the rest-house for a night or two and then on the appointed day a gang of carriers would arrive whom you would pay, probably sixpence a day, or a shilling or something of that sort. They would turn up at about five o'clock in the morning and take away everything except the camp bed you were still sleeping on. Everything had been packed by your steward the night before, so they would put it on their heads and go off to the next rest-house. At about six I would get up, get dressed in my riding breeches, mount the horse and go off with my messenger and the Emir's representative to the next port of call. My 'small boy', as we called the second steward, would then pack up the camp bed and my razor and so forth and put them on the head of the last carrier. By the time I arrived at the other end the district head or the village head would be waiting to greet one and escort one into the rest-house. Shortly after your arrival you would find, as if by magic, that breakfast had appeared and somehow hot water had been boiled so that you could get into your tin bath and have a bath. Then after breakfast you would get on with the day's work.

Further south, in true bush country, Philip Allison's work as a Forest Officer took him, sometimes for weeks or even months on end, into the heart of the dense tropical rain forests:

> Wonderful country, with attractive rocky rivers running through it and from time to time rocky hills sticking up out

of the forests, *inselbergs*, with rounded bare rocks sticking above the two hundred foot tops of the trees. It was a wonderful thing to climb out of the damp forests on to the top of one of these sunwarmed granite domes and look down on the tops of the trees you'd been sweating along underneath for so long. There was a different smell and the senses all seemed to open up and you'd look down on the tops of the trees and you'd see one of those big hornbills – one damn near as big as a goose – suddenly plunging up out of the tops of the trees like a diving bird, a cormorant rising from the sea, flying along and then plunging back, lost to sight under the canopy again.

Sometimes there were encounters with other creatures of the forest. Robert MacDonald remembers how he and a missionary doctor once went out 'on a glorious early morning, the sun shining behind us and the long line of carriers with their loads on their heads going through a sunken path down the hill from a village. The doctor and I were at the end of the line when a leopard sprang from one side of the sunken road right into the air and was spreadeagled across the heads of the carriers – and in the sun he looked as if he were made of gold. There was very little excitement aside from a gasp of astonishment. They never even let down a load, they just kept on going.' In some regions there were lesser creatures to be avoided, such as the tsetse fly in the bush country through which Bill Stubbs toured, whose bite could sometimes prove fatal:

There was an instruction that if you went into tsetse country you had to cover your arms and legs, otherwise you couldn't obtain compensation if you died of it, but it was impossible because I've even been bitten through the canvas of a deckchair. What you did was to have somebody with a fly switch brushing them off you as they settled, and you hoped for the best. They don't bite you when you're exposed to the sun, but they'll go to any point of you that is shaded, just up your sleeve or up the back of your shorts or, particularly, the shaded area at the back of one's neck.

For Bill Stubbs and for many others who went on *ulendo* or safari in Central and East Africa there was the added attraction of plentiful game: 'I was keen on big game hunting although I shot mainly for the pot rather than for the actual pleasure of shooting, but of course there was always more meat than one needed for oneself and in some cases for one's carriers, too, so you gave the headman a present of meat in which a good many people shared.'

An added pleasure for those who travelled in Central Africa was the reception given to the travelling District Officer as he neared his destination: 'The first thing you'd hear was the sound of clapping – and all the maidens of the village would come out, stripped to the waist and all they had on were a tiny little G-string in front and skirt behind, and all singing in beautiful harmony.' Where the women weren't singing they would be ululating, as Robin Short found in Northern Rhodesia:

Kaonde villages were quite small so you would have, say, ten or twelve women with their children coming out to see you, clapping their hands and ululating very loudly. But in the other districts you would have possibly two hundred women, quite a crowd, and they made a very loud noise indeed, and although it was great fun, after ten or twelve villages it did begin to wear one down just a little, particularly as the weather got hotter and hotter in the middle of the day. When one actually arrived at a village one was given a chair by the headman, who squatted on the ground or knelt, and clapped the traditional greeting, followed by his people. There was nothing servile in this. They were greeting in their particular fashion as they had always done and one replied by gently patting the place over one's heart with one's hand in acknowledgement and polite words of greeting were exchanged.

An equally stirring reception faced the District Officer as he approached a Hausa village in Northern Nigeria:

> It would be quite normal for the district head to come out with a posse of horsemen, ride up at a gallop to greet you, accompany you to your rest-house and then come in and sit with you and pass the time of day. You would refer to all the normal subjects like the state of the rains, or the state of the crops, or the health of the people and you would exchange such greetings in Hausa as *Sannu da ruwa*, which meant welcome with the rain. And he would probably say, *Ranka ya dade*, which means may your life be long, and he would almost certainly be in his best robes. After he had completed his formalities the district head would probably go back to the district headquarters and you would arrange to visit the courts or you might well visit the tax office.

In the Sudan officers would also be escorted in by the local sheikh and some of his followers, sometimes mounted on camels. They were always offered very sweet tea, and sometimes coffee as well. There were occasions, as James Robertson remembers, when the reception was truly biblical:

> Sometimes when you came to a village the sheikh would bring out a sheep and have its throat cut in front of you. Then the drill was that you had to step over this beast as it lay on the ground, to bring luck to show that you were happy with your reception at the village. At one place they even slaughtered camels and there were these great brutes sighing out their lives. Some of my colleagues used to eat a dish called *marara* which the sheikh would bring you when you arrived at his village. This consisted of raw liver and lights and always seemed to me a most disgusting thing. I would never eat it and when they complained about this I would say that I had a religious scruple about eating anything that was raw in the way of meat, and that seemed to go down well.

Much of the time of touring officers in the Sudan was taken up with the assessment and collection of taxes; herd tax, based on the number of animals owned by an individual, and produce tax based on the Islamic tithe system known as *ushur*. For the latter, rough assessments of the area under cultivation and the expected yield had to be made by pacing one's camel or one's horse. 'In this way one could very often make some rough estimate of the area. But the assessment of the yield was more difficult. I used to cut down a certain amount of the crop and have it beaten out and then multiply it so that you got some kind of rough estimate. I would then take the list and judge the whole of it by this one field.' The assessment of herd tax also presented considerable problems – particularly when the herds belonged to nomadic pastoralists. But where there were villages the assessment was relatively straightforward:

> . . . because the goats and sheep and cattle and camels and so forth and donkeys all came in in the evenings and were tethered in the village at night. I used to go out at about four o'clock in the morning with half a dozen police and surround the village and as the animals came out in the morning I collected them all together and then got the list from the sheikh of the village and crossed off 'Mahommed – three goats, two donkeys' – and so forth. At the end one still had a number of unclaimed animals and then one said to the sergeant or corporal, 'Now drag these off to the market and we'll sell them' – which meant that the owners came dashing out. Then you had to decide what to do. Did you fine all these people for not listing their livestock, or did you just put them in the list? I usually just put them in the list.

One of the principal duties of touring officers in Northern Rhodesia was the collection of taxes, a task that few officers enjoyed. 'I simply hated it,' declares William Addis, 'because it meant that all the young men had to walk five or six hundred miles up to the nearest copper town to get enough money to send home for the elders to pay their tax. And I knew that anyone who went up there with the slightest sign of leprosy would be turned back and would have to walk all the way back again, so anyone who had the slightest sign of it I'd sign off the tax register and say they were exempt.' Such direct handling of local affairs was far less typical of the African colonial territories as a whole than was the more delicate work of checking, scrutinizing and, if necessary, revising the work and decisions of the local Native Authority: 'Most of the hard work was done by the Africans themselves, who had a tribal structure of government with chiefs and headmen and courts and the whole paraphernalia of government, and the major part of one's job was to see that that functioned, as far as one could, fairly, efficiently and honestly. So the major part of one's job was really supervising them in the running of the show themselves.'

In Northern Nigeria this meant being accompanied on tour by the Emir's representative, who stood at the District Officer's elbow as he talked to the local Native Authority official. If a village headman complained, for example, that he had asked for a culvert to be built over a certain stream and nothing had been done about it, joint action could be taken:

> One could turn to the Emir's representative and say, 'You'll bring that one to the Emir's notice, won't you?' and he would say, 'Certainly, may your life be long.' At the same time you knew jolly well that if, at the end of one's tour one didn't also mention it to the provincial engineer and get him to give a prod to the Native Authority head of the Works Department, that culvert would never be built. So we would go through the motions of making it appear that it was the Native Authority that was getting it done. Nevertheless, something which had not been done for a long time would, with luck, actually get done.

The main bulwark of this system was the traditional African one of the local councils and the chiefs, many of whom were, according to Dick Stone, 'the salt of the earth, and marvellous administrators. Whenever we were on a tour of inspection of a chief's area we had the chief with us to hear our words of criticism or praise. Many of them were astonishingly good, with a deep knowledge of all that went on in their area, and they laid the foundations of a first class administration within the district.' Since the effectiveness of the District Officer depended very largely on his power to influence and control the native administration, a good working relationship with the chiefs was essential. In the Kasempa District, where Robin Short began his administrative career, the senior chief was 'in his quiet way' a complete autocrat:

> Chief Kasempa's judicial powers of course were defined by the Government, but his unofficial powers I suspect were very much greater because his people stood in awe of him. Generally because he was paid a government subsidy he worked with the Government to develop the people as much and as well as he could, but he wasn't a stooge or a stool-pigeon or a paid government employee. He stood very much in an independent position and this was particularly apparent when there were discussions leading up to the Federation of Rhodesia, when Chief Kasempa along with the other chiefs in the territory didn't hesitate to voice the very strongest opposition to the Secretary of Native Affairs and Provisional Commissioner and anyone else who came within hearing distance.

Another important local personality with whom the District Officer did well to come to terms was the witch-doctor or medicine man – 'any administrator worth his salt knew how to work not against the witch-doctors but with them.' When Charles Meek became the District Commissioner of Mbulu he found one such witch-doctor, Nade Bea, to be

> . . . a much more important chap than any of the four chiefs that we had, important though they were. If one was wanting

to get some big improvement in coffee cultivation, for example, the great thing to do was to get Nade Bea on your side. He was a remarkable old man; he was very, very old by the time that I'm talking about, white-bearded and I'm not exaggerating when I say that when he was born no European had been seen in the area and he'd never seen a wheel turn – yet he lived to be a wise adviser to a whole succession of administrative officers like myself and we rewarded him with some sights which must have been pretty astounding to him, flying him by aeroplane down to Dar es Salaam, having him shown over a big ocean-going liner and so on. He was a great ally to have going for one.

Witchcraft and the 'swirling tide of superstition which infests the African mind' were factors that administrators had always to take into account in their dealings with local people. There were still many areas of African life where the '*ju-ju* mentality' prevailed and governed every aspect of daily life: 'If a man drowned in a river it was said that a spirit held him under the water. If a tree fell on a man and killed him it was said that a spirit pushed the tree. Everything was governed by these beliefs. You found it everywhere. They had their *ju-jus* outside their houses, perhaps a pot on top of a hut to keep the evil spirits away. It might be a flute made from a human bone, it might be a wooden carving of a leopard, it might be the skull of an animal.' Such beliefs were understandable in earlier times, when men knew nothing. 'They only knew that when they went into the dark, dark forest they died of yellow fever and blackwater. What was it? They didn't know. It was the terror that seized them by night. It was evil spirits. Their men went out to sea, that cruel sea with those terrible waves coming in – and they were seized by the bar *ju-ju* and were drowned.' What was less appreciated was that these fears and taboos should linger on and be just as prevalent in the station and the *boma* as deep in the bush. A messenger would be unable to begin a journey after finding a broken twig lying on the path.

Seeing a bicycle pump lying around, a clerk would become convinced that a spell had been put on him and disappear. 'They'd suddenly get it into their heads that there was a *ju-ju*. A man would not talk for three days and on the fourth day he'd say, "Well, I'm sorry but my *ju-ju* wouldn't let me talk."' In Martin Lindsay's Nigeria Regiment, where they were very keen on sports, it was considered to be good for morale for the two battalions to race against each other:

> I remember we had a chap, a sergeant, who was leading by a hundred yards at the end of a three mile race when he suddenly stopped running and sat down. He said, 'My *ju-ju* won't let me finish.' And the Commandant said, 'We simply cannot have these *ju-jus* or else when we go to battle they'll all say "my *ju-ju* won't let me go."' So he was flogged and got twelve strokes with the *bulala*, a rawhide whip.

But there were times when the official did well to acknowledge the force of local beliefs. On safari in his early days in Tanganyika, Darrell Bates was once confronted by a group of women who asked for his help:

> For years there had been the custom that just before the rains they took chickens or pots of beer to a rain-maker in order to pray for rain, but people from the mission and people who'd been to schools said this was old-fashioned stuff and so this year they didn't do it and they got no rain and they were going to starve if they didn't get any rain. They went to the rain-maker but he said, 'You scorned me and I won't help you.' So they turned to me and said, 'We've come to you, will you help us?' It turned out that the rain-maker lived a longish way away, so I had to set off early in the morning and I walked nearly all day in the hills until at last in the evening I came to the place where he lived, which was a little hut on the edge of the forest. I found him there and I said I'd come to ask his help because the women of the valley had asked me to help them.

At first he said, 'Why should I help them? They've rejected me.' But I said, 'Well, the children will go hungry and old people will suffer so I ask you not to help them, perhaps, but to help me.' And in the end he said, 'Well, I will pray for rain.' And I spent a whole day up there, a fascinating day talking to him. I found that like a doctor in England he had a certain amount of patter and a certain technique to impress the patients but that the elements of his craft were very simple: a basic knowledge of insects and birds and a belief in prayer. I hadn't brought anything with me when I went to see him but I noticed he was wearing a very old blanket so when I got back I sent him a new blanket, and three or four days later I was sitting in my house reading at night when I suddenly heard the rain start.

Touring officers were almost invariably well received wherever they went – even if 'it was never easy to gauge the reaction of the village African to what one was doing.' In Nyasaland Pat Mullins found the most common attitude to be one of passive acceptance:

It was a tradition of the country that they were hospitable to visitors and this went for the white *bwana* as much as it did for anyone else. Much of what the DC was always on about cannot have been particularly welcome to them, particularly the enforcement of agricultural rules or the collection of taxes, and I think behind it all most of the village Africans rather wanted to be left alone and not bothered on these subjects. But there was no active resentment; I think this was mostly town-bred. The villagers were polite and attentive and one always felt a little that they weren't too sorry when you went away again.

The usual way for the District Officer to meet the villagers was at a gathering, known in East Africa as a *baraza*, 'which took the form of a local meeting – both to explain government orders and policy and to hear complaints,' explains Dick Stone. 'So you'd have all the chiefs sitting with you at the high table, so to speak, while the people would be squatting on the ground below you – perhaps three or four hundred people and even sometimes, I remember, as many as nine hundred. And this was really the greatest entertainment to them; they loved their *baraza*. They saw the DO or DC on safari and they brought out their complaints and very frequently, because these people have a great sense of humour, they'd try to pull your leg and they'd say something outrageous and this was their fun in life. If they succeeded in making the DC turn a little pink in the face or stutter with rage then this was their day and they all roared with laughter. But of course the DC was also able to pull their legs a bit, and so we carried on these proceedings with the greatest of friendship and enjoyment.'

After the meetings and at the end of the day's work there would be 'the other half of the day's romance and pleasure', as Tony Kirk-Greene saw it:

> This would come from going for a walk at between six and sunset, probably through a village and probably followed by a horde of children. You'd stop and talk to people and some-body might want to show you something; perhaps it was where there had been some guinea-fowl he'd spotted the day before, perhaps a snake that would live in a certain place, or a crocodile, or just showing you his farm. I always used to try and time my tour so that I was out the last ten days of the month, so that you got the moon rising and would be able to have your supper sitting outside, with no light on but with ample illumination from the moon.

When he toured Bill Stubbs often used to take a tribal story-teller along with him: 'In the evenings after all the work was done he would entertain the carriers, and usually the hero of the stories was *Wa Kalulu*, Mr Hare, very amusing but gen-erally pretty ribald variations on the Brer Rabbit theme.

Chandler Harris, of course, got all that stuff from Africa.' Sometimes the days would end more dramatically: 'Quite often in the evening of the second day the local people would put on a dance in one's honour, attended by several hundred young men and girls dancing away to their drums. And they often asked us to come and join them, which we did – somewhat inexpertly but very much to their amusement.'

This was an experience shared by many officers on tour. George Sinclair recalls how:

> When the drummers were inspired the call of their rhythm was irresistible and the whole village – men, women and children – were drawn into a swirling mass of dancers. We used also to listen through many nights to the Ashanti folk-stories, called *ananse* or 'spider' stories, interspersed with songs which often took the form of lampoons of some government measure or of a government servant. Occasionally, before one knew much of the language, one would find everyone roaring with laughter and then suddenly one realized it was a representation of one's own arrival in the village a day or two before.

Music and song, in one form or another, accompanied the touring officer through much of his travels. If he was touring on foot there would be songs and choruses passing up and down the line of carriers, and if he went by canoe there would be the work songs of the boatmen. Philip Allison recalls particularly 'a canoe song that a gang of canoe men used to sing taking us across the river from the forestry station to the station of the timber men. The leader sang, "You tiger, you!" and then the pullers all joined in, "You tiger, you!" – tiger was pidgin English for a leopard. Then there was another song where the chorus went, "Elder Dempster! Elder Dempster!"'

As the District Officer gained in knowledge and experience, moving from one district to another or even from one province to another, so he came to make comparisons: 'Every District Officer had his favourite tribe, that was natural. Different people got on with different tribes.' Fortunately, such tribal favouritism tended to keep pace with transfers, so that most District Officers professed to find the tribe with whom they were most closely associated to be the one whose virtues exceeded all others. For Robin Short it was the Lunda from Northern Rhodesia's extreme north-west corner who were the 'outstanding' tribe: 'They were intensely superstitious, intensely conservative, intensely secretive and spirit-ridden, but at the same time they had many attractive qualities and they produced men who by a combination of brains and character surprised one when one was in Africa at that particular time. They were courteous, well mannered, very ceremonious to their chiefs, polite and pleasant people – and they were willing to learn and willing to listen.'

For some it was the martial qualities of the tribe that were particularly attractive. This was a characteristic of the Nandis of which Dick Symes-Thompson was acutely aware:

> They were a very fine warrior people who had fought successfully against the British when we first came to Kenya, and they had dominated the surrounding tribes with their force of arms. Although they were a law-abiding people – many of them had joined the police and the army – towards the end they began to get a bit disturbed and worried about the changes that were coming and I had one rather serious piece of trouble because they sounded their war horns, which meant that every Nandi of fighting age had to drop whatever he was doing and seize his spear and his weapons and rally to the horn. On this occasion the war horn sounded and ten thousand or more fighting men marched into the neighbouring district sounding their horns and shouting and causing a good deal of terror and alarm and it was my job to try and stop them and bring them back.

In West Africa the very much larger tribal association of the Ashantis had a similarly warlike reputation. For David Allen they also had 'special qualities that set them apart. They had certainly proved themselves in wartime as being the bravest and the toughest people whom we had to deal with in coming to the Gold Coast. I'm inclined to think too that they were in some ways the nicest people in the Gold Coast, a very friendly lot indeed and very easy to get on with, and although they were volatile and could change fairly quickly they always quickly came back again to this wonderful, easy, friendly, happy people.'

Sometimes it was a certain fellow-feeling that drew the District Commissioner towards a certain tribe, as Dick Stone explains: 'Over the years the British and the Acholi got on extraordinarily well together. I think they had rather the same sense of fun, the same sense of humour; they were fond of games, fond of hunting, and we seemed to see eye to eye very well indeed. Life was rewarding with them and most of us British expatriate officers felt that we had some sort of vocation for working with these people.'

In some instances it was the very intractability of the people that provided the satisfaction. Few tribes were more difficult by reputation than the Kikuyu – with whom Frank Loyd worked for many years: 'Although as people they weren't so attractive or so easy-going and easy to get on with, nevertheless, in a different way it was much more rewarding to work with them because you did sometimes achieve results. It was much more wearing, much more difficult to do, took an immense amount of time and a great deal of patience. They were totally different in every respect to their pleasanter, quieter, more happy-go-lucky brothers in other parts of the country, but they did achieve many more results and the proof is that they are now running the country.'

Just about midway, geographically speaking, between the Acholi and the Kikuyu were the Kipsigis, who spoke what Richard Turnbull considered to be 'the most melodious, mellifluous language' he'd ever heard in Africa. 'They are a stock people – brilliant herders of cattle and devoted to them –

and, of course, stock-thieving was their métier. It was their way of improving their herds and passing the time.' This stock-thieving reached such enormous proportions in the 1930s that on one occasion the Acting Governor of Kenya came up to hold a special *baraza*, where he told them that they were ruining the economy of the country and disgracing their names: 'The leader of the Kipsigis listened to what he said very carefully and then came forward and said they recognized the error of their ways; that owing to what he'd said this blinding light had flashed upon them and from that day forward they would steal no stock and become model citizens. The Governor was really extremely pleased. He said nothing but you could see him smiling to himself and reflecting upon what a word or two from the great would do. That night the Kipsigis came into the station and stole the entire government herd.'

This close identification with a particular people and a particular area only reached its peak after several tours as an Assistant District Commissioner, when the District Officer was finally given his own district. The officer who trekked extensively got to know his district and its inhabitants so intimately that he inevitably came to identify himself with it, until 'he regarded himself as a native of the district and would stand up for his district against anybody – including the governor.' A remarkable insight into the rapport that could exist between tribesmen and their local District Officer was once afforded to Violet Bourdillon when she and her husband were touring Uganda in the early 1930s. With the District Commissioner they visited a remote district headquarters where there was only one District Officer and no other Europeans:

> In the evening they were going to do us a dance called the rag dance but they'd all got so frightfully drunk – celebrating our coming up there – that they couldn't do it. I remember the little DO, he was a wonderful man called Preston, who said, 'I'll go and get my men from jail.' So he trotted off and came

back with all these jail-birds who solemnly divested themselves of every stitch of clothing in the moonlight – I can see them now – and started to dance. And he danced with them in the middle; I could see his little bald head bobbing up and down. I'd never seen a sight like it, never! And when it was over I said to the DC, 'That was a wonderful show.' And he said, 'Yes, they absolutely adore him. They call him "Our little one" and the only punishment in the jail is that they are not allowed to dance with him on Saturday nights.'

Even though such terms as 'my people' and 'my district' were officially frowned upon, they were an honest indication of how many District Officers and Commissioners felt – especially in the inter-war years when the burden of government lay more heavily on one man's shoulders. Bill Stubbs's first district was one of the more remote districts of Northern Rhodesia, and it was not well provided with supporting services:

It was about six thousand square miles in area and there was no police, no postmaster, no veterinary service, agriculture, education or anything. You were a one-man band and it was a great life. Although the responsibilities were heavy, the pleasure one got out of it was intense; having power – in the best sense – to see that one's people lived as reasonable a life as one could get for them. It was the feeling more or less of ownership that gave one pleasure, like inheriting a large country estate, but there was more than that; one worried about one's people and one would defend them, although it was a constant battle with the Treasury to get enough money and we had desperately short supplies for improvements, development and things like that. But the loyalty of the DC to his people was something which I don't really think one can describe. You felt almost fatherly towards them and you got a lasting affection for a particular district even though that district might not have been regarded as a particularly pleasant one. I was lucky in that I had three full years at my favourite station, but it was a matter of bitter regret to me that I wasn't allowed to go back for a further three years and see schemes that I had started grow into fruition. I had many senior jobs after that but nothing could compare with the life of a DC on an out-station and the rapport that one had with the people from that district. I used to dream in the local native language, in fact I occasionally do today – and the whole life was something I can't imagine being equalled or certainly not excelled in any other walk of life. It was something really unique.

7

Men with Sand in Their Hair

The frontier had its own mystique and officers who served there were tremendously attached to it. There were huge distances, camels, nomadic peoples, great heat and a feeling of spaciousness which was absent from the rather more crowded and populous districts in the rest of the country, and it did seem to draw out the character of the people who served there.

While every district and every African province had its own remarkable qualities there was one particular group of territories that exercised a stronger hold over the British officers who served there than any other. Just as, in the days of the Raj, India's North-West Frontier maintained a strong hold over the lives and imaginations of its British frontiersmen, so the desert frontier regions of British Colonial Africa had their own unique and powerful character, drawing towards them a rather special kind of administrative and military officer. These desert lands were to be found on the fringes of Northern Nigeria and Northern Uganda, in British Somaliland and the Sudan, and along a wide belt of scrubland running across Northern Kenya.

It was this last area, Kenya's Northern Frontier District or the NFD, that had perhaps the fiercest reputation, although the term District was really rather a misnomer:

Kēnya, as we used to call it – it's now called Kĕnya – is divided
roughly into two halves, the southern half of which consists of
what we call the settled area where the white people had their
farms and the agricultural natives had plantations, and the
northern area which extends from Lake Rudolf to the Somali
border and consists of about a hundred thousand square miles
of acacia scrub, laval desert and patches of sand desert,
roughly twice the size of England. The administrators in
the southern half of Kenya thought we were mad to live there
at all, but our work was entirely different from theirs and it
called for certain qualities that produced what we thought was
a fine type of young officer.

Another desert territory that also had more than a touch of
glamour about it was the Sudan, with its vast scrub and
dunelands and its provinces each the size of France. Life here
and on the NFD was always tough and uncompromising –
'there was no softness about its nature' – and it developed
these same qualities in the people who lived there and the men
who went there. For Gerald Reece, who first came to the NFD
in 1925 and rose to become one of its almost legendary
'Officers-in-Charge', it was where 'real life' was to be found:
'Things were vivid and the people lived precarious lives and
things seemed to mean much more than they do when one
lives in a place which we regard as civilized. There was
something genuine and real about it all, something clean
and refreshing about the atmosphere, and those of us who'd
had hard lives in the war found a certain peace in the solitude
of the desert, where one is much closer to nature, getting away
from modern civilization and all the pettiness of modern
society.'

'Uncle' Reece's successor as Officer-in-Charge of the NFD
was another outstanding frontiersman, Richard Turnbull, for
whom the greatest attraction of working in these 'rugged and
desolate surroundings' was that 'one was dealing with not only
picked men in the service but with Africans who were

enormously handsome and brave and alert and quite different from the likeable but not outstanding people further south.' This attitude was shared by many in the Sudan Political Service in the lands to the north and in particular by Hugh Boustead, one of the last of a distinguished line of Englishmen drawn to the great deserts of Africa and Arabia. For him the desert country was a place that 'got a great hold on you. Always there was a feeling that you were free, untrammelled. You could go anywhere, there was nothing to stop you, and at the same time you were part of a moving family, so to speak, with the chaps who were with you.' For Hugh Boustead his 'moving family' was the Sudan Camel Corps, which he joined in 1924 – after adventurous careers in both the navy and the army – and which he eventually came to command.

Many of his early years with the Camel Corps were spent in remote corners of Kordofan Province, exercising a unique command:

> The men were enlisted by the company commander, they were trained by him and they were discharged by him. You had probably 180 men and 230 animals to look after, and you had chaps who were ready to go anywhere within four hours notice. The camels would be carrying both grain for eight days and water for four days for the man on them, so that you could go off into the blue regardless of wells. And it gave you a freedom of the uplands of the deserts which was tremendous. When you left, all the good ladies of the company would come and sort of wail – ululate – to their men, and you'd go off on marches of approximately six hundred to a thousand miles. And the chaps got thoroughly interested, they didn't worry because they had their lunch late or they hadn't had their breakfast. It wasn't a case of where's my effing breakfast? They were most pleasant chaps to command because they were always so ready for anything. They moved like trains on foot; they were very fit, tough lads and immensely cheerful, always ready for a laugh and there was damned little vice with them.

But we had to be very strict with them. If a chap going to sleep or through carelessness sat on the side of his saddle he'd give his camel a sore back and then he was not allowed to get on that camel again until it was healed. And he might have to run six hundred miles with the company. But there wasn't a court martial in the ten years I was there. It was unheard of. The worst thing you could do to a chap was discharge him – because it was just like a family.

Sometimes these camel treks were made at night 'under a tremendous forest of stars. Then you'd come in the early morning and you'd go down to a well-field to water the camels and there you'd find lines and lines of camels all waiting under the palm trees with the herdsmen all round them there and you'd have to wait your turn. Then the chaps would go down to the well and start pulling up the water with all the accompanying noises of the camels gurgling and complaining.' It was very much 'a man's life' and not one suited to marriage: 'You got swept away while you were home, then when you came back you'd say, "Christ almighty, I must be mad! What's a girl going to do out here? She won't be able to enjoy this; she'd get damned bored and tired. Am I going to chuck this and go and live in some suburb at home or in some stuffy room in a barracks, with a very limited urban sort of life around you?" I couldn't have stuck it.'

The same dedication and camaraderie was to be found in the NFD, where there was 'a tremendous *esprit de corps*. We used to have silver cufflinks made from Ethiopian coins rather like threepenny bits with Menelik II on one side, and when a person really stayed a reasonable time in the NFD as a District Commissioner and had done well we gave him these cufflinks, which was rather like getting his colours.' Part of this *esprit* expressed itself in a feeling that the NFD was quite separate from the rest of Kenya. Its officers talked of 'going down to Kenya', and 'we would always say in extenuation if a man made a complete nonsense of something, "Of course, he's a

Kenya man" – we didn't regard ourselves as part of Kenya.'
The attitude in the South was rather different:

> The North had a bad name in a certain sense; it was
> regarded by some people like joining the foreign legion
> and most officers couldn't or didn't want to stand more than
> eighteen months of it, after that they either got bored or
> their health gave way because of the heat, or they became
> nervous, so that was the average period during which an
> officer stayed in that territory. The result of course was that
> the Government in Nairobi used to have to send new
> officers fairly frequently, and very often there were not
> enough volunteers and so people used to be posted there
> and it was referred to sometimes as a sort of punishment
> station where you did your eighteen months and having got
> that over your name was erased from the list. Yes, we felt
> that in Nairobi they didn't understand.

The NFD's reputation as a punishment station was not
entirely without foundation, particularly in the days of the
one-man stations. It was to just such a station, just south of
Lake Rudolf at Kolosia, that Gerald Reece was posted in
1927:

> I took over from a man who was sleeping half in and half out of
> the door of his house. The houses in these places were just
> made of mud – you made them yourself out of local trees and
> an earth roof because there was no grass with which to thatch
> them – and this poor chap had a complete nervous breakdown
> and he found especially when it rained, which it very seldom
> did, but during the rainy season when the earth on the roof
> became heavier and the timber started to creak he was afraid
> of the house falling on him. On the other hand, he was afraid
> that if he slept outside – as a great many people did in Africa –
> his face would be eaten by hyenas. So he decided to put his
> bed half in and half out so that he could jump either way in an

emergency. The man before him had died of blackwater fever and the man before him had similarly had a nervous breakdown and had had to be brought south by an Indian sub-assistant surgeon. The District Commissioner before him had committed suicide, so it was a gloomy place to live in, and of course in those one-man stations there was not a European within a three-day march and no motor transport or wireless or anything like that.

It was not an area to which wives were made officially welcome, although married quarters were eventually provided in two or three of the more accessible stations. Even after the Second World War conditions remained spartan in the extreme. In 1946 when Dick Symes-Thompson was first posted to Isiolo – the 'gateway' to the NFD and its Provincial Headquarters – he was given a house about half a mile out in the bush:

This was a thatched *banda*-type house with white ants that had affected the roof and when one ate one's meals the earth tended to drop down from the ceiling into one's soup, so it was rather uncomfortable. The bath was made of cement which somebody had fashioned with his hands to make a sort of bath and the lavatory outside was a pit, a long drop with a thatched roof over it, and I was rather frightened of this because a previous occupant had told me that I had to be careful going out there because he had gone in once and found a spitting cobra sitting on the seat which had then spat at him, so when I arrived I was actually very careful.

Standing in for Gerald Reece as Officer-in-Charge at that time was another great and eccentric frontier character, Hugh Grant, 'a great bayonet fighter and trick pistol shot and a splendid figure', who was to die later when a Masai warrior threw a spear at him – 'he threw his spear right through him and ran round and picked it up and ran away, leaving Hugh Grant dead on the ground.' Invited to Hugh Grant's house for supper on his first evening at Isiolo, Dick Symes-Thompson was advised to think of the two great rival groups on that part of the frontier – the Somalis and the Boran – as highlanders: 'He said that they were very similar; they had these clannish attitudes and clan frictions but when the common enemy arose they clung together. If I realized they were highlanders I wouldn't go far wrong.' When the time came for Dick Symes-Thompson to return to his house that night he was handed a 'very obscure' Diets lamp and warned to beware of the snakes on the path: 'It took me a very long time to get back to the house. Later on I would have strolled down without a light with no worry at all because I realized the dangers were more imaginary than real – although lions did often kill between my house and the rest of the *boma*.'

When Richard Turnbull first came to the frontier in 1936 his chief mentor was Vincent Glenday, a 'most wonderful fellow' who 'didn't allow you to get above yourself. He would constantly say to us, "Look here, my friend" – when he said "my friend" you knew he wasn't very pleased with you – "Look here my friend, in this place I want public servants not public dictators." He wouldn't allow you to say "my district" or "my people". You could say "the district" or "the people I administer" but you had to be very careful in your choice of words. All the same he took enormous pleasure in being the master.' This was particularly sound advice in view of the strongly independent-minded nature of the local inhabitants, who regarded themselves as 'not exactly independent – but they just know they are better than you are'. This became immediately apparent to Richard Turnbull when he held his first *baraza*: 'There were only ten people present instead of the hundred one would have down-country and after I'd spoken a charming old man got up and said, "Oh Turnbull" – none of this *"bwana"* nonsense – "you have made four points, I will deal with them in reverse order." And he answered me in the most polished debating manner I'd ever heard.'

The two principal tribal groups on the NFD were the Somalis

in the east and the Galla to the west, neither of whom were the truly indigenous folk of the area:

> The Somalis were the head of a great migration which had started in the fifteenth century from right up in the Horn of Africa, and had reached Kenya or the country which later became Kenya about 1900, and the Galla had been the previous masters of the area and had been forced to the west by the Somalis and were now rather pathetically huddled in a corner of their former Kingdom. The Somalis were devout and very bigoted Muslims, and the Galla a most interesting people, pagans with a priest-king of the sort that one read of in *The Golden Bough*. The Somali was the better fighter and the dominant character in the area, but the Galla, having access to horses, could give a pretty good account of themselves. They also had a most revolting habit of castrating their enemies and handing the relics to their girlfriends who would proudly wear them round their necks.

As elsewhere in Africa, different District Officers tended to like one tribe more than another – and usually the Somali came low on the list of preferences: 'He's accused of being treacherous, avaricious, unreliable and untruthful – a generally cruel and unpleasant person.' But this was not how either Gerald Reece or Richard Turnbull saw the Somalis. The latter considered them to be 'an extraordinarily attractive people':

> They are always spoken of as being highly strung, and indeed they are, and they are spoken of as being unreliable and so they are, and they are spoken of as being constant in only one thing – their inconstancy. And all this is true. But of course they are loyal to themselves. The Somali knows what he wants and he's determined to get it and in the end he will get it. He will deploy any number of weapons and the biggest gun he has in his own armoury is that of flattery. He will come to you and

say, 'I want my son to sit outside your office,' And you will say, 'Oh, why?' He will say, 'Because my son is going to learn to ride a horse and we know that you are a great horseman and if only your shadow will fall across our son twice a day we know he will learn something.' Now I'm not a horseman, in fact I once disgraced myself by falling off a mule on the Moyale Parade Ground. So why should the Somali say this to me? Well, he has a reason. The son will sit there for a month and in the end you'll find he's got a prescriptive right to the spot – and after six months he will produce a lease signed by Queen Victoria saying the place where he is sitting is Somali property.

The Somalis were also capable of employing more direct means to get their way: 'I got to know the more sophisticated Somalis on the frontier – that is to say the Ishaak – in an extraordinary way. They had an agitation of some sort which I was compelled to oppose and they collected a considerable sum of money and gave it to a chap to shoot me. He didn't do it – he went off to Aden with the money – but it set up rather a bond between us, and years later I would discuss this ridiculous episode with those who'd contributed and we would laugh heartily about it – and have a good gossip.' Naturally, it was the Somalis on whom the attention of the administration was most directly focused:

Our main preoccupations in the NFD were to halt the great Somali drive to the south, then to prevent fighting between the Galla to the west and the encroaching Somalis to the east, for if a fracas started at one end of the line it would run like a powder trail to the other and the casualties could be serious. These conflicts could happen very easily and from the most trivial causes. A herd-boy might be insulted by another herd-boy. The herd-boy would send for his father, his father would send for his friends, and before long you might have a confrontation of half a dozen spearmen ready to fight for the particular prestige – and once the row had started it was difficult to stop it. An inter-tribal fracas amongst Somalis was fairly easily solved by calling a reconciliation ceremony where the injury suffered by either side was set off and the balance was paid in stock, either in camels or in sheep and goats or in cattle. But where you had the Galla and the Somalis each with a different tribal system and each with a different rota of penalties for everything from injured honour to the death of a man, it became much more difficult. But unless a proper peace meeting could be arranged and enforced there was a constant danger of the conflict spreading.

Maintaining law and order under these conditions was never easy. Nor did the specially adapted India Frontier Crimes Act always suit local conditions and local mores. Many officers felt, like Dick Symes-Thompson, that there was 'some conflict between the letter of the law and what one felt was justice – usually because the local custom of the tribe concerned regarded murder, perhaps, as something to be dealt with by means of compensation and the British law which insisted on bringing the offender to justice and hanging him seemed foreign to them. Nevertheless, it was very much part of our job to train people that the British law was a new law in the area which had to be obeyed and killing was wrong, and on the whole justice was done.'

Local attitudes towards British court proceedings were equally difficult to reconcile: 'The Somalis were expert at making you lose your temper. They had the most wonderful methods and unless you were very careful before long you were hopping up and down with rage. They would make you lose your temper by leaning back and laughing at you when you were speaking, meaning that what you were saying was so ridiculous, so beyond the credence of a reasonable man, that it was meant to be a joke. And if you could possibly never get cross you'd won an enormous victory.'

Hugh Boustead was faced with very similar problems when after ten years with the Camel Corps he transferred to become

District Commissioner of the Western District of Darfur, on the fringe of the North African Sahara: 'I introduced the talking stone, which was a stone that was kept in the court and the rule was that anybody who talked without that stone in his hand had to pay a five *piastre* fine. And that effectively stopped people because although they treated it as a great joke at first, when they found the five *piastres* were disappearing they treated it pretty seriously, and you stopped this great chatter going on which made the trying of cases almost impossible.' There was also the problem of getting hold of witnesses, which was solved by producing numbered metal tags: 'Anybody who received a bit of metal knew it was a sign that he was wanted in the court and if he didn't come in a few big court messengers would go out and bring him in and probably give him a couple on the bottom as they brought him in. So that was pretty effective.'

There was a strong feeling that imprisonment was not an appropriate form of punishment for a predominantly pastoral people. To Richard Turnbull 'there was something particularly horrible about locking a man up – and when you are dealing with people like the Boran and the Somalis who scarcely have been in a building all their lives, it's a terrible punishment to lock them up. I can remember old men coming into my office and sitting there sweating with fear in case the roof fell in upon them, because they'd never been in a building before.' It was an environment in which summary justice, in certain remote areas, made a great deal of sense – 'it wasn't a question of power. It wasn't a question of being a magistrate or anything else – you dealt with things on a human basis and you did what you thought was right. You couldn't consult anybody – they were too far off.' This applied particularly in the military detachments of the King's African Rifles that were stationed in the remote frontier outposts of the NFD, as Brian Montgomery explains:

Justice was rough – particularly in the context of military

discipline. The KAR *askari* were perfectly disciplined but the military law to which they were subject was not the Army Act of the British Army but the colonial forces version of it. Very seldom was there any recourse to a court martial for a serious offence because it was so difficult to create one in the sparse garrisons that were so prevalent. The necessary machinery for reference to a higher court was simply not there and the accused might have to relax in jail for two months or more before anything would happen. Therefore very severe powers were given to COs of detachments – but only for use in very exceptional cases. When a very serious case occurred, such as striking an NCO or rape, the CO would have to sentence the accused to summary physical punishment and he might award a sentence of, say, six lashes, in which case the accused would be paraded in front of the whole detachment, he would be stripped and laid down on the ground, where the sergeant would administer six lashes.

For these floggings a *kiboko* or rhinoceros-hide thong was used, with the detachment formed up on three sides of a square. But the occasion did not always go according to plan, as Anthony Lytton once witnessed on the frontier:

This particular malefactor was awarded twenty strokes with the *kiboko*. His trousers were taken down and the Sergeant-Major got ready to apply the blows – and the blows are always, by tradition, counted in Arabic. '*Wahid*' – down came the first blow. '*Thaneen*' down came the second. '*Thelata*' – as the third was coming down he picked up his bags and ran and the entire battalion broke ranks, yelling '*Kamáta, Kamáta* – Catch him, catch him.' The fellow outstripped the entire battalion but was collared round the legs by a corporal from the ration store who was a rugby footballer and caught him just as he was leaving the camp. And he was brought back and held down and the remaining eighteen were duly administered.

If justice was a little rough at times, so, too, was medical treatment if there was no trained medical practitioner on the spot. 'The first man I injected was rather sleepy with malaria,' recalls Anthony Lytton:

He was a Turkana. The dresser exposed his behind and prepared the spot with methylated spirits and so forth and gave me the syringe. After a great deal of palaver and preparation I plunged the needle into the hip of this victim, who at that moment instantly rose from the couch with the needle and syringe sticking out of his behind and hopped round the surgery until the needle fell out. He was pacified by the dresser and brought back and things were explained to him and he said to me that he had had a dream that he was being speared by his enemy. Another time, hearing of my exploits of sewing people up, a chief brought in his wife with her lips hanging in ribbons. 'How did that happen?' I asked. 'Oh, well,' she said, 'I had a fight with another lady. She bit me.' So I sewed her up and I think I only used one enormous stitch to pull the two bits of lip together and trimmed it up. I heard from the chief afterwards that he was very pleased with her appearance after my cosmetic surgery.

To assist him in the maintenance of law and order the frontier administrator had at his disposal a body of tribal police known as *dubas*:

Uncle Reece's policy was that the *dubas* should be selected from the most wealthy and distinguished families among the Somalis and the Boran so that we got the best young men in the country and they were proud and cheerful and very valuable allies if anything went wrong and in the frontier things *could* go wrong. They were very colourfully dressed in white *shukas* – which is a great white sheet – and a scarlet turban and they were really magnificent people. Their great strength was their local knowledge. When one went out on safari they were the ones who put up the tent, they were the ones who acted as interpreters, acted as messengers, acted as police, they protected the District Officer and they would be sent on various errands. For example, if there were an inter-tribal battle threatened among grazing tribes squabbling over a water-hole or over a bit of lush grazing, the *dubas* would be sent out to keep the peace.

In addition to the *dubas* there were also the *askari kanga*, government messengers who could on occasion show quite extraordinary courage and devotion to duty. While on service as a military administrator in the country south of Lake Rudolf, Anthony Lytton employed a Turkana messenger whose principal duty was to deliver the mail, including the weekly edition of *The Times* – through country which was infested with 'over-familiar' lions:

> He travelled by night because he could travel more easily in bare feet and more swiftly, and he slept, lying up some-where, during the day. He carried his two spears, as all Turkana do, and considered himself capable of dealing with any lion at any time, night or day, provided he had his spears. On one occasion he was late and explained that he had spent the night in a tree. He said, 'I don't get in a tree for a lion if I have my spears, but your newspapers are so heavy that I couldn't carry my spears and the bag, so I left my spears behind.' On a second occasion he arrived, as it were, too soon. He had travelled two nights and slept one day and he had done 124 miles. In this case he had driven a lion off its kill, put a haunch from the kill over his shoulder and left practically nothing for the lion. He was then followed during the night by the lion and arrived at break-neck speed with a damaged ankle.

Ultimately, the effectiveness of the administrator or the officer on attachment depended on his own skills and knowledge rather than on other people's. It took time to acquire such knowledge and, as always, the best way to gain it was through travelling on safari: 'The important thing was to go about simply, with animals and on foot so that you could see more of the people and talk to them and get to know them, not sticking to the roads but going to villages, however far away they were, and sitting down and talking to people. One used also to stop one's caravan whenever you met anybody, which of course is the way people in deserts do find out what's going on. It's not considered to be bad manners to stop a person and ask all about his business, it's the custom.'

Gerald Reece considered it part of his job to know everything that was going on in his district – and much of his information he gained from conversing with local people:

> For example, one day I was going along with my camel caravan and I saw a small boy herding goats and I stopped and asked him where his father was. And he said that his father had gone to the station with two cattle that he was going to sell, and so I said, 'Well, you and your father must be getting very rich because the prices now on cattle are high.' And the boy said, 'No they are not, we only get 20s. when we sell an ox.' Well now that enabled me to find out that the headman to whom the Government had entrusted the buying of these cattle was cheating, because the Government was paying 60s. for each ox. In that way – without intruding on the privacy of people or spying in a way which makes them mistrust you – you got to find out a great deal about what was going on in their lives.

It was equally important to know about the land, and about water because, as Richard Turnbull explains:

> We only had one running river in the whole hundred thousand square miles and two or possibly three seasonal rivers, which

ran in the rains and in which you would find water by digging in the dry weather. In addition there were half a dozen well systems. Then there were possibly a hundred or more seasonal waters, pools which were there by nature, or pools which had been made merely by animals rolling. Even the giraffe rolling in the sand will make a depression which, when rain falls, will take water and will feed a village's sheep and goats possibly for two or three days, which is of great importance when you are moving stock and you want a staging point. We had to know where all these waters were and we had to know, of course, which of them had filled up in the rains, because the people would all be on the permanent waters during the very dry weather, with their homestead stock, but when the rain fell there'd be a general dispersal to the small pools and we had to make certain that this dispersal did, in fact, take place. As the season advanced, so the small waters would all dry up and the people would move back on to the larger pans. Ultimately, as the dry weather became more intense the homestead stock would move off back to the permanent waters, there – if our policy and their practice had been properly followed – to find the grazing dry but still existent.

Just as important as water was vegetation, which became Richard Turnbull's special interest to the point where 'I became a fearful bore to all my young men' and eventually had a species of acacia bush named after him – 'a very squalid little shrub which grows in a howling desert'. This specialized knowledge had enormous practical advantages, because it enabled him to follow the movements of the herdsmen:

For instance, the in-calf camels would have to get salt browse immediately after the rains in order to ensure that their lactation took place properly. And as one knew the salt browse areas one knew where they were likely to be. I'm proud to say that after four or five years working on it, I got to the stage

where stock-owners found it very hard to diddle me over it.
They would say to me, 'We must go to such and such a place
and have grazing rights there,' and I would ask them why, and
they would say 'Because the *Bleforis fruticosa* is found there' –
and I would know jolly well that it wasn't!

It was mastery of such intimate details that made life on the
frontier such an 'extraordinarily rewarding job'. But at the
same time it was a 'damned hard, lonely life and we did have
difficulty in getting men to come back to it.' This was not
surprising when one considered the position of an officer in
such a place as Mandera, in the extreme north-east corner of
the territory. This was where Brian Montgomery spent the
most isolated six months of his life, speaking no other language
but Ki-Swahili:

Towards the end of my six months I can see that I was over-
conscious of small events which assumed too great a proportion in my daily thinking. For instance, we had to be very
careful over the accounting and although I had an African
clerk it was necessary to check very carefully that the amount
of sugar or flour consumed by the platoon detachment in one
week was not greater than the authorized ration. And if I
found that my computation of the amount varied from that of
the clerk by one ounce say, it tended to worry me greatly. And
more so when the camel mail arrived with a note from the
company detachment 250 miles away to say that there was a
quarter-ounce discrepancy in my accounting for sugar. This
seemed to matter a lot – which, of course, it didn't really – but
I'm sure it was caused by isolation. Curiously, however, on
safari that sense of isolation vanished and you couldn't have
been happier, even by yourself.

As in the Sudan, these long safaris were made with camels –
but baggage camels rather than riding camels – and they were
'always a delight' for officers on the frontier:

Starting off at four in the morning you went ahead of your safari, several miles ahead, of the sixty-five camels, and you were alone with your orderly, who carried your rifle, and you had probably a native tracker who knew the desert. You carried your own sporting rifle – I had a 375 Mannlicher – and of course you were out for the game shooting. You went ahead and then when it got to about eight o'clock or so it was time to go back and the tracker for some extraordinary reason was always able to find his way back to the camp, where you found the safari. We made camp, the camels were hobbled and turned into the bush to graze. It became very hot indeed about midday, nevertheless the cook produced a three-course lunch always which one was supposed to eat. I spent my time, because I was then a very zealous soldier, reading books for the Staff College examination. But I recall that very frequently I was asleep by the time lunch arrived. Then when the evening march was resumed at about four o'clock – and the sun always set at six o'clock in those latitudes – you went ahead again. But it was always absolute habit that when you came back to safari the *bwana*'s tent must be erected and his table and his bottle of whisky and his camp chair ready for him. Your bearer had your evening sundowner ready and you changed out of your bush shirt, put on clean clothes and relaxed in your chair with your evening drink until dinner was served by your bearer. The African cooks were extremely good; they had the facility of making virtually a whole meal out of one of those vulturine guinea-fowl which were so very good eating; they would make a soup out of it, followed by the most excellent cutlets and give you a savoury out of its liver, and they also were able to carve a complete bird in slices and put them together again so that you could take your slice without carving yourself. There was always a three-course meal and you then had your pipe or cigarette and your cold drink – because we used to carry the soda syphon in a *chagoul* or canvas bag which was carried on the camel

and by evaporation always remained cool. Then, as the
night went on you frequently heard the roar of a lion and
there was always the cough of a hyena and the squeal of the
jackal – all the sounds of the night in the African bush,
aided of course, by the romance of the amazing starlit sky.
You never slept in a tent but always in the open on your
camp bed – and always with your revolver under the pillow
in case of some alarm.

8

The DO's Wife and the Governor's Lady

She had been, I believe, a mannequin or something in Glasgow and she had married this young man and come out to this place with a house that was only fit for a cow to live in and no Europeans within seventy miles of them. And I said to her, 'My dear, you must have been terrified when you came here' – and she said, 'Coo, I was terrified.' 'I don't wonder,' I said. 'You must find it very strange.' And she looked at me and she said, 'I didn't mean that. I thought I shouldn't be adequate.' I said, 'Adequate? You are absolutely magnificent!'

There was a traditional condition known as feeling 'end of tourish', which was to be found in every territory quite irrespective of whether the tour lasted a year or three years. It was essentially a 'subjective condition – you thought the tour was coming to an end so you felt end of tourish', but it was still the case that towards the end of the tour most people felt run-down. This was caused not so much by sickness as by a combination of a hard climate, poor living conditions and, in particular, poor food. While such artificial stimulants as 'claret laced with soda-water to buck one up' might occasion-ally have been resorted to, the most effective remedy was an extended and generous leave: 'This was one of the glories of the service – for five months you were answerable to nobody.

If you were wise you went by boat and the Government was paying for the roof over your head and the food down your throat and you were buying cheap drinks on board. It was all tremendous fun and you had enough left over to give yourself a good quiet holiday at home and no doubt three or four splendid weeks on the Continent as well.'

It was on such leaves, of course, that most men found – and in due course married – their wives. But not, in most cases, for quite a few years: 'Marriage for administrative officers was not really entirely a matter of personal choice. One of the terms of our engagement was that for a number of years you could not, in fact, marry without the permission of the Governor or the Resident.' The absence of married quarters was not the only reason for this ban, although certainly in the early years between the wars this was a major factor. Personal finances had something to do with it since most administrators – other than the Sudan politicals – regarded themselves as badly paid. But there were other very sound reasons for requiring a junior administrative cadre to be made up entirely of bachelors: 'The first thing you had to do when you went out there was learn about the country and the people and the language, and learning about the country meant going out on tour in the bush for weeks on end in often pretty unsavoury and unpleasant conditions and there was a danger that if a youngster went out there with his wife he would say to his Resident, "Oh, I can't go to that place, it's dreadful. My wife will get ill" – and so wives were discouraged.' This ban ended with the Second World War, when 'people were coming out of the forces and joining the Colonial Service who had been married for several years and they just wouldn't stand that sort of treatment, and so although in theory they were still expected to ask permission for their wives to join them, permission was never withheld.'

The natural sequence of events that most young officers seemed to follow was to become engaged after a second or third tour and to marry on the next leave, a routine that often coincided with a promotion from Assistant District Commissioner to District Commissioner, so that officers returned to Africa not only with a bride but also to their first full district. Not surprisingly, quite a number married within the tribe, finding their wives from among the sisters of fellow-officers or – rather more typically – from among those families where the tradition of colonial service was well established and understood. Betty Moresby-White, who married in 1936, qualified on both counts; both her grandfathers had been in the Indian Civil Service and her brother was then an administrator in Southern Nigeria – although he had never met her husband, who was stationed in the North. Mavis Stone had the same Colonial Service background, which included in her case a childhood in Uganda up to the age of four, followed by that cruel separation of parents and children that was so much a part of family life in long-established colonial territories like India, but which was then far less common in Africa. For such children there may have been a 'certain glamour' in having parents in Africa, but there was always a heavy price to pay: 'The children grew up with little contact and tended not to know their parents very well, and you grew up never really belonging anywhere. I was divided between Africa and England. When in England you got very homesick for Africa and when in Africa you felt homesick for England.'

Fiancées and newly married wives with this kind of colonial background had a pretty shrewd idea of the kind of life they were letting themselves in for, but there were many others who did not. 'My husband thought I ought to see the horrors of living in West Africa,' recalls Dorothy Ruston, who got married in 1925, 'so he took me to see *White Cargo*, a play then running in London. Fortunately, life in Northern Nigeria wasn't really anything like *White Cargo*.' Even Betty Moresby-White was ill prepared: 'I used to hear stories from my brother about things but I really didn't take it in very much. I never even thought to ask what standard my husband had got to and I was quite amazed when I got a letter from him from Nigeria with "The Residency" written on it. But it wouldn't have mattered where he'd gone; I'd have been happy to go too.'

No doubt most young wives went out with very similar attitudes – coupled, perhaps, in the early days with an awareness that 'one was part of a world-wide British Empire and in some way privileged to be part of it.' This was certainly how Nancy Robertson felt when she first came out to the Sudan in 1926:

> We realized in a way that no modern girl can possibly do, that we were very privileged to be allowed to go there, because our fiancés or husbands were really the first generation after the military rule where women were completely forbidden except in Khartoum. And therefore we may have been a little bit scared but we realized that we had got to keep well and we had got to keep cheerful or else some superior government official would order us home. And therefore, I suppose we were conditioned to putting up with things that weren't very nice and enjoying things that were very nice very, very much more than more modern girls might feel called on to do – and, of course, with communications being so terrible, by the time the reply to your letter home to mother saying it was unbearable had arrived, four or five months had gone by and you were enjoying yourself.

Another quality that was still very much in evidence in the years immediately after the Great War was self-confidence – 'because in those days to be British was, in our minds anyway, to be absolutely top of the world'. Such self-confidence, together with the knowledge that 'you were much luckier than your contemporaries back home', made it easier for young innocents fresh from England to put up with the most extreme conditions. When Nancy Robertson first came to Geteina – a day and a night up-river from Khartoum – she found herself to be the only white woman in the area. This made her an immediate focus of interest, particularly among the local Sudanese women, 'very kind, very inquisitive people who knew nothing about the British. One of them said to me, "Why is it that the Turks" – and that is how they addressed us – "are always so rude, and why do they smell so bad?" And from then on I realized that to these people we smelt disgusting, because we were meat-eaters and we smelt like death. We might not like their rancid oil smell, but our smell was as bad for them as theirs was for us. And that, I think, was a great help during the next twenty or thirty years.' All the same, 'it was terribly lonely, far lonelier than anyone could understand who has never been in that situation.'

The house that she first lived in was 'exactly like a hen-house surrounded by wire-netting to keep the mosquitos and sand-flies out', which her husband had 'done his best to make as dreary as possible'. However, there were periwinkles in the garden and a few vegetables and 'just at the bottom of the garden there was the Nile – and even the name of the Nile in those days was romantic and exciting.' The same powerful aura of romance was found by Alys Reece when she first came to Marsabit, a volcanic outcrop in the heart of the Northern Frontier District of Kenya, in 1936:

> I was remembering the awful stories I'd been told by the people on the boat about how bleak and bare the whole region was and how crazy everybody went there. The journey seemed to me to be absolutely endless, along a rather vague road that had been a camel-track and had been kept up enough for motor traffic, and the further we went the bleaker it got and I began to believe all the tales I'd heard on the boat. And then we came to the foot of the mountains and that was so incredibly beautiful that all my exhaustion vanished. We came to a place where elephants had just very recently crossed the road, there were steaming heaps of elephant droppings bang in the middle of the road and this was the Africa I'd come to enjoy. The roads on the mountains went through some very beautiful windy ways, with thick forest coming right down to the road and across it in places. The harvest was nearly ripe at

the time, there was a wonderful moon and all the maize was shining in the moonlight. There were fires at each little hut as we got nearer the station, and we were passing through plantations, and it really looked too romantic and glamorous for words.

The local people were understandably curious about Gerald Reece's new bride: 'He was well known in that part of the world as a bachelor, he'd been there for years and everybody knew him. If we went out riding he'd stop and talk to anyone we met on the little hills and I can remember how embarrassing the conversation sometimes was. The usual greeting was "Is the maiden fat?" – which I didn't entirely like, but it really meant prosperous, I think – and how much had I cost, how many cows? And whatever Gerald answered it seemed to be questionable because they'd look me up and down and then they would ask me whether God had seen fit to send me an embryo yet.'

In the towns and larger stations new wives had easier and less dramatic introductions to colonial life. Communications improved rapidly during the inter-war years, with new ports and harbours being built along the coast and with better road and rail links to the interior – even, from 1930, an Imperial Airways service to both East and West Africa, with a flying boat that made the run from Poole Harbour to Lake Victoria in a series of short hops with frequent night stops. But deep in the bush and in the remote out-stations life changed very little. Certain corners and bush tracts remained permanently thirty years behind the times and never succeeded in catching up – so that the young woman who joined her husband in a bush-station in Northern Rhodesia in the 1950s could find herself in circumstances that, but for improved prophylactics and perhaps a fridge, were in no way radically different from the 'extremely primitive, very bush' life experienced by Dorothy Ruston in Nigeria twenty-five years earlier:

There was no refrigeration, no electricity, no means of keeping your food. Whatever you had was killed that morning and eaten either for lunch or dinner. The excitement was really the boat train once a fortnight when you got your papers and your mail and you could, with luck, buy fresh butter – which, of course, didn't keep for very long. You might get some sausages and real English meat and sometimes you could even buy English potatoes. Otherwise you had to make do with yam. The cooks were extremely poor because there'd been very few women to teach them so one did one's best but of course it wasn't easy. The cook used to go with his cook's mate to the market and he would buy eggs and chickens and anything that he thought might be reasonable to eat, but the only place where you could actually shop would be what was called the canteen, which was run by the European companies, and they would have all the tinned things, tinned butter, tinned cream, tinned milk – everything had to be in tins whatever it was, jam or flour or anything.

Her husband's staff was made up almost entirely of Ibos who spoke pidgin English: 'You might have a little Northerner as a tennis boy who would carry your racquet up to tennis and retrieve the balls, but usually they were Southerners. The pay doesn't sound very much – the cook would have about £3 a month, and steward boy £2, then your second steward or your gardener boy would probably get £1 a month and the little boy that you took up to tennis, he would get 5s. – but of course, they were provided with housing and everything was extremely cheap then.'

In East Africa the role of the canteen was filled by Indian stores known as *dukas*:

There was no place, however remote, where one wouldn't find a couple of small Indian shops. Their owners were bully-ragged by the local Africans but somehow they survived and made a jolly good living. They brought the produce that the

Africans brought in to them, and they sold the staples. They had in addition a most surprising range of tinned and bottled stuff. There were all those Eno's Fruit Salts in the old-fashioned wrapping with the children climbing the wall handing the grapes down to each other; there was Borwick's Baking Powder. There was Reckitts Blue – everything washed in Kenya in the early days always came out a bright blue. It was used in enormous quantities by every *dhobi* and every household had any number of Reckitts packets lying about. Ovaltine was another product which you'd find in almost every shop and when you were drinking camel's milk which had been held in a wooden container washed out with ashes it had a certain indefinable quality attached to it which didn't improve tea and didn't improve coffee, but Ovaltine went awfully well with it.

The young European housewife could always turn to more senior and experienced wives who 'took great delight in telling new wives out from England how to manage their houses and their servants', but there were always occasions when there was no one to turn to and where the housewife had to learn how to cope on her own. Here such stand-bys as *Chop and Small Chop: Practical Cookery for Nigeria* by Norah Laing and *The Kenya Settler's Cookery Book and Household Guide*, written by the ladies of St Andrew's Presbyterian Church, proved to be invaluable. The first was written by the wife of the Senior Resident of Zaria in the early 1920s and resolutely ignored all local produce ('groundnut oil is at the bottom of a great deal of indigestion'). It was superseded during the Second World War by the publication of *Living Off the Country*, which emphasized the value of such local produce as *paw-paw* leaves, for tenderizing the local *tukanda* (meat), or *yakua* leaves (roselle), to be used in place of vinegar or lemon juice when cooking greens or even as a cocktail. *The Kenya Settler's Cookery Book*, however, published in 1928, was very much in a class of its own. As well as giving all the standard recipes and a wide range of local recipes it also contained such wide-ranging household hints as how to make your own *mealie meal* soap, how to stiffen silks with gum arabic, and how to treat scaly legs in chickens or 'Nairobi eye', the bite of the Nairobi fly ('Milk, calamine lotion or soda bicarbonate applied at once will give relief'). Also included was a list of items to take on safari and, most useful of all, 'it had a vocabulary which enabled you to speak to Kikuyu-speaking gardeners and two lots of Swahili, one for good Swahili speakers, called Ki-Swahili and one known as Ki-settler, the language of the settler. All this was a tremendous help, particularly when you were new to it all and weren't too sure how to begin handling your boys.'

Learning to run an African household was fraught with all sorts of difficulties, the first of which was having to overcome a reluctance in some households to take orders from a woman, a situation that usually ended with the senior steward or house-boy quitting the household – but not always. When Betty Moresby-White came out to Nigeria the head boy, Nuku, had already been with her husband for nearly twenty years: 'Poor Nuku afterwards told me that he was sure he was going to be sacked as soon as I arrived in the country because, he said, every Missus sacked the boys when they first arrived. I told him that far from sacking him I was absolutely thankful for him, because he was so good.'

There were also language barriers to overcome and, where largely untrained servants were concerned, enormous areas of confusion that produced a rich crop of horror stories – the family silver cleaned with Vim, silk underclothes pounded on a stone, puddings decorated with toothpaste and plates dropped with the remark that 'its day had come'. Extraordinary disasters would occur during dinner parties and would be explained by the disarming apology that 'our heads went round'. 'I loved my black servants,' declares Violet Bourdillon, 'they were sweet and kind and lovely but they were dreadfully inefficient.' Even as a governor's lady she found it wise to check everything for herself, making sure that they hadn't

MISCELLANEOUS RECIPES AND HOUSE-HOLD HINTS.

Alkama Sponge Cake.

4 eggs, 3 ozs. castor sugar, 4 ozs. alkama, ¼ teaspoon baking powder, ½ teaspoon boiling water.

Beat the eggs and sugar together until very thick. Mix the baking powder with the alkama and fold lightly into the eggs and sugar. Add the *boiling* water slowly turn into a tin 5 inches in diameter. Bake for about 25 minutes in a moderate oven. When the cake is cold ice it with Zaria sugar icing.

Banana Chips.
(A substitute for potato chips with fried fish)

Peel green bananas and slice lengthways or crossways as desired. Sprinkle with pepper and salt and fry up quickly in fat or lard. Pile on a dish and serve immediately.

Bean Croquettes (Kwasi).

Soak native beans in cold water over night. In the morning remove from the water and grind finely in a food chopper or have a native woman grind them on her stone. Add enough water to make a stiff batter. Add *finely* chopped onion and salt to taste.

Drop by small spoonfuls into a saucepan which is about half full of hot fat, preferably groundnut oil. Care should be taken that the oil is not too highly seasoned with pepper or the bean cakes will be too 'hot' to eat. Remove from fat when they are brown. Serve hot with some sort of tart sauce, such as "Kukuki" jam.

Local recipes and local foodstuffs as found
in *Living off the Country*, published in Nigeria in 1942.

'turned the towels which the last gentleman cleaned his boots on inside out in order not to get new ones and so on'.

It was this inefficiency – from a Western point of view – that led to bullying and shouting, even if wives 'made a conscious effort not to behave like that'. There was what Beatrice Turnbull describes as

> . . . an almost continual battle between African servants and their employers. It wasn't from lack of sympathy on either side. The real problem was each side had entirely different basic assumptions. East Africans – the people I'm talking about – had what I must call a tribal way of thinking, and it was extremely painful for them to be made to see or to have it pointed out to them that anything they had done produced any particular result. If there was an unlucky outcome of anything it was an affair of God, or of the Government, or of the weather, or me, or an unnamed malevolent spirit – and the only possibility of getting any change in this attitude was to become a nagger and try to get a man to see by going back carefully, step by step, that what he had actually done had caused the chimney to go on fire, or the laundry to flood. And if in the end you could induce him to agree, 'yes, he had made the mistake' – from that moment on he was quite a different man.

Another source of irritation was the partiality for *ju-ju*, which usually found expression in an attempt by one servant to put a curse on another, although it could take the form of an 'affability potion', in which the opposite effect was desired. When she and her husband moved into Government House in Lagos in 1935 Violet Bourdillon inherited a cook named Mr William, who had been on the staff for twenty-five years: 'Well, we went on gaily for five years and then one day I went out into the compound and there was the most frightful screeching going on. It was a police raid and the next thing was I found that cook had been arrested;

they'd gone into his house and found ten affability potions, each labelled: "To make my master look on me with the eye of favour". In fact, for five years we'd been given affabilities in our soup and tea.'

Despite this constant battle between the two cultures, a very genuine bond of trust and affection between mistress and servants did exist in many households. The European house-wife got used to being addressed, for all her protests, as 'Ma' or 'Missus' – or as 'Memsahib' on the East African Coast – and she learnt to value her servants' honesty as far as money or valuables were concerned – while turning a blind eye to the customary perks in the way of tea and sugar and a little extra on the cook's shopping bill. She accepted responsibility for the upkeep and welfare of their families, in the African tradition, and she learnt not to visit the kitchen at the back or the staff quarters without plenty of warning. But two vital duties she always kept to herself; she supervised the washing of lettuce and other vegetables for salads in 'pot. permang.', as well as the boiling and filtering of water. A curious result of this constant boiling and filtering for Beatrice Turnbull was that when she returned to Britain she and her children were 'quite unable to drink a glass of water drawn from a tap. We could draw water from a tap into a jug and then pour it into a glass, but we could not drink water straight out of a tap.'

Even with a house full of servants it was not an easy life for a European woman and not all wives adapted themselves easily or even willingly to the colonial life. No doubt there were many housewives like Veronica Short who, when she first came to Northern Rhodesia, was fascinated by the life: 'I loved the Africans, they were all so friendly and it was a lovely climate, but after six months it began to pall and I'm afraid that for the rest of my ten and a half years out there I was just waiting for my husband to retire. And I think most wives were like I was; they'd taken on a job. We knew what we were doing when we married our husbands and although we might not

424 — Tales from the Dark Continent

English

129. An insect has eaten this.
130. Dig the garden.
131. Cut the grass.
132. Split the firewood.
133. Cultivate the soil.
134. I want to see your registration certificate and book.
135. Where have you been since you left your last master?
136. I do not give such high wages. If you work here, I will give you . . . shillings and food.
137. You are free every day from 2 o'clock till 4 o'clock, but at any other time you must be on duty on the premises. No one is allowed to come here and sleep in your hut unless I give him written permission to stay.
138. No one is allowed to come here and sleep in your hut unless I give him written permission to stay.
139. I do not allow strange boys near the house.
140. Do not be sulky.
141. You are insolent! You must look pleasant (or pleased).
142. It is better not to be sulky.

Ki-Swahili

129. Kimeliwa na dudu.
130. Lima bustani.
131. Kata nyasi.
132. Pasua kuni.
133. Palilia ardhi.
134. Nataka kutazama kipande chako no buku.
135. Umekuwa wapi tangu ulipotoka kazini ya Bwana wako wa mwishe?
136. Sitoi mshahara mwingi kama hivi. Ukifanya kazi hapa, nitakupa shillingi . . . na posho.
137. Una ruhusa kila siku kutoka saa nana hata saa kumi, lakini wakati mwingine wote lazima uwepo kazini huku.
138. Hapana awaye yote alive na ruhusa ya kuja huku na kulala nyumbani mwako (S) (or mwenu, Pl.) asippopata cheti kwangu mimi.
139. Siwapi maboi wageni ruhusa ya kukaribia nyumba.
140. Usiwe kaidi; or, Usinune.
141. Mfidhuli we! Inakupasa uso wako uwe wa furaha.
142. Ni heri kutokuwa mkaidi.

Ki-Settler

129. Dudu kwisha kula hii.
130. Chimba shamba.
131. Kata majani.
132. Pasua kuni.
133. Lima udongo.
134. Nataka kuona kipandi yako pamoja na buku yako.
135. Wewe kwenda wapi tangu siku ile wache kasi ya bwana?
136. Sitaki kutowa mshara kubwa nami hii kama wewe kuja hapa nitatoa shillingi . . . na chekula.
137. Kila siku, wapata ruhusa tangu saa nane mpaka saa kumi. Saa ingine, dasturi yako hapa nyumbani.
138. Sitaki watu wageni lala nyumbani yako hapa kama wataka ruhusa kwa wageni hapa, nitaandeka barua, (or uliza mimi andeka barua.)
139. Dasturi yangu, hapana wageni kuja karibu nyumba.
140. Usiwe mwenyi hati ya kunua.
141. Wewe jeuri! sharti wewe tezama chekalea.
142. Kutununa ni afadhali kuliko kununa.

Instructions for servants in Ki-Swahili and its corrupted form of Ki-Settler, from *The Kenya Settler's Cookery Book and Household Guide*, 1928.

have liked it we made the best of it.' Making the best of it meant living in 'rather horrid little houses' that were allocated to them which they were required to abandon at frequent intervals for other equally unhomely dwellings – 'because you were always moving on'. It often meant enduring months of appalling dry heat, when 'one had to be very careful or one ended up looking rather like a dried-up walnut,' or months of extreme humidity when shoes and dresses turned green with mould and people at cocktail parties looked as if they'd been fished out of the sea, when 'if you dropped something while you were dressing you didn't attempt to pick it up – bending down would absolutely put an end to all your preparations.' It meant having cockroaches in the linen, silver-fishes eating their way through one's books, sitting in the evenings with legs either inside a pillow-case or in hot mosquito boots – and sometimes having to chase baboons or even elephants out of the garden. It also meant snakes. 'The thing that I was most frightened of at the beginning was the snakes,' declares Alys Reece:

> The garden at Marsabit was very overgrown and there were any number of the kind of cobra that spit in your eye if you gave them a chance – and although I was terrified of them I knew that if I flicked them on to the grass with a special hoe that I'd sharpened they didn't have much chance. They were always racing for cover but with the very sharp hoe I could cut them in half before they got to it – and I became really quite vicious over them. The other snakes that we had were puff-adders. I think they were as frightened of us as we were of them, but one would find them coiled round in the cool shade beside the loo seats, which was rather disturbing – and one would also find them coiled on the path that one was walking along. On one occasion Gerald trod bang on the head of one in the dusk and I was just about to step on it too when I saw its fangs moving, with its head sticking firmly in the mud.
>
> Gerald teased me a bit about being scared stiff of snakes and

it was a little ironic that shortly after that, when he was doing an early Saturday morning tour round the township, walking through the long grass he got bitten by one. The snake-bite took effect very quickly; his temperature went to 105, he was delirious and his leg went black up to his waist. We had cut the place and done all the squeezing and all the old pot. permang. and that sort of thing, but there wasn't much I could do except try to keep the fever down by continually sponging him with lots of cold water and praying like mad – and by the Monday morning the worst was behind us. He had a very bad foot for some time and had to go around on safari in carpet-slippers, but apart from that he made a marvellous recovery.

In the larger stations such isolated horrors could be set against an active social life that centred very much on the club and the various sporting and social entertainments that went on there – the dances, fancy-dress parties, amateur theatricals, cricket weekends, gymkhanas and polo weeks as well as the private supper parties, with their endless rounds of *toasties* and small *chop*, and the weekend luncheons. While they provided a very necessary relaxation from official duties, such diversions also had their critics. Some wives found the other European women to be 'completely aloof from the people who really could have used their help. Their main topic of conversation was how frightful their servants were, how ghastly everybody was and why hadn't they been asked to the Governor's dinner the night before?' Also much criticized were the real casualties of colonial life, the wives who were 'really very unhappy in Africa and never fitted in. They hated to be parted from their children and they didn't want to be taken on safari so they had a lonely time because they were left on the station by themselves a lot. They were bothered by the lack of entertainment and facilities. They weren't interested in games or their gardens, so there was very little left to do.' For them life was perhaps 'a little dangerous, because some white women, unaccustomed to freedom from household chores and with nothing to do, assembled for elevenses in the clubs and became very easily involved in intrigues.' The fact that the men greatly outnumbered the women made Africa 'a terribly tempting place for a woman. There were lots of bachelors kicking their heels and they buzzed around married women like bees round a honey pot. Very few families hadn't got at least one man attached to the husband and wife, pathetically hanging on, hoping for crumbs that fell from the rich man's table. The husband might go off on safari and the temptation was stark. In Kenya it got to such a pitch that one used to say, "Are you married or do you live in Kenya?" '

By far the luckiest wives in Africa were those suited by health and temperament to a rough, outdoor life and who were able to become intimately involved in their husbands' jobs: 'This was the greatest satisfaction of being a colonial wife. You felt you were being constructive and productive and doing something that was well worthwhile and enjoyable.' This enjoyment was never more keenly felt than when they accompanied their husbands on tour. 'Camp life was to me the essence of Africa,' declares Mavis Stone. 'Both Dick and I felt much nearer to the heart of Africa and in much closer contact with the Africans, because somehow they were at their best then.' Touring through Northern Uganda they passed through

. . . magnificent scenery, long khaki-coloured plains with the flat-topped thorn trees and scrub bushes – and with a lot of game near the game reserves, particularly buffalo, waterbuck and elephant. You got the rather attractive little villages with woven fences, funny little granaries where they stored their food for the dry weather and chicken houses made up like little mud huts with thatched roofs and stuck up on stilts. And everywhere the children, the fat babies and the *totos*, the children that were half-grown, all legs and smiles. The men standing around on one leg leaning on spears. The women always graceful, always carrying loads on their heads – even a matchbox I've seen them carrying on their heads – never anything in their hands. And their babies on their backs, of course, with gourds over the heads of the babies and flies – flies everywhere.

One of the remarkable features of these tours was the way in which the cooks managed to produce high-quality meals cooked in *debbies*, four-gallon paraffin tins with the tops cut out and made into portable ovens. 'The cooks were marvellous,' recalls Alys Reece. 'They made bread in holes in the ground and they would carry the bread in the half-way stage in cloths on the camel and as soon as the fires were made in the evening out it would come and they would bake the bread at night in a hole in the ground, with cinders. We had one cook who used to make beautiful éclairs the same way on tour.'

It was nearly always the evenings in camp that held the greatest attraction – certainly for Mavis Stone:

We always had a camp fire which we used to sit round. It was usually lit at sunset which we would sit and watch and there was supposed to be a blue flash which you did just see as the sun disappeared and then it got dark very quickly. Then the mosquitoes came out, so you'd want to have had your bath in the back of the tent, an old-fashioned hip-bath where you had to swat at the mosquitoes while you were having your bath. But it was very refreshing and then you got into your trousers and mosquito boots and a long-sleeved shirt and you went and sat by the camp fire and had your drink. And the night sort of closed around you and you were very aware of the stars – and usually from the village that was not far away you would hear the noises of the people calling and chatting and quite often the drumming that went on. Wherever we went there was nearly always a dance laid on. In Acholi, particularly, they did the most beautiful dancing with little drums and leopard skins and those magnificent head-dresses that they wore made out of sisal, almost like long blond hair. They did this leaping and dancing and it was almost like a ballet.

There was one aspect of married life in Africa with which it was particularly difficult to come to terms. 'Until the Second World War there were no European children in Nigeria,' recalls Dorothy Ruston. 'You didn't anticipate taking your children out, so they had to be left at home. Every married couple had to face the problem of what would happen when they decided to have a family. It wasn't easy to decide that you must spend part of the time at home with the children and part of the time with your husband. Some people decided that perhaps it was better to have no children at all.' To say that there were no white children was perhaps putting it too strongly, for there were always children to be found in the settled areas and in the healthier climates and among the mission communities. And if most couples sought to have their children born and reared, as far as possible, back home in England, there were always the exceptions. Three of Alys Reece's children were born during her first few years at Marsabit:

Having a baby in those days was rather a pantomime, as one had to go all the way down to Nairobi, which meant two or three days travelling and a long stay in Nairobi. And when my first child was born it turned out to be a daughter which wasn't at all the right thing to do by local standards and poor Gerald had to put up with a lot of commiserations. All the old men called on him in a ceremonial fashion and wrung his hand and wished him better luck next time. One Somali servant that we had produced a fertility emblem that he insisted I hung over my bed. He was a bit worried about its being second-hand, but it was a dreadful thing and shrieked its message. It was a huge ostrich egg with a lot of conch shells rather representative of fertility, and this had to be hung over my bed and I used to wake and see it in the night and be terrified of it and I was very glad indeed when I could hand it back and say that, yes, it had worked and it was fine. But another daughter arrived and poor old Ibrahim thought it was partly the fault of his second-hand fertility emblem. However, the women of the place were very interested and all the young women called to see the baby and play with it and were very nice and comforting and then, some time later, our first son was born and when I came back to Marsabit I was staggered by the reception that I got. With the girls the men had just sent their wives or daughters to congratulate me, if you could call it that, but when I came back with a son it was quite a triumph, and all sorts of old men appeared with a terrific range of presents from a beautiful white ox to bunches of bananas and hens and all sorts of things like that to celebrate the birth of our son.

Bringing up small children in the tropics presented all sorts of difficulties. The most serious health risk was malaria, since the taking of quinine or methadine as a daily dose was not good for children. But even after the Second World War, when the introduction of paludrin removed the threat of malaria, there were still plenty of other dangers. Even when there were servants and, in East Africa, *ayahs* – 'a very wonderful race of women who really did love their charges and ruled them with an iron fist' – trained to look after and care for the children, the need to be on the alert was always there. Veronica Short's constant worry was the fear of rabies: 'On almost every posting we had there was a rabies scare, which meant that all the local dogs had to be tied up. But then there were always dogs that would escape from the villages and run through the *boma* and if your children were playing in the garden you were never quite sure whether they had touched the dog, because my children were fond of animals and very apt to pat any dog that came near, so this was one of the things that always haunted me while I was in Africa.' Then there were such minor hazards as – in Nyasaland – the *puttse* flies that laid their eggs on the washing as it dried in the sun. If the washing wasn't well ironed there was always the risk that the eggs would hatch and the grubs work their way into the skin. This was what happened to Noel Harvey's son Christopher when he was two years old: 'He got rather pale and complained of a sore head and we found there was a boil coming up, so we took him round to the doctor and the doctor treated it as a boil and said that we must wait until it came to a head. When it finally did we went in and the doctor said, 'This is *not* a boil.' He took his two thumbs and squeezed and out from the boil came a most revolting little maggot.'

The risk to life may not have been so acute as it had been in earlier years, but it was still a risk that on rare occasions had to be taken seriously – as Sue Bates found one night in Tabora:

> I wasn't sleeping very well and I went in to look at the youngest child and I found that his cot was completely black with ants. Soldier ants had been working their way right through the house – and his cot had been in the way. They'd got under the netting and through the netting and his ears and nose and his mouth were full of ants so he couldn't cry out. We had buckets of water so we put some in a basin and we held him more or less under and tried to pick all these things out and he started to cry and so that was all right. Then we got the other two children and we put the four legs of our iron double bed into tobacco tins full of paraffin and the five of us spent the rest of the night in the bed. And by the morning the ants had worked their way through the house and they'd eaten all the cockroaches and pretty well everything else there was to eat. It was a rather horrifying experience because if I hadn't gone in to see him he would have been killed.

But there were always compensations to be set against the privations and the risks. For the children these first years in Africa were ones of rare privilege, with love and affection lavished on them by all the household and constant attention focused upon them wherever they went. Alys Reece recalls how, when her three children were a little older, they were visited by

> . . . two stark naked warriors with their spears who came and
> sat down on the lawn just outside the house. The following day
> they came back and just took up the same position again. They
> didn't look at all hostile, so I wasn't frightened by them but I
> got a little bit curious and at last I sent a note down to the
> District Commissioner and asked him who they were. And
> they were Geluba from the far corner of the province who had
> been brought in as witnesses in a murder trial. They had heard
> rumours of a little girl with white hair who rode her own pony
> and they were waiting to see this happen. So Sarah, who had
> very blond hair at that age, obligingly and very seriously got
> on her pony and did a neat little gallop round and they shook
> hands all round and went away delighted.

This African childhood was very rarely prolonged: 'The
children couldn't stay after a certain time because the tropics
were bad for them and there was no proper schooling. They
had to go off to England to boarding school.' Then came 'the
awful choice which comes sooner or later between husband
and children', a choice that was undoubtedly 'the saddest and
most controversial part of the lot of the colonial official'. Some
wives stuck by their husbands, others went with their children.
Most tried to do a bit of both, staying in England for several
months after their husband's leave was up and coming back
early a month or two before the next leave was due. For some
parents, like the Mackays, it was 'a very, very painful choice to
make and in the end we left the Colonial Service.'

Just as the First World War effectively brought one era to a
close so the advent of the Second World War marked quite
unmistakably the ending of another. On the day that war was
declared in August 1939 Mercedes Mackay had been having
'a particularly riotous day' with the other Europeans on the
station:

We were playing a cricket match in which all the men dressed as women and all the women as men. There were some absurd costumes and some very peculiar cricket was played, and I remember going on as a soldier dressed in my husband's solar topee and carrying his rifle. Various other idiotic things happened and we were all laughing so much that we could hardly speak when suddenly a car appeared and a man got out and said, 'Come quickly to the club, the Prime Minister is about to speak.' So we beetled off in our cars round to the club and we all stood round in our ridiculous costumes and they turned on the wireless and there was that fatal announcement. And I remember looking across at the Inspector of the Public Works Department, who had dressed himself up in a long, black flowing dress with a red wig as a madam of a brothel, and he was standing there with tears pouring down his face. It was one of the most tragi-comic situations that I can ever remember.

9

Winds of Change

We have seen the awakening of national consciousness in peoples who have for centuries lived in dependence of some other power ... In different places it takes different forms but it is happening everywhere. A wind of change is blowing through this continent, whether we like it or not.

HAROLD MACMILLAN Address to the Joint Assembly of the South African Parliament 3 February 1960

When Alan Burns first went out to Nigeria in 1912 there was 'no thought in anybody's mind that Independence was to come within our lifetime, and at that time we none of us believed that the Africans were fit for self-government. It was only after the Second World War that people began to realize that sooner or later – and probably sooner rather than later – there would have to be Independence. Even then they didn't think – not even the Africans themselves – that Independence was coming as quickly as it did.'

The war and its aftermath brought about many changes, both in circumstances and attitudes, not the least of which was the sudden revelation that pith helmets need not be worn. When Philip Allison first came to Nigeria,

. . . there was usually quite a lot of discussion if you were at a drinks party during the day on a Sunday morning at somebody's house; some people thought that if you wanted to go out to relieve yourself in the compound there was just time to go out and do this without putting your hat on, but many people religiously put their topees on before they went out to relieve themselves in the garden. But during the war when British soldiers came out and walked about bareheaded and nothing terrible happened to them, people realized at last that nobody every really suffered from sunstroke. What they'd been suffering from was heat-stroke – due to wearing a heavy helmet for one thing, no doubt. But that was one of the things that the war exploded for us.

There were also sudden dramatic improvements in living conditions, such new drugs as paludrin and sulpha-guenodine became available, refrigerators became standard issue for all government servants – 'and for once they started by issuing these refrigerators to the lower paid before the senior officers were offered them' – and improved air services brought Africa and Great Britain that much closer, making it increasingly possible for wives to shuttle between husbands and children – even for the children themselves to come out and join their parents for a summer or winter holiday. The war also added a new word to the colonial vocabulary – 'development'. 'It has to be remembered that a country like Tanganyika was chronically short of money between the wars,' explains Charles Meek, 'so there was nothing whatever to spend on development. Each colony was supposed to subsist on its own and if you had very little, as Tanganyika did, in the way of primary produce in high demand, sisal, cotton, a bit of coffee, then the country was going to be hard up – and poverty-sticken it certainly was. It was only during the war with the passage of the first Colonial Development and Welfare Act that the coming of better times was signalled. They were slow in coming but slowly the momentum of development did build up and the pace got faster and faster.'

In the district this new aid expressed itself in development plans which not only 'enthused all of us white administrators but also caught the imagination of the Africans' so that comparatively small sums of money – in Charles Meek's district of Mbulu it was £90,000 spread over five years – provided the basis for ambitious self-help programmes in which the local young men were drafted in to provide free labour in the dry season.

With this development came the concept of the administrator as chairman or co-ordinator of a District Team rather than as the isolated head of a district or province. There were, too, a number of other shifts of emphasis in district work, heralded by a dramatic increase in paperwork. 'This seemed to grow and grow,' recalls Bill Stubbs, 'and towards the end of my service it was even necessary to recruit a brand new kind of officer who went in many cases even to out-stations to assist in the growing paperwork which took so much of the administrator's time and took him away from the other more important duties.' The District Officer found himself 'increasingly embroiled in political matters, not necessarily on a local level but on a regional or even a federal level'. The commonest expression of this politicization was in the introduction of democracy into the fabric of tribal life. In Tanganyika Darrell Bates found himself charged with replacing a 'rough and ready system of democracy, which largely consisted of knocking off the chief if they didn't like him' with a system of electing local representatives that accorded to some degree with English-style democracy:

> We would invite the people to a gathering to nominate two
> advisers who would sit on a council to advise a chief. And shyly
> and slowly people would come forward and say, 'We nominate
> him' – and 'We nominate him' – until I had perhaps seven or
> eight different people. Then I told those who supported them

to stand behind the candidate of their choice and then I took the person who had the least votes and said, 'Now, you are a non-starter – you go and stand behind your second choice,' and this went on until you had the two with the largest number of supporters. This was a form of democracy that was open and reasonably honest and so in this way democracy came to a small corner of Africa.

Elsewhere very similar experiments in local democracy were being carried out. 'From 1950–51 onwards life in Northern Nigeria was dominated by elections,' recalls Nigel Cooke. 'Initially there was a very indirect form of election, with hamlets electing people to go forward to a village area and a village area to a district and a district to an emirate and so on. It was all in stages and very, very indirect, but gradually with regional and federal elections the pattern changed to more and more direct elections. And of course the more direct the elections grew the more danger there was to law and order.'

In the meantime changes were taking place among the administrators themselves. Although the post-war generation came from very much the same background – the public schools and Oxbridge in most cases – the war had undoubtedly created a gulf between the two generations, a gulf accentuated by the freeze that had been put on recruitment for most of the duration of the war and by the fact that only the youngest members of the various colonial services had been allowed to join up. In Northern Rhodesia a line had simply been drawn through the Staff List and 'only those DOs under thirty were allowed to go to war.' Those who were forced to stay on – sometimes under threat of imprisonment if they attempted to join up – had served out enormously extended tours of duty, which had further accentuated their isolation. As a result these older administrators, many of whom prided themselves on their liberal outlook, were caught out by the new post-war mood of

egalitarianism. When Tony Kirk-Greene came to Nigeria in
1950 most of the senior administrators were men who had
gone out between 1920 and 1935:

> The big gap was between them and those of us who came in
> after the war. People who came out after the war were more
> likely to question the hierarchy, question why things were
> going to be done. The whole structure seemed to be very
> different after World War Two. And I think the real break-
> through came with a younger group of us recruited after
> World War Two when we decided that we would spend much
> of our time getting to know the new élite. We were convinced
> that this was where the future lay. Instead, as our seniors had
> done, of paying all the attention to the elders, the chiefs and
> senior Native Authority officials, we went for the younger
> educated élite, people who had been to secondary schools,
> occasionally to university. And this made all the difference.
> I'm not blaming people for not doing this before the war. I
> think in that kind of society – both European society and the
> Colonial Service hierarchical society – this would have been
> impossible. This easy mixing, having young educated Niger-
> ians to your house, playing Scrabble and, particularly, mixing
> them with some of the other Europeans who were also
> interested in getting to know the new Nigerian, I think this
> was the big change-over.

This difference of attitude was in no way confined either to
West Africa or to the youngest generation of administrators. In
Tanganyika Charles Meek also felt that:

> There was a gap in the thinking between young and old. The
> older men, Provincial Commissioners, members in Dar es
> Salaam under the old membership system of government,
> found it very difficult – and quite understandably so – to
> appreciate the urgency that people of my age, in their late
> thirties, felt, and the consuming feeling that it was no longer

possible to think as we used to think of handing over power in very deliberate slices. We used to believe that you could give them a little bit now and see what they made of it and in ten years time give them a little bit more. This wasn't going to work. Not in the tide of opinion that the nationalists had set up, operating against a background of world opinion, particularly American opinion and UN opinion, which was totally hostile to all our conceptions of colonialism.

There were other ways, too, in which the differences between the generations were making themselves felt. One of the principal features of district life that was disputed by the post-war generation was the importance attached to touring by their seniors. There was a feeling that perhaps some of them 'toured for touring's sake'. This was not helped by a prejudice in some quarters against touring by any means other than on foot: 'After the war ADOs were asking for advances to buy cars,' Nigel Cooke recalls. 'Now this was not commonly given and I remember one very pompous Resident saying, "No, Smith, I will give you an advance for a pair of boots, but not for a car."' To some extent the issue was resolved by the arrival of four-wheel drive and the Land-Rover, which 're-volutionized administration in East Africa. Your people were always accessible, then. You might have an exciting time getting to them, but you did get there. And it really altered things for us.'

Another new arrival in the district, and a further by-product of the war years, was an altogether new model of colonial wife. Not only was she freed from many of the constraints that had inhibited her predecessors but she also had more positive ideas about her role and was often determined to do 'as much as a woman is allowed to do in an African male Society', involving herself in local African councils of women or such organizations as the Girl Guides rather than simply offering token support to 'the charity of the Lady Governor of the time'. Even more significantly, the ending of the war also released a professional work-force of women trained in leadership for whom service in the colonies was a natural progression from their war work. One of these was Catherine Dinnick-Parr, who had served during the war in the WRNS and who was appointed in 1947 to work among the Tiv people of Northern Nigeria as an adult education officer. Although she was by no means the first woman educationalist to go to Northern Nigeria – Sylvia Leith-Ross had been appointed as the first Lady Superintendent of Education as early as 1926 – her work in the bush was as much a pioneering venture as anything that her male colleagues had been through in the earlier days:

I left by car on the road which leads from Benue Province to Ogoja Province, which is in the Western Region of Nigeria. I was told to drive to milestone 40 and then turn right. There was a path there, even though I couldn't see it, and we drove some distance down this bush path and came to a local school. Then we were told to drive back to a certain tree and to plough through the grass, which was at least six feet high, which we did, and there was this one room with a little wooden verandah and a thatched roof. There were huts in the compound for the boys and there was also a round mud hut as a kitchen. We unloaded the car and I told my steward, Sam, that I would have to go and salute the chief, who was the head of the clan. I knew I couldn't make a mistake about his compound because it was at the end of this bush path, and also it was surrounded by tall trees which signalled it was a chief's compound. There were twelve old gentlemen sitting on the ground and in front of the middle one there was a deck-chair. I had very little Tiv then, but I could salute them all, '*M sugh u*', which means, 'I greet you'. The man in the middle put his hand out for me to sit on the deck-chair, which I did, and it immediately collapsed. Eventually a dog came out and sniffed at me, then a woman came out and she put her foot by mine. I was wearing open sandals and she was obviously saying to them all, 'Well, at least her feet are the same as ours.' Then she felt me more or less all over and although I was covered she was obviously saying, 'Well, she's the same as us even though she's wearing clothes.'

Her first problem was to become accepted – by both blacks and whites. Although 'most of the Europeans I met were very kind and helpful, I think they thought I must be a little strange being on my own.' Meeting another European in the bush she asked him to join her for a drink, 'and while we were sitting drinking he kept turning round and I couldn't think what he was looking for. I asked him if he'd lost something. He said, "No, I'm just looking for your husband." So I said, "But I don't have a husband. I work here." "But", he said, "we don't have any woman working on her own in the province." And I said, "Well, at last you have met one."'

Catherine Dinnick-Parr's principal objective was to get the Tiv people interested in female education. But in order to work with the women she had first to be accepted by their menfolk:

I had to be very, very careful in case I did something which they wouldn't like and I found it very difficult at times to keep my thoughts to myself and my mouth closed. But if they thought that you were trying to wipe out all that they believed in, they would not have been willing for you to stay and work with them. The position of the women in the family has to be understood and one cannot just run in like a bull in a china shop when they are doing something which we consider is absolutely wrong according to our culture.

By walking round the village compounds every day and getting to know the people and their customs – 'whether you felt they were right or wrong that wasn't for you to judge' – Catherine Dinnick-Parr not only learnt a great deal

– 'learning by watching what the women were doing, how they worked, what foodstuffs they put in their dishes, seeing their babies, talking to the women, listening to the old men telling their stories about former days' – but also built up trust. Then she was able to start classes, first in one village and then another – 'they would wait until my car arrived and then a drum would be sounded and they would come in' – concentrating particularly on hygiene, child care and cookery. 'Always in every class there is one woman who listens. She may not agree with everything you say, but she does put some of your things into practice. The next time you go to visit her hut you find that it has been swept out, she's tied a rope between two huts and she's putting the sleeping mats and the sleeping clothes out in the sun to kill any germs there may be. She's made a little platform of mud on which to prepare her food rather than doing it all on the ground and she's covered all the pots which have food in them.'

Just as Catherine Dinnick-Parr found some of the Tiv customs hard to understand, so no doubt the Tiv people found some of her own customs equally inexplicable:

In an evening in the bush I always wore a long evening dress to keep up my morale but also one had to wear mosquito boots; there were mosquitoes and sand-flies everywhere and the long dress was a great help. I remember when I was at Mbaakon the Development Officer would come along and have dinner with me – he in a dinner suit and I in an evening dress – and we would walk along the bush path talking and everyone gathered to see us. They were all so excited. I think they wondered why we got all dressed up and covered ourselves when it was so frightfully hot. In an evening I would often play my gramophone records. I had an old-fashioned gramophone that you had to wind up and I had hundreds of records and the ones that they liked best were one by Tom Lehrer called *Pigeons in the Park* and *Dreaming of a White Christmas*. These tunes they absolutely adored and they'd ask for them to be repeated time and time again. All the village would come. We'd sit round and we would have these records on and then always there was a drummer with his drum and he would start drumming and they would start dancing. And it was absolutely beautiful, particularly by moonlight and I can't tell you how friendly they were. And although I was often on my own I was safer there than I would ever have been anywhere in England today.

Some years later Catherine Dinnick-Parr was posted to Kaduna where, as Chief Education Officer, she found herself up against 'tremendous opposition to girls' education that went on year in and year out'. There was a great difference between the education in the Muslim far North and in the Southern region of Nigeria: 'In the Southern part there was the mission influence and many girls attended school. But the mission were not permitted to work so freely in the North, where there was still tremendous opposition to female education of any kind, due partly to religious beliefs and tribal customs, particularly early marriage, or to the loss of a young wage-earner and the loss of a young pair of hands to do the chores. It was very, very hard going to get the girls into school.' The change only came in the early 1960s when it became obvious that 'if the country was to go forward then the women must go forward with the men. The modern Northern Nigerians now quote an old Arabic saying, that "a country where the women are not educated is like a bird with only one wing."'

Another teacher who came out to Northern Nigeria was Joan Everett: 'I remember being rather staggered to see a girl walk to the window, firmly grasp her nose and blow it violently out of the window, and I couldn't help thinking that this was a slight change from my girls at Sherborne.' Both for her and for Mary Allen, who came out by air to teach in Accra in 1950, 'being a single woman in a small station had enormous

advantages because one was rather in demand.' Not unex-
ectedly, this led to an alarmingly high drop-out rate among
their fellow women educationalists: 'This was a constant
source of consternation to the people in headquarters because
no sooner had they got somebody who they thought was going
to stay with them for some time, than they were smartly
snapped up and married.' Indeed, both Joan Everett and
Mary Allen followed this pattern by getting married within a
few years of their arrival in West Africa, the former to a police
officer, the latter to a District Officer.

The immediate post-war period also saw the start of a
decline in the independence of the district office, with a
corresponding growth in the power of the provincial or
central secretariat. It was to this hub of government –
sometimes referred to as the 'scratch box' on the Gold
Coast, and as the 'biscuit box' in Northern Rhodesia – that
most administrators gravitated as they rose up the ladder of
promotion: 'Most people resented going into headquarters; a
few were honest and said that they actually enjoyed life at
headquarters, and most of us once we got there found there
were certain attractions in it, but we felt we were saying
goodbye to the touring which we had enjoyed so much as
Assistant District Officers.' However, objections to working
in an office at headquarters were tempered by the knowledge that promotion came more readily to those who had
had secretariat experience:

> The District Officer who didn't want to serve anywhere but in
> a district and who had become an expert in district work had
> comparatively few opportunities of advancement. He could
> become a Senior District Commissioner and he could become
> a Provincial Commissioner in charge of a province where
> there were perhaps six or seven districts under his control, but
> he was not usually thought worthy beyond that of promotion
> to the higher reaches of government. Whereas the secretariat
> officer had his sights perhaps on becoming the Financial

Secretary or the Chief Secretary of the territory and eventually, perhaps, on a governorship.

The fact that nearly all officers were required at some time or
other to serve for a period in the secretariat did not prevent a
very wide degree of suspicion, bordering on contempt, growing
up between these two partners in government – 'the same sort
of feeling as exists between a line officer and a staff officer in the
army' – which expressed itself in mutual distrust:

> The secretariat officer didn't think that these bush-whacking
> DCs really knew much about what was going on. He thought
> that they weren't all that well endowed on top, that their letters
> were not quite up to secretariat standard and that they didn't
> understand the drift of government policy. On the other hand,
> the DCs reckoned that if you got a secretariat man away from
> his car and off a metalled road he would lose his way, and that
> he didn't understand the language or the country. He was just
> a good chap on writing letters on subjects on which he wasn't
> really fully conversant and what he really needed was to come
> out to a district and get his knees brown.

To officials who, until their most senior years, lived simply
and roughly and for whom 'money was always a preoccupation', the matter of promotion and the public recognition of
their services meant a great deal. This recognition was most
often expressed in the form of a 'c' after some twenty years
of service – with perhaps a 'K' to follow for the high-fliers.
But it was not the fact of the award but its timing that was
really significant, and this caused considerable heart-searching as every New Year's Honours List was published: 'You
tended to scan it to see whether contemporaries of yours in
other branches of the service or in other territories had
beaten you to it, and where you had been beaten to it you
tended to make allowances by saying, "Well, of course, he
was lucky. It was a small territory and therefore he got his

'C' earlier than he would have done had he served on with us here in Tanganyika or wherever." '

The peak of the administrator's career was to be found among the governorships, which came in four grades of importance. Nigeria, Kenya, the Gold Coast and Tanganyika all merited a class one governorship; Sierra Leone, Uganda and Northern Rhodesia came into the second category; Nyasaland, the Gambia, British Somaliland and Zanzibar fell into class three. A fledgling governor might serve an apprenticeship on some small Pacific island before moving on up the ladder – provided that he had satisfied his masters in London that he was the right man for the job. Just as the selection of cadets had been greatly influenced by one man, Sir Ralph Furse, so the selection of governors in the post-war period was very much the responsibility of another key figure in the Colonial Office, Dennis Garson, on whose 'A' list were to be found the names of those regarded as fit material for governorships. Kenneth Smith remembers him as a 'naturally unobtrusive chap', who spent much of his time slipping largely unnoticed in and out of various colonial territories and who 'reached the height of his influence in the early fifties when it was his job to assemble these lists for the key governorships when it became necessary for political reasons to replace a governor who had clearly run out of steam in his capacity to cope with local problems.'

The most pressing of these local problems was everywhere the dramatic rise of African nationalism, a phenomenon that could also be said to have had its roots in the war, which had given soldiers from both East and West Africa a glimpse of 'what was happening in other territories round the world – in India, Ceylon, Madagascar and so on. They saw that they all had Independence – or were about to get it – and they thought that it was time that Africans should also get Independence.' When this awakening of political consciousness was first observed in West Africa it was not viewed with undue alarm. The principle of Independence itself had never really been a major issue: 'All of us who served in the African colonies never had any doubt in our minds from the start that our job was to bring these countries forward to Independence.' But what became increasingly a matter for dispute was the question of the time-scale, because 'everyone was talking about eventual self-government – with the emphasis on the word "eventual".'

At the end of the war there was still 'very little belief that we would be called upon in the course of our careers to hand over to the people we were working with'. Even as late as 1950 – only seven years before Ghanaian Independence – recruits on the Colonial Service Course in London were being assured by a 'much-respected and not illiberal' governor of the Gold Coast, Sir Charles Arden-Clarke, that 'there would be jobs for us there during our lifetimes and the lifetimes of our sons.' This reluctance to face facts was certainly not due to personal motives, because there was undoubtedly a widespread awareness that, in principle, 'we were there to do ourselves out of a job.' But what actually happened, as Darrell Bates found, was that 'once one arrived in Africa and was actually involved in the day to day administration it seemed so remote, to be perfectly honest, that I didn't really give any thought to it. I didn't conceive that a situation would arise in which they would run their own affairs without our help in my lifetime – and how wrong I was.' David Allen, in the Gold Coast, admits to a very similar attitude towards Independence: 'The fact of the matter was that we'd all looked upon Independence – in so far as we had thought about it at all – rather like a young man thinks of old age; something that's going to happen sometime, but it's a very long way ahead and one doesn't pay much attention to it.'

It was the issue of Africans' running their own affairs – in a word, 'Africanization' – that provided the main stumbling block in every territory's progress towards self-government. It was argued that 'there were insufficient trained Africans both in the civil service and outside it to govern the country without it' – but at the same time programmes for the advancement of such a skilled work-force were not being effectively promoted. Nor was opposition to such Africanization programmes entirely one-sided. In Nigel Cooke's opinion the administrator's reluctance in Northern Nigeria to train up or advance Africans for district work could be attributed 'very largely to the deference with which they treated the chiefs' views. They did not want African administrative officers. I had an example of this when I was in Kano, when the chief complained about his African DO taking his wife in the front of his car. I had to explain to him that times had changed and that the African DO was perfectly entitled to carry his wife in the front of his car.'

This failure to build up an indigenous executive cadre was widely recognized as perhaps the greatest error of colonial rule – and, with hindsight, the 'slowness with which we brought the people to manage their own affairs' was universally and deeply regretted. Yet this failure was, in James Robertson's opinion, brought about not so much by a lack of will as by 'a lack of imagination'. In 1942 he was one of a group of senior officers in the Sudan whose opinion was sought by the Civil Secretary about the possibility of promoting Sudanese officials to the higher administrative posts: 'Practically everybody said, "No, we couldn't run our province if we had to have these chaps" – because they were not educated enough. I don't think the thing was a rearguard action; it was a wish for good government. They reckoned that they wouldn't get as good a service and as good administration as they had from British officers. They couldn't see that if a country was going to be independent you must take risks and get ahead with these things.'

In fact, Sudan's Africanization programme was in advance of that of the other African colonial territories, and in 1956 it became the first of the British-ruled territories to gain its Independence. When James Robertson was appointed Governor of Nigeria in 1955 he found the contrast between the two territories very striking. In particular he was surprised 'at the delay which had apparently occurred in Nigerianizing the services', and one of his first acts was to call for plans to bring this into rapid effect. In some institutions Africanization was already well advanced, notably in the Church, which had a long-established tradition of equal partnership. Yet even here a 'paternal attitude' among the older missionaries had been very evident to Bob MacDonald when he first came to Calabar in 1929, and what had changed his attitude was the fact that, through its mission secondary schools, Nigeria had started to produce young men who were proceeding to British universities and coming back as lawyers and doctors and teachers – 'and it was just stupid for us to patronize or be paternal to people who were just as well educated and as widely read as we were. That kind of change brought the older missionaries into line and led the way to a system of integration which gradually handed over the whole of the work and property and the control, from a mission council which was composed of white missionaries to the Senate of the Presbyterian Church of Nigeria. And it came very easily, very happily, very gently.'

Rather more surprisingly, integration in the world of West African commerce was also well advanced. There had always been a tradition of business co-operation between white and black traders that went right back to the days of slave trade, but the first real breakthrough in integration came with the 1930s slump when many European companies cut down on their white staff, thereby creating vacancies in jobs that had previously been regarded as exclusively European. When Donald Dunnet had first gone out to Nigeria in 1920 it had been taken for granted that 'the white man was superior – and I'm afraid as a young and rather cocky young man I accepted that as a fact. That's the way we lived and that's the way we thought. In those days they said an African could never be a cashier or an African could never do this or that, but, in fact, some of the Africans did the jobs a lot better than any Europeans had ever done.'

Even if they were behind the Sudan in Africanization and integration, Nigeria and the West Coast territories were still a long way ahead of East and Central Africa. The contrast was immediately apparent to Mercedes Mackay when she and her husband transferred from Tanganyika to Nigeria in 1941:

> We arrived in the docks in Lagos and the first thing that happened was that our luggage was all put into a blazing hot Customs shed and instantly up marched a very smart-looking black man all in uniform. He said, 'Open that one, please,' and started fumbling all through my underwear and generally sorting things out, and I was absolutely flabbergasted. I couldn't believe my eyes, they were popping, almost literally – that an African would dare to even dream of doing such a thing! A few days later we went to Government House for a cocktail party and there, to my equally amazed eyes, were Africans dressed in dinner jackets and black ties and moving around and being introduced as Mr So and So, Mrs So and So. And you shook hands with them, which was something quite unheard of – and I suddenly began to look at these people and heard them talking perfectly normally, and I realized that they were not only human but most charming human beings. And from that moment on my colour prejudice just faded away.

The first organized anti-Government demonstrations took place on the Gold Coast in February 1948 – 'when Nkwame Nkrumah organized a march on Government House one Saturday afternoon, a time when many people were playing cricket and others were out on the beaches bathing – a move that caught us completely by surprise'. But the one event that really shook British self-confidence more than anything else, and forced home the message that Britain's days in Africa were numbered, was not strictly to do with nationalism at all: 'Mau Mau was the most horrible experience that Kenya has suffered. All civil wars are said to be infinitely more savage than wars between nations and this was certainly true of the Mau Mau business. It was almost unbelievable that the Kikuyu could have inflicted such casualties, and with such brutality, on people of their own sort.' Beginning as sporadic outbursts of violence in the Kikuyu districts of Kenya in 1952, the Mau Mau rebellion took such a hold that eventually a state of emergency had to be declared. For Richard Turnbull, then Minister for Internal Security, quite as much as for the rest of the white population of Kenya, the Emergency had all the characteristics of a nightmare:

> The atmosphere of Mau Mau was horrible. Worse than any other civil disorder that I'd heard of, or been associated with. Long after the Emergency we were still digging up bodies in Nairobi that had been buried and, as for the forest, goodness knows how many Kikuyu are still buried there. I always think of that passage in Philip Sidney's *Sistina*: 'The scenes I hear when I do hear sweet music, the dreadful cries of murdered men in forests'. There were all kinds of interpretations, most of them, I'm afraid, face-saving from our point of view. But land was at the bottom of it and the whole Mau Mau exercise was part civil war and part rebellion. It was civil war against those Kikuyu who were comfortable as they were, who may have been keen nationalists but were moderate nationalists and were prepared to follow constitutional methods, really the Kikuyu 'haves' against the Kikuyu 'have nots'. The rebellion side of it was a determination to create such havoc in the European farm areas that the Government would have to reach accommodation with them. There wasn't a very large number of European deaths, but those seventy farmers killed were killed in the most savage and terrifying way, and they were seventy of the best.

Two other administrators who were also intimately involved in combating the Mau Mau were Frank Loyd, District Commissioner in the Kikuyu districts of Fort Hall and Kiambu, and Dick Symes-Thompson, who found himself in the thick of it when he came to Kericho in 1953:

I must say the shock of arriving in a district where dead bodies were lying about and people were living in fear of their lives under threat of attack with *pangas* – which is a large type of knife – was very frightening and for the first two or three weeks I was more frightened than I have ever been in my life and I found it difficult to sleep. I was worried about what might happen to myself and my family and I was worried about the situation and how it was to be got under control and so on. It was enormously difficult to know who was the enemy and who was not and this particular situation was tremendously impressed on me when I went round the locations which were for the most part under the charge of young District Officers, Kikuyu Guard – they were called DO's KG – who had had a little military training in the Kenya Regiment after having been at school in England or out in Africa and they were put on their own in charge of an African location of, say, twenty thousand people and given a few tribal policemen and told to recruit loyalist Kikuyu Guard to carry out their defence and to start getting control of the locations. Well, each one built his own guard post, which consisted of a little mud fort and a bamboo house in which the officer lived with his few guards and police and a big ditch around it so that they could be safe from attack at night. And when I questioned these District Officers saying, 'What is your situation, are you safe from attack?' they would say, 'Well, I think I trust three of my men, the others I think are sympathizing with the enemy but I am not quite sure.' This was a terrifying situation for me.

The fight against Mau Mau was won by taking the most drastic measures: 'We decided to concentrate the whole of the population in the district into the villages and this was done. Of course, when it was first begun it was bitterly opposed but because we put all the Kikuyu into the villages this meant that it was easier to consolidate land and once we had started doing this land consolidation, and the people themselves had seen what it actually meant on the ground, it gained in popularity and in Kiambu District we had the curious situation where there were people clamouring to get on to the priority list.'

The war against Mau Mau and the long-term effects of Mau Mau were far-reaching. Above all, 'it led to a realization of what enormous power they – the Africans – had if they but cared to use it.'

10

The Flags Come Down

One of the strange things about our presence was the reluctance with which we appeared to go in and the speed with which we came out.

For many officers in the field the late 1950s were years of 'tension and impending tragedy. One could see the clashes coming and we simply didn't know really what was going to be done about them. We thought vaguely that the Home Government was moving far too slowly and that there was this gulf fixed between the nationalist demands and the pace at which we were allowed to move. Quite clearly there was going to be trouble and we were going to be caught in the middle of it.' As far as they were concerned the wind of change had begun to blow long before Macmillan's celebrated – and belated – speech in 1960:

It was scarcely a prophetic utterance, it was something that we ourselves had realized for many years and was received pretty cynically by officers in the field. The Home Government had had one policy under Alan Lennox-Boyd as Colonial Secretary, which was a policy of a fairly rigid paternalism with talk about eventual self-government perhaps over the next generation. And then, at the end of 1959, there was a change of

Colonial Secretary and a change of policy, a belated recognition of what was going on when Iain MacLeod came in on a progressive liberal ticket and we all marched off in the opposite direction, where it was quite clear that independence for all the colonial territories in Africa was coming within the next few years.

Until that change of direction there was a strong feeling among senior administrators that successive Home Governments and British politicians were not supporting them: 'It was pathetic how little they knew and how little they cared.' However, with the advent of modern air services the phenomenon of visiting politicians became increasingly familiar: 'People came out who didn't know anything, more prepared to talk about what they thought about it than to take the word of the man on the spot.' Violet Bourdillon recalls how such visitors to Government House in Nigeria during the war 'always knew everything. I used to say to my husband, "What are you going to tell them?" He'd say, "What's the good? They know it all." ' Occasionally the politician out from home ventured up-country. When Nigel Cooke was Senior Resident in the Jos Plateau Province a 'senior cabinet minister' once dropped in and asked to see some naked pagans:

So the next day we went down the road and when we were about thirty miles outside Jos we saw an old pagan aged about sixty-five wandering along traditionally dressed, which meant to say he had nothing on at all. The politician shouted, 'Stop! Stop!' because he wished to take a photograph. So I got out of the car and went up to the man, slipped him a shilling and said, 'Do you mind if this man takes a photograph? He's an extremely important person from the UK.' So the old gentleman stopped in his tracks and stood there stolidly, while the politician got out of his car and very laboriously took a photograph. But it was from the rear view, and it was then that I realized that these people were not as unsophisticated as

I thought, because when I said to him, 'Would you turn around?' – so that this politician could take what would now be called a full-frontal – he said, 'That will be another shilling.' I felt that I had indeed fallen rather low, acting as a pimp for a visiting politician.

But it was not only the Home Government that was 'perpetually being surprised and brought up short by developments'. Almost every territory had to suffer the agony of rioting or of civil disturbance to a greater or lesser degree as it failed to come to terms with nationalist demands. In Nyasaland, so long regarded as the most pacific of territories, the crisis came in 1959 – and it began in Noel Harvey's Karonga District:

Karonga, when I'd first been there, was a very peaceful total backwater, an area of love and trust and affection, with very, very little happening. Your monthly security report was really a joke; you would struggle to think of half a page worth of things to say. Going back after a year and a half away, suddenly you found yourself being spat at, you found people afraid to talk to you, a completely different atmosphere, an atmosphere of dumbness and distrust. Now when I got back we went straight into the thick of this tension, and it built up to a point where, on a Sunday at the very beginning of March, the DC came into my house and said, 'Noel, they are holding an illegal meeting outside my house as a gesture and they want to see what I'm going to do about it.' And I said, 'Oh.' And he said, 'We'll have to do something, won't we?' And I said, 'Yes, I'm sure we shall.' Then I looked at him and said, 'What do you think we ought to do, Gordon?' Here was a toy-town situation; we had an African police officer, one sergeant and three constables on the station, and the meeting was of about three hundred people. So the DC and the African sub-inspector and myself went and arrested the leaders of the meeting, who were all sitting round a table waiting for us to come. We none of us had arms; obviously it would have been ridiculous to carry a gun. The DC came in his car because he thought that he would then take the leaders of the meeting in his car and appear to drive them right outside the area of the settlement. In fact, what he was going to do was go round in a big loop and come back to the police station and charge them. Well, all we did in fact was to leave plenty of time for the 347 people left at the meeting to get to the police station and be waiting for us when we got there. They then pressed so tightly on the police station that we couldn't get out of one office and out on to the verandah and back into the next office to get the charge papers, and we had this ludicrous situation where we had to say to them, 'Look, we know you, you know us. You are going to hear more about this, but we can't actually formally charge you on paper now. Off you go.' Meanwhile they ripped the flag off the DC's car, smashed his windscreen, planted an axe in the bonnet and bust the windows in the police station. And that actually was the first riot of the emergency.

Those caught up in such emergencies were no doubt unaware that they were part of an over-all pattern of events that was being followed with depressing consistency right across the continent and elsewhere; 'a repetitive pattern of leaders of African opinion being arrested, imprisoned and brought back as future governors of their country'. Patrick Mullins witnessed this cycle of mistakes twice, first in the Gold Coast, then in Nyasaland:

It happened to one particular colonial officer I can think of, first of all as a senior official in the Gold Coast with Nkrumah, then as Governor of Cyprus with Makarios, and finally as Governor of Nyasaland with Banda. In each case they had to graduate from prison before they could pass an essential stage in their journey towards becoming rulers of their own countries. In Ghana they wore 'PG' on their caps – 'Prison Graduate' it stood for – and they realized better than we did that before they were going to get anywhere they'd got to go to prison and then be brought out again and reinstated. And the reason for this I think was because the governors and indeed the colonial administration generally – as well as the Home Government – couldn't accustom themselves to the pace of the change that was beginning to sweep Africa. They were always holding on until too late and making their concessions too late, and then having to make much larger concessions and adopt far shorter time-scales than we thought they were going to have to do.

After the Sudan, the next African territory to complete the cycle was the Gold Coast. Its peaceful transition from Gold Coast to Ghana provided a valuable model for the others to follow. One of those who participated in the hand-over of power was George Sinclair:

The two main catalytic agents apart from Nkrumah and the two nationalist movements themselves were Sir Charles Arden-Clarke, who came as the new governor shortly after the riots, and Reginald Salaway, with his background of experience in India. Charles Arden-Clarke was completely different from the governors that we had experienced. He came to us with a realization that new forces were on the move and they'd got to be made to work constructively rather than to be held back. The phrase he used was, 'I believe in making the inevitable the basis of my policy and I believe it is better to channel water to useful purposes rather than dam it up and let it overflow and destroy the country below it.' He caught the imagination of leaders who had been in prison and got them to work with him and we then embarked on what was a real honeymoon period, with the overseas administration and all the departments working together with the politicians, and African staff coming up towards senior posts as fast as we could bring them on and as fast as they could take themselves up there. And this was for many people, I think, both African and European, a golden period.

Dressed in elaborate uniforms designed, so it was said, for the Crimean campaign – 'the white uniform was quite cool but the blue uniform was devised by the Colonial Office to kill off governors' – the retiring governors of the late 1950s made easy scapegoats as symbols of discarded policies that had been tried and found wanting. There were, indeed, diehards among them, as well as tired men who had stayed on a year or two longer than they should have, but there were others who had in their time been considered dangerously liberal. It was their fate to be replaced by a last batch of governors – realists who bulldozed their territories through into Independence – of quite exceptional quality.

Nigeria's last colonial governor was Sir James Robertson, the very antithesis of the pompous colonial official of popular imagination and 'not a chap who got excited about protocol or pomp'. Although he accepted the necessity for ceremony, 'whenever the opportunity came I used to take my glad rags off and go about in my shorts and shirt – and I don't think that did me any harm. What one heard was that the Nigerians were very pleased that one sort of got down to their level and talked to them and didn't throw one's weight about too much.' As the Governor's Lady Nancy Robertson shared the same unassuming outlook. What had most struck her when she and her husband moved into Government House in Lagos in 1956 was the fact that she now had her nightdress ironed every day:

> But I think it was probably lonelier for me than it had ever been even in the very early days because I had to be very careful about what I said. The only time I said what I thought, which was over Suez, I was indirectly ticked off. It was also very tiresome until I had a little car of my own because I couldn't go out to coffee without ordering a Rolls-Royce or its equivalent and the people who were going to be there had obviously put on stockings for the only time in six months. It didn't make for comfortable living, but from the other side I

had the privilege of meeting people and entertaining people that I would never have approached in ordinary life.

Although there were arguments over timing as well as friction and disharmony between North and South over the question of federation, the actual transition of power in Nigeria took place without a hitch. 'It is the fashion to talk about the fight for liberation but in fact there was no fight in Nigeria. The whole thing went incredibly smoothly.'

In Tanganyika, however, the situation was rapidly deteriorating when Sir Richard Turnbull took over as governor in 1958. 'Governor Turnbull, when he came to us was very different,' recalls Charles Meek. 'I remember, from the speech he made at his swearing-in, my neighbour saying, "He's come to pack us up." Well, so he had. The whole trend which he was to follow through with such skill and persistence in the next three and a half years was to speed up this process of Independence which had looked so infinitely remote to us in my early days, and which was suddenly rushing upon us at a breakneck speed – but a speed which could not be slowed down at all without the risk of the most violent bloodshed and disruption.'

Richard Turnbull began his governorship with appalling disadvantages:

I came there as the hammer of the Mau Mau, the oppressor of nationalists, the associate of the wicked Kenya settler, and all these were pretty strong factors working against me. Luckily I'd been speaking Swahili for thirty years and I spoke it with some fluency and could cap any proverb in Swahili with another proverb in Swahili, and although my accent was a horrible Kenya one, that was my trump card – that and my friendship with Julius Nyerere were the two things that saw me through. Because when I arrived in Tanganyika and recognized how extremely strong the Tanganyika African National Union was I decided that what I must do was to get in touch with the leader of TANU and find out what kind of a fellow he was and let him see what kind of a chap I was and see if we could work together. Luckily I had a very gentle, generous leader of the opposition with whom I immediately came to terms, and we became close personal friends, and that was Julius Nyerere. What the position would have been if I'd had a blundering bully-boy to work with I don't honestly know.

Governor Turnbull now accepted that in Tanganyika, as in so many other territories, 'the old axis of the administration and the Native authorities, the chiefs and chiefs in council, which previously held the country together, was disintegrating.' Instead, there was 'a very tricky path' to tread: 'I had to move fast enough with Julius Nyerere to meet the demands of the wilder element of TANU, because if I had kept Julius down to the speed that I wanted and that the Colonial Office wanted he would have been discredited. But if I went as fast as Julius's men wanted him to go then the Colonial Office would have been extremely alarmed and the administration in Tanganyika would have been horror-struck. So I had to tread this rather tricky path with the greatest care.'

It was now this question of pace that provided the major cause of heart-searching among the government officials, the great majority of whom would agree with Anthony Lytton's opinion that the hand-over of power was 'too swift at the end, too slow at the start'. In Kenya Frank Loyd feared, as did so many of his colleagues in other territories, that 'there simply wasn't going to be time to achieve an orderly Independence. This came as a great shock and surprise, and we wanted time. We were too involved and too fond of the country and our friends in Kenya to want to have to rush to Independence. We didn't think we would be able to do this in such a short time and in the event I am more than delighted that we were proved so conclusively wrong.' Another common fear was that 'in some ways the machine was going to go backwards: government was going to be less efficient, possibly more corrupt after Independence.' Yet it was also realized that this was not really the main issue: 'The important point was that they had to learn to run their own show and the time had come where there was absolutely no option at all but that they must start running it themselves.' To Joan Everett in Nigeria the African point of view was expressed in very much the same terms: 'I remember an African friend saying to me that when the Romans were ruling Britain Boadicea didn't seem to think that they were the right people to be in control and, in the same way, even if Nigeria *wasn't* up to Independence standards in the eyes of the rest of the world, they wanted Independence and if there were going to be any mistakes they'd like to make them themselves.'

After the months of feverish activity and negotiation that had led up to it, the actual hand-over of power often came as something of an anti-climax. Ceremonies, church services and parades followed in quick succession, culminating in the lowering of the old flag at midnight and the raising of the new: 'The Prime Minister and I walked out together,' recalls James Robertson:

I had to wear my uniform, feathers and hat and medals and things and we stood on a little dais and the Union Jack was illumined by searchlights and the band played 'God Save the Queen'. The lights went out and the flag was lowered and then the new Nigerian flag was hoisted to the top of the flag pole. The lights went on and the bands played the new Nigerian anthem. And I noticed the Prime Minister was really affected by this, tears were running down his face when I turned and shook him by the hand and congratulated him. But to me it was a parade, it wasn't nearly so emotive as the bit in my own house. We hadn't any official ceremony for this but I and some of my staff gathered and stood by as the Union Jack came down and I must say that this was the most moving part of the whole show for me.

Different individuals celebrated or noted the coming of Independence in different ways. 'I spent the evening of Independence Day alone,' recalls Philip Allison. 'I could have gone to various parties but somehow I never got there in the end. I sat alone in the rest-house in Abeokuta listening to the new national anthem, "Nigeria we hail thee, our home and native land" being played on the radio. I was working in the museums in a job I enjoyed and I'd have gone on longer doing this, but I wasn't so preoccupied with it that I wasn't prepared to think of a new life in England. I was comparatively young so it wasn't all that of a wrench – I can't pretend it was.' In Adamawa Province in the North Cameroons Nigel Cooke lowered the flag outside the Residency: 'I don't think that I or the other administrative officers felt any particular emotion about the occasion – and the next day we went back to work as normal.'

Inevitably the coming of Independence brought casualties in its wake. There was, in particular, 'one constant feature of development' that disturbed many administrators – 'the necessity to abandon friends who believed we were there for keeps'. Kenneth Smith saw it happening in varying degrees in all the territories in which he served, 'from Zanzibar on to the Seychelles, to Aden and the Gambia. Always the foreign servant, such as myself, has retired home to his pension and a search for another job, but he is unhappily aware that he has left friends who trusted the continuance of the British presence very dangerously exposed to the incoming regimes.' Nowhere was this concern more evident than in Kenya with its recent experience of Mau Mau: 'Naturally we were very afraid that the chiefs and the Kikuyu District officials and others, who had remained throughout staunch supporters of the Government and had done very good work with us, would be victimized in an independent Kenya. This, in the event, proved to be totally wrong and in fact many of those men either remained in the jobs they were doing in the administration or were promoted into others, and to this day have remained as some of the pillars of the Government in Kenya itself.'

Nevertheless, there were territories where such fears were indeed realized, as in Malawi, – formerly Nyasaland – where 'the Africans on the spot were categorized as stooges and traitors, having first of all been loyal to the previous régime. No provision was made for their future and many of them suffered at least professionally, if not in other ways, and we felt there had been a betrayal of them.' By contrast, European officials who chose to stay on were made very welcome: 'Those who wanted to come away were provided with pensions and with compensation for loss of their careers. Those who wanted to stay were received in a most friendly fashion by Dr Banda, who made room for European civil servants in his Government for some years after Independence and quite frankly told his Africans that they wouldn't get those jobs until they were of a standard where they could really occupy them.'

It was the same in most newly independent territories, where 'life went on much the same but the facial colour of the officers next to you changed.' A great many officials did stay on for perhaps one or two tours after Independence before beginning to feel – as Nigel Cooke did – increasingly conscious that they were becoming redundant: 'I remember saying to the Superintendent of Police on one of the rare occasions when I was in my white uniform that I felt I was an anachronism and it was about time I left.' And so in their turn they too became constitutional casualties. 'We saw our chosen careers fading away when we were all at our most vigorous,' observes Charles Meek, 'deprived of the prospects of all the glittering prizes which young men aspire to when they enter a great service like my own. Some will have felt things harder than others; there are some, I am sure, who felt that it was all wrong that Independence should have been conceded as early as it was. I believe that it was a fact of life, that it had to be.'

And so the anachronisms – 'we are now an extinct species as colonial servants; the conservationists didn't reach us in time' – began their departures, taking their leave always with mixed feelings, with hopes and fears for the future, pride and regrets about the past, and sharing the conviction – for all the prevailing mood of hostility towards anything that smacked of colonialism – that their work had been to some good purpose. Mistakes had indeed been made and, in Sir Alan Burns' opinion:

> The greatest mistake was to expect an average colony to support itself. But when one considers colonial rule one has got to remember what was there before it started. Cannibalism, slavery, human sacrifice and various other abominations all existed in Nigeria and the Gold Coast. So I'm quite certain that colonialism was a good thing from the point of view of the African native himself. It taught him respect for the law, it removed him from the constant fear of witchcraft and it taught him also that you could have a democratic government instead of the absolute rule of the chiefs.

Sir James Robertson also believes that to judge Britain's colonial record it is necessary to know about the past:

> I think a great deal is now spoken by people who don't know very much about the background to our rule in Africa. When we took over many of these countries there was very little government, there was very little civilization, there was a great deal of intertribal warfare. Our policy in these countries was, as Virgil said, *imponere paces mores*, to impose the ways of peace, and that's what we did, and we developed them as best we could. One of the things that our critics seem to forget is that we had no money. The British Government gave us nothing for many, many years. In Sudan, which I know best, when Kitchener defeated the armies of the Mahdi at Omdurman in 1898 there were no railways, there were no telegraphs, there were no schools, there were no hospitals, there was no sort of modern government with ministries or anything of that kind. And when we left the Sudan there was a system of railways, there was a system of roads, there was a police force, there was

an army, there were hospitals, there were schools, there was even a university. This was all done in the space of about fifty-eight years – and you could walk from one end of the Sudan to the other more safely than you could walk in the back streets of London, without any fear of danger. We had set up a civilization which had not existed before.

But the imposition of a *Pax Britannica* meant also the imposition of alien ways and customs that had little relevance to African life. A prime example in Sir Richard Turnbull's opinion was British parliamentary democracy: 'We always thought that the political system that happens to suit us in this northern part of Europe is suited to Africa and to the extraordinary tribal society that exists there. It is not. The single party state is what's wanted, although I must admit that we were badly shaken when we first came across the single party state. For us who grew up in the thirties and saw the dictatorships arising, the single party state and fascism are not so far apart and to us it was very distasteful.' In very much the same way there were differences of opinion as to the efficiency – or indeed the relevance – of the English legal code in the African context. Nowhere was the contrast more apparent than in Northern Nigeria, where Nigel Cooke found that 'the administration of law was seen in a very different light by Muslims and the British. We were always against native judges carrying on cases in their houses, and were all in favour of the pomp and ceremony of the law. And this was brought home to me when a new Chief Justice for Northern Nigeria came to Bida, which is the headquarters of an important emirate, and explained at length why he was building a new court-house which would add prestige to the region and increase trade and so on. And he received what I saw to be an absolutely stinging rebuff when a member of the council looked at him and said, "Can you explain what this has to do with justice?" '

Even more damaging to African sensibilities was the initial assumption of racial superiority which had long continued to be expressed in the form of benevolent paternalism: 'When the paternalistic era became a bit outmoded we perhaps weren't very clever in dropping it and adjusting ourselves to getting the right sort of relationship with the new, educated, politically minded African. We preferred dealing with the backward people who we thought were manly and honest and straight-forward – we didn't perhaps like so much dealing with the clever politician.' A very similar 'early and abiding error' was made in concentrating 'too much on the happy and progress-ive development of rural agricultural communities and too little on what was happening under our noses in the big urban centres. Your urban population was never treated with the careful analysis of its hopes and fears that events subsequently proved they required.'

These were the errors of extreme conservatism, a negative side of British colonial rule that was nevertheless, in the opinion of most of those who served in the African colonial territories, outweighed by its merits. 'In our moments of depression we would wonder whether really we were doing any good,' declares Sir Gerald Reece:

> I myself came to the conclusion that the British were doing more than perhaps most other nations would do in that we were serving a purpose. Undoubtedly we interfered with the Africans, sometimes by trying to introduce our own way of life which didn't suit them, but, on the whole, I believe that the British did set an example for them to follow if they wanted to do so. Our attitude to such things as honesty and tolerance, our belief that an absence of bribery and corruption amongst officials produced the best results, and above all the idea that if we have a responsibility and are put in charge of others, it is up to us to serve the people in any way that we can. That was a great lesson I think that the British have left behind in Africa.

And was it all, in the light of later events, a waste of time? Chris Farmer, looking back on his own experience in Nigeria, believes that it was not: 'Of course, it's easy enough looking back to be cynical and disillusioned. It's easy to say, "God, what a mess they've made of it." But then you look back over English history and you say to yourself, "Well, look, we and the Nigerians together" – and it *was* a partnership, you know – "in the course of a mere sixty years we brought Nigeria along a road which took us British unaided in this country how many hundreds of years?" And so, looking at it in its historical perspective, I don't think we did badly.'

And so the British departed, sometimes accompanied by regrets – 'because one regrets leaving the country where one's left a large chunk of one's heart, as one regrets leaving the life one lived and the job that one was doing' – sometimes with relief – 'ninety-nine per cent sheer joy – at going home, one per cent great sadness'. Some left with tears: 'I will admit to crying as I saw the Land Rover drive out of the gate carrying my personal servants, with whom I had very happy relations for many years and of whom I was very, very fond – and I much feared that they were going to have a far less happy life in the future.' Others left with a sense of satisfaction, 'from the fact that in spite of all the dire warnings before I went to Africa that I would never survive, twenty-eight years in tropical Africa didn't seem so bad.' Some 'dreaded the flatness' that lay ahead after what was 'the most vivid part' of their lives, and some faced the future rather more pragmatically: 'I loved my thirty years in Africa but when finally I came back to England I came back to the country in which I was born and which I dearly loved. I no longer have some of the joys of living in Africa and I'd love to go back, but I have no desire to go and live there again.'

With every departing ex-colonial there went 'the memories which you live on in your old age'. Perhaps the 'recollection of camels rolling in the dust around a big fire at the end of a long walk'; 'hippos surfacing and sounding like very old men laughing at jokes'; 'the herdsmen whistling to their cattle as they munched their way through the long grass'; 'the coming of the rains after a dry spell – suddenly down it comes, like thunder, and we all rush out and just stand there and get drenched in it – and then up comes the beautiful smell of grateful earth'; the sound of the African dove – 'for all the world like the bouncing of a ping-pong ball, only very musical' – and the sounds of 'house-boys chattering on the back of the verandah and laughing their lovely, fat, uninhibited laughter'; the smell of wood-smoke in camp or from village fires and the universal African sounds of cocks crowing at dawn and the drums beating at night: 'It wasn't right on the doorstep, it was down in the town, and so it used to rise up to the Residency and you could hear this going on all the time until eventually, of course, you didn't hear it at all because it was like mosquitoes – you hear the pinging to begin with and then you don't hear them any more. And the drumming was comforting in a way, it was the feeling that everybody was content, and if there hadn't been any drumming it would have been a bit sinister somehow.'

Coming home in the mid-1960s was a depressing experience for many ex-colonials and their wives. They came back to an England where the public image of colonialism and the colonial servant was very different from their own: 'I think we were viewed at home as a lot of rather superior beings who'd come along via the Somerset Maugham route, living in luxury and drinking gins in large clubs and flying their flags in large cars as they passed through their districts.' Even more wounding was the 'complete lack of interest in what had happened in Africa in the last fifty years. It was all forgotten, as though it had never been, and all that replaced it was an aura of bright optimism about how much better it was going to be without us.' Veronica Short was asked by friends what her husband had done in Africa: 'When I told them that he had been a District Officer it meant nothing to them at all, they had no idea what he had done. This I found rather sad because I felt that he and all the other people in the Colonial Service had done an extremely good job with very little reward and all that seemed to have been ignored by England and the world at large.'

There was perhaps one final consolation. With Independence the last of the barriers between the races had come down, so that now – 'We find that we can be completely at ease and talk in the friendliest possible way and there isn't, as perhaps some people might expect, a legacy of hatred or dislike. One feels that one is back with real friends and they always say, and I'm sure they mean it, "Do come back we'd love to see you."'

Elder Dempster Lines
Passenger List

Tales from the South China Seas

1

The First Sigh of the East

Suddenly a puff of wind, a puff faint and tepid and laden with strange odours of blossoms, of aromatic wood, comes out of the still night – the first sigh of the East on my face. That I can never forget. It was impalpable and enslaving, like a charm, like a whispered promise of mysterious delight.

Joseph Conrad, *Youth*

To young Britons born in the early years of this century the East was a mysterious and exotic place. Even in childhood its call was sometimes irresistible. Bill Bangs, destined to become a rubber planter and a Muslim, collected stamps as a boy and was always drawn to the Federated Malay States' stamp which showed a leaping tiger, telling himself, 'That's the country I want to go to.' As a child of four or five, Anthony Richards had a retreat in the shrubbery of his parents' country parsonage which he called 'Sarawak': 'I can only suppose that the name was picked up from some newspaper report that the Second Rajah had died. He died in 1917 and I dare say that the papers contained quite a lot about Sarawak which I got second-hand.' Twenty years later he would be embarking on the Straits steamship *Vyner Brooke* at Singapore, bound for the Sarawak Civil Service.

Other children were similarly imbued with romantic notions of life in the East. Reared on a diet of Kipling, Derek Headly had determined from an early age that India was to be the place for him, while as a teenager Edward Tokeley found himself torn between India and China: 'I had to make up my mind what I was going to do and I was introduced to a lovely old man who was a retiring partner in Bousteads in Malaya. I was sent out to dinner with him one night and when he'd finished telling me about these gin-clear seas and golden sands, and the waving casuarina trees, and the gorgeous, dusky girls with their *sarongs* and kebayas, I said, "Where is this place?"'

Then there were those with colonial connections in the family, who hoped when they grew up to follow in their fathers' or uncles' footsteps. John Forrester's father had captained tea clippers on the China run, Richard Broome's was a surgeon in the Indian Medical Service, Peter Lucy's uncle had been a ship's doctor before becoming a Medical Officer in Malaya: 'The ship called in at Singapore and they played cricket against Singapore Cricket Club. My uncle made a hundred and the Governor said, "You're the sort of man we want in the Malayan Service".'

What all these young men had in common was a British middle-class background. Like so many of their contemporaries in the Twenties and Thirties who were to take up careers in the Far East or South-East Asia, they came mostly from country homes and from the public schools, where 'the idea of service wasn't imposed on you but was intrinsic'. They found themselves subject to the traditions of their generation, which meant, in Guy Madoc's case, that his elder brother went into the armed services, 'while I, as the younger son, was expected to go overseas and make my fortune'. A career in the East, whether in government or business, offered a standard of living that could not always be guaranteed at home. And it seemed particularly attractive to those who, like Cecil Lee in 1933, had left school without any particular qualifications and without private means: 'If

you wanted to be a lawyer or an accountant in those days
you had to pay a premium. So the mercantile firms and the
Asiatic Petroleum Company and the banks were an outlet
for you. The fathers and friends of others used to say, "Go
East, young man" – that was the sort of cry.'

A career in the East also offered an outlet for men like Bill
Harrison, who had survived three years in the trenches in the
Great War: 'I wanted to escape from offices, factories, streets
of houses and the general hubbub of life in England. I was
looking forward to another kind of adventure – to seeing
foreign places, climbing mountains, sailing up rivers and
exploring.' He had already qualified as a mining engineer
before the war but with demobilization found 'millions of men
of my age also looking for employment – so I was glad to have
the first offer that came along'. Within a few months of the
ending of the war he was prospecting for tin in the jungles of
Malaya and Siam.

There were many others like Harrison for whom chance
played the decisive role in shaping their futures. It was a casual
encounter on a train that led John Theophilus to become a
rubber planter:

> I was going down to my parents in Hampshire and I had to
> change at Basingstoke Station, where I saw an extremely
> attractive young lady. When she got into the train I got into
> the same carriage. She couldn't run away because there was
> no corridor and in the course of the journey I got her name
> and address in Devonshire. And as soon as I got home I wrote
> to her, after which we used to meet in London quite fre-
> quently. After a few months she said, 'You're not getting very
> much pay here' – I was on thirty shillings a week. She had a lot
> of relations who were out in Malaya and so she spoke to one of
> them who arranged for me to have an interview with a rubber
> company, which I did in late '25.

Robert 'Perky' Perkins had a similarly fateful chance meeting:

In about Christmas 1928 I met the father of an old friend of mine and I said, 'Where's Archie?' – that was his son. 'Oh, Archie's gone out to Malaya.' And I thought of the Malay pirates with their little crinkly daggers. 'What's he doing there?' 'Rubber planting.' I thought of Archie walking along throwing seeds into the ground along set rows. 'He's having a wonderful time,' his father said. Well, I was going in for mining engineering at the time and I didn't like it much so I said, 'How did he get the job?' He says, 'You just go up to London. They're looking for new people.' So I went up to the address he gave me and a fortnight later there I was, on my way out to Malaya on the *Malwa*.

For Edward Banks, who in 1925 had just completed his degree at Oxford, it was a spur of the moment decision that decided his future: 'There were a number of my colleagues at a meeting wanting jobs and a professor said, "Well, they need a curator out in Rajah Brooke's museum in Sarawak. Does anybody want the job?" One of my colleagues said, "No, I don't want the job." And I said, "Well, I'll have it" – not knowing anything about it. I didn't even know where the place was.' In due course Banks was interviewed by the brother of the Rajah – 'a charming old gentleman' – and got the job.

The interview constituted the only real hurdle that the great majority of applicants for jobs overseas had to face. Whether for the government services or the business firms these inter-views tended to follow the same pattern: 'They wanted athletic people and as long as you could play games and mix with people that was the sort of person they wanted.' But back-ground and schooling were also important: 'There's no doubt at all that in those days they were only choosing people from public school backgrounds. They wanted people who'd al-ready experienced a degree of leadership through being a praepositor in the school, from service in the Officers' Train-ing Corps and the like. And they certainly wanted people who were accustomed to an open-air life.' Being good at games counted for a lot more than academic ability: 'They asked the sort of questions which nowadays a lot of people sneer at. You ask a chap if he plays games. If he does and he's got a reasonable academic record as well, you're not going to go far wrong, because chaps who are good at games are usually well-orientated overall.'

The larger rubber companies, in particular, took the sporting ethic very seriously. In the years before the slump in 1929 two of the biggest trading concerns in South-East Asia were Dunlops and Guthries, and both companies took on players of international standard to play in their respective rugby teams. One, a former England cap, started with Guthries but proved to be a better sportsman than he was a rubber planter. 'He took to drink and was sacked,' recalls John Theophilus, 'but he was such a good rugger player that Dunlops took him. Unfortunately, he still continued his habits so off he went.' Theophilus himself has no doubts as to why his first job interview with a Dunlops director went off so well: 'He asked me one or two questions as to where I'd been born and what my parents were and so on and then he said, "What's that tie you've got on?" I said, "It's the Harlequin Rugby Club, sir." And he said, "'You'll get some rugger out there" – and that was my interview.'

Some of the larger Eastern trading houses, as well as the two major banks – the Hongkong and Shanghai (the 'H&S' or the 'Honkers and Shankers') and the Chartered – were rather more selective. The 'nicest' people were said to go to Bousteads and the Asiatic Petroleum Company: 'We weren't snobbish about it but we used to say without any doubt at all – and we never found anybody in Malaya or Singapore who would disagree – that the chaps you found in Bousteads and APC were the best of all.' Gerald Scott was one of those who was soon to find that 'APC was a password to the whole of the Far East. Wherever you went you just signed your name and put APC after it. There was a certain arrogance. When you were picked up on it you said, "But I'm APC".' Guthries, on the other hand, was traditionally a Scots firm and most of its planters were Scots – who regarded their rivals in such firms as Bousteads as having 'not much topside and a lot of old school tie'.

Where academic ability did count was in the selection of administrators. Appointment to what were known as the 'Eastern Cadetships' was by examination as well as interview and only open to graduates. The Public Services Examination governed entry into the Diplomatic and Home Civil Services, the Indian Civil Service and the Eastern Cadetships, with selection based strictly on merit. As far as the overseas services were concerned there was an unofficial but clearly established hierarchy: 'The ICS was the supreme service, only the best people could get through. Then there were three Eastern Cadetships – Ceylon, Hong Kong and Malaya – and that was really the order of batting, with Malaya regarded as the least worthy of the three.'

Sjovald Cunyngham-Brown sat for the week-long exam in 1928 with the intention of entering the Consular Service. He passed high enough to enter – only to be told that there was a three-year waiting list:

At the same time I learned that I could join the Indian Civil Service or the – to me – hitherto unknown services known as the Eastern Cadetships. My uncles and friends who had been or were in the Indian Services said: 'Don't join the ICS, old boy, because it'll be Indianized a considerable time before you're due for retirement.' I said, 'Well, what about the Eastern Cadetships?' Their eyes brightened at once. They said, 'Good God, if you're offered that, take it. The great island empires of the East. The Eastern archipelago, Malaya, half unexplored; a land of adventure: beautiful people, charming surroundings, tigers, elephants. And further east those wonderful islands; Bali, Sumatra, Java. All the riches of the East, loaded with romance and with things still worthwhile doing. Take it if you get the chance.'

Sitting the examination three years later William Goode found that he too was a victim of political change:

> There was only one vacancy for Ceylon and I wanted to go there because I had relatives who'd been in the Ceylon Service. When the results came out and we were called up for our medical interview, I remember complaining in a very loud voice that there was only one vacancy for Ceylon this year and some bloody black man had taken it, and a voice came from behind me and said, 'Yes, it's me, and what's worse, I come from Cambridge' – I being an Oxford man. It was a very nice man from Cambridge who later became very distinguished in the Ceylon Civil Service.

A generation earlier Alan Morkill had also been forced to settle for what he had at first regarded as second best, when he joined the Malayan Civil Service (MCS): 'The state of my knowledge about Malaya was absolutely nil. So I took my mother to Kew to find out what the climate was like. We went into the first greenhouse which was nice and cool, the next one was a little bit warmer but very nice and then finally we got into a place where the steam on our glasses made it difficult to see. But we saw a palm marked *Federated Malay States*. "Alan, you can't go to a country like that!" she said.'

There was widespread ignorance about conditions overseas. As John Baxter left the London offices of his future employer after a successful interview, he met an old school friend: 'He said, "Hullo John, what are you doing?" And I said, "I've just got a job in North Borneo." He said, "Where's that?" I said, "I'm going off to get a map to see."' There were others whose knowledge of South-East Asia came principally from the works of Somerset Maugham, notably a popular film from a play of his called *The Letter*, which was based on a notorious case of adultery and murder that took place in Kuala Lumpur in 1911.

But knowledge was less important than youthful enthusiasm. 'We were young men going off abroad, doing what we

wanted to do,' was how John Davis remembers the mood at
the time. 'We had no idea of what we were going to do – and I
cannot honestly remember that worrying us in the very least.'

Davis was going out as a Police Probationer in the joint
service of the Straits Settlements and the Federated Malay
States, one of the few services that took on young men straight
from school. The business concerns generally sent their em-
ployees out at twenty-one, when they were of an age to sign
their own contracts. Until then they were taken on as 'Trainees
for the East', going the rounds of the various departments and
learning the business at the London end. Similarly, the newly-
appointed Eastern Cadets were sent on half-pay to the School
of Oriental Studies at Finsbury Circus for a six-month course,
much of it taken up with learning Malay but with a smattering
of colonial law and a rudimentary course on tropical health
and hygiene thrown in. The instructors were usually former
administrators, who 'filled us up with a great deal of romantic
stuff about Malaya and the Malays'. The students were also
subjected to a 'tone' test to see if they were suitable candidates
for a department of the Malayan Civil Service known as the
Chinese Protectorate. One of those who passed the test was
Richard Broome:

> The Chinese language being tonal, it's useless unless you have
> a slightly musical ear. I did fairly well but a great friend
> deliberately cheated so as not to do well. He was quite
> prepared to do anything so as not to go into the Chinese
> Protectorate. It was in some ways a specialist department and
> it wasn't popular with those people who wished to be gov-
> ernors and things. People who were in the Protectorate were
> always thought to be mad anyway and I think it did rather
> affect one's career to a certain extent.

In commercial circles it was not thought necessary to learn
Malay or Chinese. But one of those who took the trouble to
learn something of the language before he went out was Bill

Bangs: 'I got a Malay phrase book and a dictionary and I walked up and down the beach at Frinton learning these words and phrases by heart. Most of them I found were not used at all. I remember one of the things I learned was that champagne was called *simpkin* – and I don't think I needed that very much anyway.' However, his rudimentary Malay did prove to be surprisingly useful on the voyage out:

> When we got to Port Said it was so hot that the youngsters who were going out planting decided to take their mattresses up on the deck and sleep there. When we got up there the Lascars were closing the hatches and somebody asked them how long it was going to take. The answer was, 'No speak English. Can speak Malay.' And one of the phrases that I'd learned on the beach at Frinton-on-Sea was 'How long will it take to finish this?' And I remember shooting this out and after that everybody on the boat thought I was the finest Malay scholar possible.

But before the voyage could begin, other preparations for life out East had to be completed. Tropical kit had to be bought and contracts signed. Lists of required clothing were supplied, together with the names of recommended colonial outfitters, and friends and relatives with experience of the East came forward with such practical tips as to buy only the more formal articles of clothing in Britain and have the rest made up at half the cost by Chinese tailors and shoe-makers in such places as Singapore, where a white suit cost three dollars, a pair of shorts one dollar fifty cents and socks worked out at about a dollar for half-a-dozen: 'You didn't bother to darn them; when the holes came you just threw them away.' Shoes were equally cheap and made to measure: 'You went to your shoe-maker and you put your foot down on a piece of paper. Then he drew round your foot and you got your shoes within three or four days. Made with English leather they cost three dollars.'

Alan Morkill's mother provided him with a 'green-lined

umbrella, a special jacket with a protective strip for the spine and a steel-lined trunk which had been my aunt's in India, which we dug out from the stable where it was serving as a corn bin.' These umbrellas and spine pads – 'a thick felt pad that you had sewn into the back of your uniform with red cloth inside and khaki exterior' – and other items of protective wear, such as the Straits Settlements' *Sola Topee*, were regarded as essential prerequisites to good health in the tropics when Morkill joined the MCS in 1913. Twenty years later they were still to be found on all outfitters' lists.

Trevor Walker was one of those who bought a *topee* at Simon Artz emporium in Port Said, only to find when he got to Kuala Lumpur in 1937 that scarcely anyone was wearing one. Edward Tokeley found that he only needed to wear his *topee* when 'fielding on the boundary at cricket', and although Sjovald Cunyngham-Brown wore his for several years, he found it increasingly cumbersome:

> There was a period from 1935 or so when it was generally regarded by all the newcomers as absolutely ridiculous to wear a *sola topee* or a spine pad but that we ought to lie naked in the sun and enjoy the gorgeous, beautiful heat. This was all very well but anybody who did that, as I did, now gets skin cancer, and many of the people who had persistent sunstroke went mad or died. There was a great deal to be said for the old Civil Servants who used to shout at me, 'You'll be sorry for this one day, young fellow. You'll pay for it sooner or later.'

Some of the other items supplied by colonial outfitters seemed equally out of place. Soon after his arrival in Kuala Lumpur Walker noticed that one of his mess-mates wore undervests that were all curiously frayed at the bottom:

> I said to him, 'I understand that the laundry is pretty rough out here but that's a bit much.' He said, 'Oh no, it's nothing to do with the laundry. I had a list that must have been written in

about 1900 because it included twelve pairs of long combina-
tions which I duly bought. I wore them on the way out here
and I wore them for the first month out here and in the end I
got so fed up and so hot that I took a pair of scissors and cut
them all in two.'

Guy Madoc and John Davis, both preparing to go out to
Malaya as Police Probationers in 1931, were sent to Hawes in
Farringdon Street where, 'amongst dusty surroundings, we
were given beautiful white pipe-clayed *topees* and invited to
indulge in something called "throw-away socks", which rather
suggested that the moment you'd bought them and got sweaty
feet, which wouldn't take long in the tropics, you just threw
them away. So everything was bought in very considerable
numbers.' They were also advised that it was compulsory for
them to travel out on the P&O – 'a very high-class sort of
shipping line' – and that they would require no less than
eighteen stiff shirts – 'boiled shirts, we used to call them' – and
thirty-six stiff collars.

Then there were the contracts or letters of appointment.
Guy Madoc's was a very impressive document, informing him
that he was to be 'elected' to an appointment to the Colonial
Service at a salary of two hundred and fifty Malayan dollars a
month, just under thirty pounds. There was also a small cost-
of-living allowance – 'which was taken from us when we'd only
been out for about three months'. The letter also set out
various do's and don'ts: 'They were evidently very worried in
case I got married in a hurry, because it said, "If you marry
before reaching Malaya you will forfeit the appointment. And
if you marry during your first tour of service, the government
will not be liable to provide a passage for your wife, nor to
issue you with married quarters or a marriage allowance".'

This starting salary was virtually the same for all the young
men starting their careers and remained a fairly constant
figure throughout the inter-war period. The major exception
was the Malayan Civil Service, whose cadets received a

starting salary of just under four hundred dollars and promise of a generous pension of a thousand pounds a year for life. Edward Tokeley's terms of service were typical for those joining the mercantile trading companies:

> We didn't have contracts in Bousteads; you had a letter of appointment which was backed by a gentleman's understanding. It said that I could expect my first home leave at the expiry of five years and before the end of my sixth year of service, subject to the exigencies of the service. And that I could expect one local leave holiday of three weeks during that time. There was nothing in the letter of appointment about marriage but it was made clear to you that in order to get the partners' approval to get married you had to earn a certain sum of money a month, which took about ten years' service to achieve.

Both in government and in business new recruits were left in no doubt that marriage before the end of the second tour of service was frowned upon, and that permission had always to be sought first. In Sarawak the Second Rajah had laid down that no officer was to marry before his second tour of five years was completed. The big banks were equally specific; their young men were required to sign an agreement by which they could ask for permission to marry only after they had completed eight years' overseas service. Insufficient income and the difficulty of providing married quarters were the stated reasons for this attitude, but at the back of it was the assumption that the new men were expected to spend their early years getting to know the country and their work.

Finally the time came for embarkation on one or other of the many passenger ships that plied between Tilbury or Southampton and the East: 'In those days it was another era, when all the great shipping lines – the P&O, which was rather posh, the Blue Funnel, and Glen Line, the BI and the Bibby Line – took British men, women and children backwards and forwards across the Empire.'

For all those sailing East for the first time the month-long voyage was to be a memorable experience. Cecil Lee boarded the *Patroclus*, a Blue Funnel liner, at Birkenhead: 'I'd never been beyond Brighton Pier and suddenly here I was living in comparative luxury on this ship which only had one class, not like the P&O. It was full of planters because they felt it was more free and easy than the P&O, which took out the Indian Army officers and the rather high civil servants and was said to be rather snobby.'

One of those travelling by P&O was Guy Madoc, who sailed from Tilbury Docks on a cold, grey December morning on the *Kashgar*:

> We young officers, ten of us, were pushed three to a cabin really designed for two. And so we sailed out with the usual rough weather down the Bay of Biscay and then round by Gibraltar. By that time, we ten policemen, going out to different branches of government service for the first time, had established ourselves right up in the eye of the fo'c's'le on the ship and when you looked right over the bows down to the forefoot of the vessel cleaving through the water, there were porpoises dashing backwards and forwards. It began to feel already that you were getting towards the tropics.

By tradition, the East began not at Suez but at the coaling port of Port Said:

> The orders therefore were that all portholes had to be closed, and your door must be kept carefully sealed, not only because of the coal dust, but because of the 'gippo' thieves who we were assured would come on in great numbers. Well, we young men all decided that we'd go ashore, and of course there were plenty of doubtful touts waiting on the quayside to take us around. One of us, I remember, even slipped a very small automatic pistol into his pocket, and was evidently prepared to defend himself to the death. Of course there

Communications on this subject
should be addressed to—

THE UNDER SECRETARY OF STATE,
COLONIAL OFFICE,
LONDON, S.W.1.

and the following
Number quoted: 17545 Appts.

Downing Street,
Au~ust , 19₿0.

Sir,

       I am directed by Lord Passfield to inform
you that, subject to your being passed by the
Consulting Physician to this Department as
physically fit for service, it is proposed to
select you for appointment to the Colonial Service
as a Police Probationer in the joint service of
the Straits Settlements and Federated Malay States,
with salary at the rate of $250 a month.   On
becoming a passed Probationer, with a minimum of
two years' service your salary will be increased
to $300 a month.   In view of the high cost of
living by which Malaya, like the United Kingdom
and other countries has been affected a temporary
allowance of 10 per cent of salary in the case of
unmarried officers and 20 per cent in the case of
married officers is at present also given.   You
will be provided with free (partly furnished)
                        quarters

G.C.MADOC, ESQ.

Letter of appointment, 1930. The temporary allowance referred to
was withdrawn within three months of the recipient arriving in
Malaya. The letter went on to warn that 'if you marry before
reaching Malaya you will forfeit the appointment'.

were the gentlemen coming up under your elbow, offering you
'feelthy' pictures. But we were taken to an Arab mosque and
we were taken to the famous Simon Artz, the great big store
which lit its lights the moment the ship tied up alongside the
dock. Most of us bought queer Arab burnous and other
accoutrements, which were very useful later on in the voyage,
when we had a fancy dress ball.

Cramped or not, travelling by P&O was done in considerable style, as Sjovald Cunyngham-Brown discovered on his first
voyage out. During the daytime there was 'the fun of talking to
friends, having pre-lunch drinks, a good lunch, happy afternoons playing deck tennis or splashing in the canvas pool that
had been erected over the forehatch'. At mid-day there was the
tote on the ship's daily run, followed by lunch and a siesta – a
word that soon gave way in the newcomer's vocabulary to the
curiously nautical 'lie-off', used throughout the Far East. Then
there were more sports and outdoor entertainments until the
evening when everybody, whether in First or Second Class,
bathed and changed for dinner, wearing dinner-jackets as far as
Port Said and thereafter 'the short white jacket, worn with black
trousers, known as the bum-freezer, in which one went in to
dinner in the tropics'.

There were two sittings for dinner and at first Cunyngham-
Brown was annoyed to find that he had been put down for the
second dinner:

What I hadn't realized was that it was rather a good thing.
The first service used to get hustled down to dinner pretty
early, whereas the second service – mostly the senior officers,
strangely enough – would stay around the bar for an hour-
and-a-half until the bugle suddenly blew for the second
service. You should realize that the P&O in those days was
a very military establishment and the bugles rang at all hours,
beautifully played. And the bugle for dinner, of course,
resulted in our drinking our dry martinis as quick as we could

and descending the large companionway down into the very handsome dining-room with its great *punkahs* swinging, and all my friends in their mess-kits – Gurkhas, 11th Hussars, Indian civilians going back from furlough, whatever it might be – all of us laughing and chatting, getting to our appointed places and discussing the wines that we were to drink that evening.

Whether bound for Bombay, Colombo or beyond, the passengers were more or less of the same background. In consequence, a convivial and club-like atmosphere prevailed on board: 'Our little shipload became more and more intimately fond of each other. We became fast friends, some of which have remained to this day.' Sailing out on the P&O steamship *Carthage*, Edward Tokeley was astonished to find how 'the more seasoned of the Easterners looked after the newcomer. For meals I found myself sitting at a table with three generals, one of whom was going out to be GOC Singapore, and another to do the same job in India. But they looked after me very kindly.' On board the *Patroclus*, however, Cecil Lee found himself seated at the Chief Engineer's table:

> The stewards were Chinese and I remember one day how one came up to me and said: 'Your name Lee? My name Lee, too. Chinese.' I thought this rather funny and I told the story at the Chief Engineer's table and he growled at me: 'You should have kicked his arse!' That was rather the attitude, as I noticed later when we reached Penang from the way some of the officers set about the Tamils swarming on board as stevedores.

After dinner there was dancing, with the ship's band regaling the dancers with the tunes of Cole Porter and Ivor Novello. Those who did not wish to dance could play bridge – 'some women, who seemed very hard cases, played bridge from morning till night, as far as I can remember' – or retire to the bar and enjoy the novel experience of signing for drinks with *chits* which were then presented for payment weekly, on

'Black Monday'. Cecil Lee soon found that his small stock of money was being quickly exhausted: 'I was rather afraid of being thought "*chit*-shy" and not signing for my round but I had to draw in my horns.' Others who were on half-pay found themselves running up bar bills that could not be settled until the ship reached Penang or Singapore, where they began to draw their full salary.

Shipboard romance flourished: 'Aboard ship there is a very lovely feeling of freedom, of happiness, of quickly getting to know each other. And of course all the lovely young girls coming out East were the attraction of all the officers – and ourselves.' There were daughters going out to join their parents, fiancées coming out as brides-to-be and wives following their husbands after an extended leave: 'When we went on to the boat deck to have our cigarettes or cigars after dinner we'd select our partners for the evening and promise ourselves that, in the intervals between the dances, we'd come up on deck to have that beautiful fresh air of the Bay of Bengal blowing in our faces – whilst we underwent fierce flirtations on the boat deck.'

Like many of the youngsters on board, Cecil Lee felt himself to be 'too green and shy and callow' to make the most of the situation:

I used to look with astonishment and wonderment at some of these chaps who'd been out before and knew the ropes. I remember one particular planter, always immaculately dressed, wonderful at all games, doing quite a strong line with a very attractive French wife who was on her way to Saigon. Strangely enough, I followed the career of this man who was a prominent cricketer in Malaya and I heard later that when the Japanese overran us he got away to Java but when he discovered he was going to be taken prisoner he calmly shot himself. This seemed to be all at a piece with his character as I recall it. The life that he knew was gone and so he shot himself.

So the weeks passed – hot, listless days and 'cool, velvety nights spent gazing out over the limitless ocean', as the ship 'rolled gently over the Indian Ocean in starlight and phosphorescence'. There was often a coaling halt at Aden – where Edward Tokeley went ashore: 'I looked at the barren rock and said, "Cor, I do hope that Penang isn't like this." A little while later we landed at Colombo and I looked at this island of green and I thought, "Please, let Penang be as lovely as this. Even if it's half as lovely I shall be happy."'

One morning, as Sjovald Cunyngham-Brown remembers, a little cluster of trees appeared over the horizon. The voyage that had seemed 'as if it might go on for ever' was coming to an end:

> Brilliant sunshine, blue sea, a huge Asian sky of clouds – because Asia has skies that no other place in the world has got; higher, more grandiose, more flamboyant – and clustering under it this little block of land: South-East Asia. The very beginning of the great romantic East, the island empires of which I dreamed. All my friends left the bar and came to the starboard side of the ship as this little dot of land called Pulau Way – a tiny island at the tip of Sumatra – hove up into sight, with a great sea pounding on its beach, brilliant in the sunshine under bending palm trees. Gorgeous bathing, as I discovered later. We watched it and drank our Singapore gin-slings – or Singapore pink-gins – as it slid into the horizon behind us. Now we were east; this was the beginning.

Soon afterwards his ship made its landfall at Penang Island, the first of the British Straits Settlements: 'We watched it coming up in the early morning light. A big mound of land, a great whale lying there basking in the sea as we crept up toward it and went in between it and the mainland of Malaya. A beautiful land with high mountains, three thousand feet high, gorgeous little bays, cliffs and jungle. All under the keen light of morning and a strong wind from the northeast.'

Penang Island had already known a century and a half of trading and prosperity under the British. Rickshaws and hand-drawn carts filled the streets of George Town, and old-fashioned Chinese shops with red-tiled roofs and Chinese signs lined its bazaars. The most penetrating sounds were the cries of hawkers peddling their wares – rice-cakes ('*nasi lemak!*'), green coconuts ('*ba-cha-cha!*' – with a pleasing inflection on the last syllable) or the large noodles known as 'pig's-guts cake' ('*chee-cheong-fan!*') – and the clip-clop of the wooden clogs worn by Chinese women dressed in bright blue or white jackets and black trousers. On the outskirts of the town there were broad, tree-lined avenues dotted with elegant mansions, some dating back to the early days of the East India Company, others belonging to Chinese dollar millionaires, and shaded by flowering trees: 'the "trees of golden rain" called the *angsana*, the royal palms and the beautiful jacaranda that fell in blue drifts across the bougainvillea.'

For the old Malay and China hands this was where South Asia ended and where the Far East began, for 'it was like coming home when you hit Penang'. And its appeal was not lost on newcomers. 'It was an enchanting place,' declares Cunyngham-Brown, 'and I was so happy to be there.' For Edward Tokeley, too, there was relief and delight as he became aware that Penang – where he was to be based for the next four years – appeared to be even more beautiful than Ceylon: 'It was completely unspoilt; it was paradise enow.'

As Bill Harrison's ship, the *Futala*, anchored off the wharf at George Town, a tropical storm broke overhead:

We came up on deck early in the morning to be greeted by a terrific thunderstorm with the most vicious forked lightning I have ever seen, streaking across the sky, blue-white streaks of lightning from horizon to horizon and the most heavy down-pour of tropical rain I've ever experienced. The rain hit the deck like two shilling pieces and bounced up as high as our knees, with a white haze of spray. You couldn't see through the rain it was so heavy. Finally, that blew across as it does with some of these Sumatras – storms that come across from Sumatra. The wind carried it away and up came the sun and we looked across to the mainland and there was a row of palm trees along part of the Butterworth shore and rubber plantations and, way in the distance, the Kedah peak, standing up like a sugar loaf.

The wharf itself was like a beehive, crowded with Chinese coolies and Tamils with their bullock carts, while up along the quay were stacks of hundredweight ingots of tin waiting to be shipped out, as well as canvas bales of SRS (Smoked Ribbed Sheets) rubber and copra. These 'scented the whole atmosphere with the sweet, nutty smell of drying coconut', mingling with the stink of the monsoon drains and the scent of cloves and pepper – 'that pungent, spicy odour, so redolent of the Far East'.

The 'purple East' also began to exert its influence in other ways. Unlike most other newcomers, Bill Harrison had travelled by way of India and then sailed from Madras to Penang on a 'coolie-ship', its decks crowded with immigrant Tamil labourers coming out under contract to work on the plantations, together with their wives and children:

> I remember on our arrival we were all trimming up for going ashore and one of the young lads with us – we were nearly all young fellows coming out to join our firms in Malaya – needed a haircut, so he called over a Tamil barber who was cropping the hair for the Indians on board. 'Give me a haircut as well,' he said. But when he got up out of the chair he'd been given a Hindu haircut and his head was shaved right across the top half and the back half was long. He did look a sight. All he needed was a couple of coloured spots on the centre of his forehead and he would have been a Hindu.

Sjovald Cunyngham-Brown was among those who would be leaving the ship at George Town in order to cross by ferry to the mainland or to catch the fast Straits Steamships' service to Port Swettenham and KL (Kuala Lumpur). When his ship finally came alongside the wharf a government representative came aboard to escort him and his fellow Eastern Cadets ashore:

> We all said, 'Good morning, sir.' To which he replied, 'Don't call me sir, for heaven's sake. I'm only eighteen months senior to yourselves.' I said, 'What are we going to wear?' 'Well, of course, wear your *tutup* jackets' – that is to say, the white cotton jacket that buttons up to the neck. That and white cotton trousers, black socks – which appeared to be *de rigueur* at that time – and black shoes. On our heads, naturally, were to be the *sola topees* and behind our backs the spine pad. Then, rejoicing, we went down the gangway.

Rickshaws, with their Chinese rickshaw-pullers, were waiting on the quay: 'We sat in them, rather hot and stifling in the morning sunshine, and John Hannington, in his rickshaw beside me, with sweat dripping off his nose and the tips of his ears and pouring down his face – as indeed it was off mine – said: "I suppose we're going to feel like this for the rest of our lives".' To Guy Madoc, however, the heat seemed 'glorious. It was nice to be slightly sweaty all day.'

As Cecil Lee left the ship he was overcome by homesickness, for 'it had been a wonderful voyage and suddenly I was saying goodbye to everyone and starting a new life.' There were no customs or immigration formalities to be observed and a rickshaw carried him straight to his firm's office, where he met the European staff:

> One of them – an awfully nice fellow – took me round and gave me lunch at the main hotel there, the '*E & O*'. Then he left me to have a lie-off in the Penang Club. So I sat in this gaunt, high-ceilinged club with its great fans whirling round up above, lying in one of those long bamboo chairs with arms

for your legs and a slot for your *stengah*. The Chinese 'boys' padded silently by and it was all quiet – except for raucous laughter coming occasionally from the bar and the cry of 'Boy!'

2

Agents of Trade

The seventeenth-century traders went there for pepper, because the passion for pepper seemed to burn like a flame of love in the breast of Dutch and English adventurers about the time of James the First. The bizarre obstinacy of that desire made them defy death in a thousand shapes; the unknown seas, the loathsome and strange diseases; wounds, captivity, hunger, pestilence, and despair. To us, their less tried successors, they appear magnified, not as agents of trade but as instruments of a recorded destiny, pushing out into the unknown in obedience to an inward voice, to an impulse beating in the blood, to a dream of the future.

Joseph Conrad, *Lord Jim*

Sacred to the memory of John Baird, Junior, son of the Hon. J. Baird, Master Attendant and Midshipman of the Wellesley East Indiaman, who arrived on this Island on 27 August 1800 and died the 6 September following aged 17 years and 6 months

Inscription on tombstone,
Northam Road Cemetery, George Town, Penang

UNDER the frangipani trees in Penang's oldest cemetery lies buried Francis Light, founder of the Settlement of Prince of Wales Island – later to become Penang. For Sjovald Cunyng-

ham-Brown, still living for much of the year on the island, the
cemetery has a special significance:

> I never pass the cemetery without thinking of Francis Light in
> his completely neglected tomb. It's a melancholy place in a
> way. So many young people's graves are there, who died of
> malaria between the ages of eighteen and twenty-three; young
> cadets – masses of them – girls in childbirth, all neglected these
> days. And among them Francis Light, who died of malaria like
> nearly everybody else on this island.

In British times a ceremony was held every year in the
cemetery to mark the anniversary of the death of the settlement's founder on 21 October 1794. After *Merdeka* and the
coming of independence to Malaysia the ceremony dwindled,
until only two people were left to celebrate it: 'One was Henry
Grummit, of long descent on this island, and the other was
myself. We would come with a bottle of Cognac and discuss
Francis Light, sitting on his very grave, and as the dusk came
on we would get tipsier every minute!'

It was Francis Light, an independent 'country trader' newly
commissioned by the British East India Company with the
rank of captain, who in 1786 arrived with three ships off the
island and began clearing the sandy headland on which
George Town is built:

> The ground at the time was covered with a small hard coastal
> tree known as the *penaga*, which very soon blunted the axes that
> had been brought down from Calcutta, so the *Eliza* was sent
> down to Malacca to buy native *beliong*, as they're called – very
> small, hard iron axes from Dutch Malacca. She was away for
> about three weeks during which period, in order to keep the
> troops occupied and happy, Francis Light was in the habit of
> loading his guns on the *Prince Henry* and *Speedwell* and firing
> them off into the surrounding undergrowth of the island. He
> filled his cannon with small coinage of all descriptions – annas,

pice, even an occasional rupee – and fired them off, and in the
ensuing scramble for money more opening up of the headland
was done than could possibly have been achieved in any other
manner.

To all intents, this first scramble for money among the
penaga trees of Penang Island marked the arrival of permanent
British trading interests in the Malacca Straits. But long before
the British, there had been Portuguese and Dutch traders, and
before them other foreigners, all drawn by the lure of trade:
'From untold ages in the past South-East Asia has been the
nodal point through which the trade of the world had to go. It
has supplied the world with an essential commodity in the
form of spice.'

The spice islands also provided humanity with one of its
greatest mixing bowls:

> From the Marquesa Islands in the Pacific, right through
> South-East Asia and through Ceylon down to Madagascar
> in the shape of an enormous lozenge are the 'between the
> islands people', the *Nusantara* in Sanscrit or the *Kun Lun* people,
> as they've been known to the Chinese since pre-Christian
> times. These people have on one side of their family a
> common origin in the Western Pacific, and although they
> formed only a tiny minority among the aboriginal tribes whom
> they encountered, they intermixed and the more primitive
> people naturally took on the characteristics of the more
> advanced ones.

Over the centuries other ingredients were added; waves of
settlers from Northern India spreading east and south as far
as Bali, to leave behind a Hindu culture, and then a second,
sea-borne invasion from Southern India, bringing the new
religion of Islam to Sumatra and Malaya, which thereafter
became strongholds of Muslim teaching throughout South-
East Asia:

Islam took a very rapid and permanent root in this part of the world because it hadn't got any very strong counter-religion to sweep back again over it – and of course this Islamization had the result of bringing in new traders from Southern Arabia, the 'Sinbad the Sailor' type of distant trading venture. And these people – Sheiks and Sayids, landed and slave-owning, wealthy and strong merchant princes – carved out land in this part of the world in the twelfth, thirteenth and fourteenth centuries, and their descendants form the present-day governing aristocracy of Malaya, Sumatra and Brunei.

The most powerful of these dynasties today is the Sultanate of Brunei, whose present ruler can trace a royal ancestry that goes back nearly a thousand years. Robert Nicholl, who spent many years in Sarawak as an educationalist, now works for the Sultan of Brunei as an historian and from this unique vantage point has examined the impact of Europeans on the established trading patterns of South-East Asia:

The South China Sea may be compared to the Mediterranean in the sense that it is the cradle of ancient and affluent civilizations. Not ancient in the sense of Egypt and China but ancient in the British sense. When Alfred was burning the cakes and being ravaged by the Danes, it is recorded that the Maharajah of Shrivijiya in Palembang each morning went out onto a balcony which overlooked a pond and into the pond he threw a brick of solid gold. It was a very successful arrangement of course, because when the Maharajah's successor took office he fished up all the thousands of bricks from the pond and started off with a healthy bank balance. Or, if we come a little further, to Henry VII's time, an observer at that time noted the children of the Chief Minister of the Sultan of Malacca having a wonderful time building sandcastles. The little tots greatly enjoyed themselves, but what was interesting was that they weren't using sand, they were using gold dust. So it wasn't without reason that the Indian travellers, who were the first to explore South-East Asia, referred to it as the Land of Gold and spoke of Sumatra, Borneo and Malaya as the Islands of Gold. It was a very prosperous little world. It had a great trade with China to the north and then to the west there was the trade with India reaching far beyond to the Caliphate and so ultimately to Europe. It was an area of peace and prosperity and great affluence.

Suddenly, into this stable world there came 'an eruption' in the shape of the Portuguese, arriving not as ordinary traders but as a hostile power intent on seizing the spice trade for themselves and establishing a monopoly:

In 1498 Vasco de Gama was making his way along the East Coast of Africa and at Malindi by some extraordinary chance he encountered the greatest Arab navigator of his day, Ahmed Ibn Majid, who guided him across to Calicut in India. Calicut was at this time a great centre of the spice trade, which stretched from the Moluccas in the east to Venice in the west. Now when you talk of spices you're simply talking of curry powder and it's often forgotten that the medieval Europeans were amongst the world's greatest curry eaters. There was no means of feeding animals during the winter except at great cost and therefore you killed off all your fat animals in September and for the next six months or more you lived on salted meat. Now the attractions of salted meat pall and so the demand in Europe for anything that gave savour to salted meat was very great indeed.

But before these spices could reach Europe they had to pass through all sorts of customs barriers where levies, official and unofficial, had to be paid:

You bought your sack of pepper for five ducats in Calicut and by the time it reached the Rialto in Venice it was sold for eighty ducats – and pepper is the least valuable of the ingredients in curry. Now when Vasco de Gama arrived in Calicut he loaded up with spices and brought them straight back to Lisbon. No customs duties, no levies, no palms to be greased. The profits were such that no man had ever seen them before! And there was an immediate rush of the Portuguese out to India and beyond to secure this profitable trade.

The Portuguese quickly became the super-power of the Indian Ocean and in 1511 they captured the emporium of Malacca, which gave them control of the narrow straits between Sumatra and the Malayan mainland. But although they established a monopoly the effect on local trade was not as damaging as it might have been. It was the arrival of the Dutch in 1600 that finally brought devastation: 'The Dutch were not only powerful at sea, they were also hard-headed business men and the monopoly they fastened on the archipelago was one of iron efficiency. It really wrecked the trading pattern of the South China Sea. Native trade wasted away and by the time the British came on the scene the great ports that had been frequented by merchants from all over the east had sunk into decay and had become the nest of pirates.'

Groups of these 'pirates' helped to build up Malaya's still sparse population so that what was later to become the State of Selangor was 'largely peopled by Bugis immigrants, originally pirates, who came from the islands grouped to the south of Singapore. They settled mainly in *kampongs* along the coast and then penetrated gradually up the rivers. Similarly, the Negri Sembilan Malays came from Menangkabau in Sumatra, and they again were a sea-borne people who came in from outside and settled along the coast and gradually infiltrated up the rivers.'

The East Coast Malays had different origins. Many were immigrants from across the Gulf of Siam – but they too settled on the coast and they worked their way inland:

These people came when the whole of the land was covered
in absolutely impenetrable jungle so thick that when somebody wanted to visit what is now a tourist attraction seven
miles outside Kuala Lumpur, he had to go there by elephant
and it took him three days. Now the answer to this jungle
for your ordinary immigrant was to settle either on a sea-
shore or up a river, and there was a saying in the days when
this Malay immigration was at its height, that a cat could
walk from Port Swettenham down to Malacca without
getting its feet wet, so thick on the ground were the houses
along the beaches..

Compared with the Europeans, the impact of the Chinese
on the Eastern archipelago was less traumatic and of far
greater consequence in human terms. Living among a community that is still predominantly Chinese in origin, Sjovald
Cunyngham-Brown has learned a great deal about them both
as traders and as settlers:

There have been coastal Chinese fishing communities in the
archipelago from as far back as records go. But they became
more numerous after the taking of Malacca by the Portuguese.
Many Chinese settled there and started the *Hokkien* communities in Malaya; soft-featured, Southern Chinese from Amoy.
A preponderance of the Chinese in Penang are also of *Hokkien*
descent, who came in as fishermen or cooks during the days of
the East India Company.

Under Company and then (after 1867) under Crown rule
the Chinese in Malacca and Penang prospered. They came to
be known as the 'Queen's Chinese' and looked upon the
Straits Settlements as 'practically a county of England. They
were stoutly pro-Queen Victoria, strongly pro-British and sent
their sons to England to be educated.'
In the middle of the nineteenth century a second wave of
Chinese settlers began to arrive: the *Hakka* people, a 'notori-

ously stubborn race of hill-farmers' known throughout China as the 'stranger' people:

> They came down to Malaya in enormous numbers as a result of the Taiping Rebellion in 1851–65. They were exiled officers' families from that rebellion, which gave General Gordon his name of 'Chinese' Gordon. He was called out as a very young man to help settle that affair and it took him ten years to get them all away. They went to Manila in the Philippines, to Surabaya and Batavia in the Dutch East Indies, and to Singapore in large numbers – and from Singapore they came on to Penang.
>
> Those in Penang found themselves confronted with a highly organized community of *Hokkien* Chinese who knew not one word of their language and the two were antagonistic from the very beginning. The *Hakka* hated the *Hokkien* and the *Hokkien* were annoyed by these energetic, loud-voiced newcomers, so filled with initiative and push. Very soon they not only lived up at the top of the hill, where they opened farm lands, but they also came down into the town and began to bust up the settled *Hokkien* community.
>
> Gang warfare between the *Hakka* and *Hokkien* secret societies more or less coincided with the discovery on the mainland of huge fields of tin ore. *Hokkien* prospectors had moved up the rivers into the Malayan jungle and were excavating open-cast tin-mines in such places as Kuala Lumpur, the 'muddy estuary' at the confluence of the Klang and Gombak rivers. They couldn't get up in large boats any further than the junction of the two rivers so they made a base there at what is now called Kuala Lumpur. The survival rate was very low in those early days, from jungle fevers and what not, but they just kept on bringing Chinese workmen in faster than they were dying and they finally moved the jungle back a bit and then things opened up. The Malays established forts at the mouth of the river where they could collect tribute on everything going in and

everything coming out – and the Chinese paid the tribute and did the work.

Then came warfare between rival gangs of Malays and Chinese and there was chaos.

The intervention of the *Hakka*, equally anxious to carve out spheres of influence on the mainland, further aggravated the situation: 'The upshot was that the Malay States under their native rulers began to take sides, one against the other. And so from about 1865 the entire Malay peninsula from north to south rapidly became a murderously dangerous blood bath – and something had to be done about it.'

By now the trading monopoly of the old East India Company had long since been broken by any number of rival syndicates of merchant adventurers based in Penang and the other two principal Straits Settlements, Malacca and Singapore. Typical of these East India merchants were such firms as Guthrie and Co. and Boustead and Co., both of which had their head offices in Singapore. The first had been founded by a Scotsman, Alexander Guthrie, only two years after Stamford Raffles had leased the island of Singapore from the Sultan of Johore in 1819. Bousteads was started six years later by a China trader, Edward Boustead; 'a far-sighted chap, because he and his partners bought some prize land sites and built splendid houses on them. He also started the first club in Singapore, the Billiards Club, and edited Singapore's only newspaper.' Like most of the other *hongs* or mercantile houses in Singapore, Guthries and Bousteads were in what was traditionally known as the 'jam and pickle' business, exporting what was available and importing whatever was needed.

These trading concerns found themselves inextricably involved in the disturbances on the mainland. In some cases they even took sides, supplying the combatants with 'unconventional items of mining equipment' in the form of brass cannon, rifles and ammunition. Partly at their behest and partly to keep open the Far Eastern trade routes, the British Crown intervened. With the treaty of Pangkor, signed in 1874, peace was restored on the mainland – but at a price. The Sultan of Perak was required to accept at court a British officer whose advice was to be taken in all matters except those pertaining to Malay religion and custom. So began the direct involvement of the British Crown in the affairs of the Malay States, following the 'commercial *box-wallah* who'd gone in first and might have been in trouble if he hadn't been helped'. For here there was no question of 'Trade following the Flag': 'It was the flag that followed trade – often very reluctantly. Trade was the basis of the British endeavour in South-East Asia; trade and nothing but trade was at the bottom of the whole business.'

Nowhere was this reluctance to extend Britain's imperial domains more apparent than in the case of Borneo, where only the tiny island of Labuan was brought directly into the colonial fold, in order to provide a naval base against the pirates that infested the South China Sea. On the main island itself a large area in the north was leased in 1881 to a chartered company, the British North Borneo Company, to govern more or less as it pleased – just as the East India Company had earlier ruled India and the Straits Settlements. And further south there was the remarkable phenomenon of Sarawak, where it was said that 'the white man was held in higher regard than in any other British territory'. In 1841 the coastal strip of tropical jungle, inhabited mostly by tribal peoples, was handed over by the Sultan of Brunei to an English adventurer named James Brooke. When he died in 1868 he had already been succeeded by his nephew, Charles Brooke, who was known as the Second Rajah and was the true creator of Sarawak. Long after the Second Rajah's death in 1917 stories about him continued to be told in the longhouses of Borneo.

There was a very marked difference in the way that British North Borneo and Sarawak were governed. In the former, commercial considerations came first:

'Under the Chartered Company everything was far more simple. There weren't the rules and regulations that came with colonial government. The manager of a rubber estate was really more important than the government officer in his district. He was a law unto himself and the government really let him do more or less what he liked.' Thus when John Baxter first came to Sapong Rubber Estate, near Tenom, in 1924 he found it to be a 'very hard life' for European assistants like himself and for the estate's Javanese indented labour alike. His manager was a harsh disciplinarian of thirty years' standing in the country who was also responsible, as the local magistrate, for preserving law and order in the district. If any of the labour tried to run away he would send police after them and sentence them to be flogged as an example to the rest: 'Then in 1927 a Dutch Labour Inspector came to Sapong and for the whole day was interviewing people who had complained about the treatment they'd received. But they were frightened of speaking out on the estate, so that evening, when he was having his first beer back in Tenom, three dripping figures appeared. Despite the crocodiles, they had swum over the Padas river to put their case. That same night the Dutchman tried to cut his throat and had to be taken down to the coast.' Three months later a second Dutch Inspector came and this time succeeded in bringing charges: 'My manager was kicked out of the country and questions were asked about him in the House of Commons.'

In Sarawak, too, there were few of the rules and regulations of colonial administration. But here any attempt by outsiders to exploit either the country's natural resources or its people met with the strongest opposition:

> It was the policy of all the Rajahs, First, Second, and Third, not to develop the country. They would not have European companies in to plant rubber all over the place and mine it and work the timber. They wished that the local people should plant their own rubber gardens and work their own timber, or, if they wanted to work gold, to go and work it. They weren't wage-slaves; they were free to earn their own living. And this is

a very important point in Brooke rule, because it was almost the only country where such a thing was done. The result was that nobody was rich and nobody was poor.

The one European company that was allowed to trade in Sarawak with any degree of freedom was the Borneo Company. It had earned this privileged position by coming to the rescue in 1857 when the little township of Kuching was attacked by Chinese and the Rajah was forced to flee down-river. It was the timely arrival of the Borneo Company's steamer, the *Sir James Brooke*, with the head of the company temporarily appointed 'acting Rajah', that had saved the day. This same company went on to win for itself a rather special place in popular history when a few years later its manager, acting on behalf of the King of Siam, engaged as a governess to his Court the widow of an Indian Army major, Anna Leonowens.

But the great boost that turned the more far-sighted of the trading companies into powerful managing agency houses was the advent of rubber. The discovery that the shallow but well-drained alluvial soil between Malaya's central mountain range and its western seaboard could grow better-quality rubber than anywhere else in the world led to an explosion of planting and trading that was to dramatically alter both the landscape and the economy of the country. And with the plantations came not only hundreds of young Englishmen and Scotsmen in search of profit and adventure, but also a vast force of unskilled labour in the person of the humble coolie. Tens of thousands came in junks across the South China Sea – and hundreds of thousands from India, mostly Tamils from the south. So the last waves of migration began, and by the end of the nineteenth century the social, political and economic patterns for the next fifty years had been more or less fixed throughout the archipelago. It became a region where 'four separate communities divided by race, religion and culture lived together – generally in harmony but on the whole keeping themselves to themselves'.

On the peninsula the other eight Malay states followed Perak's example: some became Federated States – the FMS – with a British Resident and a British administrative system, while others hung on to a greater degree of independence as Unfederated Malay States – the UMS – where a British Adviser might advise the Sultan but whose powers were otherwise strictly limited: 'These states each had their own history, their own people and their own rulers, and were almost foreigners to each other. They hardly mixed and thought of themselves as being Perak Malays or Selangor Malays or whatever it was.' There was 'no such nonsense as democracy and egalitarianism and all that. The Malays accepted that the Sultans were the rulers, and the lack of politics was one of the country's great charms.'

Nevertheless, it was impressed upon young officers when they first went out that, beyond the confines of the Straits Settlements, Malaya was not to be thought of as a colony: 'It was a protectorate of Britain and we had to behave with very great respect towards the Malay rulers, who were all very dignified men indeed and carried their dignity well.' Before any European official could take up an appointment within an Unfederated Malay State his name had to be submitted to the Sultan in Council for his approval. A special courtly form of Malay had also to be used when writing to the ruler or when speaking to him: 'There was a formula you used. If you addressed the Rajah you addressed the dust below the feet of his exalted highness and so on.'

When Bill Bangs first came to Kelantan State in 1933 the ruler was Sultan Ishmail, who had been crowned in 1920. Even when it came to dealing with the British, his authority was considerable:

He got his own way in many things but according to the Treaty he was supposed to take the advice of the British Adviser in anything except *adat*, which was Malay custom and religion. However, I can remember on one occasion his sister, the *Tungku Merani*, was very angry because the Posts and Telegraphs had cut down some of her rubber branches which were interfering with the telephone line. She called the Posts and Telegraphs' man up to tick him off over this, and he rather stupidly lost his temper and used the word '*mu*' to her instead of saying '*tungku*'; '*mu*' is a very low 'you' used only to labourers. He was also in charge of Customs and he accused her of getting a lot of goods for her house in without paying duty on them. She was very, very angry and went and complained to her brother, the Sultan, and the Sultan called the British Adviser and this man, who was very senior in government service, was out of Kelantan on the next mail train.

The government officers who occupied these upper tiers of the civil administration in Malaya came from the ranks of the Malayan Civil Service. When Cunyngham-Brown joined in 1929 there were approximately three hundred such officers administering an area about the size of England and Wales – 'a small body with the greatest *esprit de corps*, with a vocation and dedication to our job – and that was one of the main and most endearing features of the MCS to anybody who belonged to it'.

Although the age of the pioneer administrators had ended long before the Great War, one or two survivors were still in evidence in the 1920s. In his first weeks in Malaya as an Eastern Cadet in 1928 Mervyn Sheppard was out in his district supervising the collection of rent:

We were carrying on the very simple, slow-moving process of collecting fifty cents or a dollar when suddenly down the road we heard a motor-car approaching – and there weren't any motor-cars in Malaya in those days. Then there was a screech of brakes and the car stopped, and down stepped a very tall figure with a rather pronounced stoop, dressed in a white uniform with a high collar – which was known in those days as a *tutup* – and long white trousers and wearing a *topee*. The village headman, who was with me, immediately recognized him and, taking absolutely no notice of me or anything else, hurried down the path and held out his hand in greeting. Then, in the Malay way, they just touched hands and exchanged the Arabic greeting: '*Salaam alaikum*; peace be with you', and the answer, '*Wa alaikum salaam*; to you be peace'. Then the tall figure started to speak, and he spoke for at least five minutes, in Malay and in the Pahang *patois*, of which I didn't understand a word. But everybody else was engrossed, enthralled by what he was saying. Then at the end of his brief address he turned round, got back into his car and was driven away.

This unexpected visitor was Sir Hugh Clifford, High Commissioner for the Malay States, who forty years earlier had come to Pahang as its first British Agent.

A rather more curious relic of the early days of British administration in Malay also existed in the person of Captain Hubert Berkeley, the 'uncrowned king of Upper Perak', who was usually to be found dressed in full Malayan costume, consisting of *sarong*, *baju* and *songkok*, in the remote jungle district of Grik, close to the Siamese border. Stories about *tuan* Berkeley were part of the folklore of Perak:

One day he was going out on an elephant ride, which he used to do very regularly. As he got up on his elephant and was about to go, the Court Clerk came running to him and said, 'Sir, you've got cases in court today.' Berkeley turned round and said, 'Blast it,' and then asked how many cases there were. The Court Clerk said, 'Twenty-five sir.' 'What are they?' said Berkeley. 'Minor offences, sir.' 'Have you read the charges?' 'Yes sir. They all plead guilty.' 'All right. Odd numbers discharged, even numbers fined five dollars.' Then he turned round and rode away.

Berkeley apparently preferred his own summary justice to the precepts laid down in the Indian Criminal Code and followed by British magistrates in Malaya. When a dispute over a boundary came before him he adjourned the court and summoned the litigants and all their witnesses to follow him to the site in question. Here he formed the disputants into two teams and held a tug-of-war contest using rotan creepers from the jungle, awarding the land to the winning team. Tales of Berkeley and his eccentricities also circulated widely among the European population on the peninsula:

> Berkeley was quite a good host, but he had a double-barrelled lavatory. And he seemed to think that it was part of being a good host to join his guests there. People with rather more delicate sensitivity used to spend a lot of time saying, 'I think I'll just take a little stroll before breakfast,' and hope that they'd be able to get into the loo without their host being there. But they very rarely succeeded. He'd come up and say, 'Oh, fancy meeting you. How nice! I've brought a spare copy of *The Times* along in case you'd like to read it.' On the opposite wall of this double-barrelled thunderbox was pinned up a large photograph of the Chief Secretary to Government of that time, Sir Frank Swettenham. Berkeley said that looking at that horrible chap made him have better motions.

It was said that Berkeley had jumped ship in Penang and had then enlisted in the police before eventually joining the MCS. He was known to come from an aristocratic Roman Catholic family in Worcestershire and 'seemed to regard himself as a combination of an English squire and a Malay chief'. Several times a week he could be seen driving off to bathe at some nearby hot springs 'in an English landau and pair, with a postillion dressed in a red and white garment that corresponded to the Berkeley family livery'. Having built up for himself an extraordinary degree of independence in his district, Berkeley was able to resist all attempts to get rid of him:

He very much disliked seeing senior officers from more civilized parts of the country coming up to inspect his district and criticizing it. And on one occasion when a very senior government official sent a telegram saying, 'Am coming up tomorrow on Inspection,' Berkeley sent a telegram back saying, 'No bridge at sixty-fourth mile.' And that thoroughly discouraged the British official. The fact was that the sixty-fourth mile ran through fine flat country with no river or bridge. But he managed to keep most visiting firemen out of his district in that way.

Alan Morkill had the unenviable task of relieving Hubert Berkeley when he finally retired in 1925 at the age of sixty-two – seven years past official retiring age:

I was received by Berkeley who was dressed in Malay costume. I took over a herd of cattle, three elephants and three or four horses. He had about fifty cattle and he warned me to be very careful when it came to the annual return. 'In order to avoid trouble with the Auditor-General, you must never alter the return,' he said. 'Calves are born and plod their weary way till they become beef in the DO's compound – but they must still go down as calves.' He showed me round and when we came to the Court House he said, 'Here we dispense justice but not law.'

Above the bench were two fox masks.

Morkill once encountered another sort of relic from the past when in temporary occupancy of an old bungalow:

It was the fashionable time, about midnight, when I heard steps coming up the drive and I assumed it was the police inspector coming to report a murder or something. I went outside and the steps continued but I didn't see anybody. I called out but there was no answer, so I thought no more about it. Then Haines, who'd had the district before me, was staying with me one Christmas and he said, 'Oh, do you ever hear Abraham Hale's ghost?' Abraham Hale was an early DO who had died out there. I said, 'No. What happens?' He said, 'Oh, he walks up the drive and on to the porch and disappears.' Well, I put a whisky and soda out in case he took it – but he never did.

Only in one other corner of the South China Sea did individualism on the Berkeley scale continue to flourish after the Great War. When Edward Banks came to Sarawak to take up his post as Museum Curator he found himself in a country that was full of eccentrics and characters drawn from all over the world:

> The Rajah rather liked having these people who weren't stuffed shirts, as he used to say. There were men there who'd been cowboys in the west – they'd been to Alaska on the Kicking Horse Pass gold rush; there were men who'd been round the Horn in sailing ships, or on the Ashanti goldfields and to Johannesburg. And, of course, men from the services. There was an RAF sea-pilot, there was a magnificent man off a destroyer, who was unable to go home on leave because he was a bigamist. Then they had chaps from the China Customs and the Burmese teak forests. They were not qualified in any scholastic way. They were simply men who'd gone out into the world and made their way. And very often they were the younger sons who had left home – as I was – and who'd gone out in the world and eventually fetched up in Sarawak. They met the young Rajah who'd had a stern father and could appreciate this type of chap who didn't want to be pushed around very much: 'Good chap, but he had to be handled carefully.' And I don't think anyone handled them as the Rajah did.

The commercial world also had its survivors from an earlier age. An outstanding figure in rubber circles was Sir Eric

Macfadyen, who continued to act as what was known as a visiting agent for such companies as Harrison and Crosfield long after his planting days were over. 'I remember standing with him on the top of a hill from where you could see the upper reaches of the Klang river,' recalls Cecil Lee. 'And he said, "I used to come up here in a small boat to collect timber for my bridges." He was a small man who wore an eyeglass. I think he'd been run over by a gun-carriage in the Boer War and one eye tended to sink in a bit and so he wore an eye-glass. But he was a strong, humorous character with great foresight.'

Another pioneer planter was Henri Fauconnier, author of *The Soul of Malaya*. Bill Bangs met him during his first weeks with the Anglo-French company Socfin:

> I was put on Rantau Panjang Estate where Henri Fauconnier was the manager. Unfortunately, he was just retiring, but I do like to think that I worked under Fauconnier. And when he published The Soul of Malaya I must have read it twenty or thirty times. I became very keen on knowing more about Malaya and learning the Malay language and trying to understand the Malays, and this was mostly due to Fauconnier's book. I remember in the book he said, 'No one will understand Malays unless they live with Malays and take the Malay religion,' which was one of the reasons why in 1928 I embraced Islam.

3

The Meeting Place of Many Races

Singapore is the meeting place of many races. The Malays, though natives of the soil, dwell uneasily in towns, and are few; and it is the Chinese, supple, alert, and industrious, who throng the streets; the dark-skinned Tamils walk on their silent, naked feet, as though they were but brief sojourners in a strange land . . . and the English in their topees and white ducks, speeding past in motorcars or at leisure in their rickshaws wear a nonchalant and careless air. The rulers of these teeming peoples take their authority with a smiling unconcern.

Somerset Maugham, *P&O*

IN the Twenties and Thirties the greater part of the small British community in the Malay archipelago was concentrated along the West Coast of the peninsula; on the rubber plantations in Lower Perak, Selangor, Negri Sembilan and Johore, and in Singapore and the capital of the FMS at Kuala Lumpur. Here the pre-war rubber boom had helped to lay down an efficient railway system and a network of rudimentary dirt roads that covered car drivers and passengers in red laterite dust and were, perhaps, more suited to bullock carts than to motor-cars:

Motoring was in its infancy then in Malaya. We had roads but they were laid out along the contours of the hills and chiefly followed bullock tracks. The surveyors and the contractors got more mileage by going round the contours and using as many bends as they could, so you could make no speed. And there was jungle everywhere. You had a road into a rubber-plantation or a road to a mine and where the rubber trees stopped the jungle began – solid jungle, so thick that you couldn't see the sky above. If you spent any time in there you came out pale-faced.

Elsewhere in Malaya, and in Sarawak and Borneo, there was still no road system worth speaking of outside the towns and *kampongs*. Instead the rivers continued to provide the main lines of communication, with fleets of shallow-draught steamers and Malay *prahus* ferrying goods and passengers along the coast and inland.

Even the railways were no match for some of the steamers that plied the Straits of Malacca. The large ocean liners only called in at Penang and Singapore, so it was left to such shipping lines as Straits Steamships to handle local traffic. Passengers who disembarked at George Town could either cross by ferry to the mainland and catch the Malay Express which carried the night mail down to KL – or continue by sea on a local steamer. Straits Steamships ran more than fifty of these steamers – known as 'the little white fleet' on account of their white hulls and blue and white funnels – all shallow-draught vessels that ran with clockwork precision between nearly eighty ports in South-East Asia. But the pride of the fleet was the *Kedah*, which at twenty-one knots outran the Malay Express. First-Class passengers – 'Europeans always travelled First Class. It was a rule; you wouldn't sell a deck passage to a European before the war' – could board the *Kedah* in Penang in the evening and land at Port Swettenham – the port for the federal capital – at dawn. On Friday nights the *Kedah* also ran punters and racehorses up from Singapore in time for the Penang races the next day.

The picture includes the text: EASTERN AND ORIENTAL HOTEL, PENANG. · STRAND HOTEL, RANGOON. · SARKIES' HOTELS. · Raffles Hotel · THE CRAG HOTEL SANITARIUM PENANG HILLS.

John Harrison was one of those who boarded the Malay Express after crossing over to the mainland from Penang Island on the ferry. Here he became aware for the first time of the manner in which the four principal races thrown together in the South-East Asian mixing-bowl coexisted while at the same time keeping each other at arm's length:

> We found that, without any orders or regulations, the First Class was used only by Europeans, the Second Class was mainly occupied by Chinese and the Third-Class compartments were occupied by Tamils. The races seemed to segregate in that manner, of their own accord. They didn't mix and they didn't mind not mixing. The Malays went according to their means. If they were of the ruling class they'd travel in the First Class. Otherwise, if they had the money they'd go in with the Chinese and take a table to themselves or if they were of the coolie class then they would go into the Third Class. But the working-class Malay never had any money in his pocket – unless he had come out of a pawn-shop.

The First Class carriages had hard sleepers but in almost every other respect proved to be comfortable: 'They were kept nicely aired by little revolving fans in the corners of the carriage and the windows were screened in that flyproof screening you used to get in the old meat safes we used.' But with coal-burning engines even these turned out to be inadequate once the train had got under way: 'The railway company was buying soft coal from Rawang collieries down in Selangor and the smuts were coming in all along the way. So every time you got up from your seat you had to shake yourself to throw off the smuts.'

As the train crossed through Province Wellesley and Perak, Bill Harrison was able to enjoy a landscape of 'beautiful *padi*-fields with the most gorgeous pale-green young *padi*, where Malays with their *sarongs* tucked up round their loins were wading, planting the *padi* in the *sawah* – the wet *padi*-fields.' Interspersed between the fields were 'clumps of banana and coconut trees and little villages where the *padi*-planters lived in their palm-thatched houses'. But at Ipoh Harrison changed trains and travelled northwards into the wilder country of Siam – where the engine ran into a herd of bullocks, which left 'their entrails draped along the first carriages of the train'.

Travellers continuing on down the peninsula were woken at dawn as the train pulled into KL's railway station – a building belonging, as one newcomer heard it described, to the 'Late Marzipan' period. 'It wasn't in the least like any railway station we'd seen before. It was designed with domes and small spires and lots of oriental arched windows – and a hotel – all combined.' But this exotic unfamiliarity was offset by much that was familiar – which, to John Davis, at least, came as a tremendous relief: 'We arrived in the very cool of the morning, there was a mist around and a few chaps who'd come down to meet us were wearing ordinary blue, public school type blazers. They seemed to be our type completely and this I think raised our morale all round.' From the station he and the other Police Probationers were taken straight up to the police mess – 'known for some reason as the "Jam Factory" ' – and given their rooms.

The station had its own hotel which, with the newly-opened

Majestic and the *Empire*, made up the sum of Kuala Lumpur's European hotels. Cecil Lee's first night in KL was spent in the *Empire*, which he found to be 'rather a come-down from the purple East' as he had envisaged it:

> There was this rather scruffy room, embrowned mosquito net, thunderbox sanitation and a generally depressing ambience. I recall on the first night having to jump under my mosquito net to avoid a bunch of flying ants that came in through the window. I also remember leaning out in the cool of the night and there below me, under a large spreading rain tree, was a Chinese rickshaw puller, resting on the shafts of his rickshaw, utterly exhausted, because it was a killing business.

Singapore, too, had its modern hotels: notably, the slightly raffish Dutch hotel, the *Van Wijk*, 'the place of assignation' for European women of easy virtue – where 'you could get French, German, Dutch or Russian girls but not an English girl. If an English girl came out on the mail boat the CID sent her back on the next one. They wouldn't have it' – the old *Hotel de l'Europe*, regarded as *the* hotel in the inter-war period, and the *Raffles*, the hotel made famous by Somerset Maugham. The last was one of a chain of hotels that three enterprising Armenian brothers had built up in the East in the 1880s which included the *Strand* in Rangoon and the *Eastern and Oriental* in Penang. Arshak Sarkies, the youngest of the brothers, was sometimes to be seen waltzing round his own ballroom in the *E & O* with a whisky and soda balanced on his head. It was said of him that when the great slump came in the late 1920s dozens of planters and tin-miners who had run up large bills in his hotels had their accounts 'overlooked' on his orders – while others in even worse straits were provided with passages home to Britain.

However, arriving at the *Raffles* after journeying across the Pacific from America, Norman Cleaveland was shocked to see how 'extremely primitive' the hotel's plumbing was. It was his first introduction to the *jamban* and the 'Shanghai jar'. The first was no more than a simple commode, popularly known among Europeans out East as a 'thunderbox,' while the 'Shanghai jar' – otherwise known as a *tong*, 'Suchow tub' or 'Siam jar' – was a 'huge ceramic receptacle from which you were supposed to ladle cold water to bathe yourself'. Like many a newly-arrived innocent, Cleaveland mistook the jar's purpose: 'I thought you were supposed to get *in* it so, much to the distress of the servants, I got in and bathed in the Shanghai jar. I thought it looked a little tight but it was kind of cosy.'

Primitive though it might have appeared, the Shanghai jar was a bathroom fixture that visitors quickly learned to appreciate. Due to evaporation through the porous clay, the water inside was always kept deliciously cold: 'One of the great delights in one's daily routine, morning and evening, was to douse oneself over with these lovely streams of cold water from a wooden scoop of large dimensions known in Malaya as a *gayong*. One would *gayong* the water over oneself with many a splash and shout and feel enormously better afterwards.' And in places where there was no refrigerator and no ice-box the Shanghai jar had another useful function: 'We used to put our beer in there.'

Another mistake that Cleaveland made was to turn up in Singapore improperly dressed in a straw hat:

> It was an obsession that the people in Malaya had at that time that you had to wear what was called a *topee* to prevent the horrible effects of the sun on your head. When I arrived at the office I was promptly taken by the secretary out shopping to get proper headgear. There was only one *topee* we could find that would fit me, a heavy cork thing and most uncomfortable to wear, but I was constantly reminded that I should wear it, and whenever I showed up in my straw hat I was admonished – because the company had after all invested quite a bit of money in getting me out there and so they had good reason to look after their company's interests.

Bill Bangs was another newcomer who disembarked in Singapore – and he, too, was soon introduced to the Eastern way of doing things. He was met by the acting manager of the rubber estate on the mainland to which he was being sent and told that he would need some working clothes:

> He took me to a tailor's shop in Singapore at ten o'clock in the morning where I was measured for six pairs of shorts, six shirts and four white drill suits. The acting manager said, 'When will they be ready?' And the man said, 'They can't be ready before two o'clock this afternoon.' So we did some more shopping elsewhere and had a very good lunch at the *Europa Hotel* and then we went to the tailor, where all my clothes were ready – and the tailor was apologizing that he hadn't been able to send them to the *dhobi*! At the end of the month I sent him a cheque, because in those days no Europeans ever carried any money; everything was signed for.

When his shopping was completed Bangs was taken by launch across the Johore Straits and then up a creek to his rubber estate.

However, for many newcomers their travels ended with their arrival in one of the three large towns – George Town, Singapore or the FMS capital, Kuala Lumpur. In KL the Eastern Cadets, as well as the Police Probationers, had their own mess. Officially designated the 'cadets' bungalow' but known to its occupants as the 'Bull's Head', it stood on a ridge overlooking the big parade ground and playing field known as the *padang*, which had originally been levelled for the police to drill on but soon became the central ground for the principal sporting activities of Kuala Lumpur.

Hanging about outside the cadets' bungalow when Mervyn Sheppard first arrived were a number of Malays, Chinese and Indians, all hoping to pick up jobs as servants: 'Very often they'd been employed a number of times before, hadn't been successful and had been discarded. There were several cadets requiring a servant so I was more or less allotted a rather elderly Malay called Mat. He had at least two letters saying he'd been in previous service and had been satisfactory, so I took him on.'

The bungalow itself consisted of about a dozen single rooms opening onto a very large central dining room:

> In our bedrooms we had no means of keeping cool and they were rather hot and mosquito-ridden, but over the dining-room there was a series of pleated fans called *punkahs* – not a Malay word but an Indian word which had been introduced from India. These hung from a wooden frame which was connected to the roof by struts. It had pleated blanks of cloth and a long rope which was pulled when required by a small boy, who was probably the son or grandson of one of the staff. He might pull it with his finger or his toe, but he would go on pulling and letting go for as long as he was required to do so. And as long as he pulled the rope and let go the fans continued to flap and thereby caused a reasonable amount of movement of air.

While there were no formal lines of demarcation, both the police and the cadets' messes in KL were sited in what amounted to a government officers' residential area west of the *padang* and overlooking the main town itself. Next door was the mercantile housing area, where the larger companies and the banks had bungalows for the senior and married staff and messes for the bachelors, concentrated mostly in the 'hilly area with its great albizia trees round the Maxwell Road'. Between them these two areas constituted the 'European quarter' of Kuala Lumpur, leaving the Chinese in control of the town and the Malays on the outskirts. Thus, Harrison and Crosfield had three staff houses up on Maxwell Road, named *Wycherley*, *Congreve* and *Farquhar* 'after the naughty dramatists of the Restoration Period', as well as a mess named *Sheridan*: 'Just below it was the Hong Kong Bank house and opposite was a

green, grassy area which was a meeting place for a flock of
Chinese *amahs* with their little European charges, who played
and gambolled around while their *amahs* chatted amongst
themselves like a sort of Chinese club.'

The mess – sometimes referred to in Singapore and the
other Straits Settlements by the Anglo-Indian term *chummery* –
provided the means by which two or three bachelors could live
together and save expenses: 'We'd have one cook and one
"boy" and one gardener. All the food that came into the house
was divided by three and all the drink and expenses, and at the
end of the month you'd have to pay your third share of
everything, which was very small. I don't think it came to more
than about a hundred and twenty dollars all in.' But not all the
companies provided a mess, in which case 'you hunted round
the various *chummeries* – maybe four engineers or sales people
or accountants or whatever there were of that particular
company – and you went and had dinner with them and if
you liked the sort of life they lived you became one of them.'
Gerald Scott was one of those who had to look for a mess when
he first came to join the Asiatic Petroleum Company in
Singapore in 1938:

> I went out to dinner to three chaps in a *chummery* who had a
> vacancy and it was eating at eleven o'clock at night – which was
> fairly normal at that time in Singapore – and a lot of drink and
> so forth. It was a totally unintellectual, practical engineers' type
> of life and it wasn't my cup of tea. So I went off on my own and I
> quickly found another chap in the Shell Company who was an
> Oxford type, and we had something in common and so we went
> off to live in a Chinese palace which was quite magnificent. It
> was run by an extraordinary woman who was a hermaphrodite
> – although we didn't know it at the time – and whenever the
> moon was full this woman used to go absolutely berserk!

Rather more representative was the Harrison and Crosfield
mess that Cecil Lee eventually moved into in KL:

It housed four of us – two Seniors and two Juniors – and we had two 'boys', a cook, a gardener or *kebun* and the Seniors had two *syces*, an Indian word for a groom for the horses which had been carried over with the advent of motor cars. The cook was said to have been with Sir Laurence Guillemard, a former governor, and one of his *pièces de résistance* was a pigeon pie. The idea was that when you cut the pie a pigeon flew out – and then he brought in the real one. Once, when we had some young girls round to dinner, one of the young topsies cut the crust and the poor little pigeon hopped out and misbehaved itself. The girl screamed and the whole thing was a bit of a flop.

The mess also had a large garden surrounded by jungle and full of such flowering exotics as Vanda Joachim orchids, purple petrea, yellow allamanda, red poinsettias and white, fleshy frangipani. There were also jacaranda trees, bushes of blue plumbago and a pomelo tree, which had inedible fruit and was mainly used as missiles in some boisterous games. It was all very exotic and in some ways so attractive, but I missed the freshness of our home flowers and even the exotic scents seemed to have a harshness and a lack of the fragrance that I'd been used to at home.

Tending this garden was an old Malay *tukang kebun*, 'a retainer of twenty-seven years' service who had followed one *tuan* after another with exemplary patience and fidelity. In the morning you'd wake up and he'd be watering the plant pots or scything the grass, which seemed to be his main task. One master after another would pass through and some would take an interest in his work, but mostly he was left to his own devices.'

Away from the messes large numbers of servants were rarely to be found in individual households. Bachelors who set up house on their own generally managed to get by with a cook-boy 'who bought the food and cooked it for you' – possibly supported by his wife and a *tukang ayer* or water-carrier 'who did the washing and scrubbed the floors'. Even with increasing seniority and marriage it was unusual to find a European household with more than three or four personal servants.

As soon as the newcomers were established there were certain formalities to be observed, the first of which was the custom of calling. 'The business of calling and card-dropping, as in India, was still in vogue when I came out. It was probably declining,' Cecil Lee recalls, 'but I still remember being taken by my host, who was a government servant, to sign the book for the Chief Secretary and the Resident and the Chief Justice, which were kept in little boxes in the bottom of their gardens. And I remember being told that I and my colleague in the mess would not be invited to the house of a certain senior member of the firm unless we dropped cards.'

Before cards could be dropped they had first to be printed and then delivered personally at each bungalow. Artificial and old-fashioned as this ritual appeared to some, it was nevertheless based on good sense – as Edward Tokeley discovered when he joined Bousteads in George Town:

> This was a very important part of life in Malaya and Singapore in those days because the British community went out of its way to look after the new arrivals and see that everything was done to make them welcome and to bring them into that community. And in order to do that, you had to have some name cards printed. Then the mentor who met you gave you a list of senior people – married people of course – upon whom you had to drop these cards. We were supposed to do it in the evening time, and not be seen. All houses in those days had a little card box at the entrance to the drive, so you waffled around with your list with your mentor, who'd be driving you to show you where everybody lived, and you dropped a card in the proper boxes, and then it became obligatory upon those people on whom you dropped a card to invite you to their houses for a meal or a drink, so that within a very short space of time a newcomer became known and knew other people as well.

In a land where 'you were on the move the whole time' and where government servants particularly could expect to be moved from one posting to another about twenty times in the course of their careers, such customs may have made sense. But, increasingly, there were newcomers who saw such social conventions in a different light. 'When I arrived in Singapore I realized very quickly that I was living in the British colonial Raj and that there were certain rules to obey,' acknowledges Gerald Scott. 'I suppose at that age I was a bit bolshie and I wasn't going to cower down to any of these rules.' So Scott decided not to drop cards on anyone – 'for the simple reason that I realized from my colleagues out there that if you did you were absolutely done for. I didn't want to be under the discipline of the good wives of the British – and so I didn't call on them. I didn't drop cards on the Governor and I didn't drop cards on the Shell Company wives – quite wrongly, looking back.' In due course, he was forced to compromise: 'I got a girl-friend and her father, who was an important chap in the MCS, said, "You don't take my daughter out unless you have the courtesy as a visitor in a colony to call on the Governor." And of course when I was talked to by such an eminent creature, naturally this was the first thing I did – but I didn't do it on the Shell Company wives.'

After the proper introductions had been made the newcomer could then turn his attention to joining the right clubs. Penang could boast the senior club in South-East Asia, the Penang Club, founded in 1858; an all-male preserve with a women's annexe attached known as the 'hen roost'. This was the *tuan besars'* (big masters') club, to which Juniors or *tuan kechils* (small masters) could not hope to gain admission – unless they happened to belong to the MCS. The club's presidents were mostly senior British businessmen but its membership included a number of leaders of the Asian community; Muslim Indian and Chinese business tycoons, as well as the Sultan of Kedah, who was automatically the patron of the club by virtue of the fact that his ancestor had leased the island to the British back in 1786.

For other Juniors in Penang, young mercantile assistants like Edward Tokeley, there was the Penang Cricket Club which, besides cricket, 'gave you absolutely everything you wanted – rugger, soccer, tennis, hockey. You also joined the Penang Swimming Club, which had a lovely swimming pool a few miles along the coast from the township.' The Swimming Club was 'strictly a European concern in those days, because no Chinese would think of swimming in the sea. Only the mad Englishmen would do that.'

Singapore and Kuala Lumpur had virtually the same set up, each with three major clubs that were 'for the Europeans and exclusive to the Europeans'. As a Junior in Singapore 'you could join the Tanglin Club and the Singapore Swimming Club, but you couldn't join the Singapore Club, which was the Seniors' club, where they all had their tiffin.' John Forrester's first visit to the Swimming Club had been as a young boy, when his ship had called at Singapore on its way back to England from China: 'It was in the sea and had nets all round it, but a shark got in and took one of the lady swimmers. This very brave man was on the raft that she'd just dived off and he dived on top of the shark and got her back to the raft, minus a leg. We were on the beach at the time and there was a terrible commotion. I remember being taken very quickly back to the ship.'

In KL there was the Golf Club, dominated by Scots, the Lake Club for the *tuan besars* and the more egalitarian Selangor Club for Juniors and Seniors alike. 'We would no more have dreamt of putting our names up for the Lake Club than flying,' asserts Trevor Walker, who joined Guthries in Kuala Lumpur in 1937. 'We should have been blackballed anyway. We joined the Selangor Club, which gave us our team games and the social outlet that we needed. There was dancing there with the daughters of senior men, but there weren't enough of them and we had to book them up about three weeks ahead.'

The Selangor Club – popularly known as the 'Spotted Dog' or simply the 'Dog' – was one of the great institutions of the

East. From modest beginnings in 1884 in a wooden hut with an *atap* thatch roof on the northern side of the *padang*, it had grown into a rambling timbered complex of bungalows that housed two bars and a number of tiffin, card, billiards and reading rooms. The Dog was the scene of such high spots in KL's social calendar as the St George's Night Ball when, to the strains of *The Roast Beef of Olde England*, beefeaters from the Royal Society of St George carried dishes of roast beef onto a dance floor surrounded by enormous blocks of ice – with frozen roses inside. Perhaps its greatest moment was the occasion of the Prince of Wales' visit in 1922, when he was said to have greatly upset the senior *mems* by dancing all night with a particularly attractive Ceylonese Eurasian.

By the 1920s the bulk of the Dog's two thousand members were planters and others living outside Selangor State, for whom the club provided a second home where they 'could come in and have their lunch and sink into one of these great long chairs with leg rests and a hole in the side where you put your *stengah* – your whisky soda'. There were a number of conflicting stories as to why the club should have come to be known as the Spotted Dog. Some said it was because of its early policy of allowing Eurasians and Asians to join, others that it went back to KL's early days when the wife of the Superintendent of Police used to drive down to the club with two Dalmatians trotting under her carriage. Sjovald Cunyngham-Brown was given a possibly more authentic version, from an old friend of his named Harry Kindersley:

He told me that his grandmother, the wife of the original Kindersley who planted a large estate not far from KL in 1885 or so, used to come up by dogcart from the estate very frequently and have a picnic with her young friends under a tree on the *padang*. Now under the dogcart were two Dalmatian dogs, and it became the habit of the young people having their picnic with this extremely attractive lady – as she was apparently – to say: 'Are you going down to the spotted dogs this morning?' And from that habitual picnic event there grew up the title 'Spotted Dog' for the club which was being built at that time.

The three European clubs were by no means the only ones in KL: 'The Chinese also had their own clubs – a well-known millionaires' club and a Chinese athletic association – and the Indians had theirs, and so had the Malays and the Eurasians. As young men we played cricket against them all – except the Chinese millionaires – but they were as exclusive as our clubs were.' There was no question of 'not wishing to mix with the other races', argues Trevor Walker. 'That was just not true. But in the privacy of our clubs we wished – and *they* wished – to follow our own way of life.'

However, if the races kept to their own clubs they did at least meet on the playing field – as Alan Morkill experienced when he was a District Officer in 1923 in Tampin:

> The wicket keeper was a Japanese photographer, the best bowler was a Sikh who took about a hundred yards' run and delivered a fearsome ball, and my Malay assistant magistrate had been at the Malay College and was a very good player. We had an Indian clerk from my office who was fielding at square leg and somebody hit a ball while he was watching a pretty girl go by on a bike, which hit him on the backside and knocked him flat. Our opponents included a former captain of Eton who was a planter and another planter who had played for Hampshire, but by stonewalling we managed to make a draw of it.

Both in the towns and in the outlying districts organized sport played a major part in the lives of the younger Europeans, because, 'when you weren't working, your life was playing games'. The year was divided into two seasons 'not for climatic reasons, because there wasn't an awful lot of difference between the months, but for sporting purposes'. Football and cricket were played from March through to the end of August and then, for the next six months, rugby football and hockey. Heat and humidity were ignored – 'although we used to sweat like hell, of course', and at the end of every game 'you first of all wrung out your shirt and shorts and then had a large glass of salt and water before getting down to more serious drinking'. The only concession to the climate was that soccer and rugger matches were five minutes shorter each half. 'When one is young one can acclimatize very quickly and so the heat didn't come into it,' Edward Tokeley maintains, 'although, if it was a particularly hot period and the ground became hard-baked, one did appreciate the activity of the fire-brigade in hosing down the field a bit beforehand – and in the Thirties they were kind enough to do that.'

Sporting tournaments – notably the *HMS Malaya* cup for rugger between the different states – as well as more local fixtures were taken seriously but not to extremes. Norman Cleaveland found prevailing attitudes towards sport in marked contrast to those that he had known in the United States. Although regarded as an 'interloper' he was a good games-player and had even played some rugby football before coming to Malaya:

I managed to get in the state side that won a couple of local championships and I found an extremely interesting contrast in the relaxed attitude that they had. In fact, I remember one important match in which we were severely criticized for questionable sportsmanship because we had been training and it was not considered proper to do that. I found that training generally consisted in not going on the field under the influence. But if you abstained from drinking and went to bed early and took exercise then you were violating the code.

However, this same social code ensured that in a small community 'the young bachelor was brought *into* the community'. Edward Tokeley in Penang found himself being asked out to dine two or three times a week. If the company was mixed, he was expected to wear a dinner jacket and a stiff collar, which was 'a bit of a bore – but not so much of a bore as it was on a dance night, because the collar that one wears with tails gets pretty limp if you're dancing in a temperature of eighty degrees, and so one had to change one's collar two or three times during the evening'. Yet, despite the discomfort, 'we managed to get through these evenings with the utmost ease and considerable pleasure.'

Some took the business of dressing for dinner very seriously, notably in KL a 'very pompous Chief Secretary with a very portly stomach, who dressed every night in a stiff shirt and black trousers and white mess jacket. All his shirts and stiff collars were sent back to the United Kingdom to be laundered – and every week a parcel used to come through from a laundry in Notting Hill Gate.' Bachelors dining on their own usually dressed much more informally. In Cecil Lee's mess it was the senior member who set the example:

> He was a bachelor and his ways were very fixed. Every night about six o'clock his car came chugging down and his *syce* took him off to the club, where he drank with his friends. He used to arrive back about seven-thirty and change into his *sarong* and *baju*, which was the Malayan equivalent of pyjamas, and then swallow a couple of whisky *pahits* and have his dinner and go to bed. We followed his custom of wearing a *sarong* and *baju* for dinner until a new member of the mess arrived who frowned upon it and regarded it as a sign of degeneracy, so then we always dressed for dinner.

To get to work Cecil Lee and his colleagues in the mess had only to jump into a rickshaw or simply 'walk across the green of the *padang* and past the government offices into Market Square, which housed the main European firms. It had tulip and jacaranda trees in little grass plots and in those days housed all the cars that were needed.' The Harrisons' office was 'an old-fashioned building with great bat-haunted Corinthian columns – and with an old *jaga*, a Sikh watchman, sitting out in front with his *charpoy* [bed]. He was generally the man who lent most of the Asian staff money, which he used to collect from them when we paid them every month.'

The Guthries' head office was in Singapore but they also had a smart new office in KL in Java Street, with a *godown* or warehouse on its ground floor – 'harking back to the days when the shopkeepers lived over the shop with their goods down below them'. Bousteads, too, had its head office in Singapore but with a branch office in George Town; an imposing building facing the harbour with a *godown* below and offices above. Across the middle of the *godown* ran iron rails for loading and unloading ingots of tin. As well as tin the warehouse housed copra, which 'smelled a bit after the heat had been on it, encouraging little copra bugs that flew around in their hundreds and got in your hair'. Another feature of the Penang office was a monsoon drain in the road outside which 'got cleared when the tide was in but left a lot of evil-smelling mud when it went out. The smell of the mud with that of the copra and some of the other spices that were being held in the *godown* – these were the romantic smells of the East!'

Offices at this time were generally large open-plan areas 'with little horse-boxes where the Seniors sat'. All the executive staff were European. 'We all had telephones and like other young men we tended to be fairly noisy and light-hearted,' recalls Trevor Walker:

> Facing us in serried ranks were our subordinate staff; Indian and Chinese accounts clerks who knew much more about the work than I did and upon whom I was very dependent in my early period. But it was a feature that the subordinate staff worked in deathly silence and in deathly earnest until they went out to have a cigarette, which they were not allowed to smoke in the office itself, or have a cup of tea, which was served to them downstairs. These clerks were generally known

as *keranis* – an Indian word that denotes clerk – and the office boys were generally Malays and were known as *peons*, which I think came from the Portuguese. In those days the more simple jobs were done by Malays, and the Indians and Chinese divided the rest of the work between them.

For the Juniors the working day began at eight-thirty with the Seniors arriving half an hour later. There was no air-conditioning until late in the 1930s; most offices had high ceilings from which hung electric fans, keeping the air circulating and at the same time 'disturbing all the papers on your desk'. Ties were worn but no coats, and only senior government servants and a few brokers still clung to the old-fashioned *tutup* jacket. 'We had jackets made of crash but we never wore them,' asserts Trevor Walker. 'You carried one over your arm and hung it up when you got to the office, and took it home in the evening without ever wearing it. So one was very free and easy in white trousers, a shirt and tie and rolled-up sleeves.' Prickly heat where one's arms rested on the desk was a common complaint but in other respects these were perfectly bearable working conditions for most Europeans, who found the climate monotonous rather than oppressive: 'You could walk across the *pandang* to have your lunch and back again and, even with your coat on, you wouldn't be perspiring that much.'

Working out of doors was a different matter. Then the full force of the equatorial sun und the accompanying humidity became almost intolerable – as Edward Tokeley experienced whenever his duties took him out to the ships discharging coal opposite George Town:

> One had always to be properly dressed in a white drill suit and tie and standing on the iron decks of these ships at mid-day you could feel the heat coming up from the soles of your feet and down through the hair on your head. Then you did sweat – and the coal dust settled all over your nice white drill suit. I

remember going back to my *tuan besar* and suggesting very politely that these suits should be a charge on the company. That produced no response that I welcomed at all.

Unlike the Dutch in their Eastern territories, who took long afternoon siestas and returned to work in the late afternoon, the British preferred to work through the day, leaving themselves an hour and a half for games and exercise before the short tropical twilight came on. It was also usual to work until one o'clock on Saturdays, with sport in the afternoon, which left them free on Sundays to enjoy a large curry lunch followed by a 'lie-off' in the afternoon. Attendance at church was not expected of anyone – but for those who did go there was one significant concession to local custom: 'you could even sign a *chit* for the collection'.

Between the leading mercantile houses there was also a distinct element of rivalry, 'dating back to the old days of the clippers, when Jardines sent their teas racing home to get them on the market before other people'. However, the 'sharp infighting' of the nineteenth century had long given way to a friendlier competitive spirit, partly because money had become scarcer in the 1920s and the slump had seriously weakened the market. Rivalry was also hard to keep up when one's competitors were also one's closest friends, for 'although we competed very hard with each other we all shared the same clubs and played rugger and cricket together and drank together. But at the same time you were very pleased if you could get a certain contract and the other chap couldn't.' It was also a fact that with the improvement of the shipping services and the telegraph a company's Eastern offices were no longer as independent from its board of directors in London as they had been in earlier times. Air-mail, however, only began to play an important role in the years immediately preceding the Second World War; companies and individuals alike were still heavily dependent on the weekly arrivals of the mail-boat, which arrived off Penang on the Thursday and left, homeward bound, on a Saturday afternoon: 'That was always a great day because you would pile on board and see your friends away who were going on leave. It also meant a certain activity beforehand in the office because the outgoing mail had to be completed in time to catch the ship.'

Juniors in the big companies were expected to toe the line. The borrowing of money was forbidden and the man who got into debt to a money-lender was regarded as beyond the pale. If his borrowing came to light he was usually bought out and packed off home. The firms were equally strict in enforcing the ban on marriage during the first tour of service. This proved to be the undoing of at least one Junior, who began his first contract in Ceylon while concealing from his employers his intention of getting married:

> I had assumed that I would work so diligently and they would be so impressed that they would waive the rules. However, the rules applied to a great many people and they weren't about to waive them for me – as it turned out when I got the sack and three months' pay, which made me richer than I had ever been before. I then found that I had to take the ship home within four weeks, otherwise a passage home would no longer be my entitlement and I would be thrown upon my own resources – which was not a very happy prospect in view of the fact that it was impossible for a Westerner to work in the ordinary sense in a colonial place. You either worked at the top or somewhere near it or not at all. Because of the social mores of the day nobody would consider taking me on. I stomped round all the offices I could think of, looking for another job, whereupon I found that the word had preceded me and every door was closed.

Europeans were expected to 'maintain the reputation of the white man' and to observe social standards: 'If a man "went native" he was frowned upon and ostracized. There was one man whom we called *Tuan Burong* – *tuan* Bird – who went and lived native in the *kampong*, but nobody knew him and he never mixed with any of the other Europeans. That was the kind of attitude; the colours kept to themselves.' Inevitably, there were difficulties when it came to relations with the opposite sex. Guy Madoc remembers how when he first came to KL there was a 'considerable shortage of feminine company. As far as we could make out there were only two unattached young English women in the whole of that big town.' At the same time, 'any relationship with a local native woman would have meant the sack'. This ban was most strictly applied in government circles but even among unofficial circles there was the same taboo. 'We weren't allowed to associate with Asian women,' declares Percy Bulbrook, at that time based in Singapore as a First Mate with Straits Steamships. 'When some poor lads broke the bonds they were just shot off home, with no redress whatsoever.' Bulbrook was one of those who married a Chinese girl:

> I said, to hell with them. This is my private life. You employ me, not my wife. But we had a hard fight to break this caste business down and that's what sent a lot of the young lads up the lines after prostitutes. It got so bad that about 1931 the Mothers' Union in the UK decided that the young fellows were all going astray out here, so out they came and made a few enquiries and went around. The brothels were down a place called Malay Street and of course the Governor ordered them all closed down, the lot of them. But the ladies of the street wouldn't be beat. They formed what the old stagers here called the 'rickshaw parade'. They used to get rickshaws from Johnson's Pier and come right up the Cathedral and Stamford Road. And we lads, of course, were all there ready – and off we went!

From the point of view of the more strait-laced Malay states, Singapore was regarded as a 'sort of Buenos Aires' of the East, a place where planters and others could take local

leave and 'come down once in a blue moon to see the races
and to beat it up'. But even in Kuala Lumpur there was
Batu Road, lined with houses of ill-repute, the best-known of
which was Mary's:

> One could go down to Mary's and pay for a young lady of
> one's choice, and, in due course, depart refreshed. But once
> some of the younger wives of a particular government depart-
> ment decided that to go down Batu Road and have a drink
> with old Mary, and a refreshing talk – heaven knows what they
> talked about – was the 'in' thing. And therefore the young and
> randy bachelor suddenly found himself faced with some lady
> whom he'd always supposed to be extremely respectable, and
> whom he had not expected to meet outside of the confines of
> the Selangor Club.

For those seeking more innocent pleasures there were the
taxi dancers in places like the *Eastern Hotel*, where 'you could go
and have a drink and have a dance by buying a book of tickets
and giving the girl a ticket and dancing away'.

So, step by step, the Junior came to terms with Asia and its
ways. He learned to sprinkle his conversation with Anglo-
Malay *argot*; to talk about *makan* for his food or meals, *barang* for
his luggage or property, *gaji* for his pay, *chop* for his company's
trade-mark. He learned to call out 'Boy!' with authority and
talk about 'coming round for *pahits*' rather than cocktails. He
grew accustomed to a monotonous climate that remained
damp and steamy throughout the year; with nights 'when you
rolled around in a mosquito net and found it difficult to get a
good night's sleep' and a rainy season in the winter when it did
nothing but rain 'buckets and buckets'. He learned to consult
the 'Birthday Book' or the Civil List, which listed the seniority,
salary and date of birth of every official in the country and all
his gazetted posts, and the equally invaluable *Straits and
Malayan Directory*, which provided the equivalent details of
commercial life – as well as offering information on everything

from '*jinriksha* (rickshaw) fares within the municipal limits of Penang' to the 'payment of savings deposits belonging to lunatics'.

The newcomer also quickly learned to know his place, which in the British community was very largely decided 'by your work and for whom you worked'. In business circles this meant that a social barrier divided mercantile from trade. Europeans working in such large stores as John Little, Robinsons or Whiteaway and Laidlaws were held to be tradesmen and were expected to stick within their own social circles and clubs, as were a handful of other salaried workers such as the British or Eurasian engine-drivers, NCOs on attachment from the British Army and jockeys.

All the same, the British in South-East Asia never adopted the rigid hierarchical system of the British Raj in India. Commercial interests were still paramount, to the extent that 'whereas in India the *box-wallahs*, as they were called, took second place to the Indian Civil Service, in Malaya the heads of commerce were really the heads of the community'. And yet, when William Goode first arrived in Kuala Lumpur in 1931 he was perplexed to learn that he and his fellow Eastern Cadets had joined the 'heaven-born'. This was an Indian term associated with the highest Hindu caste and, by extension, the ICS in India and the MCS in Malaya: 'I suppose it was because we gave ourselves such superior airs, but it wasn't a title that I particularly enjoyed – nor, I think, was it meant to be complimentary.' However, the Malayan Civil Servant was rarely the remote and authoritarian figure that popular imagination sometimes made him out to be:

> Generally speaking, the MCS officer was a mixer and did his best to get to know people of all communities. It was not at all common for a British officer to be aloof – and if he was he would be hurriedly put into the Treasury, perhaps, and kept there. There were certain jobs which were reserved, you might say, for people who didn't mix.

It was also a fact that the MCS provided the top layer of government, so that 'in the pecking order of the country they ranked above doctors and customs officers and policemen'. Its authority was inescapable, although it was less obvious in the towns than it was in the districts where, 'when you entered the club you went and said, "Good evening, sir"', if the District Officer was there, rather as you did in the army. They weren't toffee-nosed about it but they did require that little bit of deference.'

If the civil servants occupied the top rung it was generally accepted that their closest rivals were the police, whose authority was greatly strengthened by the almost complete absence of military forces in British South-East Asia. It was also left to the police in Kuala Lumpur to provide a military note with its mess nights. Young Probationers like John Davis and Guy Madoc spent their first nine months in the country in the police depot, 'learning criminal law, learning the language, learning police regulations and, almost every morning of the week, square-bashing on the parade ground'. But every evening at the mess they were required to dress in their 'pretty smart white uniforms', which on mess nights were exchanged for 'the full rig – what we called "tight-arse" trousers and a shell mess jacket, vulgarly known as a "bum-freezer" '. These mess nights invariably began as very solemn occasions:

> At the end of dinner the mess president would stand and say, 'Mr Vice, the King' – we did not say 'King-Emperor' in Malaya. Then Mr Vice would stand up and say, 'His Majesty the King'. After that came the second toast: 'Their Highnesses the Rulers' – by which we meant the ten sultans of the individual native states of the peninsula. After that, 'Gentlemen, you may smoke'. And then port – which most of us felt was just the wrong thing to drink in a hot sticky climate – and cigars.

She--You know darling. I shall never learn this beastly language Do ask the Boy for some matches.
He—Matches. Boy.

Cartoon from *Straits Produce*, 1927,
a satirical fortnightly which had been keeping Europeans
in Singapore and Malaya amused since the 1880s.

After dinner the formal atmosphere continued until the senior officers departed – which was the signal for 'all sorts of high jinks'. Motor-cycles were brought up onto the veranda that ran right round the mess building and raced up and down, vulgar songs were sung and games like 'Are you there, Moriarty?' were played, where 'you would lie on the floor blindfolded and try and hit your opponent with a rolled-up magazine'. The police mess also had its own version of the naval gun drill competition seen at military tattoos:

We had a gun which was made up entirely of wood with detachable wheels, just like a small field gun, into which a twelve-bore shotgun barrel had been cleverly inserted. You started at the back of the dining hall and you had to carry your piece of gun without touching the floor, so most of the time you were swinging from one beam of the roof to the next. At the end of it you clambered down into the port, at the front of the mess, where you quickly assembled your gun – whereupon a Malay from the armourer's staff handed you a blank twelve-bore cartridge. You shoved this up the breech and you fired it and with any luck you had beaten the other team. That was quite a favourite performance to put on when one of the sultans was invited to dine in the mess.

These essentially military rituals were being celebrated in a country that had no standing army – at least, not until 1933 when an experimental company of what was to become the Malay Regiment was formed. Even then, the expansion of this solitary 'native' regiment was very slow and only one full battalion had been formed by the time the Japanese invaded Malaya in 1941. One of its senior officers at the time of the invasion was Major George Wort, who had first come out East to Singapore as a young subaltern in the Wiltshire Regiment in 1933: 'We were the only battalion on the island. In fact, the only other battalion in the whole of Malaya was the Burma Rifles, who were stationed in Taiping. Out at Changi there were also two barrack blocks built for gunners and occasionally we went out there on company training. Little was I to know that some years later I would find myself having to enjoy the lovely views of Changi under different circumstances.'

To make up for this military deficiency there were the Volunteers – either the FMS and Straits Settlements Volunteer Forces or the MVI (Malay Volunteer Infantry) which civilians from all the races were able to join as territorial soldiers – and which Britons were certainly expected to join. 'It was suggested to you that you joined,' asserts Edward Tokeley. 'It wasn't at all compulsory but the system and the social set up was such that you would have been uncomfortable if you hadn't – and I really can't remember anyone refusing.'

Run by officers and sergeants seconded from the British Army as staff instructors, these volunteer units provided opportunities for enjoyable and expense-free get-togethers that cut across many of the barriers of race and class: 'In many ways it was the best club of the lot.' Training was never taken too seriously; the units met once a week and on occasional weekends, and there was an annual camp with a fortnight spent under canvas. Once a year the Volunteers turned out in somewhat ragged ceremonial display on the local *padang* for the King's Birthday Parade.

Edward Tokeley joined the machine-gun section of 3rd Battalion, Straits Settlements Volunteer Forces, Penang and Province Wellesley:

We had parades every Monday night and we had a superb Regimental Sergeant-Major from the Coldstream Guards who taught us how to march properly. He tore you to pieces when you were trying to mess around with the machine gun but called you 'Sir' if he saw you at any time in town. There were occasions when we had exercises over Penang Hill. A lot of them took place through the Chinese cemetery and I always suspected that they didn't bury their dead too far below the surface, because during the mid-day heat one could smell aromas of the East which were not quite as pleasant and romantic as they should have been. I also remember so vividly one exercise which was co-ordinated throughout the country by the GOC, Major-General Dobbie. When it was over he gave us a lecture – and I make no mistake in what he said then. He said, 'The enemy will be Japan and the Japanese will come down the mainland.'

4

Muster

We were all standing round the bar. The Boy never stopped pouring out whisky; bottles of soda-water opened with a rhythmic hiss like ripples in the sand. The talk was, of course, of rubber.

Henri Fauconnier, *The Soul of Malaya*

THAT 'almost extinct tropical species', the British planter, was by reputation 'whisky-swilling' and the sort of man 'who only married barmaids'. His trade was said to be 'the highest paid form of unskilled labour'. Like most reputations, this was a little wide of the mark.

Liquor was cheap and plentiful – 'a bottle of whisky in those days was three dollars and gin one dollar, sixty cents' and few planters would deny that as a group they did drink 'a tremendous amount'. However, 'This drinking was not out of hand', argues Peter Lucy:

It didn't do anybody any harm and it probably did us a lot of good. If we had a heavy night we had what's known as a prairie oyster for our early morning tea – raw eggs and Worcester sauce to settle the stomach – but at half past six we were out on the estate. The sun was hot by seven and by breakfast time the effects had all disappeared. At lunch time we certainly had such drinks as gin-slings, which in the hot climate didn't do us any harm, and in the evening we started drinking whisky and soda again, a lot of it – but always well diluted.

For some planters there was no question that 'without drink it would have been difficult to carry on' – and, as far as John Baxter was concerned, 'I don't think I could have stuck life without it'. For men like Baxter, who began working on Sapong Estate deep in the North Borneo jungle immediately after the First World War, planting was a 'very hard life'. In such remote areas the average planter was a 'very rough type; the unpopular boy who was sent out because he couldn't get a job anywhere else – a very mixed crowd indeed'. One of the reasons why estates like Sapong had more than their quota of black sheep and remittance men – 'from familes who sent them so much a month to keep them out of the country' – was the real danger to health. Baxter himself replaced a man who had died of malaria and 'there wasn't a case of a man *not* having malaria. I also had dysentery and scrub typhus, which very nearly killed me. I didn't sleep for a week and then it broke and luckily I lived. But in the early days there was continual malaria and sickness.'

A year was to pass before Baxter even got off the rubber estate and two years before he was able to visit the port of Jesselton, the headquarters of the North Borneo administration. It was a 'very narrow' existence, he recalls, with long working hours and little social life:

You got up at four-thirty in the morning, roll call was at five-thirty by lamplight and you came back at ten-thirty for breakfast. You weighed in latex from eleven till one, came back and had a two-hour lie-off. Then you went to see your tappers working in the afternoon and went to the office at four, where on work-days you worked till six – and on Wednesdays and Sundays till five. You played tennis on the Wednesday and we had a little five-hole golf course where you played on the Sunday. We had two free days a month, four free days at Christmas and four days at *Hari Raya*, the big Islamic holiday, because labour in those days was imported labour from Indonesia. There was no social life except that you went to the club every evening after six o'clock. I suppose at that time there were about eight members. We had a billiard table and you played billiards or you played bridge. Then you walked back to your house with your *tukang ayer* – your water-carrier – carrying a lamp. You were so fully employed that you were dead beat when you got back and you went to bed straight away.

Discipline on Sapong Estate was strictly enforced, following Dutch rather than British custom: 'If you were asked to the manager's house you had to take your hat off and stand outside. You always had to address him as "Sir" and he was a little king on his own. The assistants among themselves were very friendly but even there the senior assistant was on a superior stage and a junior assistant was a very unimportant man.' Dress was also more formal in those early days: 'You all wore the same – a *topee*, long trousers and *tutup* jacket with a collar. Khaki clothes in the morning and white in the afternoon.'

On the Malay peninsula working conditions were better and the quality of the planters themselves was higher. At the end of the First World War there were a great many officers on the labour market to choose from, some of whom, like Hugh Watts who spent a year after demobilization on a tropical agriculture course at Chelsea Polytechnic, were well qualified. In later years a firm like Guthries even made a point of looking for recruits with degrees in agriculture from the University of Aberdeen or with diplomas from the Edinburgh Botanical Gardens. However, technical skills were of no use to a planter who could not handle the estate's labour force: 'Literary gifts were not called for, nor any great expertise in the office side of

DEC. 25, 1922.] STRAITS PRODUCE.

MRS. A. D. O. (NEWLY ARRIVED) TO
MRS. P. W. D.: "DOES ONE CALL ON THESE RUBBER FARMERS?"

'Mrs A. D. O.' refers to the wife of the Assistant District Officer,
'Mrs P. W. D.' to the Public Works Department.
From *Straits Produce*, 1922

the business. The great thing was that he had to be good at
controlling labour.' And yet it was not a job that offered much
security: 'The trouble with a planter's life really was that one
never knew what was going to happen to the price of rubber. If
the price of rubber was high, one got quite nice bonuses and
the salary was quite good, but as soon as the price went down
that was the end of the bonus and the directors quickly
arranged for cuts in salary through their agents, and so a
planter really never knew where he was.'

Handsome sums could indeed be earned as commission
when the price of rubber was high. For every year that he
worked the assistant received a number of shares that multi-
plied in number so that by the end of six or seven years of
service he might have accumulated as many as two hundred

shares, each paying a dividend on company profits. The only trouble was that there were few years of profit. Hugh Watts' first job, on Henrietta Estate in Kedah, lasted for a year before the rubber slump of 1921. The estate was put on a 'Care and Maintenance' footing and its three junior assistants were sent home. Then the price of rubber rose again and Watts returned – but at two-thirds of his original starting salary. Worse was to come with the great slump that began in 1929, when four out of every ten planters got the sack.

Yet for young men like John Theophilus and 'Perky' Perkins, both new recruits to Dunlops in the 1920s, life on a rubber estate on a starting salary of two hundred Malay dollars a month, rising by twenty-five dollars a year and with a bonus paid as commission from the fourth year onwards, still seemed an exciting prospect.

Perkins landed at Singapore and made his way to Bahau Estate by train: 'We stopped at a station and picked up another young chap who'd been out for a year or so and he told us all about planting and soon changed our ideas about it. He said, "Have you ever heard about muster?" I said, "No." "You've got to get up at half-past-five and take muster every morning, including Sundays."'

The ceremony of muster began every planter's day. After being roused before dawn 'by the sound of tomtoms' all assistants had to make their way in the dark to the coolie lines, where the labour force would be assembled in long columns that on some of the larger estates stretched for more than half a mile. Each estate had a number of Indian conductors or *kanganis* (overseers), as well as *mandors* (foremen) and *keranis* (clerks), so that assistants were required to do little more than be present:

> The conductor does the actual calling out of names and the coolies answer if they're there. If they're not well they wait on one side and the dresser, who's fairly competent, will go and see if they're sick or pulling a line. Any labourer who's fairly ill

is pushed off to the estate hospital or maybe the government hospital in the nearest town. The tappers have fixed tasks so they pick up their buckets and off they go. Then the weeders; they have to be told where to go and what to do. And then the factory workers; they know their job and where to go. And all this we used to do in the dark – with lamps, of course.

Bahan was one of Dunlops' larger estates, with several thousand acres under rubber and employing fifteen Europeans; one manager with an equal number of senior and junior assistants: 'Each senior was in charge of a division and he had a junior under him. The coolies were mostly Tamils from South India, thousands of them, so we had to learn Tamil. In fact, it was one of the conditions of your employment.' This meant sitting down with a copy of Wells' *Coolie Tamil* on the table at mealtimes and eventually taking the Incorporated Society of Planters' Tamil exam. Those who passed received a ten-dollar a month Tamil allowance; those who failed had to sit the exam again until they did pass – or risk dismissal.

Attendance at muster seven days a week was compulsory for all junior assistants – except when it rained. Soon after his arrival Perky Perkins and a fellow-assistant mistook the sound of water from overnight rain dripping off the trees around their bungalow for fresh rain and stayed in bed: 'But in fact there was muster that morning and later we were up on the mat in front of the manager. I remember him saying, "You've come out here to work. At least, I presume you've come out here to work." So we were gated for three weeks, which meant that we weren't allowed off the estate.'

At mid-morning there was the hearty breakfast that the planters called 'brunch' – 'usually porridge, eggs and bacon, toast and marmalade'. Then it was out to the field again to supervise the tappers and the weeders. Various systems of tapping the rubber trees were employed but the crucial point was to ensure that the trees were not 'wounded': 'We were allowed an inch of bark a month to cut. If you cut too deep the tree heals the wound and this interferes with the renewal of the bark. But you must cut deep enough or you won't get the yield. The tappers start tapping the trees and putting down cups about half-past-five and at about half-past-ten they come round and collect the latex.' The latex had then to be weighed and checked for its dry rubber content – 'usually about three-and-a-half pounds of dry rubber to the gallon' – which was then recorded on the estate's check rolls. It was also necessary to see that the weeders kept the rubber trees free of under-growth: 'When I first came out the custom was complete "clean weed", not a single blade of grass to be seen. Then people began to realize that the soil was being washed away. But I remember finding on my desk one morning a clump of grass which my senior assistant had found in my division.'

By two o'clock in the afternoon the day's work was finished and the assistants could do as they liked. After lunch and a lie-off they went down to the club which on larger estates was often part of the estate itself. Bahau planters' club had a fifty-acre golf course and tennis courts where the estate's assistants could work up a thirst before repairing to the bar for their *stengahs*, gin *pahits* and beer – although not everyone drank. 'We were very keen on sport in those days,' avers Theophilus, 'so I and several of my friends never drank during the week at all. We had a good beat-up on Saturday night and Sunday and then stop. No smokes and no drink during the week – and that went on for many years.'

Theophilus started as a junior assistant on Jindaram Estate, an average-sized plantation with twelve hundred acres under rubber. His nearest club was the planters' club at Nilai, nine miles away and with a membership of sixty. It held a Club Night every Thursday when 'the local wives used to take it in turns to put up food for supper' and members of other clubs in Negri Sembilan State would drive over to play tennis or have a game of bridge. It was at this level that social drinking could present problems, because 'the great thing was that you sat in a circle of, say, ten people and each man stood a round of ten drinks. Nobody wanted ten drinks but you had to go on and do it; you couldn't jack out of that and live. And that is where, undoubtedly, we did drink too much.'

On Saturdays Theophilus and his colleagues often went further afield to the much larger Sungei Ujong Club in Seremban, the state capital, which had been founded in 1886 and was reputed to have 'the longest bar in Asia'. This was disputed by the Shanghai Club which claimed to have the longest *straight* bar in the East, whereas the Sungei Ujong Club bar was oval-shaped. The club's patron was the ruler of the state, the Yang Di-pertuan Besar, a 'fine upstanding old man with handlebar moustache' named Tuanku Muhammad, who had a great sense of humour and was very popular among the Europeans. He was in the habit of dropping in casually to play pool, which he referred to as *main bola saribu* – 'the game of a thousand balls' – but his patience was once sorely tried when a young Scots planter, a newcomer to the club and unaware of his identity, hailed him as '*Towkay*' (Chinese storeholder) and addressed him as '*Lu*', a familiar term used when speaking to inferiors.

Like other bars in the European clubs the Sungei Ujong Club bar was to all intents an all-white and all-male preserve – although on occasion it did have more unusual visitors. Coming in to Seremban early one morning to attend a meeting, Theophilus found himself alone at the bar: 'I ordered a beer and I had just taken a sip when I suddenly felt something – hardly felt it – on both shoulders. I'd already put the beer down and I looked round – straight into the face of a live tiger! Luckily, I was still young then, otherwise I'd have fallen off the stool with a heart attack.' The tiger turned out to be a pet of a local planter and was named Blang: 'He used to take pictures of Blang with empty Tiger Beer bottles and got quite a nice bit of cash for it from the Malayan Breweries. He also gave curry lunch parties on Sundays to which people came with *syces* to drive their cars and when it was time to go home in the afternoon they'd come out and call their *syces* but no one would answer; they'd all be up the nearest trees because the tiger was walking round.'

The Sunday curry tiffin was a very popular social convention among planters, given in turn by one or other of the managers or senior assistants in the district. They were boisterous and cheerful affairs where quantities of liquor were consumed before any lunch was actually served. Perkins was present at one such tiffin where 'a chap had invited a lot of people then had forgotten about it and gone out himself to another curry tiffin. We all arrived and drank everything he had in the house and then drove his chickens across the lawn and shot them with his own rifle. Then we gave them to the cook to make the curry.'

Outside working hours there was little contact with Asians on the estate, other than with one's servants in the bungalow, although Christmas, the Chinese New Year festivities at the end of January – when fireworks and firecrackers were let off – and the Tamil festival of Thaipusam soon afterwards, were occasions when fraternization between the races did take place. All the same, the planter had 'a very soft spot' for the men he called 'his *narlikis*' – the word being Tamil for 'tomorrow', with the implication, as with the Spanish *mañana*, that things would get done 'tomorrow' rather than at once. And in the dark years that were to come the Tamil labourers in their turn proved to be 'very faithful fellows', as many of their former employers were to discover: 'In 1942 they were sent up in droves by the Japanese to the railways in Siam where we were and it was very touching to see how they met and greeted their old masters – and even gave little presents and gifts to them.' Cecil Lee remembers one particular period as a prisoner of war when the Tamils and the 'white coolies' worked side by side: 'We were carrying earth in little baskets on our heads with them and dropping them on the line to build an embankment. There we were, dressed exactly as they were, in loin cloths and doing the same work, with the same mud on our heads. We would gather together during the *yasume*, the rest period, and yarn and smoke and exchange comments about the funny little monkeys that were in charge of us. It was ironic really; former masters and servants now comrades together in misfortune.'

But even at the best of times the planter's life had many drawbacks. On the smaller and more isolated estates it could be a very lonely life indeed. When he was a District Officer in Tampin in the 1920s Alan Morkill had once to make enquiries into the case of a planter who had killed himself: 'These wretched young men were living alone in bungalows with rubber trees right up to the bungalow; all they heard was the crack, crack, crack as the nuts on the rubber trees split and fell. When I went down to see what had happened to this man who had committed suicide I found six months' letters which hadn't been opened.' Some years later Guy Madoc had to face a rather similar situation in an outlying district when a planter threatened suicide:

One evening there was a hullabaloo back in the kitchen quarters and my cook came along with another Chinese whom I recognized as the cook of the neighbouring bachelor, whom I didn't know at all well. This cook was in an awful fluster and he said: 'My *tuan* has been drinking for the last two hours. He's got a pistol on the table in front of him and I'm afraid he's going to commit suicide.' I'd just come in all sweaty from a walk so I thought that the best thing was to pretend that I was passing his house and just looking in. So I went along and said, 'Hullo, Snibbs, how are you getting on?' He said, 'Both my mistresses have disappeared, I'm afraid. They've gone off to become taxi dancers. I'm desperate' – and there was the pistol. I said, 'What's that for?' He said, 'I'll deal with that when I've had enough to drink.' So I said, 'Would you like to give me a drink?' He put out a certain brand of whisky and we started drinking. This was about six o'clock and I think it was about half-past-eight before I was able to grab the pistol from him. After that I didn't bother with him anymore; I told him, rather like my headmaster at school, to have a cold bath and forget it. But since then that particular brand of whisky has seemed to me to be an absolute abortion; I just cannot touch it.

The lack of European female company was, of course, even more marked in planting circles than it was in the towns – and what few *mems* there were near at hand were almost invariably married. There was one well-known case of a young rubber assistant who, it was said, fell 'violently' in love with the wife of the local District Officer and who was so upset when the DO was transferred that he drank a bottle of white ant poison. However, 'it was found out that what would kill a white ant would not necessarily kill a European and he recovered'.

One result of this lack of unattached white women was that the strict taboos against consorting with Asian women were ignored. 'A lot of planters kept women,' recalls Perky Perkins. 'They had Siamese girls or Indian or Chinese and they used to help with the bungalow.' These kept women were widely known as 'sleeping dictionaries' and were 'not seen around'; they usually remained at the back of the bungalow when guests came to call. Japanese women were also popular and, in North Borneo, tribal women from the interior. 'You took a local girl, as I did – a Kadazan girl who's now my wife,' declares John Baxter. 'It was not really respectable but it was done by everybody.' The only Asian women who did not find employment as mistresses were Malays. This unwritten ban was particularly strong in Johore State where 'you were never allowed to have a Malay girl. If you tried, the Sultan, Ibrahim, would see to it that you were thrown out of the state straight away.' Ironically, it was the Sultan himself who provoked what was probably Malaya's greatest public scandal since the notorious 'Letter' murder case in 1911, with his own efforts to consort with European women: 'At one time he was banned from Singapore in the evenings because if he saw a pretty girl he'd stop his car and take her off to Johore.' The scandal came to a head in 1938 when the Sultana – 'a doctor's wife he'd stolen from Singapore' – arrived at the door of the British commander of the Sultan's military forces in the middle of the night begging to be sent home to Scotland.

Isolated as they were on their estates, the planters enjoyed having visitors and always entertained in style. One such visitor to Jindaram Estate in the early 1920s was the writer Somerset Maugham. A newly-arrived assistant was deputed to give him a bed for the night and take him to muster in the morning: 'So Maugham arrived and they had a jolly good evening. There was plenty of booze and dinner and brandy afterwards and then they went to bed – but never woke up in the morning and missed muster.' Maugham apparently departed in a disagreeable frame of mind, having seen nothing of the working of the estate that he had come to see.

More frequent visitors to the rubber estates were the visiting agents and planting advisors, senior men from the agency houses who came to inspect and advise – as well as younger men from the estates departments of the same agencies whose job it was to handle the day-to-day business affairs of their rubber companies. As one of Guthries' estate agents, Trevor Walker felt it important 'to be on easy terms with the estate managers with whom I was otherwise just corresponding, so I used to visit their estates in my own time as often as I could. To start with they took a perverse delight in knocking one up at half-past-four so that one could go out with them to muster – to show the young man from the town how they lived – but once they had amused themselves I found that their life and routine was really the proper way to live in the tropics.' Many of the managers that he met in this way became his firm friends:

Some were daunting – they were much older men than I was, to start with – and I remember having a brush with a redoubtable character who was in charge of our largest estate in Negri Sembilan, one Harry Thomas Piper, who looked

rather like Aubrey Smith in the old films. When I became his
agent I had occasion to write and pass on some criticisms of a
shipment of rubber that a certain firm of brokers had declared
to be 'rusty, barky and bubbly'. The phone rang early in the
morning and this well-known voice said, 'That you, Walker?
You're a bloody liar and so are the brokers.' I was not
prepared to be spoken to like this, even at the age of
twenty-two, so I hung up – which infuriated him. The phone
rang again and he said, 'Were we cut off?' I said, 'No, you
weren't. I hung up. Now what is it that you want?' – after
which we got on splendidly and never had another cross word,
because he was a very fine planter.

A manager's authority was considerable: 'The manager of
any rubber estate was very much king of the district and was
respected by everybody in the district.' The managing agency
house deferred to him and right up to the outbreak of the
Second World War a great deal of power was concentrated in
his hands:

> Due to lack of transport and communications a planter had to
> be a bit of an engineer and a medical man as well as an
> agriculturalist. If anything went wrong with the machinery he
> had to put it right on the spot and, just the same, if anybody
> got sick and it wasn't easy to send him to hospital, he had to
> know something to be able to treat him, even though each
> estate had its dresser. He also had to collaborate with the
> District Officer. There was a bit of a quarrel at one time
> because the Labour Department insisted on certain things and
> managers thought they knew what was best for their labour in
> the way of punishment, but on the whole the managers of the
> rubber estates and the administrators got on well together.

A manager's position was undoubtedly strengthened by the
fact that 'because one was an Englishman one didn't have any
difficulty in exerting one's authority; it was accepted straight

away'. But much depended on personality and between the wars many of the older managers in Malaya were considered to be outstanding men. Some of them 'weren't all that excellent from the agency's or the company's point of view' but were still 'first-class men to lead a community'. One such man was the planter C. B. Colson, whom Cecil Lee got to know through his visits to his small estate when he came to audit the books of his company, the New Crocodile Company:

> He'd been a classical scholar at Cambridge, but some love affair had sent him out East where he'd been recruited by Sir Eric Macfadyen to plant and he'd been the rest of his life on this little estate. He was the only planter I knew who actually refused a rise in salary because he said he wasn't worth it. The estate was only a small one, he said, and couldn't afford it. But eventually Sir Eric Macfadyen wrote out that he was to be paid the rise whatever he said in the matter. He grew the most lovely roses which he got every year from Australia and rather incongruously he used to display them on his dinner table in Shippam paste pots. I have memories of coming back from the Banting Club with him at night after playing pool and drinking probably too much beer, and sitting in his old open bungalow with the moon shining through the coconut palm fronds and the Tamil gardener padding through and watering the lovely maidenhair ferns and pot plants which surrounded the bungalow. Old 'Collie' would sip a few more whisky *pahits* and I, gasping for food, would be waiting for the call for the old Indian cook, '*Makan!*' – which means food. Then at dawn we used to arise and do a tour of the estates, and come back to the most delicious and gargantuan breakfasts: great piles of eggs and bacon and sausages and fried bread. I used to dream about these breakfasts afterwards when I was a prisoner of war in Siam.

Another well-known planter in Selangor was a 'tall, gangling fellow with a full prawn moustache' named H. V. Puckridge.

Known to everybody as 'Puck', he had won a DFC as a fighter pilot in the First World War, was said to come from 'an old hunting family in England' and blew a copper hunting horn 'on all possible occasions'. When Guy Madoc first knew him he owned a bull-nosed Morris – 'but to make things difficult for the police he had the tail taken off and another Morris radiator and bonnet put on at the back – so that nobody knew whether he was coming or going'. Like the great majority of planters, he was interned by the Japanese in 1942 but survived the war and was still planting in one of the loneliest and most dangerous districts in the country throughout the Malayan Emergency: 'He was given a small guard of special constables and he had them all trained so that every morning, shortly after dawn, they were paraded in front of his office, the Union Jack was raised and he blew reveille on his hunting horn.'

An even more unusual planter was Rupert Pease, a gifted amateur artist who painted water-colours that 'evoked the very soul of Malaya'. He ran his own small rubber estate of no more than three or four hundred acres near Port Dickson. 'There was no doubt whatsoever that he was a benevolent, honest, good man,' declares Sjovald Cunyngham-Brown:

> Everybody on that estate was devoted to Rupert. He had a blackboard upon which he wrote up every day the day's crop. Next to it was the current price of rubber. Next, the price of rubber per *kati* and the price of rubber per pound. They saw it before their eyes: 'Total day's profit, so much. Those working it today were so and so. Divide that number into the other and each man's earnings for the day is that much – minus two days' wages for lazy me who didn't go out into the field but have had to do this sweat for you.' I'm simplifying a bit, but they all knew exactly what he was doing – and they all loved him devotedly.

Pease also was interned by the Japanese. He happened to be a diabetic and he took with him into prison enough insulin to last him for four years:

But when he got in he discovered that there were several people also with diabetes who had not got enough. So he got a little committee together of all the diabetics and said, 'We will try to make the young survive.' Pease and a friend of his called Trevor Hughes, of the Malayan Civil Service, both gave all that they had and pooled it – and there were others, I believe. This did, in the event, entail the survival of the few who were diabetic in Changi during the war. Naturally, it also entailed the death of Trevor Hughes and Pease himself.

Even though it could hardly be compared with the terrible experiences of the war years, the depression and the slump just over a decade earlier also had a catastrophic effect on what had been till then an 'easy and very comfortable life' for most planters. When John Theophilus had first come out in 1925 the price of rubber had been about five shillings a pound: 'The next year it was down to about four shillings and from then on till the end of '29 it went down tremendously fast to about thirty cents a pound. In 1931 or '32 it went down to five cents, which was just over a penny. And it was from late '29 onwards that the planters were axed – about fifty per cent of them at that time – most of whom went home to England.'

Estates which in the early Twenties had been overstaffed with perhaps half-a-dozen assistants, were reduced to one manager and one assistant, while many of the smaller holdings were amalgamated with neighbouring estates. As the slump worsened some stopped tapping altogether and the salaries of remaining staff were further reduced. Quite a number of planters who had lost their jobs stayed on in the hope that circumstances would improve and in late 1930 the government stepped in to form a Special 'Service' Company of the FMS Volunteer Force, which was raised at Port Dickson specifically for unemployed planters and others in a similar plight. Among them was Hugh Watts. He found the training hard but in other respects 'life was very pleasant. There was plenty of company and we could swim or play tennis or go sailing.'

One of the lucky ones who kept his job was Peter Lucy, manager of the Slim River Estate on the northern borders of Selangor:

> I can remember receiving a letter from the agents saying that the company had no more money and the only way we could carry on was for us to sell our rubber to the local Chinese who would come and collect it at the factory. The wages of the labourers were to be paid out of the proceeds, and if there was anything over it would be the manager's salary. But for six months there was nothing over at all and so I had no salary whatsoever. There were other people in the district in a rather similar position and we simply got together and lived the best way we could, more or less off the jungle. We used to go shooting flying foxes, which had a rather strong meat but were not unpalatable and also mouse-deer, which provided a good meal. I remember giving a party once which was called a flying fox curry tiffin; this consisted of curried flying foxes and vegetables taken out of trees, which we had found in the jungle. We had no money to go to the club or anything of that kind so we just used to visit each other and enjoyed our life as best we could in those rather difficult circumstances.

Eventually the government was forced to take measures to stop the rubber industry from total collapse. A rubber restriction scheme was introduced and the price of rubber soon began to spiral upwards again. By 1933 most of the estates were able to resume tapping, but on a limited scale and without the large European staffs of the previous decade.

In August of that year Bill Bangs was appointed Manager of Kuala Pergau Estate in Kelantan, the most isolated and, in many ways, the most thoroughly Malay of the different Malay States. He was thirty years old: 'I think I was probably the youngest manager in Malaya and the reason was because the estate was very, very unhealthy and nobody wanted to take the job on.' Its last two managers had both caught blackwater fever; one had died and the other after recovering had refused to return to Kuala Pergau. The estate itself had been closed down for nearly four years, its Tamil and Javanese labour force had long since been paid off and it was sited a considerable distance up the Pergau river in what was known as the Ulu Pergau – 'the Malay word for anywhere up-river is *ulu*'.

At first the only way to get there was by walking in through the jungle and paddling downstream in a canoe on the return journey. Bangs found the estate completely run-down: 'Jungle had been allowed to grow up and no anti-malarial work had been done so there were considerable numbers of anopheles mosquitos around.' Within six months Bangs was himself seriously stricken with fever, which was assumed to be sub-tertian malaria but turned out to be tropical typhus. 'I became very ill indeed,' he recalls. 'At one time they came in and measured me for my coffin.' Once he had recovered Bangs turned his attention to recruiting a suitable labour force. He had been surprised to find when he first came to Kelantan that although the population was ninety-five per cent Malay all subordinate staff and labour on the railways, in the PWD and on the estates was Indian. He therefore decided to try to recruit a Malay labour force:

All the planters in the district said I was quite mad: 'Malays were useless. Malays were lazy. There was no discipline' and so on. However, I took no notice and I got a hundred per cent Malay labour, with Malay clerks, Malay conductors and Malay *mandors*. I did not have any other race on the estate and I found that if you treated them well and if you really liked them then the Malays liked you as well, and you could go very far. This paid off very well and Kuala Pergau was very successful. I also had the backing of the District Officer – he was the nearest European, forty-four miles away by river – who was very pleased when he heard that I was employing Malays.

At first there were problems of absenteeism which had to be overcome:

> They would ask for leave because a grandmother had died or a sister was ill or something like that – any excuse to get away. And I found the best way to deal with it was to recruit my labour from as far away as possible. If I took them from the *kampongs* close by they'd want to go back and see their mother or their grandmother or somebody every other day. Then when it came to the big feast days like *Hari Raya* I always gave a big feast, killing a buffalo or a bullock, and had typical Malay shows; *wayang kulit* shadow plays, *ma yong* and *ronggeng* dances or *menora*, which is a Siamese show. I would arrange for these people to come and send boats down for them. I paid fifteen dollars a night and gave them their food.

Later Bangs bought a cine-camera and a projector, making Kuala Pergau probably the first estate in Malaya to have film shows for its labour. Charlie Chaplin films were always a great hit as well as Bangs' own films showing work on the estate.

Another problem with the labour force was improving standards of hygiene:

> I had a very good water supply from a waterfall in the hills and we just blocked up the waterfall and ran a pipe down and there was water for everyone. So it was quite easy to have modern sanitation, but the great difficulty was that the Malay labourer would go in and pull the chain and then do his business and leave. It was very difficult to make him understand that you pulled the plug afterwards not before. I also used to find a lot of human waste on the grass in front of the lines where the labourers lived. No one could ever find the culprit, so I found in the stores some old powder paint which was of no more use and took this out and started to sprinkle green and red and different colours on the grass in different places, and of course it wasn't long before one of the labourers came up and asked

me what this was for. I said, 'I'll tell you if you promise not to tell anybody.' He said he wouldn't tell anybody, so I said, 'Well, the thing is this; I want to find out who is using this place as a lavatory and now whoever does use this place his behind will be one of these colours, and then I shall know immediately who it is – but *don't tell anybody*.' And from that day on there was no excreta found anywhere on the grass.

Few Europeans came up to Kuala Pergau apart from the Chief Medical Officer, who called once a month to inspect the labour force and to hunt for mosquito larvae in the surrounding ponds and streams. One other important guest who came to stay was the British Adviser in Kelantan, Captain Baker: 'I remember my "boy" coming into my room after I had had my bath and telling me that Captain Baker was outside and dressed in a dinner jacket. I hadn't thought about this and was merely putting on a white shirt, so I had to change hurriedly into a dinner jacket, which I had never worn in my bungalow, and pretend that I changed for dinner every night.' Another stickler for formality was the formidable Captain Anderson, who was Commissioner of Police in Kelantan for many years. Bangs used to go out on trips into the jungle with Malay friends and on one occasion, 'right up at the *ulu* of the Pergau river', met Captain Anderson camped outside the police station of a small village: 'He asked me to have dinner with him that night and I agreed and came along – and was rather surprised to find him fully dressed in a dinner jacket, because this was miles and miles away in the jungle. The drinks were all iced and I found out afterwards that he had prisoners from the jail in Kota Bharu running through the jungle with ice from the Cold Storage.'

Despite his isolation from other Europeans Bangs found it difficult to be lonely – 'because I surrounded myself with Malays. I don't think up the Pergau river there was ever a wedding without my advice being taken or without my being asked whether I could turn up for the wedding. I don't think

there was a circumcision ceremony ever held without them
contacting me first. I was mixed up with the Malays the whole
time.' Bangs' 'boy' was also a Malay:

> When I first came out I joined the Selangor Golf Club in
> Kuala Lumpur, and I had a Malay caddie who was aged
> about fourteen. His father had just died and his mother asked
> me if I could give him a job, so he came into the bungalow and
> just pulled the *punkah* and then learnt to be a 'boy' and then
> learnt to cook. When I became a Muslim in 1928 I promised
> him that one day we would both go to Mecca and when I went
> on the *haj* to Mecca in 1954 he came with me. He retired after
> forty years' continuous service with me – except for the time
> when I was a guest of the Japanese.

The Soul of Malaya

*As we crossed the first few hills, a new and unexpected Malaya was
disclosed, and yet one that answered to the expectations of my heart.*
Henri Fauconnier, *The Soul of Malaya*

THERE were really two Malayas. On the western side of the
peninsula the developed Malaya that most Europeans knew,
where the main activities lay and where most people lived and
worked, with its large towns, its roads and railways, its
unsightly tin-tailings and its thousands of square miles of
rubber trees – 'quite beautiful when solitary but a very dull-
looking thing in the mass when planted in neat symmetrical
rows'. Then to the east, over the mountains and beyond, an
altogether different Malaya, little developed and little visited
by the majority of Europeans – 'in fact, to many people the
thought of being moved across the mountain range to work in
states like Kelantan and Trengganu or Pahang was very
unacceptable indeed'.

But there were always Europeans who felt drawn to this
undeveloped Malaya, even though the attraction was not
easy to put into words. 'I find it difficult to describe,'
acknowledged John Davis. 'I know I wanted the jungle
and the East Coast. But there must have been others

amongst our crowd for whom it was the last thing they wanted.' In their free time and at weekends Davis and Guy Madoc, along with other like-minded police cadets, began to venture out on their motor-cycles to see what the rest of Malaya outside Kuala Lumpur had to offer: 'When we got beyond the rubber estates and saw the wilderness of the jungle, that, I think, is really what got me – that first impression of the jungle as a mysterious and almost impenetrable place. I still remember so clearly John Davis and I getting off our motor-cycles and standing on the roadside and saying, "I wonder if we could get into this".' Later there came the moment when Madoc took his motor-cycle up to the central mountain range and saw what lay beyond:

> Hundreds of miles of jungle over rolling mountains, exciting torrents coming down through the jungle, and when the torrents levelled out into smooth river, green *padi*-fields and little Malay *kampongs*, dotted around in the shade of fruit trees and coconut trees. It was all that I had imagined of a rural Malaya.

There was at that time only one road across the mountains to the East Coast and one railway line, running north to Kota Bharu. To cover the two hundred and fifty miles of laterite road from KL to Kuantan it took the best part of a day of hard driving, along 'a thin streak of red winding its way through heavy jungle for mile after mile'. Those without private transport could go with the mail car on its daily run or – if they were European – sit up front in the 'seat of privilege' alongside the driver in a local 'mosquito' bus. But there was also a third way to get to the East Coast: 'The easy way and the best way was to go by night train to Singapore and then up by sea in a small coastal steamer.'

This sea journey took three or four days, with the ships passing through clusters of islands lying off the coast, each with its own legends. The largest was Pulau Tioman, 'lying exactly like a sleeping dragon', about which a story was told of 'a princess who came voyaging south and fell in love with a dragon and settled down there – which is entirely understandable if you come across Pulau Tioman in the early dawn'. Another 'most glorious' sight were the brightly-painted boats of the Malay fishing-fleets, 'going out in the morning with the rising sun coming up over the sea, the Malay fishermen wearing their kilted *sarongs* in striking colours – yellow and black, green and black, blue and black – and sailing back in the afternoon, a whole fleet of sails in the sunlight'.

One of those who travelled by sea when he first came to Kuantan in 1931 was Bill Goode:

> We took three days, calling at various little ports on the way up, along a very lovely coconut-fringed coast with sandy beaches and these little river mouths where the ship went in and usually anchored in mid-stream and people came off – until eventually early one morning we went across the sandbar into the Kuantan river, with coconut palms on either side. There was not much sign of life but there was a little jetty against which the ship was tied up and on the jetty were two Europeans in white shorts and white pith helmets. I was hoping they had come to meet me and indeed one was the District Officer, Huggins, who met me and took me to the rest house.

On the East Coast – as in Sarawak and North Borneo – the rivers were all-important: 'The Malays came in from the sea and the only way they could move up into the country was along the rivers'. And because of the dense tropical jungle they continued to be 'the high roads along which people travelled and on the edge of which people lived'. On their opaque, coffee-coloured waters could be seen 'small, overloaded boats – just about sinking by the look of them – full of women and children and men with their wide hats to keep the sun off', and at their banks 'women washing clothes or perhaps bathing their babies, and children who would rush down to the water's edge waving madly and jumping into the river because they liked to catch the wash of the boats'. The water itself was also full of life:

> There were fish and creatures of every sort, particularly crocodiles – although it wasn't as easy as all that to see them, because they were nearly always deep under water. But they were known when they took an animal or a person and they were a real danger. They had larders deep in the mud-banks under the water where they kept their prey until it became nicely weathered before they ate it. They were in every way repulsive, repellent creatures. Yet all the Malays and Dayaks – who were the cleanest of people – regularly bathed in the rivers by the houses.

Young cadets like Bill Goode who were posted to the East Coast could usually expect a warm welcome from the local European community. In Kuantan this consisted of 'the District Officer and his wife, a Customs Officer and his wife, a Public Works Officer and his wife, a young policeman and myself – as well as three or four European planters who were scattered around at varying distances from Kuantan'.

Eastern Cadets could also expect to receive advice and guidance from the District Officer – although it was not always forthcoming. Mervyn Sheppard was placed under a notoriously difficult DO: 'After my preliminary interviews in the Secretariat there was an interval of about forty-eight hours before we were told where we were to go. When I was told that I was to go to a place called Temerloh in Pahang the senior MCS officer in the cadet bungalow reacted fairly strongly and said it was "the arse of the earth"! "Smith is the District Officer," he added, "and the combination will be undiluted purgatory."' Having got to Temerloh – 'a little village by the side of the big Pahang river' – he was allotted a 'funereal' three-roomed bungalow, 'which was raised three feet off the ground because of floods and was very unattractive because it had been painted with a kind of black creosote as an antidote to white ants'. He was then taken across to the district office to meet the DO:

> He suffered from three disabilities, none of which he could be blamed for. First of all, he came from Aberdeen. Secondly, he'd served in the war and he'd suffered shell shock. And thirdly, he was just recovering from malaria, which was extremely prevalent in Temerloh. He was just cold and dour, with a grim face and no smile. He didn't say 'welcome', or 'glad to see you' or anything like that. He merely said, 'Well, you've been sent to me to learn Malay and the rudiments of administration. You won't be able to do anything useful for me for some time to come but I hope you will get over the preliminary studies as soon as possible, so that you can be of some use to me.'

Sheppard and Goode learned their jobs by being thrown in at the deep end, but to help them there were Malay Deputy and Assistant District Officers, members of the Malay Administrative Service. 'I was really put in the charge of the Malay Assistant DO,' recalls Bill Goode:

> His name was Dato Hussain and he was a local territorial chief; a man of very considerable personality whose eldest son – then a very small boy – was later to become Prime Minister of Malaysia. But it was Dato Hussain who really taught me my job. He took me to the magistrate's court, where I sat beside him and listened to him administering justice. Because the courts produced a complete array of all the local people and all the local languages, interpreters had to translate from Malay into English and English into Chinese or possibly into an Indian language, so I got to recognize the local people and of course at the same time I was learning something of court work.

The Malay Administrative Service provided a second tier of administrators under the MCS. Its officers were all educated Malays; most had been to the Malay College, which was run on English public-school lines, and they were all fluent English-speakers. They were members of the local 'European' club and were regarded as social equals by their MCS colleagues – 'we went to each other's houses and played badminton together and they were very friendly and relaxed and excellent companions'. Further support came from the office clerks – Indian, Chinese and Malay. 'They were the best people to teach you because they knew the routine,' declares Sheppard. 'I spent the first week of my time in Temerloh simply watching and making notes from each of the chief clerks in the three different divisions: the District Office, the Land Office and the Sub-Treasury.'

But the first priority for any junior officer was to learn the local language. To encourage him to speak Malay, Goode was sent out into the district:

> One of my jobs was to go out and inspect work on making what were known as bridle paths – the beginning of communications other than by river – and I was given the job of inspecting the work and paying off those who had worked there. When I got to a rendezvous I would be met by the local *penghulu*, a sort of parish headman, who of course would speak nothing but Malay. We would talk as best we could and we'd look at the work and very often I'd have lunch in his house, so that I was gradually introduced to Malay habits and Malay people. Naturally I would eat the food that they produced, which would be rice and some form of curry – chicken, or, more likely, fish – with local vegetables, and probably a cup of very sweet coffee to finish up with. Being Muslims, of course, there was no question of their having any alcohol in their houses; life was still comparatively simple in those days and untouched by the evils of civilization.

Once the local Malay dialect had been mastered it was possible to become more closely involved with local people and their day-to-day affairs. After training in Kuala Lumpur and spending several months on short attachments, Guy Madoc was sent out for the first time as the Officer in Charge of a Police District (OCPD) in a remote area east of the central mountain range in Negri Sembilan:

> I can claim that I made great progress in Jelebu because my office orderly used to encourage me to go around with him and attend local celebrations in the villages. I went to quite a lot of Malay weddings where I had to chat with the guests. I would be told, for example, that provided I embraced the Islamic religion the person talking with me would present me with his daughter as a wife. I also learned bit by bit some of the local taboos. One that is common through most Asian countries is eating only with the right hand, because the left is concerned more with the intimacies of personal hygiene. Another one was that you must never walk behind a sitting man without first asking permission to do so, the reason being that you might have a hate on him and be preparing to stab him in the back. In the same way, if you draw a *kris* – the famous curved Malay dagger – immediately you draw it from its sheath you must touch the wall or something solid nearby, because the Malay believed that when a *kris* was drawn it had the immediate desire and intention of stabbing, so therefore you must permit it to stab something it couldn't harm. And, again, you never asked a favour direct in Malay society in those days. You always asked a third person and then the third person would pass your question on to the man you really wanted to talk to.

Madoc was a very keen bird-watcher and here, too, he learned a lot about Malay customs:

> The Malays had some very peculiar beliefs about birds. There's one which is called the spurwing plover, that was

said to lie on its back and cradle its eggs on its feet. I couldn't believe that one, although this particular bird laid its egg on the sand, which was tremendously hot, and I do know that the spurwing plover used to go into the river and wet its breast feathers and then sit over its eggs. Then there was another belief regarding the Malayan moorhen, which is almost exactly like our moorhen. They said that if you could put a moorhen's nest on your head, then you were crowned with invisibility – very useful, of course, for thieves, although I never actually saw a gentleman bent on thieving walking along the road wearing a nest on his head.

Another pursuit that helped to strengthen local ties was touring the district – not in the grand manner of their contemporaries in India, but in a more relaxed and simple style. When OCPD in Pekan, the seat of the Sultan of Pahang, John Davis did most of his touring by bicycle and on foot:

> I tried to set up a tradition that the OCPD would go and visit every single one of his stations down the coast once every month or two months. It was boyscouting in a way but it gave us a great thrill and kept us out, and it also kept our outlying stations on their toes because they never knew when this daft OCPD of theirs was going to call on them.

Part of the tour usually involved walking through the jungle but most of the distance covered was along the beach, where bicycles could be used:

> I'd probably take my orderly along with me, and one or two other police constables who were perhaps relieving stations down south, and we'd travel with about half a day's journey between police stations. The idea would be to arrive at a police station, hold an inspection there, taking a couple of hours, perhaps, and then settle down for the evening, probably having a Malayan meal with the local police and the inhabit-

ants, chatting, wandering about, seeing points of interest. Then early next day we'd set off again down to the next station, and because it was a very remote area and there were no other Europeans around you really began to become friends. You were always the boss – that was one of the inevitable things – but you felt very close to them. In those days our uniform was still rather formal, with a Wolseley helmet and a Sam Browne belt, worn with a shirt and shorts and stockings. This was necessary because you were on duty and you had to be fairly smart if you were inspecting the men, but there was no formality in conversation when we were going along together and helping each other along. It was a very happy relationship.

Touring also provided an opportunity to do a bit of shooting for the pot. Madoc would go out in the evenings 'either in the *padi*-fields shooting snipe or on the jungle edges shooting green pigeon' – which would fly over 'almost with the precision of a time clock' at about ten-to-six.

Junior administrators and other officials also toured, not always using the same means of transport but with very much the same end results. Goode did much of his touring in a Malay *prahu*, 'a native boat with a straw mat covering in which I slept and cooked and had my being'. His evenings were often spent in the local headman's house, 'sitting for hours collecting all the local gossip. One was very close to the people. One felt that one belonged and they seemed to accept one as belonging to them.'

Along with a greater sense of belonging came a greater understanding of the Malay character: 'The Malays in these rather underdeveloped areas may have been people of limited wealth and unsophisticated living but they were extremely astute in judging character. If they accepted you as being the sort of person that they could admire and like, they gave you everything that you would want. But they were quick enough to reject the meretricious and the spurious.' It was often said of the Malay that he was easy-going but 'you had only to see a Malay at work in irrigated *padi*-plots, ploughing, planting-out or reaping – or go out to sea once with the Malay fishermen to appreciate that they were in no way lazy'. Nor were they obsequious when it came to dealing with Europeans or officials: 'You were treated as an equal and they would tell you face to face where you were making a mistake and getting it wrong.'

One of the additional advantages of living in these predominantly Malay areas was the survival of traditional Malay culture, particularly in the many forms of Malay entertainment, from kite-flying and top-spinning to dancing and simple theatrical performances. What Guy Madoc particularly enjoyed was the *wayang kulit*, the 'leather theatre' shadow play performed with delicately-trimmed puppets cut out of thin leather and then brightly painted:

It always surprised me so much that they bothered to paint these leather figures because all that appeared was a black silhouette on a screen. If you were sitting out in front all you could see was a white cloth, which might have been a table cloth, with a brilliant light behind it. But the real excitement was to be allowed to go in behind stage and see what was happening. In a very remote village in Kelantan I once sat behind for, I suppose, a couple of hours. In front of me there was the operator sitting cross-legged on the ground and above his head was a brilliant pressure lamp illuminating the cloth in front of him. Then at the foot of the cloth but invisible to the audience there was a great big juicy stem of a banana-plant – something about eight inches thick – and all his puppets. He probably had about forty ranged on either side of him as if they were in the wings of an ordinary theatre, and each was mounted on a short stick, pointed so that he could stab it into the banana plant when its cue came. Some of them had movable jaws so that they appeared to be talking, particularly the comedians, and some at least one movable arm, so that they could gesticulate. This man was working in a pool of sweat, because he was telling a folk-tale – originally from the Hindu *Ramayana* but very considerably modified over the years so as to suit Mohammedan tastes – loud enough for the people on the other side of the screen to hear it and all the time he was also operating his puppets; bringing one in, making it talk, possibly making another one punch it with his fist, then pushing it back into the wings and bringing more out. Sometimes at the end of a performance like that the operator, who must have been in a trance, just fell over in a dead faint and had to be brought round with a bucket of water.

There was also a darker side to the Malay character: 'One of the dreaded things which we had heard about through Somerset Maugham and other people was the Malay business of *amok* or "running amuck". The typical *amok* involved a gentleman in a completely mad state running down the village street with a dagger in each hand and stabbing everybody who got in his path.' As policemen, both Madoc and Davis had to deal with a number of *amok* cases in their careers: 'You couldn't just stand there with your revolver and shoot the man dead, so we all felt that if we came across an *amok* we were in for real trouble.' The great difficulty for them was that 'everybody expected you to do something and what on earth could you do? There was no question of your being in any danger – unless you took action. But they were always difficult to handle simply because everybody turned to you and you didn't know what to do and you were inevitably excited like the rest of the crowd.' Davis recalls how *amok* 'seemed to create a strange, throbbing, reddish sort of atmosphere around it, with a man working himself up from beginning to seem a little strange and abrupt and then a little bit more difficult and gradually working up and working up but never becoming actively furious until perhaps he makes a lunge and tries to kill somebody. But internally they're absolutely boiling – and this boiling seems to spread over into the crowd which always encircles them. Of course, if it's at dusk and there are fires lit it's particularly dramatic in the flickering light.'

Guy Madoc had to deal with two cases of *amok* within three months of each other. 'I remember the first one very vividly,' he declares:

I dashed out in the car to the village where the man was and the corporal in charge of the local police station said, 'Well, he's up on the platform outside his house and he's got an axe in one hand and he's got a *parang*, a jungle knife, in the other. He hasn't actually injured anybody yet, but don't go anywhere near him. The moment you go within six feet of him, he's up on his feet screaming, and wielding his weapons.' So I went along and I said in Malay: 'How do you do? Nice day isn't it?' And after about ten minutes, he said, 'Come and sit on the platform with me.' So I said, 'Right.' And I got up and I sat on the platform with him, and he hadn't touched his axe and he hadn't touched his jungle knife and when I was close enough and thought that his attention was diverted, I just put my arms right round his body and his arms and held him tightly against me and the corporal came up and put the handcuffs on him and that was that. After that I didn't think that an *amok* really was such a terrible thing.

But Davis remembers one particularly 'lurid' case that left him 'horribly frightened', where a man had barricaded himself in a Malay hut, having already killed two people:

It was in the night and there were literally hundreds of people and a large number of policemen surrounding the place when I arrived. They didn't know whether there was still anybody alive in the house so that to rush him might have meant the needless death of some other person. The only thing one could do was to gradually get closer and closer until two or three Sikh policemen and myself crashed in from various directions carrying hockey sticks. The hockey stick is a most wonderful

weapon in all riots and anything like that because you can hit
hard and you can hook a man who's making a slash at you. We
rushed the man and we succeeded in overpowering him and
brought him in. That was a bad case.

For most young government servants and policemen, life on
the East Coast was rarely dull or lonely. 'It was only in the first
six or seven weeks when it poured with rain every day and I
was having such difficulty with the language and didn't know
anybody that I did feel lonely,' Goode acknowledges. 'But
once I got settled down I was too busy and the house was
always open day and night so that anybody could come and go
at any time – and they nearly always were coming and going.'

As regards female company in the bungalow, the prevailing
ethic among officials was a simple one – 'it simply wasn't
something that one did'. Early officials like Clifford and
Swettenham had approved of concubinage and disapproved
of European wives, but in later years this policy was reversed.
Goode recalls how he and other newly-arrived cadets were
handed 'a rather pompous piece of paper' which was the
notorious Secret Circular A, written by the Duke of Devon-
shire when Secretary of State for the Colonies in 1909, which
'laid down the law that cadets were not expected to live with
local ladies and that if they did they'd get the sack – about
which we all laughed. But I think we all observed self-restraint.
I certainly was conscious – and I think they were – that, if you
took a local girl into your house and into your bed, it made a
fundamental alteration in your relationship with the rest of the
people in your district.'

Guy Madoc was equally content with his lot in his isolated
district of Jelebu – 'but then I was twenty-one and proud that I
was in charge of a district of several hundred square miles'.
There was no club house as such; instead Madoc and two or
three other Europeans foregathered in the late afternoon in
one of the rooms of the Jelebu rest-house – or played a round
of golf on a 'tiny golf course which bounced from one side of a

cleared valley to the other'. After the golf they 'sat on the veranda and possibly had a whisky and soda, and usually dispersed before sunset, which all through the year occurred at precisely the same hour, about half-past-six'.

An occasional visitor to the club was *Abang* Braddon – 'the "elder brother", to distinguish him from his younger brother *Adik* Braddon, who lived the other side of the pass' – a mine-owner who had been in Malaya 'since the year dot' and enjoyed talking about his early life:

> If he had to go to Seremban, the state capital across the hills, he used to start about six o'clock in the evening in an old-fashioned bullock cart. In the back of the bullock cart he would put his chaise-longue, and a bottle of whisky and something to eat for the journey. His buffalo cart would travel all through the night, and next morning he'd wake up quite refreshed on the outskirts of Seremban. Abang Braddon also had a Chinese mistress and at that time the Chinese community seemed to disapprove very much of their women having any truck with the red-headed devils, and so she always had to be disguised as a man. She wore men's clothes and a cap, and when out in public view she would go through the motions of being the *syce*, the driver of his pony trap.

In the evenings Madoc would bring papers back to his bungalow to work on or write long letters to his parents. The bungalow was enormous – 'I just rattled around in it like a pea in a drum' – and like most old-fashioned bungalows it stood on stilts, 'for the very good reason that in a Malay *kampong* you could get tigers and panthers wandering around at night. And indeed my own bungalow had what was called a *kramat* tiger, which I was told carried the spirit or the soul of one of the former Undangs of Jelebu, a local chief. I saw its pug-marks but I never heard it moving round the bungalow at night.'

At the back of the bungalow, but at ground level, was the bathroom: 'You walked down concrete steps, three or four of them, onto the concrete floor, and there was a hole in the corner where the water could go out and a great earthenware receptacle, which some people called a Shanghai jar, others a Siam jar, full of cold water. You had to keep a wooden cover on your jar, otherwise it was a tremendous breeding place for mosquitoes.' Then at the front of the house there was the veranda:

> Now in these old-fashioned bungalows you lived on the veranda, which was probably big enough to have played a game of badminton in. It had no windows or walls – just a balustrade about three foot high and otherwise open to the elements. The only protection when the wind blew and the rain beat were the roller blinds, which were called *chicks*, and which your cook-boy was expected to lower when things became unpleasant.

These *chicks* were often lined with blue canvas cloth which cast 'a very attractive, bluish, subdued light that was extremely pleasant; it was such a relief to the eyes to come from the glare outside into the gentle blue-green lighting that suffused the bungalow'. In the evenings the *chicks* would be raised again so as to let in as much air as possible, 'although you also got the maximum number of bats, moths and flying cockroaches. And of course the smaller avifauna all concentrated on your lamp, because mostly we worked after dark with things called Aladdin lamps which shed a brilliant light and attracted every bug in the district, so about every hour the thing would go out in a cloud of smoke.'

As well as insects every bungalow had its colony of pale little lizards known as *chi-chak* – 'quite harmless and perfectly clean' – running up and down the walls and across ceilings. It was a Malay belief that the *chi-chak* would interject its voice whenever it heard a truth being uttered: 'When you and I are talking, for instance, suddenly a *chi-chak* will say "chi-chi, chi-chak". And then I would be able to say to you, "You see, the *chi-chak* agrees. It's true." '

There was also the bigger lizard known as the *gekko*: 'When the *gekko* starts his "choh, choh" the Malays like to sit quietly listening – and betting as to the number of calls he makes before he stops. Some people hold four fingers up, some perhaps nine and then if you get it right you scoop the pool.'

As night came on there would be other insect and animal noises: noisy crickets that would 'start just at sunset and had a most tremendous wild squeal – but fortunately never went on long into the night'; the 'late evening trumpet beetles that were as big as your thumb and made the most appalling noise, like a child's tin trumpet, that would go on and on until nine o'clock at night and then suddenly stop'; and sometimes, overheard from the veranda, the call of the *tock-tock* bird – another sound that appealed to the Malay gambling instinct – 'actually it was a nightjar but it really did go "tock-tock, tock-tock, tock-tock". You never knew how many times it would produce that "tock-tock" without stopping and at a party when the Malays who had driven their *tuans* over to some entertainment were all sitting outside on the mudguards of their cars, you'd hear them laying bets as to how many times the *tock-tock* bird was going to produce its call.'

Madoc's bungalow stood on the top of a hill, and from his veranda he could look out over the police barracks and across towards the mountains: 'One could see, I suppose, for a score of miles across those jungle-clad hills; sometimes they were bright green, sometimes they were almost blue, depending on the time of day and the amount of sunlight – or of storm, because the elements could be mighty boisterous at times.'

On the West Coast there was the wind called the Sumatra – 'just a sudden squall that blows up, but when it blows it blows like blazes and is very often accompanied by torrential rain. Then it was the duty of your servants at the back to come running and release all the ropes and let the *chicks* come down at a run.' On the East Coast there was the winter monsoon, which brought welcome variety to the climate and played a decisive role in the lives of its inhabitants. When Mervyn Sheppard first came to Kemaman in November 1932 the north-east monsoon was just about to break:

> The fishermen were just having their last outings before they pulled their boats high up on the beach for the next three or four months, because once the monsoon started, general communications by sea were cut off and you gave up all attempts to travel about the district. The north-east monsoon was known in Malay as *musim tutup kuala* – closed river mouth. It was a period of stagnation. The river mouth, which was the way in and out of the country and had been for perhaps a thousand years, was shut and the only way that anybody could get about was on land. So that was the time when, if you wanted to move at all, you walked.

During the monsoon period only two ships continued to battle their way up and down the coast. One was an ancient Chinese vessel known as the *Hong Ho* and the other was one of several owned and captained by Danish sea captains, who were 'very much admired and sometimes loved because they had very close contacts with the local people, particularly the Chinese businessmen in the various ports or villages where they stopped. They tried very hard never to let them down, however bad the weather was.' The most beloved and ad-mired of these Danish sea captains was Captain Mogensen, about whom many stories – both true and apocryphal – were told:

> Perhaps one of his most famous adventures was when he brought his ship into Kemaman on New Year's Eve and invited the local Malay commissioner and the local Malay shipping agent and one or two Chinese shopkeepers to come on board for a drink and dinner. Before going down to dinner he said he was going to let off a ship's rocket to entertain his guests and also the public. So he let off his rocket and it was a

very great success and the entire village of Kemaman turned out and stood along the edge of the wharf. It was such a success that the guests asked him to let off a second one, by which time every single man, woman and child in Kemaman had assembled on the edge of the wharf and there was a demand for a third. So he agreed to make it three; the third and the last before dinner. So the third rocket was fastened to an upright support on the ship and lit, but something had gone wrong and as it rose from the ship it turned at right angles and directed itself straight down the main street of Kemaman, dividing the public sharply to right and left. When it got to the first crossroads, there was a strong breeze from the sea which blew it off course and it entered the door of the leading general store, where it buried its nose in a large collection of bottles of beer, Guinness and other liquids. There was the roar of an explosion – and that was that. The captain realized that there was nothing he could do and so he hurriedly took his guests down to dinner. But the story of the rocket survived for at least a generation and more.

The weekly steamers from Singapore provided a vital link with the outside world. 'I often used to go out in the boats taking out the dried fish and have a very welcome cold beer with the Danish captain,' recalls Bill Goode. 'They really kept some of us along the coast sane, because every week they brought in some supplies and human contact.' As well as supplying duty-free drinks the steamers provided first-class meals, which could be arranged and booked in advance. It was also common for the Chief Officers on board to come to private arrangements with some of the European wives along the coast who would give them lists of shopping to be done in Singapore. But perhaps their greatest service was that they brought in goods from the Cold Storage Depot in Singapore: 'real meat, packed originally in ice – which by then had melted – and sawdust, all of which had to be washed off', but which made a welcome change from local goat and Chinese pork;

imported apples from New Zealand and such luxuries as Iceberg Butter, 'which came in a tin from Singapore and in the heat you had to put it on with a paint brush'.

The ships also kept the local Chinese stores stocked up with the kind of food that appealed to European bachelors: 'The grocers' shops in the most remote of places always kept champagne, tins of caviar, tinned salmon and tinned asparagus and one or two other things that in those days were looked upon as the height of luxury even in England.' These luxuries helped to make up the 'orthodox bachelor dinner', so that 'when you went to a bachelor's dinner party you knew what you were going to get: tomato soup, cold asparagus served with bottled salad dressing, very tough chicken roast with mashed potatoes and tinned peas, and tinned fruit salad. That was routine.'

Opportunities for escape from day-to-day routine were inevitably more limited on the East Coast than elsewhere in Malaya, particularly during the winter months, when an invitation to join the British Adviser for Christmas might mean walking a hundred miles – as was once the case for Mervyn Sheppard in Trengganu. But a fortnight's annual leave always made it possible to get away to Singapore or perhaps to one of the small hill-stations that were fast becoming a feature of European life in Malaya in the inter-war years: the largely official Fraser's Hill in the hills outside Kuala Lumpur and the more egalitarian Cameron Highlands in the higher mountains further north. But there were always a number who preferred to find escape by exploring the jungles that still covered more than three-quarters of the peninsula: the great primary rain forests of South-East Asia. 'I used to spend my weekend in the jungle,' Guy Madoc remembers. 'I also used to spend my annual leaves in the jungle and even after I was married I sometimes deserted my wife and family and went off. And I came to love the jungle and also the islands off the coast. I claim that I've been on every island off both coasts and on two occasions I sneaked over to visit some islands on the far side of the Straits of Malacca which had a special ornithological interest for me.'

Another young man who quickly came to terms with the Malayan jungle – and was later to put this familiarity to good effect – was John Davis: 'We wore gym shoes, no socks of any kind, with shorts and a shirt – and we would carry a jungle knife. This was rash because we got covered with leeches and ended up having jungle ulcers, so we learned to keep our legs covered. But this was the quality of the jungle; that you just walked into it at any time in absolute comfort and with no fear whatsoever.'

Like Davis, Sjovald Cunyngham-Brown soon realized that the jungle was far from being a dangerous place. However, it was not always easy to walk through:

> The Malayan jungle undergrowth is extremely thick and you have to cut your way through with a knife or else quietly work your way through. There are so many thorn bushes that will hold you back, one in particular known as the *nanti dahulu* or 'wait a bit' thorn, but apart from that the Malayan jungle is the kindest jungle in the world; great hardwood trees, about twenty-five or thirty feet apart, and a dense cover of foliage at two hundred and fifty to three hundred feet above your head. That's where the flowers are and where the birds and butterflies live, while down below in these dark, cool caverns there's very little life indeed.

There was plenty of wildlife but it was more often heard than seen: the ' "whoop, whoop, whoop" of the monkey which the Malays call the *wa-wa*. It lived in the high jungle trees and usually performed at dawn'; the 'rattling of woodpeckers tapping on hollow trees' and the 'whoosh of the wingbeats of the great hornbills flying over the tops of the jungle canopy'. One bird call that Madoc learned to reproduce was the sound of the hornbill, known to Malays as the 'chop down your mother-in-law' bird:

The call goes 'Roo, roo, roo – karoo, karoo – hah, hah, hah!' and the Malays say that the 'roo, roo, roo' is the sound of the axe biting into the pillars, the 'karoo' is when the house suddenly falls down, presumably with mother-in-law in it, and then you have the idiot laughter as he trails away into the jungle with his axe. One evening when we were prisoners of the Japanese in Changi prison, I was permitted by the authorities to go over and lecture on these birds in the women's camp, a very rare privilege, and I started this call in full bellow. The women thought it was marvellous but I had forgotten that I had a Japanese sentry standing immediately behind me and he came up with his bayonet and said 'Harghh!' and I rather thought I was going to get a bayonet up my backside.

The birds of the jungle were 'always calling, whistling, mocking, but seldom seen' – and the animals were equally shy. Tigers were no exception – although Cunyngham-Brown did meet one face to face:

I was pursuing a path which I must have lost and then found again. It was about five o'clock in the afternoon and the light was filtering down more and more obliquely through the tops of the trees, with the occasional lazy moth beginning to float through the sunbeams, and it was all becoming a little eerie and creepy. I wondered, 'Shall I go on or shall I try and get back before dark?' And thinking these thoughts I jumped up onto a fallen tree trunk, with a great patch of sunlight on the far side of it. And as I jumped there was the most appalling 'Aaarghh' from the other side of the tree trunk and a full-grown tiger of enormous dimensions swung round and glared at me, baring its teeth and with its yellow eyes boring into me. I stood there, with my legs turned to water, quivering on top of this tree trunk and then suddenly with a snarl it jumped – not at me, thank God, but sideways into the jungle and I fell, a quivering heap, into the sand pit where it had been basking in the sunshine. We must have been the most frightened man and the most frightened tiger in South-East Asia.

The denseness of the jungle discouraged big-game hunting but there were those who went out on shooting expeditions. Derek Headly once took a boat up-river to Ulu Pahang to hunt the Malayan wild ox known as the *seladang*. His plan was to make contact with some of the aborigines of the peninsula known as the *Sakai* or *Orang Asli* – the 'original people' of Malaya, who were usually to be found a day's journey upstream of the last Malay villages on the river: 'At the last Malay *kampong* we went ashore and drank from green coconuts with the headman, and he then went on with us up-river, where we contacted these *Orang Asli*. One of the younger ones came with us while we were stalking the *seladang* and both these men were tremendously brave and a great help in the hunt.' Seven years later the three met up again in extraordinary circumstances:

It was shortly after I dropped back into Malaya by parachute in 1945. We were moving off through the jungle very early in the morning – one of those mornings in Pahang where the night mist hung over the tops of the trees. We came to the banks of a rather cold, broad river. We could see the tops of the trees on the other side with the grey mist swirling around and we stood there on the bank not liking the idea of getting into this rather deep, cold water and saying 'Oh, go on, you go first.' Then suddenly round a bend in the river came a little bamboo raft, poled by an *Orang Asli* with a Malay in a white turban sitting at the stern – the same *Orang Asli* and the village headman with whom I'd gone shooting seven years earlier. They took one look at me and I took one look at them and they made that marvellous sign of greeting, putting both their palms together and raising them to their foreheads. It was really a very moving moment.

Living and working on the East Coast was for John Davis, as for many others, 'altogether delightful'. But for him this period of what some of his colleagues in Kuala Lumpur referred to as 'lotus eating' suddenly came to an abrupt and distressing end:

> I was a very young policeman in those days, aged twenty-one, and a great deal too big for my boots, thinking that I stood for the law and that the letter of the law must be upheld. The Sultan of Pahang was a young man of about twenty-four, a fairly ebullient, perhaps slightly provocative sultan in those days, although later on he became a very fine man indeed. But I decided against the advice of my policemen that as I had information that the Sultan's wives were gambling in the *Istana* and as this was against the law, then the law must be upheld. So I duly raided the Sultan's *Istana* – God knows why – and brought several of his wives in and I was going to have them prosecuted. I soon got instructions from my chief not to worry too much about the prosecution and that was all I heard of it for some time. Then one day my boss phoned me up and said I'd been selected to go to China to learn Chinese and should leave in two months' time. 'For heaven's sake, why?' I asked. 'I'm deliriously happy in Pekan.' And he said, 'Well, you can't stay there. You will go raiding the Sultan's wives and the Sultan has asked the Governor whether you can be removed from the state.' I was so delighted with Pahang but I suddenly realized that if I was going from Pahang I had no other interests, so I said to him on the phone, 'Well, if I've got to leave Pahang let me go to China and be done with it.' And in fact this was the most wonderful decision I ever made, because the whole of the rest of my career derived from my going to China.

All government servants knew that their postings were of limited duration, since it was not the policy of the government to allow officials to remain in one place for too long. The longest tours rarely exceeded two years and were often far shorter. After seven months in Temerloh Mervyn Sheppard received orders to report for duty in Kuala Lumpur as Private Secretary to the Chief Secretary:

This was the first occasion that I experienced what was one of the saddest parts of a civil servant's life; the infrequent but nevertheless unavoidable farewells to people with whom one has worked and for whom one has tried very hard to be of service. The more you put your efforts, your feelings, your affections into a job and into the people of the place where you were working, the harder it was to part from them and the more distressing – almost heart-rending – the experience. As time went on I came to dread this ultimate, unavoidable parting which had to come, whatever job you were allotted to.

Bill Goode felt very much the same way when, after two-and-a-half years in Trengganu, the time came for him to take his first home leave:

As I passed through Singapore, I sought an interview with the then Colonial Secretary to ask him if he could possibly see his way to arranging that I should be posted back to Besut when I came back from leave, as I hadn't been there long enough to complete a lot of things that I'd had in mind to do. But he told me in no uncertain terms that the last thing he would agree to would be that I should return to my own mess in Besut. He thought that was a very bad thing. I was upset at the time, but he was absolutely right. It would have been quite wrong for me to go back.

6

The Land of the White Rajahs

England was very far away and when at long intervals they went back was increasingly strange to them; their real home, their intimate friends, were in the land in which the better part of their lives was spent.

Somerset Maugham, *Preface*,
The Complete Short Stories, Vol III

SHORTLY before the Japanese attack on Pearl Harbor, Robert Nicholl was walking on the upper deck of the Dutch liner *The New Amsterdam*, 'somewhere East of Zanzibar' and on his way to the Middle East, when he fell into conversation with another officer: 'We started talking about British possessions in the Far East and he said to me, "You know, as the Colonial Office Auditor I have had experience of all the British possessions in the Far East and South-East Asia and the status of the white man is highest in the little state of Sarawak. There he is held in higher regard than in any other territory."' Nicholl had never heard of Sarawak and asked his companion where it was: 'He said, "Oh, it's a dreadfully jungly little place in Borneo. They had a marvellous ruler, an old man named Charles Brooke, the Second White Rajah. He ran that place extraordinarily well but he's dead now and his son rules, the Third Rajah, Charles Vyner Brooke."'

Sarawak in 1941 had just celebrated a century of Brooke rule under its three White Rajahs – yet it was still a land about which most Britons knew very little. When told by the Cambridge University Appointments Board in 1934 that Sarawak was recruiting graduates as administrative officers, Bob Snelus had to admit that he had never heard of the place. Peter Howes, training to become a missionary with the Society for the Propagation of the Gospel in 1937, mainly associated the country with the 'head-hunters of Borneo' and with 'a pop tune of the time called *Sarawaki*, which was played by a band whose leader had married one of the Rajah's daughters'. Indeed, it was probably in connection with these daughters that most people in the 1930s thought of Sarawak, if at all: 'Charles Vyner Brooke had no male heirs but he was blessed with three lovely and attractive daughters. The eldest, a very gracious lady, married Lord Inchcape. The second one married the famous Harry Roy, the band leader, and the third one married an amateur all-in-wrestler.' All this did nothing for the image of Sarawak: 'When Didi – as she was known – married the band leader she promptly became known in the British press as Princess Pearl, which was entirely false as her local title was the honorary one of *dayang*, which didn't mean princess or anything like it. And it did become a little irritating to be asked from time to time if Harry Roy was your Rajah.'

Rajah Charles Vyner Brooke himself was 'a very much respected and well-liked old gentleman' but also something of an enigma to his officers. Although he and his family lived comfortably rather than lavishly, there were those who regarded him as a bit of a playboy because, in contrast to his father who was 'not addicted to the comforts of life and a bit of a spartan', Vyner Brooke made social life in Kuching 'more lively and much more joyous, with more parties, more dancing, more trips on his yacht and Race Week twice a year, when all the outstation officers were invited down in turn and used to have a terrific time'. The Rajah could indeed be 'perfectly charming – but his personal dignity was as great as his personal charm. He was always the ruler and nobody ever dreamt of addressing him in a familiar way.' Yet when he gave orders it was never done in an authoritarian manner: 'He would talk to you quietly, chat and make a few suggestions and if you took the hint then he was delighted – and you were one of his finest officers. If, on the other hand, you thought you knew better and did something else, you were apt to end up in one of his furthest outstations.'

The fact was that the Rajah was an absolute monarch, controlling everything except foreign policy. He was the 'ruler of a country the size of England and Wales which was entirely his own. He had no connection whatever with Whitehall. The revenue was his own. He had his own stamps, his own money, his own flag. It was his to do with as he liked. He even had power of life and death over his own subjects.' Yet at the same time he had no military power to impose his will: 'He had to get his way by persuasion and by consultation with people whom he trusted and who trusted him. He was Rajah with the consent of the local population, notably the Malays, and he could not really do very much without consulting them and senior members of the other communities and of course his brother officers.' This close and informal consultation formed the basis of what was known as the 'Brooke tradition': 'The government of Sarawak was purely personal; from the Rajah downwards every government officer had to be accessible – and that's why Sarawak was unlike any other English colony. There was an intimacy between the government and the people. It was men, not a machine, and there was practically no bureaucracy at all. All you had was a handful of Europeans assisted by another group of native officers, and it was all personal government.'

The country was divided up into five divisions, each under the charge of a Resident who was, according to Bob Snelus, 'king in his own little country. The true king had almost nothing to do with the way the division was run. The Resident ran it on his own lines and those lines might differ from one

division to another depending on the nature and the character
of the individual Resident.' Supporting him in each division
were a handful of District Officers, but because of the
surrounding jungle and the lack of roads, both Resident
and District Officers were very much on their own. The latter
reported to him by letter every month and the Resident in turn
reported by letter direct to the Rajah.

The relationship between rulers and ruled was a feudal one
– based quite deliberately on 'the principle of the close
relationship between the lord of the manor and his tenants'
– and yet without a doubt it was an extraordinarily popular
regime by any standards, which flourished because Sarawak
was a colonial cul-de-sac, self-contained, self-financing and all
but cut off from the outside world.

There was only one way to get to Sarawak from the outside
world and that was by catching a steamer from Singapore,
preferably one of the Straits Steamships' boats that called in
regularly at Kuching. There was the cargoship *Circe*, which
carried 'an equal tonnage of cargo and cockroaches', or the far
smarter mail-steamer, the *Vyner Brooke*, which was 'kept spotless
like a yacht' and sailed from Singapore every ten days. The
journey across the South China Sea took two days and three
nights, with the sailings geared to the tides, so that the ship
could navigate the sand-bar at the mouth of the Sarawak river
and then go on up on the flood tide to Kuching town, some
twenty miles up-river.

'The approach was most striking,' recalls Bob Snelus:

You arrive at the coastline to find there's Santubong mountain
rising three thousand feet directly out of the sea. Then you
wind your way up between the *nipah* palms for miles and miles
and it's all rather dreary, with an occasional little native
habitation but mostly unbroken *nipah* palms, until you are a
mile or so from Kuching. You round a bend in the river which
then opens up before you and all on the left are lines of
Chinese shop-houses known as the bazaar, terminating in the

government building which in those days was known as the Court House. Then on the other side of the river, opposite the shop-houses, there's first of all an old fort, Fort Margherita, with the guns still poking through its portholes, which was erected in the days of the Dayak pirates who used to come up the Sarawak river in their huge war *prahus*, with the aim of pillaging the Chinese shops and any wealthy Malays who might be around.

As well as Fort Margherita, built in 1879, there were other forts in Sarawak, built in 'places where the Second Rajah was still having difficulty in keeping order among the Iban tribes who inhabited that part of the country. They were nearly all named after female members of the Rajah's family – his daughters or people that he had known: Fort Alice, Fort Sylvia, Fort Lily, and names like that.'

A hundred yards beyond Fort Margherita there was the *Istana*, the palace of the Rajah, a 'fine old colonial building' with broad lawns sloping down to the water's edge. It had a stone-crenellated keep at one end but its most striking feature was an enormous roof made up of *bilian* hardwood shingles and covering 'a very cool veranda and a very cool interior'.

The arrival of the mail-ship was signalled by the firing of a gun from the fort, when 'everybody who had business with the ship went down to the wharf'. The vessel then had to be turned around in the narrow river before tying up at the Straits Steamships' wharf, a risky manoeuvre that only the most skilled captains could perform: 'The way they turned was to go up so close to the *Istana* that the bow was overhanging the garden and then swing with the tide so that the stern came round.'

As well as announcing the arrival of the mail-ship the signal gun also served as a time-gun, a fact that Peter Howes was unaware of when he first arrived in the country:

I was put up in the Bishop's house where I slept like a top for my first night – to be woken up, to my astonishment, by a great explosion. I was on my feet in a moment. It was pitch dark. I thought I'd come out to a rebellion and I stood by the bed all set for a burst of firing and the frantic shouts of natives as they rushed up the hill to set the mission on fire. But after a minute or two nothing happened, so I put on a torch, to see what the time was. It was five o'clock – and nobody had bothered to tell me that the Brooke Government provided an alarm clock for the residents of Kuching in the form of a time-gun, which was fired from Fort Margherita, precisely at five o'clock each morning. Fort Margherita was on the bank of the river just opposite the Bishop's house and when the water was high the sound used to ricochet off the water, straight into the Bishop's veranda and it really felt as if the whole house was being shaken to pieces.

A second signal gun was fired every evening at eight o'clock: 'During the Rajah's time anybody, Dayak or Chinese or Malay, who liked to go and see the Rajah and put a case to him was at liberty to do so. They usually went across in the evening and if you were a Dayak you could drink the Rajah's gin and chew betelnuts and spit out of the window, and behave just as you behaved at home. But at eight o'clock the second time-gun was fired and this was the sign that the Rajah was about to have dinner and then all his visitors left.'

All new arrivals to Kuching were rowed across the river in a *sampan* to sign their names in the visitors' book kept at the bottom of the steps leading up to the *Istana*. They were not, however, expected to call on the Rajah himself. Anthony Richards' first opportunity to meet him came when the Rajah was rowed over in his state barge to the Court House to hear what were known as 'Requests' or petitions: 'He had just arrived across with the Sergeant-at-Arms carrying his yellow umbrella over him and he was carrying his spear, presented to him by the Sultan of Brunei, which was a tall staff with a silver cap over the spear-blade. He simply nodded, saying "How do you do?" and "Welcome to Sarawak" and then left me to my mentors, which seemed at first to be a bit offhand.'

Kuching was then still very much a 'man's community' from the European point of view. When Edward Banks had first arrived in 1925 to take up his curator's post at the Sarawak Museum there were no more than three or four European women in the town and practically none at all outside Kuching. A decade later there were still only twenty white women in the capital – out of a total population of about a hundred Europeans – and life continued to be 'pretty austere. You went to the club and drank and there was no alternative. The club itself was a very old-fashioned place, dingy and dark with a lot of elderly gentlemen sitting about and where you spoke only when you were spoken to. But as a junior you never signed for a drink – if you did your seniors took it away and signed the *chit* themselves, partly because they didn't want you to get into debt and partly because a young man was expected to be seen and not heard.'

However, it was not customary for cadets and other new arrivals to stay long in Kuching. Within three weeks Peter Howes found himself posted to the mission station at Betong in the second division. To get there he had first to travel in one of the many Chinese launches that plied the rivers of Sarawak with their holds filled with provisions for the up-country bazaars and with enough room on the hatches for twenty or thirty passengers:

> These passengers were a very mixed crowd; you would have some quite sophisticated types who came from houses near to a bazaar and they would be in trousers and shirts. And then you would have others who came from way up-country, wearing nothing but a loin cloth. But everybody got on extremely well together. You chatted away and they chewed betelnuts and offered you their Dayak tobacco and as you went along there were opportunities to speak to all sorts of people too, because you stopped at fish-traps where you could buy fresh fish from

the Malay fishermen. Or perhaps a log-jam would block the river and it would be necessary for the passengers to try to move one or two so that the whole log-jam gave way and let the boat through. And then the boat would put in at little bazaars perhaps ten or twenty miles apart.

At Betong mission Howes was welcomed by the priest in charge and introduced to the two other priests who made up the staff of the station: 'It was a happy place but we lived a very hard and almost monastic life.' White cassocks were worn throughout the day – 'you would never be able to afford the washing bill that this would entail today but in those days we employed a Chinese cook-cum-houseboy who also did the washing and he cost us seventeen dollars a month' – and *topees* whenever the missionaries ventured out of doors: 'We had a *topee* stand just near the door so that the moment you went outside into the dangerous, tropical sunlight you grabbed your *topee* and put it on – even if it was only for the few hundred yards between the mission house and the church.' At first his mornings were spent teaching English in the mission school and his afternoons learning Iban, the language of the tribal people in that part of Sarawak. Without Iban, Howes was told, he could be of little use to the community since the bulk of the mission's Christians were scattered over an area equal in size to an English county.

In Sarawak the Muslim Malays formed only a tiny minority and there was no ban on Christian missionary activities as there was in the Malay States. Indeed, many of the Anglican missions had been in existence since the days of the First Rajah, James Brooke, as well as a number of other churches, and in order to avoid conflict between the different denominations the country had been divided by the Rajah into various zones of influence:

Anglicans and Roman Catholics worked together in the first division and the Anglicans worked alone in the second division. The Roman Catholics and the Methodists had the third division and to this day if you go up the Rejang river all the churches on the left-hand side of the river are likely to be Methodist and all on the right Roman Catholic. The fourth division was given to the Anglicans and Roman Catholics and the fifth division was left empty and remained so until just before the war when a non-denominational mission based in Australia came there.

Within these divisions the various missions had their head-quarters, where each priest was 'given two or three rivers and was responsible for the Christians along the length of those rivers'.

The administration divided up its divisions and districts on very similar lines – and here, too, newcomers were very quickly sent out to get to grips with the country and its people. Bob Snelus was sent to the headquarters of the third division at Sibu, where he found himself one of four European officers under the command of a Resident who was very much of the old school, a man who had known the 'wilder days' of the Second Rajah: 'He was a strong character – but strong in a cheerful way; very much the country squire type of chap, a Devonian, I think, and by no means an academic. He didn't expect others to write long-winded reports about their jobs and what they'd been doing but he kept his finger on the pulse of things and generally knew what was going on in all his districts, of which there were five in his division.' Although the Resident 'was not a tyrant to his subordinates by any means', Snelus quickly learned that he was expected to toe the line:

The most important thing in those days as far as the Resident was concerned was that one should appear at the local club no later than six o'clock in the evening to engage in games of indoor bowls. So in the course of that one naturally got a good sweat up and imbibed a good deal of alcoholic refreshment. The other point was that one was not allowed to leave the club by the Resident until at the earliest nine o'clock. It was often nine-thirty before I was able to get away, by which time one felt pretty worn out and one hadn't had one's evening meal. But despite that, early in the morning, at about five-fifteen, one had to be up and about because one of the duties of the new cadet was to turn out the prisoners. I couldn't skip this early morning turnout because once or twice a week the Resident would turn up, too, on his pony, just to make sure you were there and on parade.

However, the Resident was not above letting his hair down when he was off-duty:

On one of my first Sundays in Sibu as a new boy I was invited to curry tiffin at the District Officer's house to meet the others. The curry tiffin didn't start till about three o'clock and we probably didn't rise from our chairs till after four o'clock, by which time everybody was rather jolly and I remember the Resident had a little bet with the doctor: there was one little Austin Five which the Resident was allowed to keep and run – it was the one car in Sibu in those days. There were no other cars in the whole third division, because there was only one road about seven miles long out to the golf course. The doctor and the Resident both reckoned they were good shots so they decided to take aim at the little Austin which was parked outside the bungalow. The Resident sent for his shotgun and the doctor had a revolver, and then they shot up the car until there was very little left of it; the tyres were all deflated, the windscreen was in smithereens, and when there was really no point in shooting at the body of the car any longer the Resident just swung his gun right round firing indiscriminately as he went, so that everybody was ducking and careering down the steps and hiding in ditches.

Snelus soon got down to learning the ropes as an outstation officer and, in the process, imbibing the Brooke philosophy.

Perhaps its most important single element was that all government officers had to know their districts or their divisions intimately. This meant staying in the same place for some time:

> You didn't want a man coming in and spending six months, or perhaps a year, as happened in Malaya. That would have been making nonsense of it all. Good gracious, no. He was expected to spend at least three years in that river basin, and get to know people. That was the key to the whole situation. He was on his own. He'd be days and days up-river and he had to make his own decisions. He couldn't take refuge behind some faceless bureaucracy; the most he could do would be to refer it to his Resident. And Residents weren't always easy to get at either, because there was also the Sarawak tradition of travel, which meant that all administrative officers were away from their offices for long periods each year. What happened if you wanted to contact your Resident when he himself was perhaps days upriver and completely out of reach? That meant you had to take the decision yourself, which was one of the reasons why the old Sarawak officers were men of forceful character.

Quite a number of these officers were the 'younger sons of landed gentry, a great many from the West Country because that was the Brookes' own background. They knew the sort of people they wanted – and they were just right for the job.' Until the mid-1930s few had qualifications or appropriate training. 'People who came out before then were apt to come out at the age of eighteen,' explains Anthony Richards, who was among the first of the graduate administrators:

> The list of incumbents of my office in Simanggang starts with two eighteen-year-olds in the 1850s when there were only two European officers at a time in that whole division. So these young men were faced with consultations with the locals,

fighting off the various Dayaks, building a fort, protecting themselves and living somehow – with support from head-quarters, but all by sea and very slow – at the age of eighteen. We in turn were not very much older than these people, just having a degree at twenty-three or twenty-four, and well before we were thirty we could be handing down sentences of two years' imprisonment, fines of a thousand dollars, several hundred pounds, and so on. And this without any specific training.

These long periods of service in distant outposts led almost inevitably to close identification with the people under their charge, particularly when the DOs were dealing not so much with the Malays or Chinese as with the indigenous tribal peoples of Sarawak, known to the Malays as 'Dayak' – the 'up-country' people. The largest of these tribal groups were the Sea Dayaks or Ibans who, with the Land Dayaks and the Melanaus, lived along the coastal belt and the rivers in the southern half of the country, while the Kayans, Kenyahs and Kelabits occupied the highlands further to the east. To the British who knew them they were all equally 'nature's gentle-men – a hackneyed phrase, perhaps, but nevertheless apt, since they were hardworking, very courteous and very charm-ing'. Anthony Richards spent most of his early years among the Ibans and came to regard them with great affection:

They seemed to attract a great number of European officers, perhaps because they were so open and democratic. They had their leaders but they didn't have a class system. They would acknowledge status but their social behaviour cut right across and that was very impressive. When they came into a room, for instance, there was no question of bowing or anything like that. They strode in as if they were making a stage entry, usually with a hand outstretched as one gentleman to another. Some were given to cadging, some to bragging and they got on your nerves sometimes but I found that having first associated with the Iban I stuck to the Iban, while other officers whose first contact was in the Baram river with the Kayans couldn't see anything in the Ibans at all. So we agreed that where your first love is, there you go and stay. You started by trying to get the hang of the Malays, the Chinese, the Ibans and all the rest and then you fell for one or the other.

The Ibans were also a very attractive people to look at:

Because of their poise and their immense natural dignity one was never at all conscious that they were in any way naked. The men wore their hair long, with a fringe at the front and knotted up into a sort of teapot handle at the back. They had copper-coloured skins with dark blue tattooing in the form of rosettes just inside their shoulders on the front and on their arms and legs and they wore long scarlet loin cloths which hung down at the back and front with long tasselled ends. They also wore black and silver arm and calf bracelets so that the general effect was of copper, black and red.

Many of the Iban men also carried tattoos on the backs of their hands and on their fingers, which showed not only that they had taken heads but also their exact number. Despite being vigorously suppressed by the Rajahs, in the early 1930s head-hunting had still not completely died out. One of Snelus' first duties as a cadet in Sibu was to go out after what was probably the last well-known band of rebel head-hunters in an effort to get them to surrender.

'Head-hunting is basically a fertility rite,' explains Robert Nicholl.

It was concerned with the fertility of crops and it was a religious rite. There were long prayers, and all sorts of ceremonies before the party set out. Off they went and back they came with the head which, as distinct from its owner, was always considered to be benevolent. It warded off evil spirits and it ensured the forthcoming harvest. The eyes were taken out and generally the lower jaw was taken off, and the rest of it was smoked and then hung up on a sort of circular frame in the roof. And that was the safest place in the whole longhouse, because no evil spirit would dare go near the heads, so when the guest came, he was given the place of honour under the heads.

However, with the Ibans the cult of head-hunting had developed far beyond a fertility cult:

It became an expression of valour. No young Iban could hope to win his girl unless he produced at least one head, and he would hope that his rival wouldn't come along with two. Head-hunting in this sense was obviously a menace to society. You could never have any stability if you had young men going about the country, whipping off the odd head here and there. That just wasn't the way you established any permanent order at all. So the Brookes were very effective in that they finally stamped it out completely. Even so, the ancient heads were kept because they were necessary for certain ceremonies and observances. But later, there were the odd Japanese heads to be seen hanging up. There was one that I noticed up in the Rejang river which actually had its spectacles on.

The women were just as striking in appearance and character as the men. They wore only 'a short black skirt which was very simply a short tube from waist to knee and held up by two or three canes' and confined themselves to tattoo marks on their wrists – 'usually signifying a change of name after recovery from illness'. Many of the young women were extremely attractive and in general they were anything but reserved in their behaviour: 'One tends to think of women as second-class citizens in these communities but nothing would be more remote from the truth. They really had a say and a big say, too. They would sit round with everybody else and often played a very forceful part in the discussions. They were monogamous and their moral code was very rigorous indeed – but the young people could have lots of fun before they married.'

This relaxed attitude towards sexual matters had met with the approval of the Second Rajah, who believed that the presence of too many European women in Sarawak would prevent his officers from getting to know the country: 'It would have been perfectly ridiculous to have expected young men in those extraordinary circumstances to live a monastic existence and a promiscuous one would have been even worse, so the Second Rajah encouraged the adoption of one particular attractive girl as a house-keeper-mistress. This was so eminently sensible from every point of view that it became a pretty widespread habit.'

The practice of keeping what were known as *nyai* or 'house-keepers' continued right up to the last years of Brooke rule. 'Most of us had what were known as sleeping dictionaries,' Bob Snelus confirms. 'That expresses their purpose very well because they encouraged you and enabled you to learn the language and the dialect very much better and more colloquially than you could otherwise have done – and they satisfied the natural urge of many at the same time.' However, according to Anthony Richards, there was one disadvantage to learning the language in this way: 'For some reason the source of your knowledge was immediately evident the moment you opened your mouth, because the ladies have a distinct manner of speaking. One man that I knew quite well had learnt his Malay that way and it was quite obvious where it had come from – not that it mattered or that anybody minded.'

A detailed grasp of the language was essential to an understanding of a society bound up with all sorts of complex taboos. A case in point was the understanding of Iban omens and the value they attached to them:

They have the Brahminy kite as the father of all omen birds and he has seven sons-in-law who are the principal omen birds. You go to seek omens in the proper order from the appropriate birds before undertaking such major operations as beginning a rice farm, going on the war-path, or at different stages of building a house. If you intended to build a house you would go out at dawn and seek to hear the white-rumped Shama, which is called the 'cool' bird. He sings away with a liquid song in dense trees or in the forest and he's often to be found near houses. The practice is to find an odd number of birds on the left for women and an even number on the right for men, and if you don't get these on the first day then you have to go out on another day until you do – or abandon the site.

The problems of coming to terms with these taboos could be considerable: 'When certain birds crossed your path in a certain direction then there was nothing for it but to turn back. It was not merely that you yourself might meet with disaster but that you might bring disaster on the whole of the community that you were staying with – and you didn't want that. So it could be very inconvenient indeed.' But to know and to respect these and other omens was one way of maintaining the easy relations between *tuans* and natives that was characteristic of Brooke rule, for 'it was the custom that if you just wanted a chat with the DO and a gossip, you went along to his house in the evening. The door was always open and there he was, surrounded by people from up and down the river. So you went in and you chatted and talked late into the night. It was the same with the Resident. He wasn't a sacrosanct, remote figure as was the case in other places.' This mingling of the races was most striking to outsiders. Richards recalls an occasion after the Second World War when his Division of Simanggang had a visitation from a representative of the Indonesian Embassy in Singapore:

When he arrived he was told by the guard on duty that we were all down at the bazaar having lunch, so he went off there and he found the Resident, the European District Officer, a couple of Malay and Iban officers, the policemen, the trader and his family and several others, including the boatman, all sitting round a table having a jolly good lunch. This man came in, sat down and goggled. I asked him what was the matter and he said that he'd never seen anything like it. His own people had never in a lifetime of service sat down to eat with the Dutch and he had never imagined that people of different races would sit down together – particularly Europeans sitting down with the boatman – to eat.

Another characteristic feature of Brooke rule was the emphasis placed on travel as a means by which close contact with people was maintained. This was just as important in missionary circles as it was in government, and the style of travel was really no different. 'Every month you set off with your ecclesiastical supplies and a carrier and a boatman,' explains Peter Howes:

You paddled away, making use of the tides, until you got to your first Dayak longhouse, which would always be on the bank of the river. Then you would spend at least one night and possibly two nights in the longhouse, taking an evensong while you were there and a mass, and next morning hearing confessions and also instructing people who wanted to be Christian. Then you would go back to your boat again and travel further up-river, a matter of two or three hours, to the next longhouse – until eventually you got right up to the headwaters in the hills, where the water was perfectly clear and often very shallow. Finally, when you reached your last longhouse you'd cut back down-river. A journey of that nature could take you away for ten days or even three weeks.

Similarly, at the Sarawak Museum Edward Banks made a point of travelling round the country as often as he could, either on collecting expeditions or in answer to a specific request:

A District Officer would say, 'Something's wrong with the turtles on Turtle Island this year.' They used to have about five or six million turtle eggs every year and some years there weren't any. So you trotted off and you had a look at these islands and totted it all up and you came to the conclusion that due to rough weather the turtles hadn't come up. And then there were the huge caves full of birds' nests from which the Chinese make their birds' nest soup. They were very valuable; about a pound weight of nests would fetch you a quid – so it was quite a lucrative trade to the local people. But sometimes there was a hell of a lot of them and at other times hardly any. Everybody said that the locals pinched the nests and sold them. But again it was traced to a rotten winter or a rotten summer.

But what gave Banks the greatest pleasure was going up-river to collect specimens:

You took ship up-country till you came to, say, the mouth of the Baram river, where there was a District Officer and a little fort and from there you started off by boat up-river. These were very long boats, made out of one tree trunk, perhaps thirty or forty feet long and built up on the sides with planks and I suppose they put twelve or fifteen paddles on each side, two abreast, with a fellow behind to steer. Mostly, in those days, you used to row to the next village and then men from that village would take over. They didn't exert themselves terribly hard because they'd got a long row to go, but they paddled along quietly, and they chatted among themselves. Somebody pointed out a snake or a fish or a bird or a pig or something like that, and you sat in the middle and had a chat with all and sundry. The paddlers were Muruts or Kayans. They'd got long ears with rings in them and long hair and just a little g-string round their waists and I used to give them tobacco and odds and ends; you didn't actually pay them cash because they didn't know what to do with it but they were quite pleased to come along. And so it went on from one village to the next. When you arrived in a village they pulled in alongside the bank where there was a notched tree-trunk ladder going up the bank, with the houses built on poles on top of the bank. And generally, the headman came out to greet you and say, 'Hallo, come up.' Then you whizzed up this awful notched log, if you were lucky, and you were taken in and sat down and everybody wanted to know where you came from, and where were you going to and what were you doing and how many children had you got and all the rest of it. And there you stayed the night.

The style of travel was just as important as the method. 'The Brooke tradition was very firm,' declares Robert Nicholl, who after the war became one of Sarawak's first Education Officers. 'Every officer who travelled lived with the people. There was no question here of setting up half-a-dozen tents and dressing for dinner in the jungle as the great proconsuls did in Africa. That was out as far as the Brookes were concerned. You stayed in the longhouse and you lived with the people.' The difference between Sarawak and Malaya, as Bob Snelus saw it, was that 'we behaved like natives. We accepted Dayak conditions as they were. I always insisted on having my bath in the river first and then got into my *sarong* and *baju*.'

After this evening swim the guest was expected to eat with the headman or one of the other families in the longhouse. 'They were always exceedingly kind and hospitable,' recalls Peter Howes:

They would kill fowls for you which they had running about outside the longhouse by the score and these dreadful Dayak fowls took an awful lot of getting through because one might just as well have been chewing on sticks of rubber. But plates and dishes would all be spread on great mats on the floor and if you were well up-river you would be given a fresh banana leaf and a great quantity of rice would be dished out into it for

you. Then you folded your legs so as not to prod your
neighbour to left or right and then you just reached with
your fingers out into the various bowls and selected such titbits
as you fancied. Your neighbour, if he felt particularly well
disposed towards you or if he felt that you were not doing
justice to the fare, would pick up some titbit and hand it to you
or stick it on top of your rice. Once you got more familiar with
people, the great thing was to offer them the sort of titbit that
they couldn't chew – the foot of some fowl or else its head.
You'd pick this up and hand it to your neighbour, then he'd
feel duty bound to make an effort to eat this thing, so he'd pull
the comb off it and pull the eyes out and do his best. But he
might hand you in return the foot and then you'd be caught as
well.

Once dinner was over such official business as required to
be seen to was speedily transacted so that the evening get-
together, known as the *randau*, could begin. 'All the up-river
people had one distinguishing characteristic common to them
all and that was their hospitality,' declares Snelus. 'Whenever
the Dayaks were visited by the District Officer celebrations
invariably took place.' They began with the singing of an ode
of welcome:

The whole community would be sitting in a circle and you
would go and sit beside the head of the longhouse and then his
wife or perhaps his daughter would come along with a large
glass of *borak*, rice wine, and sing an ode. The theme was
always one of welcome but translations showed just how poetic
they were. The lady would end her ode and then offer you the
borak which you were expected to down in one. Then you
would probably get another lady who would come up and do
the same thing – and so it would go on.

As well as songs of welcome from the women, the men sang
or intoned what were known as *pantuns*, 'long verses recounting

their glorious past, the object being to liken their distinguished visitor to their own heroes of the past, with some of the older men recalling the number of heads they'd taken or the battles they used to have against another village on the same river'. Then the District Officer – or the chief guest – was expected to make an offering to the spirits: 'Food of different varieties was presented to him and he would have to pile them in a certain order onto a dish, which was then put outside for the spirits to consume and to pacify them.'

Once these solemnities were over there was usually dancing and more singing, either to the melodious accompaniment of the *engkerumong* – 'an array of four or five brass gongs held in a wooden tray and varying in size from six inches to twelve inches in diameter' – or to the sound of the *sapeh*, the two-stringed mandolin favoured by the Kayans and Kenyahs. These two tribal groups produced outstanding singers – 'the only people in South-East Asia who sang naturally in harmony' – and dancers. The men concentrated on war dances – 'there used to be competitions every two years for the finest dancer on the Baram river' – while the women did such dances as the bird dance, for which they 'put on the black and white tail feathers of the hornbill with little clamps onto their fingers and imitated bird moves – a bird ballet that was very beautiful indeed to watch'. Finally there were wilder dances in which everybody joined in a long column: 'The person in front performed various gyrations and everybody else followed and you processed round the longhouse.' These dances often lasted right through the night – 'and all the time some lady would be coming up to you and insisting on singing an ode and then you would have to toss back yet another glass of powerful *borak*. It was very exhausting indeed and it only came to an end with dawn.'

For those who could sleep there were certain formalities to be observed and precautions to be taken. 'As a man you would sleep on the general *ruai*, alongside the bachelors,' recalls Howes:

Mats would be put down for you and you would be provided with pillows and blankets if they were needed. You brought with you your own mosquito net. In many of the up-river longhouses there were next to no mosquitoes because the longhouse stands high off the ground. But you really needed a mosquito net to keep dogs out of the bed – because a Dayak longhouse contains as many dogs as people and at night-time these wretched dogs charge up and down the length of the *ruai* either in sport or in battle and they are quite likely either to leap over you if you have no mosquito net or come up and nestle close to you for warmth's sake. Also, underneath the floor of the longhouse all the chickens roost, very often in bamboo cages. They scratch vigorously from time to time and you can get used to that – but in certain hours of the night and early in the morning the cocks crow furiously and in any one longhouse there may be anything from thirty to eighty or even a hundred doors – that is families – each with its own cocks and hens and pigs and things all rooting round under this house, so that the noise and the scratching and the cock-crowing and the pigs grunting and the yells and yelps of dogs and their pitter-pattering backwards and forwards across the floor do tend to make for a somewhat disturbed night. You find too in certain communities that while the first five minutes on the mat is restful you then become aware of an increasing irritation and if you switch on a torch and look at the mat you may see it covered with hundreds of bedbugs. The great aim of any traveller in a society like that is to get instantly to sleep, because if he is not asleep in the first five minutes the chances of getting to sleep afterwards are practically nil.

In 1941 the Rajah and Ranee celebrated their Silver Jubilee in Kuching:

It was a most memorable and extraordinary evening. All the *kampongs* were lit by hundreds and hundreds of little oil wick lamps made out of pieces of green bamboo and the Malays all turned out in their best clothes; the women in their gold embroidered *sarongs* and looking ravishing, like a lot of butter-flies. The Rajah and Ranee drove around through cheering crowds, all pressing against the car to make quiet but heartfelt remarks of greeting. It was a lovely evening and a lovely occasion. There was no question about it at that time; the Rajah was enormously loved.

In their turn, the Rajah and a great many of the *tuans* who served him also loved Sarawak and its people: 'When I left the country in 1963 the best known of the Dayaks was a man called Temnggong Jugah,' recalls Bob Snelus. 'I first knew him as a young *penghulu* and in some ways it could be said we grew up together. He always came on my trails of the Dayak villages in the the district of Kapit and he always insisted on accom-panying me, and eventually we went through the ceremony of becoming blood-brothers by cutting each other's fingers, making a little incision and drawing a little blood. It's a very simple little ceremony but it's rather touching – and not often done.'

7

Pax Britannica

It may be that some of those peoples, Malays, Dayaks, Chinese, were restive under the British rule, but there was no outward sign of it. The British gave them justice, provided them with hospitals and schools, and encouraged their industries. There was no more crime than anywhere else. An unarmed man could wander through the length of the Federated Malay States in perfect safety.

Somerset Maugham,
Preface The Complete Short Stories, Vol III

THE exercise of power and responsibility came easily to most young men reared in Edwardian and Georgian private schools, where 'the whole idea was that you built up petty power and then you moved a stage higher and it was knocked out of you and you started again; so that we were all already as boys well accustomed to taking on power when it was offered and to losing that power when you moved elsewhere.' What made this assumption of power even easier was that 'no difficulties were put in one's way. In those days because one was an Englishman one didn't have any difficulty in exerting one's authority. It was accepted straight away. Whether we liked it or not, they looked upon us as power points, as persons slightly apart.'

This is as true of a manager of an estate, an administrator or a captain of a Straits Steamships vessel. 'Our word was law and that was all there was about it,' declares Captain Percy Bulbrook. 'You weren't curtailed in any respect – not in those days.' It was this freedom of action that James Morice most enjoyed as an officer in the FMS Customs and Excise: 'You were your own master. If you got fed up in the office you could go away for the day to your outstations and nobody would say a word.' And it was the same sense of liberty that Bob Snelus felt when he first became a District Officer:

> Being a DO gave one an enormous boost. It is one's first real taste of power and power wielded on one's own without anybody continually breathing down your neck and wanting to know what you're doing and what you're not doing. And, in those days, the work of a District Officer was remarkably varied. The District Officer was in charge of the prisons and had to turn out the prisoners. He was also the magistrate, so that having remanded a chap in prison he then had him come up before him in court and had to decide whether he was guilty or not guilty. He was also responsible for public works, for maintaining such roads as there might be in the district and drains and so forth. And all this quite apart from his main job of generally administering the people in this area – touring around finding out their troubles, resolving their problems, settling their land disputes and collecting the head tax – which was the only tax in Sarawak in those days.

This bewildering range of responsibilities was by no means confined to Sarawak. When Richard Broome was appointed District Officer on Christmas Island – 'a little island south of Java about four days' steaming from Singapore, whose great claim to fame is that it is a wonderful deposit of phosphate from bird-droppings which have occurred over millions of years' – he was also gazetted as 'Harbour Master, District

Health Officer, Magistrate, Coroner, Chief of Police, Inspector of Machinery and a whole host of other jobs which didn't occupy one's time much but for which one had to have powers in case something cropped up'.

However, what Sjovald Cunyngham-Brown remembers as an 'idyllic noon-tide holiday on the part of the Malayan Civil Servant' – where he was 'a little king unto himself in his own district' – was slowly coming to an end. With improvements in communications and increasing centralization of government the administrator's powers were gradually being reduced. Many of his responsibilities were taken over by a fast-growing number of independent departments and services:

> We would have been nothing had it not been for the police, the Education Services, the Health and Medical Services, the Survey Department from New Zealand, the Mines Department that discovered all the areas for private interests to exploit, the Agricultural Department – who were practically the originators of the wealth of Malaya – to say nothing of that most silent, unobtrusive and generally forgotten arm of government known as the Public Works Department.

It was the PWD, 'with all their roads, their bridges and their brothers-in-arms, the Electrical Supply Department and the Wireless and Telegraph Services, that quietly brought a civilized country into being. There was nothing that the PWD did not do. They created all the furniture for the government offices and bungalows – and built the bungalows themselves.' Indeed, all the British territories in the East shared the same joke about the kapok tree being known as the 'PWD tree' – 'because it looks as if a PWD engineer had built it'.

In territories like Sarawak and British North Borneo this building-up of the infrastructure took longer to achieve, allowing some curious anomalies to persist rather longer than they did on the peninsula:

Inhabitant (pointing to Kapok) :—That's a P.W.D. Tree.

Stranger :—Why do you call it that ?

Inhabitant :—Because if the P.W.D. built a tree, they'd
build it like that !

One of the classic jokes of the East. From *Straits Produce*, 1926

That meant that in a gambling case, for instance, the chances were that you had led the police raiding party and the people caught gambling illegally had then been brought before you as a magistrate. If you put them in jail, you were in charge of the jail, and you were also the prison visitor. This system – or lack of system – was open to all kinds of abuses, but people did the best they could, and you simply changed your attitude with the different hat you were wearing. One minute you were a raiding police officer and next minute you were the magistrate, and you tried to set aside the fact that you knew the chap was guilty because you'd caught him the night before. In those days they seemed to accept all this.

In more typical circumstances an administrator's duties were in accordance with his experience and qualifications. In the MCS a cadet could expect within three-and-a-half years – having passed the required examination in law and language – to become a 'Passed Cadet'. He was then eligible to 'act' as a junior assistant in a number of jobs that were graded as Class Four posts, graduating in time to Class Three jobs. His magistrate's powers were similarly graded, with strictly defined limits as to the sort of cases he could try and the severity of the fines and sentences that he could impose. By the time he became a District Officer he would have become eligible to exercise full magistrate's powers.

However, it was rare for an officer in the Malay States to spend all his time out in the districts: 'Establishment Officers watched each man's career and his list of jobs very carefully and they would say, "That man's done enough in a district or out in the *ulu* and it's high time he came in and got some discipline and tidied up in the Secretariat." ' Spells of duty out in the field usually alternated with periods in the Federal or a State Secretariat so that in time almost every officer acquired a wide range of experience.

Almost all administrators had to spend a certain amount of time in the magistrate's court and those who found the work to their taste were encouraged to read for the English bar so that they could concentrate on court work or even transfer to the Legal Service. During his first home leave in 1935 William Goode took time off to be called to the bar at Gray's Inn and when he returned as District Officer, Raub, had much of his time taken up with court work which he rarely found tedious, 'probably because we went to the heart of the matter and reached a decision. We must have made mistakes but at least justice was quick: somebody could commit an offence on Tuesday, be hauled up in court on Friday and the whole thing would be over by Saturday afternoon.' The courthouse in Raub was typical of many district courts:

> It was a large, airy, white-washed brick building, with plenty of windows all round because we had no air conditioning, just a *punkah* being pulled over our heads, and an elevated bench on which the magistrates sat. Then in front of you, you would have the local police officer, who did the prosecuting. Very rarely in places like Pahang would there be a lawyer for the defence; the accused or the defendant had to defend himself. This meant that the magistrate on the bench had to try and make sure that the defendant's case was put as well as possible.

Only in the larger towns and the Straits Settlements was the full majesty of the law displayed – as Cunyngham-Brown experienced when he became for a spell Fourth Magistrate in Singapore:

> The whole of the old Havelock Road Police Court had so great an aura of faded dignity surrounding it that it was almost ludicrous in its grotesque formality. There was an enormous Sikh at the door, who'd salute crashingly as you stamped up the steps to the pillared, green-painted police court – and into the chambers behind it. There one waited for the appropriate moment to go up the steps into the court and behind the great big table on its dais four feet above the court itself, and as you

waited you heard the murmuring of people in the court, which would hold about five hundred people all sitting in rows and was very seldom less then crammed to the edges with people standing at the back and everyone waiting in expectation, chattering away and eating peanuts until the magistrate came in. Then a tremendous noise; the bashing of a stave on the ground by another enormous Sikh. '*Diam*,' he would shout, meaning 'silence'. Everybody stood up and there would be dead silence as you came in, bowed to left and right and then sat down. In front of the magistrate's bench there was a Mr Surattee who was the Clerk of the Court, with his own clerks sitting on a green baize table underneath one, and he would jump up and give you the right legal references to any point in doubt. At one's right hand side there was the box in which the accused or the defendant was to sit or stand, with the lawyers at the next table to Mr Suratee's own table. There were *Hokkien* translators and Cantonese. All the Indian tongues, Tamil and even Telegu were also frequently spoken in the court, Punjabi because of the Punjabis' money-lending proclivities, and Hindustani as a matter of course. Consequently, we were fairly well kitted up with linguistic ability in that court. And, as time went on, a certain relaxation would be permitted to creep into this fearful formality.

However, there was one occasion when the relaxation went too far:

I remember particularly one morning after a long weekend spent sailing my little boat across the Malacca Strait when I'd got abominably sunburnt, and so in the absolute safety and security of my seat, knowing that I had a big baize curtain hanging down over the table's other edge so that nobody could see what I did, I undid my belt; what a relief! I then listened to a long discourse on the part of the counsel for the defendant and opened a few buttons. And, when it came to a little further cross-examination with the plaintiff's lawyer, I took a bold step: I slipped off my trousers, lifted my shirt and gave myself a really good and satisfying scratch. I couldn't understand what was happening in the court. There had been a certain murmuring from earlier on but now a positive uproar suddenly broke out. I saw small boys standing on tables at the back pointing and screaming, as the three uniformed police were banging the floor, shouting '*Diam! Diam* everybody!' And Mr Surettee, turning around to see why there was all this fuss, jumped up with a face of horror, opening his jacket like wings, and said, 'Sir, they've taken the baize away to be cleaned!'

For the policeman who had to take on the prosecutor's role in the smaller courts there were also lighter moments. Guy Madoc remembers how the courthouse at Kuala Selangor had 'a roof of jungle fibre, no walls and just an earth floor. Occasionally at important moments when I was addressing the magistrate on the bench in great fluency, I would look up and staring through the roof would be the faces of three or four monkeys. Whilst scratching on the ground just in front of the dock where the prisoner was lounging, would be five or six chickens which had come in from the farm across the road.'

The language of the court was always something of a problem. 'Most of the cases were heard in the vernacular and this was a very slow and sometimes very difficult process,' declares Madoc. 'I myself spoke only Malay, in which I became sufficiently fluent to be able to deal directly in questioning witnesses and the accused person. But if you were dealing with Indians or Chinese, then you had to work through an interpreter.' With such difficulties misunderstandings of one sort or another were inevitable – as Alan Morkill once discovered when called upon as District Magistrate to hear a deposition from a man who was said to be dying:

Under the Indian Evidence Act, a dying deposition could be admitted as evidence and I was asked to go down and take one from a Chinese. I found him – an enormous Chinese – lying in a bed, apparently speechless. He'd complained that he'd been assaulted and I had to ask him whether he thought he was going to die. I don't know how the interpreter put my question to him but he obviously thought I was threatening him with death. He thereupon leapt from the bed and ran for it, pursued by the Inspector of Police.

The cases heard in the magistrate's court covered an enormous range – 'anything from riding a bicycle without a lamp or hawking without a licence to much more serious cases to do with theft or even murder, which, after the preliminary enquiry had been held, would go on to a higher court'. It was Madoc's job to investigate every sort of case before bringing it to court:

> We were expected to investigate such trivial criminal offences as the theft of five coconuts, worth about a dollar, and much more serious cases like gang robbery. In the first years of my life in Malaya gang robbery was far too prevalent an offence because we were going through a world recession and so many people, particularly Chinese, were out of work and desperate for money. Amongst the Chinese, there were also ritual murders which were quite terrifying things. I had to investigate one when I was still very raw. I was called out about three o'clock in the morning, marched for miles through semi-cultivated country and eventually came to a half-derelict hut on the bank of a stream and there was lying a poor old man who had suffered the death of a thousand cuts, which is a Chinese ritual form of murder. He had nothing like a thousand unjuries on him actually, but he was very thoroughly hacked up indeed.

Working in conjunction with the law courts in the Malay States were native courts presided over by Malay *hakims* who dealt with all matters relating to *adat*, Malay social custom and religion. For the Chinese the closest equivalent was to be found in the offices of the Protector of Chinese. 'It was a system whereby any Chinese had direct access to a senior member of the government,' explains Richard Broome. 'The Assistant Protector sat at his desk in a very large open hall with seats and benches in front of him. Then nobody could stop a Chinese coming straight in and spouting out what his trouble was. You tried to get his grievances settled and it also taught you plenty because one got a most wonderful insight into Chinese life.' The disputes that Broome and his colleagues handled could be divided into either domestic or labour cases:

The labour cases were of people who had not been paid their wages, because labour on the rubber estates and on the tin-mines was recruited through Chinese contractors and they weren't all honest men. The labour sometimes would go on working for this chap for months and then discover that he had absconded with all the money owed to them. You used to come down in the morning to the office, and see about a hundred women outside your office, and your heart sank because you knew it was an absconding contractor case. They'd say 'What about our wages?' and they always supposed that the Protector had a magic wand. Sometimes you got some money out of the contractor but very often you had to go on negotiating until you got the management to pay out a percentage.

Many of the domestic cases also followed a set pattern:

It was usually started by a woman who came in and said, 'My husband beats me and I want you to divorce me.' So you sent the husband not an official summons but a little standard letter in Chinese saying, 'Be at the office of the Protector on such and such a day' – and invariably they came. There was no legal obligation on them whatsoever, but they came and you used to have to try and sort out these things. It was like being a marriage counsellor as much as anything else. And they ended up nearly always with our either arranging a divorce, or else persuading the woman to go back. All these proceedings were conducted openly before the whole audience but the Chinese never seemed to worry about privacy in that respect at all.

The statutory powers of the Protector of Chinese were few, except in relation to the protection of women and children and in such matters as looking after the welfare of *Moi Chai*:

> *Moi Chai* means little sister and in those days girls in a Chinese family were not very highly thought of as compared with boys and if they had enough in the family they had somehow or other to dispose of the excess girls. What they did was to make arrangements with a richer family so that girls would be taken over, usually at about six or so, to be brought up as domestic servants and eventually married off. Now you could not at the stroke of a pen get rid of an ancient Chinese custom like that, so what was done was that all these *Moi Chai* were registered and every single one was visited at least once a year – and in many cases we were able to rescue girls from an extremely unpleasant existence. In the Protectorates we kept what were known as *Po Liang Kuk*, which literally translated means 'preserving virtue establishment' and these little girls were brought up in these homes and eventually married off quite successfully.

One other power available to the Protector of Chinese – 'seldom used but it was a good threat' – was the right to photograph people: 'If you got a really nasty customer or one who was truculent, you could order him to have his photograph taken. It sounds a fairly mild thing, but the Chinese hated that, because these photographs were often put up on boards with the name underneath and the reason why his photograph had been taken. It originated with the Chinese secret societies because we had to have photographs of all the chief members.'

In Sarawak the closest equivalent was the Court of Requests, where all the races could come to lay complaints or seek redress of one sort or another. Justice was also rather more informally arrayed than in Malaya; the law courts were simpler and often little distinction was made between the DO's office and the courtroom. When he travelled the court went with him: 'You *were* the court. You took a policeman with you as a matter of course and you simply went and heard disputes. You didn't keep notes on each case because the great majority of these were customary law cases where there was no point in keeping a record, although you were expected to record anything of general interest in your travelling report.'

Customary law in Sarawak – whether Chinese, Malay or Dayak – affected the DO's work to such an extent that he nearly always sat with assessors – 'prominent local people well versed in customary law' – beside him on the bench. 'The law was contained in what we knew as the Green Book, which contained orders made in almost minute detail by the Rajah,' explains Anthony Richards:

It even included such things as orders that anybody originating in Sarawak was not to appear before any European officer in a building wearing a hat of Western style – because local people do not doff hats. And with the Green Book there was a Black Book which had all the minor regulations. We used an adapted Indian Penal Code and apart from that it was said that where the law of the land was silent then English common law should apply. But of course a great many of the cases were affected by local or racial custom. You couldn't apply English law to Chinese inheritance, for instance. A case I remember particularly was that of two widows who appeared in my office one morning, two middle-aged Chinese ladies, who came the length of the office holding hands. They said, 'Sir, we have come to report the death of our husband.' One of them came from Singapore, the other from the station I was in. They had never met before, but the old man had died and they came to sort out the inheritance, in a perfectly friendly manner. I took advice from the local Chinese leader – the *kapitan China*, as he was called – and sorted it out as fairly as I could, but they were happy with it.

The main difference between the law of the land and customary law was that the latter's main function was to satisfy the parties concerned and not to administer the law for the law's sake: 'The fact that a man was killed did not affect the necessity to pay the ritual amount of brassware or money in order to perform the rites and make the peace, so it didn't really help to put a man in jail or to string him up.' There were, however, certain problems in dealing with customary cases:

The oaths or affirmations used in the court were not regarded as binding by the local people. Muslims would take oaths in the mosque and the Chinese used to take an oath by killing a black cockerel. With the Ibans you could require somebody to call down death and disease and poverty upon himself, but that wasn't really used at all; you simply had to weave your tortuous way between the tissues of lies on both sides. But the chief confusion for outsiders was that they telescoped time. They would relate something that happened five years ago as if it happened last week and so you could go very badly astray on this. But then these customary law cases were not court cases as we understand them; they were really debates and arbitration. A magistrate who knew how to do it would simply listen until everybody had talked themselves to a standstill, and then when they began to dry up he would give his decision in such a way, hopefully, that both sides would accept it. And only if they did accept it – whether it were a fine or an instruction to do something – only then would the decision stick, because if one side disagreed with it, they would simply go away in a huff and come up with the same case next week. And that was why one of our judges, who was formerly a

District Officer, laid down (probably in the club house, I think) the rules of court for longhouses. They were very simple: 'Not more than three persons shall speak at any one time, and no drinks to be served until after a decision has been made.'

Sarawak was also said to be the last country where trial by ordeal continued:

It almost always arose over land disputes or over heirlooms, where you would get such a barrage of perjury on both sides that the District Officer and his assessors were utterly unable to reach any conclusion at all. Both parties were absolutely right. If it reached a stalemate, then the parties could appeal to the trial by ordeal. Each party picked its champion, and then the whole court adjourned down to the river. A spot was picked where the river was deep, the two champions dived in and he won who could stay under water longest. And no one would ever dream of questioning the verdict.

The rich mixture of races and cultures in the Malayan archipelago inevitably meant very different views on what did or did not constitute a criminal offence – neatly exemplified by the dubious proposal that Jim Morice received in his post one morning while working in the Customs and Excise Office in Kuala Lumpur:

On opening this, out came a typewritten letter with a photograph of a young Chinese girl. It was from a Chinese lady offering me her daughter in marriage on certain conditions which she outlined. The first was that I was to give her daughter a dowry of three thousand dollars, roughly three hundred and fifty pounds. The second condition was that I should find employment for her son in the department. And the third and last condition was the mother was to live with her daughter in my bungalow! I happened to have to attend a licensing board meeting at the Chinese Protectorate later that day and, being a friend of the Protector of Chinese for Selangor, I passed over this letter and said to him, 'See what I got this morning in my post!' He had a look at it and said, 'That's nothing new. Just a minute.' And out from his drawer he produced several other letters on similar lines. 'You leave this letter with me and I will deal with the matter,' he said. Later on I heard that he'd had the pair up before the Protectorate Court. He'd admonished the mother and he'd sent the daughter to a home for the protection of young girls.

The confusion of attitudes was most obviously apparent in such sensitive issues as bribery and corruption, where 'the Asians were corrupt according to our lights, no doubt, but not necessarily according to theirs'. Here the gap between British standards and others was at its widest and – as far as the government services were concerned – not easily crossed. 'The whole basis of our education was that we should always remain completely incorruptible,' declares John Davis. 'One of the great points about the British Empire was that although we were powerful, difficult, bossy people who may have been intensely disliked by the inhabitants of the countries which we ruled, they accepted it simply because they knew we were not involved. Very, very few British people would be involved in corruption because, even if we had an inclination towards being corrupt, there was nothing really that they could offer us that would have had any great significance.'

It was said, however, that 'certain departments of government were more open to bribery than others' and there were two major scandals associated with government officers in Malaya in the 1930s. The first involved corruption in the Department of Mines and resulted in several 'very senior and respected officials being imprisoned – which was a bit of a shock to the community in those days'. The second shock came in the form of a purge on homosexuals, who were 'ruthlessly banished from the country' – provoking a number of scabrous jokes in the process. Ipoh was said to be a centre of homosexual vice where 'the Volunteers were not prepared to fall in in the front rank' and, similarly, the Blue Funnel steamer taking the victims of the purge back to England was said to have 'entered Penang harbour stern first'.

There were strict rules forbidding the ownership of land or shares where private interest might conflict with public duties, but the regulations concerning gifts and presents to government officers were less specific, so that 'the question of where to draw the line was always being discussed amongst us'. Early on in his career Guy Madoc was shown how to deal with the problem without causing offence by one of his seniors:

> Around Christmas time I was in his bungalow when up came a rickshaw with a man from the local grocery shop. He had with him a whacking great case which he brought in and said, 'This is a gift to the *tuan*.' The *tuan* looked at it very suspiciously and he turned to me and said, 'This happens every year, you know.' It contained bottles of whisky, brandy, plum-pudding and so on. 'We can't accept these things,' he said. 'But I always accept a token amount. Now here are apples and bananas which are going to deteriorate anyhow, so I'll accept them and the rest is going back.' And he handed it to the man and said, 'Take this back to your master and wish him a prosperous Christmas.'

Much of the responsibility for the prevention or control of various activities that one section or another of the community considered harmful fell to the Customs and Excise. It was they who saw to it that no licences for the sale of liquor were issued to Muslims in the FMS, who were forbidden by their religion to consume or deal in liquor. Jim Morice was once called upon to deal with a complaint from the Sultan of Selangor that a Muslim grocer's shop in KL was selling liquor to Europeans. He investigated and found that 'when the shop's European clientele ordered their groceries they also put on their list of requirements, gin, whisky and so on – and to oblige them the grocers used to purchase the liquor from a Chinese licensed retail shop opposite and then send the liquor out with the other goods to their customers'.

From time to time Morice's duties also required him to take part in various raids – against opium dens, illicit stills or smugglers:

> One of the oddest raids that I was on was when I was stationed at Muar in the State of Johore. I had a long journey to a Chinese village up-country with an informer who took me to a Chinese temple. We entered the temple premises from the back and heard a Buddhist service going on – tomtoms and gongs with a priest intoning. We had to look behind the altar which was covered by a wall and we found an illicit still with jars of *samsu*, which is Chinese wine made from yeast and molasses and rice. Having collected all these exhibits, we waited for the priest to finish his service and when he came to the back to disrobe we collared him and removed him and his exhibits without his congregation being any the wiser.

Life was in many respects 'very easy' for the British in South-East Asia in the inter-war years 'because we exercised power reasonably' – and certainly there were few challenges to British authority. When an occasional interracial dispute flared up the authorities 'sat down on it like a ton of bricks' – but otherwise there were few signs of unrest until 1937 when a series of strikes and riots – which had their roots in continuing low wages in the rubber and tin industries but were organized by the largely Chinese Malayan Communist Party – hit Kuala Lumpur and other towns. 'These riots were a shock to me and to a lot of people in the country,' declares Richard Broome, who was closely involved in events at the time. 'They were a shock because Malaya was normally a happy and peaceful place – one of the happiest countries you could think of – and there was precious little politics at all.'

Nor, to all appearances, was there much desire for self-government. Returning to Malaya after a four-year spell in South India as an emigration controller, Sjovald Cunyngham-Brown found the peninsula still remarkably untroubled by politics: 'There was not the remotest desire throughout Malaya for independence. There was certainly a sense of nationalism in the Malay States, yes, but the nationalism was to Kedah, to Perak, to Kelantan, and so on. These were the nations to which the Malays, who were in the majority in all these states, were giving their unyielding loyalty. But in the Straits Settlements nobody wanted in the least to be independent from anybody. They'd already had eight generations of belonging to Britain. More "dependence" was what they wanted.'

In 1935 King George V's Silver Jubilee was celebrated throughout the Empire. 'My colleague and I were given fifty dollars to decorate the office,' recalls Cecil Lee:

The great Corinthian columns were swathed in the Union Jack and stag-moss from an estate. When we'd done it we pushed off to Port Dickson and on the way down all the little villages and the *kampongs* had little pictures up of the King and Queen and I suppose that was happening throughout the Empire. Then in 1936 George V died. I was down on a coastal estate when we got the news and a planter and I went along to the club and solemnly lowered the flag. And I suppose that, too, was happening throughout the land and other parts of the Empire. Of course, I realize now how privileged we were – but, I must confess, I didn't realize it at the time. It was the twilight of the colonial calm and it was all so peaceful, so placid. I remember an old hand saying it was our best colony: it was healthy, there were lots of sports, there was no great internal strife. It was a halcyon, idyllic period when I look back on it and afterwards it was never quite the same. I'm afraid for me, in the words of Browning, it was 'never glad, confident morning' again.

For many of those who survived the great catastrophe that was about to break over them these years immediately before the outbreak of war would seem, in retrospect, 'golden years' – and, in Cunyngham-Brown's experience, full of strange ironies then impossible to conceive:

In the winter of 1943 I was with a collection of survivors from a vessel that had been torpedoed. We'd been dragged out of the sea after seventeen hours in a somewhat sorry condition; we hadn't any clothes on to speak of, some had none at all, and in the morning we were lined up by the Japanese to be marched to the Happy World Internment Camp in Happy Valley in Singapore, which was no more nor less than the accumulated gash heaps of the entire city. As we were marching towards this in a tropical deluge of rain, the streets running with water, our beards soaking wet and drenched, our long matted hair hanging over our faces and hardly a stitch on our bodies, we passed the Havelock Road Police Court. There, standing elegantly at ease as usual and conversing condescendingly with some minute but rather pompous captains and colonels of the Japanese Army, stood no less a person than my handsome Sikh. And as he looked somewhat contemptuously at this miserable gang of semi-human creatures shambling past in the rain, his eye caught mine. He couldn't say, or acknowledge the fact, that he knew me, obviously, but he did the one thing that restored my confidence more than anything in the whole of the war. His feet banged together in a salute as though he was killing a mosquito between them, he looked me straight in the eye, and then relaxed back to go on with his smiling conversation with the Japanese captain and colonel. When the war was over I did attempt to seek him out in order to shake him by the hand and say, 'Thanks for what you did.' Alas, I never found him.

8

Captains and Kings

I was already the man in command. In that community I stood, like a king in his country, in a class all by myself.

Joseph Conrad, *Youth*

IF there was one group of Europeans in South-East Asia and the Far East who were a breed of men apart it was the sea captains and river steamer captains: the China Coasters who commanded the ships of the Jardine Mathesons and Butterfield and Swires' fleets along the China coast and up her great rivers, and, in the South China Sea itself, the masters of the shallow-draught, coal-fired vessels of the Straits Steamship Company's 'little white fleet', based in Singapore:

Butterfield and Swires and Jardine Mathesons had an agreement with the Straits: 'You don't run in our territory, we won't run in yours.' The other place that the Straits could never get in was the Dutch Indies, Java and Sumatra. That was strictly Dutch KPM. The Straits territory was as far north as Bangkok, right across to the Philippines, Zamboanga and Manila, down to Borneo, round the Sandakan and beyond the back up along Sarawak to Singapore. And then right up the Malacca Straits, right up to Rangoon and Moulmein and Bassein. That was all our territory.

Percy Bulbrook joined Straits Steamships because of the slump in 1928 and Monty Wright some years later. Bulbrook was from an old Cornish seafaring family, with a grandfather who was a fisherman 'but also sidelined with a bit of smuggling' and a father who had left the navy to become a coastguard. After nearly a decade of sea-time in the merchant navy he found himself in a situation where 'even the sailors in the fo'c's'le all held Master-Mariner's Certificates'. The Straits offered 'security and steady employment – but, of course, you had to wait for promotions. It took me twelve years in the Straits with a Master-Mariner's Certificate before I ever went in command, and then, of course, there were quite a few old greybeards left when I joined and they resented us First and Second Officers because we were all carrying Master-Mariner's Certificates, the whole lot of us. All we were virtually doing was waiting for them to get out and we'd step in. There was quite a lot of animosity because the old greybeards had to put in a confidential report to the company every year and you didn't know what was ever said against you.'

Many of these senior Ship's Masters were 'real old salts who'd been in square-riggers round the Horn and even blackbirding' (illegally transporting Chinese to work as slave-labour in the South Pacific). One of the best-known characters was the twenty-two-stone Captain Caithness, who was said in his youth to have been either a Hudson Bay whaler or 'out of the Dundee trawlers, which was a hard affair in those days,' and whose boast it was that he could pick up a coil of ship's rope and throw it across the deck. He was said to have a tremendous capacity for beer, being capable of drinking 'a couple of cases before tiffin with a few gin *pahits* to help it down', and was widely known as 'Captain Allsopp'. A 'dear old day passenger' was said to have inadvertently given him this name: 'They asked her how she'd enjoyed the trip and she said, "Well, it was very nice, but this Captain – I think his name was Captain Allsopp – kept saying to his 'boy', 'Allsopp, boy, Allsopp'."'

At sea the Ship's Masters had almost unlimited powers: 'We were allowed complete freedom with regard to our decisions and they were never questioned by the management. For instance, sometimes you'd get an obstreperous – to use a nautical term – passenger, getting on the booze and probably interfering with the women. Well, you could send for him and say, "Right, I'm putting you ashore here." Finish!' But back in Singapore there were frequent disagreements with the management in the person of the Straits Marine Superintendent, particularly, as Bulbrook recalls, on such matters as uniforms:

We used to wear what the navy called Number Tens; long trousers of white twill, the *tutup* jacket that came up to the neck with brass buttons and the *topee* that the boy had starched up. You ordered the suits by the dozen and you could get through five or six in a day, all dirties, when you were supervising work on the cargo. Then some lad home on leave had to go to Harley Street on some trouble he had and mentioned this *topee* business and the doctor said that sunstroke came through the eyes. So then we all went into dark glasses and threw off our *topees* and reverted to our uniform cap, much to the disgust of the Marine Superintendent. But the greatest shock of all was when our navy decided that in the Eastern Station the day uniform could be white shorts and stockings and open necks. So I got half-a-dozen suits made and was very proud of them. The Marine Superintendent used to come aboard about six in the morning to do his rounds of the ships and, as Chief Officer, I went to the gangway to greet him. He looked me up and down: 'Go and get dressed,' he said. There was a hell of a row about it but we won the day.

Life was by no means made easy for the junior officers. There was no shore accommodation for bachelors and during their first term of service there was no official leave: 'We didn't get a single day's holiday in our first five years and the only way you could get any holiday was to be sick and then they put you in the hospital. We rather resented that because although we were doing all the ports we couldn't get around inside the country.'

Nor was there much mixing with the European business community in Singapore. The company provided its officers with their own club and 'if we got fed up ashore we said, "All right, the so-and-so mail's in – the German mail, the Dutch mail, our mail. Let's go down there, boys!" And we'd pile into rickshaws – because the only means of getting around was by rickshaw – and go aboard. And if the bar bloke knew you were sailors, then you'd get everything cheaper. But the *Raffles*, the *Adelphi* and the old *Europe Hotel*, they combined and got that all stopped, because we were doing them out of business.' However, with the Straits time ashore was always limited since 'the voyages were short, with short stops in port', and in consequence, 'it was a life with one foot on the gangway and one on the shore all the time'.

Starting as Second Officers, both Bulbrook and Wright spent their early years with the company getting to know the various ships' runs:

> You were put there on one run, say, for two months and then it depended on how much knowledge you could get into your head. If it was a small run, after a couple of months you were shifted to learn another run and then shifted again, until you got to be Senior Chief Officer. Then you could say, well, I'm here for about a year. So you circulated – and we had a saying that if you didn't like the ship the only way you could get a transfer was to paint your cabin and as sure as hell you'd get a shift, because you wouldn't be there to enjoy the cleanliness of it.

On most runs the ships spent a day in Singapore and then one or two days at sea, working up the east or west coast of Malaya and down again, carrying general cargo and passengers on the outward run and returning with local produce:

sheet rubber, tapioca, wood and copra. The major run was to Borneo and back:

> The ships would have a week in Singapore and then be three weeks away, calling at various ports along the Borneo coast – Miri, Labuan, Jesselton, Kudat, Sandakan and on to Tawau. The scenery from Jesselton round to Tawau was very beautiful because the Malawadi channel was strung with islands, some belonging to the Philippines, some to North Borneo; some were inhabited and some not. The channel was narrow and it was as though you were sailing on a multi-coloured sea, ranging from deep blue to green where the reefs showed through, with the islands set like jewels here and there. At the approaches to Sandakan there was an island called Berhala, which used to be the leper settlement for British North Borneo. The cliffs were red in colour and when approached just before sunrise they seemed to stand out in a vivid colour, gradually changing as the sun rose.

Some of the ports were just coves where all they had to export were a few bags of copra:

> If they wanted the ship to stop they would hoist a signal – usually a bucket on a coconut tree – and the ship would anchor off-shore and they would bring their produce out to the ship. The ships carried their own tally-clerks under the charge of a *chin-chu*, the same as a *comprador*, who on behalf of the company would purchase the produce at the market price. And where there were no banks the ships used to act as the bank. If the District Officer required some money he would give the Master a chit for the required amount and the Master would give him cash from the safe. Each port had some form of club for the European inhabitants but there was no other real diversion except the Straits ship when she came into port, so the housewives would come down and buy the bread, meat and dairy produce from the ship's cold storage and made use

of the dining facilities in the saloon. An invitation from a Master or a Senior Officer to join him for dinner was much sought after and people also used to book tables for dinner or lunch on board. And this friendliness between the ships and the local inhabitants was something that was enduring.

On these runs the stops were usually during the daylight hours with most of the sailing between ports done overnight, when 'large areas of the South China Sea, being phosphorescent, almost seemed to be alive. But there was always plenty of marine life, with the porpoise and dolphin gambolling and swimming close to the bows, almost seeking companionship. Various coastal areas, especially off the rivers, abounded with sea-snakes, all venomous and extremely lively, and very often when the ship was anchored and waiting the tide to cross a bar into a river and fishing lines were put over the side, these seasnakes seemed to be the main catch.'

The sand-bars across the river estuaries always presented a serious hazard to shipping, particularly when the north-east monsoon whipped up the smooth water of the South China Sea into a fierce 'chop' that was 'most dangerous because it came from all ways and pounded the sand hard as iron'. This was still an era when navigational aids were limited to a few lighthouses so that the Straits' captains depended to a very large extent on their own skills and experience – 'all you had were your eyes, your ears and your blinking brains'. It was their proud boast that they always performed their own pilotage: 'We in the Straits never took pilots, even in Singapore, where the junks were the bane of our existence when the tide was strong and there was no wind.' They had also to know the rivers 'like the backs of our hands, which was no mean feat as the channels were always changing. In order to turn the ship around one usually drifted six to seven miles down the river in the course of turning, a process made more hazardous by odd outcrops of rocks here and there. But everyone finished up in the putty some time. Bouncing off the bank was an accepted fact and being stuck on a bar was an accepted fact. Nobody worried.'

Every captain had his own method of gauging his ship's approach to the shore. 'You had to pick out your own distinctive landmarks and it was a bit awkward if they chopped down a few trees here and there. Some of the rubber planters used to do that. Up the Perak river there's a little creek named Daley's Creek and this chap Daley he had a big rubber place up there. He'd fallen out with old "Talky" Roberts at the club and so whilst he was away Daley cut down about five of the trees that were most important. Of course, old Talky Roberts went ashore!'

Other local aids were also enlisted – particularly at night: 'There was one point in North Borneo in particular where we used to get close to within half a mile of the shore which we could not see in the dark but were guided past by a local dog that invariably barked, and depending upon the loudness of the bark we could gauge our nearness from the shore.' Even fireflies glowing in the dark could help to show where the river banks were when the ships were travelling up- or down-river: 'These passengers used to say, "How the hell can you get down the river?" They'd step out from their cabins or the bar or the saloon and peer over, but of course we weren't in the glare of the ship's light.'

Even the smallest Straits' steamers carried a large crew drawn from several races but nearly always divided by occupation: 'The officers held British Certificates and were recruited in the UK. The crews were traditionally Chinese in the engine room and catering departments and Malay seamen on deck, as well as Chinese labour – eighty was the average on our small ships – to load your ship and unload, because we had our own crowd to discharge that ship. We used to pilot up to the wharf and if the cargo coolies on shore were too slow we'd say, "Get on with it, boys." ' As well as the crew each ship had its complement of passengers: 'Up to forty First-Class passengers, a couple of dozen Second-Class and up to three hundred

and fifty Deck-Class. We also carried on deck livestock in the
form of pigs in baskets, hump-backed cattle, chickens, fighting-
cocks and on occasion the odd circus.' Each ship also had to
have three galleys: 'One for Mohamedans, one for Chinese,
one for Europeans. The Chief Steward bought all the victuals
and Europeans in the First Class used to have eight-course
dinners – beautiful *makan*. The Master made sure he had a
damn good cook on board because that attracted the passengers – and they made their bit out of it, too.'

Although the ships' runs always followed the same pattern
and timetable there was very little monotony in the work: 'It
was always different; the wind, the tide, the currents. There
was always some factor which made the berthing of a ship
different from the time before. And whether it was an old ship
or a new one, one always had pride in whatever ship one was
appointed to.' Occasionally there were moments of drama and
even tragedy – as in the 'affair' of the *Klang* in 1930:

> That was a very bad affair. Old MacDonell was Master – a
> gentle old bible-puncher he was, a bearded bloke and fairly
> elderly, who was going to retire when he got back. The *Klang*
> called into Port Swettenham and then on to Penang, had a
> night there, and then back to Singapore. She sailed at four
> o'clock and they got out to Keppel Heads, the entrance to
> Singapore Harbour, and in the meantime the deck crowd was
> settling down. She had about six hundred deck crowd pas-
> sengers and they each had a little cane mat which they put
> down on the deck and that was their bit of space. Well, by the
> time they got out to Raffles lighthouse, some Malays decided it
> was time to say prayers to Mecca. They weren't going to wait
> for the sun to go down, they were going to do it a little in
> advance. They had lain their mats down and, unfortunately
> too, they were *Hajis* – that's to say they'd just come back from
> Mecca – and in those days they used to stain their whiskers red
> with red lead. They went to the ship's rail at the stern to *Al-
> Allah* to Mecca. I don't know how long they were, must have

been about a half-hour as usual, and back they came. But in the meantime, another fellow had picked up their mats, thrown them in the scuppers and put his down. Of course there was an argument and the next thing – out with the *kris*. And they started stabbing. The Mate was up with the old man on the bridge and they had another six miles to go before you get around Kapis to go up the Staits of Malacca. And the first intimation they got that there was something wrong down on the decks was when all these deck passengers, women, kids and all, began trying to get up on the prom deck. In the meantime, a *kemudi* – that's a Malay term for a helmsman – who was off duty having his *makan*, his food, saw all this and managed to climb up over the awning spars onto the bridge and told them that some fellows had run *amok*, and were foaming at the mouth like mad dogs. So the Mate said to the old man, 'I'll go down and see what I can do.' And the old man said, 'No, you'd better leave it to me.' So down went the old chap and he met these two coming along the deck, which was clear now because all the other passengers had crowded the other side to get out of the way. In the meantime, they'd scuppered three or four that were lying round the decks bleeding. The old man went up to one of them, put his hand on his shoulder to ease him down and this fellow just – sheesh – disembowelled him there and then. Then he and the other fellow got busy with a few more. I think there were seventeen altogether, seventeen Asians anyhow and old MacDonell. The Mate on the bridge didn't know what was happening, so he got hold of this *kemudi* and asked him to go over the awning and look down and of course he did and came back and told him, 'The old man's *sudah mati* – the old man's dead.' So the Mate put the ship hard over and came back to Singapore. They got in off Johnson's Pier and had the police flag up and it took the police nearly a good half-hour to get off. In the meantime, the two *amok* fell out with each other and one got killed by the other one. But that left one who was still roaming around and even ran down the engine room. That's where the Chief Engineer got his –

luckily he felt the knife coming in and put his knee up, so he was all right; they stitched him up. The European Inspector brought a couple with a rifle; they boarded, the Mate bawled down from the bridge what was wrong and they saw this bloke and they put four bullets into him. That didn't stop him, but they got him in the launch and he didn't die till they got him on the pier. Now, the bold European passengers had locked themselves in their cabins. Among them were a lot of army officers, too, and they had revolvers, guns. Oh, it was hushed up; it had to be, but that was the *Klang*.

Piracy was no longer a serious threat to shipping in the South China Sea but it was still a risk on the more distant runs to the Philippines and to China. Straits Steamships had a subsidiary company running three passenger-cargo vessels between Rangoon, Singapore, Swatow and Amoy – which meant passing a notorious haunt of pirates just north of Hong Kong known as Bias Bay. Since the most successful ploy used by the pirates was to infiltrate on board as passengers and then take over the ship at an opportune moment, many of the merchant fleets operating along the China coast employed White Russians as guards on the ships. The Straits preferred to arm its senior crew members instead:

The officers all had arms issued from the armoury consisting of Webley-Scott revolvers and Greener shotguns and were stationed behind grilles separating the officers' accommodation, the bridge and the engine room from the rest of the ship. Once the ship had cleared Hong Kong northward-bound, we were in contact with the Anti-Piracy Control to which all ships on the coast reported, sending our position every two hours and our expected time of arrival at the next port. If this transmission was not received then the Anti-Piracy Control was expected to take action. Despite these measures a number of ships were successfully seized and taken to Bias Bay, to be looted and their passengers held for ransom.

Few can have experienced quite as many hazards in the course of their careers as Robert Williamson, who retired in 1947 after twenty-six years with the Indo-China Steam Navigation Company. Nearly half his service was spent on the longest of China's rivers, the Yangtse:

The Chinese always refer to the Yangtse as the *Ta Chiang* or the Great River, because it is the greatest river in China and it is the great highway of China as it traverses the country from east to west. It rises in Tibet, it flows south until it reaches the mountains of Yunnan and there it is deflected and turns and flows back north again for about a hundred miles. It then skirts the base of the great Cheng-tu Basin which in past ages was an inland sea. The Yangtse flows on the southern edge of it down to Chungking and then through the generally hilly country for about two hundred miles. For about a hundred miles it flows through tremendous gorges – the Yangtse Gorges, until it leaves the mountains at the port of Ichang and then flows down through the great central plains of China right down to the sea.

The river begins to rise usually about May, but the first rise is a false rise and is due to the melting of snows in Tibet. But shortly after that the monsoon rains begin and then one gets the summer rise which begins to gradually build up. All the tributaries and the side streams are flooded, they all pour down into the main river and they build up enormous floods right up until the latter part of August. In the autumn the rains begin to ease off and the floods drain away until you get to December. Then December, February, March are the months when the river reaches its lowest level. Some years the monsoon rains are heavier than in others, but in one year – I think it was 1921, which was my first season of navigating a ship on that river – we had a very high river and at the entrance of the Wu Shang Gorge, which is the longest of the gorges and twenty-five miles in length, I recorded that the river had risen to just over two hundred feet above its winter level.

In 1921 Bob Williamson began a four-year tour as a Ship's Master on the five-hundred-and-fifty-mile stretch of rapids and gorges known as the Upper River:

The Master has to be on the bridge the whole time. He goes on the bridge when the ship gets under way at the crack of daylight and he's on the bridge until he brings the vessel into the anchorage in the evening. We carried Chinese pilots, local junkmen who knew the river intimately but only from a junkman's point of view. They knew every danger, they knew every change of level one had and they actually acted as pilots, but it wasn't safe to allow them to handle the ship, because they knew all about handling a junk but nothing about handling a steamer, and many accidents on the Upper River were due to the fact that inexperienced Masters trusted those pilots too implicitly. Of course, these pilots had probably been born in a junk. They knew the river and absolutely everything about it and they were familiar with the stories and the legends – and every mile of the river has its legend. For instance, in the Windbox Gorge there is a sheer thousand-foot cliff and running up the face of this cliff is a zig-zag row of holes from the river's bank right up to the top of the cliff. This is known as Meng Liang's Ladder and goes back to some time in the era before Christ known as the Wars of the Kingdoms. Meng Liang's army was attacking up-river but the defending general above the Windbox Gorge had stretched chains across at low level so as to bar the river from an attack by water. So Meng Liang's men cut holes in the cliffs and inserted beams into these holes and by making them zig-zag, they made a ladder right up the face of the cliff, got up to the top and attacked the defending force from the rear and defeated them.

The whole of the gorges section, particularly, is full of links with the past history of China. Every rock and every shoal has its own name. The Windbox Gorge takes its name from the fact that on the high cliffs opposite Meng Liang's Ladder there are some boxes in crevices, the square ends of which look like Chinese bellows – but how these boxes got into these crevices nobody knows. It's a mystery. Then there is the Wu Shang Gorge, which means the Witch's Mountain Gorge. Wu was a legendary wizard who lived on a mountain before the river burst through the mountains and he is said to have blasted with his breath a passage through the rocks, to allow the river to flow through – hence it being called the Wu Shang Gorge. In a steamer capable of steaming fifteen knots it took six hours to make your way up-river through that gorge under very wild conditions, because you're bucking in this current which rushes off each point and shoots across to the next point and then the next.

Of the many kinds of hazards on the river the most serious were the rapids in the gorges:

When the river gradually falls in the autumn the gorges become very quiet and placid – a joy to navigate really. But then the rapids begin to show up at places where there are reefs stretching out from the shore. They become uncovered and between the reefs and the bank you get a very narrow channel indeed and a very swift rapid. At low level there were about thirty rapids and races, of which the greatest was the Sin Tan, caused by an enormous landslide in the seventeenth century, which almost dammed up the river. That leaves only a channel between the outer rock and the bank of less than two hundred feet where the sluice runs down so hard that no steamer can surmount it. So here we had to what we called 'heave it'; the steamer would steam into the tongue of the rapid and then a wire was thrown ashore on a heaving line and made fast to a rock above the rapid. This was then taken to the windlass and as the ship steamed and sheered to and fro so they hove-in the wire and the steamer gradually worked its way over to the top of the rapid and away.

Another hazard came in the form of other traffic on the river:

> On the Lower River one could meet enormous great timber rafts coming down with a whole colony of people living on board who were handling the rafts. Then one would occasionally meet a convoy of ducks going down to Nanking where they were to be processed as Chinese ducks for export. The poor little blighters were made to swim down. They were herded together by the main junk following astern and by men in small single *sampans* who kept them going. In the evening they would herd them ashore and pen them up and in the morning they would set them afloat again and carry on. There were also convoys of salt junks coming down and above Chungking one could pass a small town where they made large pots and one would occasionally meet the potter on his way to Chungking to sell the pots. He bunged them up and made them watertight, he bound them into a raft with bamboos and then he took his place on board and travelled down to Chunking.
>
> On the Lower River you'd get quite a lot of traffic, not much on the Middle River and even less on the Upper River, where you would only meet the odd steamer coming down and the junks, always close in at the bank going up but, when they came down-river, drifting down in the middle of the stream. Yet they very seldom interfered with the steamer and the experienced Master; he knew how the currents were running and when he saw a junk coming down he knew whether it would be set towards him or away from him and handled his ship accordingly.
>
> The largest cargo junk, carrying about eighty or ninety tons of cargo, had a crew of twenty men who were called 'trackers' and these lads also handled the *yulos* – a side oar which is worked with a sculling motion, not a pulling motion. They couldn't work up any great speed but they could manoeuvre with the *yulos*, and Providence has so arranged things that in the winter at low level in the gorges you usually get an up-river

wind. The current is slack, probably not more than one or two knots, so with a good up-river wind, the junk could sail up, using one great sail which they hoisted. At the same time they worked their *yulos* with a peculiar chant that they had which was the equivalent of what we used to call in sailing ships 'whistling for the wind'. This was a wild 'Hoo-hoo-hoo' while on the smaller junks that were rowed with great sweeps they would chant 'I-eee-yah!'

Now when the junk came to a rapid, then all the trackers went ashore and they had a tow-line from the mast-head of the junk – not from the bow because of the rocks. It was hoisted about half-way up the mast and made fast and the trackers then spread themselves along the bank and then they had to haul the junk over the rapid by main force. And in a very bad rapid, like the Sin Tan or the Sin Lung Tan, the New Dragon rapid, and the Ya Tan, which was the Wild Ass rapid – and was a very wild ass indeed at times – on these very, very strong rapids, they would be reinforced by local boys who would come down and form themselves into gangs under a leader and hire themselves out to the captain of the junk, who would hire as many extra men as was necessary to haul the junk over that particular rapid. It was a hard life being a tracker; where there wasn't enough wind then they had to go ashore and haul the junk up by main force. For miles and miles they would be plodding along, and they didn't haul with the hands; they had a canvas strap built round the shoulder with a short length of line which they toggled onto the main tow rope so that they hauled with their bodies and when it got to a tough spot they would go down on hands and knees and claw themselves along from rock to rock!

The third major hazard on the river was also a human one:

China was a very wild and lawless country in those days. There were several of the so-called war-lords who, every year, were campaigning against each other, trying to get control of a principal city like Chungking or Wanhsien where the people could be taxed. These people were quite a curse and as there was no law and order, the country was infested with troops or gangs of what were actual bandits. They just went off looting all on their own and so we had to be very careful of the places where we anchored. We had a night watch that we set and we had enough rifles on board for our own use and our pistols, too. The ship's bridges were also enclosed in bullet-proof steel all round the bridge with flaps which had loop-holes in them so that we could enclose the bridge in armour. They were arranged on quick-release hooks so that the flaps could be dropped at practically a second's notice. One could come round a corner where there was fighting on between the various war-lords and if one came across a gang of them on the march, sometimes they would just shoot at the ship out of sheer wantonness!

I can remember one occasion when I was going up-river some hundred miles below Chungking. I had to cross from one side of the river to the other to avoid central dangers and on the opposite bank was a small village and there seemed to be some commotion going on. I looked through my glasses and I saw that there was a bunch of bandits looting the village. There were a couple of long-gowned gentlemen with their hands tied behind their backs – the local merchants that they were robbing – and there was quite a hoo-ha. The head of the gang was sitting on a large rock practically at the river's edge, directing the whole proceedings. As we turned across the river, heading towards the village, he looked round. Then I saw him shouting to somebody obviously asking for his gun. The gun was handed to him and as soon as I saw that I knew that he was going to have a pot-shot at us as we began to go in fairly close. So I thought I'd spoil his aim and got my own pistol ready – and sure enough, he swung round and fired a round at the ship. As soon as he had fired one round, I fired at the rock on which he was sitting and hit it and he threw up his arms and went off backwards. Before they could recover themselves and send a few stray shots after us, we'd rounded our stern and were well on our way.

During his four years on the Upper River Williamson was based on Chungking, which was still largely untouched by the outside world:

> On the first evening I arrived in Chungking with a brand new ship and I was up in the office. When I arrived back on board there were two little Chinese girls sitting in my accommodation, so I said to my boy, 'Who are these?' He indicated that the management had sent them and said, 'Well, you need a little home comfort.' So I gave the little girls *cumshaw* – which is a gift – and they went ashore again. Then we used to go in the evening through the streets in our sedan chairs – because there were no rickshaws in Chungking in those days – and with our bearers carrying a hand lantern, to the Chinese theatre. And this was real, real China, quite untouched by any outside influences, where life went on as it had done throughout Chinese history.

The Upper River was capable of offering moments of great beauty:

> There was one place in the middle of the Wu Shang Gorge where there was a side stream and in the late autumn when the gorges were quiet and the violent period was over, it was possible to anchor there. Then just at the peep of day one would heave up the anchor and ease the ship out into the mid-stream and steam up-river and you'd be in deep shadows still. But at one particular place there is a gap in the cliffs and you could see a ten-thousand-foot peak in the distance, bathed in the rosy light of early dawn, and that is a picture one never forgot – just the snoring of the waters and that glimpse of that distant peak so green and beautiful against the pearly sky.

But, inevitably, there were also moments of great tragedy – as in the story of Freddie Brandt, a British subject with a German father and a Chinese mother, who was a fellow captain on the Upper River:

Now on the Upper Yangtse there was a lot of smuggling of opium and Freddie was up to his ears in this business. I would never have anything to do with it. But Freddie, unfortunately, also became involved in an arms racket. There was a war every summer in Szechwan between the warring war-lords. The man who was in Chungking had control of all the taxes so the man who was up in Cheng Tu would bring his army down and they would have a war to see who could chase the other one out; so of course there was a great demand for arms and unfortunately Freddie became involved in the arms racket. I knew about the opium – everybody knew it – however, the arms I didn't know about. But I was in Chungking, it would be in the autumn of 1924. Freddie's little *Tzeit Swei* was anchored on the opposite shore from Chungking when I arrived in the late afternoon and I sent a *chit* across to Freddie to come and dine with us, myself and my crowd. So Freddie came over and we had dinner together and after dinner it was dark by that time and I said, 'Well, Fred, you don't want to go back to your ship, doss down on my settee and I'll send you over in my *sampan* in the morning' – because he was due to sail next morning at daylight. So he did. I got into my bunk – because it was only a small cabin in a small ship – and Fred turned in on my settee and we lay and chatted. Now he was a married man and he had two children down in Shanghai, and as we yarned I said, 'You know, Fred, I don't know why you carry on up here on this Upper River. You've got plenty of money. Why don't you chuck it and go down to Shanghai?' 'Oh,' he said, 'I must finish the season, I must finish the season.' So I said, 'Well, you must have a lot of enemies up here you know, with all these rackets.' One skipper had disappeared over the side and there had been some nasty business, so I said, 'You get back to Shanghai, man, chuck it.' 'Oh,' he said, 'I will, Bob, soon as the season's over I'll be finished.'

Well, next morning I hauled my *sampan* away and I took Fred across to his ship and I stood and I watched him while he went on the bridge and hove up his anchor and as he turned around into the river we waved to each other and that was that. Two days later I was downbound myself loaded for Ichang and I was going through the last of the gorges, called the Yellow Cat Gorge – it's about ten miles in length – and about halfway down, I saw a little steamer coming into the lower end of the gorge and it was the *Tzeit Swei*. This was Fred upward-bound again and as we passed, of course we waved. Two or three days later I was upbound again and coming on through the second half of the Ichang Gorge – I remember this sight well – in the Lampshine Gorge, when a steamer came down and as she came down I saw them with a blackboard. We hadn't time to signal to each other so we always had a big blackboard on which you put any information about the river. One wrote on the blackboard and showed it to the ship as you whizzed past each other. I saw the blackboard coming out and read on it, 'Captain Brandt was shot at Kowchochin at such and such a time.' I thought, 'Oh, Lord.' Well, I got up to Wan Sien and the British gunboat was there and the captain came on board. He said, 'I'm very sorry to have to tell you that Captain Brandt has been murdered. He was shot and thrown over the side but his body has been recovered and is lying in the Joss House in Kowchochin and I want you to stop there and pick him up and carry him on to Chungking.' I said, 'Yes, of course I will.'

I arranged my sailing from Wan Sien to arrive up there just before nightfall. I anchored and I sent my *comprador* – what we would call a purser, but they always used the old Portuguese term out there of *comprador*, the buyer – to the headman of the village, telling him that I was commissioned to carry Captain Brandt and would they kindly send him on board first thing in the morning. I said, 'Take plenty of money, *comprador*, you pay the headman all the expenses of recovering his body and fixing him up and the coffin and the *cumshaw* on top.' At daylight a terrific hoo-ha started up ashore as Fred had a really good send-off from the Joss House with firecrackers all the way down to the beach. The coffin was then put on board a big *sampan*. They brought him over to the ship and up on deck and away we went. And that was the end of poor old Freddie Brandt.

After nearly five years on the Upper River Bob Williamson moved down to Shanghai, where he served for nine years as the Indo-China Steam Navigation Company's Marine Superintendent. But the Upper River was an experience that could never be forgotten:

It was my life and I loved every minute of it. I was an Upper River Master, which was recognized as a very difficult and at times hazardous occupation. And it's a source of great pride to me that my name in Chinese was Wei Ling Soong (Williamson) and that I was known as Wei Ch'uan Ju. Ch'uan is the ship, Ju is the overlord and that is the Chinese word for a captain of the ship, so I was Wei Ch'uan Ju and I would go ashore in Chungking and I would hear the Chinese say, 'Who's that old foreigner?', and somebody would say, 'Wei Ch'uan Ju.' It meant that I was Captain Wei and that was that.

9

The Mems

They played tennis if there were people to play with, went to the club at sundown if there was a club in the vicinity, drank in moderation, and played bridge. They had their little tiffs, their little jealousies, their little flirtations, their little celebrations.

Somerset Maugham, *Preface,*
The Complete Short Stories, Vol III

As far as marriage was concerned most Europeans had little option but to follow the standard convention:

At the end of your first contract you were called in by a director in London and he said, 'I'm pleased to inform you that you are now permanent staff. You've served four years; we think therefore as directors of the company that you should get married and you've got four months' leave in which to find a wife.' This was rather difficult in those days, but you were twenty-eight or twenty-nine and you were getting a good salary by that time, so the best thing you could do would be to go to a teaching hospital in London, hang around outside and pick up a nurse. That was the quickest way of finding on four months' leave a girl with whom you might get some association going and then be able to say, 'Would you like to get married?'

If only a minority of bachelors succeeded in finding prospective brides on their first home leave, that was hardly surprising. Many more marriages took place during the second long leave or during the second term of service, often within twenty-four hours of the bride-to-be setting foot on Straits or Malay States territory. The 'export' of fiancées for these 'beach weddings' was regarded as a risky business – and not without reason: 'If you didn't take her through the Red Sea on the P&O yourself she was almost bound to fall for somebody on the ship,' declares Gerald Scott. 'So very often these chaps from the rubber companies and the tin-mines who were exporting their fiancées from England – an awful lot of characters in my day in Singapore – they'd nip up to Penang and then the girl would come down the gangplank with some shipboard romance on her arm and they'd have to give the wedding reception they'd planned as a wedding present to the girl.'

But not all the single women who landed at Penang, Port Swettenham or Singapore came out as intended brides. Increasingly, from the late 1920s onwards, single women were being recruited by the Educational and Medical Services. In 1927 Mary Culleton, who had trained as a nurse at Guy's Hospital during the First World War, joined the Malayan Nursing Service. Her first three years in Malaya were spent in Batu Gajah hospital as a nursing sister, looking after the European women's ward and dealing for the most part either with maternity cases or malaria. It was malaria that presented the most serious threat to the health of the community. Quinine-based treatment had little effect: 'You had temperatures up to one hundred and five degrees easily and you sweated so terribly that you had constantly to be changed. It was very common to get it – and that's what got me finished earlier than I would have.'

After a particularly bad bout of malaria Mary Culleton was invalided out of the service in 1930. However, in the meantime, she had met and become engaged to a rubber planter named Hugh Watts – 'We met at the Station Hotel, Ipoh, where the sisters were invited to a party. There was a group of young rubber planters also having a party and they said, "Let's all join together." ' After a period of recuperation in England she returned and was married at Port Swettenham – 'a quiet wedding with the minimum of fuss and a wedding breakfast at the Rest House'.

Tamsin Luckham and Dorothy 'Tommy' Hawkings came to Malaya as teachers. Both had relatives in the Far East: Tamsin Luckham a brother in the MCS and a sister married to a Bousteads' executive; Tommy Hawkings a cousin in Malaya but with far stronger family connections with China, where her grandfather had gone out as a missionary in 1875 and where she herself had been born and educated. At the start of the Second World War she moved down to Malaya to open a nursery boarding school for European children in the Cameron Highlands, driving up through 'great tropical rain forests with orchids hanging from the trees'. She was struck by the 'peacefulness of life' in Malaya: 'After all the tragedies I had seen in Shanghai when the Japanese entered the Chinese settlement – old men and women with stones tied to their feet being thrown into rivers, young girls being taken off to be raped over and over again and then shot – Malaya seemed so calm and quiet. Everything was running so smoothly and it really was a dramatic change from the turmoil of life in China.'

In the Cameron Highlands she met Peter Lucy, a young planter and Manager of Amhurst Estate, who was on local leave. In November 1941 she moved down to Kuala Lumpur and saw a lot more of him:

We had a wonderful time together and I remember the evening when we walked through the Malay village in Kuala Lumpur after a dance and there were great stalls of what we call *makan kechils*, small eats, and kebabs on sticks that the Malays were making over the fires. This was about four o'clock in the morning because dances in Malaya seldom finished before dawn, and it was there that Peter proposed to me and we became engaged.

Tamsin Luckham had started her teaching four years earlier in an Anglican mission school for girls in Kuala Lumpur. She too had been greatly impressed by a landscape that she

TEL. WHITEHALL 3226

SARAWAK GOVERNMENT OFFICES,
MILLBANK HOUSE,
WESTMINSTER, S.W. 1

G.635   5th June, 1946.

Dear Sir,

      With reference to your letter of the 30th May, I have received a telegram from Sarawak that your request to marry is approved.

         Yours faithfully,

J O Smith

Government Agent.

Rec & ack
7.6.+6.

In this instance leave to marry was granted three months before the required eight years of service in Sarawak had been completed.

first saw from the open cockpit of a Tiger Moth, piloted by a friend of her brother's who flew her down from Penang:

> The jungle that covered so much of Malaya wasn't very colourful. It was rather grey-green – although the new leaves were always red, surprisingly. But looking down on the tops of trees you saw bright birds and flowers that usually you saw very little of unless you went to a hill-station. The mountains looked very, very blue – I suppose because of the atmosphere – although at midday the light tended to drain all the colour from things – that flat light with the sun overhead and no shadows.

Her school had an English headmistress with a staff made up of Eurasians, Indians and Chinese and about five hundred pupils:

> This was a very well-thought-of school so we got the daughters of very well-off Chinese *towkays*, but also we had the daughters of anybody who could pay the very, very small fees that were needed, because it was a government-aided school where the government paid the staff. The majority of the girls were Chinese but there were also Sikhs, Tamils and Eurasians. There were no Malays because the school wasn't in an area where there were Malays and Malay girls tended to go to their own Islamic schools – although they thought convents were very ladylike.

After only a year at the school Tamsin Luckham found herself acting headmistress while the head went on leave. Her only moment of crisis came when a tiger was sighted near the school grounds:

> I was a bit taken aback because these schools, being in a hot climate, were completely open, so there was no way of shutting doors or anything like that without a tremendous palaver. I

thought, what happens if the tiger walks into a school of five hundred girls? But I said, 'Oh well, I don't expect it will come this way' – and it didn't come that way. The next day I saw a Baby Austin car with the girls absolutely crowding round and I said to them, 'What's all this about?' And they said, 'Oh, that tiger was shot and he's selling tiger meat. If we have that, it'll make us good and strong.' So here we were in a mission school and all the girls buying tiger meat to make themselves big and strong!

Being young and unattached in Kuala Lumpur had obvious advantages: 'I was very lucky because as an unmarried girl I was welcomed into all the clubs without paying anything. We were entirely supported by the men, who were so pleased to have some girls that I got all the facilities of the clubs for nothing, which was a big thing because I was terribly badly paid, of course, and I wouldn't have been able to afford going to the clubs otherwise.' As well as being entertained at the clubs she was also taken out to the Chinese dance-halls which were usually to be found in amusement parks. It was at one of these that she was introduced to Richard Broome, one of her brother's colleagues in the MCS, who later became her husband.

Another notable group of young single women in the Malay archipelago were the daughters of Britons already working there and who came out to join their parents as teenagers when their school-days were over. One such teenager was Una Ebden, who came out at her mother's insistence at the unusually early age of fifteen, soon after the war in Europe had started: 'I arrived in Malacca where my father was Resident Councillor and went straight from school into this glorious atmosphere of grandeur, with the sentry saluting you as you went in the front door and a car with a Union Jack and police saluting me. It seemed very grand and I was so impressed.'

Driving up from Singapore to Malacca through the Malayan countryside she had been greatly struck by the humidity and its 'encouragement to growth':

It was like a large greenhouse, so that everything was green
and of enormous growth. Then there were splashes of colour
against the green; bougainvillaea which was purple; next to
bougainvillaea, orange; next to that yellow canna lilies. Everything ought to have clashed but it didn't. It looked gorgeous,
like a great bed of azaleas. The Malay women wore the same
clashy clothes but they also looked gorgeous; where a white
skin would look simply dreadful they looked really beautiful.
Then the stars were so bright you could almost read by them
and when the moon was full you could read. The strange thing
was that the moon was sideways. Instead of a man in the moon
it was a rabbit. I remember seeing that and thinking how
funny it was. And of course swimming at night in Malacca
swimming pool, which was just a fenced off bit of sea. As you
waved your arm out of the water it dripped fire and you could
see everybody splashing around in a great mass of fire and
phosphorus.

Even at fifteen Una Ebden was able to enjoy the
advantage of being one of a greatly sought-after minority:
'I was rather lucky in having a good friend who was exactly
the same age, the daughter of the Dunlops' representative
there. We had a very good time together, because there
was no shortage of dates. We were taken out dancing,
swimming, on picnics, anything we wanted – there were
people queuing up. Oh, it was absolute heaven and very
bad for the character, I know, but being good friends we
were able to enjoy it all together and revert a little to
childhood sometimes and have a good giggle.' When the
climate became too oppressive she was able to escape with
her family to the Cameron Highlands, which was fast
becoming the premier hill-station of Malaya: 'It was five-
and-a-half thousand feet high, which meant that it was still
nice and warm during the days but that the air was fresh
and you had wood fires in the evening and blankets on the
bed, which was a treat. There was a golf course and lovely

walks and horses to ride and a dance in the hotel every Saturday night.'

It was 'a lovely, carefree, irresponsible life' for a teenager. Yet Una Ebden was very conscious of the role played by her father and others like him: 'I saw my father as a man dedicated to Malaya and to the Malays, for whom he had a lot of time – good-natured gentlemen, was how he used to describe them – and I do think that he was typical of the MCS as a whole; the country was their only interest.'

For those who came out East as newly-weds – new *mems* knowing very little about the country or what to expect – life was not quite so carefree. Nancy and Guy Madoc had grown up together on the Isle of Man: 'He then went out to Malaya and we wrote to each other. He used to write me long, glowing accounts of the country and how interesting it was and sent me wonderful photographs, and I began to get very interested, thinking it was a romantic place to live.' When Madoc returned on his first home leave the two met up again, became engaged and got married. During their honeymoon in Somerset Nancy Madoc had a foretaste of what married life in Malaya could be like when her husband had an attack of malaria: 'He had a very high temperature and would wake up shouting, and that worried me to death.'

The Madocs sailed for the East, to be met in Penang by a smell that Nancy found 'so frightful that I couldn't believe it. I said in a horrified voice to Guy, "What is that terrible smell?" And he said, "Oh, that's durian. That's this wonderful fruit that they all think so much of." Then Guy took me straight to the *Runnymede Hotel* – a lovely place with everything that could be luxurious, with fans and servants – and we had ice-cold mangosteen, which is another fruit and it really was lovely. There were no mosquitoes, and a breeze blew through the room and I thought, "Oh, this is lovely, I am going to love this country."'

They had already been told that Madoc's next posting was to Kuala Selangor:

The other officers on the boat said, 'What a dreadful place to send a young bride', so I began to wonder. However, Guy was reassuring and said, 'Oh, it's a lovely place and we'll be all right. We've got a bungalow and we've got a cook and we've got an *amah*,' and so I made up my mind that it would be all right and off we started. We drove and drove and drove, and at every little *atap* house that we passed on the way, standing way back in the jungle paddy, I would say, 'Is our bungalow like that?' and he'd say, 'Oh, yes, it's a bit better than that.' Eventually we got to Kuala Selangor and stopped at the bottom of a flight of eighty steps and that was the only way to get up to the bungalow, so we trudged up and Ah Chi, the Chinese servant, met us with his wife and small boy. It was a nice bungalow, perched on a hill, but our outlook was just the rather muddy Selangor river and the mangrove swamps really as far as you could go. The police station and *padang* were just below the hill, which was a consolation, because I could actually hear Guy sometimes in his office, but I was very homesick at first. I really was pretty miserable and it took me a long time to get used to it.

To her initial dismay this new life was not at all what Nancy Madoc had imagined it would be:

I used to wonder how I could have been so foolish as not to realize that of course it wasn't going to be a glamorous state of going to the club and being amongst a lot of other women, because Guy's letters had more or less told me that he wouldn't have liked that sort of life anyway. But we had a very old-fashioned bungalow; there were just kerosene lamps that had to be lit every night and a terrible old bathroom with slats on the floor that you could look through and see just the ground underneath – and, of course, every time I went into this place I saw snakes coming up through the slats in my imagination and it really took me a lot of courage to go into that bathroom. Then I was alone an awful lot of the time and I

used to imagine things, I suppose – in other words, I got the
jim-jams. Every terror that I could think of was there; a snake
under every chair, a spider under every cushion. And it wasn't
all imagination, because one day when we were down on the
beach, I was standing under the casuarina trees watching
other people who were still in the water surf-bathing when I
became aware of a kind of tickling on my shoulder. I was in a
sleeveless dress and I didn't think anything of it; I just reached
up and shook my shoulder and then a clammy sensation began
to grow upon my arm and I looked and there crawling from
my shoulder down my arm was a beautiful vivid green snake. I
have often heard people say they were stiff with fear and I was;
my lips stuck to my teeth and I couldn't shout, I couldn't do
anything. I just shook it off and I turned my head and there
was our faithful Majid who always came with us. He saw that I
was terrified and came running and cut the snake in half.

But as Nancy Madoc grew accustomed to her new role she
began to realize that the country was not full of terror – and
her confidence grew to the point where she could accompany
her husband into the Malayan jungle without any qualms.

An important stage in the process of cultural acclimatization
was learning the language. The tradition – particularly among
government servants – was that '*mems* spoke Malay. In those
days all servants, shopkeepers and market people, all – whatever their nationality – spoke Malay. It was a very simple type
of Malay, but that was how we communicated and in fact
servants didn't think it was correct in those days to speak
English.' This was not something that most *mems* found easy at
first – and Nancy Madoc was no exception:

Guy tried very hard to teach me the basic words to say to the
servants and I used to repeat them religiously every evening. I
got my accent more or less right but the time came when he
had to be away overnight. I was rather nervous, but he said,
'You will be quite all right with Ah Chi. All you have to do is to

tell him to lock everything that will lock,' and he told me what to say which I, faithfully, thought I knew well. So when Ah Chi came into the room and said goodnight, I said, 'You must *kenching sini, kenching sana, kenching sini, kenching sana*', and I went on saying this to Ah Chi, whose face never altered. He didn't let on by any indication at all that I was saying something quite wrong and off he went, back to his quarters, which are always at the back of a bungalow in Malaya and eventually I heard him laughing hysterically, and his family all laughing and laughing, and I thought, 'That's funny, why are they laughing?' So when Guy came home he said, 'How have you been?' And I said, 'Oh, I was all right, but when I told Ah Chi "*kenching sini, kenching sana*" they just roared with laughter.' And then, of course, Guy roared with laughter. What I should have been saying was *kunchi* which means lock, but what I was saying was *kenching sini, kenching sana*, which means, 'pee here, pee there', so no wonder they laughed.

There were many genuine and deep friendships between *mems* and their household staff but they took time to develop. One of the hoariest jokes in the Far East was about the Englishman who returned with his bride and introduced her to the servants: 'He said to his houseboy, "Boy, this lady here belong my wife," and the boy grinned and said, "Yes, master, yes, yes." But early next morning she felt her shoulders being shaken by the houseboy who said, "Missie, belong five o'clock. More better you go home now."'

Rather more typical was the close relationship that existed between Tamsin Broome and her household servants – who were all Chinese:

The nice thing about the Chinese is that they're always so sure that they are very, very superior people and therefore there's none of this difficulty which I think one got in India over servants. Our cook was marvellous, for instance. He could cook English, or Chinese, or anything you asked. He also did the marketing and that kind of thing. The *amah* knew how to bring up a newborn baby and she taught the baby nursery rhymes in English and sang to it and so on. So though I was never able to have long conversations, because my Malay was not really up to that and nor was theirs, we were still very, very great friends and I think that we both felt that we were on a par. Now it wasn't quite the same with the other servants. We used to have a gardener – nearly always a Tamil – and gardeners in Malaya were the bane of my life because I love a garden and you could have a beautiful garden in Malaya, but whatever kind of gardener you had they always said they couldn't speak a word of either English or Malay and therefore they went their own way, whatever you wanted. On Christmas Island we had a Chinese gardener but I had to do everything through my husband because he wouldn't speak a word that I could understand. When Richard said plant vegetables he would nod and then you would say, 'Why weren't they planted?' He'd say, 'Oh well, the moon wasn't right,' or something – and Tamil gardeners were exactly the same: 'We don't understand English, or Malay' – and so they went their own way, endlessly cutting little tiny beds in the middle of your back lawn and filling them with marigolds and such like. So you never really got what you wanted. But of course you moved so frequently that however hard you worked you probably never saw the advantage of your garden.

Later the Broomes took on a houseboy, Ah Chuan, whom they had first met on Christmas Island when he was working for another employer – 'because on Christmas Island we had a very nice custom where if you were ever asked out to dinner it was taken for granted that your household staff would go too'. Here, as in Sarawak and other more out of the way stations, the houseboy would help to hand round various canapés – known as *makan kechils* or 'small eats' – serve at table if he was needed and then join the host's staff for their own dinner. After the Broomes moved to Penang Ah Chuan appeared at Richard Broome's office:

> He walked in and said, 'I've come to work for you.' I said, 'But we're not employing anybody else at the moment. We've got the cook and the *amah* and we reckon that's enough.' 'Ah yes,' he said. 'But Mrs Broome is going to have a baby and then the *amah* will be fully employed and then you will want me.' Of course, he was quite right but this was, we thought, a secret – and he had worked it all out. Like most of the domestic servants he was a Hainanese and my language was Cantonese, so I was a little doubtful but in fact he spoke quite enough Cantonese and Malay and so we could get on.

When the Japanese invaded Malaya, the cook and the *amah* went to join Tamsin Broome in Singapore. Richard Broome was then asked to join a special forces unit and told Ah Chuan to go: 'I said to Ah Chuan, "You'd better get off, because you'll be quite all right if you fade into the Chinese community here." But he said, "Oh no, I want to come with you." I said, "It's dangerous, you know," and he said, "Yes, I realize that but one has to die somewhere and I'd rather die in your company, please" – which was a very delightful thing to hear anybody say, so he finally came with me when we sailed for Ceylon.' When Broome later returned to Malaya by submarine and was landed secretly on the coast, Ah Chuan was forced to stay behind in India. However, he trained as a wireless operator and made three unsuccessful trips by submarine to try to join Broome. He then got himself trained as a parachutist:

> Eventually the time came when we were to receive our first drop of men and supplies from an aeroplane, and it was a most fantastically exciting moment. We were on this dropping zone, lighting enormous fires in case they shouldn't see us, and down these bodies came. And the third one to come down was Ah

Chuan. I didn't know this, but he came marching over in full regalia, with his uniform and his parachute wings on, saluted smartly, brought out a cigarette case and said, 'Have a cigarette! I know you've been waiting for one of these for a year.'

On duty in the bungalow the servants were always immaculately turned out: 'Even if they lived in the tiniest little hovel, their clothes were starched and they always looked beautiful when they came out. The men wore these starched white *tutup* jackets, which were always tight up to the neck, and white Chinese trousers. Then the *amah* wore either a white or blue *baju*, a short-sleeved and rather long blouse, and loose Chinese trousers, sometimes patterned but usually black.' It was considered to be rather bad form for the *mem* to visit either the servants' quarters or the kitchen:

> The whole business of overseeing meals was done by word of mouth. The reason was that one trusted one's staff to be clean and reliable and to handle food properly. But also the kitchen would be one of about four or five rooms rather like cells but made quite comfortable by the boy, the cook and the water-carrier, who would be lounging about on their veranda in fairly casual clothes. When you called or summoned your boy he would be very quick to put on his trousers and jacket and come in, but he wouldn't be wearing them when he was in the kitchen quarters and so one didn't go there. Then if they had wives and children they would also be living there at the back so it was an invasion of their privacy to go and see them there.

Much of the cooking was done on the simplest wood-burning stoves, or even over open fires. Ovens were frequently shaped out of the ubiquitous and invaluable kerosene (paraffin) tin – 'a square, deep tin like a large biscuit tin which was very much a common-place item in the East'. Yet with this primitive equipment miracles in the way of cooking were performed by the better cooks – although it was also true to say that a lot of the food came from tins. There were additional drawbacks to a high standard of cuisine in the form of a climate that very quickly turned food bad and encouraged weevils and maggots: 'Flour and rice had to be spread out in the hot sunshine on a mat and these creatures would then crawl away. Then the flour would be sieved and it and your rice would be put back into their containers.' There was also a permanent battle to be waged against ants. 'The two things I found continually trying all the time I was in Malaya were ants and mosquitoes,' admits Nancy Madoc:

> The mosquitoes never stopped biting me; everywhere I went I had to have a smudge stick which is one of these coils that you light. It sends out a sort of spicy incense smell and it does keep the mosquitoes away. But it was the ants that really got me down because they were everywhere. You only had to drop a spot of sugar on the floor and in no time there was a trail of ants coming towards it and dragging it away. They got in amongst your handkerchiefs and they were in the food unless you watched like a hawk. You put the legs of your food-safe into bowls of paraffin and unless you did that the place was just a teeming mass of ants. They also went for flowers and plants and I eventually decided that Malaya was built on an antheap, with ants everywhere.

Such little difficulties were never enough to discourage the high degree of entertaining by which members of an often widely-scattered European community kept in contact with each other. On more formal luncheon and dinner parties the *mem* had to ensure that the table was properly arranged so that government officers were seated in accordance with their rank, beginning with the most senior man present being placed on his hostess's right and his wife on the host's right. But with the official and non-official worlds so closely connected, such formality was rarely taken too seriously. And, increasingly in the Thirties, the old custom of dressing for dinner no longer prevailed except for the more formal dinner parties: 'Generally all we did was to change into decent clean clothes in the evening. There had been a time when this business of changing regularly for dinner really did maintain; it had something to do with the discipline of keeping up one's self-respect. Inevitably it got simplified but still people felt that a certain standard was needed if one was not to let oneself go completely. This even happened later on in prison camp, when some of the men always managed to shave somehow, whereas others grew their beards and whiskers right away from the beginning.'

Both in the towns and in the *ulu* the most popular means of entertaining at home took the form of the Sunday curry tiffin, the only significant difference between town and country being that in the towns, where there were more women present, drinking gave way to eating a little sooner – 'but never before two o'clock'. The food was the same throughout the archipelago:

> When you went in you started off with mulligatawny soup, and then a really good hot curry with a lot of *sambals*, which were little side dishes like coconut, banana and fruit and all sorts of things like that to put on your curry, which was sometimes almost too hot but very good, a huge meal generally. After that you were expected to have your sweet, which was always a thing called *gula Malacca*, a cold sago with two sauces, one coconut cream and the other *gula*, which was palm-tree sugar of a very dark colour; an absolutely delicious sweet. After you'd had all that all you could do was long to get away and pass out on your bed for the rest of the day.

There was a very great difference between the everyday lives of the *mems* in the bigger towns and those who lived in more spartan surroundings up-country. In the former 'the community that one lived with and knew was entirely

European and one lived for entertaining, for the club, and for seeing other people'. The bungalows were more comfortable and up-to-date and there were more creature comforts and amusements to hand. In the district, by contrast, most bungalows were built to the same basic pattern by the PWD and filled with PWD furniture, so that 'if you got a house that looked rather different you felt very pleased'. Beyond putting up her own curtains – 'which were never pulled but looked pretty' – installing her own plant pots on the stairs and veranda, adding one or two of her own pieces of furniture and her own pictures on the walls, and making sure the servants kept the house clean and the floors polished 'with a mixture of beeswax and paraffin applied with a coconut husk', there was little a *mem* could do to make a real home for herself and her husband. As a junior *mem* she was expected to toe the line and to defer to the senior *mem* of the district who sometimes would 'help the younger wives under her and give them advice as regards running their homes and in the way they ought to behave towards the local people' – but who also in some instances 'made it her business to pronounce on the behaviour of others'.

When Madeline Daubeny came to Sarawak as a newly-wed in 1933 she expected to find a small European community 'full of backbiting and scratching'. Yet although 'people came from every conceivable social background – which in those days meant so much more than it does today – this was completely swallowed up in the ordinary fellowship and friendship of living in a small place together. Most of the men had made it fairly clear to their wives before they brought them out what they were coming to, so they made friends with each other and were pretty happy. Very few marriages broke up and there were almost no romantic scandals.' It was equally apparent that there were really two kinds of *mems*:

Some of the wives came from very limited backgrounds and they were usually the ones who were disturbed and upset by conditions. They'd been given no idea what to expect and they did have problems – although I don't think we had the Somerset Maugham type of *mem* who was responsible for the stories and reputation that *mems* had all over the place. Of course, there were one or two who were difficult. There was one I know who used to keep her husband from going to the club when she didn't want him to by making him change into pyjamas early for dinner. But the wives who went up-country were a different kind of woman on the whole; they were usually the ones who had some idea of what they were going to cope with and so they did cope.

Madeline Daubeny was herself one of Sarawak's first generation of 'outstation wives' who accompanied their husbands to the more remote district headquarters up-river, and her husband, Dick Daubeny, was one of that heroic cadre of administrators who had gone out to Sarawak straight from school: 'Dick was nineteen when he first went out in 1921 or 1922 and after a very few months from then on for the next eleven years he was in places where he was practically the only European. The isolation was so great for these young men and they were such boys.' She had known his parents for some time before she actually met their son:

I'd always heard about this adored son who was due to come back on leave after nearly eleven years in the Far East, but when I did meet him and he told me how isolated and lonely and cut off his areas were I didn't like the sound of the life he lived. However, I fell in love with him and it was as easy as that. He had to go back in the autumn and I arranged to come out and marry him in Penang the following year, and during the time I was engaged Dick saw that I found out as much as he could arrange for me about Sarawak. He gave me books that were highly romantic and not at all reliable but they did give me the first idea that he was anxious that I should accept the existence of native 'companions'. This was something so eminently sensible that I saw no reason to create about it. Most English wives of that time were people like myself who were not easily shocked by this sort of thing. We were sensible enough and old enough not to be romantically influenced against the notions of such an arrangement but to accept it as something that was there and had happened and was past – and I must say very strongly that I entirely approved of this attitude.

However, the custom of keeping *nyai* did take 'a little bit of sorting out' when the first European wives began to live up-country:

Very soon a sort of convention was adopted which was that if you visited a household where there was a Dayak woman in the background she didn't appear. It was rather silly but it saved a lot of embarrassment because it is awfully important to remember the climate of opinion of the day. But it was a little disconcerting sometimes if you were having lunch with two or three men by themselves and a baby started to cry not so very far away. Of course, it was always accepted that this was the cook's child that was crying – although the children of these associations were always cared for by the fathers. They took their fathers' names and when they were older they were sent to the mission boarding schools so that they were properly brought up, even if the fathers did eventually separate themselves from their children and from that life.

After a couple of days in Kuching the Daubenys set out in a government launch, which took them out to sea and then sixty miles up the Batang Lupar river in Simanggang:

The whole European content of Simanggang had arrived to meet me and was standing on the wharf; there were three of them. I was of course not only the only woman but the first

European woman ever to live there. So I was going to be a great nuisance to these men, who had never worried about their language, their behaviour, their alcohol intake or anything else and now they knew they were more or less going to have to – although they were very good about it, I must admit – because it was really awful for them to have a woman suddenly invading them. Anyway, we climbed up the steps onto the jetty and a prison gang of about eight men were then told to unload our luggage and I was appalled in my innocence and ignorance to see that two or three of the men had shackles and chains on their ankles. As I had just come from seeing a romantic film with Paul Muni in it, called 'I Was a Prisoner in a Chain Gang', this thing shook me cold. However, I soon discovered that the whole attitude towards prisoners was extremely light-hearted. There was a euphemism for being a prisoner which was *tolong perintah* meaning 'helping the government', because all the prison gang normally did was to scythe the coarse grass round the area of the station, the official part of Simanggang, and the nine-hole golf course which was only a golf course by the skin of its teeth. In fact, I very soon discovered that one of them was going to be our *tukang ayer*, the scullery boy. He was not actually chained in the ordinary way, but he was a murderer, who had been given a life sentence for killing his wife's lover. His name was Jokmin, he was Chinese, he was absolutely splendid and we adored him.

However, some time later the Rajah came on a visit to Simanggang and to mark the occasion it was customary for the Rajah to grant certain favours: 'We were so fond of our Jokmin that we asked the Rajah if his life-sentence could be quashed. It was; and within twenty-four hours Jokmin had left us to go back to a life of freedom.'

Once settled into her bungalow Madeline Daubeny soon got used to the regular daily routine that begun at six with morning tea and fruit on the veranda:

Dick went off to the office at eight, before it was too hot, and I was then supposed to speak to the cook, Ah Kit, which was a frightful problem at the beginning. However, I very soon managed to learn the basic kitchen Malay, which was a very bad kind of Malay that all wives learned to speak, so that I was able to take down the cook's shopping list. Later on, of course, I spoke quite reasonable Malay so that eventually I was able to give him complicated and elaborate instructions on new recipes.

The Daubenys would have lunch together and then while her husband went back to his office – 'rather hot and disgruntled because the afternoons were very, very hot' – Madeline Daubeny would have a lie-off: 'On our beds we had a thing called a "Dutch wife", which was used throughout the whole East Indies. It was a firm bolster which you stretched a leg over and was very comfortable and cool.' Her husband reappeared at tea time, which was followed by a game of badminton or a round of golf with the other European men on the golf course or a walk through the edge of the jungle, 'because these settlements were just tiny clearings in an endless, interminable, tall, dense, wild jungle. Sometimes a hornbill would fly across the clearing and this was a most uncanny experience because it flew with a noise exactly like a very old-fashioned self-starter.' All round the outstation was the green wall of the rain forest:

The great feeling the jungle gave one was of enclosure because if you went into it you could only walk along known paths which were very uneven and very overgrown. It was a very 'Alice in Wonderland' feeling, because every plant would have a stem perhaps three or four inches in diameter and be fifteen or twenty feet tall, so what would have been a wild flower or a weed in an ordinary woodland as we know it, was grown to an immense size. At the same time it could be so sappy that one cut with a *parang* would slash it down very easily indeed. But jungle walking was limited only to paths that were little tunnels through the jungle, something like the tunnels that a pheasant makes through an English field, with the trees themselves making a close ceiling high overhead, a hundred and fifty to two hundred feet up. Any flowers there might be were quite invisible way overhead on the jungle ceiling and the only reason you got to know that they might be there was if there were one or two dead blossoms on the floor of the jungle. It was a very strange world; a secret place and very alarming. There were always birds calling, whistling, mocking, but seldom seen. The one thing you did see fairly often were monkeys, because they travelled about in such tribes that you heard them and then you looked for them and usually saw the movement of the trees and branches as they flung themselves around.

Twilight and dusk always came with predictable regularity – and with it the visitors of the evening:

That was the signal to go and sit on the veranda and have a drink, although, as often as not, we sat in the sitting room, because of the mosquitoes. I got almost bitten to death when I first arrived. Mosquitoes love somebody new and I don't know why I should have tasted better but I clearly did, although eventually I got hardened to it and it didn't worry me too much. But these evenings had one particular highlight which terrified me that first time it happened, and always made me jump a little bit. After darkness had fallen, one could be sitting quite quietly talking or reading and suddenly there in the large open door would be a party of some six or eight Dayaks always dressed in the proper Dayak rig; a beautifully draped scarlet loincloth, black and silver calf and wrist bangles and some superb tattooing on their coffee-coloured skins. Even the old men looked fine and the young men were very striking. But when you'd no idea they were there it was extremely alarming. So they would be welcomed in and given little tots of neat gin which

went down with a smack. Then they would have a long talk
to Dick about their own troubles and worries.

Not every *mem* appreciated these visitations: 'Many years
later one of our District Officers got engaged to an English girl
from Malaya and when she saw this ceremony of the Dayaks
arriving for the evening drink and chat for the first time she
was appalled. She'd come from a rubber garden where her
planter family had always kept the "natives" at bay.'
Sometimes after the last visitors had gone the air would be
filled with the sound of drumming late into the night:

> I never got used to the drums, they were always romantic to
> me and they would be either for some wedding or perhaps
> there would be a party going down- or up-river to a celebra-
> tion with the drums going as they travelled. The drums were
> really brass gongs and the most elaborate kind was called an
> *engkerumong* which was an array of about four or five held in a
> long straight wooden tray. They varied in size and note and
> they would play the most beautiful diatonic scale on them.

There were exotic sights to be seen at night, such as 'a tree
in the grounds alive with fireflies, much more beautiful in their
flickering way than the glow-worms of England' or the
nocturnal antics of a pet honey bear that 'used to shuffle
round the bungalow at night crying for honey and attention
and which kept us awake and had to be given away.'
For Madeline Daubeny, as for many young *mems*, the 'great
problem was how to occupy my time. I hadn't yet learned to
become a gardener, which I did later on, but I did love
drawing and so I drew a great deal. But I wasn't actually
lonely. I was an only child, fairly self-contained and able to
amuse myself – but it was difficult without plenty of books. I
missed books very much indeed – far more than I missed
people. In fact, it wasn't until long afterwards that I realized
that in six months I'd never even seen another white woman.

Then, fortunately I suppose, my first pregnancy intervened and that changed the whole situation.'

Shortly before the baby was due the Daubenys were moved to a new posting in Kuching but otherwise no concessions to her condition were made or expected: 'Nobody gave me any warning whatsoever about possible snags or miscarriages. The only thing I was told was that I ought to walk as much as possible. So I was blissfully unaware of some of the things that could just possibly have happened to me, which was just as well, since the journey back to civilization took anything from a full thirty-six hours to two days and a night and there was no medical help whatsoever in our place except a partly-trained dresser who could bandage or carry out first aid.'

Another Sarawak administrator's wife was Daphne Richards, who found that pregnancy and motherhood were a great help in breaking down social barriers when her husband was away on tour and she was left on her own:

> If I was lonely and wanted to talk to someone in English I used to walk to the Roman Catholic mission which was about a mile away and I often met people from the *kampong* or the bazaar on my way and they would say to me, '*Makan angin kah?*' which means 'Are you taking the air?' or literally, 'eating the air', and I would say, 'Yes I was.' Then they would say, '*Selamat jalan*', which is 'Good luck on your path', and I would say, '*Selamat tinggal*', which means 'Good luck to you who is staying behind'. They were always very friendly, the people there, and when they saw that I was pregnant they'd always enquire about this and be very interested and want to know where and when the baby was going to be born.

Three of her children were born in Sarawak and their presence always aroused great interest:

> I remember on many occasions someone stopping me – probably a Chinese who didn't speak Malay – and asking

me a question as to whether it was a boy or a girl and either not understanding what I said or not believing it and finally undoing the baby's nappy to have a look to see whether it was a boy or a girl. They frequently commented on how big your baby was for its age or how well it looked and they would therefore ask questions as to how you fed it and they were most surprised to find that a European woman breast-fed her baby. I quite frequently visited either Malay or Chinese or Iban houses and I would feed the baby there to great interest. It was the natural thing to do and no one thought anything of it.

There were, of course, disadvantages in bringing up a European child in the tropics: 'You couldn't wrap a restless baby up; I tried this once or twice with the very thinnest of cotton sheets and found the baby absolutely covered in prickly heat next morning – but, on the other hand, it was certainly an advantage in that babies needed very few clothes.' Illnesses could be 'quite frightening because the children developed high temperatures very quickly and as for most of my time I was in an outstation where there was no doctor usually within fifty to a hundred miles, this was quite scaring because you just didn't know what might happen.' Then there were such diseases as hookworm, 'so you couldn't let your child go around barefoot, which they very much wanted to do', and the rare but ever-present risk of being bitten by a scorpion or a snake:

When my daughter was about two years old, I remember, my husband and I were having our breakfast and she'd gone down the steps just outside the house where we could hear her laughing like anything. After a minute or two we wondered what on earth she was laughing about, so we went out to have a look and outside at the bottom of the steps there was a narrow drain and she was leaning over and there was a kitten with her and the kitten was pawing at something. We went closer and saw what the kitten was pawing at was a very large scorpion and my daughter was reaching down to pick this up. Fortunately, we caught them in time because the bite of a scorpion of that size could have killed a child of her age and it certainly would have killed the kitten.

Madeline Daubeny had a very similar experience with her son: 'Instead of putting him in his cot while she prepared the bath the *amah*, for some reason, put him on a bed. When she'd finished bathing him she threw the towel on the cot and a black cobra came out of the cot and slid through the bathroom and out.'

Despite the dangers and difficulties many European children thrived in the tropics: 'My children now look back on their early lives in Sarawak with great affection and almost as a sort of paradise,' declares Daphne Richards. 'Their first language was Malay and when we spoke to them in English they would always answer in Malay, because we were frequently the only Europeans where we were living and their companions of their own age were always children who spoke Malay or possibly Iban.' There were infrequent trips to the Malayan hill-stations and more frequent visits to the palm-fringed beaches that were never far away. At Christmas the branch of a casuarina tree served as a Christmas tree and a traditional Christmas dinner would be celebrated with locally-made plum pudding and cold-storage turkey from Australia.

But a time always came when the children had to be sent away: 'When the children reached the age of seven or eight they really needed to go home to school. Although there were local mission schools in many places the standard was not very high and children who were kept out later than that found they were very behind when they got home.' Their mothers had then to make a decision between staying with their children in England or with their husbands. The choice was never easy and many compromised, spending some time in England until their children had settled into their boarding schools and then returning to their husbands. 'It seemed to us at the time that there really was no other choice,' states Daphne Richards, 'but my children took it quite for granted because their friends were doing the same sort of thing.'

The European *mem* certainly had her critics. There were those who saw her as coming between her menfolk and the land in which they had chosen to spend their working lives. But if there was 'the occasional *mem* who lived a rather frivolous life and only occupied herself with her own home and surroundings and parties and socializing', then there were also others who in increasing numbers learned to take discomfort and physical hardship in their stride, and who made an effort to 'become involved in the local community, finding voluntary work to do and getting on very well with all members of the community'. They were themselves pioneers in their own way. 'We lived through things without noticing what was happening,' declares Madeline Daubeny, 'yet there was certainly a very great drama in the way we were living when I first went out there. Looking back, it's strange how we took it all for granted.'

10

The Four Sisters

This account of childhood in Malaya between the wars was first broadcast – in a more extended version – on Radio 4 on 25 December 1982 as the last programme in the first series of Tales from the South China Seas. *The four sisters were the daughters of the rubber planter Mark John Kennaway and his wife Dorothy.*

SUSAN: There were four of us daughters actually, my sister Ann, followed by my sister Elizabeth who was born in England on leave. And then Pippa and then myself, Susan, born in 1928.

ANN: We used to laugh at my father because – coming out from England – Escot was a kingdom of its own and my father was the ruler . . . Escot was surrounded by jungle. And he was always fascinated by it. He would look at the blue hills in the distance and say what wealth was underneath . . .

SUSAN: My father, Mark John Kennaway, when he was nineteen was given the opportunity to go out to Ceylon under the manager of a tea estate and learn what he could of planting methods. He embarked for Ceylon in 1899 and the family he left behind was typical of many young men who went out to the East in those days. He was the second son of a country clergyman in Northamptonshire. They lived in a nice old rectory with old oak furniture and their days were spent, the women certainly, doing good works, attending church services and serving afternoon tea in the drawing room, and I think many men like my father must have escaped from that kind of life with relief.

ANN: Well, my father was not exactly the black sheep of the family, but he was less docile, I think, than the others. They used to pack them off to the colonies in those days. Then after about three years, he went over to Malaya, where Mr Ridley had just discovered that rubber could be grown. And my father went over to see what the chances were.

SUSAN: His devoted family came to see him off. We have a photograph in our album of him on that day. His father was wearing a clerical black hat and a black suit and his step-mother and sister with their wasp-waists and large picture hats. A Salvation Army band had also come on board to see off one of their number and my grandfather insisted that they joined in the hymns, as it would do equally well for my father. And it's easy to guess their apprehension at that time because the estate he was going to, Batu caves, was an area notorious for malaria and diseases, and they could possibly have never seen him again. About a third of the work-force had been carried off by malaria and in fact most planters reckoned to spend one week a month laid up with malaria.

Looking at our photograph albums there are so many pictures of clearings of the jungle and small rubber trees being planted and a proud young man, my father, standing looking at them. It was a very exciting time. There was a feeling of expansion and something new in the air – one can sense it from looking at the photograph albums. In 1909 he took over a small rubber estate and called it Escot Estate, after his uncle's house in Devon, whose forebears had been in the East India Company at the end of the eighteenth century.

ANN: I remember that the steps from the front door led up to the hall at Escot in Devon, there were always big pots of ferns and flowers on either side. And my father had done the same thing, in a Malayan way, at Escot Estate.

SUSAN: There was always a porch to cover you from the tropical rain and you went upstairs – the house was built on stilts – up a long flight of steps with lots of flower pots everywhere – and upstairs you went into a huge veranda room.

ELIZABETH: When we got to the top of the steps there was an enormous veranda and in the middle of it there was this very, very ornately carved Ceylonese table with elephants' tusks for feet which had been a wedding present to my mother. The doors that led off were stable doors. They swung to and fro and I never learned to shut a door for ages afterwards when I got back to England.

ANN: Escot Estate as such was simply jungle. And gradually the jungle was cut down and rubber trees were planted. And he went back to England to try and raise money later on for this wonderful new development.

SUSAN: On his leave in England he was given the chance to place so many shares in the Cecily Rubber Company, which was floated in 1904, and he did a grand tour of his relatives who were rather stiff-backed and he begged and implored them to buy but they refused to take them up, and only Jones, the family butler in his uncle's house in Devon, bought some and I'm glad to say he became later a very wealthy man.

ANN: Well, by 1910 or 1912 there was a tremendous rubber boom. And when he went back home on leave the second time, he was richer than any of his family put together.

SUSAN: It was very much a life for a man. There were no European women in the district at all. And the first woman came out and reigned, as my father said, for one year. And the second one came out and when she arrived she unpacked her things and the first lady came round to ask her if she could help her and she said no. So when the second lady had unpacked she sat back and waited for the first one to call and a tremendous row broke out in the district with all the bachelors taking sides as to whether she'd called or she hadn't and my father very much enjoyed this.

ANN: My mother came from Yorkshire. Her father was a wine merchant who had gone bankrupt when she was about sixteen. And she went up to London and tried the stage, and she was very successful. She had a lot of push.

ELIZABETH: She was very much a person of her age, the 1920s.

ANN: And she did end up once playing the lead in the West End. It was one of our bedtime stories.

SUSAN: My parents met when my father was on leave in London and they became engaged, and my father went back to Malaya.

ANN: My mother came out two or three months later, and was married on the beach, as my father used to say, and then they went back to Escot Estate, which of course was very primitive. But my mother was very happy I'm sure, in those first years. They had a very good time.

ELIZABETH: Before I was born there was a river that used to run right across the entrance to the estate, and when it rained the river used to flood the bridge and nobody could get in. My parents used to take a bearer with their evening clothes and their bathing costumes, and when the river was in flood they would swim across the river with the bearer carrying their evening dress, and dress the other side of the river and walk, scramble, up a hill where the train crossed, and stop the train and go to Kuala Lumpur and have the evening out.

SUSAN: Rubber was booming and the smart young women of the Twenties came out as brides, and sisters came out on visits and pretty English governesses came out to look after the growing families, and romances blossomed and our photograph albums are filled with weddings and visits to the races and fancy dress parties.

And my father started the rafting parties of Tanjong Malim. He would have rafts made of bamboo and early in the morning they would meet at a point up the river and sail down, two on a raft, shooting down the rapids, with cold beer laid in various corners of the river to keep cool as they went down. And at the end they would all end up with a huge curry tiffin, I believe, at the Tanjong Malim Club.

My mother enjoyed that life very much, but she said sometimes that she felt she was enclosed by a wall of rubber on the estate, as the trees were surrounding the garden and stretched for miles and miles on end in every direction.

ANN: Being very much wanted, as our parents had married late in life, I think we were very spoiled. We had *amahs* to look after us and all the servants on the estate, as I remember, doted on us. We had Chinese *amahs* mostly, although Susan had a Malay *amah* who was called Denlora Perian, which I always thought was a lovely name. And I think we had a very happy, unspoilt, uncluttered early childhood.

SUSAN: Every time a new baby was born my parents would throw another bedroom and bathroom onto the bungalow and soon it became a very sprawling, very comfortable home. The stilts down below were filled in and a dining room was made and windows with shutters and there was a huge lawn outside of very coarse grass – it was quite a pride of my father's, this lawn – and a tennis court and canna beds. The cannas in Malaya were everywhere. They grew in people's gardens; bright orange and red flowers. And we had beds of them always round the house and there were some bougainvillaea and other plants I can't remember. And beyond the garden surrounding the lawns were the rubber trees – hundreds and hundreds of them in monotonous straight rows – these long alleyways of nothing.

ANN: The jungle was there. I just accepted it, as part of my background, where animals lived. My only fear, I remember, was tigers.

ELIZABETH: One day we woke up to find in the garden the marks of a tiger, footprints; he'd been walking through the garden.

ANN: And from then on afterwards, I always had this dreadful dream that there was a tiger over my cot! I remember we walked down to the end of the garden and I kept expecting the tiger to come – I never realized these marks in the ground were anything to do with him. It was a totally happy period.

SUSAN: I can remember my father calling for the 'boy' at four o'clock every morning for his cup of tea and his 'boy' who'd been with him for thirty years would bring it to him. There was a great understanding between them and he would have his tea and get up in his *sarong* and go to his desk and write for the next two hours.

ANN: Then we'd have tea on the lawn, which was one of the nicest times of the day 'cause it was cool. My father would go off and do his rounds. And then he would come back about nine, and we'd have breakfast, and then he'd go off again. And after breakfast I suppose we played about in the morning. Everybody slept in the afternoons till four. And by five o'clock or six o'clock we were down at the tennis club and it was getting cooler. We'd play around with the other children of the Europeans while the parents played tennis or drank at the bar, and then we must have been taken home about seven or eight and put to bed. Little beds and big beds, you know, with big mosquito nets.

SUSAN: And I can remember last thing at night lying inside these great white net cages and the lights faded down and all was dark and then the sounds of the jungle outside would begin to be heard – the jungle was never far below the surface in Malaya.

SUSAN: We have a photograph of the whole household, my parents and us, and the staff in the bungalow and there seem to be quite a number of them, standing at the back.

ANN: But Hi Ho was the constant one, he had five little sons and a fat wife.

ELIZABETH: Hi Ho the houseboy was really the key figure in the home. He was the man who employed the *amahs* for my mother.

ANN: And he was the one who appeared if you shouted and he would serve the drinks and serve the food. There was Cookie, he was a Chinese. Then there was the gardener who was called the *kebun*, I remember, he'd cut the lawn with a scythe. He was usually Javanese or Malay. And the chauffeur, or *syce*, he was a Malay. Father had a car, a large Ford, but then later on he bought my mother an Austin Seven as a present and there's a photograph of us all piled in this Austin Seven; father, mother, four children and the governess.

SUSAN: It was very comfortable, but there were disadvantages. All food had to be kept in meatsafes, standing in bowls of water, otherwise the ants would have got to the food in minutes. Home leave clothes were kept in tin trunks, otherwise they would go green with mould.

Unfortunately, in 1931–32 the price of rubber fell to five cents a pound and many planters were forced out of business.

SUSAN: We had to go back to England and my father stayed on and they were very bad days I believe.

PIPPA: My mother took a very small maisonette in London into which we all piled and we were extremely hard-up. So much so that my father couldn't afford to join us.

ELIZABETH: My father, to keep the estate going, wrote out horoscopes which he bought from Woolworth's at sixpence each. These were a great success because the Chinese love anything to do with astrology and he made quite a lot of money which kept him going.

ANN: And my father came back to us every three years, or three-and-a-half years.

PIPPA: When he finally did come home I remember nanny saying to my mother, it's just as if he'd been down to the pillar box and come back; meaning that we had all accepted him so quickly and readily. He wasn't what I expected; a tall bronzed man with a *topee* who could look well on a horse. He was a little man with a keen sense of humour and a huge trunk full of trinkets and toys and dolls and snuff boxes and all sorts of treasures that he'd brought home for us.

ANN: And those were lovely times. He'd arrive from off the ship with boxes of Turkish Delight he'd got at Simon Artz in Port Said, and Japanese dolls, I remember he brought back. And the time always went too quickly. He had to cram all the treats that normal fathers would give us in three-and-a-half years, into six months. And then, sadly enough, he'd go off again, on the P&O. We'd all be very sad after he'd gone. Although we grew up in London, my mother always talked as though our home was in Malaya at Escot. And all our plans were geared towards the life we would live out there, not an English life at all.

ELIZABETH: In the summer of 1939, when the war came, my mother decided to take Ann and I back to Malaya. The other two were left behind in England.

ANN: Probably it was one of the last P&O boats in the pre-war luxury style, and my sister and I had only just stopped being schoolgirls. We thoroughly revelled in all the luxury, the great long menus which we ate our way through.

At night after Port Said, there was no more blackout, and the boat deck was lit with coloured lights, and the band played and we danced with young naval officers. I think because I was seventeen, it was very romantic. It could never come again. But the beautiful sky, the stars in the sky and the sun on the sea, and you had this feeling that you were sailing away, away from the war in Europe.

My father drove us from Penang to Escot Estate. And it was strange coming back. Things that you'd forgotten about came back to you. And many faces were looking slightly older, like Hi Ho. My sister and I ran round looking in each room – I looked at my nursery which hadn't been used for ten years and was just – just there. The dining room was the same. The silver all set out on one side and kept clean. And the veranda of course had altered rather – sort of large divans, with brightly coloured cushions, and the pictures which were Renaissance beauties. The rhythm of life hadn't altered.

Susan: And my sister Pippa and I, who were at school in
England, returned to Malaya in June–July of 1940.

Pippa: I remember how delighted Sue and I were with the
bungalow, we had no idea our family owned anything as
grand. Over the next few days my sister and I were
introduced to all the various servants round the house
and were most impressed. We had no idea our father
was so rich and important.

Susan: The boom days were over and life had changed quite
considerably when we came back. Our wooden bungalow
was definitely becoming old-fashioned, although it was still
very much part of our lives. The bathroom attached to
every bedroom was really a concrete floor with a galvanized
tin tub and a *tong* of cold water which you could dip in and
splash all over yourself, and when you wanted a bath you
called out and someone brought a bucket of hot water up
the backstairs and you could sit and wash yourself in this tin
tub and end up with a wonderful douche of cold water.

There weren't nearly so many planters in the district of
Tanjong Malim and the club had been built for so many
more people and there were rows of chairs, long cane chairs
with a hole in the arm for the glass, but they were never all
filled and the magazines would be on the side tables and
rarely read, I think.

Pippa: I think my parents must have been quite hard put to
occupy us, but my father was always very good to me in the
way that he would always give me a game of tennis, both at
home at the bungalow, and at the club. We also watched
him at work on the estate and directing operations there. I
remember saying to my father, why did he always have to
shout at his staff and why did he never praise them for what
they'd done? And he told me that if he did, they wouldn't do
anything the following day.

I was thirteen and the novelty of being in the tropics and
of being able to bathe in a jungle river and go to Kuala
Lumpur and have shoes built for me by people who drew a

line round my foot and produced them the following day – all this was terribly exciting. Our greatest treat was to go to Kuala Lumpur which we did I think most Saturdays.

SUSAN: We'd be shopping in the morning perhaps, having clothes made, taking patterns along and having them very skilfully made up into dresses and then in the afternoon perhaps we'd go to the cinema, and then drive home.

I remember one drive particularly. There was a lovely ring round the moon and these villages were bright and alive and there were children up at ten o'clock at night running about and stalls outside with people cooking and there was a smell of the East.

ELIZABETH: I can remember also the utter boredom and loneliness of it all, because I was only sixteen and like the heroine of *When The Rains Came* by Louis Bromfield, there was absolutely nothing and one had the feeling one was waiting for something to happen.

ANN: I loved the exotic flowers and the luscious fruits, and the feeling of the vast areas of jungle that man had never been in. And the rain; the storms were exciting, they came from Sumatra, with a sudden rush of hot wind.

Sometimes we would go and swim in the Slim River Pool which was a waterfall in the middle of the jungle. And we'd walk along the path with leaves, great big leaves barring our way. We'd push our way through and there, in the darkness of the jungle, was this lovely waterfall, where the water cascaded down; you could dive in and swim. That was Christmas 1940; that was the last Christmas that our family spent all together for a great number of years.

I suppose that life was never the same for me after that. It was the end of something – I never went back – and I never went back to that total family life, when I was a child in the family in my home.

So I took the night train, on 1 January 1941, down to Singapore – *very* excited because I thought my life was beginning.

ELIZABETH: When Ann went off to Singapore I was very envious and very determined to follow her.

ANN: I started off very patriotically, wanting to do war work and I did always have the war in mind so that I wasn't entirely frivolous, but you couldn't help being frivolous, there wasn't anything else but social life and very little cultural life. I'd met a young man in the Cameron Highlands and I realized that my office was going to be next to his, and of course I had fallen in love with him.

Raffles Hotel I went to quite a lot, there was always dancing on Wednesday nights and Saturday nights and although it seemed rather shabby in the daytime, at night-time it came to life with tables amongst potted palms with little individual lights, and we danced to tunes that had been hit tunes six months ago in Britain like *In the Mood*, or swayed to *Begin the Beguine*.

ELIZABETH: I used to feel terribly gauche and I remember one woman whom I saw, whom I admired very much, in a beautiful white dress one evening, and later she gave her life saving people from a ship which was full of women and children. She swam from the ship to the shore time after time with these women and eventually she sank, exhausted.

On 7 December 1941, Singapore was attacked and Malaya was at war.

ANN: Jerry and I had been at Tanglin Club all day sitting in the sun by the pool as we usually did on a Sunday, and in the evening we went to the cinema. I remember saying good night to Jerry on the mansion steps, a lovely full moon shining, and I went to bed, went to sleep. Four hours later I was in a deep sleep, and we heard the sirens; they woke us up.

My sister turned on the light and I remember spitting at her and saying, 'Turn it off, you silly, the war's begun' and she said, 'Oh no, look, the street light's on outside', and in fact everybody was saying that, saying 'Oh well it's only a practice, the street lights are on.'

ELIZABETH: At that moment there was a terrible bang and we all came running down the stairs to the hall. And we could –

as the mansion house was on a hill – look down over the town and see the lights of the cinema going round and round, coloured: *The Road to Rio*, with Dorothy Lamour, Bob Hope and Bing Crosby.

PIPPA: I can remember seeing Japanese planes circling round our garden and waving to them thinking that they were our planes and being horrified to discover that they were Japanese.

SUSAN: I can remember too how we went down to the main road to wave to the lorryloads of troops who were going up north. And they gave us a tremendous cheer when they saw us. And it was shattering a few days later to see some lorries returning with very weary, tired-looking men and it was at that time I think I realized that something was really wrong.

ELIZABETH: Even though there was a lot going on in Singapore there was also a knowledge of what was happening. And there was the mounting terror which was creeping in.

SUSAN: We left our bungalow on Christmas Eve, my mother and my sister Pippa and I, and made our way down to Singapore. I remember feeling at any rate with relief that I wasn't going to go back to school for the next term.

ANN: On New Year's Eve, my mother eventually arrived in Singapore with my two younger sisters, and an aunt in what was then Rhodesia had cabled and said, 'Send them to me and I'll look after them, the two younger ones.' My other sister, Elizabeth and I said, 'Oh, we can't leave, we've got war jobs', and at the time it seemed quite right.

SUSAN: My father had stayed behind in Tanjong Malim with the local defence corps and he was told that he was too old to fight at sixty-two, so he left Tanjong Malim. I believe he was the last European to leave there, and he then made his way down to Singapore.

PIPPA: My sister was working at army headquarters and her commanding officer asked her to send my father to see him. They were very anxious to enroll men in the army who could speak the local languages and my father went along and was delighted to be told he could falsify his age and take on the rank of captain. This pleased him particularly as he had previously been a private in the Home Guard.

ANN: By January we had air raids in the day-time as well as night-time and I remember sitting in the Cricket Club one lunch-time when the sirens went. I looked across the street and I remember seeing a poor old rickshaw coolie looking rather bewildered as the sirens went, and the next thing was, there was a bang and I saw him lying on the pavement with blood coming out of his mouth. It was the first time I had witnessed death.

PIPPA: Despite the increasing frequency of the air raids my sister Susan and I managed to enjoy ourselves. We swam a great deal at the Tanglin Club and the Swimming Club. I honestly believe that my mother was the one person in Singapore who was quite certain it was going to fall.

ANN: My mother by then was getting desperate to get these children away and a woman said to my mother, 'Whatever boat comes, I'm getting on it with my baby, and if you like I'll take your two younger ones, because I eventually want to go to South Africa, and I will deliver them to their aunt.' So my mother agreed – that was how my two young sisters went off to Australia all by themselves.

PIPPA: We sailed off happily enough, unfortunately I can't remember saying goodbye to my parents or sisters, but we eventually arrived in Fremantle, and it was only during a visit to a post office, where I heard some English voices, that I suddenly realized that we were a long way from home – and for the first time I felt homesick and afraid.

ANN: I was totally in cloud cuckoo land. I imagined that there'd be a siege of Singapore and we'd endure it hero-ically, like the people of Malta and the British in the Blitz, but that day Churchill made a speech in the House of Commons, saying that there would be no help for Singa-pore, and I think that then reality took over because the following day most of the office had been evacuated; there was just a skeleton staff there. I saw my father on the steps of the Cathay Building, and he said to me, 'You've got quarter-of-an-hour. You're to pack a suitcase, and I'm taking you to the docks.' And of course I argued, and said, 'I'm needed – I need to do war work,' and so on. And for once in his life he was absolutely firm with us and I went home; I didn't know what to pack, so I just packed the things I liked. My suitcase was stuffed with evening dresses, and my mother and sister were waiting and he drove us to the docks.

ANN: Elizabeth and I were to be put on a ship going back to England, but my mother was going to try and find a ship that was going to Australia. So I remember, we said goodbye to her and my sister and I went up the gangway of the *Duchess of Bedford* which had just been hit, and there we said goodbye to my father, which was really very sad because he looked so strange. By then, of course, he was in the army and in a very ill-fitting uniform with a holster – but no gun in it because they'd run out – and we weren't to see him until November 1945.

ELIZABETH: Ann and I walked up the gangplank into the ship and as we walked we could see my father standing in his ill-fitting army uniform waving goodbye, and my mother trudging along the edge of the dock towards the ships.

ANN: He was a prisoner of war, and spent most of the time in Changi camp. We never really found out very much about the worst things that went on there, because he always used to laugh about it and say he'd had very good food there and a very nice peaceful time and no school fees to pay.

SUSAN: He always said he must have been the worst bargain the army had ever had – three weeks' work and four years' pay!

ANN: The day we left was the day the Johore Causeway was blown up, and I remember seeing the smoke, columns of smoke going all over the island, and I remember looking to see if I could see the mansion where I'd stayed so excitedly the first day a year ago, and eventually the island disappeared altogether, and that was the last time I saw Singapore. I've never gone back.

The four sisters and their mother were eventually reunited in Southern Rhodesia. Mark John Kennaway survived his imprisonment in Changi prisoner-of-war camp and in 1946 Elizabeth, Pippa and Susan went back with their parents to Escot Estate. However, Ann never went back. Her fiancé, Gerald Scott, had managed to escape from Singapore in a small boat and had sailed to Ceylon. When the war was over they got married.

11

The Fall

*I have seen the mysterious shores, the still water, the lands of brown
nations, where a stealthy Nemesis lies in wait, pursues, overtakes so many
of the conquering race, who are proud of their wisdom, of their knowledge,
of their strength.*

Joseph Conrad, *Youth*

WHEN war broke out in 1939 there was no immediate threat to
the British in South-East Asia. The main feeling was one of
impotence: 'A lot of us young men felt uneasy; we wanted to be
in on the act if we could and we felt increasingly uncomfortable that we were still continuing our routine civil occupations
and not making any real contribution to the war effort.'
Officials and unofficials alike found themselves prohibited
from leaving their jobs and joining the armed forces, and
when a number of younger Europeans took matters into their
own hands and made their way back to England to join up
they were ordered to return to Malaya. It was made clear to
them that they would be more valuably employed in helping
to produce the vital war supplies of rubber, tin and oil.

But gradually the position changed: 'Everybody was watching Japan in the East and when Tojo the war-lord came in we
knew pretty well what was going to happen. Nobody with any

sense had any doubt that the Japanese were going to attack Malaya. The only question was when.' From the winter of 1940–41 onwards 'all ranks in Malaya in all walks of life' began to prepare for war – 'within the limits of our resources and our manpower and always giving first priority to maintaining the economy and the output of rubber and tin'. For Bill Goode this meant working in the Civil Defence Office:

> Raising air-raid wardens and organizing air-raid precautions, raising a Home Guard with schemes for coastwatching, working out with local authorities denial schemes to prevent valuable things like boats falling into the hands of an invader, getting out schemes for rice-rationing and making stores of food, deciding whether we should store rice or whether we should store unmilled rice and how we were going to mill it. This was going on at absolutely full blast, but always in parallel with the ordinary running of the country, which went on as normal. In my spare time I was a local territorial in the Singapore Volunteer forces, with most of evenings and weekends taken up by parades with them. Then for two months, in June and July 1941, we were mobilized full-time and office work fell behind.

But if there was little complacency there was widespread ignorance, both about the state of Malaya's defences and the nature of the enemy. 'We didn't know the extent of the danger or how near it was,' declares Cecil Lee:

> Nor did we know the capacity of the forces we had to resist it. Troops were coming in and it looked big but we didn't know that they were mostly raw Indian troops. So we really thought that the country was being adequately prepared – although some didn't. For instance, we had an estate up at Jitra, in Kedah, on the front line where the 11th Division had their defence works. We made arrangements with them for compensation but I remember the company board asking Jenkins,

our visiting adviser – who was an old soldier himself – to let us know what effect these defences were having on the working of the estate. And I remember that he came back and said to me, 'They're just paltry. If those are the main defences of Malaya, thank God we've got a navy.'

In fact, Malaya's strongest line of defence was then being built up on Singapore Island, where 'we were all told that there would be in some mysterious manner a wonderful defence system worked out by the military'. These defences were concentrated on the southern part of the island in anticipation of an assault from the sea.

The impression of military invulnerability was heightened by the arrival of the battleships *Prince of Wales* and *Repulse* – but without any supporting aircraft: 'One was an ancient vessel and the other was fairly new but what good would they be without air-cover? They would be sitting ducks. We hoped and prayed we might get some air-cover – but no air-cover ever came.'

Public statements, put out for the best of motives – 'to keep morale high and to prevent people from getting into a panic' – made light of the increasing 'inevitability' of Japanese attack. Gerald Scott recalls how in Singapore 'notices of exhortation' appeared in all the banks signed by the Commander-in-Chief of the British Forces to the effect that the defences of Singapore and Malaya were not wanting and that the country could not be invaded. 'We believed this,' adds Scott. 'We didn't believe that the Japs could come in through the back door in gym shoes through the jungle and knock the place sideways.'

The fighting qualities of the Japanese themselves were also ridiculed. 'All sorts of things they told us,' Guy Madoc maintains. 'That the Japanese pilots were myopic and that their planes were not airworthy; and as December 1941 approached they told us that we'd be perfectly safe for the next four or five months, because the monsoon was blowing on the East Coast and there was no possibility of a landing from the sea during a monsoon. But I had lived in the monsoon on the East Coast and I knew jolly well that sometimes there were periods of complete calm for five or six days at a time.' When ships of the Japanese fleet began gathering in the Gulf of Siam early in December the government radio still remained 'fatuously cheerful and said they were on naval exercises – although everybody at naval headquarters was perfectly well aware that this was the beginning of the attack'.

Up in Kelantan Bill Bangs had been asked to form some local Malays into a frontier force to check local smugglers' paths through the jungle, in case the Japanese were planning to attack across the border. 'This was all put onto a map and worked very well – but, unfortunately, it was the only way the Japanese *didn't* come!' With only a few days to go before the invasion of Malaya was launched Bangs was sent across into Siam to find out what the Japanese were up to. Using the cover of a Seventh Day Adventist missionary – 'because I didn't think there was any such thing as that in the Far East' – he checked into a Siamese hotel, only to be greeted shortly afterwards by a Seventh Day Adventist from Sumatra who 'was very pleased to see me and asked me if I would take the service that evening!' After this false start Bangs went on to locate several airstrips in the jungle that had been cleared of undergrowth and were awaiting the arrival of planes from Japanese aircraft carriers. Convinced that the Japanese were poised to launch their invasion near Kota Bharu, Bangs slipped back across the border with all speed:

In those days the only way to get to Kota Bharu from there was to hire a Model T Ford and drive along the beach. This was the night of 6 December 1941. The waves were very big indeed and we had to keep stopping for the waves to go out, so when I got back I went to see Brig.-General Key of 8 Brigade and told him all that I'd seen and that the Japanese were supposed to be coming that same night. But then I told him that it was quite impossible, as I'd come along the beach and

the sea was much too rough and nobody could possibly make a
landing. However, I was quite wrong and they landed that
night at one-fifteen.

Like many others on that same night of 6–7 December,
John Davis was woken by explosions as the first bombs fell on
Singapore. Even then the realization that war had begun in
earnest was accompanied by disbelief: 'We thought that this
was one isolated raid and that we wouldn't hear any more
about the war. With the wonderful fleet we had, the Japanese
wouldn't be so foolish as to attack Malaya. The next thing we
heard was that they had landed in Kelantan – but then
Kelantan was five hundred miles away from Singapore and
there were heavy forces and many airfields in between, so that
was alright.'

The Volunteers had been mobilized some days earlier.
Peter Lucy had 'just walked out of the bungalow for an
ordinary parade as I was accustomed to do once a week,
leaving the house open and everything in it – and never
returned'. He and other members of his armoured car unit
were sent over to the East Coast to defend the local aerodrome
at Kuantan. Bill Goode was manning the defences of Singapore – no longer as Assistant Commissioner of Civil Defence
but as a lance-corporal in Singapore Volunteers, 'lost in the
big army machine and with only a worm's eye view – so that
my view of affairs became very limited indeed'. For the next
two months he found himself 'mostly engaged in digging holes
in the ground then being told by an officer to fill 'em in again
or putting up miles and miles of barbed wire and sandbag
emplacements near and just behind the Singapore waterfront,
because my battalion was responsible for the defence of the
waterfront along by the swimming club.' John Forrester was
similarly employed defending Singapore's Tengah airfield:
'It's an awful thing to say but I don't think anyone took it
too seriously. We were sitting there on this airfield for day after
day after day. Nothing was happening and we thought it was

probably going to be rather like Europe, where nothing happened for a long time. So we felt very comfortable sitting in this fortress and waiting for them to come and I think we felt more sorry for the Japanese trying to come to us rather than anything else.'

But within a few days of the Japanese landing at Kota Bharu the situation took a dramatic turn for the worse. 'I was then staying with a chap called Claude Fenner,' recalls Davis. 'He came in in the morning with the newspaper and said, "Look at this, John." And there was the report of the sinking of the *Prince of Wales* and the *Repulse*. It was unbelievable. I've never been hit so hard in my life. The whole thing suddenly for the first time became terrifying, because if the Japanese could sink our fleet like that, they could do anything. I think this broke my morale and I think it broke the morale of a tremendous number of people during the campaign, from which we never properly recovered.' There were others who were affected by the news in much the same way. Perky Perkins remembers 'the utter depression which fell on us at the time when these two great ships were sunk'. In Malacca sixteen-year-old Una Ebden was sitting for her School Certificate and at first the bad news came as something of a relief, because it now seemed unlikely that she would ever get the result of the examination:

> I remember walking back from the convent from that exam, feeling rather low and rather frightened, and overhearing an Indian boy, a youth of about sixteen, saying to a Chinese boy of about the same age, 'Cheer up, man, there'll always be an England.' And that's a thing I remember, because how badly let down those two boys must have felt later on, when the Japanese just overran the whole country.

Over the next few weeks there was some valiant fighting but to little positive effect. The Japanese consolidated their positions in the north and began to advance southwards, 'never using the deep jungle but using the roadside rubber estates which had all been beautifully mapped out by all the Japanese taxidermists, botanists, brothel keepers, amateur photographers – to say nothing of the Japanese estate owners and managers – who had come to this country in hordes before the war.' The news bulletins that Gerald Scott and others read out in the Malayan Broadcasting Corporation Studios continued to sound 'always very hopeful'. There was talk of 'firm stands' followed by 'strategic retreats' until it became increasingly obvious even in Singapore that 'we were in a hell of a shambles and that the Japs were coming down Malaya at a terrific speed'.

Up in Kelantan Bill Bangs took part in a number of rearguard actions as 8 Brigade retreated south: 'We were ordered to defend the crossroads at Mulong and were told "Last man, last bullet." This was the first time that I heard these orders, although I was to hear them many times afterwards. It usually meant that within an hour we would receive an order to retire once more.' When the fighting reached Kuantan, Peter Lucy found himself caught up in this same demoralizing process:

> We never did any defending at Kuantan aerodrome. We just sat there till the Japs arrived. Somehow or other they crept up through the rubber trees and fired on us. Without firing back we merely got the order to retreat, so we jumped into our armoured cars and drove away. And this went on all through the country – retreating, retreating, although we never had any real reason for retreating. We were never defeated; we merely retreated on orders and the feeling was one of bewilderment.

Driving inland away from the coast Lucy's unit was ambushed: 'The Japs had expected us to be using that road and they were lying in wait as we passed. Their armour-piercing bullets just came into the car and whizzed around inside and everybody was hit. I was cut right across the back and another man had his leg broken. The armour-plating was just useless against the Japanese bullets.'

Meanwhile on the West Coast battle had been joined on the Jitra line in North Kedah – where after a few days Guy Madoc was ordered to gather his local police force and pull out:

> When we got to the main road the whole of the army was streaming back, not in disorder but completely and utterly worn out. Every time there was a halt for any reason – a lorry broken down or run out of petrol – the whole convoy stopped and every driver went to sleep, or so it seemed. I spent my time hammering on the bonnets of cars with my swagger cane saying 'Get on! Get on! Get on!' Until finally at about four in the morning we reached the next big town, where I found my Chief Police Officer, and I had just about told him my tale when some goon came dashing in and said, 'The Japs have reached Gurun!' That was about fourteen miles up the road and it meant that they had done a big sweep round and had broken through the retreating column, so we all leapt into our cars and fled back another thirty miles – only to find that this ass had evidently had a nightmare. The whole thing was a fiasco, because next morning we had to go back. But at intervals over the next two months these retreats continued and I never seemed to settle down in any one place for more than about a week at a time.

One calendar month after the Japanese landing at Kota Bharu the Battle of Slim River was fought and lost. Kuala Lumpur was evacuated and the European women and children joined the growing number of refugees heading for Singapore. On KL aerodrome Cecil Lee and other members of his company of the Selangor Battalion of the FMS Volunteers were joined by British anti-aircraft gunners from Penang – who left them in no doubt as to what they felt about the Malayan campaign: 'I remember one of the gunners saying to me, "As far as I'm concerned, the Japs can have bloody

Malaya" – which gives some idea of the attitude and the lack of morale. By that time there was also looting and it was a pretty sorry sight to see people in the streets with stuff on their backs and bicycles – one fellow had a piano on a cart that he was taking along.'

Lee and some of his fellow-Volunteers were then moved to Port Swettenham to make up a new armoured car company:

> We were just put in them and told to get on with it and we proceeded down the coast road. I well remember passing a *padang* with a club and thinking that this was a society in dissolution. Then the Malays started to desert. Quite naturally, they were anxious about their families. We met one chap on the road and our rather intense commander got out his pistol and menaced this poor little wretch who was merely going home to his family. I remember seeing one dear old planter, Stephen Taylor, explaining to one of these Malays by the roadside, 'We'll be back, you know. It won't be long before we're back.' Of course, it was numbing to them to see the *orang puteh* – the white men – fleeing, and I'm told that after the war when they spoke of this they used the expression *tarekh orang puteh lari* – 'the time when the *tuans* ran'.

As they retreated down the coast they often found themselves billeted in abandoned bungalows, many still fully furnished: 'I remember seeing two chaps in their army boots and full kit lying on the double bed of a planter's main bedroom.'

When they reached Johore the various volunteer units were disbanded, the Europeans being attached to one or other of the regular army units. Lee found himself fighting alongside the Argyll and Sutherland Highlanders: 'There for the first time I met the real army, because although they were much depleted and battered they were still an effective fighting force. I remember when we had an air-raid one of the young Jocks saying: "Dinna run, man, dinna run!"'

The remaining Malays and other non-Europeans in the Volunteers were discharged and allowed to return to civilian life – where attitudes towards the war differed very much according to nationality. 'The Malays were not taking any great interest and can you blame them?' asks Sjovald Cunyngham-Brown:

> It was their country that was being rolled over by two vast overseas giants, who were fighting their disgusting battles in Malaya's own garden, smashing and destroying everything. The Malays had benefited by joining Western civilization and now they realized with horror that they were about to pay for it; this was what happened if you joined the West – so they stood by. The Indians were mostly rubber estate workers who had no contact with what was going on. They lay doggo, hearing nothing, saying nothing and seeing nothing – and I don't blame them either. They were a little minority caught in a trap. The Chinese, on the other hand, were already at war with Japan. Their mother country was fighting Japan, therefore so were they, and the more virile of them were busy getting arms to go into the jungle to die fighting against the Japanese – as indeed they did.

At Johore Bahru, where Cunyngham-Brown was based while dividing his time between his work as Controller of Labour in Johore and his duties in Singapore with the Royal Navy Volunteer Reserve, 'a steady stream of old 1933 Morrises and other motor-cars, with children inside and baggage and perambulators on top' was making its way across the narrow causeway that linked Singapore to the mainland. As more refugees came south an enormous queue of cars and people developed at the bridgehead:

> During that time my friends and I in Johore Bahru met so many of our old friends and acquaintances from up-country that we had a sort of perpetual cocktail party that went on

interminably in the garden and in the house as they poured in. We were bombed every now and then, usually in the evenings and not very close to us, but enough to put us under the staircase and under the tables, while we went on talking and saying things like: 'It'll be all right when we get to fortress Singapore.' 'Thank God we've got down here. Poor old Jimmy got killed at Perak, did you know?' 'She got away all right, but poor Jack got killed, you know.' They were all a little shaken and telling those short stories and so it became a rather macabre and everlastingly prolonged cocktail party.

Singapore itself was rapidly filling up. 'It was like a scourge of population – all European, I'm afraid,' asserts Una Ebden, who had come down from Malacca with her mother: 'We went to a boarding house called the *Manor House Hotel* which started to fill up and fill up with more and more people until they were sleeping in the corridors and on the verandas. What made it even worse was that the army kept on commandeering houses to billet the troops who were also coming down into Singapore, so the civilians were hard put to know where to go. We ended up at the Swiss Club, because there was nowhere else to go.'

The numbers were further swelled by troops arriving from overseas – whose officers were allowed to use the European clubs without paying subscriptions. Gerald Scott recalls an occasion when having got an evening off from his duties as a Volunteer he went to the Tanglin Club in his uniform – only to receive 'a note from some general saying that this was an officer's club and that Other Ranks were not allowed. I sent him a note back saying that as it had been my privilege as a member of the club to vote for serving officers becoming members without paying subscriptions, I was delighted to think that he was enjoying himself there!'

Soon the last of the British fighter aircraft had been destroyed – 'these poor little Brewster Buffalos going up with the Japanese Navy Zeros coming over in great clouds and shooting them down' – and unopposed, the bombers were coming over – 'twenty-seven at a time, slowly and easily coming across the sky, fairly low down, and dropping their bombs wherever they wished'. Many were aimed at the shipping in Singapore roads – and to good effect. Trevor Walker watched the *Empress of Asia* sinking off Singapore Island, and with it all the transport and artillery for the newly-arrived 18th Indian Division, which had been trained for desert warfare but had been diverted to Singapore instead: 'They didn't know what a rubber tree looked like or what the jungle looked like. They were keen to do a job but it was all too quick and too sudden and they had barely got into position in Johore when we were told to withdraw.'

In Singapore town itself the bombing was not particularly heavy, but what was especially depressing to Tamsin Broome, who had arrived in an advanced stage of pregnancy, was the certainty that 'whenever you heard a plane you knew it was a Jap one'. On 5 January 1942 her son was born in Singapore Hospital, with a Chinese and a Malay nurse in attendance: 'It wasn't a very comfortable time to be having a baby. The Chinese nurses got terribly worked up whenever they heard bombs and rushed in saying "Take cover." But how can you take cover when you've just delivered a baby? But luckily he was very large and very healthy and nothing disturbed him.'

Richard Broome, meanwhile, had been ordered to report for special duty in Singapore a fortnight earlier:

I was told to go to a certain office which turned out to be the Secret Service. They said they wanted somebody to look after their agents in Singapore, and while they were talking there was the noise of packing going on and so I looked round and said, 'Well, what's happening here?' They said, 'Oh, we're getting out. We just want you to stay and look after the agents.' This rather took me aback and I said, 'How many agents will it be?' And they said, 'Well, we've only got one at the moment.' So I went out with my heart in my boots – and there outside the door was another gentleman who said, 'Oh, you don't want anything to do with that lot. You come with us.' Now this was the organization which was eventually to become Force 136, and what they wanted was some Chinese speaker to escort groups of Chinese Communists trained in sabotage work up to the front line and hide them in the jungle. The Communist Party of Malaya, which had done its best to sabotage the war effort for most of the war, had changed sides and offered its services to the British Government and parties of these young chaps were now being trained in sabotage and fifth-column work. So for the next few weeks my job consisted of picking up these fellows, taking them up in lorries to as near the front line as we could get, finding them a hiding place in the jungle, giving them all their stores and trying to give them a bit of spirit by making speeches in Cantonese and waving my fist.

Soon he was joined by John Davis and between them they succeeded in putting out seven 'stay-behind' parties, with each journey to and from the front line growing shorter as the Japanese advanced on Singapore. Finally, on 31 January Johore was abandoned and the causeway was blown. 'The morning came when we thought there was going to be a battle for the bridgehead,' Lee recalls. 'But there wasn't. Contact with the Japanese was broken. First the Australians and then ourselves and the Argylls were ushered across the causeway. I remember feeling particularly happy – because we hadn't had any fighting, I suppose.'

By now the evacuation of the European women from Singapore by sea, which at first had been opposed by the authorities on the grounds that it would unnecessarily demoralize the native population, was almost completed: 'They were evacuated – but right at the end – and therefore there were tremendous losses.' Tamsin Broome and her two small children left on one of the last two large passenger liners to leave Singapore, the *Empress of Japan*, which sailed in January with 'two thousand women and children and one old man who had got left behind'.

But there were still quite a number of European women left in the city – including 'Tommy' Hawkings who was working as a VAD nurse at Alexandra Military Hospital. Within a few days of her arrival in Singapore she had received word that her fiancée, Peter Lucy, had been wounded – although not seriously enough to prevent him returning to his unit when it was pulled back into Singapore. The two met up whenever they could – and decided to get married: 'We both agreed that Singapore would stand forever. Evening after evening Sir Shenton Thomas, the Governor, broadcast that we were perfectly safe where we were, that we were to stay at our posts and were not to leave, so Peter and I agreed that we would be much happier if we were married and fought out the siege as a married couple.' Because of food shortages it was difficult to find all the necessary ingredients for a wedding cake, but the problem was solved by the Bishop of Singapore:

> He and I sat in his air-raid shelter while he transferred a bag of currants into my lap for the wedding cake, which we then made in a friend's baby bath. There was no time to issue invitations so we put notices in the paper – which was still being printed just as if everything was going on as normal – asking all our friends and relations to come to Singapore Cathedral at two-thirty the afternoon of 7 February 1942, where Peter Lucy and Tommy Hawkings would welcome everybody they knew. That was exactly one week before Singapore fell.

Despite the bombing it was a 'perfectly beautiful wedding', which was followed by a reception attended by 'a whole contingent absolutely straight from the front line, some with arms bound up and some with mud on their trousers and boots. Many of the men we never saw again; either they were killed in the last few days of fighting or they died in prison camps. Many of our women friends, too, were lost at sea when their ships

were bombed and sunk by the Japanese.' The Lucys' honeymoon consisted of two nights together, the first in an air-raid
shelter and the second broken by 'the most tremendous barrage
that anybody who had been in the First World War had ever
heard. This was the Japanese crossing over onto the island.' In
the morning Peter Lucy went back to the front line and his wife
to Alexandra Hospital: 'Neither of us had any idea that it would
be four years before we saw each other again.'

For the men who were still fighting it had now become a
matter of simple survival: 'One lived literally from hour to
hour, mainly concerned with eating and sleeping and getting a
rest when you could.' From patrolling the Singapore waterfront Goode and his company were sent across to reinforce the
Australians, who were falling back after failing to hold their
defences on the north side of the island. 'We carried out a
typical Singapore Volunteers operation,' he recalls:

> We left our camp in trucks and we drove to the address we had
> been given. But when we got there we were met by our
> platoon officer, who'd gone on ahead and who flew into a
> fearful rage and told us that our approach was under enemy
> fire, so we should have got out of our trucks way back down
> the road and come up in sensible open order to avoid
> casualties. Having made such a mess of it, we would have
> to darn well go back and do it again. So we solemnly got into
> the truck, drove back to where we should have got out and
> started walking in open order along the side of the road. Of
> course, we hadn't gone very far before a Japanese aeroplane
> came over and started machine-gunning the road. All hell was
> let loose; we were all terrified out of our wits, jumped into the
> monsoon drain, got covered in water and arrived with our
> morale rather at rock bottom.

Soon they were being mortared and taking their first
casualties: 'We dug various holes, always with the mortaring
going on, always moving about as you do in the army and

going out on patrols after snipers in coconut trees and never finding them.'

On the high ground of Buona Vista Ridge overlooking the western perimeter of the city, where the Malay Regiment was dug in, George Wort first of all had a spectator's view of events. Then stragglers from various Australian and British detachments began heading back through his lines in disarray. A period of confused fighting and sniping followed until on Friday 13 February the command post in which Wort and other officers were conferring received a direct hit. Seriously wounded, he was carried up to the Gap rest house – 'a place where in the days of peace you used to take your girl friends' – to be patched up and then taken down to Alexandra Hospital, which itself was now almost in the front line. Here Tommy Lucy and the other nurses were packing up to leave: 'Everybody knew what Japanese soldiers did to nurses and so we were all ordered out by the matron.' They were driven straight down to the docks where that same day they sailed on an 'old tramper', the *Empire Star*: 'There was no food or water on board but in the *godowns* along the wharf they found cases of Guinness and cases of asparagus, so we sailed out on a brown haze of Guinness and eating asparagus. We were down in a hold with only one ladder to get out and with thousands up above and we were bombed the whole way from Singapore to Sumatra. It was a tragic journey and yet a glorious one in the spirit of the people who were on board.'

Just three hours after his wife had left Alexandra Hospital Peter Lucy was brought in, having again been wounded in an armoured car. Because the hospital wards were already full he and a number of other casualties were put into a spare room:

> That night the Japanese attacked the hospital and we just sat there and listened to the screaming that was going on, not knowing exactly what was happening until a private soldier in the room got up and said, 'In private life I am a pastor in Norfolk but now I am a private soldier. As you all know what is

going to happen very shortly I expect you would like me to say a few prayers.' So he said a few prayers along the lines that we were about to be killed and we then waited for the Japanese. The screaming went on and then it continued above us and eventually died down. We found out afterwards that our room was not a proper ward and the Japanese had thought it was a store cupboard and didn't come in – otherwise we too should have been victims of this tremendous slaughter.

George Wort also survived the Alexandra Hospital massacre: 'I woke in the morning to find that my arm had been amputated. All the doctors and orderlies had been taken away and we were on our own. I remember lying on my bed and the Japanese coming round the ward and taking whatever we'd got. They took my watch and it was all slightly tense and then they moved on.'

On the evening of the following day, 15 February, Bill Goode and his companions were given the news that they would be making a bayonet counter-attack close by in Alexandra Road: 'This filled us all with great apprehension; however, just as it was getting dark and we were getting used to this uncomfortable fact, we were summoned again and told to our amazement that we had capitulated. I was overwhelmed with emotion. I couldn't think how it could have happened. It couldn't be true. I found myself desolated by the fact, which was quite stupid because if we hadn't I should probably have been killed the next morning.'

All over the island other Britons were experiencing very similar emotions. John Forrester, whose unit of bren gun carriers had scarcely seen any action at all, greeted the news with disbelief:

We were sitting in a compound owned by a Chinese millionaire with our bren carriers all round us and thinking what a peaceful time it was when suddenly somebody said, 'Oh, we've surrendered.' We just couldn't believe it, because there was plenty of ammunition, there was plenty of water, and our bren carriers were full of petrol. We thought the man who'd brought the news about the surrender was some fifth columnist and somebody even suggested shooting him. We were particularly amazed and dumbfounded because, although we had been to various corners of Singapore Island, we had never actually seen a Japanese or fired a shot in anger. We had done nothing worthwhile to stop the capture of Singapore. We had done nothing.

After checking to see whether the news really was true Forrester and three of his friends decided to make a break for it. They made their way down to the Singapore Yacht Club, found a fourteen-foot sailing boat, rigged it with sails and worked their way through the defences and the minefields out to sea. There were others who had the same idea: Guy Madoc had been given permission to escape if he wished so he and another police officer went down to Keppel Harbour – only to find that the boat they were looking for had been scuttled; Edward Tokeley and two colleagues got a car and drove through what was now 'a ghastly scene of destruction and desolation' towards Thorneycroft United Engineers boatyard: 'There were fires all over the place. A lot of the street lighting was gas and I can remember seeing one of these gas cones broken in two, with the lighted gas spurting out.' When they reached the boatyard they came under mortar fire. There were no boats to be seen and so they were forced to turn round and drive back into the town.

Gerald Scott and some of his colleagues in APC were luckier, having already got away in their own launch a day or two earlier. John Harrison also got away – as part of a crew of a sailing boat that eventually got all the way down to Australia. Sjovald Cunyngham-Brown, Percy Bulbrook and Robert Williamson were out at sea when Singapore fell – all of them helping to ferry women and children and the wounded across to Sumatra. Bulbrook sailed on to Ceylon in the Straits steamship *Perak*, Williamson to Madras in the SS *Pahang*.

It was Cunyngham-Brown, second-in-command of a little vessel called the *Hung Jao*, who provided one of the best-known and happier rescue stories to come out of the fall of Singapore:

We were trudging along in the pitch-black night heading for Sumatra. I was leaning over the cab of the bridge when what should I hear but a voice saying, 'Going my way?' I saw something in the wash astern and yelled, 'There's a man in the water! Stop! Go astern!' My commander, Robin Henman, came up bleary-eyed from below and said, 'What's happening?' 'Man in the water,' I said, 'We're going to pick him up.' 'How do you mean? Did he say anything?' I said, 'As a matter of fact he said, "Going my way".' 'Full speed ahead,' said Robin. 'Sjovald, you're asleep, poor chap. Try to keep awake.' I said I wasn't asleep and I begged him to let me go astern for ten minutes. So we proceeded astern and finally the aldis lamps picked up something in the water. We came up alongside and what was it but a Fraser and Neave aerated water crate!

'Full speed ahead,' said Robin Henman, 'I've had enough of this bloody nonsense.' I said, 'Robin, *sir*! For God's sake let me go astern for another five minutes. There *is* someone in the water.' And sure enough, as we proceeded astern something did turn up in the water – a man sitting on a raft. We got alongside him and threw a rope over but he couldn't pick it up. So as it was my find I eased myself into the water and swam across to tie him on. As we got him alongside I looked at him and said, 'My God, Puck!' It was H. V. Puckeridge, a remarkable and well-liked character who was manager of a large rubber plantation in Selangor. He said, 'Oh, hello, Sjovald. Do be careful of my shoes, old boy, because they're practically new.' He'd got them neatly placed side by side on top of the raft as though it was outside his bedroom door.

After the sinking of their own vessel Cunyngham-Brown and Henman attempted to escape northwards in a catamaran but were eventually captured. After many months of solitary confinement Cunyngham-Brown was brought back to Singapore as a prisoner of war.

. Richard Broome and John Davis also got away to Sumatra and from there went on to India – to begin training and planning for their return to Malaya as the spearhead of Force 136.

There were some who were offered the chance to escape but refused to take it. On 13 February Bill Bangs had escorted a senior Malay official – whose life would have been at risk under the Japanese – down to the docks where a naval launch was waiting to take him away:

> An officer said, 'Get on, get on. There's no sense in staying.' But, having had a very fine time in Kelantan and loving Malaya and the Malays, I felt that if I rushed away now I would never be able to come back and face my Malay friends. So I did not get on the launch and stayed behind. It was a very silly decision because if I'd gone out I could have then been dropped back with Force 136 in the *ulu* of Kelantan and got all the Malays who knew me together and we could have done a lot of damage to the Japanese.

Elsewhere on the archipelago other groups of Britons were also surrendering to the invaders. There too, there were many – like Bill Banks in Sarawak – who had refused the chance to get away when it was offered to them: 'You can't live among the people for years and then when the danger comes drop everything and leave them. I know it sounds daft but we felt that way. So, we stayed, not knowing what was going to happen.'

The day after the surrender of Singapore all the British forces were marshalled together and made to march out to Changi, on the eastern tip of the island, where there was a civilian jail and the military barracks. 'We marched in endless line,' recalls Bill Goode:

We came snaking in to Newton Circus with the 2/29th Australians to whom we'd been attached, and immediately behind us was a regular battalion of the Gordon Highlanders who'd been a bit further up the line from us. All through the night we marched but I found it very heartening and encouraging on that long march to hear the regular tramp, tramp of the Gordons behind us and, of course, the pipes playing, which certainly helped me to keep going through that night. It was unpleasant to start with because we were moving through parts of Singapore that had been heavily bombed, where everything was in chaos, with bits of telephone line and overhead tram cables lying about in the street, vehicles damaged and overturned and the most ghastly stench of decaying corpses. It wasn't until we got out into the coconut estates and the country districts that life began to seem a bit more normal.

As they marched there was 'plenty of time to reflect upon what had happened and what could possibly happen in the future' – and there was particular sadness among those who, like Edward Tokeley, had spent nearly all their adult years in Malaya and had grown to love the country: 'The incoming soldiers had lost the battle but they didn't have the same personal involvement that we had, walking through Singapore as the vanquished, with the Asians – who didn't know what was going to happen to them – seeing you going.'

'There wasn't any jeering or anything of that sort,' Bangs recalls. 'A lot of Chinese, Malays and Eurasians along the way had tins of water and were giving the soldiers drinks as we went along – in spite of the Japanese trying to stop them. But we hadn't had any sleep for days and on this horrible march we didn't really know what we were doing.'

Some days later some two-and-a-half thousand male civilians, led by the Governor, made their own march out to Changi. 'It was a very long march and we were all ages,' remembers Madoc:

There were a certain number of schoolboys even and people up to the age of seventy. Some foolishly overburdened themselves, others somehow managed to scrounge room on a lorry for their mattress or whatever they had with them. But what moved us was that during that march the few Asians that we saw all turned their backs as we walked past them – not in disgust but because they didn't want to have any part in this.

The women were made to march, too, a couple of days later. We heard them arrive and clearly they'd put up a better show than us, because as they marched along the walls of this very grim prison we heard singing: *There'll Always Be An England*.

12

De Profundis

ADJUSTING to captivity was not easy. Feelings of relief at still being alive quickly gave way to depression and forebodings about the future: 'To begin with our main anxiety was about our relations. Many of us did not know where our wives and our families were. The second thing – and one that took up a lot of our time – was walking around and meeting friends and trying to find out what had happened to friends, whether they were still alive, whether they too were trapped or not. And in the background was this overwhelming feeling that we probably kept to ourselves; what's going to happen to us – because there's nothing we can do which will make the slightest difference to our future. That was the sort of thing that came on you as you were trying to get to sleep at night, rather than something you talked about to other people.'

Although not particularly religious – 'scarcely any of us had gone to church except for weddings' – many of the internees in Changi Jail felt the need for spiritual support, and when it was announced on the first Sunday that a service was to be held in the exercise yard Guy Madoc and his colleagues dressed in what was left of their best clothes to attend: 'We expected to get spiritual support, we expected to sing good old hymns like *Fight the Good Fight* and *Onward Christian Soldiers* and we expected a sermon which said "Well done, you good and faithful servants". Instead we were shamefully betrayed by a senior clergyman of Singapore who preached a sermon that shocked and angered us, saying that we thoroughly deserved what had come to us and that we must treat it as a penance for our sins of omission and commission in the years that we had been in Malaya. So we left that exercise yard and I personally never went to church again.'

However, both the civilian internees and the prisoners of war soon had other more pressing problems to worry about. In Changi Jail Madoc found himself crammed with two other policemen into a small cell built for one: 'In the middle was a raised block which we called a sarcophagus on which the most senior officer slept, while we two more junior men squeezed in between the walls and the sides of the sarcophagus. This was all very well until the bed bugs started to infest us, because there seemed to be far more bed bugs on the wall attacking the junior officers than there were on the sarcophagus.' Similarly, in Changi Barracks nearby thirty-seven thousand British troops and fourteen thousand Australians had been squeezed into quarters built for only a fifth of that number. 'There was at first a feeling of every man for himself,' recalls George Wort. 'People grew their hair long and grew beards and that sort of thing. But within a very short space of time people realized that without some sort of discipline and organization none of us would survive. From then on people took more pride in how they appeared and we settled down to what you might call a military organization within the camp.'

Other camps were set up in Sarawak and British North Borneo, although in time the great majority of internees ended up in Kuching: 'Into this camp went everybody: people from Sarawak and Dutch Borneo, sailors from the *Repulse* and *Prince of Wales*, White Russians who had been taken off some ship, missionaries, bigwigs, planters, all kinds of people herded together – and it was very interesting to meet such a cross-section of people like that with different ideas.' Here and in the other camps gangs of working parties were formed and put to work as coolies. For a period Edward Banks helped to pull a bullock cart through the streets of Kuching, shirtless and barefooted: 'The local people's reaction to this was one of horror. They went indoors and hid their faces; they didn't want to see it. But I'll always remember a little Chinese girl – only a sawn-off little thing – who rushed out and gave me a bunch of bananas. The guards gave a yell and chased her but she was gone like an eel!'

In Singapore, too, many acts of kindness were shown by the Asian population towards the Europeans in the work gangs. Bill Goode remembers how 'as we marched through the streets on our way to work in the docks, a Chinese would run through the ranks of a marching column and shove a two-dollar note or a piece of bread into the hands of the nearest man – at considerable risk to himself because he could be very badly beaten up by the Japanese. They needn't have done it but they did and this sort of thing formed a bond between people like myself and the people of Singapore and Malaya, which was of inestimable value when later on we returned to Malaya.'

Peter Lucy also worked in the docks, as one of a gang of two hundred and fifty men based on Blakang Mati Island:

Our job was to unload bombs from the ships as they came into Singapore harbour, then take them across the water and stack them into the armouries on the island. They were all one-hundred-pound bombs and the order was one man one bomb; we had to stack it in the armoury and then go back for more – and this went on until the ship was unloaded, irrespective of how long it took. It was sometimes forty-eight hours non-stop except for an occasional five minute rest. It was very hard work and at first a lot of planters gave up the ghost. They were elderly and not used to hard work and it was too much for some of them. We were all treated as private soldiers and we had to do the work of private soldiers. There was no alcohol and no cigarettes and food was very scarce. We had eight ounces of dried rice a day plus whatever we could pick up from the Malays or anybody who could send over a banana or something that we could mix with the rice. We were able to catch snails and snakes and mix them up with the rice to produce some protein and sometimes we were able to collect some beans or sugar which had fallen out of the sacks as the cranes were unloading them. So those who were able to look after themselves and were optimistic, as I was, managed to survive. Discipline among the working-parties was maintained by the officers: some of the other nationalities weren't so well disciplined but we had a doctor who was an officer and one or two other officers and their orders were strictly obeyed, so discipline on the whole was good. Our attitude towards the Japanese, however, was simply to ignore them as far as possible. We just looked upon them as something completely out of this world. But they were always on top of you. You were constantly being told that you should have committed suicide before being taken prisoner, that you were the lowest of the low. If you tried to retaliate you simply got beaten up, so it was difficult to retain one's dignity. The men were rather inclined to be peasant types and if they could do anything to help the prisoners they very often did but the officers were always brutal.

The civilian internees in Changi Jail were rather more fortunate. For Guy Madoc the two greatest hardships were 'the lack of news from the outside world and from loved ones – and the lack of food'. At first the inadequate rations could be made up from supplies of tinned food brought in by scrounging parties from Singapore but eventually these extra rations ran out: 'The time came when the Japanese said, "If you want to eat you've got to grow it yourself." Fortunately at about that time they transferred us from Changi Jail, where it had been impossible to grow much food, to Sime Road, which was an open camp and where we cleared the scrub off the sloping hills

and planted acres of sweet potatoes. Even so, by the end of
imprisonment we were in a very bad state.'

In both the camps on Singapore Island great efforts were
made to preserve a semblance of normality. Camp newspapers
were produced, concerts and plays were put on and a wide
variety of subjects were taught:

We had an immense number of intelligent people in Changi,
including practically the whole of the Education Department
and so all sorts of classes were set up. You could even learn
Swahili, if you wanted to. Everybody began enthusiastically by
joining too many classes but there was a shortage of paper and
pencils and gradually attendance at the classes dwindled. I
myself had a mad idea that I might be able to escape and get
up-country through Malaya and then through Siam, so I
decided to start learning Siamese and I continued to do so
right through the whole of our imprisonment of three-and-a-
half years. I also started to write a bird book and I got great
help from one of my cell mates who was put on the job of
cleaning out the Japanese commandant's office. Every time he
went in there he stole some of the best foolscap paper and
brought it back to me. Another internee had a typewriter
which he would lend me every Sunday morning and so
gradually I built up quite an extensive bird book of more
than a hundred pages. Another ornithologist who was a good
artist added some illustrations and then we found a couple of
French prisoners who were good bookbinders and they made
a beautiful job of it. And this single volume of *An Introduction to
Malayan Birds* had a very considerable circulation in Changi.

There was little direct contact between the two camps at
Changi, although for several months Mervyn Sheppard and
Bill Bangs managed to run an effective postal service between
the jail and the barracks using a hollow bamboo. Then
Sheppard was caught and tortured by the Kempeitai. As time
went on, others in the jail were also tortured: 'Some were

tortured to death, others returned to us in such a state that our doctors could only ease their last hours of life. I remember so well working on the vegetable patch one afternoon when the body of the former Colonial Secretary of Singapore was brought back by the Japanese. Although we had Japanese sentries amongst us whose duty it was to see that we didn't slack, we all put down our tools and stood to attention whilst his body went by.'

At Changi Barracks the first major crisis came at the end of August 1942 when all prisoners of war were ordered to sign a document stating that they would make no attempt to escape and that if they heard of any other prisoner planning to do so they would inform the Japanese: 'Of course, everyone refused to sign this and as a punishment all the prisoners were put into Selarang Barracks, which had been built to accommodate eight hundred Gordons in peacetime.' The punishment backfired because, as George Wort recalls, 'everyone was in terrific form. We were cheek by jowl, we'd had to bring all our belongings with us so people were pushing beds and prams and everything, water was very short, food was very difficult to get and the lavatories didn't flush so open pits were dug, but the general effect of morale was terrific. However, after three or four days there was a great risk of dysentery and so our commanding officer ordered us to sign under duress, which we did, but it was a great morale booster in spite of the appalling circumstances.'

Then in October the Japanese started sending the first parties of prisoners of war away from Singapore by train. 'The rumours were that we were going up to the Cameron Highlands to grow vegetables,' remembers Cecil Lee. 'But we discovered eventually that we were going up to Siam to build the new railway. It was a long journey, travelling twenty-six to a box-car in great discomfort, and on the first night when we arrived at Seremban station the whole of the British Army seemed to be out relieving itself.' After four days and nights the passengers reached the railhead in Siam and then began marching up to the first of the makeshift railway camps.

Among the planters who worked on the railway were Bill
Bangs, Perky Perkins and Hugh Watts. All of them had been
Volunteers – as had been Edward Tokeley, Cecil Lee and Bill
Goode:

> We built the first camp from nothing, clearing the jungle and
> putting up bamboo huts. It was a good camp site, high on the
> river bank with a marvellous view of the hills in the distance
> and the river in the foreground, in which we were allowed to
> wash. But we soon began to come up against the hardships of
> building a railway on inadequate rations. The Japanese
> communications were almost negligible so we lived for weeks
> on end on very bad rice – we thought they were sweepings
> from the floors of warehouses – and pumpkin stew. This and
> the long hours of work, coupled with the exhaustion of the
> march up, started to take their toll

The first death 'created quite a stir', remembers Lee, who
was working in the same labour battalion as Goode: 'He was
such a nice young lad, a bank clerk fresh out from home and a
Gordon Highlander – one of the poor lads shipped out to
Malaya at the last minute and wondering what the hell they
were going to do. He got dysentery on the way up and there
was nothing for him. Of course, it became a commonplace
thing but that was the first time and it struck home.' Their
camp commandant was 'a very fine old colonel of the Sher-
wood Foresters' who 'by dint of a good deal of suffering and
great courage established a domination over the Japanese
lieutenant in charge, so our losses were much lighter than was
the case with other camps higher up.'

But then came the period known as 'speedo' – because 'it
was "Speedo! Speedo! Speedo!" the whole time' – which
started just before the summer monsoon in April 1943:

> We started moving from camp to camp, to reinforce camps
> higher up which had been decimated by disease and illness,

and this was when we really came up against trial and tribulation, because by then it was the monsoon and it was pouring with rain. We lived in mud and we slept under the remnants of tents which leaked like sieves. We got up in the dark, we went to work in the dark, we worked all day long and we came back in the dark, hoping to get some rice for an evening meal. Disease, of course, was rampant: dysentery, beri beri and malaria and then – most frightening of all – cholera. This really was very hard on morale because you could leave a sick friend in the morning when you went to work and when you got back in the evening you were told he had died. With people dying of cholera and the Japanese driving us harder and harder, it was a time when we couldn't help being seized with a most awful feeling of helplessness – because of our utter inability to do anything to influence our own fate. We were completely in the hands of these crazy savages, as they seemed to us, who had no understanding of our suffering. Our being deprived of the elementary trappings of civilization, living in filth and squalor, always having dirty hands, always having wet clothes, literally walking about in excreta – these things didn't seem to bother them. That did depress us terribly and there were times when all of us began to feel that sooner or later we must succumb.

It was at this time that Edward Tokeley, who had remained in Changi suffering from loss of eyesight, was brought to work on the Siam–Burma railway as part of 'F' Force, made up of 'seven thousand half-beats – because, by and large, it was only the sick who were left in Changi'. 'F' Force had to march two hundred and fifty miles from south of Bangkok to Three Pagodas Pass:

It was a ghastly march with thousands of midges that tortured one night after night, biting everywhere – you just couldn't keep them away from you. I got malaria after about the fifth day so I had to be left at one of the staging posts and went up with another party. So I was cut off from the bulk of my Volunteer friends and found myself mainly with some Manchesters and Argylls. I've always disliked since then the noise of the gibbon – we call him the *wa-wa* in Malaya – with that soulful, whooping noise that he makes, which did nothing to cheer one up when one was walking drenched and hungry and miserable like hell out to where you had to work in the half light of morning. Of course, disease took control very quickly. A lot of people died through cerebral malaria, screaming with agony. We got to the cholera belt, where dozens died every day. I had a very bad go but managed to get over it and as a result I was asked to stay on and help out in the cholera ward. I didn't particularly want to go out on the railroad if I could avoid it so I stayed in the cholera ward and my job for a very long time was throwing chaps on the fire and burning them, because you had to get rid of the disease somehow. There were five Boustead chaps who went up with me on 'F' Force and I was the only one came out. I watched one of them die; he turned his face to the wall and said, 'Go away, don't try and annoy me. This is a mathematical affair and I am not prepared to wait.' And he just turned his face to the wall and died. It really was a ghastly period and to me it proved that the veneer of civilization is skin deep and that once you scratch away that thin veneer you're left with the basic human being, who is unpleasant in the extreme and where it's everybody for themselves. There were very few people who really acted as Christians, very few. The vast majority very much looked to themselves and for themselves.

For Bill Goode survival was living 'literally from day to day':

If you could get through the day's work without being bashed up, if you could get something to eat and if you could get to sleep then that was one more day done. And the fact that we were living so close to the earth and such a brutish life meant that your whole being was concentrated on pure existence, and so at the very bad time you simply had neither the time nor the energy to spend on mournful speculation about your fate; you only woke up now and again to think 'Good Lord, we've been here another year and we don't seem to be any nearer getting out.' Inevitably, we became increasingly filled with what was really hatred for the Japanese and for the Koreans who were our more immediate guards. The Koreans got beaten up by the Japanese and then passed it on to us with interest. But it wasn't all gloom. The ordinary British troops, drawn from all walks of life and all sorts and sizes of people, had something quite extraordinary about them when they were gathered together in a more or less disciplined body, whereby their natural spirit seemed to triumph over these appalling surroundings. So we had lots of fun at the same time, like the names that we used for identifying our guards: Arthur Askey; Joe E. Brown; the Rocking Horse; Dr Death, who needless to say was a medical orderly; the Kenyu Kid, who was a particularly vicious little officer, beautifully dressed and an absolute bastard when it came to knocking people about. These names were given partly in a spirit of morbid humour, which carried us a long way and over many months.

When the monsoon ended conditions improved and morale rose once more, but the cost in human lives was very great. Only half of 'F' Force's original work-force returned to Singapore: 'The troops there were horrified at our appearance,' recalls Edward Tokeley. 'We were absolutely emaciated and full of disease. I can't imagine that many were better clothed than I was and all I possessed was one wooden clog and a *japhappi*, which was a form of loincloth. I didn't have anything else.'

By now not all the British in Malaya were there as prisoners. In May 1943 John Davis had been set down off the coast of Perak by Dutch submarine: 'It was wonderful to come out on deck to the muddy, soft, warm smell of the Malay coast that I recognized and loved. We got into our folboat canoes, the

submarine just gently faded away and we were on our own.'
Davis and four Chinese companions rowed five miles to the
shore. 'It was a curiously uneventful way of landing on enemy
territory,' he recalls. 'We ran ashore on a sandy beach with a
jungle canopy ahead of us and it was so quiet and so desolate
that the first thing we did was to have a bathe! Then we hid the
boats and lay down on the beach and slept soundly till dawn.'
In the morning they set off into the nearby jungle and made
camp. Then the Chinese went out to gather intelligence – 'to
find out what was happening in Malaya and to see what had
happened to the Chinese Communist guerrillas that we had
planted in the country.'

While this first contact was being made Davis had nothing
to do but wait in the jungle: 'It soon became apparent that I
was really an obstruction to my people so I decided that the
best thing was for me to go back to India to report the
situation and come back as soon as I could.' Richard
Broome went out on the next submarine and the two
men met at a prearranged rendezvous: 'We put up a
periscope at the right place and immediately I saw a junk
and there was John Davis, with his backside over the stern!'
A month later Davis returned to Malaya and was followed
shortly afterwards by Broome. Contact with the Communists
was now established:

> One evening a stranger was brought into our bivouac camp, a
> young man, probably not more than twenty-two or three,
> quiet and tallish. He was the Political Commissar for Perak
> and his name was Chin Peng. He just said a few things and
> then suddenly and abruptly he brought out a watch and said,
> 'Do you know what this is?' I said, 'Yes, that's my watch and I
> gave it to your leader when I put him down in South Negri
> Sembilan at the beginning of the campaign.' He knew then
> that I was the right person and I had confidence in him
> because he had been able to bring the watch back and from
> then on we got on famously together.

The object of their return to Malaya was to organize a fifth
column behind the enemy lines in preparation for an Allied
invasion, so mutual trust between the Communists and the
British was essential: 'It was no good being suspicious of them
or antagonizing them because we were in their hands in an
enemy country and they were looking after us. Our only
chance was to show full confidence in them in the hope that
they would respond and give us their confidence – and this,
I'm happy to say, is what happened.'

The Communists took Davis and Broome on a five-day
march deep into the interior of their country where the
guerrillas had a number of camps hidden in the jungle. Here
they settled down to plan and prepare for the eventual return
of the British. An agreement was reached by which both sides
would co-operate for the duration of the war, with the British
supplying arms as soon as it was practical to do so. In the
meantime there was little to do but wait. 'We were sleepers
really,' explains Broome:

> It was no use trying to do any sabotage while the Japanese
> were in occupation. The only result of that would have been a
> lot of innocent people murdered. So ours was really a political
> operation. The main trouble was boredom, unquestionably,
> because for a whole year we were cut off. There was only a
> very small chance of being killed by the Japanese because we
> would have had ample warning of their approach, so we were
> perfectly safe. But there was a definite danger in my mind, of
> dying from disease, because we all had malaria terribly badly.
> Every now and then we had visits from one or other of the
> heads of the Communist organization but we were at a
> disadvantage at that time because we were being of no help
> whatsoever.

The one Chinese leader with whom both Broome and
Davis got on well was Chin Peng:

He was the one man whom we were always delighted to see arriving in the camp, because he was a splendid person to be dealing with. He spoke a bit of English but we usually spoke to him in Cantonese, and he was the one Communist whom we felt to be totally reliable. You felt you could rely on his word and he was also an extremely pleasant character. He said to us once, 'Our objectives, of course, are not the same. We want to run the country, you realize that? But for the duration of the war our objective is the same, which is to get rid of the Japanese.'

During this first long period of isolation in the jungle Broome made a number of unsuccessful attempts to get past the Japanese in the plains in order to rendezvous with submarines:

On one of these occasions I was suffering quite badly from malaria and Chin Peng put me on his bicycle and wheeled me for about ten miles, so I always had a pretty soft spot for him. After the war we had several lunches together. His father had a bicycle shop in Telok Anson and as everything was very scarce in those days I did my best to get a special dispensation to import bicycle parts into Malaya simply for Chin Peng's shop, because if he'd really got established in that it's quite possible that he might have chosen a different course from the one he did, which was to become the number one leader of the Communist insurrection.

After a year and a half of total silence from Broome and Davis they were given up as lost by the leaders of Force 136 in India. Finally, they were able to get a radio going using a pedal-powered transmitter and contact was re-established:

We'd been written off and furthermore we were using out-of-date codes, so our chances of getting through were slim, but it so happened that one of the FANYS (First Aid Nursing Yeomanry) who manned the radio sets in Colombo was twiddling the knobs and she heard a signal. She reported this and there was a lot of laughter but after a bit of an argument they accepted the fact and realized that we were using out-of-date codes. The assumption was that we were in the hands of the Japanese, so they started sending over security checks on their messages to us. We didn't realize this so we didn't send the right replies, which merely increased their suspicion and they decided to class this as an enemy station. But fortunately we had a great friend from the Malayan Police in headquarters and he said, 'Oh, give them another chance.' So they sent over a message which referred to 'Tightarse', which was Davis' nickname, and to Tamsin, which was my wife's name. We then realized what had happened and so we concocted a fairly ribald message about 'Tightarse', told them to 'leave my wife out of this' and finally said, 'Are you satisfied now, you bastards? If you don't believe us, come and pedal the bloody machine yourselves.' No Jap could have made up a thing like that so they had a tremendous night out in Colombo on it – and after that things went absolutely splendidly.

Early in 1944 the first supply drop took place:

We got an army of thirty or forty Sakai aboriginals and with our own men helping we built up enormous piles of timber. Then we listened and listened and suddenly we heard the drone of planes in the distance. We immediately set light to these flares and the flames leapt up twenty feet into the air – we were told that they could be seen over the Straits of Malacca and that the whole of Perak must have been roused by them. Then the planes came round and dropped the men first of all and then lovely little weapons, small carbines which we'd never seen. So from that time on the whole scene changed and something like four hundred people were dropped in over the few remaining months of the war.

Davis also became aware that during his two years in the jungle the British Government's attitude towards the Communists had changed: 'They had become the natural enemy in the eyes of the British. But these Communists in Malaya were not baddies, they were our allies and this created tension – which became apparent immediately after the ending of the war.'

Some months earlier Davis had been walking in the jungle with a third member of their group, Freddie Spencer-Chapman, when they both heard a 'tremendous booming roar in the sky. There was a clearing nearby so we dashed out to look and there, unmistakably, were about twenty or thirty American Flying Fortresses, flying over on the way to bomb Singapore.' The same aeroplanes appeared 'like silver bullets shining in the sky' to Peter Lucy and his comrades still working in Singapore docks, and even though the bombers then proceeded to unload incendiary bombs over the city it was nevertheless 'one of the greatest moments of all', because it so clearly heralded the end of the war.

Yet liberation would come too late to save many thousands of prisoners. In the POW camp in Kuching more than half the occupants had died. John Baxter remembers how 'they were burying ten a day at the end and playing the Last Post over coffins that held two bodies at a time. Those who were still alive were walking skeletons, with no backside at all; where their spines ended their legs began.' Baxter himself dropped from thirteen-and-a-half stone to eight – but he survived: 'Age didn't seem to have much to do with it as far as I could see. It was entirely mental. If you thought it was going to end all right and you didn't worry, then you survived.'

The story was repeated in Sumatra, where Cunyngham-Brown was one of the few who survived the building of a railway across the island: 'We went across to Sumatra three thousand strong and we built that railway for the Japanese. It ran for a fortnight before the end of the war in autumn 1945 by which time we were just over eight hundred strong.' Long before then the struggle for survival had become one in which both prisoners and guards were equally involved: 'The Japan-

ese were no better to their own men than they were to us and
they equally were dying at great speed from malaria and the
absence of quinine and from under-nourishment.' Having
lived in Malaya and spent time in the jungle Cunyngham-
Brown was able to profit from his experience:

> I was accustomed to the sort of food people ate and I knew
> what sort of things one could collect from the secondary
> jungle growths around the camp that could be cooked and
> eaten. I used to bring in occasional dogs, cats, frogs or snails
> and loads of ferns, which have very good little edible tips on
> them, and attempt to persuade the British Other Ranks to eat
> this – but no, they'd rather not. And I'm sorry to say that
> whereas the Cockney would give a toothless grin and shove
> into his guts anything that was going, my own great Scotsmen,
> looking so noble and splendid, would sit dreaming of the girl
> with the light brown hair and thinking of their beautiful
> Scotland and dying as quickly as they could. I was also the
> sanitary officer of the camp and they built for me very good
> closed refuse dumps with naval-fashion hatches on top so that
> everything was hermetically sealed and you didn't get flies in
> the camp and therefore we had no cholera. There was a
> quantity of bones from the kitchen in these refuse dumps and
> it was my practice to go down into these dumps at night to
> fossick about and collect them, so that I could grind them
> down and boil them to make soup for the hospital patients.
> This was a godsend as far as health was concerned and yet so
> many people said, 'No, I'm sorry' – and died as a result.
> Coming across me one night as I wallowed in the filth of one
> of these refuse dumps in my perpetual search for bones, a
> brother officer of mine turned away from me in disquiet with
> a remark, 'I'm sorry to see you like this. I only hope I don't go
> the same way.'

Here, as in many other camps, there was a secret wireless
receiver that remained undiscovered by the Japanese, so that it

was possible to follow the progress of the war in its closing stages. Then, just when it seemed as if the liberation of South-East Asia was at hand, a sinister development occurred:

> Our guards had become extremely unobtrusive over the last week and then suddenly they were withdrawn and a very savage bundle of Koreans came in who dragooned us with day-long digging of large trenches that were six-feet deep, six-feet wide and thirty-feet long. It wasn't until they started putting emplacements up at the ends of these holes for their machine guns that we realized that these were our graves that we were digging.

A last-minute reprieve came in the form of the atomic bombs dropped on Hiroshima and Nagasaki, which 'not only saved our own lives but those of millions in South-East Asia'.

In Changi POW camp Perky Perkins remembers how the hut commanders were sent for by the Japanese:

> We all waited anxiously to hear what the result was and then the hut commanders started coming back and we could hear cheers from Number One Hut and Number Two Hut and Number Three – and then our own hut, Number Four. Oh, how we cheered! The Dutch started to sing their national anthem which they'd often sung during the imprisonment, but we'd never sung ours. But then we started to sing *God Save the King* and at first the thing rather collapsed. Then we started again and sang it with great fervency.

For Peter Lucy in the Singapore docks the end came rather less dramatically: 'We got the news and so we waited for something to happen and after waiting for at least a week we took matters into our own hands. We went up and told the Japanese that the war was over, to which they immediately agreed. We then handed our tools to the Japanese soldiers and watched the Japanese doing our work.' But of the original working party that had come to Blakang Mati two hundred and fifty strong, only eighteen remained.

Over in Sumatra the surviving prisoners began to repair a nearby airfield. 'I was given the job of putting their airstrip in order with the very greatest speed with a hundred men,' recalls Cunyngham-Brown:

> The work went on from early dawn to late dusk and we made remarkable progress but on the third day some large aircraft came floating over and circled around the camp and the airstrip. The next day they came back and we realized they were the same ones because the front one of these three aircraft was a shiny, polished one which glittered in the morning sunshine. They came lower this time but again they disappeared. On the third day we were still working as hard as we possibly could, filling in these trenches across it, but the runway still wasn't hard enough. But then to our horror and surprise the front one of these three planes came in just over the palm trees and made a landing, bumping and jumping in a cloud of dust across the airstrip and on into the secondary growth at the other end, where it made a successful turn and then worked its way out of the undergrowth again. I was furious at this and rushed over – losing every stitch of clothing in the process, because I was only wearing a small loincloth – so as to shout to the pilot, 'For God's sake don't let the rest in. Wait until we're ready for you.' But no, the door opened and an extremely attractive woman, elegant in the extreme in what I thought was a WREN uniform but was actually St John's Ambulance, was standing at the top of the gangway. I stood within twelve feet of her, stark naked, and as she came down the steps I said, 'I do apologize.' 'Not at all,' she said. 'What you need is a cigarette.' She held out a gold cigarette-case and I had my first English cigarette for three-and-a-half years. 'Do tell me,' I asked, 'what is your name?' She replied, 'I'm Lady Mountbatten.'

Later that same day Cunyngham-Brown was back in Singapore, astonished by the look of the average European: 'They were pink-coloured, fat little tubs of lard, all of them shining with sweat and good health.' Other prisoners also managed to make their way into Singapore. John Theophilus and a friend got a lift from Changi down to the docks: 'We'd all kept a pair of shorts and a shirt for just such an occasion so we looked quite respectable. We then went aboard HMS *Sussex* and had our first beer for three-and-a-half years.' George Wort also went into the city and called in at the Chartered Bank: 'I asked for my account and it was handed to me straight away, just like that!'

In Kuching Edward Banks made a point of searching out the Chinese girl who had given his morale such a boost in the early days of his captivity: 'I found that kid and gave her some emergency rations and later got her a job, because she was a bright little girl. She was the slyest little crook you've ever met, but the last I saw of her was in the arms of a British soldier, gazing up into his eyes – and the best of luck to her!'

The prisoners of war and internees were all to be repatriated as soon as transport could be arranged, but after being told that he was to go home and that he could be of no possible use in the meantime, Cunyngham-Brown decided to go back to his old post in Johore Bahru. He made his way over the causeway and went to see M. C. Hay, an old friend in the MCS, who was now the Chief Civil Affairs Officer for Johore. Here he was made welcome and given a bath and a change of clothing – 'putting on the uniform of a full colonel in the British Army, which was all that M. C. Hay could let me have'. After dinner that night in the Residency, Hay gave Cunyngham-Brown a revolver and told him that transport was waiting for him outside:

> With a cigar in my mouth and seated very comfortably in the back of the car I proceeded up the road for fifteen or twenty miles until the headlights disclosed a chunky, tired Japanese

general with his forces trudging along behind in the best order they could maintain. The car stopped and they came to a halt. I got out of the car and the general walked towards me. He gave me his sword and his ADC gave me his flag. He saluted, I responded, and I took his surrender.

Epilogue – Staying On

'I wish that the critics of colonialism could have been present when the British returned to Malaya after the Japanese surrender,' declares Richard Broome. 'Their reception was totally rapturous from all sections of the population. Three weeks after the surrender it was still going on; as I drove up-country people were coming out of their houses by the road-side and waving and cheering. The obvious relief on their faces was something terrific to see.'

The defeat and subsequent humiliation of the British in 1942 had indeed had an impact on the local population but, in Bill Goode's estimation, its effect was less than was later assumed to be the case: 'The first reaction of the population was one of overwhelming joy that the Japanese occupation was over and that the people they knew and had previously trusted had come back to help them recover from the damage done by the war, because that was the first priority – to repair power stations and water supplies, to get food in so that they could eat and cloth so that people could have clothes, and to get the economy going again.'

Under the aegis of a British military administration the former British territories in South-East Asia now entered a period that was known officially as rehabilitation. Returning to

Malaya as a civilian official with the Ministry of Supply, John Forrester was flown up to Kuala Lumpur – to be met by a large contingent of Japanese troops drawn up on the airfield: 'Some very important general marched up to us and said he wanted to surrender. We said we knew nothing about it and all we were interested in was finding transport to Kuala Lumpur, so we couldn't help him.' In KL, Forrester and other officials began to take the first measures to restart the economy by getting large sums of money back into circulation and tracking down any supplies of rubber that could be exported: 'Then gradually the banks and the insurance companies came back and people returned after their internment and a period of leave and started up the plantations properly, and everything gradually came back to normal.'

All internees and prisoners of war had been repatriated to Britain after their release. Trevor Walker was one of many who returned to a family of whom he had had no word for three-and-a-half years:

> I found my family living quite close to Dorking in Surrey, where the Guthries' office had been rusticated after being moved out of their city office. I made my number with the people in the office and told them that I'd done nothing for too long and should like to do some work. My chairman said, 'When you're fit, come and work with us two or three days a week and re-engage all the planters and the office staff. But nobody is to go back until he is fit and nobody must go back until he has been at home for six months.' So we did it gently and as best we could and one of the most remarkable things was the keenness displayed by almost everybody to go back.

John Theophilus' reactions were very typical of the great majority of planters: 'I'd been a rubber planter virtually all my adult life and I knew nothing else. I wanted to come back; I liked the country and the people and I wanted to get things moving again. It took a bit of time because the

estates were mostly secondary jungle.' Returning to Sapong
Estate in North Borneo John Baxter found gruesome scenes
of devastation:

> It was completely overgrown with weeds up to the branches of
> the rubber trees and covered in Japanese graves, which the
> pigs had dug up so that that there were bones all over the
> place. There were only two buildings left standing and the
> labour remaining on the estate were skeletons, covered in
> scabies and ulcers and suffering from malaria. About ninety
> per cent of them had died. It was dreadful. But I found that my
> family, Susan and the small children, had managed to survive,
> which was really a miracle. They had managed to exist by
> fishing and planting *padi*. But it had been a real hard life for
> them and my youngest daughter had died just at the end of the
> war from malaria.

Many marriage also proved to be casualties of the war.
'Thousands of marriages broke up and it was nobody's fault,'
declares Tommy Lucy. During the long separation from her
husband she herself had often wondered how, if he survived,
she would react to him after his release. The only news she had
received during his period as a prisoner of war had been a
single postcard containing a few phrases selected from a list
drawn up by the Japanese authorities:

> It was difficult to get together again because we had lived in
> such completely different circumstances for four years. The
> women had been in authority and in positions of responsibility
> all over the world, while our husbands had been beaten and
> treated despicably by a race that had no moral code in war
> whatsoever. So we had changed as people and it was im-
> possible in many cases to readjust. Very many of our friends'
> marriages broke up and there were times when we ourselves
> thought we would have to divorce because we were not
> thinking in the same way as we had four years before. But

we persisted; we were determined that we could make a go of it once we got back to Malaya, the beautiful country that we both loved and where we had met and married. As soon as we got back and the circumstances were the same, we found our old love for each other.

Peter Lucy's bungalow was still standing but all its contents had long since disappeared: 'We had to start from scratch with two deck chairs, two camp beds and a camp table, and we had to drink our first bottle of whisky in order to get a water bottle.' The bulk of the estate's original force had died on the Siam–Burma railway, but there were enough survivors to get the estate back in working order and within a matter of months rubber was once more being tapped: 'We then had about a year of the normal rubber planter's life – not quite so good as it had been before the war but still enjoyable.'

Throughout South-East Asia the war had taken a heavy toll among the civil population. In Sarawak, where food shortages and malnutrition had led to an epidemic of the skin disease known as yaws, Robert Nicholl was horrified to see 'these awful dripping sores all over people' when he first went up-river. Hitherto western medicine had been regarded as something to be avoided:

It was very difficult to get anybody to suffer the dangers of inoculation because that was generally associated with death, as was everything in the way of European medicine. But our hospital assistants stepped in with their hypodermic syringes and penicillin and when they had injected a few people with this ghastly disease and the sores healed up, then word very quickly spread up-river. Immediately people heard there was a cure down they came, all demanding injections. And that completely transformed the attitude of the people of the interior to Western medicine. People came down-river for days to the government dispensary, demanding cures for all sorts of things – even for bad dreams.

There was also an acute shortage of clothing material, which was ameliorated to some extent by relief supplies from America. Robert Nicholl was given some of these to distribute:

> As I happened to be going up the Baram river, the District Officer said to me, 'Look, a group of Punans are coming to Long Akah; would you take up this bale of stuff and distribute it to them?' So I went up and, sure enough, in came the Punans, twenty-seven of them as far as I remember. One of the Kayans who was with me interpreted and explained that we brought this present from the people of America. Then we opened the bale and it was really quite a surprise because it consisted entirely of fur coats. However, the Punans had never seen fur coats before and were immensely thrilled by these extraordinary things, so we divided the fur coats into twenty-seven little bundles and the Punans drew lots and each was given his little bundle. And having decked themselves out in these beautiful fur coats, off they went into the jungle and that was the last we saw of them.

Another great advance was made in the eradication of malaria, using new forms of insecticide – with unexpected consequences:

> Whereas formerly when you went up-river you sat amidst clouds of smoke conversing rather as fiends do in hell, now there was not a mosquito left and you could sit and talk in comfort. When you went to bed, however, you would be bitten not by mosquitoes but by rats, because the longhouses were overrun with rats. In killing the mosquitoes the anti-malarial teams had also killed the cockroaches, which were eaten by the cats, who seemed to find the Dieldrin seasoning attractive. So, of course, the cats died, too. People were now being bitten by these wretched rats and up went the cry, 'For the love of God, send us cats.' And that was the point at which the RAF stepped in. Cats were assembled and sorted out, generally one tom and

two female cats, and put into containers to be loaded on to
planes with little parachutes attached. The planes then flew up
into the interior, circled the longhouses and out went the
container. The parachute opened and the cat container
floated to the ground. And the cats, of course, found themselves in what could only be described as a cat's terrestrial
paradise.

It was now quite obvious that the days of colonial rule were
numbered. In Sarawak and North Borneo the first steps
towards eventual self-government were taken in 1946, when
both territories ceased to be independent fiefdoms of the
Brookes and the British North Borneo Company respectively
and were brought into the orthodox colonial fold. The only
political issues that remained to be settled were the actual
timetable of events leading up to full independence and the
question of who should do the governing thereafter. In the
meantime, it was generally agreed that the process of rehabilitation had first to be completed – as speedily and as
thoroughly as possible.

The immediate post-war years were, for Trevor Walker as
for many of his colleagues, the hardest-working years that they
had ever experienced:

> Both in the office and on the estates we were bringing things
> back to the standards that we had known before the war. We
> were approaching normality again and it looked as though not
> only peace was returning but prosperity with it. The political
> scene was changing, certainly; there was an approach towards
> Independence and people were being politically more vocif-
> erous than they had been before – although in a very pleasant
> fashion – when out of the blue came the Communist uprising
> that became known as the 'Emergency'.

The Communist guerrilla forces which had co-operated
with Force 136 and the British throughout the war had been

disbanded in 1946 with 'all the face and ceremony that the army could give them'. Its leaders had assured John Davis that, even if their ultimate aim was the political control of Malaya, 'the day had ceased when they were going to fight anybody', so that the sudden outbreak of terrorism directed by these same leaders came as much as a surprise to him as to anybody else: 'We had always known that they would remain our political enemies. That seemed all right, but it was ironic that only two years later these people whom we had treated as friends should find it necessary to start the Malayan Emergency in a terrible manner with the murder of two planters up in Perak.' The rest of Davis' career in Malaya was to be spent fighting the predominantly Chinese terrorists, who had once more retreated into the jungle, and their leader, Chin Peng – 'this man who had been my greatest ally and who had always, I believe, remained a good friend'.

In many ways the Emergency proved to be an even greater test of fortitude than the Japanese invasion and occupation of Malaya. It was a long drawn-out affair, lasting for more than a decade, and if the end result was 'the only war ever won against Communists' it was certainly not won easily. But whereas in 1941 'we were all virtually pawns, admittedly giving some help to the armed forces but entirely dependent on the fortunes of the fighters for our lives, our homes, our businesses and our possessions', now the Europeans found themselves 'masters of their own fate', all actively involved in a war that 'reached into the most remote *kampongs* and affected vitally almost everyone. We were not relatively safe miles behind the front line. There was no front line; it was all round us.'

It was the rubber planters and the tin-miners who provided the easiest and the most valuable targets. 'On 6 July 1948 we woke up to the news of the killing of two of our friends in Perak,' recalls Tommy Lucy. 'We realized almost immediately that we were going to be the main targets for the Communist bandits – they were always called bandits – because if they got rid of the British influence on the plantations and in the tin-mines then the labour forces would be disrupted and the whole of the country would come to a halt.' But what the Communists had failed to take into account was that 'we were absolutely determined that we were going to stay'. After what they and nearly everybody else in the same position had gone through, the Lucys felt that there was no question of pulling out: 'I said in no circumstances would I leave,' Tommy Lucy declares. 'The Indian women have to stay and the Malay women and so the British women must stay too and take whatever is coming to us. We did not know what was coming to us, of course, but I wish people would not call it an Emergency – because it was a full-scale war.'

As far as the planters and tin-miners were concerned, the reactions of the government to the first acts of terrorism were not encouraging: 'It was simply not realized by the authorities how vulnerable we were and how simple it would have been for the Communists to get rid of us all at a blow. It was only by a miracle of misjudgement on their part that we were not all killed in the first year.' Norman Cleaveland had returned to Malaya to resume tin-mining operations just outside Kuala Lumpur, after an absence of more than a decade. For the first three years of the Emergency he remained convinced that the Communists were going to win:

> The confusion between the services and the civilians and between the state and federal governments was almost unbelievable. We were frequently admonished by the authorities not to panic and not to publicize the situation. We were very strongly told that we must not use the word Communist. They were not Communists; they were bandits. And all the while incredible things happened that made for a lack of confidence. For instance, immediately violence broke out we were told that we were on our own. I asked what would be available to us in the way of weapons and they said, 'Nothing.' The Chamber of Mines sent a signal of distress to London to get the Colonial Office to take action and the Colonial Office

came right back and said that they had made an investigation
and their records showed that there were plenty of guns and
ammunition in Malaya. We returned a message saying they
were dead right; there were plenty of guns and ammunition in
Malaya but they happened to be in the wrong hands.

When the tin-miners took steps to defend themselves they
met with government opposition:

Our Superintendent in Perak went out with a truck and an
acetylene torch and gathered up all the armoured plate from
the derelicts of the Japanese invasion and armoured some
jeeps and other vehicles, including a jeep for the Kampar
police which was promptly confiscated by higher authority.
When we got these armoured cars to Kuala Lumpur we were
told that they too were going to be confiscated and that the
government were not going to permit any private armies in the
country. I got facetious and said, 'Well, how about the
Communist army? Was that private or public?' However,
facetiousness got me nowhere so then Anglo-Oriental, which
was the largest company in Malaya, said, 'Look either we get
those armoured cars or we shut down the show' – which would
have meant blocking off twenty-five per cent of Malaya's tin
production. They then let us have the armoured cars.

After failing to get any help from the government over arms,
Cleaveland turned to America for help: 'The first two Pan-
American planes to arrive in Singapore after the war were
loaded with guns and ammunition, not only for ourselves but
also for the entire mining industry. Later we expanded our
order and got further guns and ammunition for the rubber
industry. It was an incredible situation because these two
industries at that time were supplying more hard currency
for the sterling bloc than any other.'
Vulnerable as the tin-mines were, they were not so isolated
as many of the rubber estates and it was here that the highest

casualties among the Europeans were suffered. One in five of the rubber plantation managers in the state of Pahang was murdered and over one hundred and twenty planters killed in all.

Peter Lucy's Amhurst Estate six miles outside Kuala Lumpur was attacked on innumerable occasions: 'This was a daily event and not an occasional sporadic attack, because walking past us to their store of guns in Batu caves they would take pot shots at us, either by day or by night, and this went on for weeks and months and even years.' Right from the start the Lucys had decided that maximum protection was essential: 'A splendid Canadian couple, who were missionaries, ran a school for Chinese children two miles away from us and I begged them to protect themselves in some way but they said, "Oh, no, the Lord will protect us." It wasn't long before they and their children were burnt alive in their home by the Communists.' As well as building up an armoury that they reckoned to be second to none in Malaya, the Lucys also fortified their bungalow with a barbed-wire perimeter guarded by two Alsatian dogs and floodlit at night. Finally, as the government began to respond to the pleas of the planters and tin-miners for help, they received reinforcements in the form of twenty-six armed special constables:

When the bandits attacked us the floodlights went on, we had all the guns and ammunition at the ready and we could fire and kill them before they killed us. At the first sound of a bullet my job was to rush to the telephone and see if the line was cut, then get out my bren gun and start firing. Another of my jobs was to fire a Verey light in order to get help from the Gurkhas who were stationed on a property near Kuala Lumpur.

A sight I shall never forget is when you're lying there expecting to be shot dead and suddenly an armoured car full of Gurkhas with guns blazing and tracer bullets going into the rubber trees, comes up your drive and you know that you are safe.

As the months went by the attacks on the estate became more frequent and then, to make matters more difficult, Tommy Lucy became pregnant:

> I knew I was going to have twins and as the time drew near for their arrival my greatest fear was that a bullet would go into my tummy, so towards the end I would use the bren gun only on real emergencies. Otherwise, I used to go and lie in an old steel bath at the back of the bungalow, because pregnant or not I was absolutely determined that these devils would not get us. That attitude persisted until one night when there was a really bad attack and I was forced to use the bren gun and I must have twisted the wrong way because I suddenly felt a dreadful pain and as it was near my time I knew that I was going to give birth. My husband got out the armoured car and I was carried in, but with a gun as always by my side. As we went down the drive we saw the bandits in the drive ahead of us. There was obviously no turning back so Peter put his foot down on the accelerator and we roared and bumped over this road. Why the twins didn't arrive in the armoured car I don't know, but as a final gesture of defiance I put my pistol through the louvres of the armoured car and fired a shot and yelled, 'That's for you. You devils!' But we did get through and got to the hospital where I was safely delivered of two fine boys.

Amhurst Estate was made up of four divisions that were widely separated so that Peter Lucy was often away from the bungalow. Like other wives in the same position Tommy Lucy always had to live with 'the awful fear when your husband went out in the morning to do his rounds that you would never see him again'. Her fears were well founded, for visiting one of the outlying divisions one day with a visiting agent, Peter Lucy walked straight into an ambush:

> They opened fire with their sten guns as we approached. They shot Clarkson in the stomach; the whole of the

magazine must have gone into him because he dropped dead right at my feet. But for some reason I didn't get hurt and as I had a revolver I fired back and I presume I got a bandit because I've got his hat. Then I disappeared into a ravine and it took me three hours to get home – by which time the *Malay Mail* had appeared stating that Mr Clarkson had been shot dead and that I was missing presumed dead. My wife was in the house, having read the paper and surrounded by other planters.

After surviving a second ambush in which he shot dead a prominent guerrilla leader – 'I happened to have a twelve-bore shotgun over my shoulder and I just brought it down as if I was shooting a rabbit and got him in the head' – Lucy was warned by the police that he was a marked man. On the advice of the new High Commissioner, Sir Gerald Templer, and for the sake of their children, the Lucys very reluctantly took up the offer of a job in East Africa.

There seems little doubt that the arrival of Templer dramatically changed the tempo of the struggle against the Communists. His predecessor as High Commissioner had been ambushed and murdered in his car as he drove up to Fraser's Hill; an event that had shaken all nationalities in Malaya very badly but had also had the effect of forcing the British Government to take more positive action. 'Out came somebody who was almost unheard of – but with more powers than any soldier since Cromwell,' declares Guy Madoc:

In no time at all Templer turned us upside down. He was a man who used four-letter words and he said, 'I'm going to put some ginger up—' Perhaps I'd better not say where he was going to put the ginger but he was absolutely the key figure in those years. He persuaded the Malay leaders that we were going to win and he persuaded us that we were going to win. He was a complete human dynamo; he drove himself tirelessly and he drove everybody else. Sometimes you'd feel you weren't really getting home to him; he was looking a bit tired – and then suddenly you'd say something and he'd come upright like a spring. He'd open the bottom drawer of his desk and put his feet into it and start addressing you as 'Old cock'. Well, then you knew you were really home and that you were getting somewhere with him. I found, too, that he was a very superstitious man. One thing he absolutely refused to do was to drive up the road where his predecessor had been killed. He was always ready to go places and meet members of the Special Branch, high or low, but he refused to go up that road. He said, 'Nope. If I go up that road I'll be killed. I'll come in by chopper, old cock.' However, as far as I was concerned, one of the great moves he made was to say, 'Right, Special Branch has got to be separated completely from CID and that should be done in forty-eight hours' – and I found myself head of Special Branch.

The war against the Communists was being fought on both military and political fronts – and Templer assumed personal command of both:

In the first years of the Emergency the army really wasted a tremendous amount of energy by sending random patrols into the jungle which very rarely made any contact with the terrorists. The terrorist in the jungle had become as sensitive as a wild animal. He could smell cigarette smoke half a mile away and if you used brilliantine on your hair or used too much toothpaste he could detect that too. We had great difficulty in overcoming the British soldier's desire for cleanliness. But with the build-up in the strength of the Special Branch and its efficiency we got to the stage where every unit of the army could be gainfully used, either by denying a particular area to the terrorists or by ambushes.

It had been recognized for some time before Templer's arrival that the key to defeating the Communists lay in separating them from their food supplies and their sources of intelligence, which came primarily from the Chinese squatters living on the fringes of the jungle. This was the basis of the Briggs Plan, which involved the resettlement of squatters in New Villages together with such measures as the formation of Home Guard units, food rationing and the carrying of identity cards. Although accepted by the government the plan was being implemented with considerable reluctance. Templer seized upon the Briggs Plan and gave it top priority:

> So gradually we began to starve the terrorists from the jungle, while the Special Branch took good care to arrange defects in the food denial arrangements in some operational areas, so that our secret agents amongst the New Villagers could attract their terrorist contacts. Such places we called our 'honey pots', where the military and our para-military police could pre-arrange effective ambushes.

It was Templer, too, who recognized the psychological value of what came to be known as the 'White Areas':

> Almost fortuitously, we cleared the whole of Malacca territory and Templer said, 'Aha, now if we free the people of Malacca from practically every emergency restriction, including food control and food rationing, this will encourage the civilian population in other parts of the country to work for us against the Communists. It's a carrot that we can hold out' – and how right he was. Six months later we'd cleared the whole of the State of Pahang, which is almost continuous with Malacca, and within a year we'd got a complete White Area right across Malaya so that the lines of communication between the terrorists in the north and south were cut. Starting from the original White Area we then decided to take on Communist districts and wipe them out one at a time, concentrating all our intelligence resources and the best units of the army and knocking them out at a rate that varied between four months

and nine months each. This was never done at random; always we went for a district neighbouring a new White Area, because you'd got to roll up your enemy, so that it was obvious not only to the civilians but to the terrorists, too, that there was a sort of inevitability about it.

At the same time the High Commissioner ensured that advances were maintained on the political front. The 'Malaysi-anization' of all the government services was stepped up and Whitehall was persuaded that Malaya should be granted independence sooner rather than later. In consequence, self-government in the Malay states and the other former British colonies came about 'easily and politely and gradually' and with remarkable good will on all sides. In Sarawak, for instance, 'an elite of educated people from amongst the people of the interior had been raised up who could take over from us. They were brought into government service and put to work under some experienced officer. Gradually, they took over and the experi-enced chap remained as an adviser and in the end they were on their own. The actual hand-over took place as soon as we had got them qualified.'

Malaya was the first to gain its independence in August 1957, but as the Union Jack was hauled down here and in other former British territories in South-East Asia there was little sadness among the British witnesses. Guy Madoc was one of the many Europeans who attended the *Merdeka* ceremonies in Kuala Lumpur:

> We all dressed ourselves up in our full dress uniforms and went off to the stadium and saw this really magnificent ceremony, with the Malay police and Malay regiment marching with all the dignity and precision at which they are so adept. It was a moving ceremony; one that we witnessed without sadness but really with pride in what the British had achieved in the country and with a great warmth, too, because the Malays gave us expatriates due credit for what we did for them.

After all the pomp there were other more informal parties. In Penang John Forrester recalls how first 'there were speeches, a band played, the flag was lowered and everything was very, very formal. Then everyone, including the band, came into the bar and we had the most wonderful evening, with the Resident Commissioner dancing on the table and taking his shirt off.'

As the younger men that they had trained began to take over so the British officials went into early retirement; a few moved to other colonies but the great majority returned to the United Kingdom. They went with the satisfaction that they left behind countries that were 'prosperous and peaceful and well-governed'. They had stood for 'decent, not very efficient but well-meaning government that gave the very poorest man a chance to live and enough food to eat'. And if as rulers they had been 'sometimes pompous and stupid' they had also been, by and large, 'dedicated, intrinsically good and incorruptible'.

For those in commerce, of course, life went on very much as it had done before *Merdeka*. In 1960 the State of Emergency that had existed in Malaya since 1948 was officially lifted and all sections of the community were free to enjoy an inheritance that was in many respects the envy of a great many other newly-emergent nations. In business as in government, Malaysianization programmes ensured that more native Malaysians were brought into all the big companies. And in the clubs, too, the last racial barriers were lowered. When John Theophilus became President of the Sungei Ujong Club in 1959 one of his first acts was to write a letter to all its members: 'I said that there was nothing in our rules to stop Asians from becoming members of the club and that if any member had any objections to the club being open to anyone please would they let me know before the end of the month. I never got a single reply and therefore from 1 May 1959 the club became open to anyone from any community to be put up as members. Now we have over a thousand members of the club among whom there are damn few Europeans.'

Theophilus was one of a considerable number of Europeans

who chose to stay on when the time came for them to retire. He did so quite simply because 'it was a bloody marvellous country'. Bill Bangs (now better known perhaps as Dato Haji Mohamed Yusuf Bangs) was another who had no doubts as to where his future loyalties lay: 'There was no question of my going back to England because I looked upon Malaya as my country and I had no further wish to go back to England.' He had been a Malayan citizen since 1948. Another planter who followed the same course was Perky Perkins, who built a house for himself on a promontory overlooking the Malacca Straits: 'I saw this lovely site and I thought what a wonderful place. There was a little holy place on this cape with a grave which people claim is the grave of Admiral Ricardo, a Portuguese admiral. So I had a *bomoh* come up who looked it over and said it was a lucky site and I built my house there and called it Bukit Tersenyum – Smiling Hill.'

John Baxter, Hugh Watts and Mervyn Sheppard (now Tan Sri Dato Mubin Sheppard) also became Malaysian citizens. Datuk John Baxter now lives in retirement with his family in Tenom, not far from the estate where he first began working as an assistant in the mid-1920s, taking little interest in the affairs of Britain other than following the sporting results: 'We have fifty head of cattle, a small area of cocoa and rubber and twenty acres of wet *padi* – which has been completely washed out in the last flood. I know everybody here and they know me and if I went anywhere else I couldn't possibly be as happy. All my children have turned out well and if you have a family that turns out well then you're a happy man.'

Captains Percy Bulbrook and Monty Wright became citizens of Singapore. Today Bulbrook lives with his wife in a modern apartment block overlooking a busy dual-carriageway that was no more than a bullock-cart track when he first came to Singapore. 'I just can't fit in the transformation that's taken place,' he admits. 'I had to give up driving last year: you just keep losing your way.' But he still keeps in close touch with the Straits steamers' captains who succeeded him:

I always wig the younger generation that come up here to see me. I tell them, 'Cor, you don't know what bloody weather is yet. Wait till you go foreign.' I always joke with them and tell them what my father told me, that all the real sailors were killed at the battle of Trafalgar: 'You've got radar, echo sounders, push buttons everywhere. All we had was our eyes, our ears and our heads' – but, by God, I'd go back with them tomorrow if I could.

Sjovald Cunyngham-Brown is another expatriate, still based in Penang where he was the last British President of George Town and where today he has a small part-time export business in spices and other Malayan produce.

It is one of those old perfumed trades where one has to have a bath to get the smell of cloves off one in the evening. And it often makes me laugh when I'm doing this job to think that this is where we came in, that this is exactly the way they were doing their job in 1686 on the territory of Bencoolen in Sumatra, which was our very first possession in South-East Asia – young men in the East India Company collecting the cloves as I am, supervising the export of this precious commodity. That is an additional enchantment to a life that I find perfectly satisfying.

Robert Nicholl is now employed by His Highness the Sultan of Brunei and still gets visited by old boys that he once taught in Sarawak:

It's surprising how gratifying it is to come across boys whom one first saw as urchins puffing hard at their cheroots and knocking back glasses of *borak*, and then taught in one's sixth form. Now they are very important people either in government or in commerce and so one feels that all those years in Sarawak were not only happy but fruitful. They were not wasted years.

When Guy Madoc retired from the police he returned to the United Kingdom, like the great majority of his colleagues. However, the country in which he had spent all of his working life continues to exercise a hold over him: 'At intervals a sudden urge comes to go back just to visit some particular place, such as my beloved district of Jelebu.' In 1976 he and Nancy Madoc returned to make just such a visit:

I'd promised myself a trip in the jungle and I was in all day entirely on my own watching birds, cutting my way with a jungle knife. I came to a stream where some Malay youths were bathing and I sat and watched them. When they came out of the water they carefully examined my jungle knife. Then they said, 'You speak our language,' and I said, 'Yes, of course I do, because I was the officer in charge of the police district right here about forty years ago.' 'Oh,' said they, 'How old are you?' I said I was sixty-seven, 'Umph, when our grandfathers reach that sort of age they stay peacefully at home in their *kampongs*.'

Contributors

Plain Tales from the Raj

Geoffrey ALLEN, OBE, MC; b. 1912 Cawnpore; Asst. Manager Darbangha Raj 1933; 2nd/7th Gurkha Rifles 1939; IPS, North East Frontier Agency 1945–53; stayed on Indian Tea Assoc.

Joan ALLEN (née Henry); b. 1913 Bihar; father planter; m. Geoffrey ALLEN 1937; left India 1965.

Field-Marshal Sir Claude AUCHINLECK, GCB, GCIE, CSI, DSO; b. 1884; 62nd Punjabis 1904; CO 1st/1st Punjab Rgt. 1929; Comm. Peshawar Brigade 1933; C-in-C India 1941, 1954; Supreme Comm. 1947.

Stephen BENTLEY, BEM; b. 1902; India as band boy 2nd Bttn. Seaforth Highlanders 1927; left India 1933.

Vere Lady BIRDWOOD (née Ogilvie); b. 1909; m. Capt. Christopher Birdwood, Probyn's Horse New Delhi 1931; left India 1945.

Cuthbert BOWDER; b. Bareilly 1902; Irrigation Branch, PWD, UP 1925; left India 1947.

Norah BOWDER (née Sullivan); b. 1903; m. Cuthbert BOWDER Bombay 1933; left India 1945.

Ed BROWN; b. 1904; India as band boy 2nd Bttn. Royal Warwickshire Regt. 1919; left India 1928.

Sir Olaf CAROE, KCSI, KCIE; b. 1892; Queens Regt. NWFP 1916; ICS 1920; IPS, NWFP 1923; DC Kohat 1928; For. Sec., G of I 1939; Governor NWFP 1946; left India 1947.

George CARROLL, KPM; b. 1899; Indian Police, CP 1919; guardian to minor rajahs of Khetri, Camba, Chota Udepur; tutor to prince of Jodhpur.

Marjorie CASHMORE (née Hutchinson); b. 1896; m. Thomas CASH-MORE Chota Nagpur 1919; left India 1933.

Bishop Thomas CASHMORE; b. 1892; SPG missionary, Ranchi 1917; Waziristan 1917; Lutheran Mission, Chota Nagpur 1918; Vicar, Principal St James's College, Calcutta 1924; left India 1933.

Sir Conrad CORFIELD, KCIE, CSI, MC; b. 1893; IPS 1925, Kathiawar, Baluchistan, Rajputana, Central India, Hyderabad; Pol. Dept. 1934; Resident Punjab States 1941; Pol. Adv. to Viceroy 1945–47.

Lady Sylvia CORFIELD (née Hadow); b. 1900 Dibrugarh; returned India 1919; m. Col. Daunt, Central India Horse (d. 1953); m. Sir Conrad Corfield 1961.

Sir John COTTON, KCMG, OBE; b. 1909; India 1929; 8th KGO Light Cavalry 1930; IPS 1934, Aden, Persian Gulf, Rajputana, Hyderabad, Baroda; Dep. Secy., Pol. Dept.1946–47.

Lady Mary COTTON (née Connors), b. 1910; m. Sir John Cotton 1937; left India 1947.

Col. Walter CRICHTON, CIE; b. 1896; IMS 1920; Pol. Dept. 1930; Agency Surgeon Kurram Valley 1932; MOH Simla 1934; Chief Health Officer Delhi 1936; war serv. 1941–45.

Ed DAVIES; b. 1908; India 1924 Dorset Regt.; Meerut, NWFP; left India 1932.

Brig. F. J. DILLON, OBE, MC, 7 bars Frontier M.; Indian 1919 Mountain Battery; 3rd Afghan War, Waziristan, Mahsud Campaigns; Indian Mountain Battery 1935; Army HQ 1936; war serv. 1940–45.

Edith DIXON; b. Quetta 1898; Indian railways community Rawalpindi, Saharanpore, Simla, Calcutta; left India 1914.

Lady Deborah DRING (née Cree); b. 1899; m. Maj.-Gen. John Marshall, Rattray's Sikhs (d. 1942); m. John DRING 1946.

Lt.-Col. Sir John DRING, KBE, CIE; b. Calcutta 1902; Guides Cavalry 1923; IPS 1927; Asst. PS to Viceroy; DC DIK, Peshawar; Pol. Agent S. Waziristan; Chief Secy. NWFP; left Pakistan 1952.

Irene EDWARDS (née Green), Frontier M.; b. Agra 1906; nurse St. George's Hosp. Bombay 1925; sister Lady Reading Hosp. Peshawar 1929; matron, King Edward Hosp. Indore 1935; left India 1950.

Lady Nancy FOSTER (née Godden); b. Assam 1911; childhood in Assam and Bengal with sisters Jon and Rumer; m. Ridgeby FOSTER 1937; left India 1960.

Sir Ridgeby FOSTER; b. 1907; ICI India 1927; Bihar, Calcutta, Bombay; Chairman ICI India; stayed on in India after 1927.

Lady Kathleen GRIFFITHS (née Wilkes); India as governess 1922; m. Percival GRIFFITHS 1922; left India 1960.

Sir Percival GRIFFITHS, KBE, CIE; b. 1899; ICS Bengal 1922; retired ICS to enter business 1934; MLA 1937–47; Indian Central Leg. 1946; Govt Adviser 1941; stayed on in India after 1947.

Arthur HAMILTON, CIE, OBE, MC; b. 1895; IFS Punjab 1921; Inspector-General of Forests 1945–49.

Olivia HAMILTON (née Seth-Smith); b. 1899; m. Arthur HAMILTON 1925; left India 1949.

F. C. HART; b. Amritsar 1904; educ. in India; Special Branch, CID 1934, Bihar and Orissa; Indian Army SIB 1941; left India 1946.

Maj. E. S. HUMPHRIES, MC, DCM; b. 1889; India as private Royal Scots 1909; N. India, NWFP; Indian Signal Corps 1911 and later commissioned; left India 1934.

Sir Gilbert LAITHWAITE, GCMG, KCB, KCIE; B. 1894; India Office 1919; APS to Sec. of State for India; Round Table Conf. 1931; PS to Viceroy 1936; Dep. Under-Sec. of State Burma 1945, India 1947.

Lady Rosamund LAWRENCE (née Napier); b. 1878; m. Sir Henry Lawrence 1914; Belgaum, Sind, Bombay Prov.; left India 1926.

Mrs A. LEE; b. 1886; India as wife of Band-Sergeant Lee, 2nd North Staffs Rgt 1914; Rawalpindi, NWFP; left India 1920.

Lt.-Col. Lewis LE MARCHAND; b. Guntakal 1908; 5th Royal Gurkha Rifles, NWFP 1930; ADC Governor of Punjab 1933, war service 8th Indian Div.; left India 1947.

Prof. Lt.-Col. Kenneth MASON, MC, RGS Gold Medal; RE, Survey of India 1909; Himalayan Surveys 1909–14; Indian Army 1914–18; Dep. Supt. Survey of India, Burma 1931; left India 1932.

Philip MASON, CIE, OBE; b. 1906; ICS UP 1928; Saharanpur, Bareilly, Lucknow; DC Garhwal 1936; Sect. SE Asia Command 1941; tutor and guardian to princes, Hyderabad; left India 1947.

Sir Christopher MASTERMAN, Kt. CSI, CIE; b. 1889; ICS Madras 1914; Coll. of Salt Rev. 1928; Collector Madras 1932; Educ. 1936; Rev. 1942; Chief Sec. Adviser to Governor 1946; left India 1948.

Rupert MAYNE; b. Quetta 1910; jute merchant Bengal 1932; oil company N. India 1937; stayed on in India after 1947.

Terence 'Spike' MILLIGAN; b. Ahmednagar 1918; childhood in Poona cantonments; convent educ.; left India 1927.

Sir Penderel MOON, Kt., OBE; b. 1905; ICS Punjab 1929; Multan, Gujrat, Amritsar; left ICS 1944 to serve in Bahawalpur, Himachal Pradesh, Manipur Princely State Govts; stayed on after 1947.

John MORRIS, CBE, RGS Murchison Award; b. 1895; 3rd QAO Gurkha Rifles 1916; 3rd Afghan War 1918, NW frontier campaigns; Everest Expeds. 1922 and 1936; retired army 1930.

Grace NORIE (née Reynolds), OBE; b. Roorkee 1876; returned India 1893; m. Maj.-Gen. Norie, 2nd Gurkhas, 1898; war work 1914–18; left India 1919.

Eugene PIERCE; b. Dehra Dun 1909; Indian railways community; railways and commerce; leading role in Anglo-Indian community affairs; left India 1947.

Iris PORTAL (née Butler); b. Simla 1905; returned India 1922; m. Major Gervase Portal, Gardner's Horse, 1927; Poona, Meerut, Bombay, Hyderabad; Girl Guides Commissioner; left India 1942.

Edwin PRATT; b. 1909; assistant Army & Navy Stores, Calcutta, 1928; commissioned Indian Army Service Corps 1939–45; stayed on in India after 1947.

Lt.-Col. John RIVETT-CARNAC, MC, KPM; b. E. Bengal 1888; India Police UP 1909; 13th Bengal Lancers 1914–18; police service in UP; left India 1927.

Rev. Arfon ROBERTS; b. 1906; Methodist Missionary Society W. Bengal 1928; service inc. Supt. Bankura and Raniganj Leper Homes; left India 1951.

Rosalie ROBERTS (née Harvey); b 1902; nurse W. Bengal 1926; Nursing Supt. Santal Mission Hosp., Sarenga 1926; m. Arfon ROBERTS 1932; vol. med. work till 1951.

Dorothy ROWE (née Ellen); b. 1890; India 1927 to marry John ROWE Bombay; NWFP and Punjab; left India 1946.

John ROWE; b. 1888; India 1889 as child; RE India 1910; Military Eng. NWFP; Military Engineering Service 1939–46.

Lt.-Gen. Sir Reginald SAVORY, KCIE, CB, BSO, MC; b. 1892; 14th Sikhs 1914; war service 1914; NWFP 1921; Comm. 1st/11th Sikhs 1937; Comm. 23rd Ind. Div. 1942; Dir. Inf. 1943; Adj.-Gen. 1946–47.

Radcliffe SIDEBOTTOM; b. 1907; RN and Union Castle Line; Bengal Pilot Service 1927, based in Calcutta; invalided out as Master Pilot 1946.

Lady Frances SMYTH (née Chambers); b. Quetta 1908; returned India 1925; m. Capt. Read, 4th Gurkhas, 1927; subs. m. Col. 'Jackie' SMYTH 1940; left India 1942.

Brig. Rt. Hon. Sir John SMYTH, Bt. VC, MC; b. 1893; 15th Ludhiana Sikhs 1913; VC at Gallipoli; NWF campaigns; comm. 45th Rattray's Sikhs 1935, Chitral Force 1937, 17th Ind. Div. Burma 1940–42.

Ian STEPHENS, CIE; b. 1903; Bureau of Pub. Inf., Delhi 1930; Director 1932; Asst. Ed. *Statesman* 1937; Editor 1942; left India 1951.

Anne SYMINGTON (née Harker); b. Mahableshwar 1904; m. David SYMINGTON 1929; Ratnagiri, Bombay; left India 1947.

David SYMINGTON, CSI, CIE; b. Bombay 1904; ICS Bombay 1926; Collector Ratnagiri 1937; Sec. to Governor 1943–47.

Nancy VERNEDE (née Kendal); b. Mussoorie 1914; returned to Allahabad 1934; m. Raymond VERNEDE 1937; Garhwal; left India 1947.

Raymond VERNEDE; b. 1905; ICS UP 1928; District Officer Meerut, Benares, Unao, Garhwal; Acting Commissioner Gorakhpur 1946–47.

Kenneth WARREN; b. 1886; Assam as tea planter, James Warren & Co. Agency House, 1906; war service 1914; Assam Legislative Assembly 1923; left India 1926.

Norman WATNEY; b. 1901; Asst. Loco. Supt. NW Railway 1925; Div. Mech. Eng. Karachi, Quetta; Supt. Mech. Works. Lahore 1946; Dep. Dir. Railway Board 1939; Pak. Railways after 1947.

H. T. WICKHAM; b. 1884; Indian Police, Punjab, 1904; Ambala, Kasauli; trans. NWFP 1906; Mardan, Bannu, DIK, Tank; Comm. Military Police Bttn., Peshawar, 1919; left India 1922.

Maj.-Gen. George WOOD, CB, CBE, DSO, MC; b. 1898, Dorset Regt. 1916; 1st Dorsets India 1931; Bengal, Army HQ, Khyber; comm. 2nd Dorset Regt India 1943, 25th Ind. Div. Burma 1944–46.

Mary WOOD; b. Malaya 1904; m. Capt. George WOOD 1928; Dacca, Delhi, Simla; left India 1935.

Charles WRIGHT; b. 1898; India as private Black Watch 1922; Allahabad, Multan, Meerut, Barrackpore; left India 1935.

Tales from the Dark Continent

Sir William ADDIS, KBE, CMG; b. 1901; SC Zanzibar 1931; PS to Sultan of Zanzibar 1939; Col. Sec Bermuda 1945; Gov. Seychelles 1953–58; Foreign Office

David ALLEN, MBE; b. 1916; CS Gold Coast 1938; DO Mampong 1940; DC Kumasi 1950; Secretariat 1949; Asst. Regional Off. Trans-Volta Togoland 1953; Perm. Sec. Health, Econ. Aff. 1955–59.

Mary ALLEN (née Moon); b. 1928 India; teacher Army School Accra 1950; m. David ALLEN 1953; left Gold Coast 1958.

Philip ALLISON, ISO; b. 1907; Nigeria Forest Dept. 1931; FO S. Anambra, Rivers States, Nigeria; in 'Middle Belt' 1940; Ogun, Benin 1945; ret. F Dept. 1960; Nigerian Museums 1960–62.

Sir Darrell BATES, CMG, CVO; b. 1913; CS Begamoyo Tanganyika 1935; KAR 1940; Col. Off. 1944; DC Same 1948; OAG Seychelles 1950; DCS Somaliland 1951; Col. Sec. Gibraltar 1953–68.

Lady Susan BATES; b. 1923, brother George SINCLAIR; m. Darrell BATES 1944; Tanganyika, Seychelles, Gibraltar; left Gibraltar 1968.

Lady Violet BOURDILLON; b. 1886; m. Bernard Bourdillon later Gov. Uganda, Nigeria; lived in India, Iraq, Ceylon, Uganda; Nigeria 1935–43.

Col. Sir Hugh BOUSTEAD, KBE, CMG, MC; b. 1895; RN and Army 1913; Sudan CC 1924; Comm. SCC 1931; DC W. Dist. Darfur, SPS 1931; Sudan DF 1941; Aden, Muscat & Oman, Abu Dhabi 1949–65.

Sir Alan BURNS, GCMG; b. 1887 St Kitts-Nevis; CS Leeward I. 1905;
Asst. Sec. Nigeria 1912; war serv. WA; DCS Nigeria 1929; Gov. Brit.
Honduras 1934; Col. Off. 1940; Gov. Gold Coast 1941–7.

Nigel COOKE; b. 1916; CS Maiduguri N. Nigeria 1937; war serv. 1939;
prov admin. N. Nigeria 1943; Res. Benue Prov. 1957; Sen. Res.
Adamawa Prov. 1959; Sen. Res. Jos Prov., Kano Prov. 1961–62.

Joyce DINNICK-PARR, MBE; b. 1912; WRNS 1943; Woman Educ.
Off., CES, Tiv Div. N. Nigeria 1947; Org. Home Econ. Kaduna;
touring N. Nigeria 1951; Chief. Educ. Off. (Women) N. Nigeria 1959–
63.

Donald DUNNET; b. 1899; African & Eastern Trading Corp. Lagos 1920;
trading posts Enugu-Makurdi 1926; Dist. Man. Onitsha 1931; P. Harcourt 1934; Lend-Lease 1942; Dir. UAC Motors 1946–61.

Marjorie DUNNET (née Wiles); b. 1900; m. Donald DUNNET 1928;
Nigeria 1930; Port Harcourt, Ibagwa, Onitsha, Calabar, Usambura,
Lagos; left Nigeria 1948.

Edwin EVERETT, OBE, QPM; b. 1916; Sub-Inspector Lagos, Colonial
Police Service, Nigeria 1938; RWAFF 1940; Lokoja Nigeria Police 1943;
Asst. Comm. P 1945; Comm. Prev. Serv. 1961–65.

Joan EVERETT (née Way); b. 1923; Woman Educ. Off., CES, Sokoto, N.
Nigeria 1949; m. Edwin EVERETT 1950; teacher St. Xavier's School,
Lagos 1961; left Nigeria 1965.

Christopher FARMER; b. 1921; ADO Kano, N. Nigeria CS 1942; PS to
CC N. Prov. 1946; DO Hadejia 1950; Senior DO Kabba 1957; Dep. PS
N. Region 1959; Res. and Prov. Sec. Bauchi 1961–63.

Sir Angus GILLAN, KBE, CMG; b. 1885; DI El Obeid, Sudan PS 1910;
APO Sudan WFF 1916; DC Nyala, Darfur 1917; Dep. Gov. Nubu Prov.
1921; Gov. Kordofan Prov. 1928; Civil Sec. 1934–39.

Harry GRENFELL, OBE, MC; b. 1905; Lupa goldfields Tanganyika 1932;
BSA Co. Rhodesia 1938; war serv. 1939; BSA Co. Lusaka, N. Rhodesia
1946; Exec. Dir. BSA Co. 1956–70.

Noel HARVEY, b. 1929; ADC Karonga, Nyasaland CS 1954; DC
Rumpi 1958; DC Mzuzu 1959; Admin. Off. Soche 1961; DC Blantyre
1962–64.

Anthony KIRK-GREENE, MBE; b. 1925; ADO Adamawa, N. Nigeria CS
1950; DO Bornu 1956; Inst. of Admin. Zaria 1957; Chief. Inf. Off. N.
Nigeria 1960–61; Reader, Ahmadu Bello Univ. 1961–67.

Sylvia LEITH-ROSS (née Ruxton), MBE; m. Capt. Arthur Leith-Ross,
WAFF, N. Nigeria 1906, d. Zungeru 1908; first woman Supt. of Educ.
Nigeria 1926–31; Lagos and Jos Museums 1956–69.

Sir Martin LINDSAY, Bt., CBE, DSO, King's Polar Medal; b. 1905; Army,
seconded 4th Bttn. Nigeria Regt, Ibadan 1927; exped. through Belgian
Congo to E. Africa 1929.

Sir Frank LLOYD, KCMG, OBE; b. 1916; ADO Embu, Kenya CS 1939; war serv. Ethiopia; DC Mandera 1942; DC Fort Hall 1949; Prov. Comm. C. Prov. 1956; Perm. Sec. 1961; Comm. Swaziland 1964–68.

Earl LYTTON, Noel Anthony Lytton-Millbank; b. 1900; Army seconded. 4th Bttn. King's African Rifles, Kenya 1922; Nairobi 1922; Administrator Samburu and Turkana Dist., NFD 1924–25.

Rev. Robert MACDONALD, OBE, MC; b. 1905; CMS Missionary Ikot Inyang, E. Nigeria 1929; Admin. Supt. and Chaplain, Itu leper colony 1952; left Nigeria 1967.

Mcrcedes MACKAY; b. 1905; m. Robert Mackay, mining geologist 1933; Mines Dept., Tanganyika 1934; Geological Survey, Nigeria 1941; Jos, Kaduna, Ibadan; worked in local radio; left Nigeria 1950.

Charles MEEK, CMG; b. 1920; ADO Lindi, Tanganyika CS 1941; DC Masai 1949; DC Mbulu 1950; Secretariat 1956; Perm. Sec., Sec to Cabinet 1959; Head of Civil Service 1961–62.

Nona MEEK; 1921; b. WRNS 1941; m. Charles MEEK 1947; Arusha, Masai, Dar-es-Salaam; left Tanganyika/Tanzania 1962.

Lt.-Col. Brian MONTGOMERY; b. 1903; Army seconded to 3rd Bttn. KAR, Kenya 1927; Nairobi, Wajir, Mandera, NFD; transf. Indian Army 1932.

Betty MORESBY-WHITE (née Brandt); b. 1918; brother Nigeria CS; m. Hugh MORESBY-WHITE 1936; Abeokuta, Oyu; left Nigeria 1944.

Hugh MORESBY-WHITE, CMG; b. 1891; ADC Ijebu Ode, S. Nigeria CS 1915; DC Ijebu Ode 1920; Oyo Prov. 1925; Secretariat Enugu 1927; Res. Abeokuta Prov. 1933; Sen. Res. Oyu Prov. 1941–44.

Patrick MULLINS; b. 1922; ADC Damongo, Gold Coast CS 1951; Secretariat Zomba, Nyasaland 1952; DC Chiradzulu 1958; Clerk, Leg. Assembly 1962; Prin. Sec. Pub Serv. Comm. 1963–64.

William PAGE; b. 1904; clerk and cashier, Bank of Brit. W. Africa, Accra, Gold Coast 1926; cashier, Bathurst, Gambia 1928; left Gambia 1930.

Lady Alys REECE (née Tracy), MBE; b. 1912; m. Gerald REECE 1936; Marsabit, Isolo, NFD, Kenya; Hargeisa, Somaliland 1948; left Somaliland 1953.

Sir Gerald REECE, KCMG, CBE; b. 1897; ADC Kakamega, Kenya CS, 1925; DC Mandera, NFD 1931; OIC NFD 1939; Sen. PO Borana, Ethiopia 1941; Prov. Comm. NP, Kenya 1945; Gov. Somaliland 1948–53.

Sir James ROBERTSON, Kt. GCMG, GCVO, KBE; b. 1899; ADC Rufa'a, Sudan PS 1922; DC Nahud 1933; Sub.Gov. White Nile 1937; Dep. Gov. Gezira 1939; Chief Sec. 1945; Gov.-Gen. Nigeria 1955–60.

Lady Nancy ROBERTSON (née Walker); b. 1903; m. James ROBERTSON 1926; White Nile, Fung, W. Kordofan, Gezira Prov, Sudan 1926–53; Nigeria 1955–60.

Clifford RUSTON; b. 1900; joined Lagos Stores Ltd 1919; District Manager Zaria, Kano, Jos, Makurdi 1923–39; war serv. RWAFF; Gen. Manager Benue, Plateau, Bornu, Adamawa Provs. 1940–51.

Dorothy RUSTON (née Rayner); b. 1903; m. Clifford RUSTON 1925; Zaria, Kano, Makuri, Jos; crossed Belgian Congo to S. Africa 1943; left Nigeria 1951.

Robin SHORT; b. 1927; Army, Palestine; ADO NW Prov and Copperbelt, N. Rhodesia CS 1950; DC Mwinlunga 1958; DC Lundazi 1961; Native Courts 1964; retired early 1965.

Veronica SHORT (née Vail); b. 1917; m. Robin SHORT Chingola, N. Rhodesia 1954; left Rhodesia 1965.

Sir George SINCLAIR, Kt., CMG, OBE; b. 1912; ADC Ashanti, Gold Coast CS 1937; war serv. 1940; DC Ashanti 1943; Sect. 1945; Reg. Off Trans-Volta Togoland 1952; Dep. Gov. Cyprus 1955–60.

Kenneth SMITH, CMG; b. 1918; Cadet Tanganyika CS 1940; RAF 1941; Col. Off. 1945; DC Zanzibar 1946; Res. Mag. Pemba 1949; Col. Sec. Seychelles 1949; Aden 1952; Gambia 1956–62.

Mavis STONE (née Dauncey Tongue); b. Uganda 1924; Agric. College S Africa; WRNS 1943; m. Richard STONE 1948; Acholi, Toro, Buganda 1948–62.

Richard STONE, CMG; b. Kenya 1914; ADC Toro and Lango CS 1937; war serv. KAR Abyssinia, India, Burma; DC Acholi and Toroi 1947; Perm. Sec. var. ministries 1954; Resident Buganda 1960–62.

William STUBBS, CMG, CBE; b. 1902; BSAP Rhodesia 1921; trs. N. Rhodesia P., Admin. S. 1926; Lab. Dept. 1940; Lab. Comm. 1944; Prov. Comm. 1949; Sec. Nat. Aff. 1954; Speaker LA. Somaliland 1960.

Richard SYMES-THOMPSON; b. Kenya 1923; war. Serv. ADC Isiolo Kenya CS 1946; Secretariat 1950; DO Kericho 1953; DC Embu 1956; Nandi 1958; Kiambu 1963–64.

Lady Beatrice TURNBULL (née Wilson); b. 1908; m. Richard TURN-BULL 1938; Meru, Nairobi, Kapenguria, NFD, Kenya 1939–58; Tanganyika 1958–62.

Sir Richard TURNBULL, GCMG; b. 1909; ADC Kericho, Kenya CS 1930; DC Isiolo 1936; DC Turkana 1943; PC N. Prov. 1955; Min. Def., Int. Sec. 1954; Ch.Sec. 1955; Gov. Tanganyika 1961; H. Comm. Aden 1965–67.

Tales from the South China Seas

Dato Hajji Mohamad Yusuf BANGS; b. 1903; asst. rubber plantation Johore 1926; estate manager Kelantan 1933; POW Siam–Burma 1942; Dev. Officer Kelantan 1948–54; ret. loc. 1967.

Edward BANKS; Sarawak Service 1925; Curator Sarawak Museum; interned Kuching 1941; ret. 1950.

Datuk John BAXTER, CBE; b. 1899; assistant Sapong Estate Brit. N. Borneo 1925; m. Kadazan wife Susan; manager 1938; interned Kuching 1941; ret. loc. 1954.

Richard BROOME, OBE, MC; b. 1909; MCS Canton 1932; Asst. Protector Penang 1935; DO Christmas I. 1938; Force 136 1942; Lab. Dept. 1945; Ferret Force 1948; Sec. Def. Int. Security 1955–57.

Tamsin BROOME (née Luckham); b. 1909; teacher English school KL 1936; m. Richard BROOME 1938; taught in Johore Bahru, Ipoh, Singapore 1945; left Malaysia 1957.

Capt. Percy BULBROOK; b. 1903; Straits Steamship Co. Singapore 1929; Ship's Master 1941; war service 1941; Master Red Funnel steamship co. 1948–59.

Norman CLEAVELAND; mining engineer and mine manager Malaya, Siam, Burma 1930; manager, later President Pacific Tin, Malaysia 1947–66.

Sjovald CUNYNGHAM-BROWN, OBE; b. 1905; MCS Penang 1930; Asst. Emigr. Comm. India 1932; Mag. Singapore 1937; Cont. Labour Johore 1938; POW Sumatra 1942–5; appts. Johore, Penang; ret. loc. 1957.

Madeline DAUBENY; b. 1905; m. Richard Daubeny, Sarawak CS 1933; up-country, Kushing, Limbang, Miri; husband POW 1941.

Helen DAVIS (née Duin); b. 1914; war service 1941; m. John DAVIS 1946; Malaya; left Malaya 1960.

John DAVIS, CBE, DSO; b. 1911; FMS Police 1931; Canton 1933; CID Perak 1936; Force 136 1942; MCS 1947; Ferret Force 1948; Chinese Aff. 1949; DO Wellesley, Johore, Kedah 1954–59.

John FORRESTER; b. 1914 Shanghai; Harrison and Crosfield 1937; Ceylon, Singapore, Penang; esc. Singapore 1942; Min. of Supply 1942; rejoined H&C 1947; ret. 1969.

Una FORRESTER (née Ebden) b. 1925; father MCS, Malacca, KL 1940–42; m. John FORRESTER India 1943; Malaya 1947.

Sir William GOODE, GCMG; b. 1907; MCS 1931; DO Raub 1936; Asst. Fin. Sec. Singapore 1939; POW 1942; Secretariat KL 1946; Chief Sec. Singapore 1953, Gov. 1957; Gov. N. Borneo 1960–63.

H. L. H. HARRISON; b. 1897; mining engineer Ipoh 1919, tin mine manager Siam 1921; Anglo-Oriental KL 1936; escaped Singapore 1942; rehab. mines Malaya 1955; ret. 1955.

Derek HEADLY, CMG; b. 1908; MCS Selangor 1930; DO Pekan 1937; Force 136 1944; Resident Labuan 1947; Comm. Res. E and W. Coast, N. Borneo 1948; Brit. Adviser Kelantan 1953; ret. 1957.

Bishop Peter HOWES, OBE; mission priest Betong, Sarawak, 1937; Land Dayak Dist. 1940; interned Kuching 1942; Archdeacon Kuching, Brunei, N. Sarawak 1962; Asst. Bishop 1971–81.

KENNAWAY sisters born in Malaya; Ann b. 1922, m. Gerald Scott APC 1946; Elizabeth b. 1924, m. Bernard Davis MCS 1948; Pippa b. 1927, m. Alexander Boyle 1962; Susan b. 1928, m. John Whitley 1966.

Cecil LEE; b. 1911; Harrison & Crosfield, KL 1934; POW Siam–Burma 1942; Malaya 1946; Sandakan, N. Borneo 1951–54; ret. 1961.

Dorothy LUCY (née Hawkings); b. Shanghai 1915; teacher Cameron Highlands 1940; m. Peter LUCY Feb. 1942; Amherst Estate 1946–52; Chief Comm. Girl Guides Malaya.

Peter LUCY, CPM; rubber estate Malaya 1928; manager Amhurst Estate 1938; POW Singapore 1942; trans. E Africa 1952.

Guy MADOC, CBE, KPM, CPM; b. 1911; FMS Police Jelebu 1930; OSPC Kedah; int. Singapore 1942; Bangkok 1947; comm. Special Branch 1952; Dir. Int. 1954; Dep. Sec. Sec. & Int. 1957–59.

Nancy MADOC; m. Guy MADOC 1935; Selangor, Pahang, Kedah; evac. Singapore 1942; left Malaya 1959.

James MORICE; b. 1902; Malayan Customs Service 1921; served in all FMS; interned Singapore 1942; State Reg. Officer NS 1948; retired 1952.

Alan MORKILL, OBE; b. 1890; MCS Kelantan 1913; DO Kuala Pilah 1919; Tampin 1922; Upper Perak 1925; ret. on med. grounds 1927.

Robert NICHOLL; war service Far East 1943; Education Service Sarawak 1945; Dir. of Educ., Principal Miri Coll.; state historian, Brunei 1969; ret. loc. .

R. B. PERKINS; rubber assist. Dunlops Bahau Est., Negri Sembilan 1925; POW Siam–Burma 1942; Kota Tingi Est. 1946; ret. loc. own estate Ladang Tersenyum.

Anthony RICHARDS, b. 1914; cadet Kuchin Sarawak CS 1938; DO Saribas 1941; interned Kuching 1942; DO Kanowit 1946; Res. First Div. 1955; Resident's Native Court Magist. 1961–64.

Daphne RICHARDS (née Oswell); b. 1917; m. Anthony RICHARDS 1946; Upper & Lower Rejang, Kuching Simanggang; left Sarawak 1964.

Gerald SCOTT; b. 1914; tech. eng., Asiatic Petroleum, Singapore 1939; m. Ann KENNAWAY 1942; escaped Singapore 1942.

Tan Sri Dato Mubin (Mervyn) SHEPPARD, PSM, CMG, MBE; b. 1905; MCS, Temerloh 1928; DO Alor Gajah, 1938; int. Singapore 1942; DO Klang 1947; Dir. Emerg. Food Denial 1956; Ret. loc.

Alan SNELUS, CMG; b. 1911; Sarawak CS Sibu 1934; DO Lawas 1936; interned Kuching 1942; PS to Govt. 1946; Res. Second Div. 1949; Dep. Chief. Sec. 1953; ret. 1963.

John THEOPHILUS; b. 1906; Brit. Malay Rubber, Jundaram Est. 1926; Oriental Rubber 1931; war serv. 1939; POW Singapore 1942; Bhutan Est., Nilai 1946; ret. 1966.

Edward TOKELEY; b. 1915; Bousteds, Penang 1935; Singapore office 1936; war serv. 1939; POW Siam–Burma 1942; Bousteds Penang 1946; Chairman 1966; ret. to head office 1971.

Trevor WALKER; b. 1916; Guthries, KL 1937; war serv. 1939; POW Singapore; Guthries Singapore 1946; Chairman 1963; ret. to head office 1968.

Hugh WATTS; b. 1897; Henrietta Estate 1920; MSVR Port Dickson 1930; Brown Est., Penang 1933; war serv. 1939; POW Siam–Burma 1942; Brown Est. 1945; est. Sungei Ara Est., Penang; ret. loc.

Mary WATTS (née Culleton); b. 1892; Mayalan Nursing Serv. 1927; nursing sister Batu Gajah; m. Hugh WATTS; evac. 1942; Penang 1946; ret. loc.

Capt. Robert WILLIAMSON, OBE, DSC; b. 1891; apprentice King Line 1906; RNR 1914; Indo-China SN Co. 1920; Master Upper Yangtse 1921; Marine Supt. Shanghai 1928; war serv. 1941; ret. 1955.

Brig. George WORT, CBE; b. 1921; Wilts Regt. Singapore 1933; Malay Regt. 1939; POW Singapore 1942; Col. Malay Govt. Federation Army 1956; left Malaya 1957.

Capt. Monty WRIGHT; war serv. Far East; Straits Steamship Co. 1947; Ship's Master, Deck Supt.; retired 1977.

Glossary

This glossary contains words drawn from India (I), South-East Asia (SEA) and Africa (A). In the Indian context, in addition to Indian or specifically 'Anglo-Indian' words contained in the text, I have included some of the more common Anglo-Indian expressions, as well as slang common among the British Other Ranks (BOR), and words employed by Indian servants in Anglo-Indian households (I Dom). The spelling of vernacular words given here is basic rather than academic, thus *ucha* rather than *achchha* (very well). Anglo-Indian patois or hobson-jobson comes in three basic forms. The first involved Urdu or Hindustani interspersed with English. The second involved the vernacular given a new meaning, thus a word like *koi-hai* (who's there) was also used to describe an 'old India hand'. The third and perhaps the most interesting use of Indian words involved their corruption or amalgamation with English, as in the well-known admonition said to have been delivered by an irate BOR to a native bystander: 'You *dekko*ed me *giro* in the *peenika pani* and you *cooch biwani*ed. You *soon*ed me *bolo. I swasti* I'll *gurrum* your *peechi*' – 'You saw me fall in the water and you did nothing. You heard me speak. For this I'll warm your behind'. For further enlightenment consult *Hobson-Jobson*, the nineteenth-century glossary of Anglo-Indian words and phrases.

In the context of South-East Asia, in addition to words found in the text I have included a few words and terms of special relevance where their origins or usage are of unusual interest. I have stuck with the common usage of the day, as regards spelling. The following abbreviations are used: M – Malay; Port. – Portuguese; SS – Straits Settlements; CC – China Coast and Concessions.

In the African context, in addition to those words and phrases that occur in the text, I have added others that have a particular relevance to the British colonial period. Most are derived from one or other of three main sources: pidgin in British West Africa (WA), Swahili in British East Africa (EA) – which also looked to Anglo-India for some of its argot (e.g., *ayah* for nurse) – and Afrikaans or 'kitchen-kaffir' in British Central Africa (CA). Apart from such official terms as 'district' or 'resident', few words or phrases seem to have been able to transcend these three distinct regions. Thus what in British India was known as going on tour becomes 'safari' in East Africa, *ulendo* in Central Africa, and 'going to bush' or 'going on trek' in West Africa.

A

abdar – head servant (at the club) (I)

A class – administrative officials and others of officer rank, as distinct from B or second class officials (WA, EA, CA)

act – deputize, thus 'to do an act' (I)

adat – customary law (M)

adha seer – one pound, derog. term for Eurasians (I)

admi – chap, lit. 'person' (I)

ADO, ADC – Assistant District Commissioner/Officer, junior administrative officer in a District, occasionally responsible for the administration of a Sub-Division within a District; also aide-de-camp to a Governor (I; WA, EA, CA)

Adviser – senior British official in UMS (SEA)

AFI – Auxiliary Forces India, European or Anglo-Indian civilian 'Home Guard' (I)

alkali – Muslim judge or lay magistrate administering Muslim law in N. Nigeria (WA) *almeirah* – wardrobe, der. Port. *almario*, in Malaya *almari* (I; SEA)

amah – Chinese maidservant, nurse, der. Port. *ama* (SEA; CC)

amir-parwa – defender of the rich (I)

amok – violent homicidal condition defined by Fauconnier as 'self-liberation through revolt', thus 'to run amok' (SEA)

Anglo-Indian – originally British persons in India but later specifically those of mixed blood, see 'Eurasian' (I)

anna – one-sixteenth of a rupee, thus 'twelve annas to a rupee' – derog. term for Eurasian (I)

APC – Asiatic Petroleum Company (Shell) (SEA)

apke-wasti – a toady (lit. 'at your honour's command') (I)

Ashanti chicken – dish made up of one fowl, with bones removed, stuffed inside another (WA)

askari – soldier or policeman, thus '*askari kanga*' – tribal policeman (EA)

atap – *nipah* palm-leaf thatch (M)

ayah – native nurse, lady's maid, der.Port *aia* (I; SS); in Swahili *yaha* (EA)

B

baba – baby, thus *baba-log* – 'baby people' and 'missy *baba*' – 'little miss' (I)

babu – native clerk, der. Bengali 'father'; also derog., thus '*babu* language', 'babuism' (I)

bafu – bath (EA)

baht – language, thus '*bolo* the *baht* a *tora*' – 'speak the language a little' (BOR)

baju – Malay open shirt with long sleeves (M)

bakje bajao, khabadar – 'look out!', rickshaw coolie's cry (I)

bakuli ya safari – canvas-covered basin or bath, used on tour also known as 'safari basin' (EA)

banda – thatch shelter (EA; CA)

bandook – gun, thus 'my old *bandook*' (BOR)

banya – moneylender, thus '*banya ki raj*' – rule of the money-lender (I)

barang – things, thus luggage (M)

baraza – verandah, thus official gathering or meeting, (EA)

barracki-Hausa – simplified Hausa used by Nigeria Regiment officers (EA)

base-*wallah* – brass hat, man who avoids front line (BOR)

batu – rock, thus Batu Ferringhi – 'foreigner's rock', off Penang (M)

bature – white man (WA)

bazaar – native market (I)

besar – great, thus *tuan besar* – great gentleman; firm *besar* – great firm (e.g. Guthries, Bousteads etc); boy *besar* – head servant (SEA)

bhai – see 'boy' (I)

bhai-bund – brotherhood (I)

bheesti – native water carrier (I)

bibby – kept woman, der. *bibi* – 'high-class woman', thus *bibi khana* – 'kept woman's quarters' (BOR)

bint – native woman, der. Arabic (I)

biscuit box – secretariat in N. Rhodesia (CA)

bistra – bedding roll (I)

black velvet – native woman 'comfort' (I)

Blighty – Britain, der. *billayat* – kingdom, thus *billayati pani* – English water (soda water) (I)

Blighty-ticket – service discharge; wound requiring repatriation (BOR)

blood-chit – written authorization (BOR)

bobajee – cook, der. *biwarchi*, thus bobajee-*khana* – cookhouse (I)

bobbery – angry, 'don't get bobbery', der. *bapre!* – lit. 'father!', exclamation of surprise; also 'bobbery-bob' – der. '*bapre-bap!*' (BOP)

boma – district or divisional headquarters, lit. enclosure, from early days when government outposts were enclosed in a *boma* or thorn *zariba* (EA; CA)

Bombay bowler – casual pith helmet or *sola* topee as opposed to formal cork sun-helmet (I; EA)

Bombay milk-cart – waste disposal wagon (BOR)

bomoh – Malay medicine man (M)

boneyard – area of ocean lying between Canary Islands and Sierra Leone, also known as 'Elder Dempster boneyard' (A)

book – bundle of employers' references carried by servants (WA, EA, CA)

BOR – British Other Ranks, i.e. NCOs and private soldiers

bowli-glass – finger bowl (I dom)

box-wallah – derog. term for European businessman derived from Indian door-to-door salesman (I; SS)

boy – native servant, traditionally summoned by the vocative 'boy!' Orig. der. from *bhai* – younger brother (I); also cook-boy, Number One boy, boy *besar* – personal servant ((M); also houseboy, supported by his 'small boy' or assistant and even 'small-small boy'; also 'lantern-boy', 'turney-boy' – driver's mate and engine cranker (A)

Brahmin – highest caste among Hindus (I)

browned off – overcooked, thus 'fed-up' (BOR)

BSAP – British South African Police (Rhodesia) (A)

buckshee – free, der. *baksheesh* – alms (BOR)

buddli – temporary servant (I)

bugg-bugg – insect (WA)

bukit – hill, thus Bukit Timah (M)

bulala – rawhide whip made from hippopotamus hide (WA)

bullumteer – volunteer in Indian Army (I)

Bunby – Bombay (I)

bund – raised embankment (I; SEA)

bundo – arrangement, der. '*bundobust* – tie up loose ends'; thus 'let's make a bundo' (I)

bundu – bush country, see bush (EA;CA)

bunduki – see *bandook* (EA)

bungalow – country house, der. *bangla* – country (I)

bungy – sweeper, see also *mehta* (I)

Burma Road – rice pudding (BOR)

burra – great; big, thus *burra* bungalow – manager's bungalow; *burra-din* – big day, Christmas Day; *burra-khana* – big dinner, celebration; *burra-mem* – senior lady; *hurra nam* big name; *burra*-peg – double tot of whisky; *burra*-sahib – important man; senior sahib (I)

bus – enough (I)

bush – forest and uncultivated land and provincial areas away from head-quarters (WA), thus 'going to bush' – touring; 'a bit bush' – rather wild; 'bush house' – basic rest-house as distinct from catering rest-house; 'bush happy' – state of mind engendered by prolonged isolation from civiliza-tion; 'bush-telegraph' – local communications system that precedes official communications from headquarters; also 'bush lamp', 'bush shirt', 'bush hat', 'bush allowance' (A)

bustee – native quarter, thus 'where's your *bustee*, Glasgow?' (BOR)

butcha – baby, thus *tum soor ka butcha* – 'You son of a pig' (BOR)

bwana – master, Swahili term for European; thus '*bwana* DC' and '*bwana mkubura*' – big master (EA)

C

C – Companionage, specifically Companion of the Order of St Michael and St George (CMG), the order most often conferred on senior colonial administrators, sometimes known as 'Call Me God' (*v.* 'K') (A)

Cages – Bombay red light district (I)

canteen – up-country shop or store, usually run by European or Syrian trading companies, known in early days as 'barter rooms' or 'factories' (WA)

cantonment – military area of station (pron. 'cantoonment') (I)

cash – copper coinage, der. Tamil *kasu* (SEA)

catty – unit of weight, 1⅓ lb., der. *kati* (SEA)

CES – Colonial Education Service.

cha – tea, thus '*char* and a wad' and *char-wallah* – 'tea boy' (BOR)

chagoul – canvas or leather water bag (I; EA)

chapattis – unleavened bread (I)

chapplis – sandals (I)

chaprassi – office servant; messenger, der. *chapras* – brass buckle worn on belt or sash (I) *charpoy* – wooden frame bed with webbing, thus charp – bed and *charpoy*-bashing – sleeping (BOR)

chee-chee – derog. term for Eurasians der. from their sing-song speech (I)

chelo – get a move on, der. *chalo* – 'come on' (BOR)

cheroot – native cigar (I)

chibberow – be quiet, der. *chup rao* (BOR)

chi-chak – small house lizard (M); not to be confused with larger *gecko*

chick – split bamboo screen, der. Persian ((I)

chiko – small boy, der. *chokra* (BOR)

chilumchi – canvas-covered basin or bath, used on tour (I)

China Coaster – European with Far Eastern experience, notably at sea (CC)

chin-chin – salutations, der. pidgin Chinese (SEA)

chit – letter, note, signed bill, der. '*chitti*'; thus 'chit-up' – 'approach someone in authority' (hence, possibly, 'chat up'); *chit*-shy – one who avoids paying his round (I)

chokidar – caretaker, night watchman, see *choky* (I)

chokker – fed-up, der. '*chauki*'; thus 'I'm a bit chokker' (poss. der. of 'choked') (BOR)

chokra – native boy, thus inexperienced junior sahib (I; ss)

choky – lock-up, der. *Chauki*, see *chokidar* (BOR)

cholera-belt – flannel girdle worn supposedly to prevent cholera until *c*. 1920 (I)

chop – seal, brand, der. Hind. *chap*, thus first-*chop* – top-quality goods (ss; CC); also food, thus 'palm-oil *chop*' traditionally eaten at Sunday lunches, '*chop* box' – reinforced provision box, 'small *chop*' – canapés (see '*gadgets*' and '*toasties*'), 'steamer *chop*' – shipboard meals or food newly landed, '*chop* master' – person responsible for ordering food in mess, taken in rotation, 'Pass *chop*!' – a call for food to be served (WA)

chota – small, thus *chota bungalow* – assistant's bungalow; *chota hazri* – early morning tea; *chota peg* – single tot of whisky; *chota* sahib – junior sahib or sahib's son (I)

chuckeroo – youngster, der. *chokra* (BOR)

chukka – period of play in polo (I)

chummery – shared household, usually of bachelors (I; ss)

chung – platform, thus *chung* bungalow – house on raised platform, found in Eastern India (I)

chup – be quiet (I)

civil lines – area of station inhabited by British civilians (I)

civil list – Warrant or Order of Precedence, also known as the Green, Red or Blue Book (I)

class regiment – Indian Army regiment drawn from one racial group, e.g. Gurkhas, Sikhs, as opposed to mixed regiments (I)

Club – usually a private gymkhana or polo club owned by its members and restricted in membership (I)

CNC – Chief Native Commissioner (Kenya), later MAA – Minister for African Affairs (A)

(the) Coast – usually taken to refer to West Africa generally (*v.* 'old coaster') (WA)

Collector – chief administrator of district, originally collector of revenue (see 'DO') (I)

compound – enclosed area surrounding bungalow and servants' quarters, der. M *kampong* (I)

comprador – buyer, steward, der. Port., thus Chinese manager of a *hong*

concession – Chinese treaty port open to foreign traders (CC)

condominium – joint rule as exercised in the Anglo-Egyptian Sudan (A)

conductor – head overseer on a rubber estate, der. Port. (SS)

Congress – Indian National Congress, national political party (I)

conjie-house – gaol (BOR)

coolie – native porter; labourer, thus *coolie*-catcher – labour officer (I; SS)

Corporal Forbes – *cholera morbus* (BOR)

country-born – India-born European (I)

country-bred – India-raised European, used with derog. overtones (I)

covenanted servants – those entered into formal contract with Secretary of State for India, specifically the ICS (I)

CP – Central Provinces (I)

crab – stomach pain, der. *khrab* – bad (BOR)

CS – Colonial Service

craw-craw – skin irritation (WA), said to be caused by excessive starch in laundry, see *dhobi-itch* (EA)

creeper – trainee assistant on tea or rubber estate pre-WW1, orig. Ceylon (SEA)

cummerbund – waistband (I)

cumshaw – tip, gift, der. Mandarin *kan sieh* – thanks (CC; SS)

curry and rice days – the old days, from humorous book of this title (I)

cushy – easy, der. *khush* – pleasure (BOR)

custel brun – caramel custard, traditionally served at *dak* bungalows (I dom)

D

dacoit – robber, thus *dacoity* – robbery (I)

dak – post, thus *dak-wallah* – postman; *dak-bungalow* – government staging house (I)

dal – lentils (I)

dandy – open litter, much used in the Himalayas, carried by *dandy-wallahs* (I)

dash – gift, thus 'topside *dash*' – gift for a chief; also verb 'to *dash*' (WA)

Dashera – Hindu religious festival, celebrated in October (I)

dastur – bribe, perk, lit. 'custom' (I)

dato – elder, title conferred by sultan, also *datuk* (M)

dayang – girl, honorific title (SEA)

DC – District Commissioner, generally senior District Officer responsible for administration of district within province, known in earlier days as Native Commissioner, in the Sudan as Inspector, see 'district' (WA, EA, CA)

debbie/debe – 4-gall. petrol can, serving variety of functions from roofing material to water container (WA, EA, CA)

Delhi-Simla – Central Government axis based after 1912 in Delhi (cold weather) and Simla (hot weather and rains) (I)

derzi – tailor (I)

dewan – gatekeeper (I)

dhobi – washerman, thus 'flying *dhobi*' – 'express laundry' (I; SS)

dhobi-itch – skin irritation, usually ringworm, supposedly from excessive starch in laundered underwear (BOR)

dhol – drum (I)

dhoti – loose loincloth worn by Hindus (I)

dhurri – rough cotton rug (I)

dikky – troublesome, der. *dik* – trouble (BOR)

district – area of administration within a province, in British India one of 250 units; in Nigeria, the area administered by the Native Authority official (I; SEA; A)

Diwali – Hindu festival of lights, celebrated in autumn (I)

dixie – cooking pot, der. *dekshi* (BOR)

DO – District Officer, executive head of a District, in India known also as Collector, Deputy Commissioner or District Magistrate (I); in Malaya States known as Assistant Adviser (SEA)

doki-boy – groom, der. *doki* – horse (Hausa) (N. Nigeria

dolly – tray of gifts, der. *dali*, usually offered at Christmas (I)

dome – untouchable sweeper (I)

dona – *bwana*'s wife (CA)

doob – grass grown on Indian lawns (I)

doolally – mad, said to be der. from Deolaly transit camp near Bombay, but more probably from *diwana* – 'mad'; thus 'doolally *tap*' – fever (BOR)

dooley – covered litter (I)

double *khana* – dinner-party (I)

double *roti* – English loaf of bread (I)

double *terai* – double layered felt hat, see *terai* (I; A)

dubas – lit. red turban, tribal police in Kenya NFD (EA)

dub-up – pay up (BOR)

dudh-wallah – milkman (I)

dufta – office, der. *daftur* (I)

duka – shop, store, usually run by Indian trader (EA; CA)

dunpoke – baked dish (I dom)

durai – sahib, gentleman, der. Tamil (SEA)

durbar – court; levee (I)

Dutch wife – kapok-filled bolster used to keep cool in bed (SEA)

E

Eastern Cadet – junior civil administrator recruited to the Eastern Cadetships, comprising Ceylon, Hong Kong and Malaya (SEA)

ED – Elder Dempster, shipping line dominating W. African sea route,
founded in 1868 (A)

effendi – lord, Turkish term of respect for official (EA)

ekdum – lit. 'one breath', immediately, thus 'do it *ekdum*' (BOR)

ekka – small two-wheeled pony cart (I)

engkerumong – set of small gongs making a scale (SEA)

Eurasian – person of mixed descent in India. The term was officially
replaced by 'Anglo-Indian' in 1900 but the usage continued for another
forty years (I)

F

feriadi – humble petitioner (I)

feringi – foreigner, thus European (I)

FFI – free from infection, army VD inspection, also known as 'inspection
short-arm' (BOR)

first-timer – newcomer on first African tour, also known as 'first-tour man'
(A)

first toast – starter at dinner (I)

Fishing Fleet – girls who came out to India for the Cold Weather in search of
husbands, see 'Returned Empties' (I)

fitina – bearing of false witness and accusations, Arabic (EA)

FMS – Federated Malay States, comprising Perak, Selangor, Negri Sembilan and Pahang (SEA)

foo-foo – side dish of pounded yams, served with palm-oil *chop* (WA)

furlough – home leave, nineteenth-century term maintained by missionaries
(I;A)

G

gadgets – canapés; see 'small *chop*', 'toasties' (WA)

gai-wallah – cow-man, thus milkman (I)

gaji – wages (M)

gamelan – wooden and bronze gong orchestra (SEA)

gari-moto – motor-car; see *ghari* (A)

garrum – hot, thus VD case (BOR)

ghari – cart, thus *ghora-ghari* – 'horse-cart' (I)

gharib-parwav – defender of the poor, honorific form of address (I)

ghaskutta – grass-cutter for horses (I)

gin-sling – John Collins or gin and lime cocktail topped up with liqueurs, not to be confused with Singapore sling, made with whisky (SEA)

godown – storeroom, warehouse, der. M *gudang* (I; SEA)

gonga – mad, 'up the gonga', der. *ganga* – 'river', supposedly because lunatic asylums were up-river (BOR)

goolmal – muddle, thus, 'to make a *goolmal*' (I)

goonda – bad character (hence 'goon', perhaps?) (I)

governor – usually governor of colonial territory; in Sudan, senior administrator in charge of province (A)

GRA – Government Reservation Area, section of town reserved for houses of officials and Europeans (A)

grass *bidi* – casual country prostitute (I)

grass widow – wife at hill-station temporarily separated from husband in the plains (I)

Great Game – Anglo-Russian rivalry and counter-espionage beyond the Indian Frontier (I)

Green Book – see civil list (I)

gup – gossip (I)

gussal-khana – bathroom (I)

gymkhana – sports ground, sports meeting, der. *gend-khana* – ball room (I)

H

haji – honorific; one who has made the *haj* or pilgrimage to Mecca (SEA)

hamal – house servant in W. India (I)

haram – forbidden by Islamic law (I; EA)

harambee! – hauling cry, 'let's pull together' (CA; EA)

Hari Raya Puasa – Islamic festival celebrating the breaking of the fast of Ramadan (SEA)

hath-butti – hurricane lamp (I)

hazur – 'the presence', thus honorific, sir (I)

heaven-born – honorific reserved for Brahmins, hence applied to ICS (I)

hill station – stations and sanatoria above 5,000 feet in the 'hills' (I)

Hindu pani – 'water for Hindus', station vendor's cry (I)

Hindustani – simple form of Urdu (I)

hodi – 'who's there?', the reply being '*karibu*' – 'draw near' (EA)

Holi –Hindu fertility festival, celebrated in spring (I)

hong – house of business, thus firm (CC; SS)

housey–housey – British Army numbers game, now known as bingo (I)

howa-khana – 'breathing the air', thus 'let's take a *howa-khana*' (I)

howdah – palanquin on elephant (I)

hullabaloo – uproar, der. *holo-bolo* – to make a noise (I)

hunting clan – married soldiers (BOR)

I

ICS – Indian Civil Service (I)

IFS – Indian Forestry Service (I)

IMS – Indian Medical Service (I)

IP – Indian Police (I)

IPS – Indian Political Service (I)

Istana, astana – palace (SEA)

J

jaga – watchman, usually a Sikh, der. *jaga* – to watch (M)

jamban – commode or thunderbox (M)

jambo – greetings (EA)

jemadar – junior viceroy's Commissioned Officers, also ironical title given to low-caste water carriers (I)

jhampani – rickshaw coolie (I)

jigger – *Pulex penetrans*, insect carried on (and in) naked feet, der. *chigga* (WA)

jinriksha – rickshaw (Japanese) (SEA)

jirga – tribal gathering on North-West Frontier (I)

joss – idol, luck, der. Port. *deos* – god; thus joss-house – Chinese temple; joss-stick – incense (CC; SS)

jow – go, der. *jao* (BOR)

juldi – quickly, thus 'do a *juldi* move' (BOR)

jungli – wild, uncultivated, thus 'he's a bit *jungli*' and 'jungle-*wallah*' – forest officer (I)

jungli-moorgi – wild fowl (I)

K

K – knighthood, 'to get a K', in India usually KCIE (I); in Colonial Service usually of the Order of St Michael and St George (KCMG), sometimes known as 'Kindly Call Me God' (see K)

Kadir Cup – annual pig-sticking meet held on alluvial plains near Meerut (I)

kafilah – camel caravan (I)

kala jugga – dark place, thus secluded corner off dance hall (I)

Kali – black goddess requiring propitiation through sacrifice, much worshipped in E. India (I)

kampong – area of cleared land, thus village settlement (M)

kangani – foreman of Tamil estate labour (SEA)

kapasu – chief's messenger, constable in N. Rhodesia (CA)

kapitan China – head of Chinese Community, der. Port. (SEA)

KAR – King's African Rifles, with battalions in Kenya, Uganda, Tanganyika and Nyasaland, with a detachment in Somaliland (A)

kebaya – woman's jacket (M)

kebun – gardener, estate; see *tukang kebun* (M)

kedai – shop (M)

Kempeitai – Japanese Secret Police (SEA)

kemudi – helmsman, Malay captain (SEA)

Kenya stiff – derog. term used outside Kenya to describe its prouder
European inhabitants (A)

keramat – spirit, sorcerer, thus *keramat*-tiger – tiger infested by spirit of
sorcerer (SEA)

kerani – Indian clerk, der. *kirani* (I; SEA)

khana – meal, usually dinner (I)

khansama – cook (I)

khas-khas tatti – screen made of grass matting hung round doors and windows
in hot weather (I)

khit – *khitmatgar* – butler; waiter (I)

khubber – news, thus 'what's the *khubber*?'(I)

khud – steep hillside, thus '*khud*-racing' (I)

khyfer – skirt, thus 'a bit of *khyfer*' (BOR)

kiboko – rawhide whip (EA)

Ki-settler – ungrammatical Swahili spoken by settlers in Kenya (EA)

kitchen-*kaffir* – Rhodesian equivalent of 'kitchen-Swahili' (CA)

kitchen-Swahili – Swahili as spoken with servants, see 'Swahili' (EA)

KL – Kuala Lumpur (SEA)

kling – man from Kalinga, thus term for South Indians in S.E. Asia, now
regarded as offensive (SEA)

koi-hai – 'Is anyone there?', term used when calling servants; thus 'character'
or old India hand (I)

kongsi – coolie lines, part. Chinese tin-mines, der. Mandarin *kong his* –
company (SEA)

kota – fort, thus Kota Bharu (M)

krait – small but highly-venomous snake (I)

kris – Malay wavy-bladed dagger (SEA)

kshatria – warrior caste among Hindus (I)

kuala – river mouth, thus Kuala Lumpur – muddy estuary (M)

kuku – cook, thus '*kuku matey*' – cook's mate, said to carry at all times a jar of
yeast (WA); also chicken (EA)

kulang – crane (I)

kururu – ululation (CA)

kutcha – raw, incomplete, thus '*kutcha hal*' – uncooked truth (I)

Glossary

L

lalang – coarse tropical grass (M)

Lanes – high-class brothel area of Calcutta (I)

lascar – Indian or Malay deckhand, der. Persian *lascari* – soldier

lat sahib – Lord Sahib (Governor or Governor General) (I)

lie-off – afternoon siesta (SEA)

lines – quarters of troops or plantation labour (I; SEA)

lingam – Hindu male fertility symbol (I)

liwali – headman appointed by Govt. to represent local Muslim community (EA)

load – luggage, divided into loads of no more than 56 lb. for portering, earlier 60 lb. (WA, EA, CA)

logh – people, thus 'sahib-*logh*' – Europeans (I)

loose-*wallah* – thief (BOR)

loot – plunder, der. *lut* (I)

M

ma – term of address used by servants, der. 'madam', also 'missus', 'mama' (WA); in Kenya *memsahib* (EA)

ma-bap – mother and father, honorific form of address, thus *ap mai ma-bap hai'* – 'you are my mother and father') (I)

machan – shooting platform (I)

maharanee – great queen (I)

mahout – elephant driver (I)

maidan – public land; parade ground (I)

makan – eat, thus dinner; *makan kechil* – canapés served before meal (see 'small eats'); *makan angin* – evening promenade, lit. 'eating the air'); *makan suap* – take a bribe, lit. 'eat a bribe' (M)

mali – gardener (I)

mallam – scribe or teacher of language in N. Nigeria; Arabic) (A)

malum – knowledge, thus 'do you malum? – 'do you understand?' (BOR)

mamlet – marmalade (I dom)

mammy – African woman (pidgin); thus '*mammy*-wagon' – bus much used by market women (WA); '*mammy*- clothes' – Western garments foisted on East Africans by missionaries; and *mammy*-chair – bosun's chair used for the disembarkation of passengers off Accra and (until First World War) Lagos (A)

mandor – overseer of labour, mandarin, der. Port. *mandador* – one who commands (SEA)

masalchee – scullion (I)

mata-mata – two eyes, thus police, also known as *orang-mata* (M)

matey – servant's assistant (I)

maumlet – omelette (I dom)

ma yong – Malay court entertainment combining dance, opera and drama (SEA)

MCS – Malayan Civil Service (SEA)

mehtar – prince, thus term used ironically when addressing sweeper (I)

mem – European woman, abbrev. of *memsahib* (I; SEA)

memsahib – European woman, from 'madam-sahib' (I; SEA; EA)

menora – dance drama of Kelantan State (SEA)

merdeka – freedom, thus Independence (M)

mess – military quarters; in Africa also bachelor quarters shared by several Europeans (A)

messenger – government or district messenger, regarded as DO's right-hand man (see *askari kanga; dubas; kapasu, tarashi*) (A)

minum teh – tea drink, thus tea money or small bribe (M)

mishast to barkhast – code of etiquette, der. Persian (I)

missie – European woman, der. Dutch *meisje* (SS; CC)

MMRA – miles and miles of ruddy Africa, also more commonly MMBA (A)

mofussil – up-country, the interior (I)

mohur – Mogul gold coin, also 'mohur tree' (I)

Mohurram – Muslim festival (I)

molish – polish (I dom)

monsoon – seasonal winds blowing from N.E. across South China Sea November–February, and from S.W. May–September der. Arab. *maussim* – season; see 'rains' (SEA)

moorghi – chicken, thus *moorghi-khana* – hen room, ladies' room in club (I)

mosquito boot – boot worn in the evenings, usually black leather for men and white canvas for women (EA, WA, CA)

mottongost – mutton, der. *gosh* – meat (I dom)

mozzinet – mosquito-net (BOR)

m'pishi – cook (EA)

mufti – civilian clothes; civvies (BOR)

mulaquati – visitors; petitioners (I)

mulligatawny – spicy soup, traditionally served on Sundays (I)

munshi – interpreter; language teacher of languages (I); also *guru* (SEA)

musical chair – latrine (BOR)

Mussulman pani – 'water for Muslims', station vendor's cry (I)

mut karo – 'don't do that' (I)

mzungu – white man (EA)

N

NA – Native Administration, Native Authority, operating side by side with the colonial administration as part of indirect rule (A)

Nadge – Poona red light district (BOR)

nappy – barber, der. *napi* (BOR)

narlikis – Tamil labour, derog. term der. *narlaki* – tomorrow (SEA)

native comfort – African mistress, see 'sleeping dictionary' (A)

nazir – counsellor, subordinate official (I)

ndaba – official gathering or meeting in N. Rhodesia, (see *baraza*) (A)

negri – state, thus Negri Sembilan – nine states (M)

NFD – Kenya's Northern Frontier District, extra provincial district, under an Officer-in-Charge, colonized in 1946 with Turkana to form a province (A)

ngoma drum, thus tribal dance (EA)

nyai – younger sister, thus concubine in Sarawak (SEA)

O

oil rivers – rivers of the Niger Delta used in the transportation of palm oil, initially an administrative region (A)

old coaster – experienced West Africa hand, usually trader, also known as 'palm-oil ruffian' (A)

oolta-poolta – topsy-turvy (I)

orang – people, thus *orang asli* – original people, aboriginals of Malayan peninsula; *orang mata* – eye people, policemen; *orang puteh* – white people; *orang utan* – forest people (M)

P

paan-biri – 'cigarettes and *paan*-leaf', station vendor's cry (I)

padang – open land, thus playing field or parade ground, also known as *medan* (M)

paddy – rice field, der. *padi* – growing rice (I; M)

pagan – animistic tribe in Nigeria, thus a DO in a pagan area was known as 'pagan' or 'pagan man' (WA)

pagoda tree – eighteenth-century gold coin, thus 'to shake the pagoda tree' and make a quick fortune (I)

pahit – bitter, thus gin and bitters (SEA)

palaver – talk, dispute, der. Port. *palabra*; thus *mammy-palaver* – women's talk (WA)

palka-ghari – covered cart for women in *purdah* (I)

panga – bush knife (CEA)

pani – water, thus *pani-wallah* – water-carrier scullion; also *kala pani* – black water, thus ocean (I)

parang – machete (M)

pasar – market, township (SEA)

patwari – village official (I)

pau-peg – quarter tot of whisky, der. *pau* – quarter or finger (I)

pawang – medicine man, spirit medium (M)

PC – Provincial Commissioner, the equivalent in the Sudan being the Provincial Governor and in Nigeria and Buganda the Resident (A)

peenika cheez – something to drink, thus drinks (I)

peenika-pani – drinking water (I)

peepul – Indian fig tree (I)

peg – tot, see '*chota*-peg' (I)

penghulu – parish headman (M)

peon – office messenger; orderly, der. Port. 'footman'

phal-phul rule – flowers and fruit rule, the only gifts government officials could accept (I)

phut – useless, thus to go *phut* (I)

pi dog – pariah mongrel found all over India (I)

pidgin – lingua franca developed for trading purposes using basic English and simplified grammar, sometimes known on the Gold Coast as 'Coast piggin' or 'Kru-English' (WA)

Piffers – Punjab Frontier Force (I)

pith helmet – light topee made of vegetable fibre, see *sola topee* (I)

PK – portable thunderbox, said to be derived from *piccaninkaya* – small house (CA)

planter's long sleever – verandah chair with arm and leg rests (I)

P&O – The Peninsular and Oriental Steam Navigation Company, largest and most popular shipping company for those going out East (I)

poodle-faker – womanizer, especially in hill stations, hence 'poodle-faking (I)

POSH – supposedly derived from 'Port Out, Starboard Home', these being the cooler sides of the ship (I)

poshteen – sheepskin jacket (I)

prahu – Malay boat (SEA)

puggaree – turban (I)

pukka – proper, ripe, thûs '*pukka* sahib' – real gentleman '*pukka* house' – brick as against mud and thatch; '*pukka* major' – regimental major; '*pukka* road' – metalled road (I)

pukkeroo – to grab, der. *pakrao* (BOR)

pulau – island, thus Pulau Tioman (M)

punkah – fan, properly suspended from ceiling and pulled by a *punkah-wallah* (I; EA)

purdah – curtain, thus seclusion expected of higher-class Indian women esp. Muslims (I)

PWD – Public Works Department (I; A; SEA) thus 'PWD tree' – kapok tree, said to have been designed and built by PWD engineers (SEA)

Q

qua-hai – see *koi-hai* (I)

R

rains – rainy season, in India from June to late August, see monsoon (I)

Raj – kingdom, used chiefly to denote British crown rule in India from 1858 to 1947, see *rajah* and *maharajah* (I)

Rajrifs – Rajputana Rifles (I)

Ramadan – Islamic month of fasting, known in Malaya as Puasa (fasting) (SEA)

ranee – queen (I)

rattan – *rotan* cane or creeper (M)

remittance man – a form of Kenya settler said to depend on remittance from UK sent to stop him returning (A)

remount – replacement cavalry horse (I)

Resident – senior political agent in Indian princely states (I); senior British administrator in FMS, Malay Settlement or Sarawak division; in Penang and Malacca known as Resident Councillor, later Resident Commissioner (SEA); thus Residency – official residence of above (I; SEA)

rest-house – staging house built by the PWD or local authority for officials on tour (A; I)

Rice Corps – Royal Indian Army Service Corps (I)

rissaldar – Indian cavalry equivalent of infantry *subedar*

roll on – 'roll on that boat', 'roll on the fours and sevens', referring to end of tours of Indian duty (BOR)

ronggeng – Malay dance originating from Malacca (SEA)

Roorkee chair – camp chair, orig. manufactured in Roorkee (I)

rooty-gong – long service medal, from *roti* – bread (BOR)

rumble-tumble – scrambled eggs (I dom)

rumah – house (M)

rum-johnnie – prostitute, from *ramjani* – dancing girl (BOR)

rupee – standard silver coin in India.

S

sadar – headquarters (I)

saddhu – Hindu ascetic

safari – journey, see touring (EA)

sahib – sir, thus European; also affixed to title, thus 'colonel-sahib' (I)

sakht burra mem – tough senior memsahib, from *sakht* – hard (I)

salaam – salutation, thus 'Give my salaams to . . .', also *salaam wasti* – to pay respects

sambhur – large deer (I)

sammy – holy man, from *swami* (BOR)

sampan – small boat, der. Chinese *san-pan* – three boards (SEA)

sapeh – two-stringed guitar in Sarawak (SEA)

sari – Hindu woman's dress (I)

sarki – chief in N. Nigeria (WA)

sarong – covering, thus wraparound skirt worn by Malays (M)

satyagraha – truth-force, civil disobedience based on Gandhian non-violence (I)

SCC – Sudan/Somaliland Camel Corps (EA)

Scotch club – informal club or outdoor gathering from the first phase of administration when Europeans on station supplied their own drinks, chairs and lamps (A)

scratch box – secretariat (WA)

selamat – peace, thus greeting; see *salaam* (SEA)

selat – Strait (SEA)

shabash – well done (I)

shamardan – classical Arab lantern, with large glass bowl (EA)

shamiana – marquee (I)

Shanghai jar – large water container in bathroom, also known as Siam jar, *tong* or Suchow tub (SEA)

shauq – dominant interest, hobby (I)

shikar – shooting and hunting, thus *shikari* – hunter (I)

shite-hawk – Army slang for kite-hawk, outsider, 4th Indian Div. insignia (BOR)

shroff – Indian or Chinese accountant, thus shroffage – commission; also used as a verb as in 'to shroff an account' (I; CC; s)

shufti – look, der. Arabic, thus 'take a shufti' (BOR)

siamang – large gibbon (M)

sikkins – savouries (I DOM)

simkin – champagne (I DOM)

sirdar – local chief, usually Sikh (I)

sirkar – central government (I)

sleeping dictionary – African mistress, see 'native comfort' (A)

sloth belt – derog. term for South India (I)

sola topee – sun helmet, orig. from *sola* pith, often incorrectly written 'solar' (I, SEA)

songkok – black Malay cap (SEA)

sowar – horseman, cavalry or mounted police trooper (I)

spatch-cock – grilled jungle fowl (I)

spine-pad – felt pad worn by British troops to protect spine from sun, abandoned c. 1920 (I; A; SEA)

Spotted Dog – Selangor Club in Kuala Lumpur, also known as the 'Dog' (SEA)

squeeze – inducement, customary bribe (CC; ss)

station – government post where district officials live (I); thus 'outstation', see *boma* (A)

stengah – one half, thus half measure of whisky; derog. term for Eurasian (SEA)

stinger – see *stengah*

stoep – uncovered verandah (WA; CA; EA)

Straits Settlements – British administered colonial territories of Penang Island and Province Wellesley, Malacca and Singapore, including at different periods the *Dindings* (protected areas), Perak, Labuan, Christmas Island and Cocos Keeling (SEA)

stud book – Staff or Civil Service List (WA)

subedar – senior Viceroy's Commisioned Officer, also *subedar*-major (I).

submukin – 'the whole submukin lot', from *sub* – all (BOR)

sudah mati – dead, colloquial Anglo-Malay (SEA)

sudden death – *dak* bungalow chicken (seen alive and eaten soon after) (I)

Sumatra – sudden squall blowing across Straits of Malacca from Sumatra (SEA)

sundowner – drink taken at sundown and thereafter (A)

sungei – river, thus Sungei Siput (M)

Swahili – lingua franca developed for trading purposes, supposedly from the Arabic *swahele* – man of the coast, more correctly Ki-Swahili (EA)

sweeper – latrine cleaner of untouchable caste (I)

syce – groom (I); thus chauffeur (SEA)

T

TA – travel allowance (I)

tahsa char, garumi garum – 'fresh tea, hot as hot', railway station vendor's cry (I)

tahsildar – local tax collector (I)

taipan – European head of a *hong* (CC; Singapore)

talkies – audience with local ruler or governor (I)

tamasha – display, spectacle, thus 'a great *tamasha*' (I; EA)

tambi – office messenger (M)

Tanganyika boiler – hot water system consisting of piped water from a heated 40-gallon drum (EA)

tank – artificial lake, reservoir (I)

tapper – rubber estate worker who taps rubber trees (SEA)

tarbosh – Turkish fez (A)

tat, tattoo – local pony (I)

teapoy – tripod table (I)

teen pau – three quarters, derog. term for Eurasian (I)

tent-pegging – cavalry exercise of spearing and lifting a tent-peg at a gallop (I)

terai – plains country below Himalayan foothills (I)

tetul gat shakshi – tamarind tree witness, false witness (Bengal) (I)

thunder box – earth closet (I; SEA; A)

tiffin – light luncheon (I)

tikka-ghari – four-wheeler carriage (I)

tindal – foreman of labour, boatswain in charge of *lascars*, der. Malayalam *tandu valli* – oarsman (SEA)

tin-pot bird – crimson-breasted barbet (I; SEA)

toasties – canapés, thus 'first *toasties*' before supper, 'second *toasties*' after, see also 'small *chop*', '*gadgets*' (I; SEA; EA)

topee – hat, thus sun helmet; thus *topee-wallah* – hat man or European, see *sola topee, wallah* (I)

tory peechy – 'the good ship tory peechy', delayed repatriation, from *tora peechee* – a little later (BOR)

toto – child, der. *mtoto*, thus 'cook's *toto*' – kitchen assistant (EA)

tour – practice of surveying one's district or area of responsibility, in India undertaken in cold weather months, see 'touring'; also period of service between leaves, thus 'end of tourish' – run-down and needing recuperation (A)

touring – practice of journeying on official business through one's district, in Africa known variously as 'going on safari' (EA), 'going to bush' (WA) or 'going on *ulendo*' (CA)

tree-rat – squirrel; also native prostitute (BOR)

tuak – rice wine, toddy (M)

tuan – prince, der. *tuanku*, honorific applied to men of rank, thus Europeans; thus *tuan besar* – big gentleman, boss of firm; *tuan kechik* – small gentleman, European assistant; *Tuan Kompani* – Great Company, Malay term for East India Company, later used to denote crown rule (ss)

tukang – craftsman, thus *tukang ayer* – water-carrier, scullion; *tukang kebun* – estate craftsman, thus gardener, usually known simply as *kebun* (M)

tumbo – species of fly (WA)

tumlet – glass tumbler (I dom)

tum-tum – dog-cart, der. 'tandem' (I)

tunda – cold, thus 'I'll *tunda* you' (cool you down); also *Tunda Pani Chowkidars* – Coldstream Guards (who never served in India) (I)

tundice – ice bucket, used in train compartments before air-conditioning (I)

turawa – white men in N. Nigeria (WA)

tutup – closed (M), thus *tutup* jacket – jacket buttoned up to the neck (M)

twice born – honorific term for *Brahmin*, often used to describe ICS (I)

typhoon – cyclonic tempest, orig. disputed, deriving either from Arab. *tufan* – wind-storm, or Chinese *tai-fong* – great wind (SEA)

U

ulendo – see 'touring' (CA)

ulu – headwaters of river, thus up-river region, see *penghulu* (M)

umpeschie – cook (EA)

UMS – Unfederated Malay States, comprising Kelantan, Trengganu, Kedah, Perlis and Johore (SEA)

undarzi – vague, thus 'he's a bit *undarzi*' (I)

unofficial – European other than government official (SEA)

UP – United Provinces (I)

up-country – the provinces; upper India, see *mofussil* (I)

up the line – on active duty on the North-West Frontier (BOR)

Urdu – 'language of the camp', lingua franca of upper India, see Hindustani (I)

V

vaisya – merchant caste among Hindus (I)

vakil – Indian attorney; court pleader (I)

valise – bedding roll (A)

VCO – Viceroy's Commissioned Officer, formerly Native Officer (I)

verandah – open-pillared gallery round house or bungalow, der. Port. *verandas* – balcony (I; SEA)

W

WAFF – (Royal) West Africa Frontier Force, with regiments or battalions in Sierra Leone, Gambia, Gold Coast, Nigeria and British Cameroons (A)

waler – horse imported from Australia, orig. New South Wales) (I)

wallah – man (I)

WAR – West Africa Regiment (A)

WAWA – 'West Africa Wins Again' (also Hausa for 'fool'), term used to express irritation at local ways and means, also 'YCHA' – 'You Can't Hurry Africa' (A)

wa-wa – small gibbon, known to Malays as *ungka* (SEA)

wayang – drama on stage, thus *wayang kulit* – shadow play with puppets (M)

wishi-wishi – white-faced teal found in Nigeria, also known as *wishy-washy* (A)

Y

Yellow Jack – yellow fever; the last serious outbreak occurred in W. Africa in 1927 [Although, since 1979, Yellow Fever has staged a come-back in Africa, due to a falling-off in vaccination.] (A)

yogi – Hindu ascetic (I)

Z

zaki – lion, honorific form of address in N. Nigeria (A)

zan-zar-zamin – land, gold and women, traditional objects of crime in the Sind and North-West Frontier (I)

zemindar – landowner, more correctly *zamindar*, thus *zemindari* – landowner's estate (I)

zenana – women's quarter of Indian house (I)

zubberdust – tyrannical (I)